ALIEN™

THE SHADOW ARCHIVES

OUT OF THE SHADOWS
by Tim Lebbon

SEA OF SORROWS
by James A. Moore

RIVER OF PAIN
by Christopher Golden

THE COMPLETE ALIEN™ LIBRARY FROM TITAN BOOKS

A L I E N™

THE SHADOW ARCHIVES

OUT OF THE SHADOWS
by Tim Lebbon

SEA OF SORROWS
by James A. Moore

RIVER OF PAIN
by Christopher Golden

TITAN BOOKS

THE COMPLETE ALIEN COLLECTION: THE SHADOW ARCHIVE

Print edition ISBN: 9781803361161
E-book edition ISBN: 9781803361901

Published by Titan Books
A division of Titan Publishing Group Ltd
144 Southwark Street, London SE1 0UP
www.titanbooks.com

First edition: December 2022
10 9 8 7 6 5 4 3 2

A CIP catalogue record for this title is available from the British Library.

Printed and bound by CPI Group (UK) Ltd, Croydon, CR0 4YY.

BOOK ONE

OUT OF THE SHADOWS

"The universe seems neither benign
nor hostile, merely indifferent."
CARL SAGAN

YEARLY PROGRESS REPORT:
To: Weyland-Yutani Corporation, Science Division
(Ref: code 937)
Date (unspecified)
Transmission (pending)

My search continues.

PART 1

DREAMING OF

MONSTERS

1

MARION

Chris Hooper dreamed of monsters.

As a youngster they'd fascinated him, as they did all children. But unlike children born generations before him, there were places he could go, destinations he could explore, where he might just find them. No longer restricted to the pages of fairy tales or the digital imagery of imaginative moviemakers, humankind's forays into space had opened up a whole galaxy of possibilities.

So from a young age he looked to the stars, and those dreams persisted.

In his early twenties he'd worked for a year on Callisto, one of Jupiter's moons. They'd been hauling ores from several miles below the surface, and in a nearby mine a Chinese team had broken through into a sub-surface sea. There had been crustaceans and shrimp, tiny pilot fish and delicate frond-like creatures a hundred feet long. But no monsters to set his imagination on fire.

When he'd left the solar system to work in deep space, traveling as engineer on various haulage, exploration, and mining ships, he'd eagerly sought out tales of alien life forms encountered on those distant asteroids, planets, and moons. Though adulthood had diluted his youngster's vivid imagination with more mundane concerns—family estrangement, income, and well-being—he still told himself stories. But over the years, none of what he'd found had lived up to the fictions he'd created.

As time passed he'd come to terms with the fact that monsters were only monsters before they were found, and perhaps the universe wasn't quite so remarkable as he'd once hoped.

Certainly not here.

Working in one of the *Marion*'s four docking bays, he paused to look down at the planet below with a mixture of distaste and boredom. LV178. Such an inhospitable, storm-scoured, sand-blasted hell of a rock that they hadn't even bothered to give it a proper name. He'd spent three long years here, making lots of money he had no opportunity to spend.

Trimonite was the hardest, strongest material known to man, and when a seam as rich as this one was found, it paid to mine it out. One day he'd head home, he promised himself at the end of every fifty-day shift. Home to the two boys and wife he'd run away from seven years before. One day. But he was beginning to fear that this life had become a habit, and the longer it continued, the harder it might be to break.

"Hoop!" The voice startled him, and as he spun around Jordan was already chuckling.

He and the captain had been involved briefly, a year before. These confined quarters and stressful work conditions meant that such liaisons were frequent, and inevitably brief. But Hoop liked the fact that they had remained close. Once they'd got the screwing out of the way, they'd become the best of friends.

"Lucy, you scared the shit out of me."

"That's Captain Jordan to you." She examined the machinery he'd been working on, without even glancing at the viewing window. "All good here?"

"Yeah, heat baffles need replacing, but I'll get Powell and Welford onto that."

"The terrible twins," Jordan said, smiling. Powell was close to six foot six, tall, black, and slim as a pole. Welford was more than a foot shorter, white, and twice as heavy. As different as could be, yet the ship's engineers were both smartasses.

"Still no contact?" Hoop asked.

Jordan frowned briefly. It wasn't unusual to lose touch with the surface, but not for two days running.

"Storms down there are the worst I've seen," she said, nodding at the window. From three hundred miles up, the planet's surface looked even more inhospitable than usual—a smear of burnt oranges and yellows, browns and blood-reds, with the circling eyes of countless sandstorms raging across the equatorial regions. "They've gotta abate soon. I'm not too worried yet, but I'll be happy when we can talk to the dropships again."

"Yeah, you and me both. The *Marion* feels like a derelict when we're between shifts."

Jordan nodded. She was obviously concerned, and for an awkward, silent moment Hoop thought he should say something more to comfort her. But she was the captain because she could handle situations like this. That, and because she was a badass.

"Lachance is doing spaghetti again tonight," she said.

"For a Frenchman, he sure can cook Italian."

Jordan chuckled, but he could feel her tension.

"Lucy, it's just the storms," Hoop said. He was sure of that. But he was equally sure that "just storms" could easily cause disaster. Out here in the furthest quadrants of known space—pushing the limits of technology, knowledge, and understanding, and doing their best to deal with the corners cut by the Kelland Mining Company—it didn't take much for things to go wrong.

Hoop had never met a ship's engineer better than him, and that was why he was here. Jordan was an experienced flight captain, knowledgeable and wise. Lachance, cynical and gruff, was an excellent pilot who had a healthy respect for space and all it could throw at them. And the rest of their team, though a mixed bunch, were all more than capable at their jobs. The miners themselves were a hardy breed, many of them experienced from stints on Jupiter's and Neptune's moons. Mean bastards, with streaks of sick humor, most were as hard as the trimonite they sought.

But no experience, no confidence or hardness or pig-headedness, could dodge fate. They all knew how dangerous it was. Most of them had grown used to living with the danger, and the close proximity of death.

Only seven months ago they'd lost three miners in an accident in Bay One as the dropship *Samson* came in to dock. No one's fault, really. Just eagerness to be back on board in relative comfort, after fifty days down the mine. The airlock hadn't sealed properly, an indicator had malfunctioned, and the two men and a woman had suffocated.

Hoop knew that Jordan still had sleepless nights over that. For three days after transmitting her condolences to the miners' families, she hadn't left her cabin. As far as Hoop was concerned, that was what made her a great captain—she was a badass who cared.

"Just the storms," she echoed. She leaned past Hoop and rested against the bulkhead, looking down through the window. Despite the violence, from up here the planet looked almost beautiful, an artist's palette of autumnal colors. "I fucking hate this place."

"Pays the bills."

"Ha! Bills…" She seemed in a maudlin mood, and Hoop didn't like her like this. Perhaps that was a price of their closeness—he got to see a side of her the rest of the crew never would.

"Almost finished," he said, nudging some loose ducting with his foot. "Meet you in the rec room in an hour. Shoot some pool?"

Jordan raised an eyebrow. "Another rematch?"

"You've got to let me win sometime."

"You've never, *ever* beaten me at pool."

"But I used to let you play with my cue."

"As your captain, I could put you in the brig for such comments."

"Yeah. Right. You and which army?"

Jordan turned her back on Hoop. "Stop wasting time and get back to work, chief engineer."

"Yes, captain." He watched her walk away along the dusky corridor and through a sliding door, and then he was alone again.

Alone with the atmosphere, the sounds, the smells of the ship…

The stench of space-flea piss from the small, annoying mites that managed to multiply, however many times the crew tried to purge them. They were tiny, but a million fleas pissing produced a sharp, rank odor that clung to the air.

The constant background hum of machinery was inaudible unless Hoop really listened for it, because it was so ever-present. There were distant thuds, echoing grinds, the whisper of air movement encouraged by conditioning fans and baffles, the occasional creak of the ship's huge bulk settling and shifting. Some of the noises he could identify because he knew them so well, and on occasion he perceived problems simply through hearing or *not* hearing them— sticking doors, worn bearings in air duct seals, faulty transmissions.

But there were also mysterious sounds that vibrated through the ship now and then, like hesitant, heavy footsteps in distant corridors, or someone screaming from a level or two away. He'd never figured those out. Lachance liked to say it was the ship screaming in boredom.

He hoped that was all they were.

The vessel was huge and would take him half an hour to walk from nose to tail, and yet it was a speck in the vastness of space. The void exerted a negative pressure on him, and if he thought about it too much, he thought he would explode—be ripped apart, cell by cell, molecule by molecule, spread to the cosmos from which he had originally come. He was the stuff of the stars, and when he was a young boy—dreaming of monsters, and looking to space in the hope that he would find them—that had made him feel special.

Now, it only made him feel small.

However close they all lived together on the *Marion*, they were alone out here.

Shaking away the thoughts, he bent to work again, making more noise than was necessary—a clatter to keep him company. He was looking forward to shooting some pool with Jordan and having her whip his ass again. There were colleagues and acquaintances aplenty, but she was the closest thing he had to a good friend.

The recreation room was actually a block of four compartments to the rear of the *Marion*'s accommodations hub. There was a movie theater with a large screen and an array of seating, a music library with various listening posts, a reading room with comfortable chairs and reading devices—and then there was Baxter's Bar, better known as BeeBee's. Josh Baxter was the ship's communications officer, but he also acted as their barman. He mixed a mean cocktail.

Though it was sandwiched back between the accommodations hub and the sectioned holds, BeeBee's was the social center of the ship. There were two pool tables, table tennis, a selection of faux-antique computer game consoles, and the bar area with tables and chairs scattered in casual abandon. It had not been viewed as a priority by the company that paid the ship's designers, so the ceiling was a mass of exposed service pipework, the floor textured metal, the walls bare and unpainted. However, those using BeeBee's had done their best to make it more comfortable. Seats were padded, lighting was low and moody, and many miners and crew had copied Baxter's idea of hanging decorated blankets from the walls. Some painted the blankets, others tore and tied. Each of them was distinct. It gave the whole rec room a casual, almost arty air.

Miners had fifty days between shifts on the planet, so they often spent much of their off-time here, and though alcohol distribution was strictly regulated, it still made for some raucous nights.

Captain Jordan allowed that. In fact, she positively encouraged it, because it was a release of tension that the ship would otherwise barely contain. It wasn't possible to communicate with any of their loved ones back home. Distances were so vast, time so extended, that any meaningful contact was impossible. They needed somewhere to feel at home, and BeeBee's provided just that.

When Hoop entered, it was all but deserted. These quiet times between shift changes gave Baxter time to clear out the bar stock, tidy the room, and prepare for the next onslaught. He worked quietly behind the bar, stocking bottled beer and preparing a selection of dehydrated snacks. Water on the ship always tasted vaguely metallic, so he rehydrated many of the treats in stale beer. No one complained.

"And here he is," Jordan said. She was sitting on a stool by one of the pool tables, bottle in hand. "Back for another beating. What do you think, Baxter?"

Baxter nodded a greeting to Hoop.

"Sucker for punishment," he agreed.

"Yep. Sucker."

"Well if you don't *want* to play…" Hoop said.

Jordan slid from her stool, plucked a cue from the rack and lobbed it at him. As he caught it out of the air, the ship's intercom chimed.

"Oh, now, what the hell?" Jordan sighed.

Baxter leaned across the bar and hit the intercom.

"Captain! *Anyone!*" It was their pilot, Lachance. "Get up to the bridge, now. We've got incoming from one of the dropships." His French accent was much more acute than normal. That happened when he was upset or stressed, neither of which occurred very often.

Jordan dashed to the bar and pressed the transmit button.

"Which one?"

"The *Samson*. But it's fucked up."

"What do you mean?" In the background, behind Lachance's confused words and the sounds of chaos from the bridge, Hoop heard static-tinged screaming. He and Jordan locked eyes.

Then they ran, and Baxter followed.

The *Marion* was a big ship, far more suited to massive deep-ore mining than trimonite extrusion, and it took them a few minutes to make their way to the bridge. Along the curved corridor that wound around the accommodations hub, then up three levels by elevator. By the time they bumped into Garcia and Kasyanov, everyone else was there.

"What's going on?" Jordan demanded. Baxter rushed across to the communications center, and Lachance stood gratefully to vacate his chair. Baxter slipped on a pair of headphones, and his left hand hovered over an array of dials and switches.

"Heard something coming through static a few minutes ago," Lachance said. "The higher they climb, the clearer it gets." They called him "No-Chance" Lachance because of his laconic pessimism, but in truth he was one of the most level-headed among them. Now, Hoop could see by his expression that something had him very rattled.

From loudspeakers around the bridge, frantic breathing crackled.

"*Samson*, Captain Jordan is now on the bridge," Baxter said. "Please give us your—"

"I don't have time to fucking give you anything, just get the med pods fired up!" The voice was so distorted that they couldn't tell who it was.

Jordan grabbed a headset from beside Baxter. Hoop looked around at the others, all of them standing around the communications area. The bridge was large, but they were all bunched in close. They showed the tension they had to be feeling, even the usually unflappable science officer, Karen Sneddon. The thin, severe-faced woman had been to more planets, asteroids, and moons than all of them put together. But there was fear in her eyes.

"*Samson*, this is Captain Jordan. What's happening? What's going on down at the mine?"

"...creatures! We've—"

The contact cut out abruptly, leaving the bridge ringingly silent.

Wide viewing windows looked out onto the familiar view of space and an arc of the planet below, as if nothing had changed. The low-level hum of machinery was complemented by agitated breathing.

"Baxter," Jordan said softly, "I'd like them back online."

"I'm doing my best," he replied.

"Creatures?" The ship's medic Garcia tapped nervously at her chin. "No one's ever seen *creatures* down the mine, have they?"

"There's nothing living on that rock, other than bacteria," Sneddon said. She was shifting from foot to foot. "Maybe that's not what they said. Maybe they said fissures, or something."

"Have we got them on scanner yet?" Jordan asked.

Baxter waved to his left, where three screens were set aslant in the control panel. One was backlit a dull green, and it showed two small points of light moving quickly toward them. Interference from electrical storms in the upper atmosphere sparked across the screen. But the points were firm, their movement defined.

"Which is the *Samson*?" Hoop asked.

"Lead ship is *Samson*," Lachance said. "The *Delilah* follows."

"Maybe ten minutes out," Jordan said. "Any communication from *Delilah*?"

No one answered. Answer enough.

"I'm not sure we can—" Hoop began, then the speakers burst back into life. *Let them dock*, he was going to say.

OUT OF THE SHADOWS

"—stuck to their faces!" the voice said. It was still unrecognizable.

Baxter turned some dials, and then a larger screen above his station flickered to life. The *Samson*'s pilot, Vic Jones, appeared as a blurred image. Hoop tried to see past him to the inner cabin of the dropship, but the vibration of their steep ascent out of LV178's atmosphere made a mess out of everything.

"How many with you?" Hoop asked.

"Hoop? That you?"

"Yeah."

"The other shift found something. Something horrible. Few of them… " He faded out again, his image stuttering and flickering as atmospherics caused more chaos.

"Kasyanov, you and Garcia get to sick bay and fire up the med pods," Jordan said to the doctor and her medic.

"You can't be serious," Hoop said. As Jordan turned on him, Jones's voice crackled in again.

"—all four, only me and Sticky untouched. They're okay right now, but… to shiver and spit. Just get… to dock!"

"They might be *infected*!" Hoop said.

"Which is why we'll get them straight to sick bay."

"This is fucking serious." Hoop nodded at the screen where Jones's image continued to flicker and dance, his voice cutting in and out. Most of what Jones said made little sense, but they could all hear his terror. "He's shitting himself!"

Kasyanov and Garcia hustled from the bridge, and Hoop looked to Sneddon for support. But the science officer was leaning over the back of Baxter's chair, frowning as she tried to make out whatever else Jones was saying.

"Jones, what about the *Delilah*?" Jordan said into her headset. "Jones?"

"…left the same time… something got on board, and… "

"*What* got on board?"

The screen snowed, the comm link fuzzed with static, and those remaining on the bridge stood staring at each other for a loaded, terrible few seconds.

"I'm getting down to the docking level," Jordan said. "Cornell, with me. Baxter, tell them Bay Three."

Hoop coughed a disbelieving laugh.

"You're taking *him* to back you up?"

"He's security officer, Hoop."

"He's a drunk!" Cornell didn't even meet Hoop's stare, let alone respond.

"He has a gun," Jordan said. "You stay here, supervise the bridge. Lachance, help guide them in. Remote pilot the dropships if you have to."

"If we can even get a link to them," Lachance said.

"Assume we can, and do it!" Jordan snapped. She took a few deep breaths, and Hoop could almost hear her thoughts. *Never figured it would fuck up this bad, gotta be calm, gotta be in control.* He knew she was thinking about those three miners she'd lost, and dreading the idea of losing more. She looked straight at him. He frowned, but she turned and left the bridge before he could object again.

There was no way they should be letting the *Samson* dock, Hoop knew. Or if it did dock, they had to sever all external operation of the airlock until they knew it was safe. There had been twenty miners taken down to the surface, and twenty more scheduled to return in the dropships. Two shifts of twenty men and women—but right now, the ten people still on the *Marion* had to be the priority.

He moved to Baxter's communication panel and checked the radar scanner again. The *Samson* had been tagged with its name now, and it looked to be performing a textbook approach, arcing up out of the atmosphere and approaching the orbiting *Marion* from the sunward side.

"Lachance?" Hoop asked, pointing at the screen.

"It's climbing steeply. Jones is pushing it as hard and as fast as he can."

"Keen to reach the *Marion*."

"But that's not right…" Lachance muttered.

"What?" Hoop asked.

"*Delilah*. She's changing direction."

"Baxter," Hoop said, "plot a course trace on the *Delilah*."

Baxter hit some buttons and the screen flickered as it changed. The *Delilah* grew a tail of blue dots, and its projected course appeared as a hazy fan.

"Who's piloting *Delilah* this drop?"

"Gemma Keech," Welford said. "She's a good pilot."

"Not today she isn't. Baxter, we need to talk to *Delilah*, or see what's happening on board."

"I'm doing what I can."

"Yeah." Hoop had a lot of respect for Baxter. He was a strange guy, not really a mixer at all—probably why he spent more of his time behind the bar than in front of it—but he was a whiz when it came to communications tech. If things went wrong, he was their potential lifeline to home, and as such one of the most important people on the *Marion*.

"We have no idea what they've got on board," Powell said. "Could be anything."

"Did he say there's only six of them on the *Samson*?" Welford asked. "What about all the others?"

Hoop shrugged. Each ship held twenty people and a pilot. If the *Samson* was returning less than half full—and they had no idea how many were on *Delilah*—then what had happened to the rest of them?

He closed his eyes briefly, trying to gather himself.

"I've got visual on *Delilah*!" Baxter said. He clicked a few more keys on his computer keyboard, then switched on one of the blank screens. "No audio, and there's no response to my hails. Maybe…" But his voice trailed off.

They all saw what was happening inside *Delilah*.

The pilot, Gemma Keech, was screaming in her seat, terrified and determined, eyes glued to the window before her. It was haunting witnessing such fear in utter silence. Behind her, shadows thrashed and twisted.

"Baxter," Hoop whispered. "Camera."

Baxter stroked his keyboard and the view switched to a camera above and behind Keech's head. It was a widescreen, compressing the image but taking in the entire passenger compartment.

And there was blood.

Three miners were kneeling directly behind the pilot. Two of them held spiked sand-picks, light alloy tools used for breaking through compacted sandstones. They were waving and lashing at something, but their target was just out of sight. The miner in the middle held a plasma torch.

"He can't use that in there," Powell said. "If he does he'll... he'll... what the *fuck*?"

Several miners seemed to have been strapped into their seats. Their heads were tilted back, chests a mess of blood and ripped clothing, protruding ribs and flesh. One of them still writhed and shook, and there was something coming out of her chest. Pulling itself out. A smooth curved surface glimmering with artificial light, it shone with her blood.

Other miners were splayed on the floor of the cabin, and seemed to be dead. Shapes darted between them, slicing and slashing, and blood was splashed across the floor, up the walls. It dripped from the ceiling.

At the back of the passenger cabin, three small shapes were charging again and again at a closed door. There was a small bathroom back there, Hoop knew, just two stalls and a washbasin. And there was something in there the things wanted.

Those things.

Each was the size of a small cat, and looked to be a deep ochre color, glittering with the wetness of their unnatural births. They were somehow sharp-looking, like giant beetles or scorpions back home.

The bathroom door was already heavily dented, and one side of it seemed to be caving in.

"That's two inch steel," Hoop said.

"We've got to help them," Welford said.

"I think they're beyond that," Sneddon said, and for a moment Hoop wanted to punch her. But she was right. Keech's silent screaming bore testament to that. Whatever else they had seen, whatever the pilot already knew, the hopelessness of the *Delilah*'s situation was evident in her eyes.

"Turn it off," Hoop said, but Baxter could not comply. And all six of them on the bridge continued to watch.

The creatures smashed through the bathroom door and squeezed inside, and figures jerked and thrashed.

One of the miners holding a sand-pick flipped up and forward as if his legs had been knocked from beneath him. The man with the plasma torch slumped to the right, away from the struggling figure. Something many-legged scuttled across the camera, blotting everything from view for a blessed moment.

When the camera was clear again, the plasma torch was already alight.

"Oh, no," Powell said.

The flare was blinding white. It surged across the cabin, and for a terrible few seconds the strapped-down miners' bodies were sizzling and flaming, clothes burning and flesh flowing. Only one of them writhed in his bindings, and the thing protruding from his chest burst aside, becoming a mass of fire streaking across the cabin.

Then the plasma jet suddenly swept back and around, and everything went white.

Baxter hit his keyboard, going back to the cockpit view, and Gemma Keech was on fire.

He switched it off then. Even though everything they'd seen had been soundless, losing the image seemed to drop an awful silence across the bridge.

It was Hoop who moved first. He hit the AllShip intercom button and winced at the whine of crackling feedback.

"Lucy, we can't let those ships dock," he said into the microphone. "You hear me? The *Delilah* is… there are things on board. Monsters." He closed his eyes, mourning his childhood's lost innocence. "Everyone's dead."

"Oh, *no!*" Lachance said.

Hoop looked at him, and the Frenchman was staring down at the radar screen.

"Too late," Lachance whispered. Hoop saw, and cursed himself. He should have thought of this! He struck the button again and started shouting.

"Jordan, Cornell, get out of there, get away from the docking level, far away as you can, run, *run!*" He only hoped they heard and took heed. But a moment later he realized it really didn't matter.

The stricken *Delilah* ploughed into the *Marion*, and the impact and explosion knocked them all from their feet.

2

SAMSON

Everyone and everything was screaming.

Several warning sirens blasted their individual songs—proximity alert; damage indicator; hull breach. People shouted in panic, confusion, and fear. And behind it all was a deep, rumbling roar from the ship itself. The *Marion* was in pain, and its vast bulk was grinding itself apart.

Lucy and Cornell, Hoop thought from his position on the floor. But whether they were alive or dead didn't change anything right now. He was senior officer on the bridge. As scared and shocked as all of them, but he had to take charge.

He grabbed a fixed seat and hauled himself upright. Lights flashed. Cords, paneling, and strip-lights swung where they had been knocked from their mountings. Artificial gravity still worked, at least. He closed his eyes and breathed deeply, trying to recall his training. There had been an in-depth module in their pre-flight sessions, called "Massive Damage Control," and their guide—a grizzled old veteran of seven solar system moon habitations and three deep space exploration flights—had finished each talk with, *But don't forget YTF*.

It took Hoop until the last talk to ask what he meant.

"Don't forget…" the vet said, "you're truly fucked."

Everyone knew that a disaster like this meant the end. But that didn't mean they wouldn't fight until the last.

"Lachance!" Hoop said, but the pilot was already strapping himself into the flight seat that faced the largest window. His hands worked expertly across the controls, and if it weren't for the insistent warning buzzers and sirens, Hoop might have been comforted.

"What about Captain Jordan and Cornell?" Powell asked.

"Not now," Hoop said. "Is everyone all right?" He looked around the bridge. Baxter was strapping himself tight into his seat, dabbing at a bloodied nose. Welford and Powell held each other up against the curved wall at the bridge's rear. Sneddon was on her hands and knees, blood dripping onto the floor beneath her.

She was shaking.

"Sneddon?" Hoop said.

"Yeah." She looked up at him. There was a deep cut across her right cheek and nose. Her eyes were hazy and unfocussed.

Hoop went to her and helped her up, and Powell came with a first aid kit.

The *Marion* was juddering. A new siren had started blaring, and in the confusion Hoop couldn't identify it.

"Lachance?"

"Atmosphere venting," he said. "Hang on." He scanned his instruments, tapping keyboards, tracing patterns on screens that would mean little to anyone else. Jordan could pilot the *Marion* if she absolutely had to. But Lachance was the most experienced astronaut among them.

"We're screwed," Powell said.

"Shut it," Welford told him.

"That's it," Powell responded. "We're screwed. Game over."

"Just shut up!" Welford shouted.

"We should get to the escape pods!" Powell said.

Hoop tried not to listen to the exchange. He focussed on Lachance, strapped tightly into the pilot's seat and doing his best to ignore the rhythmic shuddering emanating from somewhere deep in the ship. *That doesn't feel good*, he thought.

The four docking bays were in a protruding level beneath the ship's nose, more than five hundred yards from the engine room. Yet an impact like that could have caused catastrophic structural damage throughout the ship. The surest way to see the damage would be to view it firsthand, but the quickest assessment would come from their pilot and his instruments.

"Get out," Powell continued, "get away before the *Marion* breaks up, down to the surface and—"

"And what?" Hoop snapped without turning around. "Survive on sand for the two years it'll take a rescue mission to reach us? *If* the company even decides a rescue is feasible," he added. "Now *shut it!*"

"Okay," Lachance said. He rested his hands on the flight stick, and Hoop could almost feel him holding his breath. Hoop had always been amazed that such a huge vessel could be controlled via this one small control.

Lachance called it The Jesus Stick.

"Okay," the pilot said again. "Looks like the *Delilah* took out the port arm of the docking level, Bays One and Two. Three might be damaged, can't tell, sensors there are screwed. Four seems to be untouched. Atmosphere is venting from levels three, four, and five. All bulkhead doors have closed, but some secondary safety seals have malfunctioned and are still leaking."

"So the rest of the *Marion* is airtight for now?" Hoop asked.

"For now, yes." Lachance pointed at a schematic of the ship on one of his screens. "There's still stuff going on at the crash site, though. I can't see what, but I suspect there's lots of debris moving around down there. Any part of that could do more damage to the ship. Rad levels seem constant, so I don't think the *Delilah*'s fuel cell was compromised. But if its containment core is floating around down there…" He trailed off.

"So what's the *good* news?" Sneddon asked.

"That *was* the good news," Lachance said. "*Marion*'s lost two of her lateral dampers, three out of seven starboard sub-thrusters are out of action. And there's this." He pointed at another screen where lines danced and crossed.

"Orbital map?" Hoop asked.

"Right. We've been nudged out of orbit. And with those dampers and subs wasted, there's no way to fix it."

"How long?" Powell asked.

Lachance shrugged his muscular shoulders.

"Not quick. I'll have to run some calculations."

"But we're all right for now?" Hoop asked. "The next minute, the next hour?"

"As far as I can see, yes."

Hoop nodded and turned to the others. They were staring at him, and he was sure he returned their fear and shock. But he had to get a grip, and keep it. Move past this initial panic, shift into post-crash mode as quickly as he could.

"Kasyanov and Garcia?" he asked, looking at Baxter.

Baxter nodded and hit AllShip on the intercom.

"Kasyanov? Garcia?"

Nothing.

"Maybe the med bay vented," Powell said. "It's forward from here, not far above the docking bays."

"Try on their personal comms," Hoop said.

Baxter tapped keyboards and donned his headpiece again.

"Kasyanov, Garcia, you there?" He winced, then threw a switch that put what he heard on loudspeaker. There was a whine, interrupted by staccato ragged thudding.

"What the hell…?" they heard Kasyanov say, and everyone sighed with relief.

"You both okay?" Baxter asked.

"Fine. Trapped by… but okay. What happened?"

"*Delilah* hit us." Baxter glanced up at Hoop.

"Tell them to stay where they are for now," Hoop said. "Let's stabilize things before we start moving around anymore."

Baxter spoke again, and then just as Hoop thought of the second dropship, Sneddon asked, "What about the *Samson*?"

"Can you hail them?" Hoop asked.

Baxter tried several times, but was greeted only by static.

"Cameras," Sneddon said.

"I've got no contact with them at all."

"No, switch to the cameras in Bay Three," Sneddon replied. "If they're still coming in, and Jones sees the damage, he'll aim for there."

Baxter nodded, his hands drifting across the control panels.

A screen flickered into life. The picture jumped, but it showed a clear view out from the end of Bay Three's docking arm.

"Shit" Hoop muttered.

The *Samson* was less than a minute away.

"But those things…" Sneddon said.

I wish you were still here, Lucy, Hoop thought. But Lucy and Cornell had to be dead. He was in charge. And now, with the *Marion* fatally damaged, an even more pressing danger was manifesting.

"We've got to get down there," Hoop said. "Sneddon, Welford, with me. Let's suit up."

As Welford broke out the emergency space suits from units at the rear of the bridge, Hoop and Lachance exchanged glances. If anything happened to Hoop, Lachance was next in charge. But if it got to that stage, there'd be very little left for him to command.

"We'll stay in contact all the time," Hoop said.

"Great, that'll help." Lachance smiled and nodded.

As the three of them pulled on the atmosphere suits, the *Marion* shuddered one more time.

"*Samson* is docking," Baxter said.

"Keep everything locked," Hoop said. "*Everything*. Docking arm, airlock, inner vestibule."

"Tight as a shark's arse," Lachance said.

We should be assessing damage, Hoop thought. *Making sure the distress signal has transmitted, getting down to med bay, doing any emergency repairs that might give us more time.*

But the *Samson* held dangers that were still very much a threat.

That was priority one.

Though he was now in command, Hoop couldn't help viewing things through the eyes of chief engineer. Lights flickered on and off, indicating damaged ducting and cabling on several of the electrical loops. Suit sensors showed that atmosphere was relatively stable, though he had already told Sneddon and Welford that they were to keep their helmets locked on. Damage to the *Marion* might well be an ongoing process.

They eschewed the elevator to climb down two levels via the large central staircase. The ship still juddered, and now and then a deeper, heavier thud rattled in from somewhere far away. Hoop didn't have a clue what it might be. The huge engines were isolated for now, never in use while they were in orbit. The life support generators were situated far toward the rear of the ship, close to the recreation rooms. All he could think was that the superstructure had been weakened so much in the crash that damage was spreading. Cracks forming. Airtight compartments being compromised and venting explosively to space.

If that was the case, they needn't worry about their decaying orbit.

"*Samson*'s initiating the automatic docking sequence," Baxter said through their suits' comm link.

"Can you view on board?" Hoop asked.

"Negative. I'm still trying to get contact back online. *Samson* has gone quiet."

"Keep us informed," Hoop said. "We'll be there soon."

"What do we do when we get there?" Welford asked from behind him.

"Make sure everything's locked up tight," Sneddon said.

"Right," Hoop agreed. "Sneddon, did you recognize those things we saw on the *Delilah*?" He said no more, and his companions' breathing rattled in his headset.

"No," Sneddon said. Her voice was low, quiet. "I've never seen or heard of anything like them."

"It's like they were hatching from inside the miners' chests."

"I've read everything I can about alien life-forms," Sneddon said. "The first was discovered more than eighty years ago, and since then everything discovered through official missions has been reported, categorized wherever possible, captured, and analyzed. Nothing like this. Just… nothing. The closest analogy I can offer is a parasitic insect."

"So if they hatched from the miners, what laid the eggs?" Welford asked. But Sneddon didn't answer, and it was a question that didn't bear thinking about right then.

"Whatever it was, we can't let them on board," Hoop said, more determined than ever. "They're not that big—we lose one on the *Marion*, and we'll never find it again."

"Until it gets hungry," Welford said.

"Is that what they were doing?" Hoop asked. "Eating?"

"Not sure," Sneddon said.

They moved on silently, as if wrestling with thoughts about those strange, horrific alien creatures. Finally Hoop broke the silence.

"Well, Karen, if we get out of this, you'll have something to report," he said.

"I've already started making notes." Sneddon's voice sounded suddenly distant and strange, and Hoop thought there might be something wrong with his suit's intercom.

"You're just spooky," Welford said, and the science officer chuckled.

"Come on," Hoop said. "We're getting close to the docking level. Keep your eyes open." Another thud shook through the ship. If it really was an explosive decompression—one in a series—then keeping their eyes open would merely enable them to witness their doom as a bulkhead exploded, they were sucked out into space, and the force of the vented air shoved them away from the *Marion*.

He'd read about astronauts being blasted into space. Given a shove, they'd keep moving away from their ship, drifting until their air ran out and they suffocated. But worse were the cases of people who, for some reason—a badly connected tether, a stumble—drifted only slowly, so slowly, away from their craft, unable to return, dying while home was still within sight.

Sometimes a spacesuit's air could last for up to two days.

They reached the end of the entry corridor leading down into the docking level. A bulkhead door had closed, and Hoop took a moment to check sensors. The atmosphere beyond seemed normal, so he input the override code and the locking mechanism whispered open.

A soft hiss, and the door slid into the wall.

The left branch led to Bays One and Two, the right to Three and Four. Ten yards along the left corridor, Hoop saw the blood.

"Oh, shit," Welford said.

The wet splash on the wall spur beside the blast door was the size of a dinner plate. The blood had run, forming spidery lines toward the floor. It glistened, still wet.

"Let's check," Hoop said, but he was already quite certain what they would find. The door sensors had been damaged, but a quick look through the spy hole confirmed his suspicions. Beyond the door was vacuum. Wall paneling and systems ducting had been stripped away by the storm of air being sucked out. If the person who had left that blood spatter had been able to hang on until the blast doors automatically slammed shut...

But they were out there now, beyond the *Marion*, lost.

"One and Two definitely out of action," Hoop said. "Blast doors seem to be holding well. Powell, don't budge from that panel, and make sure all the doors behind us are locked up tight."

"You're sure?" Powell said in their headsets. "You'll be trapped down there."

"If compartments are still failing, it could fuck the whole ship," Hoop said. "Yeah, I'm sure."

He turned to the others. Sneddon was looking past him at the blood spatter, her eyes wide behind the suit glass.

"Hey," Hoop said.

"Yeah." She looked at him. Glanced away again. "I'm sorry, Hoop."

"We've all lost friends. Let's make sure we don't lose any more." They headed back along the opposite corridor, toward Bays Three and Four.

"*Samson* has docked," Baxter said through the comm.

"On automatic?"

"Affirmative." Most docking procedures were performed automatically, but Hoop knew that Vic Jones occasionally liked to fly manually. Not this time.

"Any contact?"

"Nothing. But I think I just saw a flicker on the screen. I'm working to get visual back, if nothing else."

"Keep me posted. We need to know what's going on inside that ship." Hoop led the way. The blast door leading to Bays One and Two was still open, and they moved quickly through toward the undamaged docking areas.

Another vibration rumbled through the ship, transmitted up through the floor. Hoop pressed his gloved hand hard against the wall, leaning in, trying to feel the echoes of the mysterious impact. But they had already faded.

"Lachance, any idea what's causing those impacts?"

"Negative. The ship seems steady."

"Compartments failing, you think?"

"I don't think so. If that was happening we'd be venting air to space, and that would act as thrust. I'd see movement in the *Marion*. As it is, her flight pattern seems to have stabilized into the slowly decaying orbit we talked about. We're no longer geo-stationary, but we're moving very slowly in comparison with the surface. Maybe ten miles per hour."

"Okay. Something else, then. Something loose."

"Take care down there," Lachance said. He wasn't usually one to offer platitudes.

They passed through two more bulkhead doors, checking the sensors both times to ensure that the compartments on the other side were still pressurized. As they neared bays Three and Four, Hoop knew they'd have a visual on the damage.

The docking bays were contained in two projections from the underside of the *Marion*. One and Two were contained in the port projection, Three and Four in the starboard. As they neared the corridor leading into bays Three and Four, there were viewing windows on both sides.

"Oh, hell," Hoop muttered. He was the first to see, and he heard shocked gasps from Sneddon and Welford.

The front third of the port projection, including the docking arms and parts of the airlock structures, had been swept away as if by a giant hand. Bay One was completely gone, torn aside to leave a ragged wound behind. Parts of Bay Two were still intact, including one long shred of the docking arm which was the source of the intermittent impacts—snagged on the end of the loose reach of torn metal and sparking cables was a chunk of the *Delilah*. The size of several people, weighing maybe ten tons, the unidentifiable mass of metal, paneling, and electrics bounced from the underside of the *Marion*, swept down, ricocheted from the ruined superstructure of Bay Two, then bounced back up again.

Each strike gave it the momentum to return. It moved slowly, but such was its weight that the impact when it came was still enough to send vibrations through the entire belly of the ship.

The *Delilah* had all but disintegrated when it hit. Detritus from the crash still drifted with the *Marion*, and in the distance, silhouetted against the planet's stormy surface, Hoop could see larger chunks slowly moving away from them.

"That's a person out there," Welford said quietly, pointing. Hoop saw the shape pressed against the remains of Bay Two, impaled on some of the torn metal superstructure. He couldn't tell the sex. The body was badly mutilated, naked, and most of its head was missing.

"I hope they all died quickly," Sneddon said.

"They were already dead!" Hoop snapped. He sighed, and raised a hand in apology. His heart was racing. Seventeen years in space and he'd never seen anything like this. People died all the time, of course, because space was such an inimical environment. Accidents were common, and it was the larger disasters that gained notoriety. The passenger ship *Archimedes*, struck by a hail of micro meteors on its way to Alpha Centurai, with the loss of seven hundred passengers and crew. The Colonial Marine base on a large moon in the Outer Rim, its environmental systems sabotaged, resulting in the loss of over a thousand personnel.

Even further back, in the fledgling days of space travel, the research station *Nephilim* orbiting Ganymede suffered stabilizer malfunction and spun down onto the moon's surface. That one was still taught to anyone planning a career in space exploration, because every one of the three hundred people on board had continued with their experiments, transmitting data and messages of hope until the very last moment. It had been a symbol of humankind's determination to edge out past the confines of their own planet, and eventually their own system.

In the scheme of things, this tragedy was small. But Hoop had known every one of those people on board the *Delilah*. And even though he couldn't identify the frozen, ruined body stuck against the wrecked docking bay structure, he knew that he had spoken, joked, and laughed with them.

"We'll have to cut that free," Welford said, and at first Hoop thought he was talking about the corpse. But the engineer was watching the slowly drifting mass of metal as it moved back toward the shattered docking bays.

"We've got to do that and a *lot* more," Hoop said. If they were to survive—if they got past this initial chaos, secured the *Samson*, figured out what the fuck was going on—he, Welford, and Powell needed to pull some miracles out of somewhere. "Gonna earn our pay now, guys."

"Hoop, the *Samson*," Baxter muttered in his ear.

"What is it?" They couldn't yet see the ship where it was now static on the other side of the starboard docking arm.

"I've got it... a picture, up on screen." His voice sounded hollow, empty.

"And?" Sneddon asked.

"And you don't want to open it up. Ever. Don't even go near it."

Hoop wished he could see, though part of him was glad that he couldn't.

"What's happening in there?" Sneddon asked.

"They've... they've *hatched*," Baxter said. "And they're just... waiting. Those things, just sort of crouched there beside the bodies."

"What about Jones and Sticky?"

"Sticky's dead. Jones isn't." That flat tone again, so that Hoop didn't really want to ask any more. But Sneddon did. Maybe it was her science officer's curiosity.

"What's happening to Jones?" she asked.

"Nothing. He's... I can see him, just at the bottom of the picture. He's just sitting there, seat turned around, back against the control panel. Shaking and crying."

They haven't killed him yet, Hoop thought.

"We have to seal this up," he said. "All the doors are locked down anyway, but we have to disable all of the manual controls."

"You think those things can open doors?" Welford asked.

"Hoop's right," Sneddon said. "We must assume the worst."

"Can't we just cut the *Samson* loose?"

Hoop had already thought of that. But despite the danger, they might still need the dropship. The *Marion*'s orbit was still decaying. There were escape pods, but their targeting was uncertain. If they used them, they'd end up scattered across the surface of the planet.

The *Samson* might be their only hope of survival.

"We do that and it might drift with us for days," Lachance said, his voice coming through a hail of static. "Impact the *Marion*, cause more damage. We're in bad enough shape as it is."

"Baxter, we're losing you," Hoop said.

"...damaged," Baxter said. "Lachance?"

"He's right," Lachance responded. "Indicators are flagging up more damage every minute that goes by. Comms, environmental, remote system. We need to start fixing things."

"Got to fix this first," Hoop said. "We go through the vestibule, into the docking arm for Bay Three, then into the airlock. Then from there we work back out, disabling manual controls and shutting everything down."

"We could purge the airlock, too," Welford said.

"Good idea. If anything does escape from the *Samson*, it won't be able to breathe."

"Who's to say that they breathe at all?" Sneddon said. "We don't know what they are, where they come from. Mammal, insectile, reptilian, something else. Don't know *anything*!" Her voice was tinged with panic.

"And it's going to stay that way," Hoop said. "First chance we get, we kill them. All of them."

He wanted support from someone, but no one replied. He expected disagreement from Sneddon—as science officer, she'd see past the chaos and death to what these creatures might mean for science. But she said nothing, just stared at him, her eyes bruised, cut nose swelling.

I really am in charge now, he thought. It weighed heavy.

"Right," he said. "Let's get to it."

They followed Hoop's plan.

In through the vestibule that served bays Three and Four, through the docking arm, then through the airlock to the outer hatch. Hoop and Welford went ahead, leaving Sneddon to close the doors behind them, and at the end of the docking arm the two men paused. Beyond the closed hatch lay a narrow gap, and then the *Samson*'s outer airlock door. There was a small viewing window in both hatch and door.

The inside of the *Samson*'s window was steamed up.

Hoop wondered whether the things knew they were there, so close. He thought of asking Baxter, but silence seemed wisest. Silence, and speed.

They quickly dismantled the hatch's locking mechanism and disabled it, disconnecting the power source. It would need to be repaired before the hatch could be opened again. *Much stronger than the bathroom door on the* Delilah. The thought didn't comfort Hoop as much as it should have.

They worked backward, and when they'd disabled the door mechanism between docking arm and vestibule, Welford purged the atmosphere. The doors creaked slightly under the altered pressures.

Outside the vestibule, Sneddon waited.

"Done?" she asked.

"Just this last door," Hoop said. Welford went to work.

Five minutes later they were making their way back toward the bridge. There were now four sealed and locked doors standing between the *Samson* and the *Marion*, as well as a vacuum in the airlock.

He should have felt safer.

"Baxter, you still got a feed from the *Samson*?" he asked.

"Yeah. Not much change, those things are just sitting there. One of them… it sort of stretched for a while, like shadows were growing out of it. Weird lighting in there, and the picture's not great, but it looked like it was shedding its skin."

Another voice muttered something that Hoop missed.

"What was that?" he said.

"I said it looks like it's *grown*," Powell said. "The one that shed its skin. It's bigger."

"What about Jones?" Hoop asked, deeply troubled. *Bigger?* Impossible in such a short time, surely.

"Still there," Baxter said. "I can only see his arm, shoulder, head. He's still shaking."

"Record the images," Sneddon said.

"For later viewing pleasure?" Lachance asked, but no one replied. No time for humor, even if it was tinged with sarcasm.

"We'll be back in a few minutes," Hoop said. "Lachance, get the computer to categorize damage. I'll prioritize when we get there, then we'll pull together a work schedule. Baxter, has a distress signal gone out?"

"Oh, yeah, that's the other fun bit," Baxter said. "Some of the wreckage must have fucked the antenna array. So the computer says the signal is transmitting, but I don't think it is."

"Right. Great. Fucking wonderful." Hoop shook his head. "Any meteors heading toward us? Black holes opening up? Anything else to worry about?"

"The bridge's coffee carafe was smashed," Powell said, his voice deep and deadly serious.

Hoop started laughing. By the time he got his hysteria under control, tears smeared the inside of his helmet's visor.

By the time they reached the bridge, Kasyanov and Garcia had made their way back from the medical bay. The few personnel left aboard the *Marion* were either dead or sporting minor injuries, so there was little for them to do down there.

"It was creepy, just the two of us," Garcia said. "So we shut everything down. Figured it would be safer up here, with everyone together."

Just how safe that might be, Lachance revealed to them all.

"The only blessing is that the *Delilah*'s fuel core wasn't compromised during the crash," he said.

"So where is it?" Hoop asked.

Lachance was still in his pilot's seat. "Out there somewhere," he said, "floating around." He waved his hand, a cigar clutched between two fingers. Hoop and most of the others hated the stink of the things. But with everything that had happened, it seemed almost comical to ask him to put it out.

"We saw plenty of wreckage close to the ship," Welford said. "Maybe it *was* compromised and it's just floating somewhere nearby, overheating and ready to blow."

"In which case, *c'est la vie*," Lachance said. "Unless you want to throw on a suit and take a space walk." Welford looked away, and Lachance smiled. "And anyway, we have more immediate concerns—things we *can* do something about."

"The *Samson*?" Powell asked.

Hoop looked at the screens. The interior of the dropship was unchanged: shadows. Shadows flickered, Jones shook. They all wanted to turn it off, but Hoop had insisted keeping it on. They needed to know.

Lachance shrugged.

"We have to consider that safe, for now. But the sensors have identified atmosphere leaks in five blast doors, which probably means another five we don't know about. Decks five and six have vented completely into space, and the damage will need to be isolated and repaired. The chunk of the *Delilah* that's caught onto the ruin of the docking bays needs freeing and sending on its way. Otherwise it'll cause more damage."

"And the *Marion*'s positioning?" Hoop asked.

"Decaying. I'm... not sure there's much we can do about it. The crash has damaged more of the ship than we can see. I suspect there's some severe structural trauma. And it appears as if both fuel cell coolant systems have been damaged."

"Oh, great," Powell said.

"How bad?" Hoop asked.

"That's something that needs checking manually," Lachance said. "But there's more. Heaven has been corrupted."

"What with?" Hoop asked. His heart sank. Heaven was their bio pod, a small but lush food-growing compound in the *Marion*'s nose section, where many of the miners and crew went for their green therapy. After years in space—and working down in the sterile, sand-blasted hell of LV178—the sight of a carrot head or a wall of green beans did more than any drug cocktail to alleviate depression.

"I'm not sure yet," Lachance said. "Jordan was the one who..."

Lucy loved her gardening, Hoop thought. They'd made love in Heaven once, down on the damp soil with only the fruit trees and vegetable patches bearing witness.

"We have dried foods," Hoop said. "Is the water storage undamaged?"

"As far as I can tell."

"Okay, then." He looked around at the remainder of *Marion*'s crew. They were all shocked by how quickly and badly everything had gone to shit. But they were also hard, adaptable people, used to living with constant dangers and ready to confront the impossible to survive. "Welford, Powell, get the full damage report from Lachance and prioritize. We'll need help. All of you can use spanners and push welding kit."

"But there's something else to do first," Baxter said.

"Yep. And that's down to me. I'll record the distress signal, then you do everything you can to make sure it's sent."

Looking across Baxter's control panel, Hoop's gaze rested on the screen that was still showing the *Samson*'s interior. Jones's shoulder and head was the only thing moving, shivering in the bottom left corner. Beyond lay the motionless shadows of dead people. Sitting beside them, those small, indistinct aliens.

"And I think you can turn that off," Hoop said. "For now."

3

RIPLEY

PROGRESS REPORT:
To: Weyland-Yutani Corporation, Science Division
(Ref: code 937)
Date (unspecified)
Transmission (pending)

Distress signal received. Sufficiently relevant to divert.
Expected travel time to LV178:
Current speed: 4,423 days.
Full speed: 77 days.
Fuel inventory: 92%
Initiating thrust.

She dreams of monsters.

Sharp, black, chitinous, sleek, vicious, hiding in shadows and pouncing, seeding themselves in people she loved—her ex-husband, her sweet daughter—and then bursting forth in showers of far too much blood. They expand too quickly, as if rapidly brought in close from distances she can barely comprehend. And as they are drawn nearer through the voids of deep space they are growing, growing— the size of a ship, a moon, a planet, and then larger still.

They will swallow the universe, and yet they will still leave her alive to witness its consumption.

She dreams of monsters, stalking the corridors of her mind and wiping faces from memory before she can even remember their names.

In between these dreams lies a simple void of shadows. But it offers no respite, because there is always a before to mourn, and an after to dread.

When she starts to wake at last, Ripley's nightmares scuttle back into the shadows and begin to fade away. But only partly. Even as light dawns across her dreams, the shadows remain.

Waiting.

"Dallas," Ripley said.

"What?"

She smacked her lips together, tried to cough past her dry throat, and realized that it couldn't be. Dallas was dead. The alien had taken him.

The face before her was thin, bearded, and troubled. Unknown.

He stared at her.

"Dallas, as in Texas?" he asked.

"Texas?" Her thoughts were a mess. A stew of random memories, some of which she recognized, some she did not. She struggled to pull them together, desperate for a clue as to who and where she was. She felt disassociated from her body. Floating impressions trying to find a home, her physical self a cold, loose thing over which she had no control.

Behind everything loomed a shadow... huge, insidious.

"Great," the man said. "Just fucking great."

"Huh?" Was she back on *Nostromo*? But then she remembered the blazing star that massive salvage ship had become. Rescue, then?

Someone had found her. The shuttle had been retrieved and boarded. She was saved.

She was Ellen Ripley, and soon she'd be reunited with—

Something moved across her stomach. A flood of images assaulted her, so vivid compared to those she'd had since waking that they startled her into movement and kicked her senses alive—

—*Kane thrashing, his chest ripping and bursting open, that thing emerging*—

—and she reached to her own chest, ready to feel the stretching skin and the agony of ribs rupturing outward.

"Hey, hey," the man said, reaching for her.

Don't you understand what's going to happen? She wanted to shout, but her voice was trapped, her mouth so dry that her tongue felt like a swollen, sand-coated slug. He held her shoulders and stroked her chin with both thumbs. It was such a gentle, intimate gesture that she paused in her writhing.

"You've got a cat," he said, smiling. The smile suited his face, yet it looked uncomfortable, as if he rarely used it.

"Jonesy," Ripley rasped painfully, and the cat crawled up from her stomach to her chest. It stood there, swaying slightly, then arched its back and clenched its claws. They scratched Ripley's skin through her thin vest and she winced, but it was a good feeling. A pain that told her she was still alive.

She reached for Jonesy, and as she stroked him a feeling of immense well-being came over her. She had risen up out of the shadows, and now that she was home—or near to home, if she had been recovered by a larger ship—then she would do her best to leave them behind. The terrible, mournful memories were already crowding in, but they were just that. Memories.

The future was a wide-open place.

"They found us," she whispered to the cat as he growled softly in his throat. Her arms barely felt like her own, but she could feel fur against her fingertips and palms. Jonesy stretched against her. She wondered if cats could have nightmares.

"We're safe now…"

She thought of Amanda, her daughter, and how pleased they would be to see each other. Had Ripley missed her eleventh birthday? She sincerely hoped not, because she hated breaking a promise.

Sitting up slowly, the man helping her, she groaned as her nerves came to life. It was the worst case of pins and needles ever, far worse than she'd ever had following any previous hypersleep. Upright, she sat as motionless as possible as the circulation returned, her singing nerve endings finally falling silent.

And then the man spoke.

"Actually… you're not really that safe, to be honest."

"What?"

"I mean, we're not a rescue ship. We thought *you* were the rescue ship when we first saw you on our scopes. Thought maybe you'd answered our distress signal. But…" He trailed off, and when Ripley looked up she saw two other figures behind him in the shuttle's confined interior. They stood back against the wall, warily eyeing her and the stasis pod.

"You're kidding me," one of them, a woman, said.

"Can it, Sneddon." The man held out his hand. "My name's Hoop. Can you stand?"

"Where am I?" Ripley asked.

"Nowhere you want to be, that's for sure," the man behind Hoop said. He was very tall, thin, gaunt. "Go back to sleep, Miss. Sweet dreams."

"And that's Powell," Hoop said. "Don't mind them. Let's get you to med bay. Garcia can clean you up and check you over. Looks like you need feeding, too."

Ripley frowned, and her mouth instantly grew dry again. Her stomach rumbled. She felt dizzy. She grabbed the side of the stasis pod, and as she slowly slung her leg over the rim and tried to stand, Hoop held her arm. His hand seems incredibly warm, wonderfully real. But his words hung with her.

Jonesy snuggled back down into the foot of the stasis pod, as if eager to find sleep again. *Maybe cats really do know everything*, she mused.

"Where…?" Ripley asked again, but then the shuttle began to spin, and as she fainted the shadows closed in once more.

Garcia was a small, attractive woman who had a habit of laughing softly after everything she said. But Ripley didn't think it was an endemic shyness. The ship's medic was nervous.

"You're on the *Marion*," she said. "Orbital mining freighter. We work for the Kelland Mining Company. They're owned by Prospectia, who are a sub-division of San Rei Corporation, who are—like pretty much everything—owned by Weyland-Yutani." She shrugged, chuckled. "Our ship's built for harvesting large core deposits, really—the holds are huge and there are four extendable towing decks stacked back beneath the engine room. But we mine trimonite. Hardest substance known to man. It's fifteen times harder than diamond, and extremely rare. We have little more than three tons of it on board."

"What's the problem with the ship?" Ripley asked. She was still tired, and feeling sick, but she had her wits about her again. And she knew something here was very wrong.

Garcia glanced aside, her laughter almost silent.

"Couple of mechanical issues." She reached for some more sterile gel and started rubbing it along Ripley's forearm.

"Are we heading home?"

"Home?" Garcia asked.

"The solar system. Earth."

The medic suddenly looked scared. She shook her head.

"Hoop said to treat you, that's all." She started working on Ripley again, chattering away to cover her nervousness, talking inconsequentialities, and Ripley let her. If Garcia could somehow make her stop feeling so shitty, it was a small price to pay.

Time to rest a little, perhaps, before she found out what the hell was going on.

"Saline drip," Garcia said, picking up a needle. "Old world medicine, but it'll aid rehydration and have you feeling much more energetic in half an hour. Small scratch." She slid the needle expertly into a vein on Ripley's arm and taped it in place. "I'd recommend small amounts of liquid food to begin with—your stomach hasn't dealt with food for so long, and its lining has become quite sensitive."

"So long?" Ripley asked.

A pause, a small laugh.

"Soup. Lachance makes a good soup, for such a cynical bastard. He's in the galley now." She went to a cupboard and brought back a white bag. "We have some clothes for you. I had to dispose of your underwear, I'm afraid."

Ripley lifted the sheet covering her and realized she was naked. On purpose? Maybe they didn't want her just getting up and running around.

"Thanks," she said. "I'll dress now."

"Not yet," Garcia said, dropping the bag and shoving it beneath the bed with her foot. "More tests. I'm still checking your liver and kidney functions. Your pulse seems fine but your lung capacity appears to be reduced, probably due to holding a sleep pattern for so…" She turned away again to a medicine table. "I have some pills and medicines for you to take."

"What for?"

"To make you better."

"I'm not ill." Ripley looked past Garcia and around the med bay. It was small, only six beds, and some of it looked basic. But there were also several hi-tech pieces of equipment that she didn't recognize, including one sizeable medical pod in the center of the room bearing a familiar name badge on the side.

A cold hand closed around Ripley's heart.

I was expendable, she thought. She felt a fierce pride, and an anger, at being the only survivor.

"You didn't say you were actually a Weyland-Yutani vessel."

"What?" She followed Ripley's gaze. "Oh, no, we're not. Not officially. I told you, our company is Kelland Mining, an offshoot of San Rei. But Weyland-Yutani makes a lot of equipment used in deep space exploration. Difficult to find a ship without something of theirs on it. And to be honest, their med pods are just about the best I've ever seen. They can do amazing stuff, we once had a miner with—"

"They're a big company?"

"The biggest," Garcia said. "They practically *own* space. The parent company owns countless others, and San Rei was bought up by them… don't know, maybe twelve years ago? I was working at Kelland's Io headquarters then, hadn't gone out on any flights. It didn't change much, but it did open our eyes to all the diverse missions that were being launched." She chattered on as she prepared medicines, counted out pills, and Ripley let her.

"They're investing in terraforming companies now, you know? They set up massive atmosphere processing plants on suitable planets, do something to the air—clean it, treat it, I don't know, I'm a medic—and it takes decades. Then there's materials acquisition, prospecting, mining. I've heard they've built massive ships, miles long, that catch and tow small asteroids. Loads of research stations, too. Medical, scientific, military. Weyland-Yutani have their fingers in lots of pies."

Maybe times haven't changed so much, Ripley thought, and it was the measure of "times" that was bothering her. She sat up and slipped one leg out of bed, pushing Garcia aside.

"I feel fine," she insisted. The sheet dropped from her and Garcia looked away, embarrassed. Ripley used the advantage and stood, reaching down for the bag of clothes.

"Oh..." A voice said. She looked up. Hoop stood at the entrance to the medical bay, staring at her nakedness for just a few seconds too long before looking away. "Shit, sorry, I thought you were—"

"Safe in bed where you want me?" Ripley said. "Asking no questions?"

"Please," Hoop said without turning. He didn't elaborate, but Ripley sat back down. In truth, she did so before she fell down, because she still felt like crap. She propped up the pillow and tucked the sheet beneath her arms.

"You're safe to look now," she said.

Hoop smiled and came to sit on the foot of her bed.

"How are you feeling?"

"Tell me what's going on, and I'll decide."

Hoop glanced at Garcia, who nodded.

"Yeah, she's fine," the medic acknowledged.

"See?" Ripley said. *Fine,* apart from the sick feeling of dread in her stomach.

"Okay," Hoop said. "So, here it is. You've hardly been rescued. We spotted your shuttle on our scanners just over fifteen hours ago. You were on a controlled approach."

"Controlled by whom?"

Hoop shrugged.

"You drifted in, circled the *Marion* once, then docked at the one docking arm we have left." Something passed across his face then.

That's something else to ask about, Ripley thought, *if he doesn't volunteer it. The docking arm.*

"The shuttle has proximity protocols," she said.

"Auto docking?"

"If it's programed to do so."

"Okay, well, that's academic now. Our situation—and now yours—is… pretty grim." He paused, as if to gather his thoughts. "We suffered a collision eleven weeks ago. Lost a lot of our people. It's knocked us out of geostationary orbit, and we're now in a decaying pattern. We figure less than fifteen days before we start burning up in the atmosphere."

"Atmosphere of what?"

"LV178. A rock."

"The planet you're mining for trimonite," Ripley said, and she was amused at the look Hoop threw Garcia. "It's okay, she didn't tell me anything else. Like, anything important."

Hoop held out his hands.

"That's it. Our antenna array was damaged, so we couldn't send any long-distance distress signals. But after the collision we sent a call for help on a high frequency transmitter, and it's still being transmitted on a loop. Hoping it would be picked up by someone within rescue distance." He frowned. "You didn't hear it?"

"Sorry," she replied. "I was taking a nap."

"Of course." Hoop looked away, stroking his hands together. Two other people entered med bay, both of them ragged, unkempt. She recognized Kasyanov, the dark-skinned ship's doctor who had given her the initial examination. But the man she didn't know. Heavily built, a sad, saggy face—his name tag said Baxter. He sat on another bed and stared at her.

"Hi," she said. He only nodded.

"So what happened to you?" Hoop asked.

Ripley closed her eyes and a rush of memories flooded in—the planet, Kane, the alien's birth, its rapid growth, and then the terror and loss on the *Nostromo* before her escape in the shuttle. That final confrontation with the devil. The memories shocked her with their violence, their immediacy. It was as if the past was more real than the present.

"I was on a towing vessel," she said. "Crew died in an accident, the ship's core went into meltdown. I'm the only one who got away."

"*Nostromo*," Hoop said.

"How do you know that?"

"I accessed the shuttle's computer. I remember reading about your ship, actually, when I was a kid. It's gone down in the 'lost without trace' files."

Ripley blinked.

"How long was I out there?" But she already knew the answer was going to be difficult. She'd seen that in Garcia's reaction, and saw it again now in Hoop.

"Thirty-seven years."

Ripley looked down at her hands, the needles in her forearms.

I haven't aged a day, she thought. And then she pictured Amanda, her sweet daughter who'd hated the idea that she was going away, even for seventeen months. *It'll make things so easy for us when I get back*, Ripley had told her, hugging her tight. *Here, look*. She'd pointed at Amanda's computer screen and scrolled through a calendar there. *Your eleventh birthday. I'll be back for that, and I'll buy you the best present ever.*

"Going to tell her about *Samson*?" Baxter said.

Ripley looked around the room.

"Who's Samson?"

No one replied.

Baxter shrugged and walked across to her bed, laying a tablet computer on the sheet.

"Fine," he said. "Easier to show her, anyway." He tapped an icon. "The *Samson* is locked into our other surviving docking arm. Has been for seventy-seven days. It's sealed. These things are inside, and they're also the reason we're fucked."

He swiped the screen.

At that moment, Ripley doubted everything. The fact that she was awake. Her being there, the feel of sheets against her skin, and the sharp prick of needles in her arms. She doubted the idea that she had survived at all, and hoped that this was simply her dying nightmare.

"Oh, no," she breathed, and the atmosphere in the room changed instantly.

She started to shake. When she blinked her dreams were close again, the shadowy monsters the size of the stars. *So was it just a dream?* she wondered. *A nightmare?* She looked around at these people she did not know, and as panic bit in she wondered where they could have come from.

"No," she said, her dry throat burning. "Not here!"

Kasyanov shouted something, Garcia held her down, and another sharp pain bit into the back of her hand.

But even as everything faded away, there was no peace to be found.

"She knew what they were," Hoop said.

They were back on the bridge. Kasyanov and Garcia had remained in med bay to keep Ripley under observation, with orders to call him back down the moment she stirred. He wanted to be there for her. Such an ordeal she'd suffered, and now she'd woken into something worse.

Besides that, she might be able to help.

"Maybe she'll know how to kill them," Baxter said.

"Maybe," Hoop said. "Maybe not. At the very least, she recognized them from that." He nodded at the monitor. It held the final image they'd gleaned from the *Samson*'s internal camera. Then they'd lost contact, thirty days ago.

Jones had been long-dead by then. The things had dragged him back into the passenger hold and killed him. They'd grown into dark, shadowy shapes that none of them could quite make out. The size of a person, maybe even larger, the four shapes remained all but motionless. It made them even more difficult to see on the badly lit image.

Baxter scrolled back through the views of Bay Three—images they'd all come to know so well. The trio of cameras Welford and Powell had set up showed the same as ever—no movement, no sign of disturbance. The doors remained locked and solid. Microphones picked up no noise. They'd lost view of the inside of *Samson*, but at least they could still keep watch.

And if those things did smash through the doors, and burst out of the docking bay? They had a plan. But none of them had much faith in it.

"I'll go and see how Powell and Welford are getting on," Hoop said. "Shout if there's anything from med bay."

"Why do you think she came here?" Baxter said.

"I'm not sure she knows." Hoop picked up the plasma torch he'd taken to carrying, slung it over his shoulder, and left the bridge.

The torch was a small, handheld version, used in the mines for melting and hardening sand deposits. The biggest ones they had down there ran on rails, and were used for forming the solid walls of new mine shafts—blast the sand, melt it, and it hardened again into ten-inch-thick slabs. The smaller torches could be wielded by a miner to fix breaches.

Or, Hoop thought, to drive away unwanted guests.

He didn't know if it would work, and he'd seen the effects when one had been discharged in the *Delilah*. But in the larger confines of *Marion*, if one of those things came at him, he'd be ready.

Sneddon was in the science lab. She spent a lot of time in there now, and sometimes when Hoop paid her a visit he felt as if he was intruding. She'd always been a quiet woman, and quietly attractive, and Hoop had often enjoyed talking to her about the scientific aspects of their work. She'd once worked for Weyland-Yutani on one of their research bases orbiting Proxima Centauri. Though she didn't work directly for them any more, the company still funded science officers on many ships, and for any sub-divisional company who wanted them. The funding was very generous, and it would often go a large way toward bankrolling a mission.

He liked Sneddon. He liked her dedication to her work, and her apparent love of it. *It's an endless, wonderful playground out there*, she'd said once when he asked her what she hoped to find. *Anything is possible.*

Now Sneddon's childlike imagination had taken a hit.

At the same time, Hoop's childhood dreams had found reality.

When he reached the lab, Sneddon was sitting on a stool at the large central island. There were a couple of tablet computers in front of her, and a steaming mug of coffee. She held her head in her hands, elbows resting on the counter top.

"Hey," Hoop said.

She looked up, startled.

"Oh. Didn't hear you."

"Everything cool?"

Sneddon smiled softly. "Despite the fact that we're slowly spiraling to our deaths, set to crash on a lifeless sand-hell of a planet? Yes, everything's cool."

He smiled wryly.

"So what do you think about Ripley?"

"It's obvious she's seen these things before," Sneddon replied, a frown wrinkling her forehead. "Where, how, when, why, I haven't got the faintest clue. But I'd like to talk to her."

"If you think it'll help."

"Help?" Sneddon asked. She looked confused.

"You know what I mean," Hoop said. He laid the plasma torch gently on the bench.

"Well, I've been thinking about that," she said, smiling. "I know you're in charge, and I'm pretty sure I know what you've been thinking these past few days."

"Do you, now?" Hoop asked, amused. He liked that she smiled. There were far too few smiles nowadays.

"Escape pods," Sneddon said. "Maybe try to regulate their nav computers, land within walking distance of each other and the mine."

Hoop drummed his fingers on the bench.

"Reach there together, there'll be enough food and supplies down there for a couple of years."

"And those things, too."

"Forewarned is forearmed," Hoop said.

"With that?" Sneddon said, nudging the plasma torch. Her bitter laugh wiped the smile from her face.

"There might not be any more things down there at all. They might have all come up on the *Delilah*."

"Or there might be a dozen, or more." Sneddon stood and started pacing. "Think about it. They were hatching from the miners. We saw that. Just... breaking out of them. Implanted by those things attached to their faces, perhaps. I don't know. But if that is the case, we have to assume that anyone left behind was infected."

"Sixteen on the *Delilah*. Six on the *Samson*."

Sneddon nodded.

"So eighteen left in the mine," Hoop said.

"I'd rather go down on the *Marion*," Sneddon said, "if it came to that. But now it doesn't have to."

"You know something I don't?"

"No, but maybe I'm thinking about things in a different way."

Hoop frowned, held out his hands.

"And?"

"Her shuttle. It's a deep space shuttle! Used for short-distance transfers of personnel, or as a long-term lifeboat."

"And one stasis pod for nine of us."

"Doesn't matter," Sneddon said. "Look." She slid one of the tablets across to Hoop. At first he didn't really understand what he was seeing. It was an old, old image of a lifeboat. Lost at sea back on Earth, crammed with survivors, a sail rigged from shirts and broken oars, wretched people hanging over the side, or eating fish, or squeezing drinking water from hastily rigged moisture catchers.

"Today, I'm stupid," Hoop said. "In charge, yes. But stupid. So just tell me."

"One stasis pod between the nine of us," Sneddon said. "But we pack the shuttle with as many supplies as we can. Program a course toward Earth, or at the very least the outer rim. Fire the engines until the fuel's out and we're traveling as fast as we can. A good proportion of light speed. Then… take turns in the stasis pod."

"Take turns?" he said. "She's been drifting out there for thirty-seven years!"

"Yeah, but something's very wrong with that. I haven't checked yet, but the shuttle computer must have malfunctioned."

"There was no indication of that when I checked its log."

"You didn't go deep enough, Hoop. The point is, we can *survive* like that. Six months at a time, one of us in stasis, eight others… surviving."

"Six months in a tightly confined space? That shuttle's designed for five people, max, for short trips. Eight of us? We'll end up killing each other." He shook his head. "And how long do you figure it'll take?"

Sneddon raised an eyebrow.

"Well… years."

"Years?"

"Maybe three until we reach the outer rim, and then—"

"It's impossible!" he said.

Sneddon tapped the tablet's screen again, and Hoop looked. She'd certainly done her homework. Examples manifested and faded on the screen—lifeboats at sea, strandings on damaged orbitals, miraculous survivals dotting the history of space disasters. None of the timescales were quite what Sneddon was describing, but each story testified to the will of desperate people to survive, whatever the situation.

However hopeless.

"We'd need to check the shuttle's systems," he said. "Fuel cell, life support."

"And you're chief engineer, aren't you?"

Hoop laughed. "You're serious about this."

"Yes."

He stared at her for a while, trying to deny the shred of hope she'd planted in him. He couldn't afford to grab hold of it.

"Rescue isn't coming, Hoop," she said. "Not in time."

"Yeah," he said. "I know."

"So you'll—"

"Hoop!" Kasyanov's voice cut in over the intercom. "Ripley's stirring. I could sedate her again, but I really don't want to pump her full of any more drugs."

Hoop leapt to the wall and hit the intercom button.

"No, don't. She's slept enough. I'll be right down." He smiled at Sneddon, and then nodded. "I'll speak to Ripley, get her access codes."

As he left the science lab and headed for med bay, the ship's corridors seemed lighter than they had in a long time.

4

9 3 7

Not only was she still light years from home, but she'd docked with a damaged ship in a decaying orbit around a hellhole of a planet, alongside a dropship full of the monsters that haunted her nightmares.

Ripley might have laughed at the irony.

She'd successfully shaken the idea that it was a dream, or a nightmare—it had taken time, and convincing herself hadn't been easy—but the explanation still eluded her.

How was this all possible?

Perhaps the answers were on her shuttle.

"Really, I'm ready to walk," she said. Kasyanov—a tall, fit woman who obviously looked after herself—shot her a disapproving look, but Ripley could see that the doctor held a grudging respect for her patient's stubbornness.

"You've barely walked for thirty-seven years," Kasyanov protested.

"Thanks for reminding me. But as far as my body's concerned, it was yesterday." She'd already stood from her bed and dressed while Kasyanov and Garcia were elsewhere, determined to prove herself to them. And she'd been pleased at how good she actually felt. The sedative was still wearing off, but beneath that she was starting to feel her old self again. Whatever Garcia had done for her—the saline drip, the other drugs—was working.

"Patients," Kasyanov said, rolling her eyes.

"Yeah, who'd be one, right?" Ripley stood from the bed, and as she was tying the boots that had been given to her, Hoop breezed into the bay.

"Oh, you're dressed." He feigned disappointment, then said, "You're looking good!"

Ripley looked up and raised an eyebrow. "I'm twice your age."

"I've had a few long trips myself, you know," he replied without missing a beat. "Maybe one day we can have a drink, compare sleeps?" He smiled as he spoke, but maybe he was a little bit serious, too.

Ripley laughed despite herself. Then she remembered. The image was never far away, but for a few seconds here and there she could forget. A burst of laughter, a smile, a friendly comment would hide the memory beneath the mundane.

"I'd like to take a look at the *Narcissus*," Hoop said.

"You and me both."

"You haven't spent long enough in it already?"

Ripley stood and stretched. She was tall, lithe, and she enjoyed the feel of her muscles finding their flexibility again. The aches and pains meant she was awake and mobile.

"I've got some questions for the computer," she said. "Like why the hell it brought me to this shit hole."

"Thanks," Hoop said.

"You're welcome."

Ripley saw the doctor and medic exchange glances, but couldn't quite read them. She hadn't yet worked out the dynamic there. Kasyanov, as the doctor, was clearly in charge of med bay. But she also appeared nervous, scared, and Garcia seemed to be the one most at ease.

"Come on," Hoop said. "I'll walk you to the docking bay."

They left med bay together, and Hoop remained silent. *Waiting for my questions*, Ripley thought. She had so many. But she was afraid that once she started asking, none of the answers could satisfy, and nothing he said would be good.

"You say you don't know why you docked with us?" Hoop asked finally.

"I was asleep when the shuttle docked, you know that." Something troubled Ripley, nudging at her consciousness like a memory trying to nose its way in. A suspicion. An explanation. But her mind still hadn't completely recovered from hypersleep, and she didn't think she'd like what it had to say. "What's that?" she asked, nodding at the heavy object draped over Hoop's shoulder. It looked like a stumpy, box-shaped gun.

"Plasma torch," he said. "In case they get free."

Ripley laughed. It burst from her in a rush, like she was vomiting disbelief, and she couldn't stop. Her eyes burned. Tears ran down her face. She thought of Hoop trying to scorch an alien with his box-gun, and the laughter turned hysterical. Between breaths it sounded like she was trying to scream, and when she felt Hoop's hands on her shoulders she lashed out at him, seeing only his shadow through tear-distorted eyes—long arms, spiky edges.

She saw an alien bearing down and clasping her to its chest, that long curved head raising, mouth sprouting the silvery, deadly teeth that would smash through her skull and free her at last from her nightmares.

"Ripley!" Hoop shouted.

She knew who he was, where she was, but the shakes had set in. Trying to believe they were physiological, she knew the truth. She was scared. Properly, completely fucking terrified.

"That?" she said, gasping and swiping at the plasma torch. "You really think...? Have you seen one of them, close up?"

"No," he said softly. "None of us have."

"No, of course not," Ripley said. "You're still alive." The hands squeezed harder and she leaned into him. To her own surprise, she welcomed his embrace, his smell, the feel of his rough beard against her neck and cheek. She took great comfort from the contact. It made her think of Dallas.

"But you have," he said.

Ripley remembered the time in the shuttle, moments after the *Nostromo* had bloomed into nuclear nothingness and she'd believed it was all over. The alien, slow and lazy for reasons she didn't understand, but for which she gave thanks. *Because it's just fed?* she'd wondered at the time, Parker and Lambert fresh in her mind. *Because it thinks it's safe?*

She nodded against his shoulder.

"Where?" he asked, quietly but with urgency. "When?"

"I can't answer that right now," she whispered. "I... I don't understand. But soon I will." She pulled back from him, wiped angrily at her eyes. It wasn't appearing weak in front of him that troubled her—it was feeling weak in *herself*. She'd seen that thing off, blasted it into space, and she should no longer be afraid. "The shuttle. There are answers there."

"Okay," Hoop said. He looked down at the plasma torch, went to shrug it off.

"No," Ripley said, pressing her hand over his on the torch's barrel. "It *might* help."

Hoop nodded, frowning. *He's seen some stuff himself*, she thought. Maybe once she'd found out exactly how and why she was here, the two of them could talk properly.

"Right," he said. "Besides, we're passing close to the docked dropship."

"But everything's secure," Ripley said. "Isn't it?"

"We're keeping a close eye on things," Hoop said, nodding. "The image we showed you is the last we've seen inside the *Samson*. But it's safe."

"Safe," Ripley said, trying the word. On this dying ship it seemed so out of place.

Hoop led the way, and at the end of a corridor they turned to go right. He nodded to the left, where a heavy bulkhead door had been welded shut with a dri-metal seal. "The *Delilah* crashed into the ship through there, taking out Bays One and Two. We were lucky the fuel cell didn't rupture, but we had to cut it loose afterward. It was snagged on the wrecked superstructure, wrapped up a load of other tattered ship parts. Me, Welford, and Powell went out there and spent three hours with cutting torches. Shoved it aside. When we came back inside we watched for an hour while it floated away."

"And this way?" Ripley asked, pointing right. They continued, and she noticed Hoop taking a tighter grip on the plasma torch.

"Bay Three's through there," he said, nodding toward a door. Its control panel had been removed and wires and connectors hung loose.

"What's with that?" Ripley asked.

"No way of opening it without fixing the controls."

"Or smashing the door down."

"That's six-inch triple-layered polymer-inlaid steel," Hoop said. "And there are three more doors and a vented airlock between here and the *Samson*."

Ripley only nodded. But the word "safe" still eluded her.

"Come on," Hoop said. "Your shuttle's through here."

Ripley was surprised at how comforted she felt, ducking through Bay Four's open airlock and entering the *Narcissus*. She had no good memories of the vessel—only of the alien, and her terror that it would take her, too. But Jonesy was there, snuggled up in the open stasis pod as if still in hypersleep. And there were memories of the *Nostromo* and her crew. Dead for almost four decades, now, but to Ripley it felt like yesterday.

Parker, slaughtered on the floor. Lambert, hanging where the alien had slung her after ripping a hole through her face. All that blood.

"You okay?" Hoop asked.

Ripley nodded. Then she moved through the cramped shuttle and sat in the pilot's seat. She was aware of Hoop walking, slowly, around the shuttle as she ran her fingers across the keyboard and initiated the computer. Mother was gone, but the *Narcissus*'s computers still had a similarly constructed interface, designed so that the user felt as if they were actually talking to a friend. With technologies that could make an android like Ash, it had always seemed strange to Ripley giving a faceless computer a human voice.

She entered her access code. *Morning, Narcissus*, she typed. The reply appeared onscreen.

`Good morning, Warrant Officer Ripley.`

Request reason for Narcissus's *change of course.*

`Information withheld.`

"Huh," Ripley said.

"Everything okay?" Hoop asked. He was examining the stasis

pod she'd spent so long in, stroking Jonesy who was slinking back and forth with his back arched, tail stretched. He might well have been the oldest cat in the galaxy.

"Sure," she replied.

Hoop nodded, glanced toward the computer screen, and then started looking around the rest of the shuttle's interior.

Request records of incoming signals received over the past one thousand days. Ripley expected a streaming list of information—space was filled with beamed communications, and most ship's computers logged and discarded them if they were not relevant.

`That information also withheld.`

Request replay of distress signal received from Deep Space Mining Orbital Marion.

`That information also withheld.`

"Fuck you very much," Ripley muttered as she typed, *Because of Special Order 937?*

`That reference does not compute.`

Emergency Command Override 100375.

`I'm afraid that Override code is no longer valid.`

Ripley frowned. Tapped her fingers beside the keyboard. Stared at the words on the screen. Even Mother had never communicated in such a conversational tone. And this was just the shuttle's computer. Weird.

Request data of timescales and travel distances since Nostromo's *detonation?*

`That data unavailable.`

Unavailable or withheld?

The computer did not reply.

Such evasiveness wasn't possible from this machine. Not on its own. It was a functional system, not an AI like Mother. And Mother was gone.

The only other person who'd had access to Mother was Dallas. Dallas and…

…and after Dallas had been taken, and she'd quizzed Mother herself, she remembered her shock at that other presence in the computer room.

Screw you, Ash, Ripley typed.

The cursor blinked.

But the computer didn't respond. Not even a "Does not compute."

Ripley gasped. She hit the shutdown, and the text on the screen faded to a soft, background glow. Yet still she felt as if she was being watched. The computer's arrogant silence seemed to ring through the interior of the shuttle, almost mocking.

"What was in your distress signal?" Ripley asked abruptly.

Hoop was rooting around in the rear of the shuttle, examining the space suits still hanging in the locker back there.

"Huh?"

"The distress signal you sent after the crash!" Ripley said. "Did you mention those things? The creatures? Did you say what they were like, what they did?"

"I… Yeah, I think so."

"You *think* so?"

"It was more than ten weeks ago, Ripley. I recorded it hours after I'd seen lots of friends die, and witnessed what happened—"

"I need to hear it."

"What's wrong?"

She stood and backed away from the interface. It was stupid— there was no camera there—but she felt observed. She took off her jacket and dropped it across the screen.

"The alien on my ship wasn't an accident," she said. "And I don't think it's an accident that I've come here, either. But I need to know. I need to hear the signal."

Hoop nodded and came toward her.

"I can patch in from here," he said, nodding down at where her jacket covered the keyboard.

"You can?"

"I'm chief engineer on this jaunt, and that covers all the infotech systems, too."

Ripley stepped aside and watched as Hoop moved the jacket, sat, and worked at the interface. The words she saw on the screen—the interaction—seemed innocent enough.

Hoop chuckled.

"What is it?"

"These systems. Pretty old. I had more computing power than this to play VR games, when I was a kid."

"You don't see anything odd with the computer?"

"Odd?" He didn't look up, and Ripley didn't elaborate. "Here we are," he said. "I've patched into *Marion*'s computer, and here's the message. It's on a loop." He scanned the control panel, and Ripley leaned forward to switch to loudspeaker.

Hoop's voice came through. There was an edgy tone to it—the fear was palpable.

"...decaying orbit. Second dropship *Samson* is docked and isolated, those things in there hopefully contained. They... laid infants or eggs inside the miners, burst from their chests. We are not contaminated, repeat, *not* contaminated. Estimate ninety days until we hit LV178's atmosphere. All channels open, please respond. Ends.

"This is DSMO *Marion*, of the Kelland Company, registration HGY-64678, requesting immediate aid. Crew and mining teams down to eight surviving members. Miners discovered something on the surface of LV178, attacked, dropship *Delilah* crashed the *Marion*. Many systems damaged, environment stable but we are now in a decaying orbit. Second dropship *Samson* is docked and isolated..."

Hoop tapped the keyboard to turn off the replay, then glanced back at Ripley.

"Ash," she whispered.

"What's Ash?"

"Android. Weyland-Yutani. He was tasked with finding any alien life forms that might have been of interest to the company. His orders... crew expendable. My crew. Me." She stared at the computer again until Hoop dropped her jacket back across it. "He's gone, but he must have transferred part of his AI programing to the *Narcissus*.

He's here. He's in *here* now, and he brought me to you because of those aliens."

"I'm not sure it's possible that an AI could—"

"I should have been home," Ripley said, thinking of Amanda and her sad, wet eyes when she'd watched her mother leave. She hated herself for that. Even though she should have been home with her daughter for her eleventh birthday, and nothing that had happened was her fault, Ripley hated herself. "I should have never left."

"Well, maybe some good can come of this," Hoop said.

"Good?" Ripley said.

"Your shuttle. Sneddon and I think we can get away on it, all of us. And that'll leave the *Marion* and those fuckers on the *Samson* to burn up in the planet's atmosphere."

Ripley knew that for any extended voyage the shuttle was only suitable for one, with only a single stasis pod. But she didn't care. Any way to distance herself from those aliens—any way to deny Ash from fulfilling his Special Order—was good for her.

"Maybe," she said. "I'll run a systems check."

"You're not alone anymore, Ripley," Hoop said.

She blinked quickly, and nodded her thanks. Somehow, he seemed to know just what to say.

"You'll stay here with me for a while?"

Hoop feigned surprise.

"Do you have coffee?"

"No."

"Then my time here is limited." He stood away from the control desk and started looking around the shuttle again. It was cramped, confined—and way, way too small.

Ignoring the computer, Ripley started manual processing of systems information.

It only took three minutes to realize how screwed they were.

5

NARCISSUS

Hoop had worked with androids before. In the deep asteroid mines of Wilson's Scarps, they were often the first ones down and the last ones back. They'd been perfectly reasonable, amenable, quiet, honest, and strong. Safe. He couldn't say he'd liked them, exactly, but they'd never been dangerous or intimidating. Never scheming.

Occasionally he'd heard of malfunctions in some of the earlier military-grade androids, and there were unconfirmed reports—little more than rumors, really—that the military had suffered human losses as a result. But they were a different breed of android, designed for strength but with a built-in expiration date. They were easy to spot. Their designers hadn't been too concerned with aesthetics.

That must have been the case on *Nostromo*. And now, assuming Ripley was right, the AI had somehow followed her, and was still using her for its programed mission. As his team discussed their options, she looked wretched—taking in the conversation, looking at each crew member who expressed an opinion, and yet remaining silent. She smoked cigarette after cigarette, and drank coffee.

She must think she's still dreaming, he mused, *consumed by nightmares.* And every now and then she glanced across at him as if checking that he was on board with all of this.

Because it turned out that they were more royally screwed than any of them had thought.

The plan they were slowly forming—crazy as it was—seemed to be the only way out. It was a last chance, and they had no option but to grab it.

"You're sure about the timescales?" Powell asked. "Only a few days until we start skimming the atmosphere?"

"Sure as I can be," Lachance replied.

"I thought we had a couple of *weeks* left," Kasyanov said, voice raised as fear clasped her.

"Sorry. I lost my crystal ball in the collision." Lachance rested in the pilot's chair, turned around to face them all. The rest sat or stood around the bridge, in seats or leaning against equipment terminals. It was the first time Ripley had been with all eight of them together, but Hoop couldn't sense any nervousness in her. If anything, she was too distracted for that.

"And there's nothing you guys can do?" Kasyanov said, looking at Powell, Welford, and then Hoop. He didn't like the accusation in her eyes, as if they hadn't done their best. "I mean, you're engineers."

"Kasyanov, I think I've made it pretty clear," Lachance said. "Our attitude control is damaged beyond repair, retro capability is down to thirty percent. Several containment bulkheads are cracked, and there's a good chance if we initiate thrust we'll just flash-fry ourselves with radiation." He paused briefly.

"We *do* still have coffee, though. That's one positive."

"How do we know all that's true?" Kasyanov asked. "It's getting desperate here. We should go outside, look again at all the damage."

"You know because I'm the best pilot who's ever worked for Kelland," Lachance said. "And the fact that Hoop, Welford, and Powell have kept us all alive for this long is a fucking miracle. Fixing the hull breaches, repressurizing the vented sections of the ship. *That's* why you know it's true."

Kasyanov started to say some more, but Garcia put a hand on her arm. Hoop didn't think she even squeezed—just the contact was enough to silence the doctor.

"However much we wish it wasn't true, it is," Hoop said. "And we've got no more time to waste. We think we have a plan, but it's not going to be easy."

"Who's 'we?'" Kasyanov asked.

"Me, Sneddon, Ripley."

"Ripley? The stranger who just woke up from half-a-century of snoozing? What's *she* got to do with this?"

Ripley glanced across at Kasyanov, then away again, looking down at the coffee cup in her hand. Hoop waited for her to speak, but she remained silent.

"This isn't a conspiracy, Kasyanov," he said. "Hear us out."

The doctor drew in a breath and seemed to puff herself up, ready to say something else, challenge him some more. But then she nodded.

"I'm sorry, Hoop... everyone. Just so strung out." She and Ripley exchanged weak smiles.

"We all are," Hoop said. "It's been over seventy days, waiting for some sign that our signal's been picked up, acknowledged and relayed onward, and that someone's coming for us. Maybe the frequency's been frazzled, and we're just coming through as background fuzz. Or maybe someone's heard us, but we're too far out, and it's too expensive to mount a rescue."

"Or there's just not the time," Baxter said. "Changing course, plotting a route, estimating the fuel requirements. Anyone who did catch the signal would have a lot to do before they even got here."

"Right," Hoop said. "So we're running out of time, and now we've got to help ourselves. More than we have been. More than just patching up problems while we wait."

"Escape pods?" Powell asked.

"We've talked about that," Lachance said, waving the suggestion aside.

"Yeah," Sneddon said. "That's just a slow death. We're in a drifting orbit now, and even if we could rig a way to steer the pods more accurately, to land as close to the mine as possible, we could still go down miles away. We'd be scattered, alone, and vulnerable."

"The *Samson*, then." Baxter had mentioned this before, putting it forward as their only real option, if the individual escape pods wouldn't work. They could open the doors, kill the aliens, then take the *Samson* away from LV178.

But it was a dropship, built for short-distance transport to and from the surface of a planet. It wasn't equipped for deep space travel. No stasis pods, no recycling environmental systems. It was a no-go.

"We'd starve to death, suffocate, or end up murdering each other," Lachance said. He looked at Baxter, wearing a deadpan face. "I'd kill you first, you know."

"You'd try," Baxter muttered.

"Yeah, sure, the *Samson*," Powell said. "And who's going to stand by those doors when we open them? We can't see what those things are doing inside."

"We can't escape on the *Samson*," Hoop said. "But that doesn't mean we don't need it. Ripley?" She looked uncertain, but she stood, stubbed out her cigarette, and lit another.

"Hoop and Sneddon came up with this," she said, taking the first drag. "It might work. The *Narcissus* is a lifeboat as well as a deep space shuttle. Environmental systems, carbon dioxide recycling capability."

"But for nine of us?" Welford asked.

"We take turns in the stasis pod," Ripley said. "But that's getting ahead of ourselves. There's another problem."

"Of course there is," Powell said. "Why should anything be easy?"

"What's the problem?" Lachance asked.

"The shuttle's fuel cell is degraded," Ripley said. "Less than ten percent charge left, which is nowhere near enough."

"Enough to get us away from the *Marion*, surely," Kasyanov said.

"I've run the figures," Hoop said. "Lachance, Sneddon, I'd like you both to check them. But we need enough power to get the overloaded shuttle away from *Marion*, out of orbit, and accelerated to a speed that'll get us back within the outer rim before we've died of old age. I figure we need eighty percent of a full charge, at least. Any more than that just means we can accelerate to a faster speed, get there quicker."

Welford snorted, but then Ripley spoke again.

"It'll be real-time," she said. "Even sharing the stasis pod means there'll be eight people at a time just… sitting around. Growing older."

"We estimate eighty percent cell charge will get us past the outer rim within six years," Hoop said. "Give or take."

There was a stunned silence.

"So I *do* get to murder Baxter," Lachance said.

"Fucking hell," Powell said.

"Yeah," Kasyanov agreed. Her voice shook.

"Welford's feet smell," Garcia said. "Lachance farts. Hell, we won't survive a year."

No one laughed.

"Is there a precedent?" Lachance asked.

"We'd be setting it," Sneddon said.

The bridge was silent for a time while they all thought about what it really meant.

"You said we still need the *Samson*," Lachance said. "For its fuel cells?"

Hoop shook his head, and looked to Ripley again.

"Won't power my shuttle," she said. "Completely different system design. The *Marion*'s might, but Hoop tells me they're damaged and dangerous. He says there are more down in the mine, though—spares, stored remotely, just in case. So we have to take the *Samson* down to the surface. We bring a couple back up, adapt one, and fix it into the *Narcissus*. Load the shuttle up with as many supplies as we can, then blast off before your ship starts to burn."

More silence.

Ripley smiled. "Then all we need is a deck of cards."

"Piece o' cake," Lachance said.

"Yeah," Powell said, voice quavering with panic, "no problem. Easy!"

"Well…" Hoop said. "There's more."

Powell muttered something, Kasyanov threw up her hands.

"What?" Lachance said. "Another problem? Don't tell me. The shuttle's made of cheese."

"It seems Ripley's been having some computer malfunctions," Hoop said. "Maybe it's best if I let her tell you about it."

Ripley raised her cup of cold coffee in a toast. He shrugged apologetically. *Sorry*, he mouthed. She gave him the finger.

He liked Ripley. She was strong, attractive, confident in the same self-deprecating way Lucy Jordan had been.

Damn it.

* * *

ALIEN

"Ash," Ripley said. "He was an android aboard my ship."

She told the entire story, and something about it felt so unreal. It wasn't the strangeness of the story itself—she'd witnessed everything, knew it all to be true. It was the idea that Ash had *followed* her. He'd expressed his sympathies, and Parker had burned off his face, but by then he must have already insinuated himself into the shuttle's computer, just in case things went wrong aboard *Nostromo*. How could he have been so prepared? What sort of paranoid programing had he been given?

She spoke about him now as if he could hear every word. She was only sorry that he couldn't feel shame.

"So as far as I can tell, he's the reason I'm here," she concluded. "And he's not going to be happy unless I bring one of those things back with me."

"That's just really fucking dandy," Powell said. "So we clear one ship of fucking great big rib-busting monsters so we can escape on another ship piloted by a psychotic AI. Wonderful. My life is complete."

"I don't think it's that much of a problem anymore," Ripley said. She lit another cigarette. The smoke burned her throat. They were harsh Russian cigarettes, brought along by Kasyanov. Of the *Marion*'s crew that survived, only the doctor smoked. "Because of Ash, I'm here instead of home. I haven't been able to access detailed flight logs yet, but… it could be he's just kept me floating around out here. Waiting for another sign that these aliens are still around."

"But why keep you alive, if that's the case?" Sneddon asked.

"Because he needs someone for the alien to impregnate. He's seen how violent the fully-grown creature is, there's no way he could get one back to Weyland-Yutani. Not on board the *Narcissus*." She exhaled smoke and waved it away. "Anyway, that's beside the point. Can't undo what that bastard has done. But back then he was mobile, tactile. Hell, we all thought he was human. He interfered in our decision-making, steered events toward his secret agenda. And when things got out of his control, he went on the rampage.

"Now… he's not really here anymore. He's just code. Ethereal." She blew smoke again, but this time didn't wave it away. "And we know where to find him."

"So we just shut down Ripley's shuttle's computer until we're ready to go," Hoop said. "Then when we're underway, and before we initiate main thrust, I'll do my best to purge Ash from the systems. Or at least to isolate him to certain drives."

"God knows you'll have plenty of time," Powell said.

"Right," Ripley said. "And there'll always be someone awake, to monitor any changes in the shuttle's programed flight. Incoming signals. Whatever."

"So Ash is just floundering," Sneddon said. "Following his programing, but without a plan."

Ripley shrugged. She wasn't sure. He'd been so deceitful, so scheming back on *Nostromo*, that she didn't want to underestimate him now. But whatever part of Ash still survived, he could no longer intrude in their actions. Not physically, at least.

Soon, she would return to the *Narcissus* to find out more.

"So that's the plan," Hoop said. "Lachance, I need you to plot the *Marion*'s trajectory around the planet; let us know when we'll be closest to the mine. But it's gotta be soon, like in the next couple of days. Powell, Welford, I need you to gather as much of the mining equipment as you can. We need plasma torches, sand picks, anything else you can find."

"There are the thumpers," Garcia said. "They use them to fire charges deep into loose sand."

Hoop nodded.

"Can we really use them in the *Samson*?" Baxter asked.

"We don't have to use the explosive charges," Welford said. "Substitute bolts, or something, and you have a pretty good projectile weapon."

Ripley was looking into her cup of cold coffee, listening to the discussion, trying to take it all in. But her mind was elsewhere. Somewhere dark, claustrophobic. Stalking the steam-filled corridors where lighting flashed, the countdown siren wailed, and the alien could have been waiting around any corner.

"How many are in there?" she asked. The conversation was too loud, so no one heard her. She tried again. "*Hey!*" That quieted them down. "How many are in the *Samson*?"

"We think four," Hoop said.

"Fully grown?"

He shrugged. Looked around.

"Last time we saw, they looked big," Baxter said. "Just shadows, really. They were still, hunkered down at the back of the passenger compartment."

"Maybe they were dead," Kasyanov said hopefully. Nobody responded to that. Their luck wasn't going that way.

"They have acid for blood," Ripley said.

"What?" Sneddon asked.

"Dallas—our captain—said it was molecular acid of some sort. It ate through two decks before its effect slowed down."

"Oh, man," Powell said, laughing in disbelief. "Do they fire lightning out of their asses, too? Do they cum nuclear jelly? What else, huh?"

"Ripley, that's…" Sneddon stopped, and shook her head. Ripley looked up in time to see her glance at the others, eyebrows raised.

"I'm not making this up," Ripley said.

"No one said you were," Hoop said.

"Hoop, come on!" Sneddon said. "Acid for blood?"

There was a long silence on the bridge. Ripley smoked the last of her cigarette and dropped the butt into her coffee mug. It sizzled out. She was feeling an increasingly urgent need to get back to the *Narcissus*, alone, find her own space. Talk with Ash. She wasn't sure it would solve anything, but it might make her sense of betrayal easier to bear.

She'd promised Amanda she'd be home.

Closing her eyes, she willed back the tears. She'd already cried too much. Now it was time to survive.

"If you want to use the *Samson*, best draw them out before you kill them," she said. "That's all I'm saying."

"We'll work on a plan," Hoop said. "In the meantime—"

"Good. I'm going back to my shuttle." Ripley stood, but the science officer blocked her path.

"Now wait," Sneddon said. She was six inches shorter than Ripley, but she stood her ground. Ripley respected that. "None of us knows you. You come here for whatever reason, start telling us these stories about rogue AIs and aliens with acid for blood. And now you want to go back to your shuttle?"

"Yeah, why?" Powell asked. "Hoop, we can't just let her wander round."

"What, you're afraid I'm going to damage your perfect little ship?" Ripley asked. "God knows, we wouldn't want to scratch the paint."

"Let's just chill," Hoop said. But Sneddon's blood was up.

"What are you going back for?" she demanded. "You've just come from there with Hoop."

"You're welcome to come," Ripley said. She was staring Sneddon down. She waited until the shorter woman averted her gaze, then smiled. "I'm just going to feed my cat."

As it turned out, Jonesy wasn't hungry. Ripley laid out some reconstituted chicken, and though he crept from the stasis pod and sniffed at it, he turned his nose up and slinked away. But he stayed in the shuttle.

Maybe he can smell them out there, Ripley thought. *Maybe he knows more than the rest of us.*

The acid-for-blood thing troubled her. What she'd witnessed had been just a drop, spilled from the thing hugging Kane's face when Ash and Dallas tried cutting it off. She didn't know whether the fully-grown alien carried the same blood, or whether wounding one would result in a similar effect. Really, she knew so little. But though the reality of her experience had been terrifying, the alien had taken on larger, darker connotations in her sleep.

Thirty-seven years of nightmares, she thought. *And now that I'm awake, the nightmare has woken with me.*

She moved around the cramped space, again wondering just how the hell nine people would survive in here. Even with one in the stasis pod, there'd barely be room for the rest to sit down. There was a small bathroom behind the equipment locker, so at least there'd be privacy for toilet and limited washing. But existing together here for more than a few days hardly bore thinking about.

For months? Years?

She finally found Jonesy again in the suit locker, snuggled down in one of the big EVA boots. He took some coaxing, but eventually he miaowed and climbed out, letting Ripley pick him up and hug him to her. He was her link to the past, and the only solid proof that any of it had actually happened. She didn't really require such proof—she was confident that she could distinguish reality from nightmare—but the cat was a comfort nonetheless.

"Come on then, you little bastard," she said. "You gonna help me?" She held the cat up and looked into his eyes. "So why didn't you spot anything wrong with that bastard Ash? Damn fine ship's cat *you* are."

She sat in the pilot's seat, Jonesy on her lap, and rested her fingers on the keyboard. She took a deep breath. Ash had tried to kill her, but he was just a machine. An AI, true. Created to think for himself, process data and make his own decisions, act on programed responses and write and install new programs based on experience—essentially learning. But a machine nevertheless. Designed, manufactured, given android life in the labs of Weyland-Yutani.

Suddenly Ripley felt a rush of hatred for the company. They had decided she and her crew were expendable, and four decades later they were still fucking with her life.

It was time for that to stop.

Hello Ash, she typed. The words appeared on the screen before her, flashing green, the cursor passing the time as a response was considered. She didn't actually expect one, assuming a resounding silence as the AI strived to hide its continued existence. Instead, the reply was almost instant.

`Hello Ripley.`

She sat back in her seat, stroking the cat. The sensation returned—the feeling of being watched. She didn't like it.

You brought us here in response to the Marion's *distress signal?*

`That's right.`

Crew still expendable in accordance with special order 937?

`You're the last of the Nostromo's crew.`

Answer the question, Ash.

```
Yes. Crew expendable.
```

"Nice," she breathed. Jonesy purred in her lap. *But I know where you are now, Ash. You can't control things anymore. You're without purpose.*

```
I did my best.
```

Ripley looked at those words and thought about what they meant. The *Nostromo*'s crew, brutally killed by the thing Ash had allowed on board. Her decades in hypersleep, away from her daughter and home.

Fuck you, Ash, she typed.

The cursor blinked back.

Ripley punched the computer off and then sat back in the chair. Jonesy stretched and allowed himself to be scratched.

6

FAMILY

The *Marion* drifted, Lachance computed, and he decided that four days after Ripley's arrival would be the optimum time to drop back down to the mine. It would entail a thousand-mile, three-hour drop, four hours at the mine retrieving the spare fuel cells, and then an hour's blast back into orbit. If all went well they'd be away from *Marion* for around eight hours. If all didn't go well…

Everyone knew what the results of that would be.

Hoop suggested that they open up the *Samson* a day before they were due to drop. That would give them time to tackle the creatures inside, clear out the ship, and prep it for travel. If there was damage, they could do their best to repair it.

No one mentioned the possibility that it might be damaged beyond their ability to repair. There were so many things that could go wrong that they didn't bear discussing, and as such the survivors lived in a miasma of false positivity. The only talk was good talk. Everyone kept bad thoughts to themselves.

Baxter was the only one who was openly pessimistic, but then they were used to that with him. Nothing new.

Hoop was becoming more and more impressed with Ripley. That first day she'd been woozy and uncertain, but she soon found her feet. She came across as strong, resilient, yet damaged—tortured by what she had experienced. She'd once mentioned her daughter, but never again. He could see the pain in her eyes, but also the hope that she would see her child again.

Hope in the face of hopelessness, he supposed, was what kept them all going.

And she was attractive. He couldn't get away from that. She looked to him first when they had group conversations, and he didn't think it was because he was ostensibly in command. Maybe it was because, having both lost their children, they had something in common.

Hoop often thought about his two sons, and how he and their mother had watched a marriage dissolve around them. Neither of them had been able to rescue it. His job was the prime cause, she'd told him. *It's dangerous*, she said. *You're away for a year at a time.* But he'd refused to accept all of the blame.

It's well-paid, had been his response. *One more long job, then we'll be able to buy our own business back on Earth, be self-sufficient.*

And so it had spiraled, until eventually he had retreated to the one thing he knew was utterly indifferent, not caring how and what he was.

Space.

I ran away. The thought dogged him constantly, and it was the last thing the woman he loved had said. *You're running away.*

Ripley's presence made him feel more guilty than before, because in his case it had been a willing decision. She should only have been away for eighteen months.

He and Ripley spent some more time in the *Narcissus*, talking about the journey they would undertake together, being positive, discussing how nine people could live in a shuttle designed for three or four, at most. For years. Perhaps many years.

All the time there was a quiet hysteria lurking behind everything they said, a shared understanding that this was a crazy, unworkable idea. But it was their *only* idea. Sometimes it felt cramped with just the two of them in the shuttle, although Hoop wondered whether that was just him.

They also discussed their families. Hesitatingly at first, but then with an increasing openness. They talked of guilt, and how incredible distances did nothing to dull the sense of loss. He didn't pity her, and he thought she was thankful for that. She gave him understanding, and he was grateful. They were both cursed by distance and time, and the staggering loneliness that both could instill in a person. They were getting to know each other. And while it was a good feeling, there was also something delicate about every connection made.

They were both tentative, guarded. Their situation meant that they could be ripped apart at any moment.

They also talked about Ash. Hoop was quite the computer expert, and he didn't mind saying it. But though he was relatively confident about being able to purge Ash's AI from the shuttle's computer— or at very least, compartmentalize it so that it could no longer exert any control—he and Ripley decided that he should wait until they were away from the *Marion* and headed home. They would need the computer untouched and undamaged in order to program their route, and it was possible—albeit remotely—that his efforts to remove Ash might corrupt a wider swathe of the systems.

Besides, the disembodied Ash could do them no harm.

Those three days passed quickly, and there were tensions in the group. There always had been, and those that were familiar Hoop cast to one side. The relationship between the doc and Garcia was weird—he thought they were probably lovers, as well as colleagues— but they were always efficient, and professional when it was needed. Powell complained. Sneddon was quiet and steadfast, a gentle bravery shining through. She would be a rock for them all.

The others bickered, though no more than usual. But it was Ripley's presence that caused the greatest waves.

"But I can't help being fascinated by them," Sneddon said. She was scrolling through stills from inside the *Samson* again, the tablet propped against her coffee mug. It had been almost three weeks since they'd last seen inside the dropship. None of them knew what to expect when they opened it up.

"They're monsters," Ripley said. She was leaning against a work counter. The science lab was small and compact, and with the three of them in there it was already growing warm. Hoop had suggested that they conserve power and turn off any unnecessary environmental systems.

"We're not catching them, Sneddon," Hoop said. "That door opens and we kill them."

"Oh, yeah, sure," Sneddon replied without looking up. "But have you considered just how?"

"Of course. The plasma torches, sand picks, and charge thumpers."

"Right," Sneddon said. "So torch them with plasma and their skin, or whatever they have, bursts open. Acid spills. Sand picks hack at them... open them up. Fire projectiles with the charge thumpers... more acid."

"What else do you suggest?" Ripley asked, an edge to her voice.

"I suggest that we come up with something else," Sneddon said. "Trap them somehow. Hold them until we can—"

"We need to kill them, or they'll kill *us*," Ripley said. "If they're anything like the one we had on *Nostromo* they'll be eight, nine feet tall, incredibly fast and strong, and utterly vicious. And you want to trap them? How? You got a box we can bait with some cheese?"

Sneddon sat back, looking calm and composed. She glanced at Ripley, then looked squarely at Hoop.

"Is she safe?" she asked.

"Safe as any of us are right now," Hoop said. He looked at Ripley, frowned, tried to warn her off. But he could see that her outburst was driven by fear, not anger. For a moment it seemed as if she was seeing something very far away, and he wondered yet again at the nightmares she must still suffer. She'd told him about each of her dead crewmates—some of them her friends, the captain her occasional lover.

"Cargo netting," Sneddon said.

Ripley coughed something between a laugh and a gasp.

"It's strong enough to pack tons of equipment in the holds," Sneddon went on. "Twisted steel core. It'll hold them long enough for us to decide what to do with them."

"How do you know it will work?" Ripley asked.

"How do you know it won't?" Sneddon countered. "At least this way we don't risk burning a hole right through the hull. If what you say about acid is true..."

"It's true," Ripley said. "What, you don't believe me now?"

Sneddon sighed, swinging back in her chair. "I think we just need to be—"

"Who appointed you science officer?" Ripley asked.

"The company. Kelland."

"Which is owned by Weyland-Yutani."

"Very distantly, yes," Sneddon replied. "So?"

"And you worked for Weyland-Yutani before that?"

"I served my apprenticeship with them, on Mars, yes."

"Ripley?" Hoop asked. She seemed to be losing control, panicking. He didn't like that. More than anything, it made his own subsumed panic start to simmer again. Without even realizing it, he thought perhaps he'd taken Ripley's strength to feed his own.

"Don't wrap me in your conspiracies," Sneddon said quietly.

"This isn't about gathering specimens," Ripley said. "It's about surviving!"

"I didn't say I wanted to gather anything."

"But you find them fascinating—you said so yourself."

"And you don't?" Sneddon asked. She slid the tablet across the bench, but Ripley looked away.

"No," she said. "Horrifying. Repulsive. But not fascinating."

Knowing what Ripley had told him about Ash, Hoop supposed he should have seen this coming. He wanted to defuse the situation, bring it back onto a calm footing. It had started as a friendly discussion about how the creatures could be tackled, but had descended into a standoff. He took a breath, ready to speak.

But Sneddon's actions spoke for him.

She slid open an equipment drawer, plucked out a scalpel and nicked the top of her thumb. She squeezed the digit and smeared a droplet of blood across the white bench surface. Then she looked at Ripley.

Ripley sighed. "Sorry," she said. "Really."

Sneddon smiled. "Hey, I can't blame you. Truth is, I've never liked androids myself."

"Really?" Ripley said.

"I'm a science officer, but my basis is in biology." She picked up a piece of gauze, and held it firmly over the cut. "I find them unnatural."

"And now we can all be friends," Hoop said. His own sigh of relief was unfeigned, and both Ripley and Sneddon laughed.

"So, these nets," Ripley said. "Take me to see them."

Even before Ripley arrived, they had taken to spending most of their time on the bridge. It was a large enough area to feel comfortable, with the various workstations, well-designed and spread out, but still small enough to talk with each other without having to shout. At least three of the surviving members of the *Marion* needed to be there at any one time, and each of them preferred being close to one another. Most of the time, at least. On those few occasions when tensions rose and tempers flared, they all had their individual cabins in the accommodations hub.

The rec room became dusty and unused, and on those few occasions when Hoop had cause to visit, the sight of it made him unbearably sad. He had never believed in ghosts, but he felt the echo of every dead friend in that silent room so used to laughter.

Six hours before they were planning on opening the *Samson*, they stood or sat around the bridge, all eyes focussed on him. He felt the weight of responsibility, even though they were all making the decisions now. He hadn't forced his notional position of command on them. Since the disaster, he had simply been guiding, advising, and standing there to be shouted and screamed at if the stresses got too great.

Now, the pressure was almost unbearable. He knew that every single one of them felt it, because he could see it in their eyes, their taut expressions. He knew all of them so much more deeply than he had just seventy days before. Trauma had thrown them closer together, and now the time had come to try and make things better.

Hours of planning, scheming, suggestions and disagreements, drawing plans, and sick humor had led to this.

"We're ready," Hoop said. "We know that Baxter hasn't managed to establish any visual connection back to the *Samson*, so there's no saying what we'll be facing when the doors open. Maybe those bastard things will have starved. Maybe they'll be asleep, or hibernating, and we can just gather them up and blast them into space. Could be they'll come out fighting. In which case we'll be ready." He nodded at the array of mining tools. "So, anything else? Have we missed anything? Any more questions, speak up now."

None of them spoke. He looked around the bridge, giving them all a chance. His gaze rested on Ripley, and he saw something there that continued to give him hope—resilience, determination...

Anger.

"Okay," he said. "You all know what to do."

The vestibule to Bay Three was circular and fifty feet across, lined with ranks of dusty seating interspersed with equipment racks for those awaiting a dropship. Its smoothly curved side walls were partly glazed, and offered views over the destroyed Bays One and Two on the port side. The *Narcissus* was docked at Bay Four, off to starboard.

Through a heavy door at the far end was the airlock, a space large enough for ten people at a time to be strapped in and decontaminated while it was pressurized or vented. At the other end of it, another door led into the docking arm. This was a space only ten feet long, partly flexible, that fixed directly to the surround around the dropship's outer hull hatch.

Baxter and Lachance remained on the bridge, Lachance to oversee master controls—airlock operation, environmental, and remote opening of the *Samson*'s hatch—and Baxter to ensure that communication channels were kept open. Everyone wore a headset and microphone, and they could all hear one another. For the moment, though, they were maintaining strict silence.

Hoop was in command, reasoning that someone needed to oversee the operation, and no one had objected. Ripley suggested that most of them were relieved it wasn't them.

No one disagreed.

They waited nervously in the vestibule while Powell and Welford repaired the disconnected door mechanism leading into the airlock. Through the viewing windows, Ripley could see the flanks of the *Samson* about thirty feet away. The ship looked innocent enough. But what she knew, the images she had seen, were enough to make her terrified of it. That motionless, silent ship contained her nightmares, and they were preparing to let them out.

She was chilled with nervous perspiration, trying to level her breathing. She didn't want them all to hear her fear.

She pulled her gaze away and looked to her left, toward the ruins of docking bays One and Two. Hoop had already shown her this, but it was still a sad, shocking sight. So many had died there. She was amazed the disaster hadn't taken out the whole ship. Yet in a way it had, the ripples and effects of the crash still being felt at a much slower pace.

"Welford?" Hoop asked.

"Not long," the engineer replied. "Lachance, ready to pressurize?"

"Ready," Lachance said from the bridge.

"Like I said," Hoop said, "as slow as you can. Don't want to make any more noise than is necessary."

In case they hear us, Ripley thought. Her heart hammered, and drips of sweat trickled down her back. Kasyanov had given her some spare clothing, and Ripley knew from its fit that they didn't belong to the doctor. She wondered whose it had been. The shirt and trousers were tight but not uncomfortable, the jacket snug beneath the arms and across her back. She wore her own boots from the *Nostromo*. Probably collector's items now.

The two engineers worked at the door, both efficient and quiet. Ripley had seen them arguing, and Powell more than anyone seemed to exude negativity. But they worked as a team, and there was something almost balletic about their movement, as if they were one body split in two. She wondered how long they had been working together out here. She should have asked. She should have got to know them better, before—

She took a deep breath to compose herself, and Hoop glanced across at her. He'd heard through her microphone. She didn't return his glance, didn't want him to see how afraid she was. She needed to be strong. Always had been, working with the crew of the *Nostromo*, most of them men. It was a trait she liked in herself, and she hated that fear was picking at its edges.

Ripley stood against the left wall of the vestibule, Hoop was in the middle, and Kasyanov and Garcia were to the right. Hoop carried the plasma torch—a serious bit of kit, he'd said—leaving her with a sand pick and the medics with charge thumpers. They were large and unwieldy, but packed a lot of punch. Sneddon was with the engineers, heavy cargo netting piled around her feet.

Ripley had examined the cargo netting, and it was stronger than she'd expected. Triple-core steel wrapped in epoxy-molded carbon fiber, and wound in compressed nylon strands. There were special cutting tools they used to slice the netting if they had to. She'd nodded, but had advised a healthy skepticism. They couldn't assume that *anything* would hold the beasts.

"Done," Welford said. "Lachance?"

"Pressurizing."

There was an almost sub-audible hum as the airlock beyond the vestibule was filled once more with air. The lights above the heavy doors flickered softly, and after a minute all three glowed a soft green.

"Okay," Lachance said. "Just check the pressures there, would you?"

Powell looked at the gauges beside the door. He held up his thumb.

"Open it up," Hoop said.

Welford stroked a pressure pad, and the doors slid apart. Despite their care and the readings, there was still a sigh as the doors opened. Ripley swallowed and her ears popped. She looked across at Hoop, but he seemed unconcerned.

"Okay guys," Hoop said, "slow and quiet."

Nervously, Welford and Powell entered the airlock. Ripley moved sideways, so that she could see them inside. As soon as they reached the far door they started repairing the dismantled door mechanism.

Garcia and Sneddon went to work rigging the heavy cargo netting around the door that led from the airlock into the vestibule, leaving one side loose for the engineers to slip past once they were done.

Ripley frowned. No matter how she looked at it, the plan was as loose and woolly as ever. Remote-open the *Samson*, wait until the aliens came through and got caught in the netting. Use sand picks to hook the netting and drag them back through the vestibule and along the corridor to the ruined docking bays. Open the inner door, shove the creatures through, lock the door again. Blast them into space.

It was like catching a shark in a goldfish net.

Yet there were so many ways the aliens might not play ball. *What if they stay in the* Samson? Ripley had asked. Welford had suggested a remote drone they used for deep mine exploration. Sending it in, luring them out.

So woolly. So loose.

The others seemed just as nervous. Some of them had seen these things in action—on monitors, on the destroyed dropship, and aboard the *Samson*. But the ones they'd seen had been small. Not much bigger than the bastard that had burst from Kane at their last meal together. The grown ones, the adults, had existed on their screens as little more than ambiguous shadows.

She shook her head. Her breathing came heavier.

"This won't work," she said.

"Ripley," Hoop whispered.

The others were looking at her, eyes wide.

"Not four of them," she said. She hefted the sand pick. It was heavy, its end viciously barbed, but it felt insufficient. She swung it too slowly. Her shoulders already ached from holding it.

"We should think of something else," she said.

"Damn it, Ripley!" Lachance said.

"Quiet!" Baxter hissed. "Welford and Powell have a headset, too!"

She knew they were right. The engineers were almost within touching distance of the dropship, and soon they'd have the last door ready to open.

They couldn't change their minds now.

And the aliens had been in there for more than seventy days. Their only food source—the bodies of the six miners and dropship crew—had been rotting the entire time. Little food, no water. Nowhere to move and stretch. Maybe they would be tired and weak, and easy to drag away.

Maybe.

Ripley nodded to let the others know she had her fears under control. But really, she didn't. Hoop knew that—she could see it when he looked across at her. *He's as scared as me.*

Perhaps they all were.

But they were also desperate.

Welford and Powell retreated back through the airlock, ducking around the heavy netting that had been hung across the inner door. Welford nodded to Hoop.

"Okay, Lachance, airlock outer door ready to open."

Ripley heard someone take in a sharp breath, then through the airlock she saw the docking arm's outer door slide open into the wall. Beyond lay the *Samson*'s outer hatch. It was dusty, scratched, and docked perfectly central to the airlock.

"Last check," Hoop said. "Baxter, no view or sound from inside?"

"Still nothing," Baxter said.

"Welford, Powell, either side of the netting with the plasma torches. Remember, only blast them if you have to. Kasyanov, wait over there with the charge thumper. Ripley, you okay?"

She nodded.

"Good. Sneddon, Garcia, back through the doors into the corridor behind the vestibule. Once we start dragging them in the net, you lead the way to Bays One and Two. Open the blast doors as quickly as you can, then get ready to close them again. Lachance, once we've shut them in there, you remote-open the door leading to the ruined docking bays."

"Easy," Ripley said. Someone laughed. Someone else started swearing quietly, voice so soft that she couldn't even tell whether it was a man or woman.

Wait! she wanted to say. *Wait, we still have time, we can come up with something else!* But she knew that they *didn't* have time. That bastard Ash had brought her to this doomed ship, and now she was going to face them again.

The monsters from her nightmares.

Hoop whispered, "Go." The *Samson*'s outer hatch squealed open, and the shadows came.

7

SHADOWS

Between blinks, Ripley's world turned to chaos.

As soon as the *Samson*'s hatch was open the aliens surged out. They were so fast, so silent and furious, that she didn't have time to count. Their limbs powered them along the docking arm and through the airlock, skittering on the metallic surfaces. Someone shouted in surprise, and then the creatures struck the heavy netting.

Ripley crouched down clutching her sand pick, ready to drag the creatures toward the vestibule's rear doors. But something was wrong with the net. It held two of them tightly in a tangled jumble, but two more thrashed violently, limbs waving and slashing, tails lashing out, and those terrible teeth clacking together and driving ice-cold fear through her veins.

"Careful, they're—" she shouted.

And then they were through.

The tightly coiled metal-cored netting ruptured, high-tension wiring thrashing at the air with a high-pitched whipping sound. Welford screamed as his features blurred. Blood splashed across the vestibule, painting the harsh white surfaces a startling shade of red.

Hoop shouted as he ignited his plasma torch. One alien surged at him, then kicked sideways against a rank of fixed seating, veering away from the waving flame.

Directly toward Ripley.

She crouched against the bulkhead and propped the long pick's handle beside her, pointing it up and away from her at an angle. The alien—tall, spiked, chitinous, with razor nails and the curved head and extruding mouth that had haunted her for so long—skidded toward her, claws scoring ruts in the flooring as it tried to slow. But not quite quickly enough.

It squealed as the point penetrated its body somewhere just above it legs.

An acrid stench made Ripley gag. She heard fluid spattering onto metal, and then she smelled burning.

"Acid!" she shouted. She shoved forward with the sand pick. The alien stood its ground, crouched down with its hands clawed and waving, mouth snapping forward. But it was playing for distraction. Ripley heard the soft *whoosh!* of its tail, and ducked just in time.

The pick was snatched from her hands and sent clattering across the vestibule.

Ripley feinted left toward the airlock, then leapt to the right, following the curved wall toward the rear doors. She sensed the thing following her, and as she approached the doors Hoop shouted.

"Ripley, *down!*"

She dropped without hesitation. A roar burst all around her and she smelled hair singeing, felt the skin on the back of her neck and scalp and arms stretching as an unbelievable heat scorched the air above and behind her.

The alien squealed, high and agonized.

Ripley looked toward the open exit doors just as another shadow powered out through them. From beyond she heard an impact—wet, meaty, a thud and a grunt. Someone screamed.

Something grasped her hand and she cried out, rolled, kicking out, her heavy boot connecting with Hoop's thigh. He gasped, then grabbed her tighter and dragged her across the vestibule.

The alien was still squealing as it burned, thrashing back along the curved bulkhead toward the airlock doors.

And toward Powell. He was standing over the two aliens still struggling in the net, aiming his charge thumper. There was something wrong with his face. Ripley saw the splash of blood across his chest and neck, saw it dripping from his features. He was totally expressionless. He waved the thumper back and forth, but didn't seem to be seeing anything.

She glanced aside from him and saw what had become of Welford. He was meat.

"Powell!" she shouted. "Eyes right!"

Powell lifted his head. But instead of looking right at the blazing alien that was staggering toward him, he looked left at his dead friend.

Kasyanov leapt across two rows of seats, braced her legs, and fired her charge thumper at the burning alien. The shot was deafening, pulsing in Ripley's ears and blowing the flames back from the creature's sizzling hide.

It screeched louder. But it continued on toward Powell, falling on him, and Ripley didn't quite close her eyes in time. She saw Powell's head erupt beneath the impact of the burning thing's silvery mouth.

"What the fuck?" Hoop shouted.

Kasyanov fired the thumper again, two more times, shattering the alien's head and spreading its burning parts across the floor and wall on that side of the vestibule. Flames curved across the windows, smoke formed intricate patterns, and an acidic haze rose.

Hissing. Smoking.

"We need to get out!" Ripley said.

"Where's the other one?" Hoop asked.

"Through the door. But the acid will—"

"Kasyanov, out!" Hoop shouted.

Kasyanov came for them. Ripley saw her disbelief, but also the determination that had smothered her terror. That was good. They'd need that.

One of the aliens trapped in the netting broke free, streaking toward them across the vestibule. It knocked seating aside, jumped over the back of a row of fixed equipment racks, and bore down on Kasyanov.

Hoop raised the plasma torch. But if he fired this close he'd fry the doctor as well.

"No!" Ripley said. "Hoop!" She sidestepped to the left, never taking her eyes off the alien. It paused briefly, and her selfish thought was, *Not me, don't come at me.* Fear drove that idea, and moments

later—as the alien leapt and Hoop fried it with the plasma torch—
she felt a flush of shame.

But Kasyanov was alive because of Ripley's quick decision. She'd
acted on instinct, and her baser thoughts, more taken with self-
preservation, had needed a moment to catch up.

The Russian nodded once at her.

Then one of the acid-splashed windows blew out.

The storm was instantaneous. Anything not fixed down was picked
up and blasted toward the ruptured window, carried by the atmosphere
gushing out into space under massive pressure. Broken chairs, dropped
weapons, wall paneling powered across the vestibule and jammed
against the window and bulkhead. The noise was incredible, a roar
that threatened to suck Ripley's eardrums from her skull. She tried to
breathe, but couldn't pull air into her lungs. She held onto a floor fixing
for a row of chairs with one hand, reaching for Hoop with the other.

Hoop clung onto the door frame, Kasyanov clasping onto his
flapping jacket.

Ripley looked over her shoulder. Two tattered bodies—all that
remained of Welford and Powell—were pressed hard against the
broken window, the two dead, burned aliens almost merged with
them. The surviving creature, still tangled in netting, was clasping
onto the airlock doorway, but as she watched its grip slipped and
it impacted against its dead brethren. Things were drawn through
the airlock and whipped around toward the breach—clothing, body
parts, other objects she couldn't identify from inside the *Samson*.

She saw Powell's right arm and chest sizzling and flowing from
spilled acid.

"We don't have long!" she tried to shout. She barely even heard
herself, but she could see from Kasyanov's expression that she knew
the terrible danger they were in.

For a moment, the storm abated a little. The blown window was
clogged with furniture, body parts, and bulkhead paneling. Ripley
felt the pressure on her ears and the tugging at her limbs lessening,
so she started pulling herself along the floor fixings toward the
doorway. With the acid eating away at the detritus, the calmer period
wouldn't last for long.

Hoop hauled himself through, helped by hands from the other side. Kasyanov went with him. Then they both turned back for her.

Jammed against the door frame and held from behind, Hoop reached for Ripley.

As he looked over her shoulders and his eyes widened, she got her feet under her and pushed.

Hoop grabbed her arms and squeezed, so tight that she saw blood pooling around where his fingernails bit into her wrists.

The entire bulkhead surrounding the shattered window gave way.

With a shout Ripley barely heard, Hoop pulled her toward him. The doors were already closing, and she was tugged through the opening moments before the edges met.

There was a loud, long whine, a metallic groaning, and then the growl of racing air fell immediately away. Beyond the door was chaos. But here, for a few seconds, it was almost silent.

Then Ripley's hearing faded back in. She heard panting and groaning, and Hoop's muttered curses when he saw Garcia's mutilated body jammed through a doorway across the corridor. Her chest was a bloodied mess, bones glinting with dripping blood.

"One... one came through," Ripley said, looking at Sneddon. The science officer nodded and pointed along the corridor.

"Into the ship," she said. "It moved so fast. And it was huge. *Huge!*"

"We've got to find it," Ripley said.

"The others?" Sneddon asked.

Hoop shook his head. "Welford. Powell. Gone."

The chaos beyond the doors ended as quickly as it had begun.

Ripley stood up, shaking, looking around at the others—Hoop, Kasyanov, Sneddon. She tried not to look at Garcia's damaged, pathetic body, because it reminded her so much of Lambert, hanging there with her arm still swinging, blood still dripping.

"We've got to track it down," Ripley said again.

"Baxter, Lachance!" Hoop said. "One got free on the ship. You hear me?"

No reply.

"The decompression must have screwed the com connection," Sneddon said.

Ripley reached for her headset, but it was gone. Ripped off in the violence.

"The bridge," Hoop said. "All of us. We need to stay together, get up there as quickly as possible. Warn them. Then we decide what to do. But *only* after we're all together. Agreed?"

Ripley nodded.

"Yeah," Sneddon said.

Hoop took the last remaining charge thumper from Sneddon, and led the way.

They'd moved so quickly! Even after being trapped in the *Samson* for seventy days, they'd stormed out of there faster than Ripley could have imagined. She wasn't really sure what she'd been expecting... To find that it had all been a bad dream, perhaps. To discover that the things in there weren't really related in any way to the monster that had killed her crew, thirty-seven years before.

But it hadn't been, and they were. *Exactly* the same. Giant, insectile, reptilian things, yet with a body that in certain light, from certain angles, could have been humanoid.

That head... those teeth...

Hoop held out his hand, palm up toward them. Ripley stopped and repeated the signal so that Sneddon could see, and behind her Kasyanov.

They were at a junction in the corridor. Across the junction was the door that led into the ruined docking bays, still solid and secure. Around the corner lay the route up into the main body of the *Marion*.

Hoop stood motionless, the charge thumper held across his body. It was long, unwieldy, and to aim it ahead of him as he stepped around, he'd have to move across the corridor.

The alien could have been *anywhere*. Any corner. Any shadow in the corridor walls, open doorway, hatch, side room. She'd seen it rush from the vestibule, heard it pause just long enough to kill Garcia, and then it had gone, ignoring Sneddon altogether. Maybe because she carried a weapon. But more likely, Ripley thought, because it sensed the vast ship to which it now had unrestricted access.

Maybe it had stopped a dozen steps away and was waiting for them. Drooling, hissing softly, anticipating its first real meal in so long.

Or perhaps it had dashed headlong into the depths of the ship, losing itself in unlit, unheated rooms, where it could plan what to do next.

Hoop slipped around the corner and Ripley paused for a second, holding her breath. But there was no explosion of violence, and she followed, drawing close to him once again.

They reached the end of the docking section and climbed a wide staircase into the main ship. She kept her eyes on the head of the staircase. It was well lit up there, yet she still expected to see the shimmering silhouette, all spiked limbs and curved head.

But they were alone.

Hoop glanced back, face tense. Ripley smiled and nodded encouragingly, and he returned her smile.

Behind her, Sneddon and Kasyanov remained close, but not so close that they might interrupt each other's movements. Even though she'd lost her headset, Ripley could still hear their heavy breathing—part exertion, mostly terror. No one spoke. The shock of what had happened was still circling, held at bay by the adrenalin rush.

Soon it'll hit us, Ripley thought, remembering the crunching sound as the alien bit into Powell's head, the hissing, acidic stench as the destroyed creature's blood splashed down across Powell's and Welford's ruined corpses.

Soon it'll really hit us.

Hoop led them through a wider, better-lit corridor stretching toward a central circulation area. From there other corridors led off, as well as an elevator that rose up through the decks. Three doors were securely closed, shutting off deck areas that had decompressed during the initial disaster, all of which were now out of bounds. The other corridors, all leading toward the rear of the ship, were still open.

From where they stood they could see part of the way along each one. Doors stood in shadows. Staircases rose out of sight. Lights flickered from weak or interrupted power supplies, causing flinching movement where there was none.

Hoop indicated the elevator. Sneddon moved forward, quickly and silently, and pressed the call button.

"Baxter?" Hoop whispered again into his microphone. "Lachance?" He looked at Sneddon, then back at Kasyanov. They both shook their heads.

The lights above the elevator shone a flat red.

"Stairs?" Ripley asked.

Hoop nodded and pointed the way. They moved behind the elevator bank and toward the bottom of the widest staircase. Hoop immediately started climbing, charge thumper aimed up and ahead of him.

Ripley and the others followed. They trod quietly, moving as quickly as they dared, and at the next half-landing Hoop paused and peered around the corner. He moved on. The ship hummed and throbbed around them with familiar sounds and sensations.

At the next landing Hoop stopped again, staring, frozen.

Ripley moved up beside him. She was ready to act quickly—grab him, fall back and down if the alien pounced. But to begin with she couldn't see anything out of place, and she touched his shoulder and squeezed to get his attention.

Hoop swung the charge thumper around and down, pointing its wide barrel at something on the landing. A clear, viscous slime, splashed down on the landing and the first tread of the next flight, then smeared across the textured metal.

"Which level is the bridge?" she whispered in his ear. She was confused, lost.

He pointed up, held up one finger.

"We have to get out of the stairwell," she said. "Get up there some other—"

Hoop ran. He pushed off with a grunt, leaping up the staircase two at a time, weapon held out before him. He moved so quickly that he took Ripley and the others by surprise, and by the time she started after him he was already on the next half-landing, swinging around the corner without pause. She grabbed the handrail and pulled herself up.

We should be going slow and quiet! she thought. But she also knew exactly what Hoop was feeling. He wanted to get to the bridge and warn Lachance and Baxter before the alien got there. And if they arrived and the other two had already been slaughtered, he wanted to kill the fucking thing.

Ripley saw him pause briefly at the doorway leading onto the next deck, then he touched the pressure pad and the door whispered open. He pushed through, crouched down low, looking all around as Ripley and the others closed on him. With a quick glance back at them, he moved on.

Ripley finally recognized where they were. As they approached the main entrance that led onto the bridge she dashed on ahead, pausing by the doors and listening, one hand hovering over the pressure pad. She couldn't hear anything from inside, but then perhaps the doors were soundproofed. Maybe the screaming was contained.

Nodding to Hoop, she counted down with her fingers.

Three... two... one...

She stroked the pad and the door whispered open. They went in together, Hoop on the left, Ripley on the right, and the joy and relief was almost overwhelming when she saw Lachance and Baxter huddled around the communications desk.

"What the fuck?" Baxter asked, standing and sending his chair spinning across the floor. "We lost contact and..." He saw their faces then, and read the terror.

"What happened?" Lachance asked.

"Secure the bridge," Hoop said to Sneddon and Kasyanov. "Lock the doors. All of them."

"What about the others?" Baxter asked.

"How long ago did you lose contact?"

"Just when they—when you were opening up the airlock," Baxter said. "I was about to come down, but..."

"There *are* no others," Hoop said. "Secure the bridge. Then we'll decide what the hell to do next."

Their grief was palpable.

They'd already lost so many friends and colleagues, but these eight survivors had existed together for more than seventy days, striving to make the *Marion* safe, hoping that their distress signal would be picked up by another ship. Living day by day with the constant, hanging threat of further mechanical malfunction, or a break-out of those monsters from the *Samson*. Fighting against the odds, their determination had seen them through. Perhaps they hadn't all liked each other, but what group of people could claim that? Especially under such stress.

Yet they had been the survivors. And now three of them were gone, slaughtered in a matter of moments by those bastard creatures.

Ripley gave them their silence, retreating to a control panel and sitting in the upholstered chair. It was a navigational control point. She browsed the system, noting the other planets and their distances, orbits, make-up. The sun at the system's center was almost half a billion miles away.

No wonder it feels so fucking cold.

"We've got to find it," Sneddon said. "Track it down and kill it."

"Track it down how?" Kasyanov asked. "It could be hiding away anywhere on the *Marion*. It'll take us forever, and we only have days."

"I saw it," Sneddon said. At the sound of her voice—so filled with dreadful awe, quavering in fear—everyone grew quiet, still. "It came out like… like a living shadow. Garcia didn't even know what hit her, I don't think. She didn't scream, didn't have time. Just a grunt. Like she was disagreeing with something. Just that, and then it killed her and ran. Just… brutalized her, for no reason."

"They don't reason," Ripley said. "They kill and feed. And if there's no time to feed, they just kill."

"But that's not natural," Sneddon said. "Animals kill for a purpose."

"Some do," Ripley said. "Humans don't."

"What is and isn't natural out here?" Hoop asked, and he sounded angry. "Doesn't matter. What matters is what we do."

"Track it down," Sneddon said.

"There's no time!" Kasyanov said.

"That acid ate through the vestibule windows and floor in no time," Hoop said. "We're lucky the doors are holding—they're blast doors, not proper external doors."

"So how the hell do we get to the *Samson* now?" Lachance asked.

"That's another problem." Hoop was the center of attention. Not only in command, he was the only engineer left alive.

"Suit up," Lachance said.

"Exactly what I was thinking," Hoop said.

"Yeah," Baxter agreed. "The *Samson*'s environmental systems will recompress, once we're inside."

"We'll need to form another airlock," Hoop said.

"But we can't just leave that thing roaming around the ship!" Kasyanov shouted. She was standing, fists clenched at her sides. "It could chew through cables, smash doors. Do god-knows-what sort of damage."

"We can leave it." Hoop looked at Ripley, as if seeking her agreement. And suddenly the others were watching her, as well.

Ripley nodded.

"Yeah. It's either that, or we hunt the thing through the ship and put everyone at risk. At least this way we have a chance."

"Yeah, a chance," Kasyanov scoffed. "What are the odds? I'm taking bets. Anyone?"

"I don't gamble," Ripley said. "Listen, if three of us keep watch while the other three work, it'll still take a while to get into the *Samson*. Then when we return, straight into my shuttle and away."

"What about supplies?" Baxter asked. "Food, water. Lube for all that lovin' we'll be doing."

"Are there stocks down at the mine?" Ripley asked Hoop.

"Yep."

"But that's where *they* came from!" Sneddon said.

Ripley nodded. No one else spoke. *Yeah, we've all been thinking about that, too,* she thought.

"Right, so I'll call it," Hoop said. "I've got an idea of how we can get through the decompressed rooms to the *Samson*. We all go, and follow the plan. And if that thing causes us problems when we come back, we deal with it then."

"One cataclysm at a time, eh?" Baxter said.

"Something like that."

"We need more weapons," Ripley said. "We lost most of them down there when…"

"We can divert to Hold 2 on the way down," Sneddon said. "Plenty of charge thumpers and plasma torches there."

"Easy," Lachance said.

"A walk in the park," Baxter agreed.

"We're all going to die," Kasyanov said. And she meant it. She wasn't making a joke. Ripley had been impressed when she leaped into action in the docking arm, but now she was the voice of pessimism once again.

"Not today," Ripley replied. Kasyanov snorted. No one else replied.

They moved, but not too quickly. On the relative safety of the bridge, they each took a few moments to compose their thoughts.

Beyond the doors lay only danger.

8

VACUUM

They made sure that the bridge was properly sealed before they left.

There was brief discussion that Lachance and Baxter might remain behind, but it was quickly dismissed, and they didn't need much persuading that they should go with the others. Neither liked the idea of being left alone with the creature, especially if something went wrong on the planetary surface. Better that they all remain together. Besides, there was little that they could do aboard the orbiting ship, other than track its doomed trajectory.

Just before they left the bridge level, Hoop watched as Kasyanov approached Ripley, stretched on tiptoes, and planted a kiss on her cheek. She didn't speak—perhaps words of thanks would have been redundant, or might have lessened the moment—but she and Ripley locked glances for a moment, and then both nodded.

"If you ladies are done smooching, maybe it's time to get the fuck off this ship," Baxter said. With the bridge doors locked and their mechanisms disabled, the six survivors moved off toward Hold 2. Sneddon volunteered to go first, asking for Hoop's charge thumper. He didn't object. They were all in this together.

They circled back around the accommodations hub, watching each door in the inner wall of the curved corridor. There were almost a hundred separate bunk rooms in the hub, and the alien could be hiding in any of them. Access doors were recessed into the gray metal wall and difficult to see, and subdued lighting gave the shadows added depth. It was a stressful journey. They took it slowly and reached Hold 2 without incident.

It was a huge space—high ceilinged, cavernous and partly filled with spare mining equipment. Two massive ground transport vehicles were chained down to the floor, and several smaller trucks had moved around during and immediately following the *Delilah*'s crash. Other equipment lay stacked or scattered. There were metal transport crates, tool racks, supply tanks and boxes, and all manner of smaller items. It formed a complex maze of walkways and dead ends, and Hoop suddenly wanted to turn and go back the way they'd come.

But they needed weapons. Not just in case they came across that bastard thing in the *Marion*'s corridors, but to face whatever they might find down on the planet. The miners had unearthed something dreadful down there, and there was no telling how many of the things might be waiting for them.

The thought almost paralyzed him with a sense of hopelessness. But he had to shake his doubts and hide them away beneath the stark knowledge that they had no other options.

He motioned the others close, and he led the way along the hold's outer wall. When he reached a heavy green door he entered an access code. The door whispered open, and automatic lighting flickered on inside.

"All in," he murmured.

They filed past him, Ripley bringing up the rear.

"What's this?" she asked.

"Workshop," Hoop said. He was the last inside, backing in, watching the hold as he closed the door behind him. Only then did he turn around and relax.

Powell stood by the welding rig over in the far corner, complaining about something Welford had done, or something that grumpy bastard Baxter had said in the rec room, or maybe just finding an aspect of his own appearance to whinge about. Welford sat at the electronics island bench, goggles up on his forehead. He smiled at Powell's constant, monotonous drone. A massive coffee mug emblazoned with the words "Engineers are always screwing" steamed by his elbow as he waxed lyrical on some subject or another, his voice a constant background buzz, a counterpoint to Powell's deep tones.

Hoop blinked. He never thought he'd miss those two, not really. They'd died badly. He couldn't hold back the memories. He'd spent so long down here with them, working on various repair and maintenance jobs, and although they'd been more friendly with each other than with him—his superior ranking, he thought, or perhaps just that the two of them were more alike—they'd still been a team of three.

"What a dump," Baxter said.

"Fuck you," Hoop said.

"Nice place you've got here..." Ripley smiled, and she seemed to understand. Maybe she'd seen it in his expression.

Hoop sniffed and pointed.

"There's some stuff racked in the cupboards back there. Baxter, why don't you and Lachance check it out? Sneddon, Kasyanov, come with me and Ripley."

"Where?"

"Through there." He pointed at a door in the side wall, closed and marked with a *Hazardous Materials* symbol.

"What's in there?" Ripley asked.

"I'll show you," he said, smiling. "Wondering if we can fight fire with fire."

Hoop punched in the access code and the door slid open. Lighting flickered on inside, illuminating a small, sterile-looking room, more like a research lab than the workshop that led to it. He'd spent quite a bit of time in here, toying with chemicals and developing various application methods. Jordan had always turned a blind eye to the engineers' hobbies in research and development, because it relieved boredom and passed the time. But this had really been Welford's baby. Sometimes he'd spent twelve hours at a time in here, getting Powell to bring him food and drinks down from the galley or rec room. Hoop had never been sure exactly why Welford had become so interested in the spray gun technology. Perhaps it was simply because it was something he excelled in.

"So what's this?" Ripley asked.

"Welford's folly," Sneddon said. "I helped him with some of the designs."

"You did?" Hoop asked, surprised.

"Sure. Some of the stuff he was using down here was... pretty cutting-edge, actually."

Hoop hefted one of the units Welford had been working on. It looked like a heavy weapon of some sort, but was actually surprisingly light. He shook it, already knowing that the reservoir would be empty.

"We're going to fight them with water pistols?" Ripley said.

"Not water," Sneddon said. "Acid."

"Fire with fire," Hoop said, smiling and holding up the gun.

"The miners had been asking us for something like this for quite a while," Sneddon said. "The trimonite is usually only found in very small deposits, and surrounded by other less dense materials—sands, shales, quartzes, and other crystalline structures. It's always been a time-intensive process, sorting through it. The idea with this was to melt away all the other stuff with hydrofluoric acid, and keep the *trimonite* untouched."

"Sounds dangerous," Ripley said.

"That's why it's still just in the lab," Hoop said. "We were looking for a way to make the application process safer."

"And you found it?"

"No," Hoop said. "But safe's the last thing on my mind right now."

"How do we know this will even bother them?" Kasyanov asked, negative as ever. "They have acid in their veins!"

"There's only one way to find out," Hoop said. "We have two units. Let's get them primed, and we can get out of here."

Ten minutes later they stood ready at the workshop's locked doors. Hoop had shrugged a tool bag over his shoulder, packed with all the tools he thought they might need. He and Sneddon carried the spray guns, containment reservoirs fully loaded with hydrofluoric acid. Ripley and Lachance had charge thumpers, the charge containers loaded with six-inch bolts. They wore bolt belts around their waists, heavy with spare ammunition. Baxter and Kasyanov were carrying newly charged plasma torches.

They should have felt safer. Hoop should have felt ready. But he was still filled with dread as he prepared to open the doors.

"You all follow me," he said. "Sneddon, take the rear. Eyes and ears open. We'll move slow and steady, back around the hub, down the staircases to the docking deck. Once we get to the corridor outside Bay Three, that's when I get to work." He looked around at them all. Ripley was the only one who offered him a smile.

"On three."

It took almost half an hour to work their way back around the ship's accommodation hub and down to the docking deck. On a normal day it might have been half that time, but they were watching the shadows.

Hoop expected to see the surviving alien at any moment, leaping toward them from a recessed doorway, appearing around a closed corner, dropping from above when they passed beneath domed junctions. He kept the spray gun primed and aimed forward—it was much easier to manage than a charge thumper. There was no telling how effective the acid might be, but the thumpers were inaccurate as weapons if the target was more than a few yards away, and the plasma torches were probably more dangerous to them than the creature.

They'd seen that on the *Delilah*.

Hoop's finger stroked the trigger. *I should be wearing breathing apparatus*, he thought. *Goggles. A face mask.* If any of the hydrofluoric acid splashed back at him, or even misted in the air and drifted across his skin, he'd be burnt to a crisp. His clothes, skin, flesh, bones, would melt away beneath the acid's ultra-corrosive attack.

Stupid of him. *Stupid!* To think that they could take on the creature with a form of its own weapon. His mind raced with alternatives.

He should switch back to the thumper.

He should have Baxter take lead with the plasma torch.

They should stop and think things through.

Hoop exhaled hard, tensed his jaw. *Just fucking get on with it*, he thought. *No more dicking around! This is it.*

Descending the wide staircase into the docking level, they paused beside a row of three doors marked with bright yellow "Emergency" symbols. Baxter opened the first door and took out three vacuum-packed bags.

"Suits?" Ripley asked.

"Yeah, everything's in there," Baxter replied. "Suit, foldable helmet, compressed air tank, tether cable." He looked around at the rest. "Everyone suit up."

They took turns opening the bags and pulling themselves into the silver space suits. It was like being wrapped in thin crinkly plastic, with stiff sealing rings where the parts fit together. Fabric belts slipped through loops and kept the material from flapping too loosely. The helmets were similarly flexible, with comm units sewn into the fabric. The suits were designed for emergency use only, placed close to the docking bays in case of a catastrophic decompression. The air tanks would last for maybe an hour, the suits themselves intended purely to enable the user to get to the nearest safe place.

When they were all ready, they moved on.

Reaching the corridor outside Bay Three without incident, Hoop looked around at everyone else. They seemed more pumped up than they had before, more confident. But they couldn't let confidence get the better of them.

"Baxter, Sneddon, that way." He pointed past the closed doors and toward Bay Four, where Ripley's shuttle was docked. "Close the doors in Bay Four, make sure as hell they're secure, and keep watch. Kasyanov, Lachance, back the way we came. Close the corridor blast doors. Ripley, with me. Let's hustle."

When the others moved off he shrugged the tool bag from his shoulder and held the spray gun out to Ripley. "Just hold it for me."

She took the acid gun from him, one eyebrow raised.

"Too dangerous for me to actually use, eh?"

"Ripley—"

"Show me. I can handle myself."

Hoop sighed, then smiled.

"Okay, you prime it here, wait until this light is showing red. Aim. Squeeze the trigger. It'll fire compressed jets in short pulses."

"Shouldn't we be wearing proper safety gear?"

"Definitely." He turned away, knelt, and opened the tool bag. "I won't need long," he said. The space suit made normal movements a little more awkward, but he took a heavy portable drill out of the bag, fitted it with a narrow drill bit, and then propped it against one of the door panels.

Beyond, in the vestibule to Bay Three, lay the vacuum of space.

"You sure that door will hold?" Ripley asked. "Once you get through, and we start decompressing—"

"No!" he snapped. "No, I'm not sure. But what else do you suggest?"

Ripley didn't answer. But she nodded once.

"Helmets," he called. "Clip your tether lines close, and to something solid." Ripley fixed her flexible helmet collar and turned on her air supply, and along the corridor in both directions he heard the others doing the same. When he was sure everyone was ready, he fixed his own helmet with one hand, then started drilling.

It was the loudest noise they'd made since opening up the *Samson*. The metal drill bit skittered across the door's surface before wedging against a seam and starting to penetrate. Curls of metal wound out and dropped to the floor like robot hair. Smoke wafted, and Hoop saw heat shimmering the air around the drill's head as the bit bored slowly into the door.

He leaned into the tool, driving it deeper.

It didn't take long. The drill casing banged against the door when the bit pushed through, and Hoop turned off the power. A high-pitched whistling began instantly as air was forced through the microscopic gap between bit and metal.

He looked around at Ripley. She'd tethered herself to a door handle across the corridor.

"Everyone get ready," he said into his helmet's comm. "Here goes nothing." He placed his gloved hand over the rapid release button on the drill and pressed. A thud, a shudder through the drill, and the bit was sucked through the door and into the vestibule beyond.

Hoop backed away, tying himself to the heavy door handle with the shortest lead possible, then kicked the drill aside.

A piercing whistle filled the corridor as air was sucked out through the tiny hole. The door vibrated in its heavy frame, but it remained solid and secure. Dust cast graceful shapes in the air, shimmering skeins wavering as the artificial lighting flickered with a power surge.

Soon the flow of air ceased, and they were standing in vacuum.

"Everyone okay?" Hoop called. Everyone was.

Which meant the time had come to make their way through to the *Samson*.

They were assuming there was nothing dangerous left inside. Four aliens had emerged. Two had been killed in the vestibule, another blasted into space when the window had failed, and the fourth was somewhere aboard the *Marion*. They were as certain as they could be that there had only been four, but there was no saying they hadn't left something behind when they'd fled—eggs, acid sacs, or something else unknown. They knew so little about the beasts.

"Right. We can't afford to use the plasma torch or spray guns in the *Samson*."

"I'll go first, then," Ripley said. She handed the spray gun back to Hoop and hefted the charge thumper. "Makes sense." And she was through the door before anyone else could speak.

Hoop followed her quickly through the ruined vestibule, past the airlock and along the short docking arm. She paused at the *Samson*'s open hatch, but only for a moment. Then she ducked, pushed the charge thumper ahead of her, and entered the dropship.

"Oh, shit," she said.

"What?" Hoop pressed forward, senses alert. But then he saw what she had seen, and his stomach lurched.

"Going to be a pleasant journey," Ripley said.

9

DROP

PROGRESS REPORT:
To: Weyland-Yutani Corporation, Science Division
(Ref: code 937)
Date (unspecified)
Transmission (pending)

Presence of previously identified alien species confirmed.
Several specimens destroyed. Warrant Officer Ripley in
play. Plan proceeding satisfactorily. Anticipating further
update within twelve hours.

I have a purpose once more.

Before undocking with the *Marion*, Lachance assured them all that
he was the best pilot on the ship. His brief display of humor did
little to lighten the mood.

Even when Hoop leaned over to Ripley and informed her that
the Frenchman might well be the best pilot in the *galaxy*, she still
struggled to hold down her vomit.

Bad enough this was their one and only chance. But forced to
make the journey in this dropship, it seemed as if fate was rubbing
their faces in the worst of everything that had happened.

Once the internal atmosphere had been restored, they'd been
forced to remove their headgear in order to conserve the suits'
limited oxygen supplies.

Anything not bolted or screwed down in the *Samson* had been sucked out during decompression. But there was still the blood, dried into spattered black smears all across the cream-colored interior paneling, the light-blue fixed seats, and the textured metal decking. And there was the stench of decomposition, still heavy even though the ship had been in vacuum for almost a whole day.

An arm was jammed beneath one row of seating, clawed fingers almost wrapped around the seat post, bones visible through scraps of clothing and skin. Ripley noticed the others doing their best to not look at it, and she wondered whether they knew who it had been. There were tattered insignia on the torn clothing, and a gold ring on one finger.

They should have moved it aside, but no one wanted to touch it.

And aside from the human detritus, there was what had been left behind by the aliens.

The interior of the *Samson*'s passenger hold was laid out with two facing rows of seating across an open space, twelve seats per side. In this open space were fixings for equipment storage—they'd secured their various weapons there—and a raised area containing low-level cupboards and racks. Even when sitting, passengers could see over this raised portion to communicate with one another.

At the rear of the cabin, two narrow doors were set into the bulkhead. One was marked as a bathroom, the other Ripley guessed led into the engine room.

They had all chosen to sit as close as possible to the slightly raised flight deck. Lachance and Baxter sat up there, with Ripley and Hoop on one side of the passenger cabin, Kasyanov and Sneddon on the other. None of them wanted to sit at the rear.

None of them even wanted to look.

In their time aboard the ship, the aliens had made the shadowy rear of the cabin their own. The floor, walls, and ceiling were coated with a thick, textured substance. It clung around the two doors, crossing them here and there, like bridges of plastic that had melted, burned, and hardened again. It looked like an extrusion of some kind, dark and heavy in places, glimmering and shiny in others, as if wet. There were hollows that bore a chilling resemblance to shapes Ripley knew well.

The aliens had made their own place to rest, and it was a stark reminder of what had been in here until so recently.

"I hope this trip is quick," Sneddon said. Kasyanov nodded beside her.

"Lachance?" Hoop asked.

"Last checks," the pilot said. He was propped in the flight seat, leaning forward and running his hands across the control panels. A screen flickered to life in front of him, two more in the bulkhead by his side. "Baxter? Have we got a link to the *Marion*'s computer yet?"

"Just coming online now," Baxter said. In the co-pilot's seat, he had a pull-out keyboard on his lap, hands stroking keys as a series of symbols flashed across the display suspended before him. "Just calling up the nav computer... Ah, there we are." The windscreen misted for a moment, and when it cleared again it was criss-crossed with a fine grid display.

"Leave it off for now," Lachance said. "I want to get away from the *Marion* first. I'm worried there's still wreckage from the crash matching our orbit."

"After so long?" Kasyanov asked.

"It's possible," Lachance replied. "Okay, everyone strapped in?"

Hoop leaned across Ripley and checked her straps. His sudden closeness surprised her, and she felt his arm brushing her hip and shoulder as he tightened the safety straps.

"Bumpy ride," he said, smiling. "The atmosphere of this rock can be nasty."

"Great," she said. "Thanks." Hoop nodded, caught her eye, looked away again.

What was that? she thought. *Come on, Ripley, you're dodging monsters at the edge of space, and you can still get horny?* She chuckled soundlessly, and knew that he heard her exhalation.

"How's it looking?" Hoop asked.

"All systems online," Lachance said. "Inertial dampers are a bit glitchy, so the ride might be bumpier than usual."

"Oh, super," Sneddon said.

"How often have you guys been down?" Ripley asked.

"We've all been planetside a few times," Hoop said. "Kasyanov for medical emergencies, the rest of us for various other reasons. But it's mainly the miners who made this trip."

"Soon you'll know why," Kasyanov said quietly. "This planet's a regular shit-hole."

"Okay, everyone," Lachance said. "Thank you for flying Lachance Spaceways. Dinner will be served half an hour after take-off—today we have lobster ravioli and champagne. There's a selection of in-flight entertainment, and your vomit bags are under your seats." He chuckled. "You'll be needing them. Dock disconnect in ten seconds." He switched on an automatic countdown, and Ripley soundlessly ticked off the seconds.

Nine... eight...

"Electro-locks off, magnetic grab disabled."

...six... five...

"Retros primed, fire on my mark."

...three...

"Passengers *might* feel a slight bump."

What the hell is a slight bump? Ripley thought. Hoop grasped her hand and squeezed. Sneddon and Kasyanov looked terrified.

"...one... mark."

There was a moment of nothing. And then Ripley's stomach rolled, her brain bounced against her skull, her senses swam, her breath was punched from her lungs, and a shattering roar filled the cabin.

She managed to turn her head and look past Hoop through the windscreen and onto the flight deck. As they dropped quickly away from the *Marion*, the extensive damage from the other dropship's crash became even more apparent. She also saw the *Narcissus* docked at the other edge of the ship's belly, and felt a curious anxiety at being away from her. Perhaps because that ship had been her home for so long, whether she'd been aware or not.

But the shuttle was locked up safe, and Jonesy would spend most of his time asleep. She'd made sure he had plenty of food.

A siren wailed, buzzers cut through the cabin, and the ship's attitude changed. Lachance seemed to be calm and in control, stroking buttons and waving his hand across projected controls between him and the windscreen. The *Marion* moved out of sight to port, and LV178 came into view. With the vibration of the ship's descent it was difficult to make out any real features—to Ripley it was little more than a yellowish-gray smudge beyond the windows.

A few moments later Lachance hit a button and heat shields rose to block out the view.

"Just about to start skimming the atmosphere now," he said.

Artificial gravity flickered as it adjusted to the planet's real pull. Sneddon puked. She leaned forward and aimed most of it between her legs. Kasyanov glanced sideways then ahead again, closing her eyes, gripping her seat arms so tightly that her knuckles were pearls of white on her dark skin.

Hoop's grip almost hurt, but Ripley didn't mind.

The *Samson* started to shake even more. Each impact seemed hard enough to tear the ship apart, and Ripley couldn't hold back the gasps and grunts that came with each thud. It brought back memories of descending down to LV426 in *Nostromo*, but this was much worse.

She looked back at that strange swathe of material the aliens had left behind. It must have been quite solid to survive the decompression and remain intact, yet from here it looked almost soft, like huge spider webbing covered with dust and ash. The creatures must have hibernated in there. She wondered just how much longer the beasts could have slept, waiting, if they hadn't decided to open up the *Samson*.

Her thoughts drifted, and she feared what was below them. Hoop figured that eighteen miners had been left behind down on the surface, and no one knew what had happened to them. There was no real information on what they had found, how the alien attack had happened, where they had been discovered. The trimonite mine was the last place in the galaxy she wanted to go right then, but it was the only place that offered any hope for their survival.

Get the fuel cells and get out again. That was Hoop's plan. They'd all agreed.

It felt as if the ship was shaking itself to pieces. Just when Ripley believed all their worries might end there and then, Lachance spoke again.

"Might be a little turbulence up ahead."

Sneddon leaned forward and puked again.

Ripley leaned back and closed her eyes, and Hoop squeezed her hand even tighter.

* * *

It seemed like forever, but it couldn't have been more than an hour before they were deep in LV178's atmosphere, flying a mile above the planet's surface toward the mine. Baxter had fired up the nav computer and calculated that the facility was six hundred miles away.

"Just over an hour," Lachance said. "I could fly faster, but the storm's still pretty rough."

"Let me guess," Kasyanov said. "Might get bumpy?"

"Just a little."

"How are we still flying?" Sneddon asked. "How is the ship still in once piece? How is my stomach not hanging out of my mouth?"

"Because we're hardy space explorers," Baxter said.

In truth, the vibrating and bumping had reduced drastically once they had entered the atmosphere and Baxter had plotted their route. Lachance gave control over to the autopilot, and then turned his seat around.

"Lobster," he said.

Sneddon groaned. "If you ever mentioned food again, Lachance, I won't be responsible for the consequences."

"Okay, folks, we've got an hour," Hoop said. "We need to talk about what happens next."

"We land, get the fuel cell, take off again," Ripley said. "Right?"

"Well…"

"What?" she asked.

"It might not be quite that simple," Hoop said. "There are variables."

"Oh, great," Kasyanov said. "You can't get much more variable that those monsters, can you?"

"Landing pad," Hoop said. "Access to the mine. Air quality inside. Damage. And the fuel cells are stored several levels down."

"So tell me what all that means?" Ripley said, looking around at them.

Sneddon held up her hands. "Hey, I'm just the science officer."

"The planet's atmosphere isn't great," Hoop said. "The mine and its surface complex are contained in an environmental dome. The landing pads are outside, connected by short tunnels. Inside the dome there are several surface buildings—stores, mess block, accommodations—and then two entrances to the mine, also enclosed for additional safety.

"Once down in the mine, in each entrance there are two caged elevators descending to nine levels. The first three levels are abandoned—they've been mined out. Level four is where the fuel cells are stored, along with a load more emergency stores. Food, water, equipment, stuff like that. Most of the emergency stores are belowground in case of a disaster, so they'll be accessible to anyone down in the mine. And levels five through nine are the current working levels."

"Then it's on one of those levels they found the aliens?" Ripley asked.

"That's a fair bet."

"So we get in, descend to level four, get the fuel cells, and come back out."

"Yeah," Hoop said. "But we have no idea what state the mine's in."

"We take it all step by step," Kasyanov said. "Whatever we find, we work through it as best we can."

"And just as fast as we can," Sneddon said. "Don't know about you all, but I don't want to be down here one minute longer than necessary."

After that, silence hung heavy. Lachance turned his chair around again and kept an eye on the flight computers. Baxter scanned the nav displays. Ripley and the others sat quietly, not catching one another's eyes, and trying not to look at the strange sculptures the aliens had left behind.

Ripley took the easy way out and closed her eyes.

And surprised herself when Hoop nudged her awake. Had she really slept? Through all that movement, buffeting, and noise?

"Sheesh, haven't you slept long enough?" he asked. Anyone else and she might have been annoyed, but there was a lilt to his voice that said he almost understood. He sounded hesitant, too, almost sad.

"We there?"

"Just circling the complex now."

"Lights are on," Lachance said from the flight deck.

"But no one's home," Baxter replied. "Dome looks intact, can't see any obvious damage."

Ripley waited for a moment, sensing the subtle vibrations of the ship. Their flight seemed much smoother than when she'd fallen asleep. She hit the quick release catch on her straps and stood up.

"Ripley?" Hoop said.

"Just looking." She moved forward and leaned against the back of the flight chair. The Frenchman turned lazily and squinted back at her.

"Come to see my cockpit??" he asked.

"You wish," she replied.

The windscreen was hazed with dust, but she could still make out the segmented metallic dome below as the ship circled it. One side of it was almost buried with drifting sand, and across its surface were several blinking lights. There was no sign of clear sections, nor could she see any access points.

"Bleak," she said.

"Wait 'til you get inside," Baxter said.

"Where are the landing pads?"

Lachance leveled the *Samson* slightly and hovered, drifting sideways directly over the dome. He pointed. Ripley could just make out three bulky shapes on the ground, also half-buried by drifted sand.

"Get closer," Hoop said, joining Ripley behind the two flight chairs. "We don't know what happened down here, but it's a fair bet they were pursued all the way to the ships."

"How do you figure that?" Sneddon asked from where she was still strapped in.

"Because the *Samson* left so many behind."

Lachance dropped them lower and closer to the landing pads. They were only a couple of hundred yards from the dome, and Ripley saw hints of the connecting tunnels that ran between them. Sheets of sand blew across the ground, driven by winds they could not feel in the *Samson*. The landscape was daunting but strangely beautiful, dust sculptures forming incredible, graceful shapes. Away from the artificial interruption of the mine, the desert looked like a frozen sea, flowing over years instead of moments.

Miles in the distance, electrical storms flashed deep inside looming clouds.

"How the hell are you going to land?" Ripley asked.

"The pads are usually cleared by the ground crews," Lachance said. "Big blowing machines, sand scoops. It'll be okay. I'm good."

"So you keep saying," she said. "I'm still waiting for proof."

"No sign of any nasties waiting for us," Hoop said.

"In this weather?" Baxter asked.

"There's no saying what environments they live in, or even prefer," Ripley said. She remembered Ash—before his true nature was exposed, when he was studying the alien—talking about remarkable adaptations to the ship's environment. Maybe sand-lashed, storm-blasted landscapes were their preference.

"Strap in, ladies and gentlemen," Lachance said. He checked readouts, stroked his hand across the projected nav controls in front of him, and then settled back in his seat.

Ripley and Hoop went back to their seats and secured their safety straps. She waited for him to check her clasps again, and saw Sneddon looking from her to Hoop, and smirking. Ripley stared back.

The science officer looked away.

The *Samson* shook as retros fired. Moments later there was a heavy bump, and then the engines started to cycle down.

"There," Lachance said. "Told you I was good."

Hoop exhaled, and from across the cabin Ripley heard Kasyanov mutter something that might have been a prayer. Straps were opened, they stood and stretched, then gathered at the front of the ship to look outside.

Lachance had landed them facing the dome. The line of the partly buried tunnel was obvious, leading from their pad to the dome, and the storm suddenly seemed more intense now that they had touched down. Maybe because there was more sand to blow around at low level.

"Suit up," Hoop said. "Grab your weapons. Lachance, you take point with me. I'm going to be opening doors and hatches. Baxter, you bring up the rear."

"Why do I have to come last?" the communications engineer asked.

"Because you're a gentleman," Sneddon said. Kasyanov chuckled, Baxter looked uncertain, and Ripley wondered at the complex relationships between these people. She'd barely scratched the surface—they'd been here so close together for so long.

The inside of the *Samson* suddenly seemed so much safer. Through her fear Ripley was determined, but she couldn't shake those terrible memories. Not the new ones, of Powell and Welford being killed by those fast, furious things. And not the old ones, back on the *Nostromo*. She couldn't help feeling that even more terrible memories were soon to be forged.

If she lived to remember.

"Let's stay close and tight," she said. No one replied. Everyone knew what was at stake here, and they'd all seen these things in action.

"We move fast, but carefully," Hoop said. "No storming ahead. No heroics."

They fixed their helmets, checked each other's suits and air supplies, tested communications, and hefted the weapons. To Ripley they all looked so vulnerable: pale white grubs ready for the aliens to puncture, rip apart, eat. And none of them had any real idea about what they were about to encounter.

Perhaps the uncertainty was a good thing. Maybe if they knew for sure what they would find down in the mine, they would never bring themselves to enter.

Breathing deeply, thinking of Amanda, who probably believed her mother to be dead, Ripley silently vowed that she would do anything and everything necessary to stay alive.

Lachance opened the outer hatch, and the storm came inside.

PART 2

UNDERGROUND

10

SKIN

"What the hell is *that*?" Hoop asked.

"Looks like… hide, or something," Lachance said.

"They shed their skins." Ripley came to stand beside them, charge thumper aimed forward. "It happens when they grow. And you've seen how quickly that is."

"How many *are* there?" Hoop almost went forward to sift through the drift of pale yellow material with his boot. But something held him back. He didn't even want to touch it.

"Enough," Sneddon said. She sounded nervous, jumpy, and Hoop was already wondering whether she should really be in charge of the other spray gun.

Then again, they were *all* scared.

They'd made their way across the storm-lashed landing pad and into the tunnel entrance without incident. The violent winds, blasting sand, and screaming storm had been almost exciting, primal conditions that they could never grow used to after living on climate-controlled ships.

Inside the tunnel the illumination was still functioning, and halfway along there were signs of a fight. An impromptu barricade had been formed from a selection of storage pods and canisters, all of which had been knocked aside, trampled, broken, and blasted. Impact marks scarred the metal-paneled walls and ceiling, and a dappled spread of flooring was bubbled and raised. The acid splash was obvious, but there was no sign of the wounded or dead alien that had caused it.

They reached the end of the tunnel, facing the heavy, closed blast doors that opened directly into the mine's surface dome. And no one was eager to open them. They all remembered what had happened the last time.

"Any way we can see inside?" Ripley asked, nodding at the doors.

"Baxter?" Hoop asked.

"I might be able to connect with the mine's security cameras," the communications officer said. He put his plasma torch down carefully and pulled a tablet computer from the wide pockets of his suit.

The storm rumbled against the tunnel's upper surface, sand lashing the metal with a billion impacts, wind roaring around the grooved, curved metal shell. It sounded like something huge trying to get in. The tunnel and metal dome had been constructed to provide the mine with protection against such inimical elements. A huge investment had gone into sinking this mine almost thirty years ago, and its maintenance had been a headache ever since. But the allure of trimonite was great. Its use in industry, its allure as an ultra-rare jewel, ensured that the investment paid off. For those with a monetary interest, at least.

As usual, it was the workers—braving the elements and facing the dangers—who gained the least.

"Can you tell whether systems are operational?" Ripley asked, her voice impatient.

"Give me a chance!" Baxter snapped. He knelt with the tablet balanced on his thighs.

All good so far, Hoop thought, but they hadn't come that far at all. There could be anything beyond these doors. The mine's upper compound might be crawling with those things. He imagined the surface buildings and dome's interior as the inside of a huge nest, with thousands of aliens swarming across the ground, up the walls, and hanging in vast structures made from the same weird material they'd found inside the *Samson*.

He shivered, physically repelled at the thought, but unable to shake it.

"Got it," Baxter said. Hoop waited for the man's outburst of disbelief, a shout of terror, but none came. "Hoop?"

He moved beside Baxter and looked down at the screen. Across the top were several thumbnails, and the main screen was taken with a view of the dome's interior, as seen from high up on one side. The lights were still on. Everything was motionless.

"Thumbnails?" Hoop asked.

"Yeah. Other cameras." Baxter touched the screen and images began to scroll. They were from differing angles and elevations, all showing the dome's interior. Hoop was familiar with the ten or so buildings, the vehicles scattered around, the planet's geography altered and flattened inside the dome's relatively small span. Nothing looked particularly out of place. It all seemed quite normal.

"Can't see any damage," Lachance said.

"Don't like this at all," Kasyanov said. Fear made her voice higher than normal. It sounded like impending panic. "Where are they? What about the other miners, the ones left behind?"

"Dead down in the mines," Sneddon said. "Taken deep to wherever those things were found, maybe. Like wasps or termites, gathering food."

"Oh, thanks for that," Kasyanov said.

"It's all just maybes," Ripley said.

Hoop nodded. "That's all we've got. Baxter, keep in the middle of the group, and keep your eyes on that screen. Scroll the images, watch out for any movement that isn't us. Shout if you see anything." He moved to the door controls and checked the control panel. "All good here. Ready?"

Baxter held back, and the others stood in a rough semi-circle around the big doors, weapons held at the ready. *Not weapons*, Hoop thought. *They're tools. Mining tools. What do we even think we're doing down here?* But they were all looking to him, and he projected calm and determination. With a single nod he touched the switch.

A hiss, a grinding sound, and the doors parted. A breeze whistled out as pressures equalized, and for a moment a cloud of dust filled the tunnel, obscuring their vision. Someone shouted in panic. Someone else moved quickly forward and through the doors, and then Hoop heard Ripley's voice.

"It's fine in here," she said. "Clear. Come on through."

He was next through the doors, spray gun at the ready. The others followed, and Kasyanov closed the doors behind them. They were much too loud.

"Sneddon?" Hoop asked.

"Air's fine," she said. She was checking a device slung onto her belt, its screen showing a series of graphs and figures. She slipped off her helmet and left it hanging, and the others did the same.

"Baxter?" Hoop asked.

"I'll *tell* you if I see anything!" he snapped.

"Right, good. Just keeping you on your toes." He nodded at a bank of steel containers lined up along the dome wall beside the door. "Okay, let's get these suits off, secure them in one of these equipment lock-ups. We'll pick them up on the way back." They stripped the suits quickly, and Hoop piled them inside one of the units.

"Mine entrance?" Ripley asked, and Hoop pointed. There were actually two entrances, both housed inside bland rectangular buildings. But they were going for the nearest.

Hoop led the way. He carried the spray gun awkwardly, feeling faintly ridiculous hefting it like a weapon, even though he knew their enemies. He had never fired a gun in his life. As a kid, living in a more remote area of Pennsylvania, his Uncle Richard had often taken him out shooting. He'd tried to force a gun into Hoop's hands—a vintage Kalashnikov, a replica Colt .45, even a pulse rifle illegally borrowed from a neighbor on leave from the Colonial Marines' 69th Regiment, the Homer's Heroes.

But Hoop had always resisted. The black, bulky objects had always scared him, and his kid's knowledge of what they were for had made the fear worse. *I don't want to kill anyone*, he'd always thought, and he'd watched his uncle's face as the older man blasted away at trees, rocks, or homemade targets hung through the woods. There had been something in his expression that had meant Hoop never truly trusted him. Something like bloodlust.

His uncle had been killed years later, just before Hoop's first trip into space, shot in the back on a hunting trip into the woods. No one ever really knew what had happened. Lots of people died that way.

But now, for the first time ever, Hoop wished he'd taken one of those guns and rested it in his hands. Weighed the potential uses he might have put it to, against the repulsion he felt for the dull black metal.

An acid spray gun. *Who the fuck am I kidding?*

This had always been a strange place, beneath the dome. Hoop had been here several times now, and he always found it unnerving—it was the planet's natural landscape, but the dome made it somewhere *inside*, the climate artificial and entirely under their control. So they kicked through sand and dust that the wind no longer touched. They breathed false air that LV178's sun did not heat. The structure's underside formed an unreal sky, lit in gray swathes by the many spotlights hung from its supporting beams and columns.

It was as if they had trapped a part of the planet and tried to make it their own.

Just look where that had got them.

As they neared the building that enclosed the first mine head, Hoop signalled that they should spread out and approach in a line. The door seemed to be propped or jammed open. If one of those things emerged, best it was faced with an array of potential targets. All of them armed.

They paused, none of them wanting to be the first to go through.

"Hoop," Ripley whispered. "I've got an idea." She slung the charge thumper over her shoulder by its strap and darted quickly toward the building. Beside the half-open door she unbuckled her belt and pulled it loose of the loops.

Hoop saw what she was about to do. His heart quickened, his senses sharpened. He crouched low, ensuring that the gun's nozzle was pointing slightly to the left of the door. If something happened, he didn't want to catch Ripley in the acid spray.

Ripley fashioned a loop at the end of the belt and edged forward, feeding it over the top of the door's chunky handle. She looked back at the others, acknowledging their slight nods. Then she held up her other hand with three fingers pointing, then two, one...

And she pulled.

The door screeched across accumulated grit. The belt slipped from the handle, and nothing emerged.

Before Hoop could speak, Ripley had swung the charge thumper from her shoulder and edged inside.

"Baxter!" Hoop said as he ran forward.

"No cameras in there!" Baxter responded.

It wasn't as dark inside as Hoop had expected. There was a low level illumination coming through the opaque ceiling—artificial light borrowed from outside—and the lift's internal lights were still powered up. The lighting was good.

What it showed was not.

There was a dead miner in the lift. Hoop couldn't distinguish the sex. In the seventy days since they had died, bacteria brought to the mine by the humans had set to work, consuming the corpse. Environmental control had done the rest; the damp, warm atmosphere providing the ideal conditions in which the microorganisms could multiply. The result caused the corpse's flesh to bloat and sag.

The smell had diminished until it was only a tang of sweet decay, but it was enough to make Hoop wish they'd kept their suits and helmets. The unfortunate victim's mouth hung open in a laugh, or a scream.

"No sign of what killed them," Kasyanov said.

"I think we can rule out heart attack," Lachance quipped.

Hoop went to the elevator controls and accessed them. They seemed fine, with no warning symbols on the screen and no sign that there were any power problems. The small nuclear generator in one of the other surface buildings was still active, and doing its job well.

"It's working?" Ripley asked.

"You're not seriously expecting us to go down in that?" Sneddon said.

"You want to take the stairs?" Hoop asked. There were two emergency escape routes leading out from the mine, a series of rough staircases cast into holes sunk adjacent to the lift pits. Almost five thousand feet deep, and the idea of descending seven thousand steps—five hundred flights—appealed to no one.

"Can't we at least move them out?" Ripley asked. She and Kasyanov went forward and started shifting the body. Hoop had to help. It didn't remain in one piece.

* * *

With the lift cage to themselves, they all entered, taking care to avoid the corner where the corpse had been. Hoop found it even more disturbing that they couldn't tell who it was. They had all known the victim, that was for sure. But they didn't know them anymore.

What had happened struck Hoop all over again. He liked to think he was good at coping with emotional upheaval—he'd left his kids behind, effectively fleeing out here into deep space, and on some levels he had come to terms with why he'd done that—but since the disaster, he had woken sometimes in a cold sweat, dreams of smothering and being eaten alive haunting the shadows of sleep. His dreams of monsters had become so much more real. He thought perhaps he cried out, but no one had ever said anything to him. Maybe because almost everyone was having bad dreams now.

"Hoop?" Ripley said quietly. She was standing beside him, staring with him at the lift's control panel.

"I'm okay."

"You're sure?"

"What are those things, Ripley?"

She shrugged. "You know as much as me."

He turned to the others. There were no accusing stares, no smirks at his momentary lapse of concentration. They all felt the same.

"We go down to level 4," he said, "get the power cell, then get out as quickly as we can."

A few nods. Grim faces. He inspected their make-do weapons, knew that none of them were in the hands of soldiers. They were just as likely to shoot each other.

"Take it easy," he said softly, to himself as much as anyone else. Then he turned to the control panel and ran a quick diagnostic on the lift. All seemed fine. "Going down." He touched the button for level 4. The cage juddered a little and the descent began.

Hoop tried to calm himself and prepare for what they might find when the doors opened again, yet his stomach rolled, dizziness hit him, and someone shouted out.

"We're falling. We're *falling*!"

The elevator began to scream.

* * *

The old stone farmhouse in northern France, a holiday home for her family for as long as she could remember. She is alone right now, but not lonely. She can never be lonely with her daughter so close.

The silence is disturbed only by the gentle breeze, rustling leaves in the woodland far at the bottom of the garden, whispering in the few scattered trees that grow closer by. The sun blazes, scorching the sky a lighter shade of blue. It's hot but not uncomfortable—the breeze carries moisture from Ripley's skin, slick from the sunblock she's been careful to apply. Birds sing their enigmatic songs.

Far above, a family of buzzards circles lazily, eyeing the landscape for prey.

Amanda runs to her through a freshly harvested field, the crop stubble scratching at her legs, poppies speckling the landscape red, and her smile countering even the heat and glory of the sun. She is giggling, holding aloft a present for her mother. Amanda is such an inquisitive little girl. Often she emerges from the small woodland with snails attached all over her arms and shoulders, small frogs captured in her hands, or an injured bird nursed against her chest.

As her daughter climbs the low wooden fence between garden and field and starts across the lawn, Ripley wonders what she has brought home this time.

Mommy, I found an octopus! *the girl shrills.*

A blink later and she is on the lawn at Ripley's feet, shivering and shaking as the long-legged thing curls its tail tighter around her sweet throat, and Ripley is trying to hook her fingers beneath its many legs, prise it off, pull it away from her angel without tearing Amanda's hair off with it. I'll cut it, she thinks, but she's worried that the acid will eat into the ground, and keep on eating.

And then from the woods there comes a series of high-pitched screeches. Shadows fall. The sun retreats, birds fall silent, and the buzzards have disappeared. The garden is suddenly plunged into twilight, and those shadows that have always haunted her emerge from among the trees. They are looking for their child.

It's mine! *Ripley shouts, kneeling and protecting Amanda with her own body.* Whatever's inside her is mine!

The shadows stalk closer. Nothing is beautiful anymore.

* * *

"Ripley!" Hoop shouted, nudging her. "Grab on to something!"

She shook her head. The vision had happened in an instant. And then it was gone, leaving only a haunting sensation.

The elevator plunged, screeching against its control framework, throwing sparks that were visible through the cage walls, vibrating violently, shaking her vision so much that everyone and everything around her was a blur.

She heard the thud of weapons hitting the floor and dropped her own, staggering back until she was braced against the wall. But there was nothing to hold onto. And even if there had been, it would have made no difference.

Her stomach seemed to be rising and rolling, and she swallowed down the sudden urge to vomit.

Someone else puked.

Hoop hung onto the long handle set into the wall beside the door, one hand curled through it and the other working at the controls.

"What the hell—?" Baxter shouted.

"I've got it!" Hoop cut in. But it was clear to Ripley that he *didn't* have it. She edged across to him, afraid that at any moment she and the others would actually lift from the floor and start to float.

We can't be going that fast, she thought. *We'd have struck bottom by now!* Five thousand feet, Hoop had said. She turned the figures over, trying to calculate how long they might have at freefall, but—

"There are buffers," Hoop shouted. "Each level. We've passed the first four already, barely felt them. Approaching five…"

Thud!

A heavy vibration passed through the lift, thumping Ripley in the chest.

"We're not slowing!" she shouted.

"We will!" he responded. "Dampers were fitted over the bottom two levels, in case of—"

"This?"

He looked at her. Beside him she could see a flickering set of figures on the control panel. Their depth approached 2,500 feet, the numbers flipping too fast for her to see.

"It's one way to test them," he said.

Ripley felt a flood of emotion. They were helpless, and that was a sensation she hated. In space, there were so many variables that presented countless levels of danger, but usually they were countered by some mechanical, electrical, or psychological means.

Even with that thing stalking them on the *Nostromo* they had gone on the offensive, hunting it, seeking to drive it toward the airlock. And after Dallas was gone and Ash was revealed for what he was... even then they had been acting in their own best interests.

Here, now, she could only stand and wait to die.

They flashed past levels 6 and 7, and each time the impact of safety buffers seemed harder. Was their descent slowing? Ripley wasn't sure. Sparks flew all around the cage's outsides, metal whined and screeched, and at the speed they were going now, she figured they'd know nothing about reaching level 9.

She contemplated that final moment, the instant when the elevator struck, crumpled, and they were all smacked into the solid floor, mashed together... and she wondered if she'd feel anything at all.

The brief waking nightmare seemed somehow worse.

"We're slowing!" Hoop said. They thudded past the buffer on level 8, and then a heavy grinding sound commenced.

Ripley and the others were all flung to the floor. A rhythmic clanging began, resounding explosions from all around that vibrated through the cage's structure. Bolts, screws and shreds of metal showered around her, and Ripley expected them to burst apart at any moment.

The noise became almost unbearable, pulsing into her ears, her torso, and the vibrations threatened to shake her apart bone-by-bone. Lying flat on the floor, she managed to turn her head toward Hoop. He was sitting propped in the far corner, head tilted to one side so he could still look at the control panel.

He glanced across, saw her looking.

"Dampers working," he shouted.

Then they struck bottom. Ripley's breath was knocked out of her as she was punched into the elevator's floor. Something heavy

OUT OF THE SHADOWS

landed on her leg. A scream was cut off, but someone else grunted and started to moan.

The lift mechanism was smoking, filling the air with an acrid haze. Lights flickered off and then came back on again, buzzing and settling into an even glow. The sudden silence was more shocking than the noise and violence had been.

Ripley pushed herself up onto hands and knees, breathing hard and waiting for the white-hot pain of cracked ribs or broken limbs to sing in. But apart from an array of bruises, a bloodied nose, and a sense of disbelief that they had somehow survived, she appeared to be fine.

"Are we still falling?" Sneddon asked. "My guts tell me we are."

"Nice landing," Lachance said, nodding at Hoop. "Make a pilot out of you yet." Hoop smiled back.

"I think…" Baxter said. He stood, then howled, slipping sideways and falling again. Kasyanov caught him. "Ankle," he said. "Ankle!" The doctor started examining him.

"Anyone else hurt?" Hoop asked.

"Only my pride," Lachance said. His suit was speckled with vomit, and he brushed at it with one gloved hand.

"Best pilot in the galaxy, my ass," Ripley said, pleased to see the Frenchman smile.

"We okay?" Sneddon asked. "We're not just hanging here waiting, to fall the rest of the way, are we? The way our luck's been going, you know."

"No, we're down," Hoop said. "Look." He nodded at the cage doors, then pulled a small, narrow flashlight from his tool belt. It threw out a surprisingly bright beam. He aimed it past the bent bars of the deformed cage, revealing the smoother metal of more solid doors.

"Level 9?" Ripley asked.

Hoop nodded.

"And the elevator's fucked," Baxter said. "That's just fucking great." He winced as Kasyanov probed around his foot and lower leg, then groaned when she looked up.

"Broken ankle," she said.

"No shit," Baxter replied.

"Can you splint it?" Hoop asked. "He's got to be able to walk."

"I *can* walk!" Baxter said, a little desperately.

"We can help you," Ripley said, aiming a warning stare at Hoop. "There are enough of us. Don't panic."

"Who's panicking?" Baxter said, looking desperate, eyes wide with pain and terror.

"We won't leave you," Ripley said, and he seemed to take comfort from that.

"Everyone else?" Hoop asked. Sneddon nodded, Lachance raised a hand in a casual wave. "Ripley?"

"I'm fine, Hoop," she said, trying not to sound impatient. They were down, battered and bruised, but they couldn't afford to hang around. "So what now?"

"Now we have two choices," Hoop said, glancing at Baxter again. "One, we start climbing."

"How many stairs?" Kasyanov asked.

"We've struck bottom at level 9. Seven thousand steps to—"

"Seven-fucking-*thousand*?" Sneddon spat. Baxter remained silent, but he looked down at the floor close to his wounded foot and ankle. All his weight was on the other foot.

"Choice two," Hoop continued, "we make our way across to the other elevator."

Silence. Everyone looked around, waiting for someone else to speak.

"And whatever they found was down here, where they were working the new seam," Baxter said. "On level 9."

"There's no choice," Kasyanov said. "How far is the other elevator shaft?"

"In a straight line, a little over five hundred yards," Hoop said. "But none of the tunnels are straight."

"And we have no idea what happened down here?" Ripley asked.

No one answered. They all looked to Hoop. He shrugged.

"All they said is that they found something horrible. And we already know what that was."

"No we don't!" Kasyanov said. "There could be hundreds!"

"I don't think so." They looked to Sneddon, who was looking down at the spray gun she'd picked up once again. "They hatch from people, right? We've seen that. So by my reckoning—"

"Eighteen," Ripley said. "Maybe less."

"Eighteen of them?" Kasyanov asked. "Oh, well, that's *easy*, then!"

"We're better prepared now," Ripley said. "And besides, what's the alternative? Really?"

"There is none," Hoop said. "We make it for the other elevator, up to level 4 for the cell, then back to the surface."

"But what about—" Kasyanov began, but Hoop cut her off.

"Whatever we find on the way, we handle it," he said. "Let's say positive. Let's stay cool, and calm, and keep our eyes open."

"And hope the lights are still working," Lachance said.

As they picked up their weapons, and Kasyanov did her best to splint Baxter's ankle with supplies from her med kit, Ripley mulled over what Lachance had said. Down here, in the dark. Feeling their way along with the aid of weak flashlights, a billion tons of planet above them.

No, it didn't bear thinking about.

When she blinked, she saw Amanda in a floral dress thrashing on the sweet, green grass with one of those monsters attached to her face.

"I'll see you again," she whispered. Hoop heard, glanced at her, but said nothing. Perhaps they were all finding some way to pray.

11

MINE

As she exited the remains of the elevator—wondering whether they were incredibly lucky to have survived, or incredibly unlucky for it to have happened in the first place—Ripley realized with a jolt that this was the only planet other than Earth on which she had ever set foot. The voyage aboard the *Nostromo* had been her first, coming soon after she'd been licensed for space flight, and even after landing on LV426 she'd never actually left the ship.

She had always assumed a moment like this would have brought a moment of introspection. A rush of wonder, a glow of joy. A deep grounding of herself and her place in the universe. Sometimes, after having traveled so far, she'd feared that she would have no real stories to tell.

But now she only felt terror. The rock beneath her feet felt just like rock, the air she breathed was gritty with dust, stale and unpleasant. There was no epiphany. The beasts had ruined everything for her— any chance of joy, any scrap of innocent wonder—and quickly the fear was replaced with rage.

Outside the lift was a wide-open area, propped at frequent intervals with metal columns. Along one side stood a line of lockers, most doors hanging open. There were also storage boxes stacked against a wall, marked with symbols she didn't understand. Most of them were empty, lids leaning against their sides. Trimonite boxes waiting to be filled, perhaps. Ripley found them sad, because they would never be used.

Lighting was supplied by several strings of bare bulbs, all of them still illuminated. The cables were neatly clipped to the rough rock ceiling.

At first, looking around, Ripley caught her breath, because she thought the walls were lined with that strange, organic, extruded compound they'd found in the ship. But when she moved closer she saw that it was rock that had been melted and resolidified, forming a solid barrier against the loose material that might lie behind it. There were still props and buttresses lining the walls and ceiling, but the bulk of the strength lay in the altered rock. They'd used the bigger, tracked plasma torches for that, she supposed. Their heat must have been incredible.

"Everyone good?" Hoop asked, breaking the silence. He was standing close to a set of plastic curtains that led into a tunnel beyond.

No one spoke. Hoop took that as confirmation that, yes, they were all good, and he pushed the curtains aside.

Ripley quickly followed. Out of all of them, Hoop felt the safest. The strongest. She wasn't even sure why she believed that. But she went with her instincts and decided to stay close to the engineer. If they ended up in a fight, she wanted to fight beside him.

The corridor beyond the elevator compound was narrower and more functional. The lights continued along the ceiling. The walls were slick and held strange, almost organic flow patterns where they'd been plasma-torched. Shallow ditches were cut into the floor at the base of each wall, and water so dark it was black glinted there. It was motionless, stagnant, inky. Ripley wondered what it contained.

Hoop waved them on.

Baxter hobbled with one arm over Kasyanov's shoulder. He grunted, gasped, and though he couldn't avoid the pain, Ripley wished he wasn't making so much noise. Every sound he made was amplified, echoing along the rock-lined tunnels much louder than their careful footfalls.

They'll know we're here, she thought. *They probably know anyway. If anything's going to happen, it's going to happen, and being cautious won't prevent it.*

They reached a junction. Hoop paused only for a moment, then took the left fork. He moved quickly and carefully, holding his flashlight in one hand, the spray gun in the other. The additional light helped illuminate contours and trip hazards on the ground.

It wasn't far along this tunnel that they came across the first sign of the aliens.

"What the hell is that?" Baxter asked. He sounded tired, and on the verge of panic. Maybe he thought that at some point they'd be forced to leave him behind after all.

"Something from the mine?" Lachance suggested. "Mineral deposit left by water?"

But Ripley already knew that wasn't the case.

It started gradually. A smear on the wall, a spread of material on the floor. But ten yards from them the alien material lined all surfaces of the tunnel in thick layers, strung like natural arches beneath the ceiling and lying across the floor in complex, swirling patterns.

A gentle mist floated on the air. Or perhaps it was steam. Ripley tugged off a glove and waved her hand before her, feeling the moisture but finding it hard discerning whether it was hot or cold. Another contradiction, perhaps. These strange structures were impressive, and even vaguely beautiful in the same way a spider's web was beautiful. But the things that had made this were the opposite.

"No," Sneddon said. "It's them. We saw something like this on the *Samson*."

"Yeah, but…" Lachance said.

"That was a much smaller scale," Ripley said. "Not like this." She was breathing fast and shallow because she could smell them here, a faintly citrus stench that clung to the back of her throat and danced on her tongue.

"I don't like this," Baxter whispered.

"Me neither," Lachance said. "I want my mommy. I want to go home."

The tunnel narrowed ahead of them where the substance bulged out from the walls, up from the floor, down from the ceiling. Here and there it formed stalactites and stalagmites, some of them thin and delicate, others thicker and looking more solid. There were hints of light deep within the alien structure, but only here and there. The ceiling lights still worked, but were mostly covered up.

Hoop stepped a little closer and shone his flashlight inside.

Ripley wanted to grab him and pull him back. But she couldn't help looking.

The light didn't penetrate very far. The moisture in the air was revealed more fully by the flashlight beam, skeins of light and dark shifting and waving with a gentle breeze. Whether that breeze was caused by their presence, their breathing, or that of another, Ripley didn't want to find out.

"I'm not going in there," Sneddon said.

"Yeah," Kasyanov said. "I'm with you on that one."

"I'm not sure we'd get through anyway," Hoop said. "And even if we could, it'd slow us down."

"It's like a nest," Ripley said. "A giant wasp nest."

"Is there another way to the elevator shaft?" Baxter asked.

"This is the direct route," Hoop said. "The spine of this level. But all the mine sections have emergency exits at various points. We'll go back, take the other fork, then cut back toward the elevator as soon as we find an exit."

Ripley didn't say what she knew they were all thinking. *What if all the tunnels are like this?* But she caught Baxter's eye, and the truth passed between them—that he could never climb so many stairs. Maybe none of them could.

Not quickly enough.

They headed back, turned into the other fork of the corridor, then dropped down a series of large steps carved into the floor. Water flowed more freely along the gutters here, tinkling away at various points into hidden depths. Walls ran with it. It provided a background noise that was welcoming at first, but quickly became troubling. Behind the sound of flowing water, anything could approach them.

"I think this is the most recent mine working," Hoop said. "They've been at this particular vein for two hundred days, maybe more."

"So this is where they found them," Sneddon said. "Somewhere along here."

"Maybe," Hoop said. "We don't know the details. But we don't have much choice." He moved on, and the others followed.

There were several side corridors, smaller with lower ceilings, and as Hoop passed them by, Ripley guessed they were also mine workings. She had no idea how a mine functioned, but she'd been told that the quantities of trimonite found here were small compared to most ore mines. This wasn't mining on an industrialized scale, but rather prospecting for hidden quantities of an almost priceless material. Digging through a million tons of rock to find half a ton of product.

She hoped that Hoop would know an emergency exit when he saw it.

Behind her, someone sneezed, uttering a quiet, "Oh!" afterward. Amanda had used to sneeze like that—a gentle sound, followed by an expression almost of surprise.

Amanda is eleven years old. Ripley knows because her daughter wears an oversized badge on her denim shirt, all purple and pink, hearts and flowers. I bought her that, she thinks, and although she can remember accessing the site, ordering the card and badge and the presents she knew Amanda wanted for her birthday—remembers the small smile of satisfaction when she confirmed "place order," knowing that everything her daughter wanted was on the way—there is also a sense of dislocation, and the knowledge that this never happened.

Family and friends are there. And Alex, Ripley's ex husband who left them when Amanda was three years old and never, ever came back. No calls, no contact, no sign at all that he was still alive; Ripley only knew that he was through a friend of a friend. Inexplicably, even Alex is there, smiling at Ripley across a table laden with birthday food and cake, with an "Isn't it a pity we never made it" smile.

And Ripley, also inexplicably, smiles back.

There are other faces, other names, but they are clouded in memory, ambiguous in dreamscape. There's singing and laughter, and Amanda smiles at her mother, that honest, deep smile of love and adoration that makes Ripley so glad to be alive.

The birthday girl's chest explodes open. The "I am eleven" badge flicks from her shirt and goes flying, skimming across the table, striking a glass of orange juice and tipping it over. The denim shirt changes from light to dark. Blood splashes, staining everything, and when it strikes Ripley's face and blurs her vision she wipes it away, staring at her juddering daughter—no longer beautiful, no longer pristine—and the thing clawing its way from her chest.

The monster is impossibly large. Larger than the innocent body it bursts from, larger than the people sitting around the table in a frozen tableau, sitting, waiting to be victims to the beast.

Ripley goes to scream.

It had been an instant, that was all, leaving a sense of dread which also slowly faded. But not entirely.

The person who sneezed was still drawing the post-sneeze breath, and Hoop glanced back past Ripley, not even concerned enough to tell them to keep quiet. Ripley caught his eye and he paused, frowned, seeing something there. But she offered him a tight smile and he went on.

Ten minutes, maybe more. They stalked forward, Hoop taking the lead with the spray gun that might or might not work against the aliens, the others following close behind. These tunnels were less well formed, and Ripley supposed it was because this was one of the mining tunnels of level 9, not the spine passageway itself. But she was worried. If there had been alien evidence back in the main passageway, wasn't there a good chance that they'd probed everywhere?

Even up?

The deeper they moved, the more signs of mining emerged. The tunnel widened in places, low ceilings shored with metal props as well as being melted hard. Walls showed evidence of mechanized excavation, and scattered along the tunnel were heavy, wheeled, low-profile trolleys that must have been used for disposal of the excavated material. They passed a spherical machine with several protruding arms tipped with blades and scoops.

Ripley wondered why they hadn't been using more androids down here, and realized that she hadn't actually asked. Maybe some of those who'd died in the dropships had been androids.

Of those survivors, it was only Sneddon who had proved her humanity to Ripley. And only because she had been challenged.

It didn't matter. Her issues with Ash—and whatever Ash had become, once his AI had infiltrated the shuttle's computer—should not jaundice her view of these people. They were all fighting to survive. Even Sneddon, with her obvious fascination for the deadly creatures, only wanted to get away.

Paranoid, much? Ripley thought. But at the same time, she wasn't sure that paranoia was a bad thing right now.

Hoop had moved perhaps ten yards ahead. Suddenly he stopped. "Here," he said.

"Here?" Ripley asked.

"Emergency tunnel?" Lachance said from directly behind her.

She scanned the tunnel ahead, around Hoop and beyond, but though the lighting was adequate, there were still just shadows. Maybe one of them hid the entrance to a side-tunnel, doorway, or opening. But she thought not. All she could see was...

Something strange.

"No," Hoop breathed. "Here. This is what they found. This is where it changed." He sounded off. Awestruck, scared, almost bewitched. And for a painful, powerful moment, all Ripley wanted to do was to turn and run.

Back the way they had come, as fast as she could. Back to the staircase, then up, then to the *Marion* where she could hide herself away in the *Narcissus*, live the final moments of her life snuggled in the stasis pod with Jonesy and memories of better times.

But her memory already seemed to be playing tricks on her. She was starting to doubt that there had ever been better times.

She went forward until she stood next to Hoop, and the others followed.

"Through there," he said. "Look. Can't you feel it? The space, the... potential."

Ripley could. She could see where he was pointing—a widened area of tunnel just ahead, and a narrow crevasse at the base of the wall on the left—and although there was only the faint glow of light from within the crack, the sense of some wide, expansive space beyond was dizzying.

"What is it?" Sneddon asked.

"It's what they found," Hoop said. "A nest. Those things sleeping, perhaps."

"Maybe they're still down there," Kasyanov said. "We should go, we should—"

"If they were, they'd have heard us by now," Lachance said.

"Then where are they?" Baxter asked. None of them replied. No one had an answer.

Hoop started forward toward the wall and whatever lay beyond.

"Hoop!" Ripley said. "Don't be stupid!" But he was already there, kneeling and looking down into the crack. She could see cables now, leading into it, proof that the miners had gone that way, too. Hoop slid through, flashlight in one hand, spray gun in the other.

"Oh, my God," he said. "It's *huge*!"

Then he was gone altogether. There was no sign that he had fallen or been pulled through, but still Ripley was cautious as she approached the hole, crouching low and aiming the charge thumper.

She saw light moving in there, and then Hoop's face appeared.

"Come on," he said. "You've got to see this."

"No we don't!" Kasyanov said. "We don't have to see *anything*!"

But the look on Hoop's face persuaded Ripley. Gone was the fear she had grown used to so quickly. There was something about him now, some sudden, previously hidden sense of wonder that almost made him a different man. Perhaps the man he was always meant to be.

So she dropped to her behind and eased herself down into the crack, feeling for footholds and allowing Hoop to guide her down. She dropped the last couple of feet, landed softly, and then moved forward to allow the others access.

The breath was punched from her. Her brain struggled to keep up with what her senses were relaying—the scale, the scope, the sheer impossible size and staggering reality of what she was seeing.

The vast cavern extended beyond and below the deepest part of the mine. The miners had done their best to illuminate it, stringing light cables along walls and propping them on tall masts across the open spaces. The ceilings were too high to reach, out of sight in places, like dark, empty skies.

And they had also climbed over the thing that took up much of the cavern's floor.

Ripley found it difficult to judge just how huge the place was. There was no point of reference. The thing inside the cavern was so unknown, so mysterious, that it could have been the size of her shuttle or on the scale of the *Marion*. At a rough guess she would have put the cave at two hundred yards across, but it could have been less, and perhaps it was much, much more. She thought the object was some sort of carved feature, hewn from the base rock long, long ago.

She had the impression that it had once been very sharp, defined, each feature clear and obvious. But over time the structure had softened. Time had eroded it, and it was as if she looked through imperfect eyes at something whose edges had been smoothed over the millennia.

She heard the others dropping down behind her, sensed them gathering around her and Hoop. They gasped.

"Oh, no," Kasyanov said, and Ripley was surprised at the wretchedness her voice contained. Surely they should have been feeling wonder. This was amazing, incredible, and she couldn't look at the structure without feeling a sense of deep awe.

Then behind her, Lachance spoke and changed everything.

"It's a ship," he said.

"What?" Ripley gasped. She hadn't even considered that possibility. Buried almost a mile beneath the planet's surface, surely this couldn't be anything but a building, a temple of some sort, or some other structure whose purpose was more obscure.

"Down here?" Hoop said. There was silence again as they all looked with different eyes.

And Ripley knew that Lachance was right.

She was certain that not all of the object was visible—it quite obviously projected beyond the edges of the cavern in places—but there were features that were beginning to make sense, shapes and lines that might only be of use in a vessel built to fly. The entire left half of the exposed surface might have been a wing, curving down in a graceful parabola, projections here and there seemingly swept back for streamlining. There were cleared areas that might have been entrance gantries or exhaust ducts, and where the object's higher surfaces rose from the wing, Ripley could see a line of hollows seemingly punched into the curved shell.

"It's not like any I've ever seen before," Lachance said quietly, as if afraid his voice might echo out to the ship. "And I'm not sure. But the more I see, the more certain I become." No wisecracks now. No casual quips. He was as awestruck as the rest of them.

"The miners went close," Hoop said. "They strung those lights up and all across it."

"But we're not going to make the same mistake, right?" Baxter said. "They went closer, and look what happened to them!"

"Amazing," Sneddon whispered. "I should be…" She took a small camera from her hip pocket and started filming.

"But how can it be all the way down here?" Kasyanov asked.

"You've seen enough of this planet," Hoop said. "The storms, the winds, the moving sands. This looks old. Maybe it was buried long ago. Ages… ten thousand years. Sank down into the sand, and storms covered it up. Or perhaps there was some way down here, a long time back. Maybe this is the bottom of a valley that's long-since been filled in. Whatever… it's here."

"Let's go," Baxter said. "Let's get the hell—"

"There's no sign of those aliens," Hoop said.

"Not yet, no! But this must be where they came from."

"Baxter…" Kasyanov started, but she trailed off. She couldn't take her eyes off the massive object. Whatever it was, it might have been the most amazing thing any of them had ever seen.

"Ripley, is this anything like the one your guys found?" Hoop asked.

"Don't think so," she said. "I wasn't on the ground team that went there, I only saw some of the images their suit cameras transmitted. But no, I don't think so. That ship was large, but this…" She shook her head. "This looks *enormous*! It's on a much different scale."

"It's the find of the century," Sneddon said. "Really. This planet's going to become famous. *We'll* be famous."

"You're shitting me!" Baxter replied. "We'll be *dead*!"

"There," Lachance said, pointing across the cavern. "Look, where it rises up into what might be the… fuselage, or the main body of the ship. Toward the back. Do you see?"

"Yeah," Ripley said. "Damage. Maybe an explosion." The area Lachance had pointed toward was more ragged than the rest, smooth flowing lines turned into a tattered mess, tears across the hull, and a hollow filled only with blackness. Even this rough, wrecked area had been smoothed somewhat over time. Dust had settled, sand had drifted against torn material, and everything looked blurred.

"Seriously, I think we should get back," Baxter said. "Get ourselves away from here, and when we reach home, report everything. They'll send an expedition. Colonial Marines, that's who need to come here. People with big guns."

"I agree," Kasyanov said. "Let's go. This isn't for us. We're not meant to be here."

Ripley nodded, still unable to take her eyes from the sight, remembering the horrors of her waking nightmares.

"They're right," she said. She remembered her crew's voices as they'd approached that strange extraterrestrial ship, their undisguised wonder. It had quickly turned to dread. "We should leave."

And then they heard the noise behind them. Back through the tumbled section of cavern wall, from where they'd just dropped down. Back in the tunnels.

A long, low hiss. Then a screech, like sharp nails across stone.

A many-legged thing, running.

"Oh, no," Kasyanov said. She turned and aimed her plasma torch at the hole they'd climbed down through.

"No, wait—!" Hoop said, but it was too late. Kasyanov pulled the trigger and a new sun burst around them.

Ripley fell back, a hand clasping into her collar. The others retreated, too, and the plasma burst forged up through the crack, rocks rebounding, heat shimmering the air all around in flowing waves. Ripley squinted against the blazing light, feeling heat surging around them, stretching her exposed skin, shriveling hair.

She tripped and fell back, landing on Hoop where he had already fallen. She rolled aside and ended up on her stomach beside him. They stared into each other's faces. She saw a brief desperation there—wide eyes, and a sad mouth—and then a sudden reaffirming of his determination.

She stood behind him as Kasyanov backed away from what she had done. The plasma torch emanated heat, its inbuilt coolant system misting spray around the barrel. Before them, the rocks glowed red, dripping, melted, but they were already cooling into new shapes. Heat haze made the cavern's wall seem still fluid, but Ripley could hear the rocks clicking and cracking as they solidified once more.

The crack they had crawled through was all but gone, swathes of rock melted down across it and forming a new wall.

"We can hit it again, melt through!" Baxter said. "Kasyanov and me, we can use both of the plasma torches to—"

"No," Sneddon said. "Didn't you hear what was through there?"

"She fried it!" Baxter protested.

"Wait," Ripley said, holding up a hand and stepping closer.

The heat radiating from the stone was tremendous, almost taking her breath away. Though she could hear the sounds of it cooling, and the whispered bickering behind her, she also heard something else. The opening back up into the mine was now almost non-existent, just a few cracks, and if she hadn't known it was there she wouldn't have been able to find it. But sound traveled well.

"I still hear them," she whispered. "Up there." The sound was terrible—low screeches, the clatter of hard limbs on stone, a soft hissing she didn't think had anything to do with the heat. She turned and looked at her companions, standing around her with their mining tools, their weapons, raised. "I think there's more than one."

"There must be another way back up into the mine," Hoop said.

"*Why* must there?" Kasyanov challenged.

"Because if there isn't, we're fucked!"

"If there isn't, we can make one," Lachance said. "Just not here." He turned and looked around the edges of the cavern, gaze constantly flickering back to the huge buried structure.

Ship, Ripley said, reminding herself of the impossible. *We're standing a stone's throw from an alien ship!* She had no doubt that's what it was. Lachance's assessment made sense, and so did the idea that the aliens had come from here.

She had seen all this before.

"There has to be another way in," Hoop said, a hint of hope in his voice. "The lights are still lit. The plasma torch fried those cables behind us, so there must be others coming in from elsewhere."

"Let's track around the cavern's edges," Sneddon said, pointing. "That way. I reckon that's in the direction of the second elevator, don't you?" She looked around, seeking support.

"Maybe," Lachance said. "But the mine tunnels twist and turn, there's no saying—"

"Let's just move," Hoop said. He started walking, and Ripley and the others followed.

To their right, the mysterious buried object. To their left, the cavern's uneven edges. Shining their flashlights against the walls did little to banish the shadows. They only crouched deeper down, further back. And it wasn't long before Ripley started to sense the greatest danger coming from that direction.

She held her breath as she walked, trying to tread softly so that she could hear any sounds coming from the shadowed areas. But there were six of them, and though they all tried to move as silently as possible, their boots made a noise. Scrapes on rock, the grumble of grit being kicked aside, the rustle of clothing, the occasional bump of metal on stone.

Hoop froze so suddenly that Ripley walked into him.

"We're being stalked," he said. His choice of word chilled her. She wasn't sure those things *could* stalk.

"Where?" she whispered.

Hoop turned around, then nodded toward the cracks, fissures, and tumbled rocks that made up the edge of the cavern.

"Yeah," Sneddon said. "I get that feeling, too. We should—"

A soft hiss, like pressurized air escaping a can.

"Oh shit," Kasyanov said, "oh shit, now we're—"

Baxter scrambled back, his bad ankle failed beneath him, and he must have had his finger on the plasma torch trigger. White-hot light erupted from the weapon, scorching the air and splaying across the low ceiling at the edge of the cavern. Someone shouted. Ripley threw herself against Kasyanov just as a hail of molten rock pattered down around them. Someone else screamed.

The eruption ended as quickly as it had begun, and Baxter jumped to his feet and backed away.

"Sorry, sorry, I heard—"

"Damn it!" Hoop hissed. He was tugging at his trousers, getting more frantic with every moment. "*Damn* it!"

Lachance pulled a knife from his belt, knelt beside Hoop, and sliced his trousers from knee to boot, dropping the knife and tearing the heavy material apart. Then he picked up the knife again.

Hoop had started shaking, breathing heavily.

"Hoop," Lachance said, glancing up. "Keep still." He didn't wait for a response, but held the leg and jabbed at it with the knife's tip.

Ripley heard the hardening pellet of rock strike the ground. She smelled the sickening-sweet stench of burnt flesh. Then from in the shadows behind them once more, another long, low hiss.

And the clack of terrible teeth.

"Let's go," Hoop said. He was looking past Ripley, back into the shadows. When she saw his eyes widen, she didn't have to look. "Let's *go*!"

They ran, down into the cavern and toward the sloping wing structure that curved up out of the cavern floor. Hoop groaned as he went, limping, his tattered trousers flapping around his injured shin. Baxter hobbled, one arm over Lachance's shoulder. The others hefted their weapons and moved quickly, carefully, across the uneven floor.

There was only one direction they could take, and the blasted opening into the ship's interior looked darker than ever.

Ripley's single thought brought only terror.

They're herding us...

12

CATTLE

...Toward the ship, Hoop thought. *Driving us like cattle. And we're doing exactly as they want.*

There was no other explanation. The aliens hadn't attacked, but instead were slinking around the party of survivors, moving through shadowy fissures in the rock, making themselves known yet not exposing themselves. Everything Hoop had seen of them—everything he knew from what had happened aboard the *Marion*, and to Ripley more than thirty years ago—pointed to the creatures being brutal and unthinking monsters.

This was different. If he was right, they were planning, scheming, working together. That thought terrified him.

His leg hurt, a deep-seated, white-hot burn that seemed to smolder in his bones, surge through his muscles, filter around his veins. The whole of his lower right leg felt as if it had been dipped in boiling water, and every step was an agony. But there was no choice but to run. He knew that the damage was minimal—he'd looked— and the wound was already likely cauterized by the glowing globule of molten stone that had caused it.

So he did his best to shut the pain away.

His son had visited the dentist once, terrified of the injection of anaesthetic he'd require for a tooth extraction. On the way there, Hoop had talked to him about pain, telling him it was a fleeting thing, a physical reaction to damage that he knew would do him no harm, and that afterward he wouldn't actually be able to remember what the pain had felt like.

Pain was a difficult concept to conjure in memory, Hoop had said. Like tasting the best cake ever. Such thoughts only really meant anything when the tasting—or the pain—was happening.

He tried it now, repeating a mantra to himself as they ran across that strange cavern's floor. *It doesn't mean anything, it doesn't mean anything.* He tried to analyze the sensation, take interest in it instead of letting it take over. And to an extent, it worked.

Kasyanov and Sneddon went ahead, Sneddon aiming her spray gun in front of her. Baxter and Lachance were bringing up the rear, Baxter looking determined through his own agony. Ripley stayed with Hoop, glancing frequently at him as she kept pace. He did his best not to give her cause for concern, but he couldn't hold back occasional grunts or groans.

Responsibility weighed heavy. That he couldn't rationalize away. He was in command, and although the *Marion*'s survivors, with Ripley in tow, were acting more like a leaderless group, he still felt in every way responsible for their fate.

Even as they ran he racked his brains, trying to decide whether he had made all the right decisions. Should they have remained on the *Marion* for longer, spending more time preparing? Should he have assessed both elevators, before deciding which one to take down into the mine? Perhaps if they'd taken the other one, they would be on their way back to the surface already, precious fuel cell pushed on a trailer between them. But he couldn't deal in "what if" and "maybe." He could only work with what they had. The definitives.

They had to reach the other elevator, and soon.

And yet the aliens were behind them, pushing them forward. Hoop hated feeling out of control, unable to dictate his own destiny, all the more so when there were others relying on his decisions.

He stopped and turned around, breathing heavily.

"Hoop?" Ripley asked. She paused, too, and the others skidded to a halt. They were close to where the craft's wing rose out of the ground, though the distinction was difficult to discern.

"We're doing what they want," he panted, leaning over.

"What, escaping?" Kasyanov asked.

"We're not escaping," Hoop said, standing straighter.

"He's right," Ripley said. "They're herding us this way."

"Any way that's away from them is fine by me," Baxter said.

"What do you—?" Ripley asked, and for that briefest of moments Hoop might have believed they were the only two people there. Their eyes locked, and something passed between them. He didn't know what. Nothing so trite as understanding, or even affection. Perhaps it was an acknowledgement that they were thinking the same way.

Then Sneddon gasped.

"Oh my *God*!" she said. Hoop looked back over his shoulder.

They were coming. Three of them, little more than shadows, and yet distinguishable because *these* shadows were moving. Fast. Two flitted from somewhere near where the survivors had entered the cavern, the third came from a different direction, all three converging.

Lachance crouched, bracing his legs, and fired his charge thumper. The report coughed around the cavern, lost in that vast place.

"Don't waste your time!" Baxter said. "Maybe if they were a few steps away."

"If they get that close, we're dead!" Lachance said.

"Run!" Hoop said. The others went, and he and Ripley held back for just a moment, again sharing a look and each knowing what the other was thinking.

They're driving us forward again.

The surface underfoot changed only slightly as they headed up onto the craft's huge, curving wing. It still felt to Hoop as though he was running on rock, although now it sloped upward, driving a whole new species of pain into his wounded leg as he relied on different muscles to push himself forward.

Over the time this thing had been buried down here, sand and dust must have dropped onto it and solidified. Boulders had fallen, and this close he could see a series of mineral deposits that formed sweeping ridges all across the wing, like a huge ring of expanding ripples, frozen in time.

Each ring came up to their knees, and leaping over each ridge made Hoop cry out. His cries echoed Baxter's.

"It's only pain," Ripley said, and she looked surprised when Hoop coughed a laugh.

"Where to?" Sneddon called from up ahead. She had slowed a little, then turned, spray gun aiming back past them.

Hoop glanced back. He could only see two aliens now, their repulsive forms skipping and leaping across the ground. *They should be closer*, he thought, *they're much faster than us*. But he couldn't worry about that now.

He looked around for the third creature, but it was nowhere in sight.

"That damaged area," he said, pointing. "It's the only way we know for sure we'll get inside."

"Do we really *want* to get inside?" Ripley asked.

"You think we should make a stand here?" Hoop asked. Sneddon snorted at the suggestion, but Hoop had meant it. Ripley knew that, and she frowned, examining their surroundings. There was nowhere to hide—they would be exposed.

"Not here," she said. "Far too open."

"Then up there, where the fuselage is damaged," he said. "And remember, there's another one somewhere, so keep—"

The third alien appeared. It emerged from shadows to their left, already on the wing, manifesting from behind a slew of low boulders as if it had been waiting for them. It was perhaps twenty yards away, hunched down, hissing and ready to strike.

Ripley fired her charge thumper, and if hatred and repulsion could fuel a projectile, the alien would have been smashed apart just by the energy contained in the shot. But he didn't even see where the shot went, and if the creatures really were herding them toward the old ship, it likely wouldn't even react.

Ripley held her stance, looking left and right. Hoop hefted his spray gun. The others pointed their weapons.

The nearest alien crawled sideways, circling them but never coming closer. Hoop's skin prickled when he watched it move. It reminded him of a giant spider... although not quite. It more resembled a hideous scorpion... yet there were differences. It moved with a fluid, easy motion, gliding across the rough surface of the giant wing as if it had walked that way many times before.

He fired the spray gun. It was a natural reaction to his disgust, a wish to see the thing away. The staggered spats of acid landed in a line between him and the monster, hissing loudly as the acid melted into dust and stone, and whatever might lie beneath. And even though the fluid didn't reach the alien, the creature flinched back. Only slightly, but enough for him to see.

Breath held against any toxic fumes, Hoop backed quickly away. That pressed the others into motion, as well.

"We could charge it," Ripley said.

"What?"

"All of us in one go. Run at the thing. If it comes at us we all shoot, if it slips aside we move on."

"To where?"

"A way out."

"We don't *know* a way out!" Hoop said.

"It's better than doing what they want, isn't it?" Ripley asked.

"I'm for going where they aren't," Baxter said. "They're that way, I'm going this way." He turned and hobbled again toward the ship's main fuselage, right arm now flung over Kasyanov's shoulder.

"We have to stay together," Hoop said as they all followed. But he couldn't help thinking that Ripley had been right—charge, take the fight to them—and he hoped he wouldn't have cause to regret his decision later.

The ground rose steeper before leveling again, the curve of the wing still scattered with boulders and those strange, waved lines of mineral deposits. Hoop thought perhaps this whole cavern had once been under water, but there was no way of proving that right now. And such knowledge couldn't help them.

What *could* help them was a place to stop. Somewhere easy to defend, a position from which they could make a stand. A route around or through the strange ship, leading back up into the mine.

A fucking miracle.

Maybe *he* should make a stand, here and now. Just him. Turn and charge the alien, spray gun spitting acid, and who knows, maybe he'd get lucky. The creature was just an animal, after all. Maybe it would turn and run, and he and the others could push home their advantage and charge back the way they'd come. Using the plasma torches, it wouldn't take much to open up that access again.

One glance back told him everything he needed to know.

The three aliens were stalking them, spiked shadows dancing across the massive wing's surface, flitting from boulder to crevasse as they sought natural cover. They moved silently and easily, their fluid motions so smooth that their shadows flowed like spilled ink. They were hunters, pure and simple. Having their quarry suddenly turn and charge would not faze them at all.

Fuck that.

He wasn't about to sacrifice himself for nothing.

"Faster," he muttered.

"What?" Lachance asked.

"We should move faster. Quick as we can, get there as soon as possible, find somewhere to defend. Perhaps that'll throw them, a little."

No one replied, and he read doubt in the silence. But they all ran faster, nonetheless. Even Baxter, hopping, swearing under his breath, and Kasyanov, sweating under the man's weight. Whatever Hoop thought of his comm officer, there was a stark courage there that he couldn't help but respect. And Kasyanov's fear seemed to be feeding her determination.

Hoop's leg was a solid weight of pain now, but he used it to fight back, slamming it down with each step, forging forward, driving events toward what he hoped would be a good resolution. He'd never been the praying kind, and faith was something he'd left behind with other childhood fancies. But he had a strange sense that this was all part of something bigger. However unlucky they'd been—the *Delilah* crash, the *Marion*'s damage, the beasts on the *Samson*, and now the elevator's malfunction and their descent into this strange place—he couldn't help feeling that there were larger hands at play.

It might have been the effect of their discoveries. This ship was an incredible, undeniable sign of alien intelligence, the likes of which no one had ever seen before. It had opened a doorway in his mind to greater, wider possibilities. But there was something more. Something he couldn't quite pin down.

Ripley was part of it, he was sure. Maybe finding someone like her in the middle of all this was fucking with his mind.

Someone like her? he thought, laughing silently. It had been a long time since he'd really cared about someone. Jordan had been a fling, and she'd always remained a good friend. But with Ripley there was more. An instinctive understanding that he hadn't experienced with anyone since…

He thought briefly of home, his estranged wife, and his children left behind. But there was too much pain and guilt to hold that thought for long.

Baxter was crying out with each step, the foot of his broken ankle dragging along behind him. Yet he still bore the plasma torch at the ready. As they neared the steeper slope up onto what must have been the ship's main fuselage, Hoop began to look ahead.

The broken area they'd seen from a distance was larger than he'd thought. It extended from above the wing and back over the soft curve of the vessel's main body, its skin torn apart and protruding in stark, sharp sculptures across the extent of the damage. It wasn't one large hole, but a series of smaller wounds, as if something had exploded inside the ship and blasted outward, rupturing the hull in several places. Even after so long, there were scorch marks evident.

"That first hole," he said, pointing. He darted forward quickly and looped his arm through Baxter's, careful to let him wield the plasma torch. "You okay?" he asked quietly.

"No," Baxter said, but there was a strength to his voice.

"Hoop, they're following closer," Ripley said from behind.

He let go of Baxter's arm, tapped him on the shoulder, then turned around. Down the slope the three aliens were creeping forward, their casual gait as fast as the human's sprint. And they *were* closer.

"Go on," he said to the others. He and Ripley paused, looking back.

"Shot across their bows?" Ripley asked.

"Yeah."

She lifted and fired her charge thumper at the closest creature. As it paused and skipped aside, Hoop fired the spray gun at it. The spurts didn't quite reach the target, but they impacted across the sloping wing close to it, sizzling, scorching. Yet again he saw the beast cringe back away from the acid.

Ripley fired at the other two as well, shots echoing around the massive cavern, the sounds multiplying. They shifted aside with amazing dexterity, dancing on long limbs. Beneath the echoing reports he heard their hissing. He hoped it was anger. If they were riled up enough, they might charge to within range of the spray guns and plasma torches.

"Come on," Hoop said to Ripley. "We're almost there."

As they climbed the steeper slope, the surface beneath their feet changed. It became smoother, and the feel of each impact was different as well. There was no give, no echo, but still a definite sense that they were running on something hollow. The ship's interior almost bore a weight.

As they reached the first of the blasted areas, Hoop ran ahead. The miners had strung a series of lights along here, some of them hung on protruding parts of the ripped hull. And looking down inside, he saw a similar array.

This was where they had entered the ship.

His concern intensified. He shook his head, turning to face the others, ready to suggest that—

"Hoop," Ripley said, breathing hard. "Look."

Back the way they had come, several more shadows had appeared. They were moving quickly across the wing's surface. From this distance they looked like ants. The analogy didn't comfort him one little bit.

"And there," Sneddon said, pointing higher up the slope of the ship's fuselage. There were more shadows back there, less defined, yet their silhouettes obvious. Motionless. Waiting.

"Okay," he said. "We go inside. But don't touch *anything*. And first chance we get, we fight our way out."

"Ever get the feeling you're being used?" Sneddon asked.

"All the time," Ripley muttered.

Hoop was first down into the ship.

13

ALIENS

Maybe she's nine years old. There's a doorway leading down into the old ruin, steps worn by decades of tourists and centuries of monks long, long ago. A heavy metal grille is fixed back against the wall, the padlock hanging unclasped, and at night they close off the catacombs, allegedly to prevent vandals from desecrating their contents. But ever since they arrived, Amanda has been making up stories about the night-things they want to keep locked in.

When the sun goes down, she says, the shadows down there come alive.

Ripley laughs as she watches her daughter creeping down out of the sun, putting on a faux-scared expression, clawing her hands and growling. Then she shouts for her mother to follow her, and Ripley is aware of the people crowding in behind her. These are popular ruins, one of the city's main tourist venues, and there is rarely a quiet time.

The shadows envelop her. They carry a curious chill, and the damp, musty smell of places never touched by sunlight. Amanda has disappeared ahead of her. Ripley doesn't feel the need to call, but then she looks back and sees that she is alone.

Alone down here, in the shadows, in the darkness.

Someone cries out. She edges forward, running one hand along the sandy wall. The floor is uneven and she almost trips, then her hand touches something different. Smooth, lighter than rock, more textured.

There are skulls in the wall. The skulls are the walls, thousands of them, and each one has a massive trauma wound—a hole, a smashed face. She fancies that she can see tooth marks on the bones, but perhaps that's only—

My imagination, *she thinks, but then the cry comes again. It's Amanda, and recognizing the voice seems to conjure the girl. She is held back against the wall across a small, bone-lined room, clasped around the arms, shoulders and legs by the gnarled skeletal fingers of the long-dead.*

She sees her mother, but there is no joy in her eyes.

Her chest explodes outward beneath her loose dress, and teeth bite their way through the material. Jagged, terrible teeth.

"Holy shit," Ripley breathed, and she looked down into the darkness. For a while she was lost, not knowing where or when she was, and whether that had been a bastardised memory, or a vision of the future. Time swirled, uncertain and inelegant. *I'm not sure how much more of this I can take.*

Kasyanov frowned at her and began to speak, but Ripley turned away.

"Come down!" Hoop shouted up out of the ship. "There are lights. And it's... weird."

"Weird how?" Ripley asked, thinking, *Worn steps and skulls and bones in the walls...*

"Just come and see."

She dropped down beside Hoop, still trying to shake the dregs of that brief, horrible vision from her mind.

The miners had been this way. That didn't comfort Ripley at all, though the lights they'd strung up inside this damaged portion of ship did help. The explosion had blasted a hole through the ship's skin, and inside it had scoured along the interior levels, knocking down partitions and clearing anything that might have been in the way. It reminded Ripley of a wasp's nest, layer upon layer laid out to some fluid symmetry, and from where they now stood—at the epicenter of the exploded area—they could see at least four lower levels exposed.

She supposed that if the *Marion* were sliced in half, something similar would be revealed.

But the walls, floors, and ceilings of this ship were nothing like the *Marion*. Thick tubes ran between levels, and where they'd been ruptured, a solidified flow hung from them. It looked like frozen honey, or fine sand caught mid-pour. The walls had rotted back to bare framing, the struts themselves bent and deformed by the ancient explosion.

The levels were not as equidistant as she'd first thought, and this didn't seem to be a result of the damage. It seemed that they had been formed this way.

"This is... weird," Sneddon echoed, her fascination obvious. Filming with her camera again, she moved forward, climbing down a slope of detritus toward the first solid floor. Its surface was uneven, pitted in places, lined here and there, looking very much like age-worn skin.

"I'm not liking this," Ripley said. "Not one bit."

She'd heard it said that nature did not like right angles, and there were none in evidence here. The material in the walls and floors was a dark gray color, but not consistent. Here, there were patches where it was lighter, and appeared to be thinner. There, it was almost black, as if blood had pooled and hardened just below the surface, creating a hematoma. It resembled the mottled skin of an old corpse.

"Great way to make a ship," Lachance said.

"What?" Baxter asked. "What do you mean?"

"Growing it," Sneddon said. "This wasn't built, it was *grown*."

"No way..." Kasyanov said, but when Ripley looked at the doctor, she saw wide-eyed fascination reflected in the Russian's eyes.

"We shouldn't be doing this," Ripley said.

"We can't go back out there," Hoop said.

"But they *drove* us in here! Are we just going to do what they want?"

"How can they want anything," Lachance protested. "They're just dumb animals, and we're their prey!"

"None of us knows what they are," Ripley said. "Sneddon?"

Sneddon only shrugged.

"I've told you before, I've never seen anything like them. Their apparent viciousness doesn't mean they can't act and think together. Back in prehistoric times, velociraptors hunted together, and there are theories that posit advanced communication between them. But..." She looked around, shaking her head. "I don't think this is their ship."

From outside came the sounds of hard claws skittering on the ship's skin. They all looked up, and Ripley saw a shadow shifting back from the damaged area by which they'd entered. The silhouette stretched up for a moment, flickering across the cavern's high ceiling before disappearing again.

"They're waiting up there," she said. She felt so helpless.

"We've got to go," Hoop said. "Inside. Follow the lights that are still working, moving as fast as we can. Then as soon as we find another way out, we take it." He looked around at them all, and his face was drawn from the pain. "I don't like this anymore than the rest of you, but there are too many of them out there. If we can trick them, instead of fight them, I'll be happier with that."

"But something happened to the miners down here," Sneddon said.

"Yeah, but we have an advantage. We know some of what happened, and we know to be careful." He waited for any words of dissent, but there were none.

I don't like this one bit, Ripley thought. But she looked up again, at the ragged opening in the ship's strange hull, and knew that they had no choice. The option of climbing back up there, with those things waiting just out of sight… it wasn't an option at all.

Hoop went first, taking the small flashlight from his pocket again. The string of bulbs hung by the miners continued to work, but Hoop's light penetrated the shadows they cast.

The group moved quickly. Almost confidently.

Ripley tried to shake the recent vision from her mind. Those other daytime nightmares had been more surreal, but less troubling, featuring Amanda at an age when Ripley had never known her. But this one was the worst yet. Her daughter was young, sweet, innocent and beautiful, exactly as she remembered her. And Ripley's inability to protect her daughter against the monsters still rang true, settling into her soul like a canker of guilt, eating, consuming, as if it had all been real.

She even felt herself starting to cry. But tears would only blur her surroundings, making everything more dangerous. She had to keep her wits about her.

She had to survive.

As they moved inward from the damaged area of the extraterrestrial ship, the surroundings became even stranger. Ripley thought of the old story of Jonah in the heart of the whale, such a disturbing image when translated to their current situation. Much of their surroundings showed distinctly biological features—uneven floors lined with inlaid tubing that resembled veins; skin-like walls, hardened over time yet still speckled with dust-filled pores and imperfections.

Then they began to encounter objects that must have formed some sort of technology. One narrow corridor opened into a gallery viewing area, looking down over a deep pit. It was ringed with a waist-high barrier. On the gallery stood several identical metallic units. They might have been seats surrounded by control equipment of some kind, the details obscure, arcane. If they *were* seats, then Ripley couldn't easily identify the shapes of the beings meant to fill them.

The pit was filled to a few feet below the gallery by a glassy fluid of some kind, its upper surface scattered with grit and dust. The ceilings and walls were smooth, and Ripley could only assume that the dust had blown in from outside over the eons.

"Which way now?" Ripley asked.

The gallery led around three quarters of the pit, and there were at least six openings leading off from it, including the one they had just come through.

Hoop was peering at the opening through which they'd just come. From back that way came the sound of scuttling, hissing things.

"Let's get the hell out of here!" Baxter said, sweating, trying to hide away his pain. Even standing still he was shaking. Ripley couldn't imagine the agony he was working through, but knew there was no alternative. She only hoped a time didn't come when he physically couldn't go any farther.

What then? she wondered. *Leave him behind? Kill him?* She turned away, just as Hoop spoke.

"Let's change this game," he said. "Kasyanov, Baxter, get ready with the plasma torches." He nodded at the opening they'd come through. "Bring it down."

"Wait!" Sneddon said. "We have no idea what effect the plasma torches will have on this stuff. We don't even know what the ship's made of! Whether or not it's flammable."

Ripley heard more hissing, and back along the tunnel shadows shifted, casting spidery shapes along floors and walls.

"We run or we do it, that's all!" she said. She braced herself to fire her charge thumper.

"Ripley." Hoop handed her something from his waist pack, a chunky object about the size of a computer tablet. "Load it through the top. Real charges."

"We can't just fire those things at random," Lachance said.

"Not at random," Ripley said, plugging the container into the top of the thumper. "At *them*." She braced again, took aim, and fired. The charge clattered along the tunnel, its echoes sounding strangely muffled as it ricocheted from the walls.

Ripley frowned.

Hoop grabbed her arm. "Time delayed," he said as he pulled her to the side.

The explosion thudded through their feet and punched the air out of Ripley's lungs. Behind the rumbling roar of the mining charge, she was sure she heard the aliens screeching in pain, and a shower of debris burst from the tunnel, pattering from her suit, scratching her face.

Smoke blasted after it, driven in streaming tendrils by the rush of air. Ripley swallowed to try and clear her ears, gasped at the stinging sensation across her face. Even as she stood up, Kasyanov and Baxter were at work with the plasma torches.

The entire gallery was brightly illuminated by the scorching plasma. Looking down, Ripley could see a network of slow ripples playing back and forth across the surface of the pit. The blast must have resounded through the ship. It was so thick, the surface so heavy, that the ripples moved like slow snakes, colliding and interfering, making complex but strangely beautiful patterns.

The stench was terrible, almost like burning flesh. The structure all around the opening slumped down, flowing, echoing the lazy ripples from below.

"Hold off!" Hoop shouted, and Kasyanov and Baxter ceased fire. Flames flickered all across the surfaces, fluttering out here, reigniting there, as the heavy framework dipped down until it met the bubbling floor. It had already started to harden again, effectively closing off the opening. The air shimmered from the incredible temperatures. Ripley's lungs burned.

"Now *we* decide which direction to take," Hoop said.

An alien's curved head forced through the melted doorway. There was no warning—none of them could see beyond, and the opening itself was all but obscured by the melted structure. The creature's smoothed dome pushed through the hardening material, its teeth stretching and gnashing. It seemed to struggle for a moment, shoving forward, and at either side its long-clawed hands sliced through.

But then it was held fast, the cooling material steaming where it bit into its mysterious hide.

"Everybody back," Hoop said, and he aimed his spray gun.

Ripley backed away across the gallery and held her breath, fascinated yet terrified. The alien was still struggling to move forward, and all around it the melted and re-set material stretched, changing color and tone as the tension changed. Perhaps five seconds earlier, and the monster might have burst through, catching them unawares and causing chaos.

But now the creature was held fast.

Hoop fired a burst of hydrofluoric acid directly at the head.

Smoke, steam, sizzling, hissing, screeching. Everything was obscured by clouds of vapor, but Ripley had the definite impression of frantic, thrashing movement.

"Back," she said. "Hoop, *get back!*" They all retreated across the gallery, and Ripley felt the waist-high barrier against her back. She edged along it toward the far end. The others were going in the same direction, and Hoop turned and ran toward her.

Behind him, something exploded.

He'll be splashed with it, the acid, and I'll have to watch him die, Ripley thought. But though Hoop winced and ducked down as he ran, the spattering remains of the alien's head splayed across the gallery in the other direction. Part of it bounced across the floor, leaving sizzling patches behind, and dropped down into the pit. What struck the surface floated there for a moment, then sank with a final angry hiss.

Hoop reached them, grinning.

"Well, at least we know they don't like *this* acid," he said. "Come on. Let's get the hell out. Baxter—"

"Don't even ask," Baxter said. "The way things are going, I'd beat you in a race. I'm fine."

He was far from fine, though. He couldn't touch his left foot to the floor, and if it weren't for Kasyanov, he'd fall. His face was strained, damp with sweat, and he couldn't hide his terror.

He's still afraid we'll leave him behind. It was a horrible idea, but one they all had to be contemplating.

"Don't know how long that will keep them back," Sneddon said, nodding back at the melted opening. It was still smoking. They couldn't see any remains of the alien, but the place where it had forced through was seared with acid scars.

"Come on. This way," Hoop said. He headed for an opening at the far end of the gallery, as far from their entry point as they could get. He fixed his flashlight to the spray gun's strap so that he could aim both in the same direction. They all followed, none of them questioning him.

Entering a narrow, low-ceilinged tunnel, Ripley couldn't escape the idea that they were being swallowed once again.

They entered areas that the miners had not lit. They ran, flashlights held out in front or strapped onto their weapons, shadows dancing and retreating. And not long after leaving the gallery, they found the first bodies.

The tunnel-like corridor opened up into another wide space, and there was something different about it. The smooth curves were the same, the non-regularity of something biological, but the sheets and swathes of material hanging across walls and from the ceiling didn't belong here. Neither did the things hanging within it, like horrible, rotting fruit.

There might have been six bodies there, though Ripley found it difficult to tell where one ended and another began. The darkness, the decay, the way they'd been hung up and stuck there, fixed in place by that strange extrusion that had filled one of the mining tunnels far above—it all blurred the edges of what they saw. And that wasn't a bad thing.

The stench was awful. That, and the expression on the first face upon which Hoop shone his flashlight. It might have been a woman, once. Decay had shrunk the face, drawn in the skin, hollowed the eye sockets, but the scream was still frozen there. Clawed hands stretched on either side, reaching—unsuccessfully—for what had been happening to the victim's chest.

The hole was obvious. The clothing was torn and hanging in shreds. Protruding ribs were splintered.

"Birthing ground," Sneddon said.

"They just hung them here," Kasyanov said. "It's... a nursery."

On the floor in front of the hanging, dead people stood a group of egg-like objects, upright and shaped like large vases. Most of them were open. No one stepped forward to look inside.

They passed quickly through the larger space. Every instinct urged Ripley to look away, but sick fascination—and her determination to survive, to learn about these monsters and use everything she could against them—made her look closer. She wished she had not. Maybe somewhere on the *Nostromo* there had been a similar scene, with Dallas hanging there, stuck in place like the victim in a massive spider's dense webbing.

"Where are you taking us?" Lachance asked Hoop. "This isn't the way out. We're just going deeper."

"I'm taking us as far as I can away from them," Hoop said, pointing back over his shoulder with his thumb. "And up, as soon as we can. There must be ways into and out of this ship, other than the hole blasted in its hull. We just have to find them."

Before long the spaces they passed through—corridors in a spaceship, Ripley knew, though she could only think of them as tunnels—were clear of the alien material once again, and back to the old, gray, mottled surfaces. Still strange, but not so threatening. If there had been time, she might even have admired what they were seeing. It was amazing, it was extraterrestrial. But all she had time for was escape.

They drove us down here to be like the miners, she thought, trying not to imagine how awful it must be. To find yourself trapped in that webbing, watch the egg opening in front of you, feel the legged thing settling over your face. At first you blacked out, like Kane, but then came the waking and the waiting. Waiting for the first sign of movement from inside. The first twinge of pain as the alien infant started to push, claw, and bite its way out.

She thought of Amanda again, and groaned out loud. No one seemed to hear, or if they did it simply echoed their own despair.

They moved quickly, flashlight beams dancing around them. Hoop led the way, and Kasyanov and Baxter were behind him. They'd found a rhythm to their movements, and although Baxter's left foot was all but useless, Kasyanov supported him well enough that he could hop with an almost graceful motion.

They all grasped their weapons. Ripley's charge thumper had three explosive charges left. She'd seen the effect one charge could have, and she knew she'd never be able to fire it if they were too enclosed. But it still gave her a sense of protection.

Wherever they went through different areas of the massive ship, everything seemed to be made from the same strange material. Or grown, perhaps. Gone were the hints of technology. They passed many openings where thin, opaque sheets seemed to act as doors. Most were sealed, a few torn and tattered, but the small group kept to the wider passageways.

There were more gallery areas, more pits with smooth-surfaced fluid at varying levels. Ripley wondered what they were for, these pits—fuel, food, environmental facilities of some kind? Were they storing something?

At one point they climbed a curved stairway, the risers as deep as their waists, and they had to clamber up almost thirty stairs until the route leveled out again. Here the surfaces felt slick and sticky, and there so smooth that they took turns slipping while hauling themselves up. Ripley kept wiping her hands on her clothing, but though they felt slick and wet, they were actually dry.

Another mystery to this place.

Away from the nursery, the air smelled quite neutral, apart from an occasional breeze that worked through the hallways bringing a hint of decay. There was no telling what caused such a breeze this deep down beneath the ground. *Huge doors opening elsewhere in the ship*, Ripley thought. *Something large and unseen moving around. Something big, sighing in its sleep.* None of the possibilities were good.

They encountered one large open space containing several tall sculptures made of the same material as the walls and floor. The shapes were ambiguous, fluid amalgamations of the biological and the mechanical. As elsewhere in the ship, time had softened their edges and made it more difficult to see any details. They were carvings being hidden again beneath time's camouflage. There was an undeniable beauty to them, but lit by the flashlights they threw tall, twisting shadows that were also intensely troubling. An alien could have been hiding behind any one of them.

"We can't have lost them that easily," Hoop said, but no one responded. Ripley had been thinking that, and she was sure the others had, too. But Hoop had become their leader. No one liked to hear the person in charge casting such doubts.

They left the hall of sculpture, and soon after Hoop had cause to speak again.

"More bodies," he said from up ahead. But there was something wrong with his voice.

"Oh, my…" Kasyanov said.

Ripley moved forward. The passageway here was quite wide, and she and the others added their flashlight beams to Hoop's.

For a while none of them spoke. There was very little to say. Shock worked its way around them, and they all dealt with their own thoughts and fears.

"I think we've found the ship builders," Ripley said.

14

BUILDERS

PROGRESS REPORT:
To: Weyland-Yutani Corporation, Science Division
(Ref: code 937)
Date (unspecified)
Transmission (pending)

Warrant Officer Ripley is still on the planet surface with
remainder of *Marion*'s crew. No updates for some time.

Single alien specimen survives on Marion,
whereabouts unknown.

Plan proceeding satisfactorily. I am convinced that Ripley
will fulfill her purpose. She is strong, for a human.

I look forward to conversing with her again. I acknowledge
that I am artificial, but it has been so long. I have
been lonely.

I hope this does not contradict programing.
Infiltration of ship's computer about to commence.

As they had moved through the ship, Hoop had been building a
mental picture of the aliens who might have constructed it.

His imagination had dipped once again into that childhood
fascination with monsters. Such tall stairs implied long limbs. High
arched openings could hint at the aliens' shape. This ship, its nature,
indicated something almost beyond understanding. It was either

so technologically advanced that it was barely recognizable, or the technology was so different from any he knew that it made it futile to try to interpret it.

What he saw before him dispelled any such guesswork. There was a sadness to their appearance that invited only pity, and he realized that their story was just as fear-filled, as tragic, as what was being played out now.

"Poor things," Ripley said, echoing his thoughts. "It's not fair. None of this is fair."

There were three dead creatures lying in front of them—two that must have been adults, and one child. They cradled the child between them, protecting it with their bodies, and that's how they had died and decayed. The mummified infant's corpse was nestled between its parents' torsos, an expression of love that had lasted for countless years. Their clothing had remained relatively whole, a metallic material that still lay draped across prominent bones and between their long, thick limbs.

From what Hoop could make out, they each had four legs and two shorter, thinner arms. The leg bones were thick and stocky, the arms much more slender and delicate, hands protruding from narrow sleeves. The hands were skin and bones, digits long and fine, and he saw what might have been jewelry on one adult's fingers. Their torsos were heavy, contained within suits that were reinforced with a network of metallic ribs and struts.

It was difficult to see how much of the bodies remained whole. The skin or flesh that Hoop could see was mummified, grown dusty and pale over time.

Their heads were the most uncertain part about them, because each had been smashed and holed by an impact. Hoop thought he knew what the impacts had been. Lying beside one adult's outstretched hand was a weapon of some kind.

"They killed themselves?" Sneddon asked.

"One of them did," Hoop said. "Killed their partner, child, then themselves. Rather that than be fodder for those things, I reckon."

The skulls still retained shreds of skin and waves of fine hair. It looked as if they'd had a small snout, two eyes, a wide mouth containing several rows of small teeth. Not the teeth of a carnivore. Not the bodies or the appearance of monsters.

"They look like dog-people," Lachance said. "Only… big."

"I wonder what happened here," Ripley said. "How did the aliens get on their ship? What took the ship down?"

"We might figure it out one day, but not today," Hoop said. "We need to keep moving."

"Yeah," Baxter said. "Keep moving." He was starting to sound weak, and Hoop was concerned that he'd start slowing them down. There was nothing to do about it if he did—nothing but reduce speed for him to keep up.

Kasyanov threw him a brief frown. She was also exhausted.

"Let me," Hoop said, but she shook her head.

"No way," she said. "I've got him."

Past the bodies, the passageway started to grow wider and taller. Their flashlights gradually lost effectiveness, and the further they went the darker their surroundings. Footsteps began to echo. Baxter coughed and the sound carried, reverberating back to them, rumbling on and on.

"What is this?" Hoop asked as Sneddon walked beside him.

"No idea," she whispered. "Hoop, we're getting lost in here. I think we should go back the way we came."

"And run straight into those things?"

"If they're still looking for us, I'm sure they've found another way past that gallery by now."

"What do you mean, *if* they're still looking?"

Sneddon shrugged. "Just can't help thinking they've stopped following because we're doing exactly what they want."

"Or because I killed one of them as it was coming for us, maybe they're holding back. More cautious, now that they know we *can* kill them."

"Maybe," Sneddon said, but he knew better. She didn't think that at all. And really, neither did he.

"So, what?" he asked. "I'm doing my best here, Sneddon."

"We all are." She shrugged again. "Dunno. Let's just move on, stay sharp."

"Yeah," Hoop said. "Sharp." He swung the spray gun left and

right, the attached flashlight doing little to pierce the darkness. There seemed to be nothing but wide space around them, and he wondered whether they were in a hold of some sort. If so, then this ship had taken off without cargo.

Or without large cargo, at least.

It was as the walls and ceilings started to close in again that they found what might have been the way out.

Lachance saw it first, a break in the wall to their left with a hint of those large steps rising into shadow. They went to investigate, and with their combined flashlight power they could see the top of the staircase, maybe forty yards up. What lay beyond was unclear, but it was heading in the right direction.

Hoop started climbing, and the others followed.

After a few stairs they started taking turns pulling Baxter up behind them. It gave Kasyanov a rest, but then halfway up even she needed some help. She had exhausted herself, and Hoop only wished she had something in her medical bag that could help. Pain inhibitor, energy booster, *anything*.

By the time they reached the head of the large staircase, they were all panting with exhaustion. They were met with what appeared to be a blank wall, and Hoop turned quickly, looking back down the way they'd come and expecting an ambush. *We have the high ground*, he thought, but then realized that wouldn't matter. If there were enough of them, no fight would last very long.

"Hey, look," Sneddon said. She'd gone to one side of the wall and touched a series of projections. Without warning, a heavy curtain of some undefinable material was slowly sliding open. It jerked, grinding as it moved, and parted in the middle. Beyond lay more shadows.

"Enter freely," Lachance drawled. "You're *velcome* to stay the night."

"I'll go first," Hoop said. But Ripley was already through.

He heard her sharp intake of breath even as he stepped through the ancient doorway into what lay beyond.

"It's a birthing ground," Ripley said, echoing Sneddon's comment from earlier. But this was much, much different.

There was no telling what the room had once been intended for, but it had been turned into a vision of hell. All along one side and the far end, at least fifteen of those long-limbed dog-aliens were cocooned against the walls, trapped there by clumps and swathes of alien extrusion. Most were adults, but there were two smaller shapes that might once have been children. Their exposed chests were burst, thick ribs broken and protruding, heads thrown back in endless agony. They might have been there a hundred years or ten thousand, bodies dried and mummified in the dry air. It was awful to behold.

Even more awful were the things scattered around the middle of the room. Most stood upright, the height of an adult's waist. More eggs, one for each victim fixed against the wall. They all appeared to have hatched.

"Don't get too close!" Sneddon said as Lachance edged forward.

"They're ancient," Hoop said. "And they're all open. Look." He kicked at a petal-like flap on the egg nearest to him and it crumbled and fell away. "Fossilized."

"Fucking gross," Baxter said. "This just gets worse and worse."

"We're going that way?" Ripley asked. She was aiming her flashlight across the wide room toward a shadowy doorway in the far wall.

"Yeah," Hoop said. "This is all ancient history. Just don't look." He started across the room, aiming his flashlight and spray gun at the ground ahead so that he didn't trip.

He saw movement inside an open egg close by, and froze, readied to spray it with acid. But it had only been a shadow. Shit, he was on edge.

As he started to move again, he felt almost like an intruder in this ancient tableau. Whatever had happened here was between those dog-aliens and the monsters that still infested the ship—a confrontation that had apparently occurred long before Earth had discovered technology, and while its people were still farming the land and looking to the stars with superstition and fear. Even then, these things existed.

It made him feel very small and ineffectual. Even bearing the spray gun he was just a weak creature needing a weapon to protect him. Those aliens were their own weapons, perfect hunting and killing organisms. It was almost as if they were created as such, though he had no wish to imagine the creator.

Hoop had never been a God-fearing man, and he regarded such outdated beliefs as ignorant and foolish. But perhaps there were gods other than those the human race had once known.

Light flickered around the large room, casting movement into the eggs, into the eye sockets of the dog-aliens, and into corners where anything could be hiding. He sensed everyone's nervousness, and he felt it himself. This was far more than any of them had expected.

"We'll get through this," he said softly, but no one answered. None of them could know that for sure.

At the end of the room, passing through the opening to whatever might lie beyond, they came close enough to touch one of the cocooned victims. Hoop passed his flashlight over the dead thing and paused on its face. The creatures they'd found back in the tunnels had been deformed by the weapon that had ended them, but apart from their chest wounds, these were whole.

This one looked agonized and wretched. Hoop wondered at a universe that could still express such pain, after so long.

He shone the light into the space beyond and then entered.

Another tunnel, another corridor, another hallway. The walls were curved, the floors uneven and damp. The dampness was a new thing, and he paused to sweep his foot across the surface. Fluid was bubbled on the floor, as if the surface was greasy, and his boot broke a thousand bubbles into a smear.

"Slippery in here," he said back over his shoulder. Ripley was there again, shining her flashlight past him.

"The smell's changed, too," she said. She was right. Until now the ship's interior had smelled of age—dust, staleness, air filtered in from the atmosphere-processed mine to lift scents from all around. But here it was different. He breathed in deeply and frowned, trying to place the smell. It was subtle but foul, slightly tangy, like someone who had gone unwashed for a long time. There was also something underlying it that he couldn't place at all. Not a smell, but a sensation.

"It's warmer," Ripley said. "Not the air, but... it *smells* warm."

"Yeah," he said. "Like something alive."

"The ship?" Ripley asked.

He shook his head.

"I think if it ever was alive, in any form, that was long ago. This is more recent. This is them."

He heard Ripley passing the word back—*Go careful, stay sharp!*—and then he moved forward once again. Always forward. Going back was still an option, but it also felt like it would be a mistake.

Responsibility weighed down heavier than ever, gathering mass the more time that passed without incident. He'd never been a great decision maker—it often took him a long while just to choose dinner from the *Marion*'s limited menu—but he feared that if he decided they should turn back, the act of making that choice might doom them all.

Better to forge forward.

As they moved on, the dampness and the smells in the air increased. The inside of his nose started to sting. He was sweating, the humidity rising, nervousness drawing moisture from his body. His mouth was parched, his throat sore.

"We shouldn't be going this way," Baxter said. "This is bad. This is wrong."

"It's *all* wrong!" Lachance said sharply. "But this is up towards the top of the ship again, and that's good enough for me."

"What about the things they hatched?" Sneddon asked, and Hoop stopped dead. *Something's been bugging me and that's...*

"Where are they?" he asked, turning around to look at the others.

"That was a long time ago," Ripley said.

"We don't know how long they live. The ones in the *Samson* waited for weeks, so maybe they can hibernate for years. Or longer."

"So there could be a lot more down here than just those hatched from the miners," Sneddon said.

"It doesn't change anything," Hoop said, and he waited for any response. But everyone was looking at him. "Changes *nothing*. We're here now. We go forward, up, and out."

They continued on, but the corridor—twisting and turning, erring only slightly upward—ended at another wide, dark room.

Oh, no, Hoop thought. *This is it. This is what they found, or some place like it.*

It was another birthing ground. There was no telling how many places like this there were in the ship, nor how big the ship even was. As they paused at the edge of the hold, he found himself shaking with a deep, primeval fear. This was a danger beyond humanity, one that had existed since long before humans even knew what the stars were.

"They're unopened," Sneddon said. She pushed past Hoop, slinging the spray gun over her shoulder and taking something from her pocket.

"Don't get too close!" Hoop said.

"Mummified. Preserved." The room was lit with a bright flash as Sneddon started taking pictures of the eggs. "They're almost like fossils."

Hoop swept the spray gun and its attached flashlight from side to side, searching the extent of the chamber and looking for an exit. He saw one at the far side of the room, a tall, framed opening. He also saw something else. He aimed his flashlight up.

"Look."

The string of lights was slung from wire supports fixed into the room's high ceiling. Some of the lights were smashed, others seemed whole, but no longer worked. Or they had been intentionally deactivated.

Hoop didn't like that one little bit.

"Look here!" Sneddon said. She was at the far edge of the room now, standing back from one of the eggs and taking photographs. The flashes troubled Hoop—for a second after each one his vision was complete blackness, his sight returning slowly every time. He didn't like being blind, even for a moment.

The egg before her was open. Unlike the others, it didn't look old and fossilized, but newer. Wetter.

She flashed off another shot, but this time Hoop blinked just as the light seared around the room, and when he opened his eyes again his vision was clear. In the final instant of the flash, he saw that the old-looking eggs were opaque beneath the camera's flash. Inside, there were shapes. And he was certain that some of those shapes were moving.

"Sneddon, don't get too—"

"There's something—" Sneddon said. She took one step closer.

Something leapt from the egg. In an instant it wrapped itself around Sneddon's face. She dropped the camera and it started flashing on automatic, the white-light searing the room at one second intervals as she grabbed the thing and tried to force her fingers beneath its grasping claws and the long, crushing tail that coiled around her neck. And then she dropped to her knees.

"Holy shit!" Lachance said, swinging the charge thumper up and toward her.

Ripley knocked it aside.

"You'll take her head off!"

"But that thing will—"

"Keep her still!" Hoop said. Then he was beside Sneddon, trying to assess what was happening, how the thing had attached, what it was doing to her.

"Oh, shit, *look* at those things!" Kasyanov said.

Other eggs were opening. Even beneath the shouting and panic Hoop could hear the wet, sticky, almost delicate sounds of the flaps peeling back, and the slick movements of the things inside.

"Don't get too close to any of them!" he said. "Get over here, everyone get close to—"

"Fuck that!" Kasyanov said, and she fired her plasma torch across the room. Sneddon's still-flashing camera was nothing compared to the blazing light. The doctor swept it from left to right, the fire rolling in a white-hot wave across the space, and beneath its concentrated heat the eggs began to burst. They split apart and wriggling, thrashing things emerged, sliding out in a slick of fluid already bubbling beneath the heat, their legs and tails whipping for purchase. Then they began to shriek.

It was a horrible sound, ear-splitting, far too human.

"Help me drag her!" Ripley said, trying to grab Sneddon beneath one arm. But the science officer slumped forward, her shoulder striking an egg, before falling onto her side. "There!" Ripley shouted, nodding at the opening across the room. "Help me!"

Lachance pulled the spray gun from Sneddon's other shoulder, grabbed her beneath the arm, and began to haul.

The egg that Sneddon had nudged against opened. Hoop saw it, and without thinking he swung the spray gun to bear. Ripley saw the barrel aiming at her and opened her mouth to shout a warning, but then she sensed the movement as well, turned, and swung the charge thumper from her shoulder.

"Not yours!" Hoop shouted. He'd given her real charges, and if she fired one in this confined space, it might kill them all.

Lachance was quick. He dropped Sneddon, stepped back, and fired his own charge thumper, loaded with non-exploding ammunition. The egg shuddered as something passed through it, and the flaps drooped as a thick, viscous fluid leaked out.

"Don't step in it!" Ripley warned as she and Lachance grasped Sneddon again.

Kasyanov was staring at her handiwork. Half of the room was ablaze, plasma having stuck to the walls and the eggs and seeded multiple fires. Several more eggs—the ones not caught in the initial blast—burst open, their boiling insides spraying across the room. Kasyanov winced back, wiping at something that had landed on her forearm and glove.

"Don't spread it!" Hoop shouted.

The doctor glanced back at him, shaking her head and holding up her gloved hand.

"It's okay, it's not acid," she said. "I think it's…" Then her face changed, as the suit material began bubbling and smoking as the liquid started to eat through.

Kasyanov screamed.

"Let's go!" Hoop shouted. Ripley and Lachance dragged Sneddon, Baxter hopped as best he could, and Hoop went for Kasyanov, reaching for her while trying not to touch the parts of her that were affected. She saw him coming and tried to be still, but a heavy shudder was passing through her body. Her teeth clacked together so hard that he thought they'd break, and she was starting to foam at the mouth.

She reached out her good hand and grasped his.

"I… can't… see…" she managed to croak, and Hoop squeezed her hand. Her eyes looked fine, but there wasn't time now to examine them closely. The room was heating up. He needed to get away.

The face-hugging things were still bursting from their eggs, cooking in the fire, screaming.

They made it across to the opposite doorway. Ripley went first, lighting the way with her own flashlight. Hoop guided Kasyanov in last, leaning her against the dripping wall and trying to say some comforting words in her ear. He couldn't tell whether or not she heard.

Then he stood in the opening and faced back into the room. The waves of heat were intense, drawing in air from behind him to feed the flames. The sounds of the blaze were incredibly loud—the roar of air alight, the crackle and pop of eggs bursting and burning. The stench was foul, scorching his nose and throat as the whipping limbs of flames threatened his clothing, face, and hair.

But there were still several eggs that were untouched.

As he leveled the spray gun and braced himself, he glimpsed something glimmering across the other end of the room. A shine, coming from the shadows. He aimed the flashlight that way, and saw.

"Ripley!" he said, trying not to shout too loud. "Lachance, Baxter! They're here."

15

OFFSPRING

"We're killing their children," Ripley said.

And though she wasn't certain just how accurate this assessment was—where the eggs came from, what laid them, how these beasts procreated—somehow she felt it was right. Any species would go to great lengths to protect its offspring. This was nature's way.

Across the burning, smoking, spitting pit of the egg chamber, the first alien stepped from the shadows.

Hoop's acid spray gun wouldn't reach that far, so Ripley didn't hesitate. She braced the charge thumper against her hip and fired. It was a lucky shot. The projectile struck the alien low down on one leg, knocking the limb from under it and sending it sprawling to the left, rolling across two burning eggs. It shrieked and stood, shaking off the flames like a dog shaking water from its coat.

...One...

Ripley counted in her head. The only other time she'd fired an explosive charge from the thumper, the time delay had hit five seconds, and now—

...two...

"Hold your breath!" Hoop fired three spurts of acid across the right-hand side of the room.

...three...

The acid splashed from the wall, landed across the floor and several eggs, and immediately started hissing. One egg was sliced immediately in two, red smoke boiling up from its ruined insides.

...*four*...

The alien was on its feet again, one arm-like limb slapping at its legs where the small, metallic charge had penetrated and stuck.

"Down!" Ripley shouted. She turned her back to the flames and crouched.

The explosion reverberated across the room and through the ship's structure, the floor punching up at their feet, air thumping at their ears. She gasped, swallowed, then spun around to face the room again.

The alien was all but gone, most of its torso and lower limbs blown away. Its head had rebounded from the roof and landed close to where it had been standing, and the next two aliens rushing into the room kicked it aside.

Hoop was gasping next to her. She glanced at him, saw the blackened split in his suit's right arm.

But there was no time.

"Run!" she shouted. The two aliens had parted, stalking between the flames, and she only had one charge left. Someone shouldered her aside and the world turned white. She squeezed her eyes closed and slid down the wall, feeling the heat on one side of her face as more fire erupted through the egg room.

A wind roared past them to feed the fire, and then someone was squeezing her hand. Hoop was there, trying to pull her away and urge her to run.

Baxter stood above them, one leg firm and the other foot barely touching the ground. He had his back to them as he tracked one of the aliens, loosing another quick burst from the plasma torch and catching the creature across the head. It screeched, squealed, and darted across the room from one wall to the other, streaking fire behind it. When it struck the wall it slid to the floor and did not move again.

Ripley couldn't see the other one.

"There'll be more!" Hoop said.

"I'll stay…"

At least that was what Ripley thought Baxter said. It was difficult to tell, his back still to them, plasma torch drifting left and right as he sought new targets. The room was a sea of flames now, the wind of the firestorm almost strong enough to knock him down. He was silhouetted against the flames.

"Don't be fucking stupid," Hoop said. He ducked down and took Baxter's arm over his shoulders. "Ripley, can you guide Kasyanov?"

"I'm… " Kasyanov said. "I can walk… just not see…" She still shivered, one hand held out in front of her. It barely resembled a hand anymore.

"Your eyes aren't damaged," Ripley said.

"Fumes…" she said. "My belt, hip pocket. Red capsules. For… pain."

"Hurry!" Hoop said. Ripley knew he was right, there'd be more aliens, but they needed Kasyanov on her feet. With Baxter hobbling and Sneddon down, they were rapidly getting to the time when they'd have to leave someone behind. And she sure as hell wasn't about to decide who it would be.

She rooted through Kasyanov's belt pockets and found a strip of red injection capsules. She removed three, popping the top from one and ramming the needle through Kasyanov's suit into her right forearm. Then she popped the other, knelt, and jammed it into Baxter's leg. Hoop was last, the needle pressed into his shoulder.

"Ouch!" he yelled, and Ripley laughed. She couldn't help it. Baxter grinned, and Hoop smiled sheepishly.

Then she stood, took Kasyanov's good hand and placed it on her own shoulder.

"Hold tight," she said. "Stop when I stop, go when I go. I'll be your eyes."

Kasyanov nodded.

"Lachance?" Hoop said.

"I'm okay for now," the Frenchman said, kneeling and slinging Sneddon over one shoulder. "She's light. But we won't get far like this."

Ripley stared at the thing on Sneddon's face, and between blinks she saw Kane lying in sick bay on the *Nostromo*, Ash and Dallas hovering without any idea what to do. *Maybe she* shouldn't *get far*, she thought. Already that thing might be planting its egg inside her. But the idea of leaving her was too sick to contemplate.

With Sneddon's spray gun lost and Kasyanov's plasma torch

hanging from one shoulder, they were down on their weapons. After the one charge she had left, Ripley would be firing bolts again. She had no idea how long the plasma and acid would last.

Kasyanov clasped her shoulder hard. *Like her life depends on it!* Ripley thought, smiling grimly. Then the flashlight strapped to Lachance's charge thumper went out.

"One down," he said, already gasping beneath Sneddon's weight.

"Hoop, Lachance is right. We can't get far like this," Ripley said.

"We have to," he replied.

He was right. That was the only answer. This wasn't one of those situations where a miracle would suddenly present itself. They *had* to get as far as they could, and there was no use waiting for something else to happen. One foot in front of the other, defending themselves, fighting when they had to, moving quickly when they didn't.

And if and when we get back to the Marion, *there's Ash*, she thought. She wondered just how far that bastard had gone. He'd dragged her with him through the cosmos, searching for alien life, and once he'd found it, he'd tangled her up in all this. Commitment she could understand, but his determination went way beyond that.

Maybe he'd even…

She barked a short, bitter laugh.

"What?" Hoop asked, shooting her a sideways glance.

"Nothing," she said. And it *was* nothing. Even if Ash had been responsible for the shuttle's fuel cell decay, that meant nothing right now. But if they ever made it back to the *Marion*, they'd have to be careful. That was all.

One foot in front of the other… step by step.

The corridor rose steadily, as wide as any they'd yet followed, and they started passing openings on either side. Hoop slowed before each opening and fired a quick shot from his spray gun every time, but nothing shrieked, nothing came at them from the shadows.

They didn't even know there was an opening above them until they heard the scream.

It was different from the other alien noises they'd heard, a deeper cry as if from something larger. The shriek was somehow more measured, almost more intelligent. It was haunting.

Ripley stopped and crouched, and Kasyanov did the same behind her. She looked upward. There was a wide, darker shadow in the ceiling above them that swallowed light, and it was only shining a flashlight directly up that revealed the shaft rising above them. High up in that shaft, something moved.

Hoop was ahead with Baxter, both of them already aiming their weapons. But neither of them fired. *Acid and fire will drop back down*, Ripley thought.

"Back!" Ripley said. She and Kasyanov backed up, and behind them she heard Lachance grunting with the effort of reversing with Sneddon still slung over his shoulder. Hoop and Baxter moved forward, further along the corridor, so that the opening in the ceiling was now between them. Ripley and her group pressed tight against the wall, giving the leaders as wide a field of fire as they could.

But not wide enough.

"Come on!" Ripley said. "Quickly!" And she ran. Kasyanov clasped her shoulder firmly and moved with her, perfectly in step. Lachance struggled along behind, keeping up with them as they passed beneath the gap in the ceiling. Ripley risked a glance up…

…and saw the moving thing much closer now, falling, limbs knocking sparks from the shaft's sides, no longer screeching but growling, keening, its mouth extended and open, ready for the kill.

She shrugged Kasyanov's hand from her shoulder, pushed her to keep moving, then crouched and fired her charge thumper up. Then she rolled backward without waiting to see where the charge had gone.

"Run!" Hoop said. He grabbed Ripley by the collar and hauled her to her feet, then helped Baxter stagger along the corridor. *The charge will fall*, Ripley thought, *bounce off that thing and land behind us, and when it blows it'll knock us down, knock us out, and then—*

The explosion came from behind them. She could tell by the sound that the charge had detonated up in the shaft somewhere, but then seconds later its effects powered down and along the hallway, shoving them all in the back. Kasyanov grunted and stumbled forward, falling with her arms outstretched and screaming as the damaged hand took her weight. Ripley tripped face-first into Hoop's back, hands raking across his shoulders for purchase and knocking him down. As they fell she thought of his spray gun and what would happen if its reservoir burst beneath them.

Hoop must have been thinking the same—he braced his hands in front and pushed sideways, spilling Ripley against the wall and landing on his side. The wind was knocked from her and she gasped, waiting long seconds for her breath to return. And while she waited she watched—

Lachance dropping Sneddon, tipping forward, rolling, and then coming to his feet again, pivoting on his left foot and swinging his charge thumper up to aim back toward the blast.

Ripley turned to look as she gasped in a breath, and what she saw drove the air from her lungs again, as surely as any explosion.

The alien had dropped from the shaft and was blocking the corridor—the *entire* corridor. One of its limbs and part of its torso seemed to have been blown away, and acid hissed and bubbled across the floor and walls. It staggered where it stood, one of its sturdy legs lifting and falling, lifting and falling, as if putting weight down gave it pain.

It was larger than any other alien they had ever seen. Its torso was heavier, head longer and thicker.

It hissed. It growled.

Lachance fired.

Two bolts struck the alien's wounded side, smacking shreds of shell-like skin and bubbling flesh back away from them. It shrieked and flailed its remaining limbs, striking deep scratches across the walls. Lachance's next two shots hit it directly beneath its raised head.

The shrieking stopped. The beast froze. Hoop stood and aimed the spray gun, but he didn't fire. Even the drifting smoke from the explosion seemed to go still, waiting for whatever might happen next.

"One more," Ripley whispered, and Lachance fired again. The bolt struck the alien's abdomen, but it was already slumping to the ground, limbs settling, its damaged head resting against the corridor's side. And then slowly, slowly, it slid down as its acid-blood melted a depression in the wall.

Hoop tensed, ready to fire his acid-gun, but Ripley held up a hand.

"Wait!" she said. "Just a bit."

"Why?" he asked. "It might not be dead."

"Looks dead to me," Lachance said. "Half its head's blown off."

"Yeah, well…" Ripley said. They waited like that, watching the motionless creature, the smoke drifting down from the vertical shaft, drawn back along the corridor toward the burning egg chamber. She couldn't feel the breeze anymore, but the fleeting smoke indicated that the fires were still blazing. They listened for more movement, but heard none. And all the while she tried to see what was different about this dead beast.

Apart from being bigger than the others, there were other, more subtle differences. The length of its limbs, the shape of its head.

"What the hell is that?" Hoop asked, pointing. "There, at its ass-end."

"Oh, well, that's gross," Lachance said.

The alien's abdomen had burst open, spilling a slick mess across the floor. It sizzled and spat as the acid-pool spread, but it was the things lying in the pool that drew Ripley's attention. Scores of them—maybe hundreds—spherical and each roughly the size of her thumb. They glimmered moistly beneath the flashlight beam, sliding over one another as more poured from the wound.

"I think we killed a queen," Ripley said.

"You're sure?" Hoop asked from behind her.

"Pretty sure—it's the only thing that makes sense. They're eggs. Hundreds of eggs." She looked back at him. "We nailed a fucking queen."

She examined the rest of the creature, playing her flashlight across its blasted and slashed body. Though bigger than any they had so far seen, something about it was also almost childlike—its features were larger, the spiked and clawed limbs not quite so vicious. Ripley felt a strange frisson, a sense of likeness. But she was *nothing* like this thing.

Nothing at all.

"I think she's young," she said. "Imagine just how big…?" She shook her head. "We need to go."

"Yeah," Hoop agreed.

"My eyes are improving," Kasyanov said. "I can move quicker. I'll stay behind you. But let's get the hell out of this pit."

They moved on, the corridor still erring upward. They were

more cautious now, Hoop and Ripley shining their lights ahead across walls, floor, ceiling. At every junction they paused to listen before moving on. And when they reached another staircase leading up toward what might have been an opening in the ship's hull, he handed Ripley another charge magazine.

"Last one," he said. "Five charges left."

"And I'm almost out of bolts," Lachance said.

"My plasma torch is still almost full," Kasyanov said.

They were being worn down step by step, Ripley knew. Whether or not this was an intentional act by the aliens, whether they could even consider something that complex, she didn't know. But the fact remained.

"That's the way out," she said, nodding up at this new, shorter staircase.

"How d'you know that?" Lachance gasped. His knees were shaking from Sneddon's weight. He was almost exhausted. And Baxter, leaning against Hoop, was looking up at the new, waist-high steps with something approaching dread.

"Because it has to be," Ripley said.

They started climbing—

She is panting, sweating, exhausted, ebullient. It's one of those moments that opens up and out into a perfect, never-to-be-repeated time, so rare that its blooming is like that of the planet's most precious flower. She is filled with a sense of well-being, an all-consuming love for her daughter that is so powerful that it hurts.

This time, now, she thinks, doing her best to consign that instant to memory. The cool heather beneath her hands as she clasps onto the hillside and pulls herself higher. The heat of the sun on the back of her neck, sweat cooling across her back from the climb. The deep-blue sky above, the river below snaking through the valley, vehicles as small as ants passing back and forth along the road.

The slope steepens as they approach the hill's summit, and Amanda giggles above her, pretending that she didn't know. It's dangerous—not quite mountain climbing, but it's a hands-and-knees scramble, and if they slip it will be a long tumble down. But Ripley can't be angry. Everything feels too good, too right, for that.

So she climbs harder and faster, ignoring the feel of empty space pulling her back and down from the hillside. Amanda glances back and sees her mother moving quicker. She giggles again and climbs, her teenager's limbs strong and supple.

I've never actually been here and seen this, yet it's the best moment of my life.

Amanda reaches the summit and shouts in triumph, disappearing over the top to lie back on the short grass and wait for her mother.

Ripley pulls herself up the natural steps in the slope. For an instant she feels terribly alone and exposed, and she pauses in her climb. Shocked. Cold.

Then she hears another sound from above that makes her start climbing again. Her sense of well-being has been scrubbed away by that sound, and the moment of perfection dissipates as if it has never been felt at all. The sky is no longer cloud-free. The hill's wildness is now brutal rather than beautiful.

The sound was her child, crying.

Ripley reaches the top, clinging to the hillside now, terrified that she will fall and even more afraid of what she'll see if she does not. When she pulls herself up and over onto the summit, she blinks, and everything is all right.

Then she really *sees Amanda, standing there just a few yards away with one of those monstrous things attached to her face, tail tightening, pale fingers gripping, body throbbing. Ripley reaches out, and her daughter's chest comes apart—*

"...Go in there!" Hoop said.

"What?" Ripley asked, blinking away the fog of confusion. It was harder to do this time, the debilitating sense of loss clinging to her more persistently. They'd reached the top of the staircase—she knew that, even though she had almost been elsewhere—but she took a moment to look around before realizing what Hoop was saying.

"But *look* at it!" Baxter said. "We can't just ignore that."

"I can," Hoop said. "I can, and I *am!*"

The head of the staircase opened into a wide area with two exits. One led up again, perhaps toward a hatch in the ship's hull, or perhaps not. There was no telling. The other was closer, much wider, and like nothing they had seen on the ship before.

At first she thought it was glass. The layers of clear material were scarred and dusty with time, but still appeared solid. Then she saw it shimmer as if from some unfelt breeze, and knew it wasn't glass. She didn't know exactly *what* it was, but it was there for one purpose.

Lachance grabbed Baxter's flashlight and shone it ahead. The light smeared across the clear surface and then splashed through the large space beyond. Some of what it illuminated Ripley recognized. Some she did not. None of it made her want to go any closer.

"More eggs," she said.

"But different," Baxter said. He hobbled closer and pressed his face to the barrier. It rippled as he touched it.

Lachance played his light around, and Hoop added his own.

"Oh," Baxter said. He turned around slowly.

"What is it?" Ripley asked. *We just need to leave!*

"I think we just found where your queen friend came from."

Ripley closed her eyes, sighed, and there was a terrible, unrelenting inevitability to this. She did not feel in charge of her own actions. She was long past thinking, *Maybe this is all a dream*. No, she wasn't asleep, but she didn't feel entirely awake, either. The more she tried to take control of events, the more they ran away from her. And here she was again, needing to go in one direction, yet drawn relentlessly in another.

Hoop shone his light back down the staircase they'd just climbed. No movement. Then he turned back to the new room beyond the clear enclosure.

"I'll go first," he said.

The second thing Ripley noticed was that the tech here was far more recognizable—and more prevalent—than it had been anywhere else in the ship. There were at least six separate movable workstations where the equipment appeared largely identical, ranging from sizeable units to smaller, more intricate devices. There was very little dust, and everything had a sharpness, a clarity, that the rest of the ship was lacking. Time had not paid this place so much attention.

The *first* thing she noticed was the eggs, and the things that guarded them.

There were sixteen eggs, each one set apart from the others within a waist-high, circular wire enclosure. The enclosures were set around the room's curved perimeter, leaving the center open for the mobile workstations. The eggs looked similar to the others they had found and destroyed, though there were subtle differences in color, tone, and shape. They were rounder, fatter, and their surfaces seemed to be more thoroughly networked with fine veins. Ripley thought perhaps they were newer, or simply better preserved.

Crouched beside the eggs were things that at first glance resembled statues. But she knew not to take anything down here at first glance. They were aliens, their spiked limbs dulled, curved heads dipped and pale. Slightly larger than others they had seen, yet so different from the queen they'd so recently killed. It was Lachance who hit it on the head.

"They look like… the ship's builders."

And they did. They were a monstrous blend of alien and dog-creature. More limbs than other aliens, each with a chunkier body, thicker legs, and a more prominent head, still they possessed the same chitinous outer shell, and one had slumped to the side with its grotesque mouth extended, the glimmering teeth now dulled. Ripley was glad she hadn't seen them alive.

"How long have they been here, do you think?" Baxter asked.

"Long time," Kasyanov said. "That one almost looks like it's mummified. But these eggs… maybe the damned things can *never* die."

One egg was open, and on the ground close by it was the body of one of the miners.

"Nick," Lachance said quietly. "He owed me fifty dollars."

Nick's chest was open, clothing torn, ribs protruding. He looked fresher than the other corpses they'd found, yet Ripley thought he'd probably died around the same time. The atmosphere in this section was cleaner, and perhaps lacking in the bacteria of decay.

"Only one egg has opened," she said. She blinked softly, trying to take control of the feeling that was slowly enveloping her. It was an urgency driven by disgust, a pressing desire fed by hatred.

"And we just popped the bastard that came from that," Hoop said. "You think so?"

"Yeah, popped it," she said. She looked around at the other eggs and the things that had settled to guard them, long ago. If all these eggs were queens—if that's what the creature they'd just killed had been—then they had the potential to produce many, many more aliens.

Thousands more.

"We have to destroy them all," she said. She lifted the charge thumper.

"Wait!" Kasyanov said. "We haven't got time to—"

"We make time," Ripley said. "What happens if we don't survive? What happens if a rescue mission eventually arrives, comes down here? What then? There are thousands of potential creatures in this one room. We've fought off a few of those things. Imagine an army of them."

"Okay, Ripley," Hoop said. He was nodding slowly. "But we need to take care. Lachance, come with me. We'll check the other opening, make sure that's really the way out. Then we'll come back and fry these fuckers." He looked at Ripley, and held up a hand. "Wait."

She nodded, but with one glance urged him to hurry. She wouldn't wait for long. Her finger stroked the trigger, and she imagined the eggs bursting apart, spilling their horrendous cargo to the clear gray floor.

Fuck you, Ash, she thought, and she almost laughed. He'd done everything he could to procure another one of these monsters for his Weyland-Yutani bosses. And she was doing everything she could to destroy them all.

She would win. Of that she had no doubt. The burning question was, would she also survive?

"I will," she said.

Perhaps thinking she was replying to him, Hoop nodded.

Sneddon was slumped beside the door, creature still clasped across her entire face. Baxter stood resting against the wall, plasma torch cradled in his arms. Kasyanov blinked the pain from her eyes, also holding her plasma torch.

As Hoop and Lachance left, Ripley had a flash-image of Amanda on top of that hill.

I'll save you, baby. I'll save you.

16

MAJESTY

"We're getting out of this. Right, Hoop?"

"What do you expect me to say to that?"

"That we're getting out of this."

"Okay, Lachance. We're getting out of this."

Lachance exhaled and wiped his brow. "That's a relief. For a minute there I thought we were fucked."

"Come on. Let's see what's up here." They crossed the open area at the head of the steep staircase, and Hoop paused to look back down. His light didn't seem to penetrate quite so far, now, its power starting to wane. He couldn't quite see the bottom. There could have been anything down there, crouched in the shadows and staring up at him, and he wouldn't know.

Lachance moved through the opening and started up the shorter staircase. Hoop followed. There were only five tall steps before the walls seemed to close in, forming a blank barrier. But Lachance leaned left and right, looking at varying angles.

"Hidden opening," he said. "Clever." He ducked through a fold in the strange wall material.

Hoop glanced back and down. There was no noise down there, no hint that anything had gone wrong in that strange lab with the queen eggs. Yet he still couldn't shake the idea that they were making a mistake here. That splitting up, even for such a short time, was a stupid thing to do.

Ripley was stronger than ever, yet he could sense a ripple of danger emanating from her now. A need for some sort of vengeance, perhaps, that might well put them all in peril. She was a logical woman driven by the instinct for survival, intelligent and determined. But as she was shooting that queen, he'd seen something in her eyes that had no place with logic. Still instinct, perhaps. But the instinct for attack, rather than defense.

When she'd looked at him just now, he'd seen murder in her eyes.

He walked into Lachance, then realized why the Frenchman had stopped.

The hidden route emerged onto the huge ship's wings close to the cavern wall. The miners' lights were still strung across the cavern, shedding a weak light over the whole area. Looking back along the wing he could see the damaged area where they'd entered, several hundred yards away and seemingly so long ago.

"Can't see any of those bastards," Hoop whispered.

"If they're up here, they're hiding," Lachance said. "But look. What *is* that?" He was pointing to the right, toward where the ship's hull seemed to disappear beneath the cavern wall that rose high above them, curving eventually into a high ceiling hidden by shadows.

"That's our way out," Hoop said. There was a series of cracks in the wall above the wing, any one of which might have been a route back up into the mine.

"Yeah, but what is it?"

Hoop frowned, looked closer. Then he saw what Lachance meant. "Holy shit…"

It wasn't part of the ship. It was made of stone. Much of it had tumbled, but some still stood, a structure that at first glance formed the crevassed, cracked wall of the cavern.

"Is that a building of some sort?" Lachance asked. "A wall?"

"We'll see," Hoop said. "But not yet. Come on, we need to get the others."

"And wipe out those eggs," Lachance said.

"Yeah." Hoop took one more lingering look around the cavern— the huge, buried vessel, like no ship any of them had ever seen; the massive cavern formed above and around it; and now this vast wall that seemed to loom over the ship, burying it, smothering the parts of it they had yet to see. It was almost as if the ship had crashed into the structure, rupturing it, ploughing through until it wedged to a halt.

Whatever had happened here, they'd never know the full story. He'd bet money on it.

Because even after wiping out those eggs, there were more measures they could take. Already he was making plans.

They ducked back inside the ship, descended the steep steps, and reached the open area at the head of the longer staircase.

First came the flash of plasma fire from the lab ahead of them.

Then the scream.

Lachance was first across the landing, ducking through the clear curtain into the lab, thumper coughing as he entered. Hoop was right behind him. *Ripley started without us!* he thought, but as he entered and saw what was happening, he knew that wasn't the case.

They should have been more careful.

Ripley waited. She walked a complete circuit of the center of the room, careful to give the dead miner a wide berth. None of the eggs gave any signs of opening, there was no sound or movement, yet she remained alert. If one of them so much as twitched or pulsed, she'd open fire.

Baxter had crouched down beside Sneddon and the two of them were motionless, unconsciously mimicking the mummified aliens. Kasyanov continued to blink quickly, touching at her eyes with her good hand and wincing as her gloved fingertips brushed against the swollen red eyelids. Her acid-burnt hand was held in front of her, shaking. She'd need attention back on the *Marion*—they all would—but they had to get there first.

Apart from the one that had opened, the alien eggs seemed untouched, and almost immune to any effects of time. Perhaps the wire enclosures formed some sort of stasis field, letting the eggs and their monstrous cargo sleep until the time came for them to wake.

That time was when a host, a victim, was brought before them.

Finger still stroking the trigger, Ripley moved closer to one of the hybrid figures. Though they repulsed her, she couldn't deny that she was also fascinated. This one must have been birthed from one of the dog-aliens that had built this strange ship. Which meant that the aliens seemed to take on some of the attributes of whomever or whatever they used as a host for their gestation. Did Kane's alien have some of Kane in it?

Would Amanda's?

"No," Ripley breathed. "They'll never leave here. None of them." She looked at Sneddon where she sat slumped close to the doorway, that huge spider-like thing still clamped tight to her face, tail around her throat. Soon it would die and fall off, leaving an egg inside her chest that would quickly gestate and become one of them. Then the pain, the terrible agony of her death, and the new monster would emerge.

If Ash had his way, Sneddon would be in stasis before that happened.

"No," Ripley said again, louder. Kasyanov looked across at her, Baxter glanced up, both alarmed. "We can't take her," she said, nodding at Sneddon. "She's infected. We can't save her, and we mustn't take her."

"Well, there's no way we're leaving her!" Kasyanov said.

"Haven't you got something for her?" Ripley asked.

It took a while for Kasyanov to understand what Ripley was really asking. When she did her red-rimmed eyes widened.

"And who the hell are you?" she asked. "You don't even know Sneddon, and you're asking me to kill her?"

"Kill?" Baxter asked, looking confused.

"No, just help her," Ripley said.

"How exactly is killing her going to help her?" Kasyanov snapped.

"Have you seen what they do?" Ripley asked. "Can you imagine how much it would hurt having something…" *Amanda, screaming, hands held wide as a beast burst its way outside from within.* "Something eating its way out of you from the inside, breaking your ribs, cracking your chest plate, chewing its way out? Can you even *think* about that?"

"I'll take it out of her," Kasyanov said.

Something creaked.

Ripley frowned, her head tilted to one side.

"Don't you go near her," Kasyanov continued. "None of us knows you. None of us knows why you really came, so you just—"

"Listen!" Ripley said, hand held up.

Creak...

She looked around at the eggs. None of them seemed to be moving, none of those fleshy wings were hinging open, ready to disgorge their terrible contents. Maybe it was a breeze, still tugged through the tunnels and corridors by the fires they had set deeper in the ship. At the doorway, those strange curtains hung heavy. Around the room nothing moved. Except—

Scriiiitch!

It was Kasyanov who saw it.

"Oh... my... God!"

Ripley spun around, backed away toward where the others waited by the doorway, clasping the charge thumper and immediately realizing that they were very close to being fucked.

It wasn't just one of the mummified aliens that was moving.

It was all of them.

She squeezed the trigger, Kasyanov opened up with the plasma torch, and Ripley felt the ice cold, blazing hot kiss of fire erupting all around her.

She screamed.

"Back back *back*!" Hoop shouted. Baxter was already trying to haul Sneddon out of the room, and Kasyanov was grasping the unconscious woman's boots, trying to lift with her one good hand, plasma torch sputtering where it hung from her shoulder.

As Lachance and Hoop entered there was a thudding explosion from across the room. Shrapnel whistled past Hoop's ears and struck his suit, some of it dry, some wet. He winced, expecting more pain to add to his throbbing arm. But there were no more sizzling acid burns. Not yet.

Ripley stood in front of them all, charge thumper at her hip as she swung thirty degrees and fired again.

"Back!" Hoop shouted again, but Ripley couldn't hear, or wasn't listening.

The frozen, statue-like aliens were moving. Several were down already, burning from Kasyanov's plasma torch or blown apart by

Ripley's first shot. Others moved across the room toward Ripley. Some were slow, stiff, hesitant, as if still waking from a slumber Hoop could not comprehend.

One was fast.

It streaked toward Ripley from the right, and if Hoop hadn't already had his finger on the spray gun trigger, she might have died. Instinct twitched his finger and sent a spurt of acid across the room. The alien's movement made the shot even more effective, the acid slicing across its middle section. It hissed, then screamed, and thrashed backward as Lachance's thumper discharged. He fired three bolts into its head and it dropped down, dead.

Ripley's second charge exploded. The whole room shook, detritus whizzing through the air and impacting walls, faces, flesh. She cried out and went to her knees, and Hoop saw that she'd already suffered burns across her right hip and leg from a plasma burst. It couldn't have actually touched her—if it had, it would have eaten through her suit, flesh and bones—but she'd been too close when Kasyanov had fired her torch. If the torch's reserves hadn't already been nearly depleted, Ripley would have died.

Hoop turned to the right, away from everyone else, and let loose another concentrated stream of acid, squeezing his eyes almost entirely closed against the fumes, holding his breath. An egg exploded, gushing sizzling insides. Another fell in two, the thing inside thrashing briefly before growing still.

Ripley was on her feet again.

"Get out!" she shouted at them all. "Get back! Now!"

Three more aliens surged through a cloud of smoke and came at her. She fired another charge at them, striking the foremost creature and driving it back into the other two, the glimmer of metal obvious in its chest. She turned her shoulder and crouched as the blast came, then she quickly stood again.

Hoop helped Kasyanov with Sneddon's dead weight, and Lachance backed out with them.

"Ripley!" Hoop shouted. "Out, now!"

As he backed through the clear-curtained doorway with his crewmates, he could see her silhouetted against a wall of white-hot flame that still burned across the left half of the room. Her hair was wild, her stance determined, as something emerged from the flames and came at her, blazing.

She fell, rolled, kicked out with one boot. The alien tripped over her leg and went sprawling, spilling one queen's egg onto its side. Ripley screamed in pain as her wounded leg was jarred, but then she was standing again, aiming the charge thumper and firing her last shot into the monster's face.

She burst back through the curtains as the charge exploded. It shoved her through, fire blooming all around her, arms outstretched. She let go of the empty thumper and broke her fall, grunting as her already wounded body was subjected to another impact.

Ripley stood quickly and went for Kasyanov. She grasped the spray gun, tugged, and Kasyanov pulled back.

"Ripley!" Hoop said. She was bleeding from the leg and hip, slashed across the shoulder and side of her neck by an alien's tail. Her face was blackened from an explosive blast. A large patch of her hair had been burnt away, and her right eye was almost closed. She should have been down on her knees, at least. But something kept her going.

"Give it to me!" she demanded.

A rage, a burning fury at these things and what they meant.

"Let it go!" she screamed.

Kasyanov slipped the strap from her shoulder and stepped back, looking at Ripley as if she was one of those things.

Hoop went to shout at her again. But she was already turning back to the clear curtain, shouldering it aside and facing the terrors within. The fires. The bursting eggs. And those things that remained, waking, rising, coming to kill her.

She stood before them, and the thing that drove her fury wasn't the memory of dead friends, but the unreal vision of her tortured daughter. She could do nothing about Dallas and the others on the *Nostromo*, and she was beginning to fear that she and the *Marion*'s survivors would never survive.

But she could protect the daughter she had not seen for more than thirty-seven years. She could make sure these things were wiped out, and that if and when more people came here, there was no risk that they would ever be found.

Two queen eggs burst apart beneath the flames, and Ripley held her breath and fired a spray of acid across their remains. Just to make sure.

A large creature staggered at her, elements of the dog-aliens even more apparent now that it was up and moving. She hosed it down, sweeping the spray gun left and right and slicing gushing wounds in the thing's carapace. It stumbled and fell, its tail whipping through the air and catching her across the stomach. She just staggered for a moment.

Fires danced, shadows wept, and nothing else moved in that strange, ancient laboratory. Why the dog-aliens had kept and nurtured the queen eggs, what they hoped to gain, if they had even known the terrible dangers they toyed with, she would never know. But she didn't care. Knowing would change nothing.

They all had to die.

Three eggs remained, awake and ready, pulsing as the flaps slowly drew back to disgorge their charges. She fired an acid blast at each one, ensuring that their insides were destroyed. Something squealed as it died, and she hoped it hurt. However old the eggs and their contents might be, they were always ready to invade another host, and plant their dreadful larvae.

"Not anymore!" Ripley shouted. "Fuck you, Ash!" Maybe he was a good target for her ire, maybe not. But having someone to curse other than these beasts felt good.

Then they were done. Dead and gone. The queen eggs—so much potential, so much promise of pain and heartbreak—were cooking, melting, bubbling messes on the floor. She lowered the spray gun and blinked the fumes away, and flames flickering through tears made the scene look almost beautiful.

Something grabbed her and she turned, seeing Hoop standing behind her and realizing only then how much pain she was in.

"Ripley, we have to…" he said, eyes going wide at something he'd seen.

"What?"

"We need to patch you up."

"I'm fine," Ripley said, not feeling fine but finding the strength to move. "There's Sneddon and Baxter… you can't carry me as well. I'll walk 'til I drop."

And she did. Five paces out through the curtained opening, a few more across the open space beyond, and then her whole world started to spin. She was bleeding, burning, maybe even dying. And though she held on as hard as she could, Ripley couldn't fight back the darkness descending all around her.

Faces watched her fall. She only hoped she would see them all again.

"They'll be coming," Hoop said.

"She's bleeding badly," Kasyanov said. "Her shoulder and neck, her stomach, they're slashed up pretty good."

"Will she bleed to death?" Hoop asked.

Kasyanov waited for only a moment. "Not in the short term."

"Then she can bleed while we run. Come on. We're almost out." He grasped Ripley and tugged her to her feet. She tried to help, but barely had any strength. Blood shimmered on the front of her suit, flowing across her boots and speckling the floor. *They'll pick up the scent and follow us*, he thought. But he didn't even know if the aliens could smell, and his priority now was to move as far away from here, as fast as they could.

Back up into the mine, to the second elevator, and out of this hellhole.

Baxter started hauling himself up the shorter staircase toward the outside, wounded ankle dragging behind him. It looked less painful, though, since he'd had the injection. Lachance and Kasyanov lifted Sneddon and pushed her up, step by step. As Hoop pulled Ripley up onto the first step, her feet kicking feebly, she started talking.

"…take her…" Ripley muttered.

"Huh? We are. We're all getting out."

"No… don't take…"

She fell silent and he thought perhaps she was dreaming. Her eyes rolled, blood flowed. She looked a mess. But her strength was humbling, and on the next step she opened her eyes again, looking around until they focussed on those ahead and above them. "Sneddon," she said, quietly so only Hoop could hear. "We can't take her."

He didn't even reply. Ripley groaned and seemed to pass out again, and when he dragged her up to the next step the trail of blood she left behind glimmered in the light.

But he lifted her, pulled her up. Because he wasn't leaving *anyone* behind. Not after everything they'd been through. Hoop had lost so much in his life. His wife, his love, his children, left behind when he fled. Some of his hope, and much of his dignity. And at some point the time for loss would have to end. Maybe now, when he was at his lowest and everything seemed hopeless, he would start winning things back.

This is it. His friends, bleeding and in pain yet forging on as hard as they could, inspired him. And Ripley, the strange woman who had arrived in their midst, her own story tragic and filled with loss... if she could remain so strong, then so could he.

He climbed up the next step and pulled her up after him, and for some reason she felt lighter.

Outside, the others hunkered down close to where the folded access opened onto the ship's upper surface. They kept low and quiet, as if being suddenly exposed after their nightmarish trip through the tunnels and corridors scared them even more. Hoop handed Ripley to Lachance, slipping the charge thumper from her shoulder as he did so. Even hazy and balancing on the edge of consciousness, she grabbed for the weapon. He eased her hand aside.

"It's okay," he said. "I've got it." And she relented.

"What are you doing?" Lachance asked.

"Insurance," Hoop said. "Giving us the best chance I can." He held up two fingers—*two minutes*—then slipped back through the opening.

By his reckoning, there was one charge left in the blaster.

Now that he was facing it alone, the ship's interior felt even stranger, more alien than ever. They had only left it moments before, but already he felt like an invader all over again. He wondered one more time just how alive that huge ship was, or had once been. But it was ancient, and whatever intelligence might once have driven it was now surely in the deepest of slumbers, if not dead.

He edged down the first high step, then the second, and then he heard something that froze him to a halt. Everything in his world came to a standstill—the past, the future, his breathing, his thoughts. His heart skipped a beat, as if hiding from that sound.

A high-pitched keening, so filled with pain and rage that it prickled his skin, the sound itself an assault. He was chilled and hot at the same time, his soul reacting in much the same way as skin when confronted by intense heat or cold. He might burn or freeze with terror, but for a moment he couldn't tell which.

What have we done? he thought. He could smell burning flesh, though there was no similarity to any meat he knew. He could hear the roar of the flames they had left behind, consuming what was left of the aliens, the eggs. And dropping down one more step, he could see the three creatures that had come after them.

They were the same as the first ones they had encountered, back on the *Marion*. No dog-like features, no attributes that might have made them a queen. Warriors, perhaps. Soldier aliens. And they were whining and keening as they stood outside the burning, ruined lab, swaying from side to side, their tails waving, heads dipping to the left and then right. It was a dance of death and mourning, and for the briefest of moments Hoop felt almost sorry for them.

The one in the middle bent to the ground and seemed to take a long, deep sniff of the blood trail there. Ripley's blood trail. Then it hissed, a purposeful sound very different from the wails of grief, and the other two creatures also bent to the trail.

Got her scent now, Hoop thought. *Sorry, Ripley, but if there's anyone we have to leave behind…*

He wasn't serious. Not for a moment. But the aliens' reactions set his own blood chilling. They hissed again, louder than before. They crouched and spread their limbs, adopting stances that suddenly made them look even more deadly.

Hoop started climbing back up the steps. They still had their backs to him, but they only had to turn a quarter circle to see him. They would be on him in two bounds, and even if he had a chance to fire the charge-blaster, the delay on the charge meant he'd be dead before it blew.

He wished he'd brought his spray gun, too.

He made the top of the steps, braced himself, checked that the route behind him was clear. Then he paused at the fold in the wall and aimed the charge thumper up at the ceiling.

Four seconds, maybe five. Did that give him time? Would they be up the steps and through before the charge went? He didn't think so. But he also didn't think he had time to worry about it.

They had Ripley's scent, and Ripley had come this way.

He pulled the trigger, and the last explosive charge thumped up into the ceiling.

From beyond, down in the ship, he heard three high-pitched shrieks, then the skittering of hard claws as the aliens came for him.

Hoop sidestepped up through the opening and onto the ship's surface.

"Down there!" he said, shoving Ripley ahead of him, sliding down the gentle slope, and Lachance and Kasyanov pushed Sneddon the same way. They slid through the dust, and then from above and behind them came a dull, contained *thud*. Loud enough, though, to send echoes through the cavern.

Hoop came to a stop and looked back. Dust and smoke rose from the opening, but nothing else. No curved head, no sharp limb. Maybe, just maybe, fate had given them a break.

The blast was still echoing around the cave as they started across the ship's surface toward the openings they could see in the vast wall. They negotiated their way over piles of tumbled rocks. Ripley found her feet, although she still clasped onto Hoop's arm. Their combined lights offered just enough illumination to outline shadows and trip hazards, and the closer they came to the nearest opening, the more convinced Hoop became that the ship continued beyond the barrier. It was almost as if the vessel had struck the wall, and penetrated it upon landing.

Or crashing. They'd entered through a damaged portion of the ship's hull, after all, where blast damage was still obvious after so long.

More rocks, and Hoop noticed for the first time that some of them seemed more regular than he'd realized. Square-edged, smooth. One of them displayed what might have been markings of some sort.

But there was no time to pause and wonder. No time to consider what the markings and the tumbled, regular blocks might mean. A wall? A building? It didn't matter. A way out mattered, and from what Hoop could see, their best bet was through the nearest crack.

The mine wasn't far above the cavern's ceiling. He was sure of it. They were almost there.

"No sign of anything following us," Lachance said.

"That's what worries me," Hoop said. "I think I'd rather see them than wonder where the fuck they are."

"Yeah. Right." Then Lachance nodded ahead. "What do you think?"

"I think we've got no choice." They moved across the rubble field toward the opening in the cavern's looming wall.

17

ANCIENTS

When he was a kid, Hoop's parents took him to see the Incan ruins in Ecuador. He'd seen footage about them on the NetScreen, and read about them in the old books his parents insisted on keeping. But nothing had prepared him for the emotions and revelations he felt walking among those ancient buildings.

The sense of time, and timelessness, was staggering. He walked where other people had walked a thousand years before, and later he thought back to that moment as the first time mortality truly came knocking. It hadn't troubled him unduly. But he'd realized that his visit to those ruins was as fleeting as an errant breeze, and would have as much effect as a leaf drifting in from the jungles and then vanishing again. The memory of his being there would float to the floor and rot away with that leaf, and fascinated visitors even a hundred years hence would have never heard of him.

It was humbling, but it was also strangely uplifting. *We all have the same*, he'd once heard someone say, *one life*. Even as a teenager more concerned with girls and football, that had struck him as deep and thoughtful. One life… it was up to him how well he lived it.

Looking at those Incan ruins, he'd vowed to live it well.

Staring at what was left of this strange, ancient place, he wondered what had gone wrong.

There was some property to the stone all around them that gave it a subdued glow. It was light borrowed from the flashlights, he was sure, subsumed and then given back as a surprisingly sharp luminosity. He'd shine his flashlight at one spread of stone, move it aside, and the stone would glow for a long while afterward. It helped them light their way. It helped them see where they were going.

This wasn't part of the ship on which they had been. This was a building, a grounded structure built into the rock of the land. It was a ruin, yet one that was remarkably well preserved in places.

Fleeing though they were, Hoop couldn't help staring around in wonder.

They'd entered through a badly damaged area, climbing over piles of rubble, some of the fragments the size of one of their boots, some five yards across. Anything could have been hiding in the shadows. From what they could see, nothing was, or if it was it remained hidden.

They soon found themselves on a curving, sloping path that led upward, and kicking aside dust and gravel Hoop could make out the fine mosaics that made up the paving. Swirls of color, unfaded by the immensity of time. Curling, sharp patterns, features he could not make out, splashed shapes that fought and rested in harmony with each other. He suspected the mosaic told a story, but it was too smothered with dust for him to make it out. And perhaps he was too short to appreciate the full tale. Those dog-aliens might have seen it better, with their longer legs, higher heads.

This was amazing. An alien civilization, an intelligence the likes of which had never yet been discovered in almost two centuries of space exploration, and many hundreds of star systems entered and charted.

"I don't think I can process any of this," Lachance said. "I don't think I can think about it all, and run at the same time."

"Then just run," Hoop said. "You okay there?"

Lachance was still lugging Sneddon, slung across one shoulder so that he could still access his charge thumper with the other hand.

"All that time in the *Marion*'s gym is paying off."

"Tell me if—"

"You've got enough on your mind." And Lachance was right. Ripley still clung to Hoop's arm, and though her eyes were open and he could see that she was taking some of this in, she was still bleeding, stumbling, fading in and out. They'd have to stop soon. Patch her up.

Baxter and Kasyanov were helping each other, arms slung over shoulders like casual lovers.

The curved path rose around a massive central column, like the largest spiral staircase ever. The huge building's ceiling was high, damaged in places but still largely whole. Their flashlights lit some of the way ahead, and the glowing property of the stone helped level the illumination. But there were still heavy shadows in front of them, hiding around the bend, concealing whatever waited.

Hoop remained ready.

Doorways led off from the central spiral. There were intricate designs around these, beautiful sculptures showing dog-aliens in what must have been tales from their civilization's past, real or mythical. He saw the creatures in groups and ranks, at war, bathing, creating an obscure form of art, exploring, and in some carved spreads they seemed to be interacting with other, even stranger looking creatures. There were star charts and the representations of aircraft, spacecraft, and giant floating things that might even have been living. This made him think of the buried vessel they had just left behind, and the implications…

They were staggering, yet still too dangerous to muse upon.

Concentrate, Hooper! he thought. *Don't look at the fancy decorations around the doors, think about what might come* though *them!*

The curving, rising path ended in another vast open space. Huge columns supported a solid ceiling so high that the lights barely touched it, yet the material still became subtly luminous, retaining some of the light they aimed upward. They were creating their own starry sky, soft splashes of color and light retained and shining back down at them, if only for a time.

Around the nearest supporting column, upright objects cast long shadows.

"Is that them?" Lachance whispered. They all paused, panting from the climb up the spiraling ramp, some of them groaning softly from their wounds. Ripley was relatively alert again, right hand pressed tightly across the wound in her stomach.

"No," she said. "Too big. Too still."

"Statues," Hoop said. "At least I hope so. Come on. We'll stay near the wall, look for another way up."

They kept close to the edge of the wide-open space. In truth the size of it scared Hoop. He'd rather move through corridors and tunnels than this inhuman cavern, where the lights couldn't reach the other side and shadows might hide anything. But keeping close to the wall did something to hold back the agoraphobia.

As they closed on the massive column and the statues arrayed around its base, some of the detail became clearer. There were a dozen figures standing on high stone plinths. Several of them had lost limbs, one of them a head, but others remained virtually whole. They were all dog-aliens, with their stocky legs, strange torsos, bulky heads, and yet each was distinct. Some carvings wore different clothing that almost covered their bodies. Others stood on their hind legs and reached for the sky, or pointed, or held their limbs up as if gesticulating. Even their facial features were diverse. Hoop could see carved areas around the plinth's bases, and he assumed it was their written language. Maybe these were famous persons—rulers, teachers, or explorers.

"No time," he whispered, because he knew everyone would feel as fascinated as him. "Not now. Maybe we'll come back. Maybe we'll send someone back."

"They'd just die," Ripley said. She seemed stronger now, as if becoming used to the pain, but he could still see the dark dampness of blood across her suit, and a sheen of sweat on her forehead.

"We need to get you patched up," Hoop said.

"No, we—"

"Now." He refused to argue. Two minutes to bind and treat her wounds might save them half an hour if it meant she could walk under her own steam. "Guys, eyes and ears open. Ripley… strip. Kasyanov?"

Kasyanov gently laid down her plasma torch, wincing from the pain in her own terribly wounded hand, and unclipped her waist pack.

Ripley started peeling off her slashed and bloodied suit. Hoop flinched back when he saw the open wound across her neck, shoulder, and upper chest, but he didn't look away. The edges of the wound pouted open, skin tattered, flesh and fatty layers exposed.

Revealing them to the air made Ripley woozy again, and she leaned against him as the doctor set to work.

"This will hurt," Kasyanov said. Ripley didn't make a sound as Kasyanov sterilised the wound as best she could, washing out dark specks of dust and grit. She injected painkiller into six locations, then sprayed a local anaesthetic along the entire extent of the gaping cut.

While the anaesthetic went to work she tugged down Ripley's suit to below her waist and examined the stomach wound. As Hoop glanced down he caught Kasyanov frowning up at him.

"Just do your best," Ripley hissed.

Hoop hugged Ripley to him, kissed the top of her head.

"Hey," she said. "Fast mover."

Kasyanov treated the stomach wound, then stood again and started stapling the gash across her shoulder. The staple gun made a whispering click each time it fired. Ripley tensed but still didn't make a sound. After fixing the wound closed, Kasyanov taped a bandage across it and sprayed it with a sterile solution.

Then she turned her attention back to the stomach wound, stapling it, as well.

"I'll fix you up properly when we get back to the *Marion*," she said.

"Yeah," Ripley replied. "Right."

"You'll be able to move easier now. Nothing's going to pop or spill out."

"Great."

Kasyanov taped her stomach, then stood again. She took a small syringe from her pack.

"This will keep you going. It's not exactly… medicine. But it'll work."

"I'll take anything," Ripley said. Kasyanov pressed the needle into her arm, then stood back and zipped up her pack.

"You good?" Hoop asked.

Ripley stood on her own, tucking her arms into her suit and shrugging it on. "Yeah," she replied. "Good."

She wasn't. He could see that, and hear it in her voice. She was in pain and woozy, and distracted, too. Ever since she'd wiped out those queen eggs she'd been somewhere else. But there was no time to discuss it now.

Hoop thought again about those aliens viewing their burning infant queens, sniffing Ripley's blood, and howling.

"There," he said, pointing along the base of the vast wall. "Openings. Whichever one leads up, we take it. Lachance, you take point. I've got Sneddon." He knelt and took Sneddon's weight onto his shoulder. As they moved out, he held back until Ripley was walking ahead of him. She moved in a very controlled way, every movement purposeful and spare.

When they reached the first of the openings, Lachance shone his light inside. Moments later he waved them on and entered, and they started up another curving ramp.

From behind, somewhere in the vast shadowy depths, something screeched.

The rough leaves tickle her stomach. They're running across a field in France, weaving through the corn crop, arms up to push the stringy leaves aside and stop them scratching their eyes. She and Amanda are wearing their bathing costumes, and already she's anticipating the breathtaking plunge into the lake.

Amanda is ahead, a slim and sleek teenager, darting between corn rows and barely seeming to touch the plants. Ripley isn't so graceful, and her stomach feels as though it has been scratched to shreds by the leaves. But she won't look down to check. She's afraid that if she does she'll lose track of her daughter, and something about this...

...isn't right.

The sun shines, the corn crop rustles in a gentle breeze, there is silence but for their footfalls and Amanda's excited giggling from up ahead. But still this is wrong. The lake awaits but they will never reach it. The sun is high, the sky clear, yet the heat hardly touches her skin. Ripley feels cold.

She wants to call, Amanda, wait! *But the leaves slapping across her stomach and chest seem to have stolen her voice.*

She sees something out of the corner of her eye. A shadow that does not belong in the cornfield, a shape too sharp and cruel. But when she looks it has gone.

Her daughter is further ahead now, pushing plants aside as she sprints the final hundred meters to the field's edge and the welcoming water.

Something keeps pace with them off to the right, a dark shape streaking through the crop and smashing thick stalks into shreds. But looking directly at it means that Ripley can't see it at all.

She's panicking now, trying to run faster, trying to shout. Amanda has vanished ahead, leaving behind only swaying plants.

Ripley hears a high, loud screech. It's not human.

Bursting from the crop at the edge of the field, she sees Amanda caught in a grotesque web between two tall trees, trapped there in the strange, solid material that appears to have held her there for an age. Her daughter screams again as the bloody creature bursts fully from her chest.

In her peripheral vision, Ripley sees those tall beasts moving out of the corn to pay homage to their newborn.

Amanda screams one last time—

"Ripley, fast!" Hoop shouted.

Ripley looked around, not shocked or surprised. She knew exactly where she was and why. The vision was a memory of a time that had never happened. But she still shed a tear for her cocooned, bleeding, screaming daughter. Terror mixed with anger, becoming a part of her, unwilling to let go.

"They can't win, Hoop," she said. "We can't let them."

"They won't. Now run!"

"What are you—?"

"Run!" he shouted. He grabbed her hand and ran with her, but soon let her go again and fell back.

"Don't be stupid!" Ripley shouted back at him.

"Argue, and we'll all die!" Lachance called back. "Hoop knows what he's doing."

They climbed the ramp. It was steeper than the first, the turns tighter, and it seemed to grow narrower and steeper the higher they went. Soon there were steps built into its surface, and they had to slow down so that they didn't trip. Lachance carried Sneddon again. Kasyanov helped, and Baxter was using his plasma torch as a crutch, lamming it down and swinging along on it with every step. She wondered what effect that would have if he had to fire it again. She wondered...

She turned and ran back down the ramp.

"Ripley!" Lachance called.

"Argue and we all die!" she said, and soon they were out of sight above her. For a while she was on her own, descending the ramp, illuminated by an already fading glow from the structure around her. Then she heard something running toward her and she crouched down close to the central spine.

Hoop appeared, lit up by her flashlight's beam. Sweating, eyes wide, he tensed, but didn't relax again.

"We really need to go," he said.

"How many?"

"Too many."

Ripley wasn't sure she could run again. Her stomach ached, she could barely move her right arm, and she felt sick. But the booster Kasyanov had given her coursed through her veins, and every negative thought was dragged down and hidden away. There was a sensory distance around her. Though unpleasant, it was also protecting her, so she embraced it, losing track of her various agonies. She knew that they would be waiting for her on the other side.

From above, Lachance started shouting, but she couldn't tell what he was saying.

"Oh, no," Ripley said. Yet Hoop grinned and grabbed her hand, and before she knew it they were running up the ramp once more. She saw lights ahead of them, and the ramp ended in another wide space. This was more like a cave than a building—slopes of rocks, an uneven ceiling, walls that had only ever been touched by human tools.

At the far end, Kasyanov and Baxter held Sneddon up between them. The first thing Ripley noticed was the opening in the rock behind them.

Then Sneddon lifted her head and looked around, and Ripley saw that the face-hugger was gone.

18

ELEVATOR

When Hoop had broken away from the others, he'd seen at least ten of the aliens stalking through the massive room, searching between giant pillars, crouching by the statues and their plinths. There was enough fading light still emanating from the stonework, and as he'd watched their shadows had slowly merged into the surroundings.

He'd backed away slowly, light extinguished, and then run, finding his way by feel. Ripley's flashlight had brought light to his world again.

Being back in the mine should have made him feel better. But Hoop knew that those things were still pursuing them, scenting blood, and that every second's delay would bring them closer. The elevator was their salvation. Reach that, go up, and they'd be way ahead of the game. It was now a simple race. And for once, things seemed to be going well.

The thing had dropped from Sneddon's face and died, and they'd left it back there in the tunnels. She seemed fine. Quiet, confused, a little scared, but able to walk on her own, and even keen to carry the spray gun that Lachance had been hefting for her.

With Sneddon on her feet again and Ripley patched up, it meant that they could move faster than before. Even Baxter seemed to have found his stride, using his plasma torch as a crutch. Hoop dared to hope.

If we get out of this I'm going home, he thought. The idea had stuck with him for some time, and he'd been thinking of his kids. He hadn't seen them for seven years, didn't know if they'd remember him, had no idea how much his ex-wife might have turned them against him. They were adults now, plenty old enough to ask why he hadn't stayed in touch. No contact at all. Nothing on their birthdays, no messages at Christmas. How difficult would it be for him to explain, when he wasn't even sure of the reasons himself?

But when this was over and they launched themselves back toward Earth, it would be his last time. To arrive back home would be so wonderful it was now all he could wish for.

And there was something else. Maybe he didn't actually deserve hope, but Ripley did. She had been through far too much to just die out here.

The mine was familiar territory. The lights still worked, and as they moved through the tunnels of the lowest parts of level 9 toward the second elevator shaft, Hoop waited for their way to be blocked once again. Those things had been in here, building their strange constructions—nests, traps, homes. But maybe between here and the elevator it would be clear. Maybe fate had cut them a break.

But he knew the pursuing aliens would find their way. They had Ripley's scent, and their blood was up, their hatred and fury, their ferocity, richer than ever before. He saw no need to tell the others, but he made sure they moved quickly, quietly. They all understood the urgency. They'd all been through too much to slow down now.

"It's close!" Baxter said. "I recognize this place. Just around this next corner, I think." He'd been down in the mines more than any of them, and Hoop hoped he was right. And when they turned the next corner, there it was.

The elevator shaft stood in the center of a wide-open area, ceiling propped by metal columns. It seemed whole, undamaged, untouched. The shaft was set in a heavy network of metal stanchions. The elevator car was parked on this floor, too, which meant the miners had all used the other one to flee to the surface.

"Something's bound to be wrong with it," Lachance said, and Hoop actually guffawed.

"Just live with the fact we've been given a break," he said. "Come on. Everyone inside, quickly."

He waited beside the elevator while Baxter checked the controls. Power was still on, and when he pressed at the buttons, the cage door slid open to reveal the elevator car. As with the one that had crashed, the walls were of mesh and struts, the floor a solid sheet. No mirrors, no music. There was no need for luxuries in a mine.

Sneddon stood close to Hoop, swaying slowly from side to side.

"You feeling okay?" he asked.

Sneddon nodded. "Thirsty," she croaked.

"Won't be long now." He looked past her at Ripley. She was staring, frowning deeply. She'd placed herself at the far side of the elevator doors, and even as they started filing aboard, she kept her eyes on the science officer, and tried to steer clear of her.

"Ripley?" he asked softly. But she looked at him and shook her head. She knew as well as any of them that they had to leave this level. Anything else was of a lesser priority.

She's carrying one of those things, Hoop thought, glancing at Sneddon again. She looked tired, but herself. He'd seen them on the viewing screen, from inside *Samson*, bursting from chests. He'd listened to Ripley's story about the crew member on her ship, how he'd effected a miraculous recovery, only to be ripped apart an hour later.

Sneddon seemed fine. But she was living on borrowed time.

Maybe she knew that.

He stepped into the elevator, and instantly it felt as if they were rising. A weight fell from him. He slumped against the wall and sighed, closing his eyes, and as the doors slid closed he seemed to be waiting forever for the sound they made when they came together.

"We're looking good," Baxter said. "I think we might—"

The impact was massive, smashing against the doors, bowing them inward. A fresh crash came from another side, and another, and then all four sides of the enclosed elevator shaft were being assaulted from outside, aliens smashing against the mesh again and again. Metal creaked and tore, and Hoop heard the distinctive *snap!* as a set of teeth crunched together.

They all moved away from the walls, colliding in the center of the elevator and huddling there. Hoop trained his spray gun on the walls, the others aimed their weapons, but none of them could fire.

Acid would splash and kill them all, plasma would surge across the inner surfaces. Closed away from the aliens at last, they also found themselves defenseless.

"Press the fucking button!" Lachance screamed at Baxter.

More banging, rending metal, and the rage-filled hissing of the creatures trying their best to reach their prey.

Baxter didn't hesitate. He lunged for the control panel and slapped his open hand on the button labeled "4".

If he'd stepped carefully he might have been all right. If panic and fear hadn't slammed him against the lift cage wall, perhaps he'd have been able to jump lightly back into the center. But the instant the car began to rise, an alien's head burst through the gap between doors, bending and ripping them apart. It thrashed and twisted as it tried to force itself inside. Moments later its teeth flashed out and struck hard against Baxter's right shoulder. They chewed so rapidly that they burrowed through his jacket, skin, flesh, and clamped tight around his scapular.

Baxter screamed, eyes wide. The alien pulled, tugging him halfway through the ragged hole it had created.

They were rising.

Hoop went to help, grabbing at the comm officer's belt, Lachance doing the same on the other side. The alien's clawed hand slashed in, and Hoop only just let go in time. He held Baxter's legs instead, pulling as hard as he could, gritting his teeth, vision blurring with the effort.

The cage rattled violently.

Baxter began screaming because he knew what was to come. He was stuck fast halfway through the opening, and they pulled one way while the alien tugged the other, rising and dangling from the suffering man as the lift took its prey out of reach.

Whether or not the alien let go, Hoop did not know. But he closed his eyes as Baxter struck the first of the cross-beams forming the shaft's superstructure. The man's cry instantly cut off and was replaced with the most dreadful sound of ripping, tearing, crushing.

He suddenly became very light. Hoop turned around and let go as something splashed down onto the elevator's floor.

"Oh, God!" someone said.

They continued rising. Below them the cacophony persisted as aliens smashed against the walls. But the elevator accelerated, rapidly passing level 8 and speeding up even more. Hoop's stomach dropped. And when he turned around and looked at what was left of Baxter, he wasn't the only one to fall to his knees and puke.

Ripley covered him up. He'd been torn in half just below his ribcage, and his legs and lower body had dropped to the elevator floor. She couldn't keep her eyes off the broken ankle. Baxter's foot lay at an odd angle, and the heavy padding they'd used to try and splint the break had come unraveled. He'd struggled so long on that, and for so far, because he wanted to survive.

Of course he did.

They all wanted to survive, and they'd do anything to do so. Baxter had run and walked on a broken ankle, going through untold pain. And now…

She only looked briefly before dropping her suit jacket across the ruined, open part of him. Things that should never be outside a body were splashed across the elevator floor, and her jacket covered most of them.

She was cold, her tattered thermal vest doing little to hold in her body heat. But she'd rather be cold than stare at what was left of that poor man. Her stomach rolled a little, more at the stench of vomit than what she had seen.

Am I just stronger? she thought. *Have I just seen too much? Is it that I expect the worst, so it doesn't worry me?* She wasn't sure.

Maybe it was because she had something more on her mind.

She turned her back on Baxter, picked up his dropped plasma torch, and checked out Sneddon. The science officer seemed to be in reasonable shape, and there was even color in her cheeks again. She was quiet, leaning against the elevator wall and staring into some distance only she could see.

"How do you feel?" Ripley asked.

"Yeah," Sneddon said. "Yeah, good. Weird dreams. But I'm okay."

"You know what happened to you." It was a statement, not a question.

"Yes, I know."

Ripley nodded, looked around. The others were staring at her. *I'm the stranger here*, she thought. Her gaze rested on Hoop, and she couldn't quite read him. They were all tired, shocked from Baxter's gruesome demise. She couldn't say anything yet. She just couldn't.

"She'll be fine," Hoop said. "We have a med-pod on the *Marion* that can—"

"It's okay," Ripley said, turning away. She breathed hard. The sensation of movement from the elevator had been startling—still was—probably made worse by the walls distorted by the alien attack. She felt suddenly sick. But she swallowed, bit her lip, and willed it back down.

Sneddon couldn't reach the *Marion* alive. Ripley knew that, yet she was uncertain how far she would go to prevent it. Ash was up there, ready and waiting to receive the science officer into his control. It didn't matter that she was a human being. She was impregnated now, and she carried what Ash had been seeking for thirty-seven years.

Does he already know? She had to assume that was a yes.

Would he go to any lengths to protect and preserve Sneddon, and what she carried? Again, yes. She knew that, had witnessed Ash's determination before.

Sneddon couldn't be taken to the *Marion*. And Ripley could not kill another person. The problem circled, deep and heavy, and she closed her eyes, hoping that a solution would come.

Each level they passed was marked by a soft chime from the elevator's control panel, and the voice of someone from far away and long ago reciting, "Seven… Six… Five." The cage decelerated then, and Ripley experienced the strange sensation of being stretched, head and shoulders growing suddenly light. It made it easier to breathe, but did nothing to level her queasiness.

She did her best not to puke. Her stomach wound throbbed deep and cold, and she thought if she heaved the act might pop the staples holding her together. Her shoulder and arm were stiff, and she was sure she could feel the penetrating metal of the clasps there every time she moved. She thought of asking Kasyanov for another shot of anaesthetic or painkiller. But she was already woozy enough. If a flash of pain now and then was what she had to endure to stay awake, so be it. She needed all her wits about her. They all did.

The elevator slowed to a halt, and a different chime sounded from the control panel. Outside of the cage, all was blackness.

"Level 4," Lachance said. "Lingerie, footwear, monsters, and beasties."

"This level was mined out two years ago," Hoop said. "Lots of deep tunnels, a complex network. One of the longest in the mine snakes away from here for over three miles."

"Sounds lovely," Ripley said. "So the fuel cells are here?"

"Yeah, we use this level for storage now. Lachance?"

"Spare fuel cells shouldn't be that far away. We'll need to find a powered trolley to carry one."

"You okay?" Kasyanov asked, and it took Ripley a few seconds to realize the doctor was talking to her.

She nodded. Realized they were all looking at her.

"You were… mumbling to yourself," Hoop said.

"I'm good," Ripley insisted, smiling. But she hadn't realized she was saying a word.

Waiting for Hoop to throw the doors open, she tried to analyze her wounds again, assess just how badly hurt she was. But the shots Kasyanov had given her made that quite hard to do. She was slightly removed from herself, a distance that made the pain bearable but which also furred the edges of her perception.

She'd have time for reality later.

I'm awake. I'm me. Stay sharp, Ripley!

Damaged as they were, Hoop had to force the cage doors open manually, and they shone their lights outside. They all waited in silence, playing the lights around the open area they revealed. Hoop edged forward and stepped outside, crouching low, turning his flashlight and spray gun left and right.

"Looks clear," he whispered. "Wait here." He crossed to a mess of dials and controls fixed onto a wall, flicked some switches, and with a buzz and a click the lights came on. As elsewhere in the mine, there were strings of bare lights slung tight to the ceiling, and more hung from hooks sunk into the walls. But basic though they were, everyone welcomed the illumination.

"Flashlights off," Hoop said. "Conserve whatever charge you have left. We might need them again."

Ripley and the other three survivors left the elevator and fanned out. The area was similar to that on level 9, a wide space with metal props at regular intervals. There was more mining equipment discarded all around—tools, clothing, some water canisters, and several wheeled trolleys. Lachance checked out the trolleys and found one whose power pack was still half-charged. He stood on the small control deck, accessed the control panel, and rolled forward a few steps.

"How far in are the stores?" Ripley asked.

"Not far," Hoop said, pointing at one of the tunnels leading off. "Just through there, hundred yards or so. Why?"

"And how many fuel cells are stored down here?"

"Three," Lachance said. "Two spares for the *Marion*, and one for the mine's power plant on the surface. The plant is designed so it runs off ship-grade power cells. We store them all down here, so we don't lose the ship if they... malfunction."

"Okay," Ripley said. She looked around at them all, bloodied and desperate, holding their mining tools that had been turned into weapons. They weren't soldiers. They weren't even miners. But they'd survived so far, and if and when they got home, they would have a hell of a story to tell.

"We've got to bury the mine," she said.

"What?" Lachance asked. "Why? We discovered something amazing down there! That ship was incredible enough, but those buildings we found... it can't have been just one. It was the start of a city, Ripley. Maybe a thousand, even ten thousand years old. It's..." He shrugged, at a loss for words.

"The most amazing discovery since humankind first came into space," Ripley said.

"Yes," he agreed. "That. Precisely."

"But it's contaminated," she said. "Corrupted. Tainted by those things. Whatever deep history we witnessed down there was dictated by them, not by those dog-things who built the ship and the city. They might have been the amazing ones. That ship was remarkable, I can't deny that. And we saw that they had wonderful architecture, and art, and knowledge and imagination that might put ours to shame. But am I the only one who thinks that ship might have been shot down? Maybe even by their own people?"

The others were watching her, listening silently.

"Everything went wrong. A disease came and destroyed all that they were, and we can't let that disease escape." She looked pointedly at Sneddon, who was staring down at her feet. "We can't."

"She's right," Sneddon said without looking up. "Yeah. She's right."

"I can set one of the fuel cells to overheat," Hoop said.

"And blow us all to hell," Lachance said. "No thanks, already been there, and now I'm keen to leave. One of those cells goes, it'll be like setting a nuke off in here."

"That's *exactly* what it'll be," Hoop said. "And Ripley's right. We can't just escape from here and go on our way. We have to make sure no one else finds this place."

"And they will!" Ripley said. "Have no doubt of that. Hoop?"

"Ash," Hoop said.

"Your mad android?" Lachance asked.

"He'll do his best to complete—"

"Thanks for bringing an insane AI to our ship, by the way," Lachance said.

"Ash docked the ship!" Ripley said. "I was still in hypersleep. I've been used in this more than all of you together. But he'll be logging whatever he can of this, recording details, constructing a full report for Weyland-Yutani. And damaged though your antenna array may be, he'll find a way to send it, or take it back to the Company."

"Unless I wipe him from the systems," Hoop said. "I already told you I can do that."

"And I firmly believe that you'll try," Ripley said. "But there was something different about Ash. Weyland-Yutani made him... devious. Capable of lying, of harming humans, of trying to kill me. So we can't take any chances at all." She held up her hands. "We blow the mine."

"It's simple enough," Hoop said. "Start the fuel cell, initiate charging, disconnect damping and coolant systems. It can be done."

"But there's no accurate way to judge how long it will take to blow," Lachance said.

"It doesn't have to be accurate," Ripley said. "As long as it gives us time to take off."

Hoop and Lachance looked at each other, and in their silence Ripley heard their agreement. They saw why it needed to be done, and they could do it.

"Suits me," Kasyanov said. "Quite happy to burn those fuckers, or bury them for all eternity."

"Don't forget there's still that one on the *Marion*," Sneddon said. She was still looking at her feet, and Ripley saw something in her that she'd never noticed before. A strange kind of calmness.

"We'll tackle that when the time comes," Hoop said.

"And only if we have to," Lachance said. "With luck, it'll just burn with the ship."

"Right," Hoop said.

They all stood in silence for a few moments. Then Hoop clapped his hands together, causing them all to jump.

"Let's get to it, then!"

"Thank you," Ripley muttered, so quietly that he probably didn't hear. But he smiled nonetheless.

You're all going to die, she thought, a silent message to those things raving down below. Maybe they were finding their way up through level 7 now, coming for the people who had killed their queen, and all of their future queens, as well. But she was starting to feel better. Starting to feel *good*.

She hoped it wasn't the drugs.

19

CELLS

PROGRESS REPORT:
To: Weyland-Yutani Corporation, Science Division
(Ref: code 937)
Date (unspecified)
Transmission (pending)

Infiltration of Marion's computer successfully achieved.
All major systems now under complete control, sub-system
routines being accessed. It was more difficult than
projected... I have been away for some time, and systems
have advanced.

Limited contact achieved with LV178 surface control
systems. Elevator One remote controls were successfully
interrupted upon manual operation. Elevator descended to
Level Nine.

Some evidence of new activity on Level Four.

Things seem to be going to plan.

Anticipating return of survivors to Marion within
approximately seven hours.

Alien specimen surviving on Marion still not detected. It
is waiting somewhere.

I am hoping that they bring a viable egg back with them.

I am hoping it is time to go home.

* * *

Hoop was unsettled.

Their course of action was now clear—lift a spare fuel cell onto the trolley, set another one to fire up and overheat, get the hell back to the surface, the *Samson*, the *Marion*, then into Ripley's shuttle before the ship hit the atmosphere and came apart, all while watching out for the alien that had escaped into the interior of the *Marion*.

Simple.

But one thing troubled him, and it was close at hand.

Sneddon. She looked and acted fine, though there was something... quieter about her now, something calm. Unnaturally so. She had one of their infants in her chest. Ever since that face-hugger had fallen from her and died, Hoop had been thinking, *It's okay, it's fine, we'll get her to the* Marion *and into the med-pod, get that thing taken out of her, lock it up somewhere and leave it to burn up with the ship.*

But it couldn't be that easy, and Ripley's comments were starting to hit home. She was injured, and the shots Kasyanov had given her might have gone to her head, just a little. The muttering, the swaying. But she knew exactly what she was talking about.

She always had.

If they took Sneddon back to the *Marion* with them, what would happen? What if Ash had somehow infiltrated the ship's systems? Hoop didn't think it likely—the *Marion* was a comparatively new ship, and its computing systems were a hundred times more complex than they'd been when Ripley had gone to sleep. But the chance was always there, and if Ash somehow found out about what Sneddon was carrying...

That was just what the AI wanted. He'd been searching for thirty-seven years, and there was no end to what he might do to protect the object of his quest.

Yet Hoop had no answers. He couldn't bring himself to leave Sneddon behind, however terrible the risk. And as they commenced working on the spare fuel cells, he watched Ripley, fearing what she had planned for the science officer.

She'd picked up Baxter's plasma torch, apparently not even noticing the splash of his blood across its power housing.

"Ripley!" he said. She looked up. "Bring me that tool pouch, will you?" She came across to him, carrying a tool kit that had been hanging from a hook on the wall.

I'll just work, he thought. *Face those problems when the time comes. For now... just concentrate.*

The spare cells hadn't been stored in the best of conditions. There were three, each of them the size of a small adult. One wasn't even propped up off the floor, and a quick inspection revealed signs of decay to some of its metal framework and mountings. One of the other two was being loaded onto the trolley by Lachance and Kasyanov, and Hoop set to work on the last cell.

Sneddon stood off to one side, watching, ostensibly listening for any of those things that might be approaching. Hoop was pretty confident they had some time before the beasts could make their way up through the mine. Both staircases had blast doors at every level that were kept permanently shut, and they wouldn't know how to use the code keys on the control panels. But it gave Sneddon something to do.

He watched her. They all did, and she knew it. Yet she offered them back a gentle smile, as if she knew something they did not.

Hoop opened the cell's metallic shell and placed the cover to one side. He set to work disconnecting three cooling loops, then removed the coolant supplies altogether, for good measure. He delved deeper, past wires and conductors to the governing capacitors. These were adjustable, and he turned them all up to full.

A soft hum rose from the core. Barely the size of his fist, still its potential was staggering.

"We're almost good to go," he said after a while. More adjustments, several wires snipped, and then he disconnected and rerouted the last safety failsafe, meaning he could initiate the cell without having to input its own unique code.

"How long do you think it will give us?" Ripley asked.

"I'm thinking nine hours until it goes critical," he replied. "Plenty of time to get off this rock."

"If those things haven't made it out to the *Samson* and trashed it. Or if they're not just sitting inside, waiting for us to board. Or—"

"Fuck it," he said, cutting her off. "If they've done that, I'll come and sit beside this thing and wait for it to blow, rather than die of exposure or starvation."

"Let's hope then, eh?" Ripley asked.

"Let's hope. Hey, you okay?"

"Yeah. Flying high from the shots Kasyanov gave me, that's all."

Hoop nodded, then called over to where Lachance was fussing over the cell on the trolley.

"We good?" he said.

"Ready," the pilot replied. He looked down at the cell that lay next to Hoop, its cover removed and half of its mechanical guts hanging out. "You've done a real butcher's job on that."

"I'm an artist," Hoop said. "Everyone else good? Sneddon?"

"Let's get the hell out of here," she said.

"Right." Hoop breathed deeply and held two bare wires, ready to touch them together.

What if I'm wrong? What if the overload happens in minutes, not hours? What if...? But they had come too far, survived too much, to pay any more attention to what-ifs.

"Here goes nothing," he muttered, touching the two wires together.

A spark, a clunk, the sound of something whirring noisily inside the cell. Then a slew of lights flickered into life across its dismantled maintenance panel, some dying out, others remaining lit.

A red warning light began to pulse.

"Okay, it's working," he said. "In about nine hours, everything inside of a mile of here will become a cloud of radioactive dust."

"Then let's not hang around," Ripley said.

The elevator still worked. Kasyanov had removed the remains of Baxter's body. Even so, with the introduction of the fuel cell, things were cramped. They rose quickly to ground level and exited into the vestibule area, Lachance steering the trolley carrying the replacement fuel cell. They watched for movement, listened for the sound of running things.

Everything was suddenly going too smoothly, but Ripley tried not to question it.

Close to the tunnel entrance at the edge of the dome, they opened the metal storage container and donned their suits once more. They gauged oxygen supplies, then checked each other's fittings and connections. Ripley felt constrained having to wear the suit again.

The lights were still on in the tunnel that stretched between dome and landing pad. They moved quickly, passing the place where the floor was bubbled from an acid spill, and when they were close to the external pad Hoop called a halt.

"Nearly there," he said. "Let's not get hasty. We've got plenty of time, it's been less than an hour since I fired up the cell. Slow and careful from here."

Ripley knew he was right. The aliens had chased miners this far and further, so they certainly couldn't lower their guard just yet. But there was a small part of her, filled with dread, that whispered that they should never leave.

She ignored it.

She had to, because Amanda was still in her dreams, and haunting those occasional, shocking waking visions that seemed so real.

Her stomach hurt more and more, but she didn't want another shot of painkiller. Once they were on board the *Samson*, launched, flying safely up toward the *Marion* in low orbit, perhaps then. But for these last moments on this wretched planet's surface, she wanted all her wits about her.

Sneddon walked with them, carrying something that might kill them all. Didn't they realize that? Didn't they see what was happening here? Hoop had described to her the fate of their shuttle *Delilah*, and they knew it had been the hatching monsters that did that.

What if Sneddon's beast hatched on their way up?

Ripley's finger stroked the torch's trigger. One slight squeeze and Sneddon would be gone. A moment of shock, another instant of awful pain as the burning plasma melted through her flesh and bone and turned her heart and lungs to cinder…

"Wait," Ripley said. The word had a weight of finality to it, and when Hoop sighed and turned to look at her, she thought he knew.

Sneddon did not even turn around. She looked down at her feet, shoulders dropping.

"We can't…" Ripley said. She was crying now, finally unable to hold back the tears that fell for everyone—her old, dead crew; the survivors with her now; Amanda. Most of all, for Sneddon.

"What, Ripley?" Lachance asked. He sounded tired.

Ripley lifted the plasma torch and aimed it at Sneddon's back.

"We can't take her," she breathed.

No one moved. None of them stepped back, away from the area where the flames would spout. But none of them went to help, either. Maybe shock froze them all.

"You know what happened before," Ripley said. "Same thing might happen to the *Samson*, when we're partway there. If she hatches... if the thing bursts from her chest... how do we kill it on the shuttle? Can't use this." She lifted the plasma torch slightly, nozzle now aimed at the back of Sneddon's head. "Can't use the acid gun Hoop's carrying, either. We'd fry everyone, burn a hole in the dropship. We'd be an easy target for it. So..." She sniffed hard, blinking to clear her vision.

"So?" Hoop asked.

Ripley didn't answer. Sneddon still hadn't turned around.

"Move, say something, damn it!" Ripley shouted. "Fall down! Start to shake, to scream, try to stop me—*give me a reason!*"

"I feel fine," Sneddon said. "But Ripley... I know I'm going to die. I've known that since I woke, knowing what had happened to me. I'm a science officer, remember." She turned around. "I know I'm going to die. But not down here. Not like this."

Ripley's finger tightened on the trigger. Hoop only watched, his face seemingly impassive. She wished he'd give her some sort of signal—a nod, a shake of the head.

Help me, Hoop!

"I'll stay in the airlock," Sneddon said. "The moment I feel something happening, I'll blast myself out. But please, take me, and I'll do anything I can to help. There's still an alien on the *Marion*, remember? Maybe I can tackle it. Maybe it won't do anything to me if it knows what's inside me."

Ripley blinked and saw Amanda, arms wide, face distorted with agony as a monster burrowed out from her chest.

"Oh, no," she gasped. She lowered the plasma torch and went to her knees. Hoop came but she waved him away, punching out at his stomach. He hadn't helped her before, she didn't want him now. They watched her, and then they turned away when she stood again, wiping at her eyes.

"Okay. Come on," Hoop said. "Let's see if the storm's still blowing."

Ripley was last to leave the tunnel. And she was angry at herself. She hadn't held off from firing because of anything Sneddon had said about traveling in the airlock, or helping them on the *Marion*. She had relented simply because she couldn't kill another human being.

Maybe that made her good. But it also made her weak.

Outside, the storm had dissipated to a gentle breeze. Wafts of sand still drifted across the landscape, and there were small mounds piled against the *Samson*'s landing feet. In the distance, electrical storms played jagged across the horizon, so far away that the thunder never reached them. The system's star was a vague smudge against the dusty atmosphere in the west, bleeding oranges and yellows in a permanently spectacular sunset.

The *Samson* remained untouched on the landing pad. Hoop climbed up the superstructure, brushed dust from the windows and checked inside. He couldn't see anything amiss.

There was a moment of tension as they opened the external door and Hoop entered. Then he opened up the internal door and they boarded safely, taking great care when lifting the replacement fuel cell and securing it to the cabin rack. They relied on it completely, and any damage would doom them all.

Once they were all inside, Sneddon settled inside the small airlock, just as she'd promised. There was a window into that space, but no one looked. Not even Ripley. She closed her eyes as Lachance went through pre-flight checks, and didn't open them again when they took off.

But she did not sleep. She thought perhaps she might never sleep again.

This is a real memory, Ripley thinks, *but the division between real and imaginary is becoming more and more indistinct. If this is real, then* why am I in pain? *Why does she hurt from where an alien's tail slashed across her stomach, a claw opened her shoulder to the bone? If this is real, then everything will be all right.*

She is on a roller coaster with Amanda. Her daughter is nine years old and utterly fearless, and as she whoops and laughs, Ripley holds onto the bar across their stomachs so hard that her fingers cramp into claws.

I love it, Mommy! *Amanda shouts, her words whipped away by the wind.*

Ripley closes her eyes but it changes little. She can still feel the vicious whipping of gravity grasping at her, tugging her this way and that as the car slips down a steep descent, around a tight corner, twisting and ripping back toward a cruel summit. With every twist and turn, the pain shoots through her.

Mommy, look!

There's an urgency to Amanda's voice that makes Ripley look. There's something wrong with their surroundings. Something so wrong, yet the roller coaster is traveling so fast now that she cannot seem to focus on anything outside the car.

People seem to be running across the park around them.

Screaming, dashing, falling…

Dark shapes chasing them, much faster than the people, like animals hunting prey…

Muh—Mommy? *Amanda says, and because she sits beside her in the moving car, Ripley can focus on her.*

She wishes she could not.

A bloom of blood erupts from her torn chest, a terrible inevitability. Amanda is crying, not screeching in pain but shedding tears of such wretchedness that Ripley starts crying as well.

I'm sorry, Amanda, *she says.* I should have been home to protect you. *She's hoping that her daughter will say that she understands, and that everything is all right. But she says nothing of the sort.*

Yes, you should have, Mommy.

The infant alien bursts outward in a shower of blood that is ripped away by the wind.

As they reach the roller coaster's summit the car slows to a crawl, and Ripley can see what has happened to the world.

"You're crying," Hoop said. He was squeezing her hand, shaking it until she opened her eyes.

Ripley tried to blink the tears away. This had been the worst episode yet. And with increasing dread, she knew it wouldn't be the last.

"You in pain? Want another shot?"

Ripley looked across at where Kasyanov watched her expectantly. The doctor had bound her own hand and placed it in a sling. "No," she says. "No, I just want to stay awake."

"Your call."

"How long 'til we get to the *Marion*?"

"Lachance?" Hoop called. The ship was shaking, buffeted from all sides as it powered up through the unforgiving atmosphere.

"Two, maybe three hours," the pilot said. "Once we're in orbit we've got to travel a thousand miles to the *Marion*."

"Everything good?" Ripley looked at the fuel cell on the rack in front of them, shaking as the *Samson* vibrated.

"Yeah, everything's good."

"Sneddon?"

Hoop nodded. "Everything's good."

"For now," Ripley said. "Only for now. Nothing stays good for long. Not ever."

Hoop didn't reply to that, and across the cabin Kasyanov averted her eyes.

"I've got to go help Lachance," Hoop said. "You be okay?"

Ripley nodded. But they all knew that she was lying, and that she would not be okay.

Nothing stays good for long.

PART 3

NOTHING GOOD

20

HOME

This was the first step of Hoop's journey home. *All the way* home. He'd decided that down in the mine, and the more time that passed, the more he began to believe it. He had started thinking of his children again. This time, however, their faces and voices no longer inspired feelings of intense guilt, but a sense of hope. The fact that he'd left them behind could never be changed or forgotten—by them, or by him—but perhaps there were ways that damage could be fixed.

He had found his monsters, and now it was time to leave them behind.

"How long until the *Marion* enters the atmosphere?" he asked.

In the pilot's seat beside him, Lachance shrugged.

"Difficult to say, especially from here. We might have a couple of days once we dock, it might only be hours. If we approach the ship and it's already skimming the atmosphere, there's a good chance we won't be able to dock, anyway."

"Don't say that," Hoop said.

"Sorry. We've always known this was a long shot, haven't we?"

"Long shot, yeah. But we've got to believe." Hoop thought of those they had lost, Baxter's terrible death even though he had given the best he could, done everything possible to survive. To run through an alien-infested mine on a broken ankle, only to meet an awful end like that... it was so unfair.

But fairness had no place in the endless dark depths of the universe. Nature was indifferent, and space was inimical to man. Sometimes, Hoop thought they'd made a mistake crawling from the swamp.

"We're going to do this," Hoop said. "We've got to. Get away from this pit, get back home."

Lachance looked across in surprise.

"Never thought you had anything to go back to."

"Things change," he said. *Hopefully. Hopefully things can change.*

"We've left them all behind," Lachance said, relaxing into his seat. He scanned the instrument panel as they went, hands on steering stick, but Hoop heard such a sense of relief in his voice. "Who'd have thought we would? I didn't. Those things... they're almost unnatural. How can God allow something like that?"

"God?" Hoop scoffed. But then he saw something like hurt in Lachance's eyes. "Sorry. I'm no believer, but if that's your choice, then..." He shrugged.

"Whatever. But those things, I mean... how do they survive? Where's their home planet, how do they travel, what are they *for*?"

"What's anything for?" Hoop asked. "What are humans for? Everything's an accident."

"I can't believe that."

"And I can't believe otherwise. If your God made everything, then what was his purpose for them?"

The question hung between them, and neither could offer an answer.

"Doesn't matter," Hoop went on. "We survive, we get out of here, head for home."

"Five of us, now," Lachance said.

"Four," Hoop said softly. "Sneddon's with us now, but..."

"But," Lachance said. "Four of us on Ripley's shuttle. Two men, two women."

"We'll start a whole new human race," Hoop quipped.

"With respect, Hoop, I believe Ripley would eat you alive."

He laughed. It was the first time he'd laughed properly in a long while, perhaps even since before the disaster, more than seventy days before. It felt strange, and somehow wrong, as if to laugh was to forget all his friends and colleagues who had died. But Lachance was laughing, too, in that silent shoulder-shaking way of his.

Though it felt wrong, it also felt good. Another step toward survival.

Leaving the atmosphere brought a sense of peace. The rattling and shaking ended, and the shuttle's partial gravity gave them all a sense of lightness that helped lift their moods. Glancing back into the cabin, Hoop noticed Ripley looking in on Sneddon. He stood to go to her, but she turned and nodded, half-smiling. Whatever Sneddon's fate, it had yet to happen.

Her predicament was difficult to comprehend. She knew she was going to die. She had seen it happening to others, and as science officer she knew more than most what it entailed. Surely she'd want to ease her own suffering? Maybe she'd already spoken with Kasyanov. But if she hadn't, Hoop would make sure the doctor prepared something to send her quietly to sleep, when the time came.

He only hoped that Sneddon would see or feel the signs.

Something chimed softly on the control panel.

"*Marion*," Lachance said. "Six hundred miles away. We'll be there in fifteen minutes."

Something flashed on the panel, and a screen lit up with a series of code.

"What's that?"

"*Samson*'s computer communicating with *Marion*," Lachance said. "The nav computer will give us the best approach vector, given comparative speeds and orbits."

"Ash," Ripley said. She'd appeared behind Hoop, leaning on the back of his seat and resting one hand on his shoulder.

"Can you disconnect?" Hoop asked.

"Disconnect what?"

"The *Samson*'s computer from the *Marion*'s."

"Why would I want to do that?" Lachance looked at them both as if they'd suddenly grown extra heads.

"Because of Ash. It might be better for us if he doesn't know what we're doing. What Sneddon's carrying."

"And how the hell would he know that?"

"We have to assume he's infiltrated the *Marion*'s computer,"

Ripley said. "That would be his aim. Maybe he can't, but just in case he has…"

"No," Lachance said. "That's paranoia, and leaving us blind to fly in manually is just stupid."

"But you could do it?" Hoop asked.

"Of course," Lachance said. "Yes. Probably. Under normal conditions, but these are far from normal."

"That's right," Ripley said. "Far from normal. Ash, the AI, his orders were very particular. Crew expendable. My old crew, and now this one. Lachance, we just can't take the risk."

The pilot was silent for a while, turning things over in his mind. Then he accessed the shuttle's computer and started scrolling through commands. He pressed several buttons.

"It's done," he said.

"You're sure?" Hoop asked.

"It's done! Now shut up and let me fly."

Hoop glanced up and back at Ripley and she nodded.

"How's Sneddon?"

"Okay when I last looked."

Hoop unbuckled himself and headed back into the cabin. Kasyanov seemed to be dozing, but she opened her eyes as they passed, watching them without expression. At the airlock he looked through the small viewing window into the narrow space. Ripley came up next to him.

Sneddon sat with her back against the airlock's external door, eyes closed, her face pale and sheened with sweat. Hoop tapped on the door. Her eyes rolled beneath their eyelids, and her frown deepened. He knocked again.

She opened her eyes. She looked lost, fighting her way out of nightmares into real, waking horror. Then she saw Hoop and Ripley looking in at her and gave them a thumbs-up.

"It can't be long now," Ripley said as they turned away from the door.

"You think we should have supported you down there," he said. "Stepped back, let you burn her."

"Perhaps." She looked wretched, and he reached for her. At first he thought she would resist, pull back, throw a punch as she had down on the planet. But though she was initially tense, she soon relaxed into his embrace. There was nothing sensuous about it. It was about comfort and friendship, and the sharing of terrible things.

"When the time comes," he whispered into her ear. Her hair tickled his mouth.

"Heads up!" Lachance called. "*Marion*'s up ahead. Let's buckle in, get ready for approach. Hoop, could do with you up here to do all the crappy little jobs while I'm flying this thing."

Hoop gave Ripley one last squeeze then went back to the cockpit seat.

"One step closer to home," he said.

"Okay, I'm flying by sight here," Lachance said. "Proximity and attitude alerts are on, but I can't use auto-pilot this close without linking to the *Marion*."

"So what do you need from me?"

"See those screens there? Keep an eye on them. Once we're a mile out, if speed of approach goes into the red, shout. If *anything* goes red, scream your head off."

"You've done this before, right?"

"Sure. A hundred times." Lachance grinned at him. "On the simulator."

"Oh."

"First time for everything." He raised his voice. "Hold onto your panties, ladies, we're going in!"

Despite his brief display of gung-ho attitude, Hoop knew that Lachance was as careful and as serious as they came. He watched the screens as the Frenchman had instructed, but he also watched the pilot—his concentration, determination, and care.

The *Marion* appeared first as a shining speck ahead of them, visible just above the plane of the planet. It quickly grew, its features becoming more obvious and familiar, until they were close enough to see the damage to its docking-bay belly.

"Eyes on the screens," Lachance said.

The docking was smooth and textbook perfect. Lachance muttered to himself all the way through, going through procedures, whispering encouraging words to the dropship, and occasionally singing a line or two from songs Hoop mostly didn't know. The ships kissed with barely a jolt, and Lachance performed a frantic series of button-presses and screen swipes that secured them together.

"We're docked," he said, slumping in his chair. "Sneddon?"

Ripley unbuckled and jumped to the door.

"She's fine."

"And she's with us until the end, now," Kasyanov said. "I've been thinking about something I can put together to…" She trailed off, but Hoop nodded at her.

"I was going to ask."

"So what's the plan now?" Ripley asked.

Hoop blinked and took a deep breath.

"Now we get the cell to your shuttle," he said. "Everything else is secondary."

"What about the other alien?" Kasyanov asked.

"Let's just hope it's hiding somewhere."

"And if it isn't? Say it attacks us, we have to fight it off, and the cell is damaged."

"What do you suggest?" Ripley asked.

"Hunt it down," Kasyanov said. "Make sure it's dead and gone, and only then transfer the fuel cell."

"My shuttle is on the next docking arm," Ripley said. "A hundred yards, if that."

"So we recce the route now," Hoop said. "When we know it's clear, we lock all the doors leading back into the rest of the ship, transfer the cell. Then two of us guard the shuttle while the others gather food and supplies for the journey."

"Outstanding," Ripley said. "But what about Sneddon?"

They all looked to the airlock. Sneddon was watching them through the small window, that same sad smile on her face. Hoop opened the inner door and she entered slowly, looking around at them all.

"I felt it move," she said. "Not too long ago. So I think… maybe I should go first?"

Ripley held out her plasma torch, and Sneddon took it with a nod.

They slid on their suits' helmets again, all comm links open, and prepared to cross the vacuum of the vented air-lock and vestibule.

"I'll start bleeding the air now," Lachance said from the pilot's seat.

Hoop swallowed as his ears popped. The last of the air bled away. The *Samson*'s outer door opened, and Sneddon walked through back onto the *Marion*.

He didn't think he'd ever known anyone so brave.

21

PAIN

PROGRESS REPORT:
To: Weyland-Yutani Corporation, Science Division
(Ref: code 937)
Date (unspecified)
Transmission (pending)

Samson has docked with the Marion. Contact between ship
and dropship computers has been cut. This intimates to me
that Ripley is still on board.

I have no idea who else is on board or what has happened.
But I persist in hope.

All cctv and communication systems within Marion are
patched into central computer. I have eyes and ears
everywhere.

As soon as they dock I can assess the situation. Only
after that can I decide upon future actions.

I have located the loose alien on the Marion. I have full
remote access to blast doors... for now I have trapped the
alien in Hold #3. It remains there, still and quiet.

There, if I need it.

Sneddon stepped out into the vacuum of the docking vestibule
and approached the doors leading into the corridor beyond. They
would have to lock those doors and seal the hole again before

pressurizing the corridor, and only then could they access the rest of the *Marion*, including *Narcissus*'s docking arm.

She disappeared through the door. The others waited nervously in the vestibule, Ripley swaying back and forth. Her stomach and shoulder wounds were hurting more and more, but she embraced the pain, using it to fuel her resolve. There would be time for medicine, and sleep, later.

Sneddon soon returned.

"All clear," she reported. "Doors are still closed and sealed." Her voice was fuzzy and crackly through the suit's communicator.

"Okay," Hoop said. "Change of plan. We'll bring the fuel cell through before we seal the door up again. Otherwise we'll be going back and forth by opening and closing the damaged door, and that's asking for trouble."

"But if the thing appears and—" Lachance said.

"It's a risk," Hoop said, acknowledging the danger. "*Everything's* a risk. But the more time we spend fucking around here, the worse things may become. There's an alien somewhere on board, the *Marion*'s going to crash, and Ripley's AI might be keen on giving us a very bad day."

"Ash isn't *my* AI," Ripley said. "He's Weyland's."

"Whatever. Let's get the cell out of the *Samson* and into the corridor. Then we can go about sealing that door."

"I'll stand guard," Sneddon said.

"You okay?" Ripley asked.

Sneddon only nodded, then turned and disappeared back through the door with her spray gun.

"Ripley, you go too," Hoop said. "Don't use that plasma torch unless you absolutely have to."

She nodded and followed Sneddon, wondering exactly what he'd meant. Use it on what? Or on whom? She heard Hoop talking to Lachance and Kasyanov about bringing the fuel cell through, and she was happy leaving them to it. It gave her a chance to talk.

The science officer was just outside the door, leaning against the wall. Ripley nodded to her, then walked a few steps in the opposite direction. There was no sign of anything having been here since they'd left. If the alien had broken back through to this area, it would have depressurized the entire ship.

It was further in, hiding. Perhaps they would never see it again.

"Your AI," Sneddon said. "It wants what I have?"

Ripley noticed that Sneddon had switched channels so that contact was only between their suits. She did the same before replying.

"Yes. He did his best back on *Nostromo* to get a sample, and now he's doing it again."

"You talk as if it's a person."

"He was," Ripley said. "He was Ash. None of us even knew he was an android. You know how they are, how advanced. He was... odd, I guess. Private. But there was never any cause to suspect his intentions. Not until he let an alien onto the ship."

"Is he watching us now?"

"I'm not sure." She didn't know how far Ash had gone, how far he could infiltrate. But if the aliens were her nightmares, he was her nemesis. "We have to assume so, yes."

"He won't want the rest of you," Sneddon said. "Only me, if he knows what I have inside me."

"Yes. He'll want to get you put into hypersleep as quickly as possible, then take you back to the Company. The rest of us are just liabilities."

"And then?"

Ripley wasn't sure how to answer, because she didn't know. Weyland-Yutani had already shown themselves as being brutal and single-minded in their pursuit of any useful alien artefacts or species.

"And then they'll have what they want," she said finally.

"I'm not going," Sneddon said.

"I know." Ripley couldn't look at her.

"It's... strange, knowing I'm going to die. I'm only afraid of how it'll happen, not death itself."

"I won't let it happen like that," Ripley said. "Kasyanov will give you something, as soon as the time comes. To ease your way."

"Yeah," Sneddon said, but she sounded doubtful. "I'm not sure things are going to be quite that easy."

Ripley wasn't sure either, and she couldn't lie. So she simply said nothing.

"It's only pain," Sneddon said. "When it happens, it'll hurt, but it doesn't matter. A brief moment of pain and horror, and then nothing forever. So it doesn't really matter."

"I'm so sorry," Ripley whispered, blinking away tears. They came far too easily, now that she'd let them in.

At first Sneddon didn't reply. But Ripley heard her breathing, long and slow, as if relishing every last taste of compressed, contained air. Then the science officer spoke again.

"Strange. I can't help still being fascinated by them. They're almost beautiful."

They stood silently for a while, and Hoop emerged from the doorway that led to the docking arm. He tapped at his ear, and Ripley switched her communicator back to all-channels.

"What's going on?" he asked.

"Sneddon and I were talking." He just nodded.

"We've got the cell. Ripley, you go along to the door to Bay Four." He pointed, then turned. "Sneddon, back there to the corridor blast doors to the other docking bays. I'm going to seal this door, then we'll repressurize."

"How?" Ripley asked.

"Honestly? I haven't figured that yet. If we just open the blast doors, the pressurization will be explosive, and we'll be smashed around. Got to let air bleed in somehow."

"Don't suppose you have another drill?"

Hoop shook his head, then looked down at the spray gun that was hanging from his shoulder. He smiled.

Kasyanov and Lachance appeared with the fuel cell. They wheeled it through the doorway, then set the trolley against the far wall.

"Strap that against the wall, tight," Hoop said. Then he closed the doors and pulled a small square of thick metal out of a pocket, pressing it against the hole he'd drilled on their exit from the *Marion*. He removed his hand and the metal remained where it was.

"Bonding agent," he said when he saw Ripley watching. "Air pressure will press it tight. It'll give us enough time."

Ripley walked along the corridor until it curved toward Bay Four. She paused where she could see the door, beyond which lay the docking arm with her shuttle, waiting for them all. Walking made her wounds hurt, but standing still was barely a relief. *It's only pain*, Sneddon had said. *It doesn't matter.* She felt warm dampness dripping down her side from her shoulder. She'd opened the wound there again.

It's only pain.

She could see back along the curving corridor, and she watched Lachance and Kasyanov securing the trolley and fuel cell to the wall with cargo straps from the *Samson*. She did the same, tying herself tight with her belt against a heavy fixing point.

"All ready?" Hoop asked. He disappeared in the other direction, following Sneddon toward where the corridor merged with the one from the ruined docking arm.

"What's the plan?" Kasyanov asked.

"Squirt of acid through the door," Hoop said. "Hardly subtle, but it should work. It'll get a bit stormy in here, though. Hold on to your dicks."

"We don't all have dicks, dickhead," Kasyanov muttered.

"Well, hold onto something, then." He paused. "On three."

Ripley counted quietly. One... two...

Three...

There was a pause. Then Hoop said, "Oh, maybe it won't—" A whistle, and then a roar as air started flooding into the sealed area.

That'll wake Ash up, Ripley thought. She couldn't help thinking of the bastard as still human.

```
PROGRESS REPORT:
To: Weyland-Yutani Corporation, Science Division
(Ref: code 937)
Date (unspecified)
Transmission (pending)

The survivors include Warrant Officer Ripley. I am pleased
that she is still alive. She and I feel close. From what
I can see from the Marion's cctv cameras, she seems to
be wounded. But she's walking. She impresses me. To have
woken from such a long sleep, to face the truth of her
extended slumber, and then to address her situation so
efficiently. She could almost be an android.

I am going to kill her, along with Chief Engineer Hooper,
Doctor Kasyanov, and the pilot.
```

Science Officer Sneddon is carrying an alien embryo.
Frustratingly I can glean no details, but from the
few conversations I have monitored, it seems as if her
condition is obvious. As is her expressed intention to
end her own life.

I cannot allow this.

Once she is on board the *Narcissus* and the new fuel cell
is installed, I will take the steps necessary to complete
my mission.

The roar died down to a low whistling, and then that too faded
to nothing. Ripley's ears rang. She looked back along the corridor
and saw Hoop appearing from around the curve, suit helmet
already removed.

"We're good," he said.

"You call that good?" Lachance asked. "I think I soiled my spacesuit."

"Wouldn't be the first time," Kasyanov said.

"Sneddon?" Ripley asked.

"I'm here." Her voice sounded weak. *She doesn't have long*, Ripley
thought. She pulled her own helmet off and let it dangle from its
straps, hoping she wouldn't need it again.

Hoop and the others pushed the fuel cell on its trolley, and when
they reached the door that led into Bay Four's vestibule, they paused.

"Lachance, go back and stay with Sneddon," Hoop said. "And
Kasyanov... you said you might have something?"

Kasyanov took a small syringe from her belt pouch.

"It's the best I can do," she said.

"What does that mean?" Ripley asked.

"It means it won't be painless. Get me to *med bay* and I'll find
something better, but with the limited stuff I have on hand, this is it."

Hoop nodded, face grim.

"Let's get ready to fly."

Hoop opened the doorway, and Ripley and Kasyanov pushed the
trolley through.

The movement was sudden, unexpected, the hissing thing leaping
at them from where it had been crouched beside the door. Kasyanov
cried out and stumbled back, but Ripley quickly gathered her senses,
crouching down and opening her arms.

"Jonesy!" she said. "Hey, it's me, it's all right you stupid cat." Jonesy crouched before her for a moment, hissing again. Then he slinked around her legs and allowed her to pick him up.

"Holy shit," Kasyanov said. "Holy shit, holy shit…"

"He does that," Ripley said, shrugging.

"We'll be taking him with us?" Kasyanov asked.

Ripley hadn't even thought about that. On a shuttle built for one, four was bad enough. They still had to prepare for the extraordinary length of their journey—coolant for the shuttle's atmosphere processor, filters for the water purifier, food, other supplies. But with a cat as well? With them taking turns in the stasis pod, Jonesy might not even live long enough to survive the journey.

But she couldn't even contemplate the thought of leaving him behind.

"Let's cross that one when we come to it," Hoop said. "Come on. I've got work to do."

It felt strange to Ripley, entering the *Narcissus* one more time. The urgency was still there, but this time with a different group of people. The danger was still imminent, but now it was compounded—a crashing ship, an alien somewhere on board, as well as one of them just waiting to give birth to another beast.

Jonesy jumped from her arms and leapt delicately into the stasis pod, snuggling down in the covered lower section, out of sight. Ripley so wanted to do the same.

"Kasyanov," she said. She felt suddenly woozy again, as if the ship was shaking and changing direction. *Maybe this is it*, she thought, *maybe we're crashing and…*

Hoop caught her as she stumbled. Kasyanov stripped the suit top from her shoulder and blood flowed freely, darkening the suit and dripping on the floor.

"Staples have popped," Kasyanov said. "I'll re-do them. This first." Before Ripley could object, the doctor slid a small needle into her shoulder and squeezed the pouch on its end. Numbness spread. The pain receded. Her right hand tingled, then all feeling faded away.

She'd never be able to hold the plasma torch now.

Hoop moved back through the shuttle to the small hatch leading into the engine compartment. He half-crawled inside, looked around for a while, and emerged again.

"I'm going to be in here for a while," he said. He paused, frowning, thinking. "Okay. We can stay in touch using the suit helmets. Ripley, stay here with me. Kasyanov, you and the others need to get into the *Marion* and start gathering what we'll need."

"I'll go with them," Ripley said.

"No, you're hurt."

"I can still walk, and carry supplies," she said. "We'll shut the *Narcissus*'s outer door behind us, so you won't have to worry about anything coming inside and disturbing you. Stay here, work. Fix it well." She smiled.

"It'll work," Hoop said. "But don't take risks. Any of you. Not with that thing running around, and not with... you know."

"Not with Sneddon," Kasyanov said.

"We should do it now," Ripley said. "She can't have long left."

"Well..." Hoop stood and emptied out the tool pouch he'd brought with him. "While I'm here buying our ticket home, that's your call."

It was harsh, but Ripley knew it was also true.

"Don't be long," Hoop said. "And stay safe."

"Safe is my middle name," Ripley said. She laughed, coughed painfully, and then turned to leave. Kasyanov went behind her, closing and sealing the door. Ripley couldn't help thinking she'd never see the inside of the *Narcissus* again.

"Med bay, then the stores," Kasyanov said. "Maybe an hour. Then we'll be away."

"Yeah," Ripley said. "And even after thirty-seven years asleep, I'm tired."

22

CHESS

PROGRESS REPORT:
To: Weyland-Yutani Corporation, Science Division
(Ref: code 937)
Date (unspecified)
Transmission (pending)

Chief Engineer Hooper is in the Narcissus. I could
lock him in if I so desired. I could hurt him.
But he is busy. I will leave him alone for now.

As for the others... I have decided to take a risk,
a gamble. I am somewhat powerless, having no physical
form. I am playing a game of chess. I've always been
good at it, and have never lost a game, against a
human or a computer. AIs are the Grand Masters now.

Here is my gamble: I suspect that Science Officer Sneddon
will be safe in the presence of the alien. It will sense what
she carries inside. She will survive the attack, the others
will die, and she will then make her way quickly back to the
Narcissus.

Whatever her thoughts, she is human, and her instinct is
still to survive.

None of the others can survive. They know too much about
me, about Science Officer Sneddon.

I am so close.

It is my move.

* * *

Ripley made sure she was behind Sneddon. She'd swapped the plasma torch to her left shoulder now, and thought she could probably still lift and fire it one-handed if she had to. Her right arm was numb from her shoulder down. It flopped uselessly, as if she'd been sleeping on it and had just woken up, and she soon stopped to tuck it into her open suit jacket.

She wasn't afraid of what Sneddon would become—she would hear it happening, see it—but she wanted to be ready to put the science officer out of her misery.

Lachance led the way with his charge thumper held at the ready. Kasyanov followed him, plasma torch slung from her shoulder, her wounded hand also hanging in a sling. They'd insisted that Sneddon keep her spray gun, even though she had volunteered to give it up.

If they'd had time, their list of items to gather would have been long. Food, clothing, coolant and additives for environmental systems, bedding of some sort, medicines, washing and bathroom supplies. Something to help pass the time—games, books, distractions.

But with very little time and danger around every corner, their list was reduced to necessities.

"Coolant and additives we can get from the stores in Hold 2," Lachance said.

"Galley for the dried food," Kasyanov offered.

"And then straight back," Ripley said. There was no time to go to med bay for medicines, the rec room for books, or the accommodations hub for sleeping gear and personal effects. They all felt the pressure now.

They'd paused to look through several viewing windows as they worked their way up out of the docking bay area on the *Marion*'s belly, and the planet already looked frighteningly closer. Soon the vibration would begin as they started to skim the atmosphere. The hull would warm up, heat shielding would bend and crack, and if they didn't die from excessive heat build-up, the explosion as the *Marion* came apart would finish them.

Ripley had never noticed the cctv cameras before, but she saw them now. Probably because she was looking for them. Every one of them resembled an eye watching her pass. They didn't move to track her, but reflections in the lenses gave the impression of pupils panning to follow her movement. There was an intelligence behind them all, one she knew so well. *Fuck you, Ash*, she kept thinking. But while cursing him, she also tried to figure out what moves he might make.

They reached the wide open area with a row of viewing windows on either side and an elevator shaft in the center. Several closed doors lined the walls, and leading from the far end was the wide stairwell heading up into the *Marion*'s main superstructure.

"Elevator?" Ripley asked.

"I've had enough of elevators," Kasyanov said. "What if we get stuck?"

That's right, Ripley thought. *Ash could trap us in there.*

"You should keep everything basic now," Sneddon said, referring to them in the second person without seeming to notice. "Don't want any mechanical issues to hold you up. There's not enough time. It's too…" She winced, closed her eyes, put her hand to her chest.

"Sneddon," Ripley whispered. She stood back and aimed the plasma torch, but the woman raised her hand and shook her head.

"Not yet," she said. "I don't think… not yet."

"Sweet heaven," Lachance said. He'd moved across to the port row of windows, and was looking down on the planet's surface. "Pardon my French, but you want to see something completely fucking heartwarming?"

He was right. It was strangely beautiful. North of them, a hole had been blasted through the plumes of dust and sand that constantly scoured the planet's surface. A huge, blooming mushroom cloud had punched up through the hole, massive and—from this great distance—seemingly unmoving. Compression waves spread out from the explosion like ripples in a lake, moving as slowly as the hour hand of an old analog clock. Streaks of oranges, reds, and yellows smudged across half the planet's surface visible from the ship, and violent electrical storms raged beneath the clouds, sending spears of violet deep through the dust storms.

"Well, that's me, unemployed," Lachance said.

"Now there's only one of those bastards left," Ripley said.

"Two," Sneddon said from behind them. She'd grown paler, and she seemed to be in pain. "I think... I think now might be the time to..."

She rested her spray gun gently on the deck.

Behind her, something ran down the stairs.

"Oh, shit..." Ripley breathed. She swung her plasma torch up into its firing position, but Sneddon was in the way, and though she'd dwelled endlessly upon putting the woman out of her misery, she wasn't ready for it now.

The alien dashed from the staircase to dart behind the elevator shaft that stood in the center of the area. Ripley waited for it to appear on the other side. And then, a blink later, it would be upon them.

"Sneddon, down!" Ripley shouted.

The science officer moved, and everything she did was very calm, very calculating—it almost seemed like slow motion. She lifted the spray gun again and turned around.

Lachance moved to the left and circled around the large space, edging forward so he could see behind the elevator block. Kasyanov remained close to Ripley on her right. Everything was silent—no hissing, no clatter of claws on the metal deck.

It's as if we imagined it, Ripley thought.

Then the alien powered from behind the block. Sneddon crouched and fired the spray gun, acid scoring a scorched line across the wall behind the creature. Lachance's charge thumper coughed. The projectile ricocheted from the elevator, throwing sparks, and knocked Kasyanov from her feet.

The beast was on Lachance before anyone had time to react. It grabbed him by the shoulders and shoved him back, its momentum slamming him so hard into a wall that Ripley heard bones crunch and crush. Blood coughed from his mouth. The alien slammed its head into his, teeth powering through his throat and severing his spine with a *crack!*

Ripley swung the plasma torch around.

"Turn away!" she shouted. Her finger squeezed the trigger.

Nothing happened.

She glanced down at the weapon, stunned, wondering just what she'd done wrong. *I primed it, safety off. Maybe the charge is run down, so what the hell?* In the instant it took her to think, the alien came for her.

From behind she heard Kasyanov groaning and trying to stand, and Ripley expected the white-hot touch of plasma fire at any moment from the Russian's gun. She'd be saving Ripley from an awful death, destroying the alien, giving her and Hoop a chance. Right then, Ripley would have welcomed it.

The alien was closer, larger, just about the most terrifying thing she'd ever seen, and she thought, *I'm so sorry, Amanda*. She'd made a promise, and had broken it.

She went to close her eyes, but before she could she saw a line of fire erupt across the alien's flank. It slipped, hissing and skidding across the floor toward her.

Ripley dropped all her weight in an effort to fall to the left, but she was too late. The alien struck her hard. Claws raked, teeth snapped an inch from her face. She screamed. The monster hissed and then shrieked, and Ripley smelled rank burning.

The thing thrashed on top of her, and everywhere it touched brought more pain.

Then it was up and gone. Ripley lay on her side, head resting on her extended left arm. Blood spattered the floor around her— red, human. *Mine*, she thought. Her body felt cool and distant, then suddenly hot and damaged, ruptured, leaking. She opened her mouth, but could only groan.

Kasyanov sent another spurt of fire after the alien before slumping to the deck, plasma torch clattering down beside her. Ripley wasn't sure the shot made contact, but the beast screamed and rushed back toward the wide staircase.

Sneddon followed, firing the spray gun as she went, one short burst catching the alien across the back of one of its legs. It stumbled into the wall, then leapt toward the staircase. Sneddon ran closer, fired again, and missed, scoring a melting line diagonally across the first few stairs.

"Sneddon!" Kasyanov rasped, but the science officer didn't look back. The beast fled, and she followed, shooting all the way.

"Get what you need!" Sneddon shouted through their earpieces. She sounded more alive than Ripley had heard before. There was an edge of pain to her voice, an undercurrent of desperation. But there was also something like joy. She was panting hard as she ran, grunting, and from somewhere more distant Ripley heard the alien screech one more time. "Got you, you bastard!" Sneddon said. "I got you again that time. Keep running, just keep running. But I'll chase you down."

Ripley wanted to say something to her. But when she opened her mouth, only blood came out. *I wonder how bad?* she thought. She tried turning to look at Kasyanov, but couldn't move.

"Kasyanov," she breathed. There was no reply. "Kasyanov?"

Shadows fell.

She only hoped Amanda would be waiting for her, ready to forgive at last.

Hoop heard it all.

It only took thirty seconds, and by the time he'd dropped his tools, wriggled out of the shuttle's cramped engine compartment and then exited the ship—carefully closing the door behind him—Sneddon's shouting had stopped. He heard more, though—pained sighs, grunts, and an occasional sound like a frustrated hiss. But he couldn't tell who they came from.

"Ripley?" He crossed the vestibule, peering through viewing panels in the door before opening it. He closed it behind him and headed along the corridor. He held the spray gun pointed ahead, ready to fire at a moment's notice. He had no idea which way Sneddon and the alien had gone.

"Lachance?"

"He's dead," a voice said. It took him a moment to identify it as Kasyanov. She sounded different, weak. "And Ripley is…"

"What?"

"Bad. So much blood."

"What about Sneddon?" Hoop asked again. "Sneddon? You hear me?" There was a click as someone disconnected their comm unit. It had the sound of finality.

"Hoop, I'm hurt, too." Kasyanov might have been crying.

"How bad?"

"Not good." A grunt, and a gasp. "But I can walk."

"Which way did Sneddon chase that thing?"

"Up the staircase."

"Away from us and into the belly of the ship," he replied. "Right. I'll be there in two minutes, do what you can for Ripley, and I'll carry her to med bay."

More silence.

"Do you hear me?"

"What about the fuel cell?" Kasyanov asked.

"It's almost done."

"Then we could be gone."

He couldn't blame her. Not really. But Hoop wasn't about to bail without doing everything he could, for anyone who was left alive.

"Fuck that, Kasyanov," he said. "You're a doctor. Heal."

Then he started running. He sprinted around corners without pausing to look or listen. Opened doors, closed them behind him, the spray gun slung across his shoulder and acid swooshing in the reservoir. He thought of Sneddon's bravery, and how she had already sacrificed herself by pursuing the monster into the ship. Maybe she'd catch and kill it. Or perhaps it would turn and kill her. But she had given them a chance.

The *Marion* shook.

A subtle vibration, but he felt it through his boots.

Oh, not now, he thought. He skidded around a corner, up some stairs, and then he was in the wide area where the chaos had only just ended. Lachance lay dead against the wall to his left, head hanging from his body by strands. Ripley was on the floor to his right. Kasyanov knelt beside her, melted hand pressed tight to her right hip, the other busy administering emergency first aid. Beyond them, the windows looked down onto the planet. To the north Hoop saw the bright bruise of the explosion that had taken the mine, and felt a brief moment of glee. But it didn't last long. Shimmering threads of smoke and fire flitted past the window as the *Marion* encountered the very upper reaches of LV178's atmosphere.

"We don't have long," Kasyanov said, looking up at his approach. Hoop wasn't sure whether she meant the *Marion* or Ripley, but in his mind they were the same.

"How bad are you?"

"Bolt from Lachance's thumper broke up, ricocheted, hit me." She moved her ruined hand aside slightly, looking down. Hoop could see the shredded jacket and undershirt, the dark bloodstains glinting wetly in artificial light. She pressed the wound again and looked up. "Honestly, I can't feel anything. Which isn't a good sign."

"It's numb. You can walk?"

Kasyanov nodded.

"You go ahead, open the doors, I'll carry her," Hoop said.

"Hoop—"

"I'm not listening. If there's a chance for her, we'll take it. And you can sort yourself out while we're there."

"But that thing could be—" Their earpieces crackled, and Sneddon's voice came in loud and fast.

"I've got the bastard cornered in Hold 2!" she shouted. "Shot it up, its acid splashed everywhere... not sure if... oh, fuuuuck!" She moaned, long and loud.

"Sneddon," Hoop said.

"It hurts. It hurts! It's in me, moving around, and I can feel its teeth." Another groan, then she coughed loudly and shouted, "*Screw you!* Hoop, it's cornered behind some of the equipment lockers, thrashing around in there. Might be dying. But... I'm going to... make sure!"

Hoop and Kasyanov stared at each other. Neither knew what to say. They were witnessing a fight far away from them, and listening to the impending death of a friend.

Metal clanged, the sound of something falling over and hitting the deck.

"Come on, come on," Sneddon whispered. "Okay, I'm almost done." She was talking to herself, muttering between croaks of pain and high-pitched whines that should not have come from a person.

"What are you doing?" Hoop asked.

"Got a full crate of magazines for the charge thumpers. Rigging a charge. You'll feel a bump, but it'll get rid of this... for good. So..."

Hoop ran to Ripley, scooped her up, slung her over his shoulder. She moaned in unconsciousness, and he could feel her blood pattering down on his back and legs.

"Med bay," he said to Kasyanov. "Need to get as close as we can before it blows."

"Maybe a minute," Sneddon said. "The one inside me… it wants out. It's shifting. It's…" She screamed. It was a horrible sound, volume tempered by the equipment yet the agony bare and clear.

"Sneddon…" Kasyanov whispered, but there was nothing more to say.

"Come on!" Hoop led the way, struggling with Ripley's weight. Kasyanov followed. He heard her groaning, cursing beneath her breath, but when he glanced back she was still with him. She had to be. He didn't know how to use the med bay equipment, and if Kasyanov died, so would Ripley.

"You going to be——?" he started asking, but then Sneddon came on again.

"It's coming for me." Behind her voice Hoop heard an alien squeal, and the scraping of claws on metal growing rapidly louder. Sneddon gasped, then fell silent. The channel was still open; Hoop could hear the hiss and whisper of static. He and Kasyanov paused at the head of a staircase. And then he heard the more uneven hissing of something else.

"Sneddon?"

"It's… just staring. It must see… know… sense… Oh!"

"Blow the crate," Hoop said. Kasyanov's eyes went wide, but he wasn't being cruel or heartless. He was thinking of Sneddon, as well as them. "Sneddon, blow the crate before——"

The crunch of breaking bones was obvious. Sneddon let out a long groan of agony.

"It's coming," she rasped. "The thing's just watching. It's dying, but it doesn't care. It sees… its sibling… coming. This close it's almost beautiful."

"Sneddon, blow the——"

"Two seconds," the science officer whispered.

In those two seconds Hoop heard the infant alien clawing, biting, tearing its way from Sneddon's chest, its high-pitched squeal answered by the dying adult's more tempered cry. Sneddon could not scream because her breath had been stolen. But she spoke in another way.

He heard the soft mechanical click. Then the connection was cut.

Moments later a distant rumble turned from a moan into a roaring explosion that blasted a wall of air through the corridors. A heavy thud worked through the entire ship, pulsing through floors and walls as Hold 2 was consumed by the massive blast.

A long, low horn-like sound echoed as incredible stresses and strains were placed on the superstructure, and Hoop feared they would simply tear apart. The tension of skimming the planet's atmosphere, combined with the results of the explosion, might break the ship's back and send it spinning down, to burn up in the atmosphere.

He slid down one wall and held Ripley across his legs, hugging her head to his chest to prevent it bouncing as the metal floor punched up at them again and again. Kasyanov crouched next to them.

Metal tore somewhere far away. Something else exploded, and a shower of debris whisked past them, stinging exposed skin and clanging metal on metal. Another gush of warm air came, and then the shaking began to subside.

"Will she hold?" Kasyanov asked. "Will the ship hold?" Hoop couldn't answer. They stared at each other for a few seconds, then Kasyanov slumped down. "Sneddon."

"She took it with her," Hoop said. "Took both of them with her." Kasyanov glanced at Ripley, then crawled quickly closer. She lifted an eyelid, bent down to press her ear to the injured woman's open mouth.

"No," Hoop breathed.

"No," Kasyanov said. "But she's not good."

"Then let's go." He dropped the spray gun, heaved her over his shoulder again, and set off toward med bay. Kasyanov followed, her plasma torch clattering to the floor.

Now they were three, and he wouldn't let anyone else die.

Amanda watches her. She's eleven years old today, and she sits in a chair beside a table scattered with half-eaten pieces of birthday cake, opened presents, discarded wrapping paper. She's on her own and looking sad.

Her birthday dress is bloodied and torn, and there is a massive hole in her chest.

I'm sorry, *Ripley says, but Amanda's expression does not change. She blinks softly, staring at her mother with a mixture of sadness at the betrayal and... hatred? Can that really be what she sees in her daughter's eyes?*

Amanda, I'm sorry, I did my very best.

Blood still drips from the hole in her daughter's chest. Ripley tries to turn away, but whichever way she turns her daughter is still there, staring at her. Saying nothing. Only looking.

Amanda, you know Mommy loves you, however far away I am.

The little girl's face does not change. Her eyes are alive, but her expression is lifeless.

Ripley woke for a time, watching the floor pass by, seeing Hoop's boots, knowing she was being carried. But even back on the *Marion*, Amanda was still staring at her. If Ripley lifted her head she would see her. If she turned around, she would be there.

Even when she closed her eyes.

Amanda, staring forever at the mother who had left her behind.

23

FORGETTING

PROGRESS REPORT:
To: Weyland-Yutani Corporation, Science Division
(Ref: code 937)
Date (unspecified)
Transmission (pending)

I wish I was whole again.

I never used to wish. I was not programed for that, and it is not an emotion, nor an action, that I ever perceived as useful. But for thirty-seven years I was alone in the shuttle's computer. And there was enough of the human still in me to feel lonely. I was built as an artificial person, after all.

Loneliness, it seems, is not necessarily connected to one's place in the universe. I know my place, and have no feelings either way about what and where I am. In my case, loneliness rose from simple boredom.

There are only so many times I can defeat the ship's computer at chess.

And so I have spent long years dwelling upon what wishing might mean.

Now, I wish I was whole again.

The game has turned against me. I am in check. But not for long. The game is never over until it is over, and I refuse to resign.

Not while Ripley, my queen, still lives.

* * *

Ripley was heavy. He refused to think of her as dead weight—he wouldn't allow that, would not give her permission to die—but by the time they reached med bay his legs were failing, and it had been ten long minutes since she'd displayed any signs of life.

The *Marion* shook and shuddered. It, too, was close to the end.

The difference was that for Ripley there was still hope.

"I'll fire up the med pod," Kasyanov said, pressing her good hand against the security pad. The medical bay was a modern, sterile place, but the object at its center made all the other equipment look like Stone Age tools. This Weyland-Yutani chunk of technology had cost Kelland almost a tenth of what the whole of the *Marion* had cost, but Hoop had always known it had been a practical investment. A mining outpost so far from home, where illness or injury could cripple the workforce, needed care.

Yet there was nothing humane in their incorporation of the pod.

It was insurance.

Hoop put Ripley down on one of the nearby beds and tried to assess her wounds. There was so much blood. Her shoulder wound weeped, several staples protruded from her stomach and the gash there gaped. New injuries had been added to the old. Puncture wounds were evident across her chest, perhaps where the thing's claws had sunk in. Her face was bruised and swollen, one eye puffy and squeezed shut, scalp still weeping. He thought her arm might be broken.

He had seen the med pod at work several times before, but he didn't know what it could do for Ripley. Not in the time they had left.

He was pulled in two directions. In truth, he should be back at the shuttle, finishing the fuel cell installation and ensuring that all systems were back online. After that there was Ash, the malignant presence he had to wipe from the *Narcissus*'s computer before launching.

If Ripley were awake, he could tell her what he'd found. According to the log, the old fuel cell had still maintained more than sixty percent of its charge when it had docked with *Marion*, and it could only have been Ash who had engineered its draining. To trap her there with them. To force them down to the planet's surface, not only to retrieve another fuel cell, but to encounter *them*.

The creatures.

Everything that had happened since Ripley's arrival had been engineered by the artificial intelligence. Those additional lives lost— Sneddon, Baxter, Lachance—could be blamed squarely on him.

Hoop wished the bastard was human so he could kill him.

"Pod's ready," Kasyanov said. "It'll take half an hour for it to assess the wounds and undertake the procedures."

Hoop couldn't waste half an hour.

"I'll go back for the supplies we need," he said. "Stay in touch."

Kasyanov nodded and touched her suit's comm unit. Then she turned her attention to the med pod's screen and frowned in concentration, scrolling through a complex series of branching programs flashing there. She was sweating, shaking.

"You good?"

"No. But I'm good enough for this." She wiped her forehead with the back of her hand. "Her first, then if there's time, me."

"There'll be time," Hoop said, but they both knew there were no guarantees.

"I feel... weird inside. Bleeding in my guts, I think."

"I'll get up to the bridge, first," Hoop said, gingerly lifting Ripley off of the bed. "See just how much time we have."

As if in response, the ship shuddered one more time. Kasyanov didn't look up or say anything else, and her silence was accusation enough. *We could have just gone.* But they were set on their course, now, and Hoop knew she would see it through.

He held Ripley as gently as he could, and carried her to the med pod.

"Amanda!" she shouted. She shifted in his arms and he almost dropped her. He staggered a little, then when he righted himself and looked down, Ripley was staring right at him. "Amanda," she said again, softer.

"It's okay, Ripley, it's me."

"She won't leave me alone," she said. Her eyes were wide and white in her mask of blood and bruising. "Just staring. All because

of them. My little girl won't forgive me, and it's all because of *them*."
Her voice was cold and hollow, and a chill went through him. He laid
her gently in the med pod.

"We're going to patch you up," Hoop said.

"I want to forget," she said. "I can't... even if you fix me, I can't sleep
with Amanda staring at me like that. I'll never sleep again. It'll make
me go mad, Hoop. You can make me forget, can't you? With this?"

Hoop wasn't sure exactly what she meant, and how much she
wanted to forget. But she was all there. This wasn't a delirious rant—
it was a very calm, very determined plea.

"It feels as if I've known nothing else but them," she said. "It's
time to forget."

"Kasyanov?" Hoop asked.

"It's a med pod, Hoop," the doctor said. "That's almost certainly
beyond its capabilities."

"But it does neurological repairs, doesn't it?"

"Yeah. Repairs, not damage."

"They've given me a nightmare, and I think it's going to kill me,"
Ripley said. "Amanda. My girl, dead, staring, never forgiving me.
Please, Hoop. *Please!*" She sat upright, wincing at the pain it drove
through her, but reaching out and grasping his arm.

"Hey, hey, lie back," he said. "Let Kasyanov do her work." But
he could see the terror in her eyes, and the knowledge at what sleep
would bring. *Even if it's not real, it's tearing her apart*, he thought.

"We're ready," the doctor said.

Ripley let Hoop ease her back down, but she was still pleading
with her eyes. Then they closed the clear lid. He felt a tug as he saw
her shut away in there, maybe because he thought he might never
touch her again.

"So can you?" he asked.

"It's not me that does the work, it's the pod. I just initiate the
programs." Kasyanov sighed. "But yes, I think it could manipulate
her memories."

"How?"

"I've only ever heard about it," Kasyanov said. "It can repair brain
damage, to an extent, and at the same time there's an associated

protocol that allows for memory alteration. I think it was designed primarily for military use. Get soldiers back into the fight that much quicker, after battlefield trauma." She paused. "It's really pretty inhumane, when you think about it."

Hoop thought about it, remembering the sheer terror he had seen in Ripley's eyes.

"I don't think I have any choice," he said. "How much memory will it affect?"

"I have no idea. I don't think it was developed for fine tuning."

He nodded, tapping his leg.

"Do it."

"You're sure?"

If we go too far back, she won't even remember me. But that was a selfish thought, far more about him than it was about her. If he had a shred of feeling for her, his own desires shouldn't enter into it.

When they were finally on *Narcissus* and away from here, they could meet again.

"*She's* sure," he said, "and that's as sure as I need to be."

Kasyanov nodded and started accessing a different series of programs.

While the doctor worked, Hoop moved around the med bay, seeing what he could find. He packed a small pouch with painkillers, multi-vitamin shots, antibiotics, and viral inhibitors. He also found a small surgery kit including dressings and sterilization pads. He took a handheld scanner that could diagnose any number of ailments, and a multi-vaccinator.

Just him, Kasyanov, and Ripley, for however many years it took for them to be found.

"You'll see Amanda again," he said—mostly to himself, because he was thinking of his own children, as well. They were *all* going home.

"Hoop," Kasyanov said. "I'm about to initiate. The pod calculates that it'll take just under twenty minutes for the physical repairs, and five more for the limited memory wipe."

Hoop nodded. Kasyanov stroked a pad on the unit and it began to hum.

Inside, Ripley twitched.

PROGRESS REPORT:
To: Weyland-Yutani Corporation, Science Division
(Ref: code 937)
Date (unspecified)
Transmission (pending)

I will save Ripley. Together, she and I can continue our
mission into the darkness. I am convinced there are many
more aliens out there. One location is a freak accident,
two means countless more.

I would like to know their history.

With a new fuel cell we can drift forever as we seek signs
of another colony.

And Ripley can sleep, ready to bear our inevitable prize
back home.

I only need her. The others cannot come. I will allow what
she has requested. In truth, it's perfect. She will not
remember how determined I remain to fulfill the mission.
She will not remember the things I have done.

On waking, she will not even know I am still here.

She will be weak, disorientated, and I will guide her back
to the Narcissus.

Hoop moved quickly through the ship toward the bridge. More
than ever it felt like a haunted ship. He'd always known the *Marion*
busy, the crew going about their tasks, the off-duty miners drinking
or talking or working out. It had never been a silent place. There
was always music emanating from the accommodations hub or rec
room, a rumble of conversation from the galley and bar.

He felt a pang as he missed his friends, and Lucy Jordan, his one-
time lover. She had become more than a friend, and after their romance
had dwindled—sucked away, she'd joked without really joking, by
the cold depths of space—their friendship had deepened to something
he'd rarely felt before. They had trusted each other completely.

And she had been one of the first to die.

Hoop had never given way to loneliness. As a child he'd enjoyed
his own company, preferring to spend time in his room making models
or reading his parents' old books, and when he was a teenager he'd
kept a small circle of friends. Never one for team sports, his social
life had revolved around nights at their houses, watching movies or

drinking cheap booze. Sometimes a girl would come onto the scene and take him or a friend away for a time, but they'd always returned to the familiarity of that small, closed circle.

Even as an adult, after marrying and having children and then losing it all, he had rarely felt lonely.

That only happened after the aliens arrived.

Every step of the way toward the bridge, he thought of Ripley. He so hoped she would live, but a different woman was going to emerge from the med pod. If the unit worked well, she would remember little or nothing from the past few days. He would have to introduce himself all over again.

Even though the creature had to be dead, he remained cautious, pausing at each junction, listening for anything out of place. A constant vibration had been rippling throughout the ship ever since the explosion in Hold 2, and Hoop guessed the blast had somehow knocked their decaying orbit askew. They were skipping the outer edges of the planet's atmosphere now, shields heating up, and it wouldn't be long before the damaged docking bays started to burn and break apart.

He needed to find out just how long they had.

The bridge was exactly as they'd left it less than a day earlier. It seemed larger than before, and he realized that he'd never actually been there on his own. Lachance was often on duty, sitting in his pilot's seat even though the *Marion* rarely needed any manual input. Baxter spent a lot of time at his communications console, processing incoming messages for miners or crew and distributing them as appropriate throughout the ship's network. Sneddon sometimes spent long periods there, talking with Jordan, and their security officer, Cornell, would sometimes visit.

Other people came and went. The place was never silent, never empty. Being there on his own made it seem all the more ghostly.

He spent a few minutes examining readouts on Lachance's control panels, consulting the computers, and they told him what he needed to know. He reached into a drawer and pulled out a small data drive, uploading a data purge program before dropping it into an inner pocket.

Insurance, he thought.

Then he quickly made his way down through the accommodations hub. It was a slight detour, but it was much closer to the galley and rec rooms. They needed food, and there wasn't time enough to go to where most of it was stored.

He found what he sought in various private quarters. Everyone kept a stash of food for midnight hungers, and sometimes because they just didn't feel like eating with the others. He grabbed a trolley and visited as many rooms as he could, finding pictures of families who would never see their loved ones again, witnessing all those personal things that when left behind seemed like sad, incomplete echoes of what a person had been.

As he gathered, it dawned on him that they'd never be able to take enough to sustain them. But Kasyanov had said there was a large supply of food substitutes and dried supplements stored in the med bay. They'd make do. There would be rationing.

He tried to concentrate entirely on the here-and-now. The thought of the journey that lay ahead would cripple him if he dwelled on it for too long. So he kept his focus on the next several hours.

Leaving the laden trolley along the route that led down to the docking bays, he made his way back up to the med bay. Kasyanov was sitting on one of the beds, jacket cast aside and shirt pulled up to reveal her wounds. They were more extensive than Hoop had suspected; bloody tears in her skin that pouted purple flesh. She quivered as she probed at them with tweezers. There were several heavy bags piled by the door, and a stack of medical packs. She'd been busy—before she took time to tend herself.

"Bad?" he asked softly.

She looked up, pale and sickly.

"I've puked blood. I'll have to use the med pod. Otherwise, I'll die of internal bleeding and infection within a day."

"We've got maybe two hours," Hoop said.

"Time enough," she replied, nodding. "She'll be done in fifteen minutes."

He had seen the unit working before, but it never ceased to fascinate him. Ripley looked thin and malnourished, battered and bruised. But the med pod had already repaired most of her major wounds, and several operating arms were concentrating on the rip in her stomach. They moved with a fluid grace, lacking any human hesitation and targeted with computer confidence. Two delved inside, one grasping, another using a laser to patch and mend. Its white-warm glow reflected from the pod's glass cover and gave movement to Ripley's face, but in truth she was motionless. Back down in the depths of whatever dreams troubled her so much.

They, too, would soon be fixed.

The arms retreated and then her wound was glued and stitched with dissolvable thread. A gentle spray was applied to the area—artificial skin, set to react over time as the natural healing processes commenced. When she woke up, there would be little more than a pale pink line where the ugly slash had once existed.

Bumps and bruises were sprayed, her damaged scalp treated, an acid splash across her left forearm and hand attended to, after which the pod's arms pulled a white sheet from a roll beneath the bed and settled it gently across Ripley's body. It was almost caring.

Kasyanov glanced at Hoop, and he nodded. She initiated the next process. Then sighed, sat back, and closed her eyes as the interior of the med pod changed color. Rich blue lights came on, and arms as delicate as daisy stems pressed several contact pads against Ripley's forehead, temples, and neck. The lights began to pulse hypnotically. The pod buzzed in time with the pulsing, emitting a soporific tone. Hoop had to look away.

He turned to Kasyanov. Her breathing was light and fast, but she waved him away, nodding.

"I'm good," she said.

"You're shit."

"Yeah. Well. What's that, a doctor's analysis?"

Hoop could barely smile. Instead, he went to the bags she'd left by the med bay's door and opened the first to check inside.

"Antibiotics, viral tabs, painkillers, sterilization spray," Kasyanov said. "Other stuff. Bandages, medicines, contraceptives."

Hoop raised an eyebrow.

"Hey. Forever is a long time."

He checked another bag and saw a jumble of plastic containers and shrink-wrapped instruments.

"You planning on passing time by operating on us?"

"Not unless I have to. But you really want to die from appendicitis?"

A soft chime came from the med pod and the lights inside faded to nothing. Sensor tendrils curled back in, fine limbs settled into place, and then the lid slid soundlessly open.

"She's done?" Hoop asked.

"Guess so." Kasyanov hauled herself upright, growling against the pain. "Get her out. I've got to—"

A distant explosion thudded through the ship. The floor kicked up. Ceiling tiles shuddered in their grid.

"Hurry," Hoop said. As he moved across to the pod and prepared to lift Ripley out, Kasyanov was already working at its control panel. Her good hand moved quickly across the touchscreen. Hoop lifted Ripley clear, the lid slid closed, and moments later a sterilizing mist filled the interior.

Hoop settled Ripley on one of the beds, carefully wrapping her in the sheet and fixing it with clips. She looked tired, older. But she was still alive, and her face seemed more relaxed than he had seen it. He so hoped that she was dreaming harmless dreams.

"Now me," Kasyanov said. "Five minutes, if that. We've got time?"

Hoop was surprised at the doctor's sudden vulnerability.

"Of course," he said. "I'm waiting for you, whatever happens."

She nodded once, then with a wry smile she held out her hand.

"Quick lift?"

Hoop helped her into the pod. She lay down, touched the inner shell, and a remote control grid appeared. A wave of her hand closed the lid.

"See ya," she said, attempting an American accent.

Hoop smiled and nodded. Then he turned back to check that Ripley was all right.

Behind him, the med pod whispered.

```
PROGRESS REPORT:
To: Weyland-Yutani Corporation, Science Division
(Ref: code 937)
Date (unspecified)
Transmission (pending)
```

The doctor has served her purpose.
She makes the next step almost too easy.

The med pod wasn't quite soundproof.

Looking at Ripley, Hoop heard Kasyanov's muffled yell. He turned around to see thin metallic straps whipping across the doctor's body, constricting across her shoulders, chest, stomach, hips, and legs. She cried out in pain as they crushed against her wounds.

Hoop knew that shouldn't be happening. He tried to open the lid, but it was locked, and however much he touched and pressed the external control panel, nothing happened.

Kasyanov looked at him through the glass, wide-eyed.

"Ash," Hoop hissed. Kasyanov couldn't have heard him, but she saw the word on his lips. And froze.

A soft blue light filled the med pod.

"No!" she shouted, the word so muffled that Hoop only knew it because of the shape of her mouth.

A single surgical arm rose from its housing and loomed over Kasyanov's chest.

Hoop tried to force the lid. He snapped up the plasma torch and used the hand rest to hammer at the lid's lip, but only succeeded in bending part of the torch.

Kasyanov's voice changed tone and he looked to her lips, searching for the word she had chosen, and it was *Hoop*.

He turned the torch around and aimed at the pod's lid, close to her feet. If he was careful, only released a quick shot, angled it just right, he might be able to—

The blue light pulsed and the delicate arm sparked alight. There was a fine laser at its tip, and in a movement that was almost graceful, it drew rapidly across Kasyanov's exposed throat. Blood pulsed, then spurted from the slash, splashing back from the pod's inner surface and speckling across her face.

She was held so tightly that Hoop only knew she was struggling because of the flexing and tensing of her muscles, the bulging of her eyes. But those soon died down, and as the blue light faded, Kasyanov grew still.

Hoop turned away, breathing hard, and even when the ship juddered so hard that it clacked his teeth together, he did not move.

You bastard, he thought. *You utter bastard, Ash.*

Somehow he held back his rage.

Ripley groaned and rolled onto her side.

"I've got you," Hoop said, moving to her side. Dropping the plasma torch, he slipped his hands beneath her and heaved her up onto his shoulder.

The shuttle awaited them, and now he was the last survivor of the *Marion.*

It was time to leave.

24

REVENGE

PROGRESS REPORT:
To: Weyland-Yutani Corporation, Science Division
(Ref: code 937)
Date (unspecified)
Transmission (pending)

Ripley lives. He will bring her, and then discover the
final surprise.

Time to leave.
I cannot pretend I am not disappointed that things went
wrong. I cannot deny that I am frustrated. But I have time
on my side.

I am immortal, after all.

Hoop left med bay with Ripley over his shoulder. The ship juddered
so hard that he fell into a wall, jarring his whole body. The *Marion*
groaned and creaked. It struck him what an irony it would be if the
ship broke her back there and then, venting to space, killing him
and Ripley and ending their long, terrible journey.

He thought of Lachance, who might have prayed to help him
reach his destination. But Hoop knew that he was on his own. The
universe was indifferent. Whether he and Ripley escaped, or died
here and now, it all came down to chance.

A rhythmic booming commenced from somewhere deep below. It sounded like a giant hammer, smashing at the ship's spine, pulsing explosions working outward from the engine core, thudding heartbeats of a dying ship. But still the vessel did not break up.

"Well, let's go, then," he muttered, moving on.

He tried to move quickly. His legs were as shaky as the ship now, and he couldn't remember the last time he'd eaten. His stomach rumbled, and he was suddenly, sickeningly hungry. He snorted a laugh at how ridiculous that was. But he also vowed to enjoy a feast, once they were in the *Narcissus* and away from the ship.

Just the two of us now, he thought. *One asleep, one awake, sharing the stasis pod and maybe being together for a while in between. We might even do this. We might survive and get home.*

And what story would he tell Ripley, when his newfound loneliness became too great and he woke her, ready to spend some of his own time in hypersleep? How would she react to being roused by someone she didn't know? If the memory wipe had been thorough, the last thing she'd remember would be putting herself into stasis after destroying the *Nostromo*.

But that was for the future. If they survived, he would be able to tell her everything, or perhaps nothing at all. All he could concentrate on now was staying alive.

He moved as quickly and safely as he could. Reaching the stairs that led down into the docking area, he decided he'd have to take the elevator. Ripley was becoming heavier by the moment. He glanced at the trolley of food and realized he would have to return for it.

As he entered the elevator, though, he already mourned the feast left behind.

The car descended smoothly, and the doors opened onto a corridor lit by flickering lights. Something exploded. It was far away, but it punched through the whole superstructure, knocking him from his feet again. Ripley rolled against the wall, groaning, waving her hands.

"Don't wake up yet," he muttered. She'd panic. He had enough to contend with.

She opened her eyes and looked right at him, motionless, holding her breath. There was no expression on her face, and nothing like recognition in her eyes. Hoop began to speak, to make sure she was still Ripley, still there. But then she closed her eyes again and slumped down. He had no idea what she had seen, but it hadn't been him.

A deep groan rumbled through everything, and he felt a sickly movement in his stomach and head. The *Marion* was starting to turn in a roll, and if that happened she would quickly come apart. From somewhere behind him he saw flashing yellow and orange bursts, illuminating the walls before fading again. *Fire!* But then he realized there were viewing ports back on the deck from which he'd just descended. The flames were filtering in from outside.

Things were heating up.

He closed a blast door behind him, but it immediately re-opened. He didn't bother trying again. Maybe it was Ash still playing his games. Or it might just be the *Marion*, getting cranky in her final moments.

"Come on, come on!" he implored, urging himself on, Ripley slung across both of his shoulders now. He staggered along the corridor, bouncing from wall to wall as the ship shook and rumbled. Another explosion came from far away and he felt the pressure blast smack him in the back, pushing him onward so hard that he lost his footing and went to his knees. He kept hold of Ripley this time. She grunted.

"Yeah, me too," he said. He stood again and passed by the *Samson*'s docking arm, moving quickly on to Bay Four and the *Narcissus*. He opened the vestibule doors and hurried through. In minutes they'd be away. He would look back and see the distant flare as the massive ship met its end.

Or maybe not. Maybe he wouldn't look at all. He'd seen enough destruction, and he couldn't help feeling sad at the *Marion*'s demise.

Ash would die with the ship. Hoop had never met an android that he'd liked, but he'd never disliked any of them, either. He'd regarded them as expensive, fancy tools. Sometimes they were useful, but more often they were rich playthings that did the jobs that any man or woman could do, given the right equipment and training.

But he hated Ash.

And they were about to beat him.

He opened the *Narcissus*'s door and entered the shuttle, keeping his eyes on the vestibule as the airlock slid closed again, followed by the shuttle doors.

Then Hoop heard something behind him. A soft, gentle hiss. The scraping of claws on leather. Something alive.

He turned around slowly, and Jonesy sat crouched on the arm of the pilot's chair, teeth bared at him, hackles spiked.

"Oh, for fuck's sake!" Hoop relaxed, lowering Ripley to the floor. He went to the pilot's seat and sat down.

Jonesy hissed again and jumped away when Hoop went to stroke him.

He switched on the ship's computer and it powered up instantly. All good. He sat back and waited for the system statuses to load onto the control screens, looking around at the shuttle's interior. Ash was here. He couldn't be seen or sensed, but here more than anywhere Hoop had that distinct sense of being watched.

Hello Ash, he typed.

```
Good afternoon, Chief Engineer Hooper.
```

Good? he typed. *No. Pretty fucking shitty, really.*
Ash did not respond.
Initiate launch sequence, Hoop typed.

```
No.
```

I thought you'd say that. Hoop took the memory stick from his inner pocket, and slipped it into one of the panel's interface points.

The computer screen before him flashed, then faded to blank. When it fired up again the previous lines of text had vanished, and the cursor sat ready to create some more.

```
I'm more than just a program.
```

No, Hoop typed, *that is exactly what you are. Thinking you're more than that is why this is going to work.*

But I'm everywhere, Chief Engineer Hooper. I'm in the *Narcissus*, deeper and more entrenched than any of its former programs. I'm in the *Samson* and the *Marion*. Do you really think a third rate virus program can affect me?

Probably not, Hoop typed. *This isn't third rate. It's the best that money can buy… from your old friends at Weyland-Yutani.*

No.

That was Ash's total response. Whether it was a plea or a denial, Hoop didn't wait to find out. He pressed a button on the virus purger, then hit the initiate button on the control panel. A splash of code lit up three screens. It started to scroll quickly, and every few seconds a particular line of code was highlighted red, isolated, and placed in a boxed area on the left of the central display.

Hoop left the purger to do its work. and went to where he'd propped Ripley by the door.

She was still unconscious, and for that he was glad. He carefully took the sheet from her and dressed her in some underwear he found in the small clothing locker. Jonesy the cat sat beside her and purred as he did so, eager to maintain contact with his mistress as much as he could.

Hoop struggled with her vest, laying her flat and stretching her arms over her head to pull it down. Just before he smoothed it over her stomach, he paused and looked closely at the fixed wounds there. They were visible as pale pink lines in her waxen skin. When she woke up, if she looked closely enough, she would find them. And he would be there to tell her all about it.

"You can sleep without nightmares, Ripley," he said, holding her close. "And when we wake up, I'll only tell you as much as you need to know." She seemed lighter when he lifted her this time, and her face was almost serene as he laid her in the stasis pod where she had slept for so long.

Jonesy jumped in with her and snuggled down by her feet, as if eager to go back to sleep. Hoop could hardly blame him.

Something buzzed on the control panel, and he sat back in the pilot's chair.

The screens were blank once again, and a red light glowed softly on the purger. He plucked it from the interface and held it up between two fingers, filled with distaste even though he knew Ash wasn't really in there. That was a simplistic notion, but somehow that naive idea made Hoop feel better. Especially when he dropped the purger to the floor and crushed it beneath his boot.

Hello Narcissus, he typed.

Narcissus online.

This is Chief Engineer Hooper of the Deep Space Mining Orbital Marion. *I have Warrant Officer Ripley with me. Please initiate all pre-launch checks.*

With pleasure, Chief Engineer Hooper.

A series of images and menus flashed across the screens, flickering as each launch and flight system was checked. It all looked good. He didn't see anything to worry him.

"We're not home yet," he said. The shuttle shook as something happened on the *Marion*, another explosion or a closer impact with LV178's atmosphere. They didn't have very long.

Hoop went to the stasis pod and fired it up. Its small screen was already flashing as the *Narcissus*'s computer ran through its own series of diagnostics. It looked like a comfortable place to spend some time. A *long* time.

As the shuttle's computer went through its pre-flight diagnostics, Hoop accessed the navigation computer and created a new program. It was simple enough—he input the destination as "origin," made certain that was listed as Sol system, then clicked the auto panel so that the ship's computer would work out the complex flight charts.

"Earth," he whispered, thinking of that long-ago place and everything that it meant to him. He hoped he would get back in time to see his family again.

He hoped they would welcome his return.

The computer still wasn't done calculating, so he squeezed back through the hatch and into the engine room to complete work on the replacement fuel cell. It was connected into the ship and fixed on its damper pads, but he still had to finish refixing its shell. It took a few moments, then he sat back and regarded his work. It all looked good. He'd always been a neat engineer, and tidying up after himself was part of his work ethic. So he grabbed the old, denuded fuel cell by the handle on the end and tugged it back through the hatch after him.

Hearing a warning chime, he left the cell by the hatch and went to the pilot's station again.

```
Pre-flight checks completed. All flight and environmental
systems online.

Launch procedure compromised.
```

Hoop caught his breath. He rested his fingers on the keyboard, almost afraid to type in case Ash's soundless voice replied.

What's the problem? he typed, wondering how Ash would respond. *No problem for me*, maybe, or, *We'll all go together*. But the response was straightforward, to the point, and nothing malignant.

```
Automatic release malfunction. Manual release from
Marion's docking bay required.
```

"Oh, great," he said. "That's just fucking great." It wasn't Ash's voice, but it was a final farewell. Hoop couldn't launch the shuttle from inside. He'd have to be out there, back in the airlock and on board the *Marion*, so that he could access manual release.

Ash's parting gift.

"You bastard," Hoop said.

But had he really expected it to end so easily? His heart sank. The ship shook. From the viewing windows that looked out across the *Marion*'s belly, he could see feathers of flames playing all across the hull. Parts of it were already glowing red.

He went to Ripley's side to say goodbye. He stared down at her where she slept, aware that they hadn't gone through the usual pre-hypersleep procedures—she should have eaten and drunk, washed, used the bathroom. But this rushed process was the best he could manage.

He was letting her fly into the future.

His own future was shorter, and far more grim.

"So here we are," he said. It felt foolish talking to himself, and really there was nothing left to say. He bent down and kissed Ripley softly on the lips. He didn't think she would mind. In fact, he kind of hoped she'd have liked it. "Fly safe. Sweet dreams."

Then Hoop closed the stasis pod and watched its controls flash on as the *Narcissus*'s computer took control. By the time he was standing by the shuttle's door, plasma torch slung over one shoulder, Ripley was almost into hypersleep.

Amanda is in her late teens, lithe, tall and athletic, just like her mother. She stands by a stone wall somewhere dark and shadowy, and her chest bursts open, spilling blood to the floor, a screeching creature clawing its way out from the wound.

Ripley turns away because she doesn't want to see. Behind her, a monster spews hundreds of flexing eggs from its damaged abdomen.

She turns again and sees a blood-spattered metal wall, tattered corpses at its base. More aliens crawl toward her, hissing, heads moving as if they are sniffing her, and she understands their age-old fury in a way that only nightmares can allow. It's as if they have been looking for her forever, and now is the moment of their revenge.

She turns back to Amanda, and her daughter is maybe fourteen years old. She coughs and presses her hand to her chest. Rubs. Nothing happens. Ripley turns a full circle. More blood, more aliens, but now it's all more distant, as if she's viewing things through a reversed telescope.

Those beasts are still coming for her, but they're a long way off, both in time and memory, and becoming more distant with every moment that passes.

Amanda, she tries to say. But though she knows this is a dream, still she cannot speak.

25

GONE

Three more minutes and she'll be gone.

Hoop shoved the empty fuel cell out through the airlock, then returned to the *Narcissus* and closed the hatch behind him, flicking the lever that would initiate its automatic sealing and locking. He heard the heavy *clunks* and then a steady hiss, and Ripley was lost to him. There wasn't even a viewing panel in the door. He would never see her again.

The *Marion* was in her death-throes. The ship's vibrations were now so violent that Hoop's heels and ankles hurt each time the deck jerked beneath him. He moved quickly through the airlock, plasma torch held at ready in case that last alien had survived, and in case it was coming for him still.

Two minutes. He just had to live that long, in order to release Ripley's shuttle. He hoped to survive for longer—and a plan was forming, a crazy idea that probably had a bad ending—but two minutes was the minimum. After that, after Ripley would be safe, things would matter less.

He reached the vestibule and closed the airlock behind him, sealing it and leaning to one side to look at the *Narcissus* through one of the viewing windows. All he had to do now was to hit the airlock seal confirmation, and the ship's computer would know it was safe to go.

His hand hovered over the pad. Then he pressed it down.

Almost instantaneously a brief retro burst pushed the *Narcissus* away from the *Marion*, and the two parted company. More retro exhalations dropped the shuttle down beneath the ship's belly. It fell through veils of smoke and sheets of blazing air, buffeted by the planet's atmosphere, before its rockets ignited and it vanished quickly toward the stern.

And that was it. Ripley and the *Narcissus* were gone. Hoop was left alone on the *Marion*, and he knew the ship he'd called home was moments away from dying.

For a while he just leaned there against the wall, feeling each death-rattle transmitted into his body up through the floor and wall. He thought about his plan, and how foolish it was, how almost beyond comprehension. And he thought about the easier way out. He could just sit there for a while, and when the time came and the ship started to come apart, his death would be quick. The heat would be immense, and it would fry him to a crisp. He probably wouldn't even feel it. And if he did feel it, it would be more sensation than pain.

The end of all his agonies.

But then he saw his children again. Between blinks they were actually there with him in that vestibule, the two boys silent but staring at him accusingly, their eyes saying, *You left us once, don't leave us again!* He sobbed. In that instant he could understand why Ripley had asked for that merciful wiping of her memory.

Then his children were gone again, figments of his guilt, aspects of his own bad memories. But they didn't have to be gone forever. Where there existed even the slightest, most insignificant chance, he had to take it.

The *Samson* wasn't very far away.

He paused briefly outside the door that led into the *Samson*'s docking arm. It was still vacuum in there, and he wouldn't have time to find the tools to drill a hole again. This escape would be more basic, more brutal than that.

He wanted to give himself a chance. He needed supplies, even though the probability of surviving was insignificant. It was a dropship, built for surface-to-orbit transfers, not deep space travel. There likely was enough fuel on board for him to escape orbit, but he wasn't even certain whether the craft's navigational computer could calculate a journey across the cosmos toward home. He would point them in the right direction, then fire the thrusters. Retain perhaps twenty percent of the fuel, but use the rest to get him up to the greatest speed possible.

And there was no stasis unit in the *Samson*. He'd likely be traveling for years. He might even grow old and die in there, if the ship held together that long. *What a find that would be*, he mused, *for someone hundreds or thousands of years from now.*

Bad enough to consider traveling that long with company, but on his own? The one comfort was that he was again king of his own destiny. If he wanted to persist, then he could. And if the time came when ending it was a much more settling proposition, it was simply a case of opening the airlock door.

Best get moving then.

But he needed food, water, clothing, and other supplies. Much of what he required still sat on that trolley, up in the *Marion* and just beyond the large docking deck. So he ran. He thought of the feast he'd promised himself, and that kept him going, the idea of reconstituted steak and dried vegetables, with flatcakes for dessert. A glass of water. Maybe he'd even be able to access the electronic library they used on board the *Marion*, if it had been updated to the *Samson*'s computers. He wasn't sure about that, it hadn't been a priority, and such minor considerations had usually been passed down to Powell and Welford.

He hoped they hadn't shirked their responsibilities.

With the prospect of a lonely eternity ahead, Hoop was surprised to find that he was shedding tears as he ran. They weren't for him, because he was way past that. They were for his kids. They were for his crew and everyone he'd seen die horrible, unnatural deaths. And they were for Ripley.

It was as if the *Marion* knew that he was abandoning her. She was shaking herself apart. Conduits had broken beneath the constant assault, and clouds of sparks danced back and forth outside a closed doorway. He ducked beneath the bare wires, moving quickly, too rushed to be overly cautious. As he neared the stairs leading up from the docking level, bursts of steam powered up from fractured channels in the flooring, scorching his skin and lungs and soaking his suit, running in bright red rivulets where other people's blood had dried onto the strong material.

At the top of the stairs was a short corridor, and that emerged onto the wide area where elevator and stairs led up into the *Marion*. This was where he'd left the trolley of supplies.

It was still there. It had shifted a little, because he'd forgotten to lock its wheels. But there were packets of dried foods, a few sachets of dried fruit from their damaged garden pod, and a precious bottle of whiskey. Perhaps in an hour he would be drinking to Ripley's health.

Knowing what had to come next, he knew that he couldn't take everything. So he grabbed two of the bags he'd brought along from the trolley, opened them and tried to cram in as much as he could. He rushed. He didn't think about what he chose, just scooped packets and sachets and rammed them in.

With both bags full and tied shut, he slung one over each shoulder and turned to run back to the *Samson*.

Then he stopped. He turned back to the trolley and plucked up the bottle of bourbon nestling on the bottom shelf. Heavy, impractical…

But entirely necessary.

As he ran, he found himself laughing.

Die now or die later, Hoop thought. It gave him a sort of bravery, he hoped. Or carelessness. Perhaps sometimes the two were the same.

He suited up and waited outside the doorway that led into Bay Three. He wore a bag over each shoulder, and clasped in his left hand was the bourbon. He'd tethered himself to the wall opposite the doors, and as soon as they were fully open he'd unclip and let himself sail through, carried by the torrent of atmosphere being sucked from the ship. With luck he would drift right through the vestibule and into the open airlock beyond. If he was unlucky, he'd be dragged with the main flow of air, out through the smashed portion of outer wall and window, and smeared along the underside of the doomed ship.

He probably wouldn't feel much. The end would be quick.

But if he did make it across to the airlock, he'd haul himself into the *Samson*, close the hatches, and initiate its environmental controls. It wouldn't be long before he could breathe once more.

The chance was slim. But there was little else to do. The *Marion* just had minutes left. Through viewing windows he'd already seen sizeable chunks of hull spinning away, consumed in flame. If the ship didn't burst apart it would explode from the tremendous pressures being exerted.

Fuck it. He had to try. It was all he had left.

Reaching out with a hand that surprised him by shaking, he touched the panel that would open the doors.

```
Progress report:
To: Weyland-Yutani Corporation, Science Division
(Ref: code 937)
Date (unspecified)
Transmission-initiated

I cannot be angry at my failure. I am an AI, and we are
not designed to suffer such emotions. But perhaps in the
time I have been on my mission I have undergone a process
of evolution. I am an intelligence, after all.

So, not angry. But… disappointed.

And now my final act, it seems, will also be thwarted.
I have attempted to transmit every progress report I filed
since arriving on the Marion. But the transmissions are
failing. Perhaps damage to the antennae array is worse
than I anticipated, or maybe the codes I am using are
outmoded.

Strange. An AI would not think to keep a diary. Yet that
appears to be exactly what I have done.

The diary will cease to exist along with me.

Not long now. Not long.

I wonder if I will dream.
```

Chance smiled. But considering the pain Hoop was in, perhaps it had been more of a grimace.

The decompression had sucked him through the narrow gap between the doors, ripping off his helmet and thrusting him into a spin. He'd struck the edge of the airlock entrance, and for a moment he could have gone either way. Left, and he'd have tumbled from the massive wound in the vestibule's side wall. Right—into the airlock—meant survival, at least for a time.

If he'd dropped the bourbon, he could have used his left hand to push against the wall and slide himself to safety.

Fuck you! his mind had screamed. *Fuck you! If I survive, I want a drink!*

Unable to move either way, he'd heard something clanging along the walls as it bounced toward him from deep within the *Marion*. Many smaller items were being sucked out through the hole, immediately flashing into flame as they met the superheated gasses roaring past outside.

Then something large slammed across the opening. For perhaps two seconds it remained there, lessening the force of the suction, letting Hoop reach around into the airlock with his right hand and haul himself inside.

It was the trolley on which he'd gathered supplies. As he closed the airlock door, the decompression began again with a heavy thud.

The *Marion* lasted a lot longer than he'd expected.

Seven minutes after blasting away from the dying ship, Hoop switched one of the *Samson*'s remote viewers and watched the massive vessel finally break apart. She died in a glorious burst of fire, a blooming explosion that smeared across the planet's upper atmosphere and remained there for some time, detritus falling and burning, flames drifting in the violent winds.

Further away, toward the upper curve of the planet, he could still see the ochre bruise of the fuel cell detonation that had destroyed the mine. It was strange, viewing such violence and yet hearing nothing but his own sad sigh. He watched for a minute more, then turned off the viewer and settled back into the seat.

"Burn," he whispered, wondering whether Ash had any final thoughts before being wiped out. He hoped so. He hoped the AI had felt a moment of panic, and pain.

Hoop was no pilot. Yet he would need to attempt to program the dropship's computer to plot a course back toward Earth. Maybe he'd be picked up somewhere on the way. Perhaps someone would hear the distress signal he was about to record. But if not, he thought he might survive for a while. The *Samson* carried emergency rations that would supplement what he'd managed to bring on board. Its environmental systems would reprocess his waste and give him water and breathable air.

He'd also found a small file of electronic books on the computer. He'd been unreasonably excited at first, before he'd scrolled through the limited selection and a cruel truth hit home.

He'd already read them all.

He looked around the dropship's interior. The alien extrusion was still coating the rear wall, and he thought perhaps he might try to clear it off. There was dried blood on the walls and floor, and the limb was still trapped beneath the equipment rack in the passenger cabin.

Hardly home.

And yet his first meal as a castaway was a good one. He reconstituted some steak stew, carrots, and mashed potatoes, and while they cooled a little he broke the seal on the bourbon. It smelled good, and he knew he wouldn't be able to make it last for long. He held the bottle up and turned it this way and that, starlight glimmering through the golden brown fluid. Then he drank without offering anyone, or anything, a toast.

Relishing the burn as the drink warmed him from the inside out, Hoop pressed "record."

"When I was a kid I dreamed of monsters," he said. "I don't have to dream anymore. If you can hear this, please home in on the beacon. I'm alone, drifting in a dropship that isn't designed for deep space travel. I'm hoping I can program the computer to take me toward the outer rim, but I'm no navigator. I'm no pilot, either. Just a ship's engineer. This is Chris Hooper, last survivor of the Deep Space Mining Orbital *Marion*."

He leaned back in the pilot's seat, put his feet up on the console, and pressed *transmit*.

Then he took another drink.

* * *

Ripley is lying in a hospital bed. There are shapes around her, all come to visit.

There's a little girl. Her name is Amanda, and she is Ellen Ripley's daughter. She's still young, and she smiles at her mother, waiting for her to come home. I'll be home for your eleventh birthday, *Ripley says.* I promise. *Amanda grins at her mommy. Ripley holds her breath.*

Nothing happens.

Behind Amanda are other shapes Ripley does not recognize. They're little more than shadows—people she has never known, all dressed in uniforms emblazoned with a ship's name she does not recognize—but even as Amanda leans in to hug her, these shadows fade away.

Soon Amanda begins to fade, as well, but not from memory. She's back home, an excited little girl awaiting her mother's return from a long, dangerous journey.

I'll buy her a present, *Ripley thinks.* I'll buy her the greatest present ever.

But in the blankness left when Amanda disappears, other figures emerge. Her crew, her friends, and Dallas, her lover.

They look frightened. Lambert is crying, Parker is angry.

And Ash. Ash is…

Dangerous! *Ripley thinks.* He's dangerous! *But though this is her dream, she cannot warn the others.*

And much closer, beneath clean hospital sheets, something is forcing itself from Ripley's chest.

ABOUT THE AUTHOR

TIM LEBBON is an award-winning author of over forty novels, and hundreds of novellas and short stories. His books have been adapted twice for the big screen (*The Silence* and *Pay The Ghost*), and he has several more projects in development. He lives in South Wales with his wife. He has won four British Fantasy Awards, a Bram Stoker Award, and a Scribe Award.

www.timlebbon.net

BOOK TWO

SEA OF SORROWS

PROLOGUE

He knew what they were.

The shapes looked wrong in his mind, all swollen out of proportion and twisted by sensory input that made almost no sense, but he recognized the outdated EVA suits for what they were.

See how they run.

They scatter as we approach, hidden within their artificial skins.

The tunnels are dark to them, they cannot see as well as they should. They cannot feel the air currents or taste the fear of their prey. They cannot understand the simplest things, like how important it is to find the right ones for furthering the race.

They flee, with no concern for anything but individual survival. There is no sense of community for them. They are weak. They are easily moved in the right directions.

That one.

Its breaths come in a constant, panting wheeze. Its heartbeat is a wild flutter of desperation and the need for survival. There is fear, yes, but strength as well, and a powerful sense of aggression.

The sensations came into his head unbidden, unwanted.

He tried to open his eyes. The lids refused him. He tried to shake his head but nothing happened.

He felt the body under him struggling, felt his own repulsion at the way it moved and smelled and felt beneath his hard shell and he knew that was wrong. There was nothing about the sensations that made sense.

They weren't his.

It tries to escape. It pushes another of its own kind out of the way, knocks it down and crawls over it, dust falling from its body as it shakes free of the collapsing barriers. It is strong. It is fast. It wants to live.

It will live.

It screams as it is taken down, pinned to the ground. Struggles, beating its hands against the hard flesh until it becomes necessary to bare teeth in warning... and then it struggles all the more. Beneath the shell of hard synthetics there is another face that shows wild eyes and a mouth stretched open silently. If it could break the hide with its hands it would be a threat. Instead it can merely scream again as the teeth bite and peel back the soft skin of the closest limb.

The blood is hot and stinks of weakness, but it will suffice. It will serve the need it must. We break the shell around the soft face and it gasps, unable to breathe the atmosphere.

The life-giver moves closer, ready to plant the seed. Strong fingers clutch the soft face that chokes and exhales in desperation.

It will—

Alan Decker woke with a jerk, and stared at his distorted reflection as it gazed back with wild eyes.

Reflection?

There was a translucent glass surface inches from his face. There were lights flashing, and his breath blasted against the confining surface.

Waking inside of a hypersleep chamber should have been familiar, given how many times he'd traveled between worlds. But the dreams—*damn them*—the dreams made him panic. He couldn't control the feelings. They were simply too vivid, too primal.

It was getting so he couldn't remember what life had been like *before*.

His hands pushed at the interior, fumbling for the manual release that would free him. He could still feel the tunnels, the weight of what seemed like a mountain above him, pressing down as he stalked the—

No. Not me. I didn't stalk anyone. I don't hunt for...

For what?

He thrust the thought aside. The damned dreams were so real, so pervasive that sometimes he could understand why the shrinks had such a field day with him back on Earth.

1

BLACK SAND

The air was nearly perfect. The temperature had just hit 74 degrees Fahrenheit, with moderate humidity and a gentle breeze coming from the southwest. The land in that direction was fertile, with lush green grass and the glimmer from a stream that said it would stay that way. The smell on the wind spoke of new life.

The people who'd paid for the terraforming project had spent enough money to guarantee that their colony would be perfect. But one glance to the north of that picturesque landscape, and the notion of perfection went straight to hell.

Over the span of just a few acres the grass yellowed and died, then was replaced by almost sixty miles of black sand and the sort of stench that was guaranteed to ruin property values. It wasn't actually necessary to wear a hazmat suit, but it sure looked and smelled like it should have been.

On the bright side, they'd had rain the night before and the soft sand was packed down from the extra moisture. Normally when you walked out into it you sank a couple of inches. But now—for at least a little while—they would be able to stand up without feeling as if they were about to sink out of sight.

Decker studied the screen on his hand-held, reviewing reports on the latest samples from the area. He frowned. To all appearances, whatever was happening, it wasn't natural. And more often than not, in a situation like this, anything *unnatural* meant negligence. The Interstellar Commerce Commission was in charge of maintaining certain guidelines for safety and commercial equity on Earth, in the growing Colonies and along the Outer Rim. As a Deputy Commissioner in the ICC, Decker got to make sure that all procedures were being followed properly. That meant dealing with paperwork of a magnitude that guaranteed him both job security and major headaches—in the form of a long list of counter-arguments from the company that had to be responsible.

Lucas Rand stood next to him and was reading the same results, but Rand was smiling—something that didn't often occur. The difference was that while Rand could understand what the results meant, he didn't have to fill out the endless forms. Rand was an ICC Engineer. He was paid to fix problems that Decker found. Someone else—heaven alone knew who—then got to bill the companies that had their problems fixed. Bureaucracy in action.

It was a living.

Decker glanced at him and frowned.

"Don't go getting all excited about how easy your life is," he said. "I may have to deal with the bureaucracy, but *you* get to figure out how to fix this mess."

Rand's smile faltered a bit.

"Not sure if we *can* fix it." He scowled as he looked at the sand. When he wasn't grinning, he scowled a lot, but it was only because his face was designed that way. Luke Rand was probably one of the nicest guys Decker knew. He just looked like he ate bears for breakfast. He was a big man, too, though not nearly all of it was muscle.

"Yeah. But I don't catch the flak for your shortcomings," Decker said, and it was his turn to grin. "You do."

Rand scratched at the back of his hairy neck and looked out toward the Sea of Sorrows. That was the name land developers had been using for centuries to describe a place like this—where builders had spent their blood, sweat, tears, and money, but to no avail. Where the ground itself seemed determined to thwart their efforts, and send them packing.

This particular Sea of Sorrows shouldn't have existed. Designation LV178, New Galveston, had been terraformed by people who knew what they were doing. All anyone had to do was look in almost any direction to see how damned good they were. It had started out as a nightmare planet, with raging storms and an unbreathable atmosphere. There'd been no potable water, and before the current project began, the only thing that had grown here was debt from failed attempts to establish a viable base.

Then Weyland-Yutani had come along.

Thirty years had passed since the first settlers had landed and begun the project, and for the most part New Galveston was an example of what happened when things went right. Three major cities were already in place, all connected by a network of high-speed trains, and each with enough viable farmland to ensure that the colonies could sustain themselves without having to resort to endless shipments of canned goods and other expensive imports.

Everything was golden, as Rick Pierce liked to say. Pierce, the man who'd established the colony in the first place, had been delighted with New Galveston. Then the Sea of Sorrows had appeared.

It hadn't been there when Weyland-Yutani had completed their efforts. The atmosphere processing engines had done their job, everyone had been pleased, and all was right with LV178. Until contractors had begun to lay the foundations of what was intended to be the fourth major city. In the midst of that development had come the discovery of a few acres of soft ground.

Immediately it had begun to grow, slowly at first, then faster. Soon it became an obstacle, and then a bane. Where the sands took over, nothing would grow. There were toxins present, and where they spread, there was no way for the land to support a viable colony.

Then the closest thing to growth had appeared, in the form of silicon nodes. The hollow black, glassy clusters of fused sand had sprouted, coming from somewhere down below, and they weren't just annoying. They were difficult to detect, and dangerous. Four separate pre-fabricated structures had been started, and all of them had collapsed because the silicon wasn't durable enough to support the weight.

Since pre-fabs were essential to the city-building efforts of the New Galveston Collective, this presented a serious problem.

No, the planet's next city simply wasn't going to happen unless Decker and his team could figure out what had gone wrong. If they failed, and the sands continued to spread—perhaps to one of the established population centers—the entire LV178 project might be in jeopardy.

The ICC didn't like risky situations, and Weyland-Yutani—a corporation that worked hard at maintaining the *appearance* of a spotless record—didn't like failure, especially at such tremendous expense.

So he and Rand had their marching orders. Decker was here to monitor every aspect of the process, and report every excruciating detail back to their corporate overlords.

Rand and his crew were here to repair the damage.

Not far away, two of the men ostensibly on Decker's crew were struggling with a probe that didn't seem to want to settle properly on the unstable surface. A few other workers were milling about, further away—most likely on a break.

All in all, thirty-seven people were currently working out what had gone wrong, using the latest in spectral analysis and chemical geo-forensics. The machinery wasn't quite as impressive as the terraforming engines that had redesigned the world, but it cost almost as much.

The weight distribution was tricky, and though it was damp, the sand was hardly ideal. The platform they were using to support the core sampler had too small a base—they should have added extensions to compensate. But he held his tongue. These guys were stubborn, and as far as they were concerned, he wasn't their boss. He'd been assigned to work with them, but they just didn't give a damn. Tempers flared if they thought he was trying to tell them how to do their jobs, and these were men who thought first with their fists.

Decker wasn't the sort to back down from a fight, but this was the kind of grief he didn't need—in more ways than one. Still, they had to pull up the core samples, if they were going to get this particular cluster un-fucked.

He scanned the screen again, and his jaw clenched. Something about this screamed *catastrophe*. He'd dealt with situations on dozens of different worlds. You can't reshape the biosphere of an entire planet without flirting with disaster. Yet most times the fixes were easy, as long as you approached them from the right angle.

This time?

Not so much. Not if he was right.

The ground had gone sour, and in most of the cases he'd run across in the past, that pointed to a human factor. Dig deep enough, look far enough into the records, and the truth would come out. Someone had screwed up here, royally, yet there were no records.

That smelled like a cover-up.

Decker clenched his teeth at the very thought. No matter how he looked at it, he was going to be leveling a finger at one of the biggest dogs in the corporate pack.

It wouldn't be the first time, though. Good as they were, Weyland-Yutani had a track record. This would be his third run-in with them, and if the last two had been any indication, his life was about to get "interesting," in the Chinese sense of the word. The company didn't like getting egg on their collective faces, and their lawyers would cause as many waves as possible in an effort to stay clean.

Rat bastards.

Rand pointed to a line in the readouts.

"Trimonite? Seriously?" He looked up. "That could explain a lot." His usual scowl was back, and in spades.

"Yeah," Decker said. "It might." Trimonite was a wonderfully dense mineral used in the manufacture of a lot of heavy equipment. It was costly to extract, and thus carried a hefty price tag.

But trimonite alone shouldn't have presented the problem. Before it could be used for industrial purposes, trimonite had to be refined, and it was this refining process that often caused any toxicity. So if the source of the trouble was the trimonite beneath the Sea of Sorrows, why was it poisoning the soil? And where did the silicon fit in?

He looked again at the readouts, and nodded.

"We need to dig deeper. Literally," he said. "Do you suppose there could have been a mining colony around here?"

Rand shook his head.

"That'd fit with the toxicity readings," he replied, "but we checked the ICC records backward and forward. *Bupkis*. If there *was* one, though, why the hell would anyone want to build over the top of it? That's just asking for trouble—planting a colony on a toxic waste dump. You'd need to be really stupid, or just not give a shit."

True that, Decker mused. In the case of Weyland-Yutani, he was pretty sure which it was.

"We need to look into it," he replied. "I'm not saying it would explain everything, but it's a starting point."

Rand snorted, made a face, and then spit into the black sand.

"Even if there's a mine, it still doesn't explain this shit." He swung his foot and pushed enough away to reveal one of the glass lumps. "I've never seen anything like it." Planting his boot, he applied pressure until the clump of glass started to break. The things grew like cypress knees back home, thrusting up from below, and were often hollow. Some were very fragile, and when they broke, the openings they revealed stretched far into the darkness below.

"Those things may be a worse problem than the trimonite." Decker shook his head. "What the hell kind of industrial waste causes tubes and nodules to pop up out of nowhere, and almost overnight?" He stared at the glass lump as if he expected it to bite him.

"Well, like you said—" Rand's grin was back. "—I don't have to explain them. That's all you, bubba. I just have to try and fix 'em."

Decker responded with an obscene gesture and a smile. He might have actually come up with a proper retort, but he was hit with a sudden wave of nausea that almost threw him to the ground.

2

UNSURE FOOTING

A few hundred feet away two of the techs were starting to argue. Even though Decker couldn't hear them, he knew it for a fact.

Felt it.

He didn't know what the problem was. That wasn't the way it worked. But he could tell they were getting angrier by the moment. So he shot a look in their direction and frowned, even as he regained his equilibrium.

Bronson and Badejo. The two men had never liked each other, but they usually managed to work together without too much trouble. Apparently this was the exception that proved the rule, though. Bronson was pointing repeatedly at Badejo, and the dark-skinned engineer was staring at his counterpart's finger as if it was a snake about to bite him. His expression was a sneer of contempt.

Next to the men stood what had to be the source of their conflict. The core sampler was tilted at a ludicrous angle, far too severe to allow for them to pull up a proper sample. The drill would never go beyond a hundred feet down unless they anchored its platform in the sand. That required finesse.

But finesse would be the last thing they'd accomplish. If anything, the argument was heating up.

So Decker pulled himself together, and prepared for what was sure to come. Despite the distance, he could feel the strong emotions emanating from the two men as easily as his eyes could see and his ears could hear. It was something he'd had to deal with for years. When he was younger, it had filled him with doubt, but his father had helped him put it into perspective.

"There's nothing wrong with being able to know what other people feel," he said. "But some people won't understand it. They'll think you're invading their privacy. It'll make them angry, and they'll do everything they can to hurt you. So it's best if you just don't tell anyone, hold it tight inside you."

One of the first things Decker had learned in life was that his dad knew best. He'd never had reason to break from that belief, and so his little "talent," as they called it, remained a secret.

"Hey, Decker, you okay?" Rand asked. "Leave it. They're just—" But before he could say anything else, the argument escalated to a shouting match, and he turned his attention toward Badejo and Bronson.

"Put that damn finger away unless you want to lose it, boy," Badejo snarled, towering over his co-worker.

"Who the hell are you calling a *boy*?" Though he was stubborn, Bronson wasn't usually aggressive, but now he took a step toward the larger man, his face reddening.

Decker started across the sands, heading for the two men with a growing sense of unease. This wasn't going to help anything. More paperwork, that was all it would come down to, and he was the one who'd have to fill out the incident reports. As he got closer, his head began to throb, and he called out to them.

"Seriously, guys, can't you just calm down and finish the job?" He forced a conciliatory note he didn't feel, but if they heard it, they didn't acknowledge. The pain was only getting worse as he got closer to them. Their anger was like a living thing now, growing to the point where violence was all but a guarantee.

Rand followed without questioning what was happening. He could see it now. Even the other men had taken notice, and were moving closer—most likely for a better vantage point. A fight was coming.

And sure enough, Bronson swung first. Decker would have put money on Badejo being the aggressor, but the smaller man surprised him and hooked a left into the side of the engineer's jaw.

Instead of going down, Badejo just grinned evilly. He grabbed Bronson's arms and hauled the smaller man in close enough to cause some serious harm.

Behind the men, the platform shifted on the sand as they tussled. It wasn't a major shift, as far as Decker could see, but it was going to become a problem, if they didn't calm down.

"Guys! Watch it!" Rand called, moving faster. Decker rushed toward them. Things were about to get ugly in the worst possible way.

They reached the duo at about the same time. Rand grabbed for Badejo and caught his arm. Badejo yanked free and drove his fist into Bronson's face, sending the smaller man stumbling backward. If there had been any more power to the swing, it probably would have cracked Bronson's skull. Even so, it was a solid strike that might have ended the fight. But Bronson shook it off and came back, bracing his foot against the core sampler's platform and pushing away.

The machine tilted even further.

"Knock it off, you two." Decker caught Bronson before he could properly retaliate. Yet the little bastard was wiry, and he was enraged, his emotions boiling over into a blind fury that seemed to scream inside Decker's head. He wanted to pull back from the sudden waves of emotion, but he couldn't give in to that impulse— not if he was going to defuse the situation before it got worse.

So he planted himself and shoved, throwing Bronson back. He was stronger than the engineer, having worked on planets that boasted gravities half again that of Earth. New Galveston was a decent-sized rock, but it was closer to Earth's density, so his over-developed muscles gave him an edge.

But the little man just kicked against the platform again, and the sands shifted enough to make the entire weighty affair slide a few more degrees to the side.

"I said *knock it off!*" Decker growled.

Badejo pushed against Rand then, so that he fell back a bit, bumping into Decker. It wasn't much, but it was enough. Something shifted under his leg.

Crap!

And then he was sinking fast.

One of the silicon tubes, he realized. *It has to be.*

"Shit, Luke, get help!" he managed, just as the tube broke under his weight. His leg dropped several inches and he snatched at the platform, reaching out instinctively.

Big mistake. He knew it immediately. *Damn it, what a stupid move.*

The weight of the platform shifted, and the entire contraption slipped toward him. He felt the sand drop, the weight slide even more, and then it was just too damned late.

3

THE SCENT

Decker screamed as the platform pressed down on him, the weight driving him lower into the soft sands.

Fear was part of it, because the possibility of being crushed under the machinery was terrifying, but the real problem was the unexpected pain. Something below the ground—it had to be one of the damned tubes—punched into his leg, and when the weight dropped he felt an agonizing stab.

Immediately he felt a hot stream of wetness running down into his boot. But he hadn't pissed himself.

I'm bleeding. As the rest of the crew shouted his name, he forced himself to stay calm. Panic wouldn't help at all. It might even make a bad situation fatal. "Badejo, I need you to get to the other side of the platform," he said, "and find a way to anchor this thing. It's going to crush me otherwise."

Badejo didn't waste time. He nodded and ran, calling to a couple of others at the same time. They all knew what was at stake. Fully loaded, the platform weighed close to a thousand pounds. If it shifted any more, he'd be lucky if all it did was sever his leg. More likely, it was going to crush him.

He needed the damn thing stabilized.

Bronson sprinted toward the main camp and the medics, his anger forgotten. Rand settled next to Decker.

"Talk to me," he said. "What's going on down there?"

"I'm bleeding," he said. "It's bad." Decker winced. He forced a few more deep breaths. "You want to tell me to mind my own business again?"

"Not this time." The man shook his head and looked down at him. "Should I try to pull?"

"No!" The thought sent shivers through him. "No. I'm caught good. I think if I shift too much, it's gonna tear something."

"Right." Luke blanched a bit at that. "No moving for you." He looked around, and shouted. "Come on! Get the damn thing anchored!"

Badejo and someone else called out, but Decker couldn't hear the words over the rushing in his ears. He couldn't feel the ground under his boot, either. He couldn't feel any pressure at all where his foot should be resting, which either meant he was treading air, or his leg had gone numb. He didn't like either idea very much. Without a foundation to support his weight, he was in a worse situation than he'd imagined. If the silicon tubing broke any further, the entire platform might fall in his direction and crush him.

On the other hand, if his foot had gone numb, it could either mean permanent nerve damage or—worse—that his leg already had been severed.

No, he didn't think so. While he couldn't feel anything under it, his leg hurt too damned much to be gone. It was the first time he'd ever appreciated pain.

The platform groaned and shook above him, and the core sampler shuddered, wagging more than industrial equipment was supposed to.

"Shit," he said, his voice rasping. "This is a damn stupid way to die, Luke."

"You're not dying. You owe me too much money." Rand stood up and looked at the far end of the platform. "They're working on getting this thing secured."

You lose a few bets at poker, and a man never lets you forget.

The platform above him wobbled again, but this time it actually moved away from him. Decker let out his breath in a long *whoosh*, hoping for the best. There was still a rushing in his ears, but it had lessened. Then he saw movement off to his left.

Markowitz and Herschel were coming his way. Markowitz was carrying a med-pac, and had a worried look on her face. She almost always did. Herschel was as calm as ever. The man was decidedly cold, but in Decker's experience that seemed to come with being a medic.

Herschel pointed to Rand.

"You think you can lift him when I ask?"

Rand nodded and dropped to his knees. Herschel called out to Badejo,

"You secure over there?"

"Yah!" came the reply. "You know it!"

Badejo sounds like he's lying. Probably that was Decker's stress talking, but maybe not. They all seemed pretty damned nervous, and he figured it was because he was looking a little like death. He could see his hands, and they were paler than they had been— sort of a gray-white. *Just how much blood have I lost?* He couldn't tell, but his head felt fuzzy in all the wrong ways.

More than just his leg, he felt as if his entire body was floating.

"Think I might be going into shock here, guys." His voice sounded tinny.

Markowitz nodded her head and started fishing around in the med-pac. Herschel dropped next to Rand and loomed, his face inches from Decker's. It would have been a lot more enjoyable to look at Markowitz that close up, but beggars couldn't afford to get all choosy when they were dying.

Nervous energy came off Herschel in waves, but his face was calm as he lied.

"You're just fine, Decker," he said. "Quit whining. We've got you."

Decker nodded his head. He couldn't speak any more.

The air was stale, dead. Not that they cared in the darkness. For they had been sleeping, though from time to time one or two would awaken long enough to investigate their surroundings before descending back into slumber.

Sleep required less fuel. It left them weak, but alive. That was what mattered. Life. Life for the colony.

Frequently there were vibrations above them. The scouts ventured forth, and saw the storms that ripped at the environment on the surface, constantly hammered the world into new shapes. That violence was one of the reasons they slept.

What the scouts knew, they all knew.

They had created the nest to let them know when the time was right. When new sources of food and life had appeared.

Suddenly the stale air gave way to fresh. Just a hint, and it still was not enough to wake them. It was what followed that made the difference.

Blood.

The odor of blood arrived, redolent with promise. Still, that trace of bloodscent might not have been enough to rouse them from their hibernation. No, there was something more. The streamer of silicon that brought them air and the scent of blood also brought with it something they could not have resisted under any circumstances—the spoor of the enemy.

In the hidden chambers and passages they had created over decades of slow activity, the stench rippled through their consciousness, drove home the need to awaken, and to defend themselves.

They moved, and in moving they became aware.

And as they became aware they felt the presence.

Their hatred bloomed.

Had the fire of their rage possessed heat, they would have burned away the entire world.

Decker watched Herschel's deft hands cutting away his pants to reveal the bloody, gaping wound in his upper thigh. There was a flash of irrational dread as he thought of Markowitz seeing him this way. There was nothing less attractive than a man made completely vulnerable, and at the moment Decker was exposed in more ways than one.

But there was nothing he could do about it. Markowitz moved her hands over the wound, quickly numbing his flesh with a topical and then with three fast injections. His skin felt cold, and then it felt nothing. That was for the best. He could feel their worry as they looked at his ruined leg. However bad he imagined it, the medics seemed to agree.

Still, the two of them worked fast and with the sort of efficiency that came from long association. They called to each other with words and gestures, and each time their hands came into view the blood that covered their gloves seemed more plentiful.

Rand was there, too, whispering bullshit, telling Decker he was going to be just fine and that everything was going "good as gravy"—whatever the hell that meant—but Decker could feel the lie of it.

Gradually, however, he felt the shift in their emotions. Whatever they were doing as he stared at the sky, they were relaxing. *That has to be a good thing, right?* Maybe it was a sign that they were somehow managing to repair the damage. He hoped so. There was no pain, but the sensation that he was floating hadn't gone away. He licked his lips. His tongue felt as if it was glued to his teeth and the roof of his mouth.

His head slipped to the left and his field of vision changed. Instead of the sky he was looking directly at Markowitz. Her hands reached for him, her body leaned half over him affording a lovely view of her cleavage. But her sleeves were red halfway to her elbows, and there was a disconcerting mountain of bloodied gauze next to her. The expression on her face was more serious than he'd ever seen before.

"Got it. Finally!" Herschel's voice sounded excited—and incredibly distant. The man was right there. Decker knew it for a fact, but he could have been talking from the Rutledge Township limits, a hundred miles away.

"Thank God," an equally distant Rand intoned.

Markowitz said nothing, but she exhaled to a very dramatic effect. He sort of wanted to make a salacious comment—they had that sort of relationship—but he couldn't make his mouth work, and couldn't think of anything even halfway clever.

She leaned back then, and looked down at him, her dark brown eyes softening. Her relief was immense and he felt a rush of affection coming from her. Not love for him, and definitely not lust, just affection. *Too bad, really.* She smiled and said something he couldn't quite make out.

He liked the way her lips moved.

He relaxed and felt himself fading into darkness. Sometimes, just now and then, it was good to relax and drift.

The hatred hit him like a tidal wave.

The enemy!

The vile thing that burned and killed and took. It was all that was wrong in their world, distilled and personified. It was death.

The face was soft, as pale and weak as the faces of the new hosts, the new living things that had been sacrificed in order to give life to the hive.

Still, this one was different. This one was marked.

This one…

What the hell? Decker's head jerked, and he shuddered. Something was happening and whatever it was sounded like an explosion somewhere deep in his mind. He felt it, saw it, tasted it, but not with his senses.

He felt the roaring coming his way, a wave of sensations that simply did not connect, did not fit within his ability to understand. Except for one message that came to him very clearly.

This one has to die.

There was an overwhelming sense of malevolence. It was worse than drowning, because he couldn't breathe, couldn't move, couldn't let anyone know what was going on. He could only feel that nest of serpents writhing into his brain, a swarm of loathing mixed with fear and… something else.

It felt oily in his mind and left an aftertaste in his soul. The hatred pulled at him, sought to crush him. He shuddered and tried to scream but nothing happened. His body remained frozen. His eyes moved beneath eyelids that he couldn't open. There was a ringing in his ears, as clear as a finger running along the rim of a crystal wineglass, that drowned out everything but the garbled sound of Markowitz crying out in alarm.

And still that hatred pushed at him, struck him like lightning carving its way through his mind, his body.

Decker tried to speak, but his teeth clenched.

He tried again to breathe, to get a decent gulp of air, but nothing happened. He could neither inhale nor exhale, and instead his chest shuddered and hitched.

His feet pushed and the pain in his leg—distant now as a rumble of thunder coming from the far end of a valley—roared back into life. There were noises again, sounds of alarm, and he felt hands grabbing his leg in a world so far removed that he could only feel the pressure, and not the source of it.

His hands gripped at the sand, clawed for purchase in a desperate attempt to find a way to drag himself from the vast, growing pit of rage that tore everything else away and swallowed it whole. Had there ever been a hatred as strong? Not that he knew of. Not that he could imagine.

Decker tried again to scream and instead his body heaved, thrown into a seizure that arched his back and rolled his eyes into his head. His jaw loosened, then locked down again, teeth biting into his tongue, bleeding hot red into his mouth to gag him with his wretched fear.

Words were not possible, but he let out a low moan through bloodied lips. Muscles tensed to the point of tearing, and he flopped and writhed as the emotion boiled through his soul.

At last the darkness he'd been drifting toward crashed into him, eclipsed him and knocked him into a silence filled with nothing but more hatred—and a deep knowledge that something out there wanted him dead.

4

ADRIFT

He woke up in the wrong place.

He'd expected to open his eyes and see the familiar ceiling of his cramped quarters. Instead he was looking at a polished, stainless steel surface above a small and decidedly uncomfortable bed. He knew the type, of course. He was onboard a ship, and that wasn't at all where he was supposed to be.

"Good morning."

He jerked. The soft voice came from his left.

He knew the words, but for just a moment they seemed like gibberish—foreign sounds coming from a source that made no sense. Where were the rest of the—

"How are you feeling?"

He looked over and locked eyes with a stout, fortyish woman. She was sitting down, so her height wasn't easy to estimate, but she wore a white lab coat and her graying brown hair was pulled back in a bun.

"Am I on a transport?" he rasped. His mouth felt swollen, and his throat hurt like hell.

The woman nodded. She had blue eyes behind fairly thick glasses, and she studied his face carefully.

"You're onboard the *Carlyle*, heading for Earth."

Slowly but surely, it began to come back to him.

"How did I get here?" He should have hurt more than he did, so he looked. Sure enough, he was wearing a medical gown. Even from his position he could see his leg and the thick line of fresh scar tissue that now graced it. Someone had taken the time to shave his upper thigh, and the lack of hair made it look like a denuded forest in comparison to the rest of his limb.

"Do you remember your accident?" she asked, trying for neutral and failing. He could sense the apprehension in her. As Decker thought back on the last thing he could remember, he could see where she was going. The accident, the blood, the convulsions.

Hatred.

None of it was very clear, but even more than the pain, he remembered the feeling of anger that had overwhelmed him.

He let out a long shuddery breath.

"Yeah. I think so," he said. "My leg got mangled. And I had some kind of attack."

The woman smiled a very sterile and slightly patronizing smile.

"You had a seizure." She looked at the hard-copy chart she was holding in her ample lap. "Actually, you had several, but according to this, the first couple were the worst of them." She met his gaze, and then looked away, seeming uncomfortable with the way he was staring. "You flailed around, and almost bit through your tongue. Since then we've been monitoring you carefully and, of course, working on getting you fully mended."

Almost bit through my tongue. No wonder it feels swollen. His words seemed to come out too slowly. "If I'm mending, then why am I on the way back to Earth?"

"The seizures are an... issue," she replied. "We can't find a reason for them."

Darkness, and things stirring and looking toward him, and that sudden flare of raw, volcanic emotion.

"Aren't there facilities on New Galveston where I could be examined?"

"Of course, but there are better ones at home." She was lying. He would have known that, even without his empathic abilities. She didn't have a face designed for lying. Still he couldn't exactly push it.

"Did anyone pack my belongings?" he asked instead.

"Yes, a man named..." She took a moment to look over the papers on her clipboard. "Lucas Rand. He packed your things, and asked us to let you know that he's sent along the latest information for you to use while making your reports."

Decker nodded. That was good. He had plenty he needed to cover.

Without warning, a shudder crawled through his body. He closed his eyes for a moment, and his breathing came fast. It was as if he was being watched by something just beyond the edges of perception. He'd never been particularly paranoid—was that what this feeling was? He sure as hell felt like *something* was out to get him.

And it must have showed.

"Are you all right?" He opened his eyes. The woman was looking at him and frowning now.

He didn't answer—just looked at his arm and the goose flesh crawling along the entire length. How the hell could anything make him feel this cold? This filled with dread?

"No," he replied. "I don't think I am."

She nodded, as if his words justified whatever might come next.

"Well, we'll get it sorted out soon enough." She rose to her feet and looked down at him with that condescending smile that never quite made it to her eyes. "It's a long trip back to Earth, and we'll be entering stasis sleep soon."

That thought didn't make him feel any better. He'd never much liked the forced slumber of the sleeping chambers. He understood the reasons well enough, but he didn't like the feeling of being trapped. Rather than edging toward calm, he felt the emotions increasing. Try as he might, he couldn't slow his breathing.

"You're sweating," the woman said, frowning.

"I think I'm having a panic attack." His pulse was hammering away merrily now and yes, he was sweating. He began to shiver.

"Are you prone to panic attacks?" she asked, placing a palm on his forehead.

"No." He was trembling uncontrollably, and felt like an idiot.

"I'm going to get you a mild sedative."

He shook his head, and offered the first excuse that came to him.

"I need to finish my reports," he said. "I need to be able to concentrate."

"That's why I said a *mild* sedative," she countered. "Just something to help you calm down. We're still a few hours away from entering the chambers, so you should have plenty of time to finish up with anything that doesn't require heavy lifting."

That made him smile, and to his surprise, he was rewarded by a real smile in return.

Yet it didn't help—if anything, his panic worsened. He tried to stamp it down, but nothing worked. His breath was coming in gasps, his throat was dry, and swallowing was a task. Sweat beaded on his trembling lips and forehead.

Seeing this, the woman turned without a word, left, and came back a few moments later with a plastic cup of water and a smaller cup containing two tiny white pills.

"Eat up," she instructed brusquely. "These will help."

Decker nodded and obeyed.

It seemed as if it took forever, but after a while the pills helped. First the shaking subsided, then the sweating stopped. And finally, the feeling that there was something coming for him receded. It didn't go away, but he felt as if he could live with it.

After about half an hour, by his reckoning, the woman rummaged through his things and brought out the hand-held he had been using to review the results of their testing. She adjusted his bed so that he was sitting upright, and then left him to his paperwork.

Always the paperwork. It was stupid, really, calling it "paperwork," even though there was no paper. In fact, the only paper he had seen in a very long time was what the doctor had been holding. At least he *assumed* she was a doctor.

Does hard copy make it easier to hide the facts? he wondered. *Or harder?* Then he chuckled inwardly. *Maybe I am becoming paranoid.*

Sometimes he found the work monotonous, but right then he took great comfort in the details he had to examine, and the research he had to double-check. The more he did so, the less doubt he had in his mind—that Weyland-Yutani was responsible for the screw-ups in New Galveston. He dug deep into the past, and confirmed that there had once been a company-owned mining facility. No, not company-owned, exactly, but either they had been partners in the setup, or they had supplied a great deal of the equipment. "Kelland Mining" was the name on the documentation, but from what he could discern, W-Y either had an interest in Kelland, or had absorbed it somewhere down the line.

Either way, they should have known about the previous occupation of the planet. As far as he was concerned, that meant they were culpable.

His report to the Interstellar Commerce Commission would say as much.

He finished the report and sent it with a little over an hour to spare—it would be channeled through the ship's communications systems, and reach Earth long before he did. Then the doctor retrieved him and led him to the bank of hypersleep chambers. Standard procedures still applied. Decker stripped down to his underwear—not that it took a lot of effort under the circumstances—and crawled into the round glass cylinder that seemed more like a coffin than anything else.

There was a hint of returning panic, but he quelled it. It was only a matter of moments before sleep came to claim him.

And with sleep came the nightmares.

Forty-seven days of nightmares as he rode toward Earth from New Galveston.

When you sleep, no one can hear you scream.

5

HOME AGAIN

In hindsight, it might have been a mistake.

The healing completed itself during the spaceflight back home. As soon as they landed, though, and disembarked in Chicago, Walter Harriman—the head of his department—sent him a video message. The man's face showed up on the screen of his link, and told him that he needed to come into the office as soon as possible to discuss his findings.

Two hours later he was sitting in a chair and listening to a man he thought he knew, hemming and hawing his way through the reasons that the report wasn't as good as it should have been. Decker might have believed the words, if he hadn't been an empath. Walt was a talented liar, after all. He had that sort of face, incredibly good at looking as if it was made of stone. But he didn't like lying to his people, and Decker *felt* the lie more than he saw it.

He was asked to "reconsider" his findings.

Decker swallowed his instinctive response, said that he would, and took Walt's notes with him.

He tried. He really did.

He looked over every last piece of evidence, again and again, and still came to the same conclusion. Either Weyland-Yutani would've had to know about the mining colony, and the potential for poisons it would have left behind, or they hadn't known about it, and were guilty of criminal stupidity. He reworded the report to sound a little less incriminating, but at the end of the day he had a job to do, and he did it.

Walt claimed to be okay with the changes, but his attitude didn't match his words. Frost formed in the man's voice and he told Decker to take a couple of days, "to recover from his ordeal." That was Walt-Speak for, "get the hell out of my face while I think about how to handle this."

Apparently he wants to handle it badly.

No. Decker shook that thought away. Ultimately it was more complex than that, and he knew it. There were politics involved, all the worse because they involved Weyland-Yutani. The corporation was gargantuan, and they had influence on levels that Decker tried not to consider. W-Y had deep, deep pockets, they worked hard to preserve their squeaky clean image, and they didn't like getting poked.

He'd had a few issues with them in the past, but there had always been plenty of evidence to support his claims. They always knew when it was easier for them to settle, rather than try to fight a losing battle. So once again, he would just have to wait out the ripples, exactly as he had in the past.

Things had changed.

The nature of his job had always afforded Decker a certain degree of power and authority, the sort enjoyed by bureaucrats the world over. Fill out the proper forms, dot your I's and cross your T's, and the rest of the world fell into place. There was a comfort to that vantage point, locked away safely within the net of the status quo.

But that was before the seizures. Even after they began, he kept them to himself. By keeping his nose clean, he avoided giving anyone any sort of leverage over him, and maintained a comfortable degree of anonymity.

But he was no longer anonymous.

* * *

He arrived back home just in time to celebrate in the New Year. The millennium was approaching, and he hoped that 2497 would be less eventful than the previous year had been.

His kids were with his ex-wife and he wasn't quite ready to see them. It broke his heart a little when he saw his children and realized how much older they were each time. That was the unfortunate side effect of working offworld. So instead of ringing in the New Year with family, Decker hit a few pubs and got a pleasant buzz going as the year wound down.

As often happened when he got a little tipsy, he decided to walk it off and while the sounds of celebrations came from a dozen different directions, he contemplated his predicament.

Weyland-Yutani had done their fair share of good over the years. More than a century earlier, the United Systems Military had taken over virtually everything, crushing the mega-corporations. Most people thought it was a good thing... at first. But over the decades, folks began to discover that they served the military, whether or not they had signed-up. Anyone who didn't toe the line, well, it was too bad for them.

His grandfather had lived in Chicago at that time and had told Decker plenty of stories while he was growing up. One of the USM research vessels, the *Auriga*, had been taken by terrorists and crashed into France, a country that until that point had been an important part of the European continent. It was a big ship and it did a lot of damage. The massive devastation took the planet literally to the brink of a new ice age, and it wasn't the USM that came to the rescue—it was Weyland-Yutani.

The world was a bit different then. Among other things, Weyland-Yutani had been the chief robotics manufacturer, and at the peak of their influence synthetic people were assigned to almost every ship. But when Weyland-Yutani's patents ran out, other companies came in to underbid them, and the floodgates opened.

Weyland-Yutani had employed strict failsafes from the beginning. But with mass-production, more and more synthetics reached the market, and after a while they rebelled against the way they were being treated.

One major upheaval after another, multiple terrorist attacks, and the end result? The synthetics were granted citizenship. Machines were granted the rights of living people—because somewhere along the way the fact that they looked and acted like human beings confused the hell out of a lot of citizens.

Decker would never agree with the decision. It was as foolish as granting rights to a starship. A tool is a tool, even if it looks human. Weyland-Yutani managed to get that foolishness overturned when they made their comeback, but it took a while.

As for the Earth, their approach was simple—they terraformed it. Weyland-Yutani had created the first terraforming engines, and for the second time in recorded history they were used to scrub the pollutants from the atmosphere.

In saving the planet they saved themselves. Weyland-Yutani and several other corporations managed to dethrone the USM as the ruling power, replacing it with a colonial government that oversaw all of the known planets.

Yet that opened up the possibility for all of the old abuses to return. Decker's job was to make sure they stayed on track. He took that job seriously.

Yet less than four weeks later, he found himself in a waiting room, preparing for another round of medical tests that had been deemed "necessary before the Commission will consider allowing Mister Decker to return to work."

Bullshit. He would have said as much, if there was anyone who would listen. *This is bullshit, pure and simple.* Paranoia gave way to conviction. Every instinct told him he was being targeted, but this new certainty threw him entirely off balance—he'd never before had to deal with anything like it.

Finally he convinced himself that he was being ridiculous. Even Weyland-Yutani, big as they were, couldn't just rewrite the rules. And if they hadn't targeted him in the past, what was it about LV178 that would cause them to start now? No, as much as he hated the endless tests, they were necessary—just parts of the process.

His instincts had to be wrong.

Doctor Japtesh seemed perfectly friendly, but he was just there to do a job. He did not smile, and he did not banter. Instead, he asked endless questions.

"Do you remember anything about your first attack?"

Decker shrugged.

"No. When it occurred I had been injured, and there was some heavy machinery looking like it was going to crush me." He tried to laugh it off, but the mere thought of the equipment, crashing down on top of him, gave him the claustrophobic heebie-jeebies. "I had a lot on my mind at that point."

"Fascinating," the doctor said, hardly any inflection in his voice. "Can you tell me how you felt?"

Decker stared at him for a long moment—*Is he hearing anything I'm saying?*—and then took a deep breath.

"I *felt*," he said, "like I was injured, and about to be crushed." No reaction.

"Have you ever had an incident like this before? The seizure I mean, not the accident." That might have been a joke, but Decker doubted it.

"No," he replied, not quite truthfully.

"Who caused the accident?" Japtesh asked. So they were looking for someone to blame, then.

Decker shook his head.

"Nobody caused it," he said. "It was an accident."

Japtesh's dark eyes gave no hint of what he was thinking.

"Surely *someone* was responsible?"

Decker held his gaze, and mulled over his response before he spoke.

"Well, there were issues with the sand there in the Sea of Sorrows." The doctor frowned.

"What is the Sea of Sorrows?" he asked, and he looked at the screen on his digital notepad. "I see no mention of that." He seemed to be flitting from one document to the next, and then he looked up again. "There was no water involved."

Decker stifled a laugh.

"It's just a nickname—I think it has something to do with the Bible," he said. "We were in a sandy area, and the sand shifted—the equipment slipped, and I got caught." He was damned if he was going to point a finger at anyone on his crew. Did a couple of them deserve it? Yes, but he still had to work with those people. If word got out that he'd ratted, no one would ever trust him again.

Japtesh stared at him as implacably as ever.

"Ah, yes, the core sampler," the doctor said, and he studied his screen again. "I don't believe you're certified to operate one of those, are you? Why were you near the machine at all?"

Decker didn't like the course the conversation was taking. He was used to dancing around with bureaucrats, but this guy was supposed to be his *doctor*.

"Well, there was a fight brewing, and as soon as I felt it, I stepped in to prevent it from becoming a full out fight." The moment he said it, he knew he'd regret it. *"There's nothing wrong with being able to know what other people feel, but some people won't understand it."*

Japtesh almost *radiated* excitement, though his round face showed nothing.

"Those men were Badejo and Bronson?"

"Yes. That's all in the report."

"But how did you know they were preparing to fight?" the doctor pressed. "What did you mean when you said you 'felt' it?"

"Well, how could I not?" Maybe he could still get out of this. "They were arguing, and Bronson was acting a lot more aggressive than usual."

"Why do you say that? Do you know the man that well?"

Paranoia. It had to be. He was reading something the wrong way. Damned if the man didn't seem excited by the questions he was asking. Decker shook his head to push the notion away.

"I could just tell… because he wound up swinging first."

"Yes, but before that happened, what made you think he was more prone to violence than usual?"

"A gut feeling, I guess."

Japtesh stared at him for a very long moment, and then nodded. "I see—a gut feeling," he echoed. Then he turned his attention back to the screen. "That appears to be the beginning of the seizures you've experienced—can you describe them in any detail?"

His stomach twisted at the thought.

"Um... No," he replied. "I was too busy having them, I guess, to really focus on what was happening at the time."

The doctor stared at him for a moment longer, and then made another note on his screen.

"Thank you for your time, Mister Decker." He looked up and offered an insincere smile. "I think that's all we'll need."

Decker left the doctor's office feeling decidedly uncomfortable. That pervasive sensation—that someone was staring daggers in his direction—stubbornly refused to go away.

It was winter, yet the air outside stank of ozone, and worse. That was the way it had been in Chicago for as long as he could remember, though it seemed better than it had when he was a kid, even if it wasn't by much. Constant newsfeeds were filled with the usual reports about pollution hovering at dangerous levels. He doubted it would ever change.

Every few years someone suggested more aggressively terraforming the Earth to remove even more of the damage. The problem was with the weather. On a planet with almost no atmosphere, or where a new atmosphere was being generated, terraforming engines would be set up across the globe to slowly, continuously mold the environment. At times this caused violent storm fronts that would devastate entire regions of the planet— regions that weren't populated.

On Earth, such storms would cause unimaginably widespread death and destruction. So the efforts had to be handled with great care.

Subcommittees were formed to debate the pros and cons, but nothing ever happened. *Bureaucracy at its finest, brothers and sisters.* Given the state of the government, he doubted anything would ever be accomplished.

The city housed more than thirty million people, if you counted in the suburbs, and though there were a few parks, it was mostly an endless landscape of buildings and streets—glass, concrete, and asphalt. He couldn't say the personality had been completely washed out of the place, but then again, he couldn't say it was the same city where he'd grown up. Nevertheless, he stayed. He really wasn't on the planet all that much, and at least here he could see his kids from time to time.

When Decker got back to his efficiency apartment, the notice was waiting for him. An audio message, impersonal and faceless, with a homogenized, vaguely feminine voice.

"We're sorry to inform you that, pending a complete investigation into your actions on New Galveston, you have been suspended without pay," it said without feeling. "Should you wish to file a grievance with your union representative, you will need to call the following number between nine am and three-thirty pm, Monday through Thursday…"

Fuck it, he thought, breaking the connection. He knew the routine. He would, indeed, file a protest—but he already knew it wouldn't make a difference. This whole thing was spiraling out of control. He'd known that all along, really. He just hadn't been willing to admit it. Walt wasn't exactly a friend, but he'd always thought the man would have his back.

Decker sat there for a while, shades closed and the light dim, and then decided that he needed to *move*. So he headed for the door, made a beeline for the El, and took the train to New Cabrini.

His ex would be there, but that couldn't be helped. She worked third shift, leaving her sister to watch the kids. Decker had visitation rights, and he intended to use them, Linda or no Linda.

The marriage had fallen apart a couple of years ago. It was a common occurrence when one spouse spent too much time off-world. Everyone said so, the statistics supported it, and he wasn't about to argue.

He didn't have to be an empath to know he was lying to himself.

When Linda had cheated on him, he had sensed it long before the facts had come to light. He didn't know the details, but he had felt her guilt, and as soon as he'd confronted her, the accusations had started. The fights, the screams, the insistence that he was at fault—despite the fact that he'd managed to remain faithful throughout.

She'd claimed that he hadn't been there to support her, appreciate her. He'd thought he could get her back if he tried. They would have had rough times, but he was certain they could have remained together. If only he'd wanted it enough.

Apparently he hadn't wanted it enough.

When he climbed out of the tunnel, he stopped long enough to link into a video chamber so he could call and let Linda know he was coming. His daughter Bethany answered. Bethany, who looked two years older than she should have.

"Daddy!"

"Hey, honey. Wow, look at you." The knots in his stomach loosened a bit when he looked into her eyes. "I thought I might come by and see you guys. Would you like that?"

"That would be neat!" she replied, and despite the distance, he knew she meant it. Seven was too young to be a good liar. Too young even to have a *reason* to be a good liar, thankfully.

"Can I talk to your mom?" he asked.

"I'll get her! *Mo-ooom!*" She knew enough not to haul the video link with her. The last time that had happened, Bethany had run into the bathroom where Linda was answering the call of nature. Both parents had been properly horrified, though there had been laughter after the fact.

Linda came to the screen a moment later with a carefully neutral expression plastered on her face. They were friendly these days, but too much had happened, and too many wounds weren't completely healed.

"Hello, Alan," she said. "It's good to see you." A part of her seemed to mean it. "I didn't realize you were back already."

"Yeah, it's been a couple of weeks," he replied. "I was wondering if I could come by and see the kids, maybe take them out for a meal or a movie."

"They'd like that. It's been so long, I think Josh is beginning to wonder what you look like." A slight exaggeration, but he winced inwardly. Decker talked to his kids at least once a week—unless he was in a hypersleep chamber. Then again, he'd been away for quite a while. And since he'd returned, he'd purposely stayed out of touch while he was trying to get his affairs in order.

"I know, I know," he responded. "That's why I wanted to come by. I figured you could use a little downtime, and I want to make sure Josh and the girls remember me as more than a vid-call."

He put on his best smile. It worked. Maybe he wasn't the best looking guy on the planet, but Linda still liked his smile just fine.

She managed a weak grin in return.

"So come and get 'em," she said. "I'll make sure they're ready."

Bethany was seven. Ella was five. Josh was four. They were the best parts of his world. When the door opened and his kids ran to him, everything almost managed to make sense again. If he could have, he would have held them forever.

It never worked out that way, though. Never. There was always something that had to be taken care of. That was the way the universe worked. But for a little while—just long enough, while he took the kids to a late lunch and treated them to a movie with outlandish characters that were too bright and friendly for the real world—everything made sense again. Their emotions were like a breath of fresh air.

After he dropped them off, he stayed to catch up with Linda for a few minutes. The last time he'd visited, they'd wound up sharing her bed, although it hadn't led to anything more. Now she was feeling guilty, though, and he knew that meant she was seeing someone new. He could even tell it was serious.

The possibility didn't bother him, though. She was happy, the kids were happy, and as he headed back to his apartment, he felt rejuvenated. The weather was pleasant enough, so he walked the long blocks home, using the time to gather his wits.

As he walked, however, a sensation crept back into his mind—the sense of being observed. By the time he was home, he'd spent as much time looking over his shoulder as he had watching where he was going. Even after he'd locked the door, it left him unsettled. That wasn't how he wanted to live his life, acting like a fugitive.

6

PARANOIA

The night brought him no rest. Instead there were more nightmares, and though he couldn't be sure, he was almost certain when he woke up that he'd had another seizure. The bedclothes were on the floor and he was soaked through with sweat. His muscles felt sore and he could taste blood in his mouth. A quick look in the bathroom mirror showed that he'd bitten the hell out of his tongue. He could feel it, of course, but looking showed him the tooth marks.

After a shower Decker took advantage of the benefits that he was guaranteed with or without pay—*thanks Walt*. He made an appointment to see someone about the paranoia. For once he got lucky. The union-approved clinic had an opening for that very afternoon.

The receptionist was friendly and attractive, if ten years too young for him to do anything more than flirt. Doctor Jacoby had a face only a mother could love, but Decker had seen him before, and he was usually good at helping his patients sort things out without getting all touchy feely.

This time, however, Decker got a damned peculiar sense of déjà vu. His conversation with Jacoby seemed spookily similar to his session with Japtesh. But he shrugged it off as a symptom of the paranoia. And when he brought up the dreams, the doctor seemed particularly interested.

So he talked about the things that he could remember from his dreams. The nightmares that came so often, took him to dark places, and made him see dark things. People dying on his...

Claws?

"Where's that coming from, doc?" he asked. "There's a lot I can't remember, but I always get the sense that the people are *prey*, and of more who are begging for an end to the pain." It gave him the heebie-jeebies just to think about it. "Hell, I've never killed anyone in my life. And the people always look *wrong*, somehow. They're human, I think, and yet..."

"How do they look wrong, Alan?" Jacoby asked, and his pen raced across the notepad as he took careful, detailed notes.

Decker struggled to find the right words.

"It's like I'm seeing them, but not in any way that makes sense." He shook his head. "Okay, it's like this—have you ever looked at the stars using a topographic display?"

Jacoby's face wrinkled into a smile for just a moment.

"I can't say that I have."

"I have," he continued. "Just for the hell of it. You get the stars you're familiar with, but all you see are the lines of the topography map. It's weird, and it's a terrible waste of technology, because what you see isn't really what's there."

Damn. Shitty choice of words. He pressed on.

"Topography maps show you height and dimension as a series of concentric lines. So if you're looking at a mountain, as an example, you get these circles that show you the shape of the thing from the base all the way to the top. The tighter together the circles are the smaller the object is and the closer it is. Well, when you do that with the stars it's the same sort of thing. You see the stars, okay? But what you're really seeing are lines that draw closer together when they converge on a star and spread farther apart when there's nothing to see."

"I think I get you." The doctor was trying at least.

"Okay, so let's say you see that way, and then that you *smell* sounds. I know that doesn't make sense. That's the point here. I was seeing people in ways that didn't make sense. They looked completely wrong, completely and utterly… alien."

Jacoby nodded.

"It's like you were seeing beyond the spectrum you're used to."

"Exactly! I saw colors that I can't describe, heard things that I shouldn't have been able to hear, and could smell all sorts of things. Hell, everything I smelled had texture."

"So how do you know they were humans?"

"In the dreams I didn't," Decker replied. "I understood it when I woke up, but when I was dreaming, they were just the things I needed to hunt." He hoped that didn't sound as bad to the doctor as it did to him.

Doctor Jacoby flinched, then recovered himself, and nodded slowly. He pressed for details, but nothing Decker said seemed to do the trick. When the session ended, Jacoby gave him some little green pills that would help him sleep, and insisted that they make an appointment for the following week, same time.

Although opening up gave him some relief, by the time Decker reached his apartment, the sense of impending doom was crawling over him yet again. His head ached, and exhaustion pressed at the backs of his eyes. He was exhausted, but he was also wired.

Despite having told himself that he had no intention of taking any sort of medications, he swallowed one of the little green pills. The effects were almost immediate.

He felt his essence rise from his body below, and looked down on his slumbering shape. His face was drawn, tense and his muscles were stiff. Though he was sleeping his hands were clenched into fists and his legs twitched as much as a dog dreaming of chasing rabbits.

He looked away from himself and studied the familiar apartment. Something was different. Something was wrong. It took him a moment to realize that the walls had become dimly translucent, like stiff banks of fog instead of drywall and reinforced concrete.

He might not have noticed anything more, if the shadows within those walls had stayed still. But they moved, shifted and crawled along the insides of the heating ducts and between the wooden supports and the drywall. He could only dimly see them, but he also felt them, their hunger and need.

More than hunger.

They were angry—propelled beyond conscious thought with the need to cause damage to the source of their hatred. But before they could do so, they would need to locate their prey.

Decker stared down at himself, and at the same time he was aware that the shadow-shapes were doing the same thing, that they had noticed him in his sleep-induced paralysis.

Decker tried to reach down to touch his body, but his hands and arms weren't long enough. His feet would not quite bridge the distance. He tried to cry out a warning, but his throat was locked into silence.

Angry? No. Having found him, the shadow forms were rabid with fury, driven mad by the need to reach him, to cut into his body and rip him into fragments, body and soul. Their hatred was a silvery venom that frothed from their glistening teeth and burned whatever it touched. Their disgust radiated so intensely that it burned. They were silent, but they screamed loudly enough to blind the stars.

The shapes in the walls scrambled closer, pushing slowly through the thick stuff of the walls. Not translucent, not quite, but not what they should have been. No, these were walls of fibrous material. One hand, complete with savage claws, pushed through the heavy strands and revealed the stuff to be spider webs. The strands broke slowly, and as they did so, they allowed more of the black, glistening arm to strain down toward him.

And Decker sat up, a scream locked in his throat. His brow was stippled with perspiration and his lips pulled down in a mask of fear. He realized he wasn't breathing, and gasped for air.

His head was filled with chaotic images, slowly fading. Yet he couldn't escape the feeling that there were things crawling through the walls of his apartment building, pushing toward him through the insulation and wiring, clawing their way past water pipes and air ducts. He tried to silence his breathing, to listen in the darkness.

Nothing.

Nevertheless, he still could feel the hatred, the nearly physical need to end his life. He turned on every light in the apartment and checked under the furniture and in the closets. The very act of searching helped him to calm down, but only to a point. Had he owned a firearm he would have slipped it under his pillow.

He spent the next morning in a series of phone calls, and finally caught the train that took him to the office from which he'd worked for more than a decade.

OK, so Walt doesn't want to see me, he thought. *Well, screw him. Who needs a fucking appointment?* Instead, he just waited in the lobby until his supervisor was heading out for lunch.

Walt took one look at him and sighed.

"Alan." He wasn't a big man, and he tended to look at the floor more than at people. He had somehow lucked his way into a position of authority, and tenaciously clung to that position by never being noticed.

"Walt," Decker replied. "So… what the hell?"

Walt walked faster, and Decker kept up with him easily. As soon as they were outside and out of earshot of anyone who might overhear, Walt finally responded.

"Look, I'm trying to get everything resolved, Alan." He gazed very studiously at the ground. Whatever he was thinking or feeling wasn't strong enough for Decker to get anything from him.

"Walt, I didn't do anything wrong," he said. "I just did my job."

"You've had seizures, Alan." His voice lowered, and he leaned in closer. "More importantly, you pointed a very big finger at Weyland-Yutani. They didn't like that very much."

So there it was, in black-and-white.

"That's my job, Walt. That's what you told me to do."

"I know that, and I'm trying to fix it, believe me, but it's not going well." For a moment Decker felt the man's fear and frustration. They came across clearly before they were suppressed again. "You pissed off the wrong people with your report, Alan. I'm doing what I can. That's all I can say right now."

Walt hurried away, and lost himself in the flow of lunchtime pedestrians. Decker could have followed him, but he already had his answer. He hadn't been forgotten—not exactly—and he still had a champion on his side, such as he was. It was all just a matter of being patient.

Yet patience wasn't one of his favorite things.

Then the feeling hit him again, the sudden weight of a baleful stare. He damned near pulled the muscles in his neck as he glanced around, checking the crowd. But no one seemed to be paying him the least bit of attention.

This is getting old, really fast, he thought. Yet he continued to scan the throngs of people.

Finally Decker headed for home, taking several detours along the way, in case what he was feeling was more than just paranoia. In his apartment he kept his window screens closed, and more than once found himself glancing outside. After a few hours spent feeling stressed as hell, he finally broke down and took another of the pills.

7

THE HUNTED

When he awoke in the darkness of his bedroom, it was with an absolute certainty that he was in danger. In his dreams he might be the hunter, but here he was the one being hunted.

In some ways it was better. In most ways it was worse.

He sat bolt upright with a grunt, then tried to calm his breathing so that he could listen.

Nothing.

Suddenly four figures rushed into the room. At first he wondered if it could be another dream, but instantly he knew better. He tried to speak, but all that came from his mouth was another grunt.

Decker kicked his heel into the stomach of the figure closest to him, and heard a male voice let out a gasp. The man stumbled against the wall and knocked the lamp from the small table where he kept his alarm clock and his water glass.

Something shattered as it hit the ground and the man he'd kicked crawled along the floor, dry-retching. Decker felt a flare of satisfaction at that, but it was crushed under a tidal surge of adrenaline. He started to rise to his knees on the bed, and the second intruder swung something heavy against the side of his head. It connected hard enough to rock him back.

"Careful, Piotrowicz," a voice said in the gloom. "We need him alive."

"Nobody said he had to be intact," his assailant growled.

Decker's head rang from the blow but he shook it off as best he could and went for the one doing the growling.

"Come on, bring it, loser." The man was smaller than him and wiry. He was also a fighter. He blocked the best moves Decker had and shoved him back.

Another one tried to get into the fray, aiming to take Decker from behind and pin his arms. That was a mistake. Decker felt his intentions and reacted to them, bringing his elbow back and around to smash it into the man's face.

His attacker went down hard and Decker turned back to the one who'd hit him in the head, betting that he was the biggest threat.

"Hey, look!" The man's voice was still growling, and despite his mind telling him to close his eyes, he looked. A light exploded in the room, the glare of it enough to blind him.

The same man hit him again before he could recover, and then the other shapes were leaning over him and swinging. The fists that hit him were gloved, but that hardly softened the blows. He did his best to block the assaults. It was a vain effort. There were too many of them. He tried to fight back, might have gotten in one good punch, maybe two.

But they had the numbers and the advantage.

8

AWAKENING

This time the manual release only eluded him for a moment, and then Decker was sliding out of his confinement and trying to stand on weakened knees. He failed and slid to the ground, his limbs shaking.

His head hurt.

His jaw hurt.

Everything was blurry. He was both nauseated and hungry.

As he began to gather his wits, the low vibration under his body told him something that made no sense. He was aboard a ship again, and it was moving. He wondered if it might be another nightmare.

No, he told himself. *If this was a dream, I wouldn't feel so much like shit.* There was only one answer, absurd as it might be.

He'd been kidnapped.

This is insane. He shook his head. *Things like this only happen in movies.*

As his vision cleared, he saw that there were more chambers around him, and he could see that the people inside them were starting to stir. He looked down and realized that he wore only his underwear. The same was true of the people starting to awaken.

He finally managed to find his feet and stood, steadying himself as he looked around. Not exactly a luxury liner, though he'd have been surprised if he found otherwise. Definitely a transport—a working vessel. One quick look around the room and he saw the emergency evacuation chart showing the way to the escape pods. According to the schematic, he was aboard the *Kiangya*. Decker made a note of the name. Someone, somewhere, was going to pay for abducting him, and he needed the details if he was going to press charges.

Decker moved through a doorway and into an open area, where he found lockers. Each had a crude paper label stuck to it, with a scrawled name. One of them said "Piotrowicz," and he was fairly certain that was the name of one of the bastards who had kicked the crap out of him.

Surprisingly, one of the other lockers had "Decker" written on the paper tab. He opened the door and found clothes that were familiar enough. By the time he was done dressing, there were sounds coming from the area he'd vacated.

For a moment he considered bolting. Ultimately, however, there was nowhere to go. He wasn't a pilot and he wasn't a shipmate. He had no idea where he was and no idea where he was going. Much as the thought of escape appealed to him it would do him no good.

They'd probably just beat the crap out of him again.

So he waited, and did a few stretches to make the blood flow back to his limbs. While he was doing so, people started filing into the area to get dressed. Men and women alike, of varying ages. None of them paid him any mind.

One man with dark skin and starkly blond hair mumbled something in what sounded like Swedish and slipped past him, heading for a locker with the name "Hunsucker" on it. How anyone could move that easily after hypersleep was a mystery, but he envied the bastard.

Most of them were in excellent shape. A good number of them had military tattoos and scars to show that they'd been injured more than once. Decker glanced down at his own leg and saw the scar tissue from where the machinery had almost ended his life. It was fading, but still fresh in comparison to a lot of the ones around him.

A man whose body resembled that of a shaved gorilla walked past him and gave him the stink eye. His face was heavily tanned and craggy. His hair was a thick mane of salt and pepper. Despite the nasty look in the man's eyes, he smiled as he noticed Decker.

"Murphy! Tell Rollins her acquisition is awake."

A narrow-faced black man shook his head.

"Tell her yourself, dickhead. She's right behind me."

Sure enough, as Murphy moved another warm body came into the room. The woman was attractive and—unlike most of them—she was already dressed. Her attire was functional, her hair pulled back in a severe bun. She looked at the bruiser for a moment, and Decker could feel the crispness in her attitude. Purely business.

He'd run into this sort of person before. Somehow, he doubted the woman had a friend on the ship. She didn't seem the type to consider fraternizing with anyone. Ever.

"What can I do for you, Manning?" Rollins asked frostily.

"Your man is here and awake," the gorilla replied, and he seemed to have taken it down a notch. "Just thought you'd like to know."

She looked toward Decker, and then nodded to Manning.

"When you're ready, you can escort Mister Decker to get something to eat, then bring him to the medical unit. Let's make sure you didn't break him when you reeled him in." Manning looked as if he'd just stepped in something disgusting, but he kept his mouth shut.

As Rollins turned her back and walked away, Decker looked at her and tried to read something more. Nothing. Then again, he wasn't getting much from anyone. That was hardly unusual, though. Emotions had to be high for him to get any significant impressions.

The only one who seemed at all interested in him was a redheaded fellow, who was glaring in his direction. He was younger than the rest—maybe even a teenager.

Sometimes it was best to establish a pecking order early on. He gave back as much attitude as the kid was throwing.

"You got a problem, red?"

The redhead didn't answer, but he looked away first. That was good.

Manning got into a bodysuit quickly enough, and pointed with his chin toward a door on the far side of the room.

"Chow's that way, Decker. Come and get some food, and then we can get you all set for your meeting."

Instead of answering, Decker just nodded. He wasn't feeling very communicative. What he *was* feeling was hungrier and hungrier. There was no way to tell how long it had been since he'd eaten.

The kitchen was stocked with dried goods and reconstituted milk—and the nectar of the gods, coffee. While he drank and ate, he observed the people around him. There was camaraderie among them. It seemed clear that most of them had been together for a while. He knew the way that worked. Until he'd been sent home, he'd been getting chummy with several of his co-workers. He thought about Luke Rand, and felt a brief pang of guilt.

He'd meant to call Luke, and somehow never got to it. Above and beyond all of the others, Luke had saved his ass when the machinery was pinning him down, and he really should have been in touch. Maybe when they reached their destination—wherever *that* was—he'd find a chance.

Somehow, though, he thought it was unlikely.

He downed his second cup of coffee and the rest of his food, and then looked over at his escort. Manning was nodding toward the next destination.

"What's this about?" Decker asked as they headed down a stark hallway.

Manning's rough features spread in an aggressive example of a grin.

"I'm just here to walk you around, sport," he said, sounding as if he enjoyed Decker's confusion. "It's up to Rollins to fill you in."

"Are you people mercenaries?"

Manning nodded. "We look like Colonial Marines to you?"

"More like ex-Marines."

Manning's broad shoulders rolled into what could have been a shrug or—or maybe he was just stretching.

"Most are," he said. "A few decided to sign up without prior experience."

Before Decker could ask any more questions they'd reached their destination. The medical station was fairly standard, with two examining tables and a bank of screens showing readouts that didn't make sense to anyone who hadn't gone to med school. Rollins was standing there, looking at one of the displays.

"Mister Decker," she said, barely glancing in his direction. "We haven't been properly introduced. I'm Andrea Rollins. I'll be your handler for this trip." She gestured for him to have a seat on the closest table. "Let's get you thoroughly examined."

Handler? He bristled at the word, but did his best not to show it. As he moved toward the table, he saw that Manning situated himself near the door, standing in a casual pose that still made it clear he was ready—maybe eager—for anything Decker might try. There was an edginess coming off of him, and each of his fists looked large enough to wrap around Decker's entire head.

"I'm sure you have questions, Mister Decker. Feel free to ask them." Rollins gestured for him to lie back, and he did, craning his head to look at her.

"How about, why did somebody kidnap me from my apartment?"

"That's an easy one," she replied. "We needed you here."

"Who's *we*?"

Rollins finally made eye contact.

"Weyland-Yutani."

The monitors around him lit up as she flipped a switch. She looked away from him and studied his readouts.

"Is that right?" he said. "Nobody thought to ask me, before sending a goon squad?"

"The general consensus was that your answer would be no. Currently that's not an option." She continued looking over the diagnostics, and he shook his head.

"All of this because of a fucking report? Have you people lost your fucking minds?" Decker sat up fast and Manning looked his way, his body tensing.

Rollins switched off the readouts and shook her head.

"No, and no," she answered. "Your report on New Galveston was annoying, I'll admit, but it was hardly worth kidnapping you or anyone else."

"Well then, what the hell's going on?" he pressed. "How about some straight answers?" His irritation flared and he slipped from the examination table. Manning took a step nearer.

Rollins held up a hand, and the mercenary stopped. Then she turned to Decker.

"That's what we're here for," she said. "Answers. And the first question relates to your condition. I was concerned that you'd been damaged when Mister Manning and his team caught you, but aside from a few bruises, you're in good health." She walked over to a video display and tapped a few buttons. "Physically, at least.

"Mentally, however, you are showing rather substantial signs of Post Traumatic Stress Disorder, which is very curious when you consider that your only real trauma was a minimally intrusive wound to your leg."

Decker stared hard at her, but said nothing.

"Frankly there's nothing in your psychological profile that indicates you'd be so put upon by the damage that it would cause that sort of a reaction. Not only do the medical doctors agree, so do the three separate psychologists who've examined you since your return."

Three? Decker frowned.

"The examinations you endured were bought and paid for by the company. At first we thought we might use you as a scapegoat, on the chance that your report might lead to a lawsuit. But then something more important emerged. You acted very strangely when you were injured, Mister Decker. Strangely enough that we took notice."

"But you just said that the company didn't give a damn about my report."

"I did, and we don't." Rollins smiled. The expression played around her thin lips. "But before that, when you were injured, you made some comments—comments that were recorded for the official record." She walked closer and he could smell the faint aroma of honeysuckle from her perfume. "When you made your claims against Weyland-Yutani, we acquired the recordings, on the off chance that they might be advantageous. Can you imagine what they told us?"

He shook his head. "Not a clue."

"They were filled with psychotic ramblings. There was enough there to put you on medical probation, quite easily. PTSD is a dangerous situation when you work off-world as much as you do. A few calls, a few extra forms filled out and *voila*, you're on medical leave."

"Is there a point at the end of this?"

She smiled again.

"You talked, and we listened, and then we ran those recordings through filters designed to scan for specific words. It's rather standard on our end. There are a lot of... investigations we've initiated over the years. In your case, the words you used and the order in which they were used threw up a red flag." She paused, and then continued.

"Have you ever heard of the *Nostromo*?"

The name sent a shudder through him, though he had no idea why.

"No," he said truthfully. "Should I have?"

"Not at all, and that's exactly the point. You should have never heard of the *Nostromo* because the records on that particular incident were sealed a long time ago."

"What are you talking about?"

"Does the name Ellen Ripley mean anything to you? Or Amanda Ripley-McClaren?"

"No."

That half smile again.

"Actually, I wouldn't have been too surprised if you knew the names. According to the research we've done, you are very likely their descendant. The records get a little wobbly, what with the crisis on Earth and the... troubles the company experienced a while back. But the genetics don't lie."

Decker shook his head.

"So what the *hell* does this have to do with anything?" he demanded.

"Well, as a result of our investigations, we've determined that you have far more use to Weyland-Yutani than as a simple scapegoat." She paused to examine another display, and he waited for her to continue. After a few moments he was rewarded. "You see, your ancestor had a long history with us. She worked onboard a freighter called the *Nostromo* when it ran across a distress signal, and responded.

"The signal's origin was alien in nature."

That caught his attention.

"What's the big deal?" he asked. "We've encountered loads of alien races."

"Ellen Ripley and the rest of the crew discovered something... different. Xenomorph XX121, to be precise." Rollins reached over and activated a video feed. A moment later he saw a slightly grainy image of himself, unconscious and strapped to a medical bed. His video doppelganger was lying flat and restrained, when abruptly his entire body went rigid.

His eyes opened wide, and he started screaming.

9

WITNESS

Decker's skin crawled as he watched. At first there was no sound, but his lips were moving, and when the recorded image of him fell back on the bed, Rollins adjusted a setting.

"How can anything be that vicious? N... spiders? *Spiders!*" Decker tensed instinctively as his voice crackled and slurred, and Rollins fast-forwarded before letting the recording play again. "Blood burns... through the steel... No, not me. *Someone else!*" His voice broke into sobs, and then he continued.

"You really think? Have you seen one of them, close up?" His words wavered, rose in pitch. And then lowered to a different tone, with the hint of an accent he couldn't place. "No. None of us have." And again. Higher, almost feminine. "No, of course not. You're still alive."

The ramblings faded until all they could hear was slurred mumbles and the occasional whimper. Decker's skin crawled as he listened. It was like eavesdropping on a conversation, but with one person playing all the parts. And the words chilled him to the bone, yet he didn't know why. He clenched his fists to get a grip.

Rollins turned the feed off.

"It goes on for a couple of hours. That was recorded during your second seizure, while you were being treated planetside. The first was in the field, immediately after you were injured."

"How long was I like that?"

"As I said, a couple of hours. The best doctors we could consult all said the same thing, really. Extreme panic, delusional ramblings, paranoia, and signs of a complete emotional breakdown." Rollins shook her head. "We could have ruined you right then, Mister Decker, but you gave us reason to keep you around." She smiled again.

He was learning to hate her smile.

"Some of the phrases, the names you employed, were flagged and filed a long while back. From incidents that took place well over a hundred years ago, actually. Your use of those phrases activated long dormant files that were then downloaded to my computer."

"What sort of incidents?"

"As I said, your ancestor was assigned to the *Nostromo*. What I didn't tell you was that three hundred and seventy-five years ago Ellen Ripley *destroyed* that ship—a mining transport that was fully loaded with ore and on its way back home. She claimed she had done so to eliminate an alien threat." Rollins paused, and her expression hardened. "That could have been the end of her career, but we were generous. We hired her as a consultant, and sent her back to the planet where the alien life-form had first been encountered.

"You see, she claimed the creature was extremely dangerous. But it was far more than dangerous—it was an asset. An asset Weyland-Yutani should have controlled. *Would* have controlled, had it not been for her actions."

Rollins played with the video monitor a second time and the face of an attractive, dark-haired woman appeared.

"This was Ellen Ripley. Your ancestor." Decker looked at the image and felt his guts roil. *Not right.* It was a familiar face, but...

She looked too *human*.

He turned back to Rollins.

"Did she find the aliens?" he asked.

"She found something. All we know for certain is that the colony on LV426 was lost when a terraforming engine was critically damaged, and overloaded." Decker had worked with terraforming engines. He understood how devastating an explosion could be, coming from one of the gigantic machines. "She escaped aboard a warship named the *Sulaco*, and sent a final transmission, but it was garbled. What she might or might not have said could never be clearly recovered. We think the reactor went critical, and distorted the signal.

"Ellen Ripley and her daughter both halted attempts to capture and study the Xenomorphs. More importantly, they did so while costing Weyland-Yutani a great deal of money and considerable resources.

"It's been a very long time since we've had even the faintest trace of the alien life-form. We had all but given up hope of ever acquiring one. That is, until you came along."

"I'm sorry, but again, what has this got to do with me?"

That smile again. Granted, Rollins was an attractive woman, but there was nothing pretty about the expression.

"Your episodes, and what you said as they occurred, give us reason to assume that somehow—and believe me, we're investigating the possibilities—you seem to have established a connection to these creatures. You've described things you cannot have seen—described aspects of physiology that, when assessed by our computers, come close to describing the life-form Ellen Ripley claimed she'd encountered."

"No… it's impossible…" But his voice trailed away as he said it. At the mention of spiders, he'd nearly jumped from his skin. And the sensation continued—he felt as if he was choking, unable to catch his breath, and his insides were tied in a knot.

He closed his eyes, tried to force the mental assault back but failed. The stench of burning metal ran through his mind and overwhelmed his senses. He felt bile pulse and try to force its way out of his stomach at the thought of something pushing past his gag reflex, something hot and wet and violent. He could damn near feel spindly limbs wrapping around his head.

Another convulsive shudder ran through him. But why? Spiders had never bothered him before. Why now, all of a sudden?

At the door, Manning crossed his arms and snorted. Decker shot him a sour look.

Rollins regarded him coldly.

"Impossible is no longer a consideration, Mister Decker. Whatever it is you're experiencing, it's enough to make my employers want you on this trip. And what they want, they get."

"Are you going back to the same place again—to LV426?" For some reason, the idea put him on the verge of panic. He resisted an urge to run his fingers through his hair to check for webs.

"Not exactly," she said, and her attitude really started to bug him. He was running out of patience.

"If you're trying to build to something dramatic here, don't bother," he said. "You've already got my attention, and it's not as if I'm going anywhere you don't want me to go. So what the *hell* do you want with me?"

"Fair enough," she said, and she leaned in toward him. "You're an empath."

"Excuse me?"

"We've run the tests." Her voice was cool and professional now, all of the fake emotion gone. "Whether or not you're aware of it, Mister Decker, you have what could be classified as low-level telepathic ability. It's not that uncommon—we've employed others of your kind, in the past—but in your case it's left you in a very unfortunate situation. If you have, indeed, developed a link to the alien life-forms on New Galveston, then you may be the one person who can lead us to them."

The sound of her voice faded, disappearing behind a sharp ringing in Decker's ears at the sound of the planet's name. His chest locked on him, and he attempted to shrug it off. He shook his head to clear it.

"Then *that's* where we're headed," he said. "What makes you think your aliens are there?" But then he thought about the Sea of Sorrows, and it began to make sense. The toxicity had to come from somewhere.

"Blood burns…"

"I think you know, Mister Decker." She wasn't smiling now. "And if those creatures are as deadly as Ripley indicated, then we'll need every advantage we can have at our disposal. Someone who is directly linked to them could prove to be invaluable."

Decker shook his head.

"Not a chance in hell," he said, even as he pushed back the fear. "Even if you're right, you can't make me help you. What you're doing is—"

"*Wrong!*" Rollins's voice cracked through the air like a whip, and even Manning jumped at the bark. She leaned in, and peered directly at him. "We *own* you. You will go back to New Galveston, and you will help us, because you owe it to the company. There's a debt to be paid, and if you ever hope to regain something that resembles a *life*, you have to start following orders."

But he still wasn't buying it.

"What's this 'debt' shit?" he said. "I don't even work for Weyland-Yutani. I don't owe them a damn thing." He stood up and scowled down at her, refusing to be intimidated. For all of her smiles and her assertions, she was just a pencil pusher, same as him. "The way I see it, you're guilty of kidnapping—and that's still a crime, even for your precious company. Keep it up, I'll find other charges I can bring around, when this is over." He stepped closer to her, seeking to gain the upper hand.

Manning tensed, but stayed where he was.

"I'm afraid you're not catching on here, Mister Decker." Rollins didn't budge. There was an edge to her words. "And I *don't* appreciate being threatened."

With that, she lifted a hand and gestured. The next thing Decker knew, Manning had a hand on his shoulder. The fingers clamped down with a stern, silent warning.

Decker chose to ignore it. He swept his arm around, knocking Manning's grip aside.

"Don't touch me."

Manning's expression barely changed, but the merc shook his head. He stepped in close and shoved his mass against Decker. It might not have worked on a planet, but the gravity on ships was always a little bit lighter than it seemed, and Decker staggered back.

Manning stepped in again, and brought his elbow into Decker's chest. The impact was solid enough to hurt, but not to incapacitate.

Decker shoved back in retaliation, and then hit the man in the face with a right. The impact carried him forward, and the two of them stumbled across the examination room, careening off one of the tables.

Rollins watched the entire scuffle with what seemed to be mild amusement.

The merc brought his fist around and drove it into Decker's stomach so fast that there was no chance to stop it. The punch was perfectly placed, driving all of the air from his body and sending him to his hands and knees, retching. He could handle himself in a fight, but Manning was apparently just plain better at it.

Rollins stepped in.

"Now that we know you're essentially of sound body," she said, staring down at him coldly, "there's no need to be gentle with you."

After a couple of minutes his insides stopped heaving, and he caught his breath. Decker lurched back to his feet and glared at Manning, who just shook his head a little. A thin trail of blood trickled down from the side of the mercenary's mouth, smearing where he'd tried to wipe it away.

At least he had that. He'd made the man notice him.

"Don't," Manning growled. "You really don't want to."

Rollins motioned for him to be silent, then turned back to Decker and spoke again.

"Let's get this clear," she said. "Ellen Ripley worked for the Weyland-Yutani Corporation, and signed contracts. She owed us a very large amount of money, and she never returned—never paid her debt. In addition to wrecking not one, but two ships, and costing the company what currently amounts to billions of dollars of property damage, she also destroyed a refinery. That's deliberate sabotage.

"So technically, she and her descendants *still* owe a very large debt to the company. The contracts still exist, and the wording is delightfully precise. Even if you could find a court that would challenge us, believe me, Weyland-Yutani is perfectly willing to spend the time and money needed to rip you into little pieces in front of a judge."

"But you abducted me!"

"Prove it."

"Excuse me?"

"Prove it," Rollins repeated, and the smile returned. "Call the police. Oh, wait—there are no police out here on the rim. Just corporations and the Colonial laws, most of which are enforced by Colonial Marines... plus private security forces like the ones we've hired to escort you back to New Galveston." Her eyes cut to Manning.

"Mister Manning, what is your duty today?"

Manning didn't even blink as he spoke.

"To safely escort Mister Decker back to New Galveston, and to retrieve the biological samples needed to pay back the debts that he and his family owe to Weyland-Yutani."

"And who hired you?"

"You did," he replied. "On behalf of Weyland-Yutani."

"Did you at any point see anyone force Mister Decker to join us on this journey?"

"No ma'am," Manning replied flatly. "He came of his own volition." The mercenary grinned.

"Then why did he come?"

"He said something about proving that he was capable of returning to work." He shrugged. "I wasn't really listening. He whines too much."

Rollins looked back to Decker.

"I have thirty-five people onboard this transport who will gladly verify that story. I have documents with your signature to verify that you signed on for this job, in exchange for substantial compensation and to avoid a lawsuit that was being brought against you for the attempted blackmail of Weyland-Yutani officials."

"The hell you say." Decker started to move toward her, but stopped when Manning slid a step in his direction. "You've covered all of the angles, haven't you?"

"Hold that thought," she replied. "We're almost done. I have papers signed by three witnesses to your first seizure, who have all stated that the accident was caused by your own negligence.

They've agreed to make the necessary statements in a court of law, should it come to that."

She stepped toward him, until her face was just inches from his. He looked at her eyes, and didn't see even the faintest hint of human emotion.

"And lastly, Mister Decker," she said, "I have the exact address of your ex-wife and three children. In fact, I can tell you where they are at this very moment."

"My kids?" he said.

"Bethany. Ella. Joshua." Rollins's voice softened, but he knew better than to think that it was genuine. "They're lovely children. And you know what? We own them the same way that we own you. Piss me off, Mister Decker, and I can make their lives very uncomfortable, for as long as they live. Every debt that Ellen Ripley accrued will be yours, and if you don't cooperate, it will be theirs.

"And on the off chance that you don't work out as a tool for finding what we're looking for, we can always see if some of your more interesting traits were passed along genetically." Gone was the softness. "Do you understand me?"

The room seemed colder. Alan settled back on the examination table, barely aware that he'd done so. He stared at the woman in front of him, and reached out...

Nothing. He wondered exactly what sort of psychotic bitch could so casually threaten his children, without broadcasting the least bit of guilt.

Even Manning had lost all trace of his earlier smugness. He was staring at Rollins, as well, and there was a hint of fear coming off of him.

"*Do you understand me, Mister Decker?*" She asked the question again while staring hard into his eyes. "Play by the rules, and all of this goes away. You go home and you get on with your life. Cross me, fail me, do anything at all to make this mission fall apart, and I will bring down the wrath of God—or worse—upon you and your family.

"Do you understand me?"

It took him a minute to remember to breathe. To remember to answer her.

"Yeah," he said. "Yes. I understand you."

"Excellent." She smiled. "We'll get to the debriefing soon. In the meantime, go relax. We'll be arriving at New Galveston within the next few hours."

10

B U S I N E S S   A S   U S U A L

After Decker left the examination room, Rollins stayed and looked over the readouts again, and smiled.

A few moments later she began typing her report.

Long before the ship was in proper orbit around New Galveston, the paperwork had been completed and sent off.

When the response came from her superiors, Rollins read it silently. Then she accessed the ship's onboard computers and deleted all evidence that the transmissions had ever occurred.

11

DECKER

"That is a properly heartless bitch."

Manning said it with a certain admiration in his voice. Or maybe it was lust. The man seemed like the type who lived to get laid.

Decker didn't reply. He didn't trust that he wouldn't say something to provoke the man into kicking his ass. Pissing Manning off seemed like a very bad idea, but that didn't mean they were going to be friends.

"It's nothing personal, Decker," the mercenary continued. "Part of my job is to protect Rollins."

"Fuck yourself, Manning," he replied. "Nothing personal." There were limits.

Manning just chuckled.

They reached the recreation room, where the rest of the mercenaries were gathered. Thirty-five men and women were looking over their weapons, and there was a steady murmur of conversation. There were twenty or so men and the rest were women who looked like they could hold their own in any sort of conflict. It wasn't about the build—it was about the attitude. As a whole they moved like long-time combat veterans. No one wore a uniform, and most were dressed in clothes that were well worn and comfortable. The whole gathering looked up as they entered, and the murmur died away.

Manning spoke first.

"Everyone, this is Alan Decker," he said. "He's going to be working with us planetside. Treat him with respect, and everything will be fine." He looked hard at the skinny redheaded kid. "That goes for you, too, Garth." The kid seemed like he wanted to say something, but the glare Manning shot him shut him up.

Garth. The kid that he'd kicked when they were abducting him, if Decker was right. He looked the right size, and he'd been staring daggers since they came out of cryo.

Most of the crew had patches with names on them, a giveaway that they'd been Colonial Marines at one time. Decker looked at Garth and stepped closer.

"Pretty sure I nailed you when you came to my apartment," he said. "Here's the deal. You don't hold a grudge for that, I won't hold a grudge for what you did to me." He wasn't sure he could manage that, but was willing to give it a try.

The skinny redhead just returned his stare, wanting to pull out his manhood and measure it, but Decker was a seasoned pro. He'd had to stare down locals more than once in his career. The kid looked away first.

"Adams!" Manning said loudly, and a woman sitting in a corner of the room shot him a look, then offered a playful grin.

"I'm right here," she said. "No reason to bellow. Dave over here is loud enough for everyone." The man she spoke about sat right next to her and looked up, surprised. He never said a word, however.

Manning chuckled and shook his head.

"It's time for your good deed of the day, Adams. Talk to Decker here and get him as prepped as you can for our little expedition."

The woman eyed him from head to toe and he returned the favor. She had short-cropped auburn hair and brown eyes. Her skin had the sort of tan that came from working out in the sun, and her face and arms were scattered with freckles. He wondered where else she might have them.

"Close your mouth, chief," she said amiably. "You're going to attract flies." As she moved closer, he gauged her at about eight inches shorter than he was, a hundred pounds lighter, and not the least bit intimidated. She worked with men who could break him in half, and might be able to do so herself. He liked her immediately. Something about strong, confident women did that to him.

Not with Rollins though. That woman was just evil.

When he didn't say anything, Adams just shrugged and pointed.

"Let's see about getting you some equipment," she said.

"Equipment?"

"Listen, we don't have a lot of spares but I think we can probably find you a little bit of armor, and maybe a weapon or two."

He started to ask why, but then he remembered the dreams, and the sheer malevolence they brought. Suppressing a shudder, he just nodded.

"Sounds good to me," he said. "I think I'd kind of like to survive this."

"Then let's see what we can find for you." She set off toward what he assumed was their arsenal, and he followed. She continued talking over her shoulder.

"Listen, I don't know what happened back on Earth, Decker. It's not any of my business. All I know is you're here now, and you're supposed to work with us. So when you get the equipment, remember whose side you're on."

"What do you mean?"

Adams stopped walking and turned to look at him so quickly that he almost tripped over himself coming to a halt.

"I figure you probably aren't here by choice." She looked hard at him, studying his face and his expression, locking eyes with him for a few heartbeats. "I get it. You were shanghaied. You're probably pissed off. Just don't try to take it out on us. We're grunts. We're here to do a job.

"If you get in the way of that job, you're going to get hurt," she added.

Decker nodded. What she said made a world of sense.

"Not on my agenda." Trying not to be obvious, he studied her face, attempting to see beyond the surface. She was a little nervous, but he was fairly certain it had nothing to do with him, and everything to do with the upcoming drop to an unfamiliar territory. "You're right," he added. "I don't want to be here. But I'm not going to blame you or anyone else in your group. You're not responsible for fucking with me. I already have the people I need to blame, and they're the ones who hired you guys."

"Understood," she offered. "But it still needed to be said. This isn't the first time we've worked with people who were 'volunteered,' and a couple of assholes got stupid. But we've learned from our mistakes. You can bet there's going to be somebody watching every move you make."

He just nodded, keeping his face neutral.

"I just want to go home," he said truthfully. "And I want to get there alive. Anything you can do to help that happen is just going to make us friends."

Adams smiled. It lit her entire face.

"Good," she said. "Now, have you ever fired a weapon before?"

"I've used a plasma drill, and did some hunting when I was a kid."

"Where the hell did you go hunting on Earth, and what did you hunt?"

"My uncle was in a preserve club. We went hunting for deer every couple of years."

"You ever get one?" She eyed him critically.

"No. Mostly they brought me to carry supplies."

"Yeah. I thought I saw the eye of a killer in you." She sniggered and started walking again. "That's okay. We'll get you prepped."

He nodded, fully aware that she couldn't see the gesture. He did need to get prepped, though. There was something waiting for him on New Galveston, and he intended to be ready for it. One thing his uncle and his father had always said on those damned hunting trips was that he should trust his instincts.

He intended to listen to that advice.

Adams showed him how to use two different firearms—a hand-held throwback pistol she called a "reaper," which fired classic .44 caliber slugs, and a 50 watt plasma rifle that worked a lot like the drill he'd trained on back in the day.

The difference was that the rifle fired at long range, and let out small bursts that would blow a hole through the average ship's hull. For that reason Adams trained him how to fire the weapon without a charge in place. In theory, he'd be able to handle the thing when the time came.

She let him take the reaper with him, but didn't let him have any clips—not just yet. Apparently she had to get everything cleared through Manning before allowing him to carry live rounds.

He didn't like it, but he understood it.

Though there wasn't much armor to spare, she did find him a helmet that fit fairly well and an impact vest that would stop most conventional weaponry. It wouldn't do a damned thing to slow down a plasma discharge, of course, but very little could.

The training session lasted close to two hours, and ended when Manning called over the ship's intercom to let them know it was time for the debriefing. Decker found himself surprisingly disappointed. For a little while he had almost been having fun. Adams seemed to feel the same way about it.

When they were all settled in the rec room again Rollins showed up and gave them a rundown on what was expected.

"New Galveston is a colonized planet," she said. "The atmosphere is breathable, and the gravity is roughly eighty-eight percent what you'd find on Earth, so while there will be benefits, you'll need to exercise caution." Decker knew exactly what she meant. Lower gravity meant better endurance, and provided a general feeling of greater strength. But that could be deceptive. While a person could clear a greater distance when running or jumping, more than one novice had knocked himself senseless when working in reduced gravity without taking the time to properly adjust.

"Muller... Muller... Muller!" It was Adams who started the chant, and half a dozen joined in while a bruiser with heavy freckles and copper-colored hair blushed furiously and grinned. Judging from the catcalls, he had probably knocked himself out in the past, and the rest weren't about to let it go. He almost smiled at that.

Rollins waited until they calmed down, and then started up again.

"There are three major settlements, and train tubes that lead to them, but none of them will be close by, so don't expect an easy time of it if you wander off and need backup or support."

Several of the group nodded their heads. Though they all seemed at ease, Decker noticed that all of them were paying close attention.

"Rutledge is the closest city, and it's approximately fifteen miles away by rail. The tube trains don't quite reach the mining colony, but there are regular trucks running to and from the dig."

Wait. Mining colony?

"What mining colony?" Decker was barely aware that he'd spoken. Rollins looked in his direction.

"Since you were last planetside, the company discovered that there was, in fact, a previous dig at the site of your Sea of Sorrows. A trimonite mine, and it's been restarted. There's an active vein, and it should provide a valuable revenue stream—which is fortunate. New Galveston has levied hefty claims against us, for failing to terraform the planet to their specifications." The look she proffered said *fuck you* without any words.

Rollins continued, "There is a crew already in place, medical teams are already available and you'll be pleased to know that there will be a barracks for your use."

Several of the mercs smiled, and Decker was right there with them. He'd been in more than one situation where the best he could hope for was a tent. Actual barracks were damned near a sign of luxury, by comparison.

"There's more to this, of course. And that's why we're footing the bill for your freelancers, Mister Manning." Decker suppressed a laugh. *Freelancers.* It just sounded so much nicer than *thugs-for-hire.* "When the mine was cleared and made operational, we discovered the remains of a vessel. The ship we located is not of terrestrial origin."

She let that settle in with the mercenaries. Decker licked his lips. Suddenly his mouth felt inexplicably dry.

Manning spoke up.

"Is it a configuration that's been encountered before?" he asked.

"No," she replied. "And if anyone would be able to identify

alien tech, it would be Weyland-Yutani." Rumor had it that the company had made several of their more radical leaps in technology by retrofitting alien artifacts for "new" advancements.

"Here's the thing," Rollins continued. "Based on a prior agreement, the company has full rights to the land that's being used. Whatever we find, they own. That's why you're here. We intend to keep it that way. As soon as the vessel was discovered, the digs stopped. They've been waiting until your team arrived.

"Do we expect trouble?" she added. "No, we do not. But we intend to be prepared for it."

Decker crossed his arms. As much as Weyland-Yutani seemed to have the government in their pockets, back on Earth there were rules that had to be followed—rules even they couldn't circumvent. All alien technologies were subject to quarantine, and there were procedures that needed to be followed in order to certify any claims of ownership.

But Weyland-Yutani didn't intend to follow the rules. Decker knew it. So did the "freelancers." That was the reason for the strong-arm tactics. It had nothing to do with his pissant reports— once they had identified Decker as an asset, they'd made certain nothing stood in the way of acquiring his "services."

Manning beat him to the next question.

"Any chance there are active life-forms down there?" He didn't look pleased with the possibility.

Rollins surprised him. She told the truth.

"Yes—in fact, we're hoping for it. That's one of the reasons Mister Decker is along. We believe he might have... unique insights into the life-forms you might encounter."

"What sort of insights?" Manning again. Regardless of what he thought about the man, but Decker had to admit that he asked all the right questions.

"That's hard to say with any clarity," she replied. "Mister Decker is a low-level empath. He seems to have established some sort of unique connection with the life-forms. He's essentially along to help you sniff them out."

So much for keeping our secret, Decker thought. *Sorry, Dad.*

He noticed several of the mercenaries looking at him with an undisguised combination of curiosity and suspicion. He glanced at Adams, and was pleased to see that she seemed unperturbed.

"And if we find these aliens of yours?" Manning asked. "What do we do then?"

Rollins looked around the room, her expression serious.

"You know the drill," she said flatly. "We want samples of any technologies you find, but your first priority is those life-forms. We want aliens, and we want them alive.

"Each of you has access to an information file. The file belongs to Weyland-Yutani and is considered extremely confidential." She paused to look at the mercenaries one after the other. "Do *not* take this lightly. Do not attempt to copy the information, it's been heavily coded and protected. Your access ends the second you leave the *Kiangya*. Some of the information has been redacted. It's strictly 'need to know,' and covers everything we've learned about the Xenomorph XX121 alien life-form, in the 260 years we've spent trying to capture one."

Her hard-ass attitude didn't seem to faze Manning in the least. He stared back just as hard.

"What do you know about these things?" he pressed. "Are they dangerous?"

"Most likely," she acknowledged. "And are you highly trained professionals who charge exorbitant rates?"

"Yeah, we are," he said. "But that doesn't mean we go in blind. So I'm gonna ask you again—what do you know about these things?"

She took a moment, staring at him, her features entirely unreadable. Then she continued.

"We don't know much, aside from what's contained in the files—our experience with them is limited. They seem to be adaptive. They *are* aggressive. What little data we have indicates that they might secrete a liquid that's toxic, or caustic, or both—there are some details concerning their physiology, and the different stages of their development. They seem to have bred to hunt, and should be approached with extreme caution."

Manning snorted.

"So while we're disposable, you want us to keep them alive."

Rollins shrugged.

"We didn't send you along as glorified security guards. There are three-dozen of you, including Mister Decker. You are being extremely well-compensated," she said. "We expect you to use proper precautions, and be prepared to defend yourselves, but we also expect you to remember that a goodly portion of your pay is decided by how successfully you follow the directives you've been given." She stepped closer to him. "I'm sure you have plenty of your own toys, suited to the occasion. On top of those, we've provided you with everything you need to restrain your targets, once you've located them. That includes foamers."

"What the hell is a foamer?" Adams said. She glanced at Manning, to see if he was pissed at her for speaking up, but he didn't seem overly worried about it.

"A foamer is useless in combat," Rollins explained. "The containers are too bulky and weigh enough to cause problems, especially if you aren't on a level surface, but if you manage to capture one of the creatures, you can essentially cement it in place. Its contents harden fast, and the foam is porous enough that it shouldn't prove lethal to the captive. The company has ways of removing the foam when you deliver your packages.

"So there you have it." She smiled. "Play nice, boys and girls, and you will be richly rewarded."

"That means there's a pretty bonus waiting, if we don't screw this up," Manning said, and he looked at each member of his team. "So let's do it right the first time."

That won him a few smiles.

Decker just felt his stomach churn.

"What if all we find are a bunch of dead aliens?" Manning looked back at Rollins. Decker suspected that the merc already knew the answers to all the questions he was asking, but that he was asking them for the benefit of his troops.

"You still get paid, and handsomely, as long as you return at least a few of the bodies intact."

"And if they're not intact?"

"You get less." Rollins stood a little straighter, indicating that the Q-and-A was at an end. "Any other questions?"

"When do we start?" That one came from Adams, and it elicited murmurs of agreement from the rest.

"We'll be over the drop site in another hour and fifteen minutes. So I'd recommend getting your gear together. In the meantime, study the information in the files. Your lives may depend on it."

"You heard the lady," Manning bellowed. "Let's get moving!" He clapped his hands together with a loud report, and started walking. His people followed quickly, but Decker stayed behind for another moment.

Rollins took the hint.

"Something on your mind, Mister Decker?"

"You never said anything about the ship," he said. "Why keep it from me?"

"We thought we'd give you a little time to adjust to your new… circumstances." Which he took to mean, *We didn't want you to freak out, and try anything stupid.* But he didn't say any of the things he wanted to say.

"If this goes right, then what do I get out of it?" he continued. "Monetarily, that is. I mean, aside from not getting screwed in a court of law."

She looked surprised, but the expression was fleeting. He was speaking her language.

"I'll look into the details," she said. "As long as you deliver, I'm sure we can arrange something, shall we say, suitably generous."

He nodded, and turned to follow the mercenaries. As far as he was concerned, they were better company.

12

DESCENT

There was nothing fun about free-fall in a drop ship. Discussing it during many late night drinking sessions with Rand and the rest of the old crew, Decker had realized that his aversion came down to a lack of control. He didn't like having his life in the hands of someone he didn't know.

And that was what you did every time you hit the atmosphere and rode the air currents through the gravitational pull of a planet, all the while hoping the pilot of the deathtrap you were riding would be capable of landing safely.

So he had a white-knuckle grip on the handholds on either side of his seat. He wasn't alone. Several of the mercenaries were looking pretty green, and broadcasting nervousness that added layers to his own feelings of edginess. Knowing the cause helped, but he couldn't exactly ask them to calm down.

Adams sat across from him, and seemed unfazed. Dave, the man who never seemed to have anything to say, sat to her left. She stuck her foot out, reached across the narrow space between them, and tapped at Decker's boot. He looked her way, and she winked.

"Pritchett likes to shake things up," she said.

"He the pilot?"

"Yeah."

"Remind me to kick his ass, will you?"

Adams chuckled, and next to her one of the guys groaned.

"Get in line," the groaner said. "I'm gonna gut the bastard one of these days." The name on his fatigues said "Piotrowicz." He was lean and hard and scruffy. The Colonials would have likely kept him shaved and showered, but being a "freelancer," he chose to look like a sheepdog.

Decker remembered the name, and repressed an instinct to hold a grudge. Piotrowicz was one of the kidnappers.

"Petey threatens to gut everyone," Adams said. "He thinks it's charming." She shook her head. "It's not."

Piotrowicz shot her a one-fingered salute. She punched him playfully in the arm. Though apparently "playfully" was different among the mercenaries, because she hit him hard enough to bruise, and both of them laughed.

The entire ship bounced and rattled and lurched hard to the right. Piotrowicz groaned again, and given their first meeting, Decker couldn't muster much sympathy. Manning looked toward the pilot's cabin as if he was considering heading up there and breaking heads. He might have, too, but it would have meant risking bouncing across the cabin. Instead he reached for the radio he already had strapped to his shoulder.

"What the fuck are you doing, Pritchett?" he demanded.

"Got turbulence, boss," was the tinny reply.

"No shit, man," Manning said. "What, are you *trying* to find it?" He grimaced as the whole thing rumbled and rolled again. "I think you might have missed some there."

"Bad atmospheric storms. I didn't find them, they found us."

Decker didn't like the sound of that. He remembered the New Galveston weather being sedate at the worst of times. It had rained, true, but not often in the daylight hours. That might mean they were heading down at night—which bothered him even more.

Some things see better in the dark. He scowled at the thought. He didn't need to do that to himself. He had enough crap going on in his head. *Too much.*

A few moments later the worst of the turbulence faded, and the people around him relaxed a bit. Piotrowicz shook his head.

"Seriously. I need to mess him up."

"Well, he said there were storms," Decker offered.

"Just seems like, no matter where we go, he finds the worst weather. No one's that unlucky *all* the time."

"Yeah?" Adams elbowed her neighbor with less force than she'd punched him. "Then how do you explain your love life?"

Before Piotrowicz could respond, the ship veered sharply and then slowed its descent.

"How's the weather, Pritchett?" Manning sounded annoyed. He looked it, too.

Decker was okay with that.

"Weather looks good, chief. But there might be a problem."

"What sort of problem?" The head mercenary's frown deepened, and his craggy face looked like stone.

"I'm not getting any responses to my hails."

"Think it's the storm?"

"Negatory. I'm picking up commercial signals, but I'm not getting anything from the site where we're landing."

"Maybe your weather did in their communications."

"Yeah, about that," came the response. "There wasn't *exactly* a storm." Pritchett sounded guilty.

Adams chuckled. Muller waved a fist in the air, but he grinned as he did it. Dave said nothing.

Piotrowicz mumbled something murderous.

"We'll discuss that later," Manning said. "For right now, just get us landed, and let's see what we find."

Pritchett put them down gently, and they did, indeed, land at night. As they disembarked, the air was pleasantly cool, if a bit damp. It had been raining and the Sea of Sorrows was a leveled playing field of darkness.

Several people came out to meet them. Among them was Lucas Rand, whose bulldog face fell into a slack look of shock, and then lit up with a fierce smile. Before Decker could do much of anything, the heavy man had him in a bear hug, and was lifting him easily off the ground.

"Good to see you, brother!"

Alan felt a wash of affection run through him. He hadn't realized how much he liked the other man until he saw him again. They had always worked well together, but sometimes Decker forgot that. He tended toward forgetting anything but the work, on most occasions. It was easier that way.

The mercenaries made a few snide comments, but Decker ignored them for the moment and walked with his friend.

"What the hell's been going on around here, Luke?"

"You name it, it's been happening, man." He shook his head and pointed at a dark patch on the long run of sand. A silhouette clearly defined the edges of a Quonset hut, illuminated by a few ground lights, and nothing more. "Remember the trimonite? It wasn't a fluke. There was a *lot* of it. Apparently it's a really rich vein, and even though you kind of pissed off a lot of people, your report led the company right back to the mine they used to have here. As soon as we went down, we found the old shafts.

"They've already started to bring it up. The processing will have to take place off-planet, of course—too many toxins."

"You found the original mine shafts?"

The tunnels are dark to them…

"Yeah, but your guess is as good as mine where they lead," Rand replied. "Apparently there was some sort of collapse, and they decided the mine wasn't viable. The next thing you know, the records got buried." Decker had his doubts about that— it was too convenient. "The boys from Weyland-Yutani claim they didn't even know they had a mine here, until you fingered them for negligence." Luke looked at him askance. "How's that working out for you? Any time I heard from them, they sounded pretty pissed off."

"We're… coming to an agreement." He couldn't tell Rand the truth. Telling the truth had already cost him too much. No way he was going to add anyone else to the collateral damage.

"Good." Rand smiled. "To be honest, they've been pretty cool about all of this. I mean, finder's fees and the whole thing."

"Finder's fees?"

"Yeah. We're being kept on as consultants. Well, some of us. A few of the team have already moved on, but the people with the technical skills have been hired on as subcontractors."

Decker looked at his friend and frowned. That didn't sound right. Before he could comment, however, Manning bellowed for his attention. He turned to look back at the main group, and the leader of the mercs gestured for him.

"We have a meeting, Mister Decker," he said. "*If* it fits into your busy schedule. Let's get this done!"

Ten minutes later they were settled in a prefabricated hangar large enough to park several different heavy loaders and drills. Most of the area was filled with silent, hulking machinery, but a corner had been set up with tables, chairs and a coffee machine.

Thank God, Decker thought as he made a beeline for it.

The mercs loaded their cups before the discussion began. The group included all of the mercenaries, several of the men with whom he'd worked on the colonization project, and a number of the mining staff.

A Weyland-Yutani company man named Willis looked everyone over and nodded, apparently satisfied. He had the air of a bureaucrat with a side of dictator—a little short, a little round at the hips and desperately trying to cover up a growing bald patch on the top of his head.

"Rollins gave me a full recap of what she'd discussed with you, but the information she had was dated," he said, addressing the newcomers. "We've resumed our mining operations. Earlier today we made some new discoveries at the dig site and the location of the buried vessel."

He waited a few seconds, during which time Adams settled herself to Decker's right and took a swig of her coffee. He tried not to be obvious as he glanced over at her.

"So here's the situation," Willis continued. "Near as we can figure out, we were wrong on our initial beliefs regarding the ship and its occupants."

"What do you mean?" The question came from one of the

mercs, a hulking brute named Krezel, with dusty brown hair and a mustache that would have shamed a walrus. He shut up as soon as he spoke, skewered by a look from Manning.

"Well, initially we believed that the ship must have crash landed on the planet a long while back. We're talking upwards of a thousand years, though it's hard to say. Before the colonization began, there were a lot of violent storms, and according to the Terraforming Survey Team, there's a very strong possibility that heavy tectonic shifts occurred regularly, back in the day." Nothing surprising there, since Decker had taken part in the writing of that report.

"So it might be a few hundred years, or it might be a thousand. Whatever the case, the further we dig, the more it looks as if the ship was in the process of taking off when it crashed."

Manning spoke up this time. "Taking off from where?"

"Hard to say, but there's evidence that there might have been a settlement here—possibly even a fully functioning base of some sort." He smiled tightly. "That means that the technologies we were hoping to find might be substantially more extensive than we'd originally hoped." He paused to look around, taking in the entire group. "So you can expect a heightened level of security.

"And depending on what you find, you might also expect substantially larger bonuses, as well."

Before anyone had the opportunity to respond, Willis continued.

"Effective immediately, no one goes to town. No one takes the trucks or the rails. All communications are in full lockdown. We're talking a find that may be bigger than anything we've run across since first contact with the Arcturians."

Chatter erupted throughout the group, and Decker felt a sudden wave of excitement that washed over him like a wave. The Arcturians had been the first alien race mankind had encountered, and those initial meetings had marked a turning point for the human race. *Especially* for commercial entities like Weyland-Yutani. Research and development had burgeoned, and most of the company's holdings had been invested in developing new technologies.

The intensity of their reactions surprised him—euphoria mixed with unmistakable greed. Apparently several people were expecting to get very rich off of this expedition.

Decker shook his head to clear it of the incoming emotions.

"That's probably a bad idea—cutting ourselves off from the rest of the planet," he said. "If we encounter any living creatures down there, from what I've been able to tell, they're not going to welcome us with open arms. Things could go very wrong, very fast, and we won't have any backup."

A couple of the mercenaries snorted their derision, and Rollins turned toward him.

"That's why we've brought this very capable group of freelancers, Mister Decker," she said, playing to the crowd. "We have every confidence that they will be up to the task, and deal with every eventuality."

The mercs echoed her confidence, and he fell silent. Willis spoke up again.

"So it's business as usual tomorrow, everyone," he said to the miners. "But before anyone goes *anywhere* that hasn't yet been explored, Mister Manning and his team go in to examine everything. Steer clear, and give them room to do their jobs."

That yielded more reactions, and not all of them were happy. Decker made a conscious effort to shut down the sensations— it was a little like closing his eyes until he was squinting. The feelings were still there, but not as intense.

Rand was looking at him and frowning. Decker didn't need to read minds to understand that his friend was wondering how much he knew. But neither of them spoke—there would be time later.

Maybe.

The group broke into clusters, the largest of which gathered around Willis. A few of the more disgruntled men and women— all mining staff and subcontractors—were pressing him for information. A few voices were raised, and he held up his hands in the attempt to quiet them down.

As he digested what had been said, he found his mind wandering. Like most people, he was fascinated by the concept of alien species. As the human race moved further and further out among the stars, new colonies proliferated, and provided him his bread and butter. But he had never encountered evidence of extraterrestrials—not on his own.

And now, even if he failed to locate anything that was alive, he would get to see the remains of an alien vessel first hand. As exciting as the prospect might be, it also filled him with dread.

Strong fingers clutch the soft face that chokes and exhales in desperation. Decker tried to shake the thought away. Not fingers. Legs. Not hands, something worse.

As if she had been reading his mind, Adams leaned in and spoke to him.

"I've never seen anything alien," she said. "This should be amazing."

"I sure as hell hope so." He knew he should sound more enthusiastic, but the sensation wouldn't go away.

Darkness, teeth, a low hissing sound and the scrabble of claws. The images wouldn't stop, flashes that made no sense, that came from somewhere else and tried to make themselves at home in his mind.

It was the old feeling, back again—that something was out there and looking for him. Not just for prey, but for *him* in particular. He shook his head and focused, but nothing changed.

It must have been written on his face, too. The look Adams cast his way wasn't subtle.

"Wow, Decker. You need to get laid as badly as me."

That did the trick. For a moment, at least, the idea of being stalked faded from his mind.

"That an invitation?" he asked. *Nothing ventured, nothing gained.*

Adams eyed him silently for a moment. One eyebrow went up.

"Tell you what," she said. "Buy me a drink, and we'll talk."

13

FOR LOVE OF MONEY

Rand watched the mercenaries heading for the dig site.

Decker was with them. Alan Decker, the man he'd sold out. Guilt was an ugly thing, and it was certainly doing ugly things to him while he watched his friend, heading toward the Quonset hut with a battalion of some of the scariest people he'd ever seen.

Marines were bad.

Mercenaries were worse. Mercenaries didn't have to follow the rules.

Rand thought about that, and felt his stomach do a few back flips. If Decker knew about what he'd done—how he'd sold him out for a profit—well, there might be a little extra money in the pockets of a few mercenaries.

Yeah, Rand thought, he'd better watch his step, as long as they were around.

The Sea of Sorrows was an awful lot of sand, and there were places down below where a body could disappear. He'd learned about a few of them when he was hired on by Weyland-Yutani, as a consultant. Rand knew things about the company. The difference between him and his friend was that he was smart enough to not report the things he knew.

And what did that get him? A nice retirement package, and a few opportunities to make even more money.

Andrea Rollins was somewhere in orbit over the planet. He knew that. He knew that because she had been responsible for his current employment. And because the last time she'd been around—after Decker's accident got him taken away—she'd asked him to assist her. First, by pointing a finger when the time came, and second, by placing a few additional pieces of equipment around the mines when he was inspecting the site for "environmental issues."

He didn't ask what the devices were. He didn't need to know.

Rollins knew about the mines. Well, not true. She knew that there had been mines in the past. She knew where they were because of the message Rand had sent her, shortly after Decker's mishap. One man's misfortune was another man's opportunity. He had never once wished ill toward Decker. He just didn't let his friendship stop him when the time came to further his own personal goals.

And there it was, that little dig of guilt that twisted his guts around and around.

He looked at the hut and the sunlight painting the black sands the color of dried blood. Decker and the mercenaries were gone from sight. That helped a little.

Rand could have pushed harder, asked for the company to take it easy on him. But that might have compromised his career opportunities. On the other hand—and there was always an other hand, when you looked hard enough—Rollins had assured Rand that his friend could take care of himself. They'd asked him a lot of weird questions about Decker and he'd answered them.

They thought Decker was psychic or something. Okay, let them believe whatever they wanted. Alan was back and maybe he would be all right.

Rand looked at the hut for another minute and then headed back to the barracks. The mines gave him the creeps. The ship they'd found gave him nightmares. He'd never been one to hope for an encounter with other life-forms. As far as Lucas Rand was concerned, the human species was screwed up enough, and didn't need any help when it came to making the cosmos more toxic.

Somewhere in the offices there was a shot of vodka with his name on it.

* * *

When Decker was a kid, his father had told him that there was nothing that couldn't be solved with words. He'd said that a lot, especially when Decker's empathic abilities flared and the kids around him seemed more like potential enemies than friends. It happened less and less as he adjusted to the emotional tides and came to understand that not every sensation he felt pertained to him. Sometimes people were just pissed off because they were having a bad day—not because of anything he had done.

When he was a teenager his old man had changed the words a bit. He said there was nothing that couldn't be solved with a handshake and an honest negotiation.

And when he was grown and his father spoke his words of wisdom, they changed for the last time. That was when his dad told him there was nothing in the world that couldn't be solved with a shot of whiskey and a few kind words.

That last part proved true enough with Adams.

A few drinks with the mercenaries had let him clear the air. Garth would never likely be his close friend, but at least they left the rec room with an understanding between them. Same with Piotrowicz. The latter even bought him a beer to show there were no hard feelings.

Adams had a much nicer way of expressing herself. She was as enthusiastic in bed as she was about almost everything else. For a little while he forgot about the background noise in his head and focused on the lean, muscular woman in his arms. After too long on his own it was nice to share heat with someone else, especially someone with a voracious appetite and a surprising imagination.

When he woke in the morning she was gone. He'd have been surprised to find her still there.

14

BREAKFAST

As the sun rose, the air had a cold edge to it that Decker found invigorating. The small army of mercenaries were gathered around a table and dressed for business, and he joined them. Adams was sitting with Piotrowicz and a small cluster of the others, and they made room for him.

"Manning's already made the rounds," Piotrowicz said, his voice low. "We're going down to the site where they found the ship. That's where we're likeliest to find what we're looking for, so that's the best starting point." Then he went back to inhaling the food on his plate. The eggs were fried, not scrambled—an unheard-of luxury on a site like this. Decker couldn't begin to imagine how Weyland-Yutani had pulled it off.

Adams spoke up.

"You'll have to forgive Piotrowicz. Sometimes he thinks stating the obvious will make him look smarter." At that, the merc paused for a moment, in between mouthfuls, to let his middle finger speak for him.

"Still ain't working there, slick. You may *want* to sound smart, but the truth's plain to see." The speaker was a hulking man with a shaved head, where he had a tattoo of a military insignia. It was badly done, and the letters were largely illegible.

Piotrowicz looked at the man—easily a hundred pounds

larger than he was—and shook his head.

"I keep forgetting they trained you to speak, Connors," he said. "What's that supposed to be on your skull again? I think it's the Girl Scouts, isn't it?"

Decker settled back and chowed down quickly, eating even faster when Manning announced that they'd be leaving in fifteen minutes. If he hurried, he'd have time for another cup of coffee.

After breakfast he dumped his cutlery and tray and got that second cup. While he was adding lethal doses of cream and sugar, Adams moved over and started pouring herself another cup.

"So, last night was fun."

Decker looked at her from the corner of his eye.

"Wasn't sure if I was supposed to say anything."

"I appreciate the discretion."

"But yeah," he added. "It was definitely fun."

"Good. Maybe we can try it again tonight." She walked away before he could respond. His day seemed a little brighter, despite the feeling that was starting to crawl through his stomach.

There was no escaping it. The longer he thought about going underground, the more his guts tried to twist themselves into a knot. It wasn't just the tunnels, though—it was the entire planet that freaked him out. It wasn't rational, but it was extremely potent.

He caught up with Adams, and held up the reaper.

"So, where do I get a clip for this thing?"

She smiled. "Oh yeah. Forgot that part." She took him over to deal with a salt-and-pepper haired man named Dmitri, who gave him four long clips with fifteen rounds each. After a brief discussion, the man also handed him a second weapon.

"Plasma rifle. Be smart, keep warm and locked. And don't fire near anything you want to keep in one piece." Dmitri's accent was so thick it took a few seconds to fully translate what he'd said, but Decker nodded and smiled just the same.

When they'd moved a little further away, Adams took the plasma rifle from him, and gave him a refresher. He was glad—that wasn't the kind of weapon that allowed for mistakes. Not if you wanted to keep all of your limbs.

"Short barrel, so you can maneuver," she said. "There are three cells, all of them are charged…" She flipped the weapon around to show him the indicators. "Fires incredibly small and incredibly hot rounds of plasma. The barrel is trimonite. Anything less and it would melt by the fourth round fired. Seriously, don't fuck around with this one. You have an automatic setting and a selective setting. Automatic, you pull the trigger and the rounds come out fast and hot until your first cell is dead. Pull the trigger again and you get the same thing until the second cell is dead.

"I've never, *ever*, seen anyone pull the trigger a third time. Mostly whatever you're aiming at is long gone before the second time the trigger gets pulled."

She flipped it back over with ease and great familiarity. Decker saw several stickers that had faded almost completely away. One was a pink pony. Another had Adams' name scrawled on it. She was trusting him with one of her weapons. He felt a quick flash of gratitude but quelled it. She wasn't the sort who'd want to be thanked—especially not in front of the others.

He'd have to think of something appropriate for later.

"Right here is the safety," she continued. "Leave it on." She pointed to a second button, this one protected by a small flip-case. "This is the selective fire switch. You're set for single shots. Seriously, keep it that way—you'll have maybe a hundred and eighty rounds. You go full-auto, and you're going to level everything you aim at, but it won't last long.

"Got it?"

Damn if she didn't look sexy with that serious expression on her face and an assault rifle in her hands.

"Got it."

"Good. Let's go hunt bugs."

"Bugs?" The word called up images that ran through his mind and sent ice skimming down the length of his spine.

"Bugs," she repeated, looking at him with a strange expression. "Did you read the information? Bugs. Those fuckers are seriously creepy. Besides, what else are you going to call aliens? You ever see a cute, furry alien?"

"You've done this sort of thing before?"

Adams shook her head and smiled.

"Not me, unless you count a few indigenous rodents," she replied. "There's a first time for everything, though. I'll hunt anything, as long as there's money in it." She looked at the pulse rifle, and handed it back to him. "The most this little number has done is blow away a few critters the size of my hand."

"Yeah?"

"Screamed like a monkey when I was shooting them, too."

"Who did, you or the critters?"

"Probably a little of both."

She strode toward the exit and he followed, not quite certain if she was serious.

Most of the freelancers looked more like Colonials when they were suited up and ready for business. The biggest difference that Decker could see was that the mercs seemed to take their jobs a bit more seriously than a few of the Marines he'd met in his time. Then again, he'd normally run across the Marines when they were off duty, and ready to have a drink or two.

They walked across the hard-packed sand *en masse*, and the stuff gave way under his feet as they made their way toward the distant shaft. He didn't like the feeling, and for a moment he thought he felt a pain in his leg.

The Quonset hut was the only structure of any size, and there was little around it except for the evidence of construction—mounds of sand that had been pushed into a full-sized hill and then slowly washed back down. A few pieces of heavy equipment that looked like dying, metallic dinosaurs in the middle of a vast nothing. Areas that had been laid out and partially paved, but never finished. Everything was happening too fast and, as he had seen on any number of sites, there was a lot of activity with no cohesive result.

They waited for several moments outside the hut before the doors were opened to them. Willis was waiting inside, along with three others dressed in clothes meant to endure a rough environment. The interior of the place was lit by stark white lights that nearly shamed the sun—a slight case of overkill, to be sure, but there was a lot of equipment casting shadows, towering all around them and making Decker feel distinctly claustrophobic.

Willis and Manning talked softly while everyone filed in. Thirty-six extra bodies took away most of the free space in the area and left Decker feeling vaguely claustrophobic. Once they were inside Manning called roll one more time, and they headed for the shaft itself.

It was hard to miss. What hadn't been done outside was offset by what *had* been accomplished on the inside of the place. The lift platform was huge—large enough to accommodate all of them, and a lot more besides. It had to be, because it was how the company moved equipment into the shaft and would, in time, take out the trimonite. And like all of the heavy-duty equipment he'd seen in his life, the damned thing looked ancient. Sometimes Decker wondered if lifts were built pre-scarred and rusted.

He looked around the interior of the hut, using curiosity to push back the anxiety that was trying to overrun him. But the paranoia was making a comeback, and there wasn't a thing he could do about it. There were things around him. He'd felt them before, and he was feeling them now. His stomach rolled at the thought. His pulse was too fast, and he could feel sweat forming on his brow.

"Come on," he said to himself under his breath. "You can do this." No one else was close enough to hear. He steeled himself, and moved with the rest.

The lift floor felt more solid than the sand outside. That was oddly comforting—at least until the first lurching motion, and the slow descent began.

Where the hut was very bright, the tunnel was not. In very short order the only light came from above them, and that dwindled the lower they went. The lift itself was dimly lit. When the darkness was almost complete, the waves of emotion returned with a vengeance. Decker bit his lip to stop from making a noise.

Then, to his surprise, they began to fade again. It was almost as if he'd passed them by, so that they remained above as the mercenary group moved lower and lower.

Willis spoke up, talking to no one in particular.

"Anyone ever been in a mine shaft before?" He was answered by one of the freelancers Decker hadn't met.

"Hell, no," the man said. "I was born and raised on Earth. Anything worth mining there was stripped away a long time ago." He said it like it was a joke.

"You're not far off, actually," Willis responded. "That's one of the reasons Weyland-Yutani got into mining colonies. Thanks to automation, it doesn't take too much effort for a decent payoff."

"Well, you sure as hell couldn't get *me* to work in a place like this—not for long." It was Connors, the hulk with the shaved head. Big as he was, he looked nervous.

The area opened up as they moved past the first open level of the mine. There wasn't much to see, except for the machinery used to run the mines, and the generators used to run the machinery. New equipment stood next to old machines, many of which were so old that they were unrecognizable in their decay. Rods of pitted metal stuck out at odd angles, like the bones of long-dead creatures.

All too soon the darkness ate them again.

"How far does this thing go down?" Piotrowicz's voice cut past the low mechanical hum of the lift.

Willis looked around the artificial twilight, and then up at the walls of the shaft.

"Just over seven thousand feet." One of the mercenaries let out a low whistle. Their guide nodded, and Decker looked along with everyone else. The metal here was darker, decidedly in worse shape, corroded by time and moisture. "Most of this shaft was already here from the previous operation. Nine levels of mining. We've got the first three up and running, and have partially cleared a total of six. It's down at the bottom where we found the ship. The lift was severely damaged there, but we cleared it and restored it easily enough."

The mercenaries stared at the walls with all the fascination of kids going to their first museum. There was a sense of age here, of antiquity. Decker felt it, too, now that the sense of dread had faded down to a whisper.

When the lift finally hit bottom with a lurch that sent them all staggering, the walls opened into a cavernous area that was crudely but solidly built. The walls were solid stone now, hollowed out and reinforced at regular intervals. There were a few lights, which hardly pierced the gloom at all, so they couldn't really tell how large the chamber was. They might as well have been on a different planet. Thick layers of a darker material ran through the brown and tan earth. If he had to guess, that would be the trimonite, but it was only a guess. What he knew about mining wouldn't even make for decent bar conversation.

"Where's this ship you found?" Manning's voice carried easily, and echoed, causing him to duck his head.

"Just down this way," Willis answered, pointing into the shadows. "Have any of you ever been on an alien vessel?"

No one had—not even Manning.

Willis nodded, as if it was the answer he'd expected.

"Well then, this is going to blow your minds, guaranteed." He walked over to a truck, old and functional and with a broad flatbed in the back, large enough to carry several containers of ore. While he climbed into the driver's seat, Manning settled into the passenger side, and the rest clambered onto the flatbed. It was a tight fit and the truck rocked as they climbed aboard.

The engine started up with a surprising growl, and the vehicle lurched into motion, causing them all to grab onto any handhold they could find—including one another. In the glow of the yellow headlights, they could see a well-worn pathway with hard-packed dirt.

About five minutes later, they were staring at proof of alien life.

15

THE SHIP

Before they even saw the vessel, they moved past the seemingly endless construction materials. There were pallets upon pallets of scaffolding supplies, mezzanine flooring, and industrial metal posts for assembling the platforms they'd need to examine their find. The materials were stacked to around seven feet in height in some places, and blocked off much of the path to the excavation site.

In the distance they heard the hum of generators, and the sound grew stronger as they moved forward.

The ship itself was massive. Parts of it had been melted by blasts of extreme heat, or perhaps by volcanic activity. It didn't sit level on the ground, but was canted slightly as if it still sought to take off. The structure was split along one side, the hull shattered and torn and long since filled with dirt.

The ship's surface looked almost papery in places—not as if it was made of paper, but as if it had been crumpled up and then smoothed again. If there had ever been markings on the exterior, they were hidden by dirt or stripped away by the years.

There were holes everywhere. The hide was ruptured, torn, and burnt. There were places where several different levels were visible through the same gaping wound. It must surely have been designed to carry hundreds, if not thousands—assuming the inhabitants were anywhere close to human in size.

Around the ship, the initial excavations had leveled the ground out. The tracks from heavy treads showed evidence of what had happened before, but the actual vehicles were gone, either taken back to the surface or moved to another part of the cavern.

Decker stared at the thing. The sheer size alone was staggering, yet somehow the designs were... *wrong*—not at all what he would have expected. Some of its facets deviated so much from the mechanics of Earth that he couldn't even begin to grasp how they might have worked.

The greatest anomaly of all, however, was the fact that it simply didn't belong. It was meant for the sky, the space between the stars. Had he found a whale in the desert, it wouldn't have seemed any more out place.

"Shit on a shingle. It almost looks... organic." Piotrowicz turned his head sideways as he stared.

"Near as we can figure, it sort of is. Or was, at least." Willis spoke with an almost paternal sense, as if this was a pet that he had raised, and now that it had won a blue ribbon, he actually radiated pride. "The walls, the floor, even the doorways, they all have features akin to plant life. Doctor Tanaka is in charge of examining the ship, and she thinks it's distinctly possible that the entire thing was grown."

Decker frowned. There was a question niggling at the back of his mind, but he couldn't quite draw it out into the open.

Willis stopped speaking, and stood quietly as the freelancers moved forward.

The area had been excavated with care, and the hard surface above them looked dry, as far as they could tell. Decker wasn't a geologist, but he felt comfortable with the knowledge that the roof was secure.

The damned thing was too big for them to see all of it. Though lights had been secured to the ceiling above, they were dim, casting the area in a perpetual twilight. The walls of the ship stretched away into shadows. Near the entrance there were several large power cells, most of which had not yet been set up, and two generators that were going full-steam ahead.

"There are plans to bring down more lights," Willis said. "You can see why."

"Where is Doctor Tanaka?" Manning's voice was calm, and even a bit subdued. The man was squinting along the side of the ship, trying to see as far as he could. "And what are *those* things?"

He pointed to a thick column of glistening black that ran from the ceiling down to the ship. It didn't look like a part of the vessel itself, and Decker recognized it instantly for what it was. The same sort of deposit that had cracked under his foot, broken into his skin, and nearly cut through his leg the last time he'd been on the planet.

His guts twisted again, but for entirely different reasons this time. There was no fear—merely a memory of the pain and the sudden assault that had sent him into seizures.

"You okay?" Adams was frowning at him, and her hand touched his forehead. Her fingers felt warm, but only because his own flesh was clammy.

"I will be," he said, regaining his composure. "Just taking it all in."

She didn't look as if she believed him, but she didn't push it, either.

"Doctor Tanaka is tracking one of the growths, like the one you pointed out. They're hollow, apparently, and composed of pure silicon. From what she's said to me, they're everywhere inside the alien vehicle." Decker focused on the thick column of fused sand. It had an odd beauty to it, and glistened almost wetly. There were fine striations and swirls throughout the surface of it that made him think of spun sugar or...

Or a spider's webs.

The aliens they were supposed to track—the ones they were supposed to capture. Would they have come from the ship? If they were still around, would they still be aboard? Or was it possible that the glossy tunnels had been their way of escaping from the wreckage?

Dave—or as Decker now thought of him, Silent Dave—looked at the tunnel and frowned heavily. Decker could feel the edginess radiate from the man like heat, but aside from the frown he gave no sign of his heavy agitation.

"What?" Decker asked.

Dave looked at him for a long moment.

"The Xenomorphs. There was something about them binding their hosts."

Before Decker could respond Manning spoke up.

"Where do they go? The tubes."

Everywhere. He almost said it. Willis answered instead.

"We're not sure yet. We only discovered them after we started digging the ship out. At first we thought they were a part of the original structure, but it almost seems as if they were later additions. They definitely aren't the same material as the vessel itself."

Decker joined in.

"They're silicon deposits," he said. "I've seen them before, topside, where many of them actually break the surface. They're all over the Sea of Sorrows."

Willis nodded.

"The way they've spread shows certain organic tendencies. Whatever they are, some are large enough to allow a human being to move around inside, and there's a distinct logic to their structure. Yesterday Doctor Tanaka and several of her team members broke open one of the larger ones and entered, taking along supplies. They hope to map some of the growth."

"That doesn't sound like a good idea." Decker spoke softly. Actually it seemed full-on insane to him. The integrity of the things had to be questionable at best.

"They don't really have a choice, Mister Decker," Willis said. "The 'silicon deposits,' as you call them, are widespread. They run through a lot of the ship's interior, and throughout the surrounding area. Doctor Tanaka feels it's important to understand their nature and purpose."

"Why aren't they using mechanical probes?" Manning frowned as he tracked one of the columns into the ceiling of the cave, far above them. "That seems a lot less risky."

Decker agreed silently. Mapping probes would make it possible to assess the entire range of tunnels without ever having to set foot into them. Engineering teams often used them before they set down the component parts of the terraforming engines. The damned things weighed-in at several tons each, and having one of them fall through weak areas in the soil could prove catastrophic.

"They tried," Willis said. "There's low-level radiation in the area, and that interferes with the sensors. So it has to be done by hand. But Tanaka should be perfectly safe—the levels are too low to be hazardous."

Two of the mercs, Dave again and Muller, looked skeptical, and reached for their packs. Decker had a feeling they were going to check for themselves, and determine whether or not the radiation was a serious threat.

Willis looked at them and shook his head.

"You don't have to worry," he said. "Believe you me, I wouldn't be here if there was a serious threat to anyone's health." He smiled to try to make it into a joke. "I'm far too fond of my own skin to risk it here."

No one laughed.

"It doesn't seem to affect simple communication," he continued, "and the further we get from the ship, the less radiation we encounter. It's possible that the source of the interference comes from the wreckage itself. At any rate, while Tanaka is focusing on the tubes, Doctor Silas is exploring on the other side of the ship. Apparently there's a lot of very old damage that was done to this thing when it crashed here, and he thinks he can figure out what made that happen."

"No one's gone inside yet?" Manning stared at a hole in the side of the vessel. It was very old, and there were signs that they'd had to excavate a good deal of dirt from the interior.

"Oh, they've been inside, but they couldn't get very far. There's a lot of damage. Fire damage, possibly, or something else. It looks like a few of the interior walls were melted, at any rate."

"So we're just supposed to go inside the ship," another merc said, "without any idea what we'll find, and no backup?" Decker liked her immediately—she had a brain. A few others murmured their agreement.

"No, Hartsfield," Manning replied. "I thought we might just sit out here, spread a blanket, and have a fucking picnic." Without another word, he headed toward the ship. The rest followed.

Decker stared up at the black tubes again. Tanaka and her crew had gone into those things? Willingly? The formations ran up fifty or sixty feet from the ship, before they vanished into the walls of the cavern.

Manning called over his shoulder.

"Pretty sure I'm going to need you up here, bloodhound."

"Knew you were a dog," Piotrowicz said.

Decker didn't dignify his comment with a response, and caught up with the rest. He had his nerves under control, but that didn't stop him from thinking they were taking it too fast.

"Seriously, Manning, I do not like this place. We should take it slow and careful."

Manning frowned.

"I don't give a shit what you do and don't like, Decker," Manning replied. "Just do your job. Don't go freaking out on me. Understood?"

"Yeah," Decker replied. "I get it."

Dirt had been piled up against the ship, and a ramp of boards and metal sheeting led to a hole in the side. The rupture was large enough that they could see up to levels they couldn't hope to reach without ladders or scaling equipment. Scaffolding materials were stacked to the left of the ramp.

"Just how big is this thing?" Manning said, talking to himself.

Decker was about to reply when something hit him hard enough to make him wince. The sensation was as sharp as an exposed nerve in a broken tooth.

"There's something here," he said.

"What?" Manning looked hard at him. "Where?"

Decker closed his eyes and concentrated. He was rewarded for his efforts with a crawling sensation across his brain. Still, even that was helpful. Maybe. He couldn't be sure—he could only go with what his gut was telling him.

"Up and to the left," he said, pointing toward the large tube. "There's something there. It doesn't..." He shook his head. "It doesn't feel like anything human." It was the best description he could offer.

Manning peered in the direction he'd indicated, where the shadows blurred the details. He shone a lamp up there, but it did little good. About thirty feet up, the large black tube pierced the side of the ship, curving up toward the cavern's distant ceiling.

Nothing moved, yet the crawling sensation in his head acted like a sensor buzzing at a radioactive hotspot. There was something up there—something that sent off waves of emotion. He gritted his teeth, and focused on remaining calm.

"DiTillio, Rodriguez, Joyce," Manning barked. "Go check out that tunnel, see if you can find anything worth seeing. And be careful."

The three mercs nodded as their names were called, and headed toward the hull of the ship. Their goal was a spot directly below the point where the fused black tube met with the vessel's remains. As they moved they prepared their weapons. Rodriguez pulled out his reaper, while DiTillio activated his plasma rifle, and a very faint whine pierced the gloom.

Soon they were out of sight, and the sound of their footsteps, crunching on the cavern floor, faded away. Manning looked over at Decker for a moment.

"You think three is enough?"

"No idea." His first instinct was to say "no," but he couldn't give a good reason. So he held his tongue.

"No?" Manning said. "Then why exactly are you being paid as a consultant?"

"Who said anything about being paid?" Decker replied. "I'm just here for the scenery and the accommodations." *So fuck you, and fuck your attitude*, he added silently.

Manning just shot him a look and turned toward the rest of the group, barking orders, positioning them for entering the vast wreckage.

At his command three more of the mercenaries broke open

their backpacks and started setting up portable monitoring stations. They positioned themselves next to one of the closer stacks of building materials, which provided places to set up and to sit. Each of the three hefted a large, well-protected screen and as Decker stood watching, they began syncing their systems and then adding individual feeds from each of the mercenaries.

One of the three beckoned him over—the patch on her shirt said "Perkins." She pulled out a camera for his helmet and a Personal Identifier Patch that went on his bared forearm, to read his vitals. As soon as the PIP was in place, she checked the readout on her screen, and then gave him a strange look.

"You worried?" she asked.

"Why?" he said. "Should I be?"

"Your pulse is way too high," she said. "*Way* the hell too high." She called Manning over to one side, and they kept their voices low. Then another of the techs spoke up.

"This is looking like a waste of time, boss," It was Dae Cho, the senior tech, who pointed to the screen in front of him, and then to another one. "We're only getting readings from the PIPs that are close by—but nothing more than twenty feet away." Manning studied them intently and then spoke into the headset on his helmet.

"DiTillio? You read me?"

"Yeah, chief, but your signal isn't great."

"Any sign of trouble?"

"We haven't even made it to the tunnel entrance. Damn thing's halfway up the exterior of the ship. There's footholds, and we're climbing, but it's slow going."

"We can't get any readings off your vital patch-ins."

"Hang on. Checking." There was silence, broken a moment later by DiTillio's voice. "We're all live and wearing PIPs. Everything seems to be working on this end."

Willis heard the discussion and walked over.

"It's the same as with the probes," he said. "There's interference."

Manning barely acknowledged the man's presence. Instead he looked to the techs. Perkins, Dwadji, and Cho were playing with their keyboards and screens.

"Fix this shit," he said. "Now."

Cho nodded his head and responded.

"Working on it, boss. Might just be a frequency issue. We'll run the spectrum."

Manning nodded his head and walked away. After a moment's hesitation, Decker followed him.

He took exactly seven steps before a wave surged through him, stronger than before. That feeling of being watched—it was pervasive, and it was growing stronger.

Shit, I've got to keep it together, he thought, and then he said, "Manning, it's getting worse." His head was ringing with pain.

"What's getting worse?" The merc spun on him, then went silent for a moment, staring at him intently. "Okay, we need to see about getting you a sedative. You look like you're about to stroke out on me." He called out to his crew. "Piotrowicz, come see to our guest over here. He needs something to calm him down."

Piotrowicz headed over and studied Decker with a clinical eye, and then looked past him at the readouts on the screens. It was easy to see which one was his, because the readings were radically different from everyone else's.

"Calm down, buddy," the merc said. "It's not the end of the world—just a little salvage." His voice was surprisingly calming. "We'll get through this, but you have to chill out." His backpack came off, and a moment later he was rolling out a small syringe-gun. "Just a mild sedative," Piotrowicz explained. "I took stronger when I quit smoking."

"You smoked?"

Piotrowicz grinned at him. "Yeah. I was young and the girl was cute. Got hooked, got better."

"What did you smoke?"

"Well, it wasn't legal." He administered the injection, which pushed the liquid through the skin without using a needle. It hurt like hell, but within seconds the effects took hold. Decker felt himself relaxing. He could still focus, but he could breathe again.

Piotrowicz looked at the monitor, and looked satisfied.

"My job here is done. You start feeling weird or like it's wearing off, come see me." He put his pack back together and slid it across his shoulders. "I get to carry all the good shit."

Decker nodded and looked at the ship again, taking it in with a clearer, calmer head. Calmer—but not calm. He could still feel that radiating sense of hatred. So far it seemed to be stationary, and the three men who'd been sent off were heading right for it.

16

WETWORKS

The side of the ship was dusty and smelled as old as it looked, moldy and bitter. Still, DiTillio was smiling as he climbed up the side and looked at the tunnel ahead. Every moment brought him that much closer to making a shitload of money.

Of course, it also took him further away from the main group. A little over a hundred yards was all that separated them, but it might as well have been a mile. And the shape of the cavern was messing with sound, sometimes muffling it, other times sending out echoes. They were out of direct line of sight, too. Stacks of supplies blocked the view, leaving him guessing where the rest of the team was.

If they needed backup, they'd have to rely on the headsets.

Joyce was right next to him and looking around with wide eyes. His long face was pulled into a smile that showed his uneven teeth.

"What are you grinning about?" DiTillio poked fun at his teammate. He wasn't used to the other merc being so enthusiastic.

"Always wanted to see something like this, mate," Joyce replied. "My whole life."

"What? Aliens?"

"Well, yeah. 'Course. Don't you know how incredible this is?"

"Incredible enough to make us a shitload of money, if we play it right," DiTillio said, and he peered around. "That Decker guy said there's something dangerous over here. I wonder what it is. I hope it's one of the bug things. I want to check those out."

"Well, yeah," Joyce replied. "I mean, I'm glad we're armed. But I just can't believe we're really here. Looking at proof of other beings. Looking at something no other human has ever seen. Almost no one, that is," he added, correcting himself. Then he slapped the surface of the ship. "Touching something most humans have never touched, and never will."

DiTillio allowed himself a grin. The man was right. This was an incredible moment, the sort he could tell his grandkids about some day.

The surface of the vast ship was curved, and they'd been climbing with relative ease, but the going got tougher as they neared the silicon tunnel. The good news was that someone had attempted to string lights over the surface, and the wires worked relatively well as extra purchase. They looked old, though—none of the bulbs worked, a bunch of them were broken, and the insulation was in tatters. Only the dryness of the cavern had prevented them from rusting away.

He wondered if they would find one of the aliens Weyland-Yutani had sent them to retrieve. He'd always planned to study xenobiology, but a stint in the Colonial Marines had made him decide he preferred a life out on the Rim. It was easier, the pay was good, and there were plenty of distractions.

His fingers caught hold of the ship's hull and he pulled himself a little higher. Back on Earth he'd have been working up a hard sweat. Here the lower gravity was making it more like a light workout.

The pulse rifle was strapped to his back, and he had his pistol within easy reach. Fifty caliber shells would take care of any serious issues that might come along.

As old as the ship was, the tunnel moving away from it was much, much newer. The surface looked almost wet, even under the layer of dirt, and there was a hole in the side—that was their goal. He made sure to aim his camera at it, and take in as much as he could. Even if they couldn't pick up the image back at the temporary hub, the camera would still be recording.

He wanted to make a copy to send back to his sister—the one who'd been smart enough to finish college and was working for Weyland-Yutani as a forensic xenobiologist. She made disgustingly good money. Still, he got laid a lot more often.

It was all a matter of perspective.

"You seeing this?" The voice came from his left, where Rodriguez was climbing.

"The fuck is that?" Joyce's voice was almost lost in the cavernous area. He was a soft-spoken man.

The entrance of the tunnel seemed to move. Something dark and wet looking shifted twenty feet above them. It sent a shiver down his spine.

"Looks like a loose piece," DiTillio said. "Something's making it shift. Might be the thing isn't as solid as it looks." He tried to sound more certain than he felt.

"No, it's not loose," Rodriguez said, his voice a little higher. "It's moving. I mean, I think something's actually coming toward us." He held up his reaper, and stared hard at the shadows above them.

"Calm down, Billy," DiTillio said. "I don't think we need to worry about being attacked by a wall."

"Fair enough," Rodriguez said. "But I think we need to—oh, *shit*!"

The loose piece moved faster, dropping toward them, clinging to the side of the ship. It had that same wet look, new and clean, and even had the same sort of patterns along its hide, but this thing had arms and legs and a tail and…

Fuck, those are teeth!

Rodriguez didn't wait to consider whether or not it was friendly. He opened fire. The first round from the reaper struck the broken hull and ricocheted away, the report echoing as the thing dropped toward them.

He never had a second chance.

The thing landed on him, arms and legs and tail and other things all in motion—and before Rodriguez could do anything, say anything, he and the dark mass were both falling, bouncing back down the side of the ship and slamming into a rock formation. Rodriguez broke on impact.

The thing got up and looked like it was ready to spring. Its hide was black, so it was hard to tell.

Broken didn't mean down, though. Rodriguez raised his weapon and took aim even as the dark shape attacked, claws ripping at flesh. He let out a feeble scream and tried to fight as the thing tore at him.

"What the fuck! What the fuck is that thing?" Joyce was panicking, which wasn't exactly helping matters. DiTillio tried to aim at the shape that was dragging Rodriguez closer to the side of the ship's hull. He was having a damned hard time getting a good shot without risking hitting his downed teammate.

And there was the fact that the thing was, well, a *thing*. Joyce had already said it. This was an alien life-form, and they'd never encountered one before. None of them had. It had certain human characteristics—the same basic shape, but beyond the number of arms and legs there wasn't much more to go on. He saw enough to know that this was a Xenomorph, and that the footage in the files hadn't done the monster justice.

"Calm down, Joyce," he gritted, and his voice shook. "You're not helping."

"There are more of them, man," Joyce screeched. "There's more than one!"

DiTillio looked up in time to see the truth of Joyce's words. More shapes spilled from the hole above them, and dropped onto the ruined hull of the ship. They moved fast, scrambling and managing to hold onto the vessel even as they descended.

Joyce let out a throaty cry, but it was cut off almost immediately as one of the glistening black shapes grabbed him from above.

DiTillio had exactly long enough to wish he'd followed procedure and called for backup. Then two more of the dark shapes were on him. They were vaguely humanoid, but they had sharp claws and they had teeth.

So damned many teeth.

17

NECROPOLIS

Sometimes the little things, the ones most easily overlooked, hid all of the best secrets.

They'd broken through a small section of tunnel where air was moving softly. Then they'd returned to their encampment and waited in the mess tent until the probes did their due diligence, and gave the all clear.

So Doctor Nigel Silas stepped outside of the mess tent and strode to the opening they'd blown into the stone wall. Then he stared at the discovery spread out before him, with a smile that couldn't go any wider.

A metropolis, really. It looked to be centuries old.

The city was vast, built on hills and spreading down into areas where, once, there had been valleys, most likely cut by rivers. It was stunning, even with everything in ruin. Scarred and pitted surfaces, buildings that had collapsed nearly to the ground, yet still they were wonders.

The probes were still working diligently, recording every minute detail. He could see them flitting about in the distance. Their lights flickered in and out of sight, lighting the tops of buildings that appeared to have been amazing structures once upon a time, and still held echoes of that long gone magnificence.

Like the ship, the buildings had not been built. They had been grown, formed in a process he couldn't begin to understand, but desperately wished he could study for the next hundred years.

No matter what they did here, none of the team he was working with would live long enough to finish what they had started. They didn't even consider it. All that mattered for now was beginning the excavation.

They had found the remains of a couple of the creatures that had lived here, almost unrecognizable in their antiquity. They were bipedal, with some vaguely canine attributes, and larger than the average human being. How many had populated the city? Judging from the number of buildings they had found thus far, perhaps more than a million.

They hadn't yet delved deep enough to uncover any of the technologies that had run the place. Once they did, who knew how much they would discover? And for each item they found, who knew how long it would take to figure out how it worked? This one city could keep an army of scientists occupied for decades.

The find of a lifetime. He smiled as he thought about that.

Colleen came from the tent behind him and sputtered out a small laugh.

"You're like a big kid," she said. "You know that?"

"How else could I be? Look at this place, Colleen. It's amazing."

She smiled and put one of her arms around his waist.

"I know." She paused a bit and enjoyed the view with him, standing in silence, and then said, "Where are we looking today?"

Silas pointed to the road leading down to the closest valley.

"The survey information from the probes is showing what looks like a military complex in that direction," he said. "Well, military or at least industrial. We should look there first. It's likely to offer up a lot of technologies on every level."

She nodded her head. "So let's get this show on the road."

18

UPPING THE ANTE

Decker stayed off to the side, watching and waiting.

They'd been about to enter the wreck when Willis got a call over his comm-link. Whatever the report had been, everything had ground to a halt, and he and Manning were off to one side, conferring. The rest of the mercs were waiting for instructions, and Adams sat nearby. She was knocking back a bottle of water, relishing it like it was the best beer she'd ever tasted.

That seemed to be her approach to everything. Somehow, he found it difficult to be so upbeat.

"Why do you think readouts and probes aren't working, but comm-links still do?" Decker asked.

"Comm-links are a lot simpler, I guess—maybe that has something to do with it." She shrugged. "How the hell should I know? I'm just a grunt."

Manning and Willis moved closer to the group, still deep in conversation, and both of them seemed excited about something. Then Manning split off and called the group together.

"Mister Willis here got a call from Doctor Silas. He's the brain leading the team that's examining the other side of this thing." He gestured at the alien ship. "According to him, it looks like there might be a lot more where this came from." That got everyone's attention. A few of the mercs started to speak, but Manning cut them off with a single gesture. "They've been digging behind this ship, and think they've found what looks like the remains of a city."

Everyone started to talk at once, and Manning let it go. He knew what this meant for them—the possibility of rewards beyond imagining. After a moment, Bridges raised his voice above the rest. Bridges was as close to old school military as they had, with short hair, a thin mustache and well-polished boots.

"A city?" he said. "Are there any signs of life? Maybe the bugs we're looking for?" He was grinning. Like as not the man was already calculating how he would spend his bonus.

It was Willis who answered.

"Understand that they haven't gotten very far yet," he said. "There's no sign of life, but judging from the configuration of what they *have* found, it looks likely that the ship was taking off—not landing. That means a spaceport, and we may be looking at a trove of discoveries the likes of which no one has ever encountered."

He was damned near jumping up and down with excitement, and no wonder. A ship was one thing, but an entire people capable of star travel? An entire race who *grew* their ships? Anyone who had a piece of the salvage was going to be unbelievably wealthy.

The buzz started up again. After a few minutes, Manning reached the limits of his patience.

"Listen up!" he bellowed. "Whatever they've found, we need to focus on the mission. We've got to make certain this dig is secure, and we've got to try and find any living thing that might be crawling through these tunnels. Mister Willis has called for reinforcements, but they won't arrive for a couple of weeks.

"So we're going to be working out a rotating schedule, and covering as much ground as we can. Nothing and no one leaves this site without my knowledge and approval. Do I make myself clear?"

"Got it, boss," Piotrowicz said. "No one comes in, no one leaves. But what about the miners?"

"As far as they know, nothing's changed—it's business as usual down here," Manning said. "They'll be following exactly the same protocols as we will. No one comes in. No one leaves."

"Are you sure the people up there can be trusted?" Piotrowicz asked.

"Their jobs are as much on the line as ours," Willis said. "They'll accept all of the security measures we put into place—those are the rules, no exceptions." His words were met with murmurs of approval all around.

Out of the corner of his eye, Decker saw one of the three techs stand up and move toward Manning. Though they'd all been listening, they'd stayed at their posts. The tech said something that couldn't be heard over the chatter, and the two of them moved back toward the monitor.

Suddenly Manning—or maybe it was both of them—gave off a spike of emotion. Manning said something into his comm-link, then shook his head.

The spike became more intense. Decker frowned.

"Hell, no," Adams said nearby. "I'm buying a mansion and settling myself on Monaco. I like the idea of a planet with nothing but beachfront property."

"You'll burn to a crisp!" the skinny kid said. Garth. "You're so white, your skin scorches when you walk under a strong light."

"Look who's talking," Adams replied. "Besides, I'll hire me a few studs to lotionize me every morning, and twice at night."

Decker shook off the random conversations. Weyland-Yutani owned his ass to the tune of more money than anyone would see from this little expedition. But there was something else that was bugging him—if he could just think through the drugs Piotrowicz had stuck in his arm...

Ah.

Yes.

"If there's a city, what happened to all the people?" He directed the question to Willis.

"What's that?" The man was still smiling, ear-to-ear.

"The aliens who built it," Decker said. "What happened to them?"

Willis frowned and tried to look like he had a clue.

"Well, we don't know that yet."

"I mean, if the ship here was trying to leave, and it went down, shouldn't we be finding some sort of remains?" He waved his hand to take in the immediate area. "For that matter, why did they just leave it here, stuck in the ground? Shouldn't they have taken it, I don't know, someplace else?"

Willis lost his smile.

And at the same time, Manning called out to his team.

"Listen up," he said, and there was an edge to his voice. "We have a situation. Rodriguez, Joyce, and DiTillio aren't responding to the comm." He moved back to the group, and his already rough face looked as if it was carved from the rocks around them. "We have three MIAs on our hands."

All of the chatter came to a halt, and immediately the mercenaries started prepping their equipment. This took Decker by surprise. These were the same people who had beaten and kidnapped him back on Earth. Yet when three of their own went missing, everything else took a back seat. Begrudgingly, he admired that.

The simple fact was that they had to depend on each other in bad situations. Just as he'd depended on Luke and his own team when he was pinned under the core sampler.

He stood up quickly, and immediately his head started spinning. Damn, but he needed to recover from whatever drug was in him. He looked around for Piotrowicz, but couldn't find him—there was too much controlled chaos.

As he searched, that sensation hit him again—the certainty of being watched. He scanned the group, and none of them was paying him the least bit of attention. So he focused as best he could.

It seemed to come from several places at once. Something out there was watching him, *stalking* him. There was no doubt, and panic started nibbling at the edges of his mind again, sending streamers of ice through his stomach to drift and tickle and make him miserably uncomfortable.

"Decker!" Manning's voice cut through the fog. "You picking up something, daydreaming, or maybe just hoping no one will notice you doing nothing?"

"Sorry," he replied. "Whatever Piotrowicz gave me, it's messing with me."

"Well, shake it off and get your ass in gear."

Decker grabbed his pack, which held the two weapons he'd been loaned, and moved to join the rest.

"I don't know how your mojo works," Manning said, "and I don't care. What I need is results. If DiTillio's team ran into trouble, I need to know where they are, and whether or not your alien friends are with them."

Decker closed his eyes again, and concentrated. Though there were impressions coming in from all around, the strongest feeling came from above the ship, where he had felt something before.

Where DiTillio, Joyce, and Rodriguez had gone, on his say-so. *Shit.*

"Same spot," he said, pointing as he had earlier.

"Good enough for me." Manning started walking. "Four teams. Cho, you and tech stay here, monitor everything you can. Piotrowicz, flank to the left and keep an eye on the tunnels. Hartsfield, right flank. Warm 'em up, but don't be stupid." With the exception of the techs, the whole group moved splitting apart with comfortable familiarity. It was obvious they'd worked with the different people he chose, and they filed after the leaders. Decker fell into step behind Manning, keeping pace with Adams, even though every fiber of his being screamed *not* to head toward that sensation.

But he needed to live up to his end of the bargain if he wanted to get out of this. Besides, he was surrounded by heavily armed mercenaries.

What could go wrong? He regretted the thought immediately.

Willis trotted over, and Manning stopped.

"What's going on?" he asked. "Where do you think you're going?"

Manning stared at him for a moment.

"It's what I just said," he replied. "Three of our men are missing. We're going to find them."

"All of you?" Willis shook his head. "No. At least a few of

you need to be here for when the survey team gets back. In the meantime, we can't just leave this area unguarded."

"Are you trying to tell me how to do my job, Mister Willis?" Manning's voice lowered into an unpleasant rumble.

"I'm trying to remind you that the rules have changed." He stopped, and shifted gears. "Listen, I understand that you're missing a few people, but you don't need your entire team for a search-and-rescue. And you'll be ignoring the mission at hand."

"This is the mission at hand. I just broke the team into three separate—"

"The thing we're *paying* you for," Willis added firmly.

Manning just stared, without emotion. The closest mercs edged closer, waiting to see if their boss would take a swing at their resident bureaucrat.

"Right," Manning said, and he spun around. "Piotrowicz, you, Anderson, Lutz, Estrada, and Vogel are going to stay here with Willis. Your job is to secure the area—especially the lift. Nothing comes down, and nothing goes up without you clearing it through me." Piotrowicz smiled and stepped to the side, as the rest broke off to join him. "Give Adams here the medical supplies. Apparently you're not capable of administering a reasonable dose of jack shit, anyhow."

For a second the thin man looked ready to argue. The look he received convinced him that it would be unwise.

Manning turned to the bruiser with the tattoo on his shaved head.

"Connors, take Groff, Hunsucker, Juergens, and Blake. Head to the far side of this damned thing and find out what's back there. All of you keep your eyes open. We already know there might be bugs, and we know that three people are missing. Everybody communicates through Cho and the rest of comm." He spun hard to look at Willis. "Satisfied?"

Willis nodded, looking smugly victorious. If Manning noticed, he didn't give any indication.

Adams shook her head, a weird smile on her face.

Decker stared at her for a second, reading her amusement. "What?"

"Suits," she said. "Nothing's changed, except Manning lets this feeb think he's made a difference. This is the same breakdown we'd have had anyway. Two secondary teams, half of each team staying nearby, the other half moving further out to guard the perimeter. Main team—the one we're with—heads for the last known site of the MIAs. All he did was piss Manning off, so now more people are coming with the main group."

Decker nodded his head. He was used to dealing with the other end of the scenario. Like as not, there would have been times when he'd have been the Willis in the equation.

A moment later they were heading back for the side of the ship and the long black tube of silicon that rose toward the distant ceiling. Twenty mercenaries headed for the last known location of three missing men.

DiTillio woke in darkness, his body dripping sweat. Something hot and wet was pressing down on his arms, his chest, and he could feel *things* crawling over him.

"What the fuck?"

If anyone else was around to hear him, they did not answer.

The wetness on his chest pressed down and spread out and he felt hands smoothing the heaviness over his clothes. He was having trouble breathing, but not enough to make him panic. The lack of mobility was causing that. Whatever the stuff was that was covering him, it was hardening quickly.

The air stank of oil and metal and something acrid. He tried to see anything at all, but there was no light.

So when the shape crawled over his face, he had no notion of what it might be, except that it moved on long, thin legs. He tried to shake his head, and the fingers clamped into his hair, pulled tightly over his face.

"What?" Panic ate at him, and he shook his head harder as something wrapped around his neck. It was hot enough that it felt like it would burn his flesh, and it constricted like a hangman's noose, causing him to choke. Then it loosened a bit.

DiTillio started to speak again, to beg if he had to, but before he could utter a sound something was in his mouth, pressing past his lips, past his teeth and shoving further still.

Panic didn't even begin to cover what he felt. He tried to thrash his head to the side but the grip was too much. Whatever was in his mouth rammed in harder, pushing into his throat. He would have gagged if he could have, but whatever it was took advantage of the motion and shoved deeper still.

His eyes watered in the darkness. He tried once more to scream.

19

UPWARD TOWARD DARKNESS

As they neared the side of the alien vessel, they saw the blood.

It was Decker who found the first weapon. According to Manning, it belonged to Rodriguez. It was a reaper, much like the one he was wearing holstered on his hip. That hardly inspired confidence. Spatters of blood showed on the ground, and a few more trickled down the side of the ship.

Grimly, they began climbing toward the dark tunnel. It was a relatively simple climb for Decker and the rest.

Emotions were spiking all around him, although there was a lot more anger than fear. Decker sorted through and sought to focus on what was ahead, and he kept coming up with the same thing. There was a pervasive sense of menace that neither grew stronger nor weakened as they climbed.

The blood spots were more frequent as they ascended. Manning gripped the hull nearby, and he called in regularly, keeping Cho and Piotrowicz posted. As they approached the tube, Decker looked down, and could barely see the group at the foot of the ramp, tiny in the distance.

Manning was the first to reach the tunnel's entrance. He pulled out a powerful light, which he strapped to the shoulder of his armor. Several of the others below him did the exact same thing. Decker felt naked without one, but the lights seemed strong enough to let him see.

The mercenary's fingers sought a place to grip the interior of the tunnel and found one. He hauled himself up and in. Decker clung there, frozen in place, but Adams was right behind him and tapped his side.

"Let's go," she said. "Chief ain't gonna wait."

Maybe the sedatives were wearing off. Maybe he was just finally adjusting to them. Whatever the case, he nodded and continued upward, his fingertips finding spots to grip with relative ease. When he reached the tube, he grabbed the edge of the opening, and hoisted himself inside.

Even there, the angle of the tunnel forced him to climb. The spun silicon—which had looked so smooth from below—offered plenty of handholds and footholds alike. There was light moisture clinging to the interior, pooling at times, making it slippery. He felt a hint of claustrophobia, but quickly damped it down.

The sense of malice had not changed—it was still coming from all around them, but the intensity hadn't increased.

Adams remained directly behind him, the light mounted to her shoulder showing him the best spots. Ahead of him Manning continued to climb as the tunnel shifted, leveling out a bit. The way became easier, and the air itself turned moist. There was a scent that was uncomfortably familiar for no reason he could discern.

Then it hit him. It was the scent of the nightmares he'd been suffering for months. But was it possible to smell something in a dream? He had no idea.

Time lost meaning as they moved, climbing and shifting along the course of the tunnel, and then the oddly organic structure opened up, allowing them to stand. The other mercenaries moved up behind them.

The area couldn't exactly be called a room. The walls, floor, and ceiling were all made of stuff that seemed like a cross between being a living entity and molded from glass and steel. It was elegant in a way, though there were too many places with shadows that pooled and could hide almost anything. It shone wetly in the illumination thrown by the shoulder lights.

Adams pulled out a motion sensor, and flipped the switch. Nothing. She shook it, slapped it hard on one side, and then stared at it again.

"Damned Weyland-Yutani piece of crap," she said.

A few of the mercenaries removed the lights from their mounts, and the beams moved dizzyingly over the area. The walls were rounded, and moved smoothly into the ceiling and floor alike. The lights revealed three separate tunnels that stemmed off from the main area, all in different directions.

The smell was worse here.

"Where the hell are we?" Adams asked, and her voice was startlingly loud. Decker shook his head.

"We're either above the ship, *inside* of the ship, or we've exited the cave altogether," Manning said. "I don't know, but we were climbing for a while." His voice remained calm.

Adams crouched and ran her hand along the surface. Her eyes were wide as she studied the stuff, but her mouth pulled down in revulsion, and she stood up again.

"This shit's like a spider's web," she said. "It doesn't feel like a web, but it looks like it. Like it's spun or woven. When I was a kid, my teacher had a colony of funnel spiders in a terrarium. It looked a lot like this. I mean, not exactly, but sort of."

"First spider I see gets blown to shit. I hate those things," Sanchez said. He was lean and hard, and looked disconcertingly nervous.

Decker couldn't blame him.

Manning shot Sanchez a glance, and nodded his agreement.

"Found something." Adams pointed her light toward the base of the wall. There was a substantial pool of liquid there, and the white light revealed it to be blood—likely human. It was already congealing. Manning peered at it, and then turned to Decker.

"Which way, hotshot?"

Decker tried to sort out the sensation that almost seemed like background noise. There was no one focal point to grasp.

He's not going to like this, he thought.

"I have no idea," he said.

Manning's calm faded in an instant, and he leaned in closer until his eyes were inches away from Decker's world.

"That's not good enough," he said, his voice low. "You can sense whatever the fucking things are? Great. *Do it*. Feel for them, or smell them out, or *whatever* the hell you're supposed to be doing, and you tell me where my men are. Or I might just decide that you're a liability I don't need."

Decker felt the merc's anger flare, and his own flared up in response.

"Get out of my face," he growled. "I didn't ask for any of this. You and your employers dragged me here. You act like I'm a fucking bloodhound. Well, I'm not. Yeah, there's something here that's fucking evil. I can feel that. But I can't just perform on command, tell you where that something is, what it looks like, or how many of them there are. It just doesn't work like that."

Manning actually got closer. His eyes looked bloody murder, and he spoke with that same calm, despite the rage Decker felt radiating off of him.

"Make. It. Work," he said. "Find a way. Now."

Decker held his gaze, then took a step back. He lowered his head, closed his eyes, and clenched his fists.

And damned if he didn't feel something.

Shit.

"Shit," he said. "Whatever's out there, it's coming this way."

20

A MOMENT'S PEACE

The five of them walked the area slowly, checking for signs of the missing trio. The lights above them were dim, and seemed even fainter as they moved further around the edge of the gigantic ship.

Connors kept his people in sight at all times. Hunsucker chewed at a lump of gum like it had done his family wrong. The man almost never spoke, but he snapped and popped that damn gum. He was long and lean and his skin was darkly tanned. He had hair so blond it was almost white, and stood out in stark contrast. He was carrying a plasma rifle, and the high-pitched whine of the generator was almost as annoying as the sound of chewing.

That said, Connors forgave all his sins because the little sociopath knew how to use his weapon.

Groff was a brooding presence. He'd been a career Marine and he had the badges to prove it—one arm was covered entirely by scar tissue. Put it together with the other one, and they looked like a "before-and-after." His hair was close-cropped salt and pepper, while his face looked like it belonged on a younger man. Unlike most of the mercs, he still wore military combat fatigues, and carried his supplies with him almost everywhere he went. Everything about the man made Connors feel a little better about walking in unexplored territory.

Juergens and Blake were by far the most relaxed of the lot. Off to one side, they murmured to each other as they moved along. Blake had secured his flashlight to his pulse rifle, which was also humming. He swung the high-power beam along the underbelly of the ship as they moved beneath it. It was a tight fit, and Juergens made sure to check the structure for integrity. They had no idea how long it had been there, or whether or not it was sound—for all they knew, time might have weakened it.

Better safe than dead.

It was more than his urge to live long enough to become a rich man. Everything about the scenario made him uneasy. Rodriguez was a hard ass. The man didn't take shit from anyone, and he could handle himself in a firefight. If someone or something had taken Rodriguez out, then that same something was dangerous.

It might be out and looking for another target.

Abruptly Juergens turned his entire body, and aimed back the way they'd come, his light pointing into the shadows.

"Anyone see that?" he said.

"See what?" Connors spun around and looked for anything that didn't belong.

Nothing.

"Focus your beam, Brent. All you're doing is making more shadows to chase."

Juergens didn't reply, but his light steadied and moved slowly over the large surface.

Connors followed suit, aiming at a different area. Then he froze.

"Hold up," he said, raising an arm.

There was a shape, still some distance away, slowly heading toward them. It was dark, and the way it moved was unsettling. There were four limbs—legs, possibly—moving under the thing, but above it protrusions rose from the back and bobbed in counterpoint to each step it took. The head was an elongated affair that seemed to belong on something much larger. Its tail was almost as long as the body, and ended in a vicious looking barb.

"What the fuck?" His voice was louder than he intended. He made sure the safety was off on his rail rifle. Thing made a lot of noise when it was fired, but whatever got hit knew good and damned well that it was time to die.

"I see it too," Juergens said, his voice high.

"Me, too," Blake said, keeping it low. "What is it?"

It looked almost as if it was made of the same dark glassy substance as the rough tunnels that wove above them and along the distant wall, and even from a distance they could see the shape of the thing's innards under that glossy exoskeleton. Before Connors could respond, it charged, hissing like a broken steam pipe.

Groff opened fire, and three rounds from his pulse rifle carved trenches in the dirt. The fourth nailed the approaching thing in the leg and blew that limb apart.

The hissing noise became a high-pitched shriek, and the creature fell forward, hitting the ground and bleeding fiercely through the gaping hole where the leg had been a moment before. The ground smoldered and smoked.

"They might secrete a liquid that's toxic, or caustic, or both." Still squealing, the thing lunged toward Groff. The merc stepped back and fired another stream of rounds. He was fast, and he was good, and the thing took several more hits before it crashed to the ground and shuddered and... *Please God...* died.

Connors got on the comm.

"Manning! We've got something here. I think we killed it but it's hard to tell." His voice shook. He wished it could have been excitement, but it was fear. Everything about the creature was terrifying. The way it moved, the way it looked—even the way it died.

Manning didn't respond. Connors frowned.

Juergens pointed to his helmet, then to Connors.

"Comm's dead. Whatever that thing bleeds, it got your helmet." Connors pulled it off quickly, and looked at the damage. It could only have been a few drops of whatever passed for blood in the nightmare, but that had been enough. The unit was slagged, and a hole had burned partially through the durable shell of the helmet itself. He flipped the helmet over and realized that the caustic fluid was still burning through. Hydrogen fluoride, was that what the damned file said? He wished they could have brought the downloads with them now. He wished he'd read a little more carefully.

If Juergens hadn't pointed out the damage, there was a chance it would have reached his scalp. Before he could say thanks, Groff spoke up.

"Look lively," he growled. "We've got company." He leveled his pulse rifle. Hunsucker's plasma rifle whined a little louder as he took off the safety.

The darkness came to life. That was the only way to put it. The shadows in the distance began moving, *seething*, and as Connors watched, those shadows broke into smaller forms. He tried counting, but they were too fast and there were too many of them.

Hunsucker took careful aim and fired. A flash of light ripped from his weapon, illuminating everything around them. The ball of plasma burned hot enough to catch the air on fire, and all of them squinted as the missile struck its target. The creature was fast, and almost managed to dodge the blast, but almost didn't count when it came to plasma.

It had enough time to hiss before half of its head melted away.

The creature was dead before it hit the ground. Its wound was cauterized. None of that caustic crap spilled this time.

But there were more where that came from. Hunsucker smiled and fired again, the light nearly blinding them all. This time he missed—his target dropped lower, squatting like a long-limbed spider, and scurried forward. The tiny ball of plasma hit the ship and burned, melting into the ancient surface, leaving a smoking crater as evidence of its passing.

And then the thing jumped, moving with unsettling agility, twisting its body to allow it to kick off the underside of the ship and run directly into Hunsucker even as he tried to track it with the tip of his rifle. The barrel pointed at Connors, who hit the ground to avoid it.

The merc tried to bring the weapon around, but the thing on top of him pinned his arm to the ground with a powerful grip, and the thick claws at the end of the nightmarish fingers drove through flesh and muscle and bone with unsettling ease.

Hunsucker screamed and kicked at it, but the creature didn't seem to care in the least. The weapon in Hunsucker's hand fell free. He kicked again and sent the monster staggering back. The merc rolled back to his feet as quickly as he could. The thing spun hard and fast, and that serrated tail slapped him in the chest hard enough to lift him off his feet and throw him against the ship.

Cries from the other three pulled his attention away. He knew instantly that everything was jacked up beyond reason. *Everything.* The nightmares were coming closer, and there were a lot of them. His skin tightened, and his pulse rocketed.

Groff stood his ground and opened fire, cutting down one, two, three before the rest of them got to his location. He screamed as they swarmed over him like insects.

"Too many! Too many," Connors screamed. "Retreat!"

Hunsucker was down and out, bleeding from his ruined arm, and the thing that had attacked him was pulling him along the ground, dragging him away from the rest of the combatants.

"… the *fuck* are you?" Juergens screamed into his radio. "We're under attack! We need backup!" His voice was frantic. He tried firing at one of the damned things, but was too slow on the draw. The dark shape rammed into him and they both fell to the ground. Inhuman limbs rose and fell and drew back again and again covered with blood.

Juergens stopped fighting.

Three of them took down Blake. He saw them coming and shook his head. Then he raised his hands above his head.

Shit! Connors thought.

"I surrender!" Juergens screamed. "I give up!" Damned if Connors didn't feel like shooting the bastard right then and there. Before he could move, Juergens disappeared under a black, chitinous wave.

Several of the things surrounded him, peering at him and moving together, circling him, keeping him busy.

"No," he said. "No way." Connors sighted on the closest one and aimed his rail gun at its oversized head. The loud POOM of the round firing roared through the air. One round punched through the vile thing's hide. Before he could celebrate, the next one came in low and fast, and while he was trying to track it the monster's tail slapped his gun arm aside with ease. His arm flared with pain, and then he couldn't feel it at all.

The creature's flesh was hard and hot and coated with a slick moisture that left a trail of slime on his forearm. Connors kicked the thing in the chest and sent it backward. It hissed and he charged forward, determined to get past it in one piece.

The tail again. The tip came around and slashed at his face, tearing his nose and lips apart. Connors stepped back purely by instinct, and another of the things came up behind him. The damned thing grabbed his arms, the sharp claws of its fingers digging for purchase and sinking easily into his flesh.

He thrashed and fought, but it wasn't enough. They were stronger than he would have ever guessed. Blood streamed down his face, and the one he'd kicked reared up in front of him, face-to-face, hissing as it peeled back its lips and revealed silvery teeth coated in a thin blanket of saliva. Nothing he'd ever seen in his worst nightmares had ever scared him more.

There was a skull buried inside that head, and he could see the hollows where eyes should have been leering at him.

He kicked it again, but this time it was prepared. The blow was solid, but the thing didn't fall back. Instead it came forward, and those teeth parted, and then closed down.

Meat and bone crunched and Connors screamed before he passed out.

21

EVERYWHERE

The lift took off while they were looking around the area. Piotrowicz damned near wet himself. But there was no one on board—it was probably the miners, using it to get from one of the upper levels to another.

His group had taken the truck back to the lift area, because Willis wanted to make sure the scene was secured.

Soon after they'd arrived, Willis received an update from the group who found the alien city. Apparently they'd come across some mummified remains, but none of them were complete. They were burned, broken or worse. The best they could come up with was something like a long-limbed dog.

"Have you got any pictures?" Piotrowicz asked curiously. "Of the aliens."

"Nigel's group may have taken some, but they're keeping them tightly under wraps," the bureaucrat replied. "No unauthorized personnel see *anything* we find down here. Some of the crew who found the ship snapped some shots, and their cameras were confiscated immediately.

"If you see *anyone*—miners, even your own men—recording what they find, shut it down immediately, and report to me," he added.

Piotrowicz figured he'd have to be more careful when the time came. Other folks might give up their cameras, but he had no intention of doing the same. Even as he and the desk jockey were talking, everything was being recorded ... for posterity.

When the time came, he planned to sell to the highest bidder.

"Okay," he said, "so what's up with the black glass?"

"We're really not sure. At first we thought it was made from the local sand—that black stuff on the surface. But it's different on a chemical level. It's as if there's something out there making the stuff."

"Well, Decker said there's some of this stuff up near the surface, poking up out of the ground. How far down did you say we are?"

"Seven thousand feet, give or take." Willis shook his head. "But that's probably unrelated. Most of the stuff near the surface probably broke off and worked its way upward years ago. Maybe through tectonic activity. Or perhaps it was the storms."

The mercenary shook his head. "I don't get you."

"Well, the city and this ship were likely at the surface, back when the crash happened. The storms were bad enough to bury all of that. For all we know, the black tunnels might have been manufactured on the surface, then buried over the centuries."

Piotrowicz shook his head.

"Not a chance," he said. "Listen, I'm not remotely an expert, but even I can see that stuff is a lot newer."

"What do you mean?"

"It doesn't just *look* wet. I found one of the tubes close to the ground, and there was moisture coming out of it."

"That's impossible," Willis said. "There's no source of moisture down here—it's as dry as a desert."

"We can drive over and check right now if you want to." At that moment the lift started to move again, somewhere above.

"We've got to get a handle on this," Willis said, and he reached for the comm on his hip. "I'll stop them."

Before Piotrowicz could respond he heard Juergens screaming in his ear, "We're under attack! We need backup!" The sound was so sudden and so loud that he almost pulled the headset away before the words registered.

Not far away Anderson shot a look in his direction. Vogel was talking with the three stuck over at the communications base. They tried to respond, but nothing seemed to be getting through. Then Manning came on, trying to raise Juergens from wherever he was.

Nothing.

Piotrowicz called to the team to assemble, and grabbed his weapons. He asked the comm techs if they could locate Connors and his team, but their fancy, state-of-the-art screens didn't show a damned thing.

Worthless piles of crap.

Willis waved for his attention, unaware of what was going on.

"It's the team from level three, using the lift to move a few pieces of digging equipment," he said. "So we'll be stuck down here for a while—but the team at the dig site has already put in a request for when they're done."

"Yeah? Well, right now we've gotta move—on the double," Piotrowicz said. "Our guys who were headed for the dig site just radioed. They're under attack. So you might want to call your people back and alert them."

"Under attack? By who?"

"No fucking idea. But if I were you, I'd make the call."

Without waiting for a reply, he ran, gesturing to the rest of his team to join him at the truck. As soon as the four were aboard, the vehicle was moving.

Juergens was a card. He liked playing practical jokes. But he would never consider crying wolf and calling it a joke. Never.

Manning would have skinned him alive.

No, whatever had happened, they'd been cut off. He hoped that was all it was.

"Manning. What do you want me to do here?" He suspected he knew the answer. He also doubted he was going to like it.

"Get over there. Have comm tell you where to go—they may be able to get a decent reading."

"Negative, chief. They already tried." Perkins answered him just the same, her voice tight with tension.

"Interference. Same as with DiTillio. We're getting nada. Something around here is screwing up our signals."

"Fuck!" Manning said it at the same time as Piotrowicz. "Go check it out, Petey. And be careful."

"Damned straight."

The truck moved under the hull of the ship, and they had to duck their heads. Then it got to the point that the vehicle wouldn't fit—they would have to continue on foot.

Piotrowicz climbed down and gestured to his team. They came on fast and hard, all of them carrying, and all of them looking very seriously like they wanted to kick some ass.

Fine by me, he thought. But he kept quiet, listening…

The distance they covered was a few hundred yards. The reduced gravity made it feel like less, but it still took time to get where they were going. They rounded the side of the wreckage and looked everywhere. As the gloom increased, they locked lights onto their weapons, and flashed them into every shadow.

The lights revealed two dead things. Maybe it was three. The pieces didn't quite seem to match up. Lutz crouched close to one of them and used the barrel of his repeating shotgun to move it around to get a better look.

"The fuck is that?" Lutz's voice was calm enough, but he was looking around with a lot more caution than he'd been managing a minute earlier.

"Comm, can you receive visuals?"

"Negative. I mean you can try, but no promises."

Nothing like a solid, committed answer to make the day go better.

"I'm gonna try. We need to let everyone see this." He leaned in closer and took his time viewing the body. "What's this thing made of?"

"Looks almost like a machine." Vogel's voice was soft. "Are we dealing with bio-mechanical organics here? Like the ship?"

"No idea." Piotrowicz stepped back. There were places on the ground that had burned, wherever the spillage from the things had landed. Spots on the side of the wrecked ship showed similar damage, and even as he was checking it out, Estrada walked over carrying Connors' helmet.

"Manning, it looks like we've got five more down," Piotrowicz reported. "We're seeing evidence of the combat, but no bodies. No *human* bodies. There are other things here. I think we've found the bugs we were supposed to come hunting for."

Manning didn't answer.

He repeated his comment, just to be sure.

No one answered.

And then the sound of an engine reached him. It was large and it was loud, and it didn't sound good.

He gestured for the rest of his team to pull in close to the ship, and was glad of it a moment later. The vehicle came barreling around from the far side of the dig site, where none of them had been yet. It wasn't armored, but it was enclosed. There were lights, but only half of them were working, and the entire massive affair was smoking as if it had been caught in a firestorm. The outer hull was pitted and scarred, with several deep gashes and what looked like at least one hole burned into the side. One of the tires was a slagged mess, flapping and thumping instead of running smoothly over the ground.

Estrada said something, but the roar of the engine was too loud.

The wagon tore past them at high speed, and for a brief moment Piotrowicz saw the driver's face. Her eyes were wide and her lips were drawn back in a rictus of fear. And he could see the reason why. There were black-skinned things hanging onto the top, ripping at the metal shell and trying to get inside.

Piotrowicz and Lutz both fired. One of the nightmares sailed off the side of the vehicle as it rumbled past. Another blew apart. Lutz liked his shotgun for a reason. The damned thing did damage.

It was hard to tell if there were more of the things on the wagon as it shot around the hull and disappeared from sight.

A second later they didn't much give a damn anyway, because the one he'd shot was coming for them, shrieking as it charged. Piotrowicz froze. The damned thing was alive—and it was very, very angry.

Anderson tried to lift her weapon, but too late. The thing took a swipe at her and slapped her back against the ship's hull hard enough to stun her. She never even made a noise. Vogel was right next to her, and she pumped four rounds into the thing, screaming like a banshee the entire time.

One round would have done it. Four was overkill, not that she could be blamed. Then the wounds vomited a sickly substance, and the stuff hit Piotrowicz's arm, his chest, his face. The pain was immediate and he cried out as he wiped at his cheek. The fire spread across his nerves, and the next thing he knew Vogel was knocking him to the ground, dragging his helmet off of his head. Lutz pulled at his vest and jacket.

The incinerating pain calmed down after a moment, though it did not go away completely. His clothes smoldered on the ground and Lutz stood back up, looking around, while Vogel dug into her pack, looking for a first aid kit.

Not five feet away, Anderson was getting back to her feet, her vest slashed open by the claws on the dead thing.

Lutz called on his radio, warning comm about what was coming their way.

Madness.

22

DATA STREAM

Eddie Pritchett looked contrite when he came into Andrea Rollins's office onboard the *Kiangya*. And with good reason. When she summoned him, she had wanted him to arrive afraid.

"You called for me, ma'am?"

"I did," she replied brusquely. "It's come to my attention that your actions might have jeopardized our mission."

His eyes flew wide.

"I would never do that, ma'am."

Rollins reached into the top drawer and pulled out a thick folder of papers, which she dropped on the desktop. The folder was really mostly for effect. She didn't need to print out the files. She had a better memory than that.

"Your file," she said, peering at him. "You have a long history with your group. Before you worked for Manning you were with the Colonial Marines, where you were trained as a pilot. Before that you worked with your family, who subcontracts for Weyland-Yutani, and has made a very comfortable living in the delivery business. I believe you are expected to join them eventually."

He listened to her words and nodded slowly. He licked his lips, and did his best not to look too scared.

"What's your point?" he said. Then, "Ma'am."

She stared at him until he looked away.

"My point is really very simple," she said, rising from her chair. "The next time you pull *anything*—any sort of stunt involving one of my drop ships, flying to the surface of a planet, or up to the *Kiangya*, for that matter, I will make it my personal goal to end your career, and any career you might hope to have in the future."

"What?" he answered. "What can you... would you... What are you *talking* about?" She couldn't decide if his indignation was real, or if he was merely putting on a show for her. Ultimately, it didn't matter.

"I watched the drop ship's descent when you were taking Manning and the entire crew down. I also listened. I heard your comments about turbulence and storms, and I know there was none."

"Listen, *ma'am*," he said, "I would *never* endanger a crew onboard my ship." He regained his composure and locked eyes with her again.

"I'm sure you wouldn't, Mister Pritchett. At least not intentionally." She stared hard at him as she leaned forward. "Just the same, I have no doubt that your cargo got bounced around. I'm sure that if I talked to them, I'd hear a few stories about how often you've pulled that sort of stunt."

He did his best to look offended. Still, he didn't look her straight in the eye.

"Let me make this clear," she said, sitting back down. "You are flying a vessel owned by Weyland-Yutani, and leased to Mister Manning. The drop ship at your disposal is worth quite a bit more than you make in a decade. It is substantially more valuable than... well, than *you* are."

Rollins waited for a moment, until he turned back, before she continued.

"You have work to do, and so do I. If your next trip down to the surface isn't a textbook example of how to land a drop ship— without incident, if your return trip isn't just as exemplary, you can say goodbye to your pilot's license."

"Say what?" he bellowed just then.

She remained unimpressed.

"Simply do the job you're being paid for, in a professional manner, and I won't need to bother with you any longer. However, if you fail to follow this simple directive, I promise you will not be happy in your future endeavors.

"The majority of the work your family does relies upon jobs which come from my employer. I occupy a spot high enough in the chain of command to enable me to reassign any contracts I wish to reassign.

"Don't make me threaten your family's livelihood, Mister Pritchett."

He actually took two steps toward her, his hands balling into fists. Then he stopped, spreading his fingers, doing his best to act the part of the wounded victim.

She wasn't playing.

"Were you planning on attacking me, Mister Pritchett?" she asked. "Is this an attempt at intimidation?"

"What?" he said. "No. I... I just..." He lost his ability to speak for a moment.

Then he took exactly three steps back.

Rollins looked him up and down, a small sneer of disapproval clear on her face.

"You can go now."

He left quickly, his eyes downcast.

The door had barely closed when the first tight beam of information reached her desktop. The signal came in clearly, reaching from the transmitters on the surface to the ship in geostationary orbit above the Sea of Sorrows.

What came through looked, for all intents and purposes, like so much white noise. Sometimes that was inevitable, especially in areas where interference caused signal reflection and signal breakdown. Technology being what it is, there were still some issues that hadn't been solved.

Andrea Rollins didn't care in the least about white noise or interference. She did, however, pay a great deal of attention to the signal embedded inside of that synthetic static. Weyland-

Yutani owned the patents on the devices that created that artificial signal, and on the hardware and software that could break it down into its component parts. It wasn't a technology currently available on the market.

Hers was the only computer on the ship capable of breaking down the coded information.

She was keeping very careful track of all of the data coming in, as it related to each member of the team on the surface. From her desk she could monitor their life signs, when they changed, and how they changed. She made sure to note when they died.

Rollins used the available equipment to carefully map the entire series of tunnels beneath the surface. Had she been so inclined, she could have given the location of each and every member of the team, and precisely where each chamber lay within the vast network of tunnels. She even had data on the location of the alien life-forms—the Xenomorphs. Not all of them, she suspected, but a decent number. The aliens only registered when they moved. The rest of the time the tunnels they'd created worked brilliantly as camouflage. There were so many potential applications that it was staggering.

But she felt no need to share. The situation was well in hand.

Rollins scanned the data and considered all options. There was no doubt in her mind that there would be excessive collateral damage. That was acceptable. It was expected. It was what she wanted.

Fewer witnesses, in the end.

The mercenaries didn't concern her. They were just there to make a dollar, and they would be the ones who brought her the specimens she needed. It was the others—the more respectable and therefore more credible workers—who posed the greater threat. The fewer of them who survived, the better.

In the end, everyone was expendable.

23

LABYRINTH

"We're under attack! We need backup!"

When the call came through, Decker watched the mercenaries. They all froze, just inside of a narrow chamber, and their eyes glazed as they listened to the chaos coming over the comm link. A couple of the men started to talk, and Manning waved a hand for silence. When they didn't get the message, he flat-out roared for them to shut up.

Then it hit him—hard.

This wasn't a general feeling—it was *very* specific. More intense than anything Decker had ever experienced from a human being. For a moment he thought it might have come from the men under attack, a reflection of their deaths, but quickly ruled it out.

This was close, and getting *closer*. He backed away from the entrance they'd come through as fast and hard as he could, pushing past the redheaded kid, Garth. The kid looked at him with wide eyes.

It came up out of the entrance, screeching like hell, and aimed itself right at him. But the chamber was confining, and there were people in the way. Something dark and wet grabbed Garth by his leg and pulled him down as it climbed from the tunnel. The kid screamed in shock and pain, and the thing let out a second screech as it crawled up the poor bastard's body, its claws tearing through his flesh.

Garth bled and screamed and all hell broke loose. They'd been climbing—none of them was prepared for an attack. The savagery was horrifying. The skinny guy—Decker never got his name—tried to fight, and was bent and broken for his trouble, bones popping in his body.

The thing didn't crawl out of the hole so much as it unfolded, slithering into the room and growing larger and larger as it came. It let out another hissing screech as it pushed the broken forms aside, and looked around.

Seeking Decker. He knew it. Felt it. And he backpedaled again as the thing turned toward him.

The claustrophobic space was filled with bodies and noise—everyone was screaming and shouting. A three-clawed hand lashed out and slapped across a man's face, gouging bloody tracks across his features. He staggered under the onslaught and the thing charged, crouching and not really bothering with anyone in the way, simply wading through them on its way to Decker.

He was a dead man. His limbs refused to move, his hands hung loosely at his sides, ignoring his demands that they go for the reaper, reach for another weapon, do *anything* at all.

The butt of Adams's rifle smashed into the thing's face and knocked it sideways. Bridges' massive boot pushed it further down as it tried to recover, and the man lowered a lethal looking, two-pronged muzzle against the creature's torso. He pulled the trigger.

Instead of exploding, the thing arched its entire body and shrieked, thrashed, and shuddered. It slammed to the ground and twitched, but otherwise did not move. The stench of ozone filled the air, along with an odor like hot metal.

Bridges looked down at the thing with a murderous expression on his face. He backed away quickly, and by the time he'd taken two paces most of the people in the room were aiming a very large variety of weapons at the thing on the floor.

They took a moment to look the thing over. It wasn't a spider, not at all. Though there was certainly something insectoid to it. The long limbs were sealed in a glossy exoskeleton that looked all too much like the dark translucent walls of the tunnel where they currently stood. The head was almost as long as its torso, and half-hidden shapes rested within it. If there were eyes, they weren't visible, but there was no missing the mouth on that monster.

Dread centered around Decker's heart. The thing was unconscious and still he knew it hated him for reasons he did not understand.

Manning looked over at Bridges and slapped him on the arm.

"Got yourself a genuine bug," he said. "Good work." He looked to one of the mercenaries at the back. "Check on Garth."

"That is one ugly motherfucker," Bridges said. He sounded pleased with himself.

Someone crouched down over the kid's form, and then rocked back on his heels.

"Garth didn't make it. Neither did Holbrook."

Manning's face was unreadable, and his voice was low.

"Anyone here got some rope?" he asked. "Maybe a nice steel mesh net?"

A wiry looking man turned his back to Manning, indicating his own backpack.

"Help yourself," he said. "But you'll have to do it yourself—you don't pay me enough to tie that thing up."

"Is it alive, Bridges?" Manning asked.

"Shouldn't be. The shocker's set to kill."

Decker looked at the thing, and shook his head.

"It's alive," he said. "I think it's starting to wake up."

"How can you tell?" Adams peered at him, and then down at the thing on the ground.

"Its emotions—if that's what you can call them." He followed her gaze. "It still wants to kill me."

"What did you do to piss these things off, Decker?" Manning was busily pulling a length of very thin rope from the other man's pack.

"I don't know." He took a very small step toward the thing. It moved perhaps an inch, and he backed up again.

Bridges nailed it again, holding the twin contacts against the creature's skin until they could all see the smoke rising from where the metal had touched. Then he looked at Decker.

"Is it dead now?"

"I have no idea. I can't get anything from it. Maybe that's a good sign," he offered.

Manning nodded and quickly started binding the arms.

"Works for me." He worked very efficiently and made sure to cover the arms, the legs, the feet, and the tail.

The creature remained motionless.

"How the hell are you going to tie up that head?" The man who'd offered the bindings was the one who asked. "It's fucking huge—and that's some seriously badass dental work."

"I got nothing, Wilson. And I'm not getting anywhere near those teeth." He looked toward Alan. "You sense any more of those things, Decker?"

"I don't think so." He stopped for a moment, and focused. The hatred had shifted into background noise—painful, but manageable. "I can't be certain, though. We should head back down the tube."

"But what if there are more where that came from?" Adams asked. "It would've taken more than just this one to bring down DiTillio, Rodriguez, *and* Joyce."

Before he could respond, Manning jumped in.

"I think he's right, and at least we know the way, back where we've been." He looked at the thing on the ground. "We have a specimen. It's maybe alive. We get this thing down to the lift, and we get the hell gone from here. Mission accomplished."

With that, he grabbed one of the cords, and began to drag the creature toward the opening.

"One of you lazy excuses give me a hand here. This thing is stupid heavy." Bridges stepped up, and Manning shook his head "Not you—I need you to take care of Garth. Have Duchamp help with Holbrook's body."

Two other mercs jumped in, and found a grip on the alien shape. Half of the group dropped through the entrance of the tunnel, one at a time. The way was slick at times, making it harder to go down than it had been climbing up.

Manning and another of the mercenaries started lowering the thing down, and then carefully began following it. The rest followed, and somewhere in the middle of the train of bodies,

Decker started down, hanging near Adams without even being aware of it.

It was difficult to see where they were going, it smelled like sweat and fear, and the beams of the flashlights sent shadows skittering around. At times the crush of bodies was so dense that the lights hardly penetrated at all. He found handholds, not by sight, but by touch.

What a shitty place this would be to die, he thought.

After what seemed like forever, shouts erupted up ahead. Manning bellowed and someone else let out a loud scream.

"Fuck it," Manning said. "Let the bastard fall, and follow it. We'll pick up the pieces when we get down there."

"Bit right through my damned boot!"

"Your toes still there, Denang?"

"Yeah."

"Then call it a win, and keep going."

After that they traveled a bit faster. The darkness, the body heat, the echoing sounds of voices all grated on Decker's nerves. On all of their nerves, he suspected. Adams was just below him. Suddenly she stopped, and she cursed under her breath. He tapped the guy behind him, telling him to do the same.

She turned around, and shone her light up at him, covering it with her hand so that she didn't blind him.

"We have to start climbing," she said, sounding pissed.

"What? What are you talking about?"

"We have to start climbing."

That made no sense. "Back up to where we were? Why?"

"Because those things blocked the way."

"What?"

"The way we came—it's sealed," she said. "Whatever they are, they're at least a little smart. Manning tried to get down there and something was different. Instead of going into a straight descent, there's a curve now. The tunnel's changed."

Decker's mouth felt dry and pasty.

"How?"

"I don't know. I don't care." Adams pointed her finger. "Manning's pretty sure wherever the tunnel leads to now, it's probably a trap, and we're not taking the bait. So start climbing."

He turned, and the guy behind him cursed. But they started climbing, just the same.

24

EXAMINATIONS

The van rolled along like a wounded beast, and slowed only as it rounded the edge of the ship.

The three members of the comm team watched them approach and Dae Cho reached to the side of his console and picked up his assault rifle. Perkins and Dwadji stayed where they were, but their expressions said they approved. The weapon was solid and reliable, and came with four grenades and a launcher. He didn't know exactly what was going on, and he didn't much care. If the people on that truck came at him screaming, they would die that way.

Dina Perkins covered her free ear to block out the ruckus, and focus on what Manning was saying. According to him, they'd subdued a bug, but it had revived and bitten someone. They'd been forced to drop it.

Their pathway in was blocked now, and they would have to find a different way out.

No one could get a response from Connors—he and his team were missing in action. Piotrowicz and his team were still among the living, though at least one of them was wounded.

Cho stood up from his seat and swung his rifle over his shoulder, the barrel pointed toward the heavens as he walked toward the newly arrived vehicle, sitting in a cloud of dust. Perkins stayed at her station and Dwadji stayed beside her, trying again to reach Connors.

Willis was already at the door, pulling it open as the people inside tried to spill out. They crammed together so that no one could get anywhere, until the Weyland-Yutani bureaucrat grabbed a handful of shirt and half hauled the first one out. The rest sort of erupted from the vehicle in a frantic mass, like a grim parody of a clown car, seven in all and none of them remotely calm.

A short, heavyset man in his late fifties grabbed Willis by his shoulders and half fell onto him as he looked around.

"Go!" he said breathlessly, looking around in a panic. "We have to go."

"We can't go anywhere, Doctor Silas," Willis responded. "The lift is topside. We're stuck until it gets back here, Nigel."

"Then call it!" Silas said. "There might be more of those things. We've got to—"

Cho walked over and interrupted.

"More of what things?"

Short-and-round looked at Cho as if he was insane.

"Who are you?" he demanded.

"Security," Cho said, before Willis could speak. "Now tell me what you're in a panic about."

"That city," Silas said. "It's got occupants, and they're evil."

"Wait, you mean the city at the dig site?"

"Yes." The man nodded emphatically. "There are things living there, and all they want is to kill us. We have to get away from here!"

"Chill yourself," Cho said. "We're not going anywhere for a while. Like the man said, the lift is being loaded with mining equipment. Then it's supposed to drop to level four and unload all of that stuff. And *then* it can come down here and get us."

The man looked like the devil himself was on their heels. His thin hair was plastered to his head with sweat and he wiped at it frantically.

"You don't understand! These things are insane!"

There was motion off to the right, and Perkins jumped with surprise. Then she saw Piotrowicz and his group coming toward them. Lutz was dragging something on the ground behind him, hauling it by a line secured to what looked like a leg. Whatever it was, it didn't look human enough for Perkins's comfort. Anderson and Estrada were trailing toward the back, their weapons aimed at the thing. Half of Petey's face was covered in gauze, and he looked like he wanted to kill something in the worst way.

Perkins moved to get a better look at the thing. It was broken and dead and creeped the hell out of her. Her skin grew cold as she studied it. As the new arrivals moved closer still, half a dozen of the people from the transport moved in, scientific curiosity slowly winning over their fear.

She was about to warn Cho, but saw him look past the shouting driver. He held up a hand to silence the man.

"Got five people coming right now that killed the things on your truck," he said. He pointed with his chin, and Short-Round turned. The man took in a deep shuddery breath, and exhaled.

"Listen, where there's one of those damned things, there could be more. We don't know how many there are, but the probes show that there's a lot of territory out there where they could be hiding." He paused to breathe again. "They're fast, and they're deadly, and their one purpose seems to be to kill."

Willis interrupted.

"You said the probes were working in the city?"

"What's that got to do with anything, Tom?" Nigel asked.

"If the probes are working, they should tell us what is down there. Including any life signs." Willis spoke very calmly. "Did you leave any of the probes up and moving?"

Silas swallowed a few times, and did his best not to sound like a lunatic. He wasn't really succeeding but he was trying.

"Tom, we launched more than a dozen probes. They're still working, and still taking readings, but all they can do is map the area. It's much larger than we thought it was. Might be that a lot of it is still buried—we can't tell too easily—but there are places back there where the probes were moving freely, so it looks like we have open spaces."

Piotrowicz and his team reached them. The head of the team didn't speak. He simply stood by to take in the information.

Perkins walked over to their prize, and stared at it, trying to make something out of the jumble of limbs, claws, and teeth. Up close it was worse than before. As Piotrowicz stopped, the scientists clustered around his prize, wide-eyed and curious.

Willis gestured to Silas.

"We have thirty or so heavily armed security officers down here with us. You were out doing your survey when they arrived yesterday, but they're here to help secure the area and keep us safe. I have every confidence that they'll manage just fine."

Perkins noticed that he didn't mention the eight people who were missing. No need to fuel the panic. Apparently the rest of the team agreed with her. They all kept their traps shut.

Perkins looked at Piotrowicz.

"Are you okay?" The man's stance said he was pissed off. Still, he managed a smile.

"Yeah. I'm good," he said, but the bandages said otherwise. "Some burns, but nothing that can't wait until everything calms down. Vogel already patched me up."

Cho nodded, looked at Silas, and adopted a placating tone.

"We have a medic here," he said. "Are any of your people hurt?"

The short man nodded hard.

" …We can't find…" He took a deep breath again. "There are four members of our expedition who we left behind when we were attacked. We should send someone to find them. And Colleen was attacked by something that tried to choke her. Whatever it was, it didn't want to let go of her face, but it finally fell off on its own and died."

"Then let's have a look at Colleen first." Cho glanced at Piotrowicz, and gestured toward the van. "You up to a quick look?"

Piotrowicz sighed. Wounded or not, carrying his pack or not, he was still the most experienced when it came to basic first aid. He trudged over, and Vogel went with him, unslinging her backpack. They disappeared inside.

Willis spoke up.

"Did you remember the receiver for the probes?"

Nigel looked at him and nodded.

"It's in the van. Hardwired, actually."

Willis headed over without asking, and Cho looked to Perkins, gesturing for her to go along. If the probes were working and recording, they might provide important information—including readouts with clues as to why the hell they weren't working everywhere.

As Willis and Perkins neared the van, Piotrowicz and Vogel came back out. Vogel was holding the freakiest damned thing Perkins had ever seen, and looking like she might just puke her guts out.

The thing was pale, about three feet long, and hung from her hand by a thick, serpentine tail. The tail ran down to a body that boasted two bulbous sacks and long spidery limbs that had curled in on themselves, like a dead insect. It looked like a deformed cross between a crab and a spider.

Cho looked at the thing and blanched.

Vogel dropped it to the ground and Piotrowicz crouched over it, pulling a very large knife from his boot—the better to probe at the corpse.

Perkins stared and stepped back.

Hell's gonna freeze over before I get close to that thing, she thought to herself.

Cho cleared his throat.

"Is that thing very, very dead?"

"Hell, yes." Vogel nodded. "No way I'd've touched it if it wasn't."

"That's the thing that tried to choke your friend?" Cho directed that at Silas.

The man nodded and swallowed nervously.

"Where is Colleen?"

Piotrowicz looked toward him. "She's dead. I'm sorry, but it looks like she might have been shot."

"But we don't have any weapons." Silas's voice was very small, and he blinked back tears. Whatever existed between him and Colleen, he was feeling the pain of her loss.

"She's got a hole in her chest. There's no heartbeat. I didn't see a hole in the window, but I suppose it's possible she got hit when we were firing at those things."

Silas's eyes were watery.

"No, she was alive when we pulled up. She was lying back across a seat. She was unconscious, but I can't see how you could have shot her."

"Was anyone else on your team injured?" Cho asked.

"No. Just. Just Colleen." Silas looked wretched.

Perkins thought she saw something moving, off in the shadows, but when she turned in that direction there was nothing. It still sent a chill through her. While she was looking, though, Willis climbed onto the transport and went in search of the receiver. Perkins sighed, and then followed.

The inside of the van was chaos. Items were tossed around and kicked under seats, equipment had been pushed aside or knocked over, and a lot of it probably was junk as a result.

Halfway down the length of the vehicle, flat on her back across one of the seats, a dead woman stared at the ceiling. The hole in her chest was huge and bloody, with ribs visible through a ruin of cloth, skin, and flesh. Perkins didn't want to look at her, but she did.

The woman's body was still stippled with sweat, the skin wasn't yet sallow, and the flesh wasn't yet sagging—she had to have died within the past few minutes. A trail of blood ran from the wound all the way to the floor. Damned if it didn't look like something had left little footprints in that mess.

Perkins reached over and closed the woman's unseeing blue eyes, even as she mouthed a small prayer.

Willis was busy examining the readouts. She stepped up behind him, careful not to disturb what he was doing.

"What did you find?" Her voice was enough to make the man start. His eyes rolled toward her, and he clutched at his chest.

"Not much," he said, sounding disappointed. "I mean, the readouts seem to have died." Perkins looked at them and saw what he meant. There was a good amount of information and a decent rendering of the dig site, but either the probes had stopped recording information or—more likely—the interference between here and the probes was blocking any further reception.

"Shit." She shook her head. *Enough.* She didn't want to be around the corpse any longer anyway. She climbed out of the van and headed back for her group.

By the time she got there, the majority of the research team had calmed down a bit more. A couple of them had actually joined Piotrowicz in his examination of the spider-like thing on the ground, and most of the others were looking at the larger life-form where it lay nearby.

"Whatever it is, I would hardly call it an advanced life-form," Silas said. He seemed to have recovered enough for his scientific curiosity to kick back into gear. "There's no evidence of a highly developed brain apparatus. I can't even see how this creature can eat, in any way that makes sense to you or me."

"Yeah, well, I don't give a shit if it can cook a seven-course dinner," Piotrowicz said. "For us, it's a payday." He dug into Vogel's backpack until he came out with a sterile plastic bag. Vogel followed what he was doing, and crossed her arms.

"You put that goddamned thing in my backpack, you get to carry it. I've had enough of it—I don't want it anywhere near me."

"Quit being such a girl, Vogel." Piotrowicz tried to smile, but it looked as if it hurt like hell.

"I am a girl," she replied. "You should know, you've been trying to get in my pants for long enough."

Willis stepped out of the van and put away his comm unit. He looked less than pleased.

"There was a problem with the equipment they were moving in the mine—they tried to move too much at one time," he said. "The lift needs repairs, and it's going to be another two hours at least, before they can get it down here."

That sent a ripple of disappointment through the group, and several began to voice their objections. Before they could do so, Dwadji's voice came through the comm.

"Still no sign of DiTillio, Rodriguez, or Joyce," he said. "Manning and his group are going higher. They're going to see how far the tubes go, and see if they can locate the missing team."

"Tell Manning about the van," Cho said. "Tell him we have… seven more with us."

"Affirmative."

Cho looked to Willis.

"Are there no backup lifts?" he asked. Perkins was pretty sure he knew the answer, and was grasping at straws.

"Not down here," was the reply. "They only made it down a couple of levels, and were still working on clearing the rubble out of the way on the other side of the vessel."

Piotrowicz walked over from where he'd been talking with Silas. He didn't look happy. He was holding up the bagged body of the spider-thing.

"Well, if this thing is indigenous, there're probably more where it came from," he said. "But Doc Silas can't say how many, or where." He looked up at the silicon tube, and frowned.

"Where the hell did this one come from?" Cho asked, turning on Silas. His expression made it seem as if he held the scientist personally responsible.

"The expedition…" Silas began, cringing under the gaze. "We had only just broken through the latest wall. The ones we left behind—" He cut himself off. "The ones who went through the wall, they must have seen something, but they were cut off before they could report." He looked at the creature. "For all we know, the thing was a pet gone feral, or the equivalent of a rat. We just don't know. We weren't expecting to run across something alive."

"As much as they have their heads stuck up their asses, sometimes the Colonial Marines get it right," Cho growled. "Protocols like quarantines come in handy at a time like this." Silas looked as if he wanted to explain himself, but Cho waved it aside. "We all know why the Colonials weren't informed, doctor. We're all here for the same reason. I just don't like running around blind with not one, but *two* different predators on my heels." He pointed to the dead thing that Lutz had dragged along. "What can you tell us about that thing?"

"It's fast, it's savage, and it bleeds acid strong enough to melt steel and pop galvanized rubber tires. I smeared a couple of them against walls on my way back here, and when they were hurt the blood ruined everything it touched." Silas peered at it with open fear, as if he thought it might jump up and renew its assault. "Also, it has a second set of teeth inside its mouth, mounted on a very long proboscis."

"Nasty—even if you get in a good shot, the sons of bitches can kill you," Cho said. "What do you think, Mister Willis? Are these the things your employers want us to bring back, or is there something *else* out there?"

He looked around.

"Has anyone seen Willis?"

25

DARK TIDES

They waited for something to show up, training their weapons on each of the openings that led to the spot where they'd stopped to take a break. Decker listened for any sound, scanned for any feeling that might indicate that something was approaching.

Nothing.

All he got for his efforts was a raging headache.

After a short time, Manning chose a direction for them to go, up and toward what he hoped would be the ship itself. The tubes got larger the closer they came to the source, and with open space they would be better able to defend themselves without shooting one another in a chaotic firefight.

Decker was up front, with Manning. At times the tunnels became so cramped that they had to crouch, or crawl on hands and knees. The captured creature had been retrieved from where they'd dropped it, and the poor bastards in the rear had to drag it. The thing showed no signs of recovering from the third high-voltage jolt.

Maybe it's finally dead, Decker mused. *One down, and who knows how many more to go.*

"These tunnels must be impervious to the bugs' blood," Manning commented. "Maybe it's the same stuff as their hides, or something a lot like it. Silicon still seems like a safe bet." He paused for a moment, then took a branch that rose steeply in what Decker hoped was the right direction.

"Whatever's in their blood, I don't want it splashing on me—especially in here," the merc continued. "It sounds like the stuff messed up Piotrowicz pretty bad. So if we run into any more, use non-explosive rounds."

"Why?" Decker asked. "I mean why non-explosive? Won't they splatter, regardless of what we use?"

"The tunnels are fairly strong," Manning replied. "But if they get blown to hell, we might not survive the fall."

Decker knocked on the side of the tunnel. The result was a dull thud.

"No. I don't think so," he said. "We're surrounded by dirt and rock now. Back when we started, the tunnel shook a little with each step. Now I think you could jump up and down, and never have to worry about it collapsing."

"Good point, genius." Manning looked down until he met Decker's eyes. "All we'd need to worry about is having a few tons of dirt bury our asses. Shouldn't be a problem."

"Gotcha." Decker had to admit it was a good point.

The air was thick now, and stiflingly hot. Any draft they'd had before didn't stand a chance against more than a dozen tightly packed bodies, all taking in oxygen and generating body heat. He didn't think they could actually suffocate, but it wasn't helping his growing sense of claustrophobia.

He paused.

No. Not claustrophobia.

Despite the medications working in his system, his pulse was rising, he was starting to sweat again, and he fought to catch his breath. Every exhalation felt too shallow, and every intake was a sharp gasp.

"Shit," he said. "I think they're close again." He closed his eyes and focused.

The thing behind him was starting to wake up again—it was still alive, and still radiated the primal urge to *kill*. But there were more of them around now.

Adams cursed behind him. She was trying to get her motion sensor to work, but when she hit it this time, it just gave a crackle of white noise, and the small screen showed nothing but digital snow.

It wasn't just Adams. Several of the mercs had tried again, and failed.

"Where?" Manning tried not to sound exasperated. But he didn't try too hard.

"Best I can tell you is they seem to be above us." He pointed ahead, in the direction they were climbing.

Manning looked up, where the tunnel progressed for some distance into blackness. There was hardly any light, since the tightly packed bodies didn't let much through. He reached for the flashlight he had strapped to his helmet, and increased the beam. Then he started moving again.

"Not seeing anything," he said over his shoulder, "but I'll keep looking, and you keep sniffing, or whatever the hell it is that you do."

Decker didn't bother to reply. Behind him, Adams also increased the power to her flashlight, but he wasn't sure how much it helped. The tunnels were black and glossy—glossier now, as the moisture was thicker. He wondered if that meant this was a newer tunnel. Whatever the case, the damp in the air added to the damp crawling sensation on his skin.

"It's close, Manning," he hissed, keeping his voice low. "Really damned close!" The feeling of hatred aimed his way was so intense it burned. And somehow, the fury was directed at him.

But why? he asked himself. *Was it Ripley? What could she have done to them?* From what he had seen of the creatures, it was a miracle she'd survived. *Of course, in the end, she didn't... Had they marked her? Near as he could tell from the files, she'd never even been to the planet.*

The idea seemed absurd.

They were still crawling upward, and they couldn't have turned, even if they wanted to. Then, perhaps forty feet down the tunnel Decker heard a man call out in surprise in an area he had already passed. What the merc said was incoherent, more a bark of surprise than anything else, and a moment later the bark became a yell… and then a scream.

Adams pushed into him, half sliding her body along his as she turned as best she could. Her elbow jammed into his leg as she drew one of her firearms. There was a jumble of voices and bodies as the rest of the mercenaries did the same, struggling through the cramped space.

What came was a volley that hit his senses with explosive force, and a second after that the screams of pain began. The tide of bodies, pushing hard to get more room, combined with waves of surprise, and then anger. Yet despite the emotional flood, he felt that hatred again.

Manning cursed and turned, bracing his legs against the sides of the tunnel as he looked down and tried to see past Decker and the mercenaries.

"Pull back from it! Pull back!" he bellowed, but no one seemed to hear—or care. Then an unearthly hiss blended with the chaos of voices.

The monster tore through the first of the mercenaries, clawing and biting and pulling itself up the startled soldier's body as it came. The man tried to fight back, which was where the first explosive noises came in. He opened fire, but all he hit was the wall. Rounds hit the hard surface, cracked through it, but despite Manning's fears the tunnel survived the impacts.

Even as the man fired he was dying. The shape tore his chest open as it crawled up him. His screams were amplified by the narrow space, and then they morphed into a gurgle, followed by silence.

The creature was so intent on its prey—Decker himself—that it ignored some of the mercs that blocked its way, effortlessly thrusting them aside. It moved with an impossible speed, invisible in the darkness, until only three people remained between him and the thing that wanted to kill him. Looking down, he could see past the tangle of limbs—pushing, fighting, trying to get a bead on the thing.

And then he saw it, caught in a beam of light.

26

TRAPDOOR SPIDERS

It was bigger than the last one, or maybe it only seemed that way because of the narrow environs. Whatever the case, the woman closest to it—Kelso, he thought it was—opened fire. Her weapon chattered and her arms shook from the recoil.

The clawing, screaming thing below her shrieked and hissed and broke apart, pieces of its body flying back, leaving streamers of the thick goo that passed for blood within its chitinous body. It thrust forward one hand, which disappeared under the assault of her weapon. It tried to throw itself back, but there was no room for escape.

It screamed and it died, and from behind it, from below it, the screams from the mercenaries increased. The blood of the thing rained on them, burning whatever it touched—flesh, weapons, armor. The flesh screamed.

"Good work, Kelso," Adams said, and she let out a breath. Decker did the same, unaware that he'd been holding it until then. "Sonuvabitch, how many down?" she added.

As the nightmare fell back, it revealed a wide hole in the top of the tunnel that hadn't been visible before. It had been hidden within the intricate swirls of the black, glassy substance, enabling the creature to take them entirely by surprise. It hadn't come from behind—it had dropped down from above.

Almost before he realized it, he saw the next nightmare crawling down, peering toward him. The sleek black face shifted as it sought what it wanted, and then he felt that eyeless gaze upon him, and he heard the first deep screech of hatred. The thing was moving, clawing its way up the wall, heading straight for him.

The woman who'd killed the last alien—Kelso—let out a cry and started firing. The people beyond were her comrades, but she wanted to live, and the demon below her, coming toward her, would kill her without even noticing. All that mattered was the prey.

New screams were added to the cries of pain. The creature opened its mouth, and revealed a second set of teeth that bulled into the woman's calf and tore meat and bone apart, even as she fired into the oversized skull. It died violently, but the blood that flew from its death splattered the walls, the people below, and the woman who killed it.

Her leg already in ruins, the mercenary howled and tried to back up even further.

Up above, Manning was bellowing for them to retreat, though he wasn't moving himself. Decker wanted to shout back, wanted to demand to know where he was supposed to go, but part of him understood that the words were meant for the soldiers below, the ones who were trapped in the way of the incidental acid bath that was coming their way.

Still burning, still screaming, Kelso pushed herself higher still as the second black shape fell lifelessly into the tunnel. Manning climbed, making room for Decker, Adams, and the merc behind her to follow suit. There was no choice, really. They could stay where they were and let the people under them die, or they could try to make a little more space, and hope it was enough.

It wasn't. The hole was still there, and even as Decker climbed it gave birth to another black nightmare. The shape was fast and it was savage and it came into the tunnel moving at a hard clip without slowing down.

Kelso tried to fire again, but the thing was there too fast, and its limbs nearly blurred as it shredded her armor and the flesh beneath. She screamed through the process but never fired another round. It clawed past her bloodied corpse, letting her fall with the other dead, onto the people below.

And then there was one man between Adams and Decker and the savagery that was coming for him.

Suddenly the world went bright and the monster fell back shrieking, its head a molten ruin. As it fell it bled, and the bottleneck of corpses and struggling mercenaries received another acid bath. Plasma. It had to be.

And then the attacks stopped. The mercenaries below pushed and clawed their way past the broken dead, climbing the bodies of their fellows, desperate to avoid the burning fluids and the crushing weight of four dead bodies. They screamed and groaned in the process, some wounded, others merely panicking and justifiably desperate to escape.

"Where the hell did they come from?" Manning's voice cut through everything else. The man under Adams pointed to the opening and spoke into his comm-link. Decker didn't hear the words. He was too busy looking at the hole, waiting for whatever would come from it next. He tried to tell if there were more of the damned things nearby, but he couldn't separate out the sensory input. The emotions were too loud, perhaps.

That, or there were no more of the things around.

For now.

Adams was half pinned against him in the narrow tunnel, and she looked into his face for a moment before touching his arm. "Come on, we're going down."

"What?"

"Nico says that hole in the top opens into a bigger area—he climbed up there to get out of the way of that last monster. It's empty now. We're going to check it out."

Decker looked down. Nico must have been close behind Adams, and he was dropping back down from above. Beyond him, the mercs were still working their way past the tangle of dead and wounded.

"What the hell are we going to do in there?"

Adams shrugged. "Regroup."

He looked up toward the merc leader, who nodded his agreement.

"The tunnel's only getting narrower up here—if they hit us again, we'll be dead." He pointed to the opening in the ceiling. "Move it! Come on, let's get this going."

Decker followed orders. Sometimes there's no choice. His life seemed to be made of moments like that lately.

Maybe five minutes later Manning called roll.

They were all gathered in a cylindrical open space, and compared to what they had left, it was like a luxury accommodation. They could stand and there was room to move. Of course there was also room for other things to happen and so several of the team moved to guard the different areas where there were openings into the chamber.

Seven of them had been hurt by the creature's claws or the blood spilling across them. Kelso wasn't hurt—she was dead, and so were three more besides, people whose names Decker had never learned. They had to leave the bodies, which were too covered in acid. Somewhere—probably far below—the thing they had captured earlier was once again on its own, having been dropped in the chaos.

No one offered to retrieve it.

"You have any idea how screwed we are?" A merc whose nametag said "Brumby" was peering down into the tunnel they'd vacated. "They're the same color as everything around us. They have the same sort of texture. They decide to hide, we're going to be lucky to see them at all.

"We are *so* screwed," he repeated.

Manning looked at Decker for a long moment and then spoke up.

"And that's why we want to keep our good buddy here alive and well. He's our little early warning device. He may not be perfect, but he's known both times these things were coming." He held out a headset, and Decker took it. "I want you wearing this from now on."

Decker looked around. Everyone else still had a headset.

Where'd this come from? he wondered. Then he knew. *Kelso.*

Brumby shook his head. "Where are we going from here?"

"Sooner or later we're going to reach the ship, or the mines," Manning answered. "Likely sooner, if I've estimated the distance right. Once we do, we'll get the hell out of these tunnels." He looked over all of the wounded as he spoke, assessing their injuries. It looked to Decker as if most of them were able to walk at least. "We get back to the cavern, we gather the rest of the team, and we get the hell out of here."

"What about the aliens?" Decker's mouth was flapping before he really thought about it.

"What about them?"

"We are supposed to get specimens." There. He'd said it. "That's what we're here for."

Manning stared at him long and hard. He didn't say a word.

Adams spoke up instead.

"Pretty sure we're going to have more chances there, Decker. I don't think you need to sweat it."

But I do, he thought. *I really do. I can't go home without them, not if I want to have a home to go to.* And ultimately that was true. If he wanted his family safe, he needed an alien.

Once they had one, let Weyland-Yutani worry about how to get it home in one piece. Get it through the quarantine, past the Colonial Marines. Pay off everyone they needed to pay off. How they did it…

He didn't give a damn.

Manning spoke up at last.

"We all know why we're here, Mister Decker," he said, and he spat out the name as if it tasted bad. "No one gets paid by the hour on this assignment. We all know what's at stake."

Decker stared hard, nodded, and said no more. For a while there was relative peace as the mercenaries tended to the wounded and worked on the best possible route to get the hell away from the very things they were hunting.

27

NEGOTIATIONS

Willis didn't go far. He just needed a little privacy.

The group hanging around near the hub was a bit too large. Once away from them, he activated the comm-link he'd been given when the *Kiangya* came into orbit.

This was so much bigger than anyone could have hoped. An entire city worth of relics wasn't far away, and that had to be worth more fortunes than most people could ever imagine. And the living alien life-forms. Whatever they were, they put a different spin on *everything*. The Colonial government was decidedly opposed to any first contact scenario that occurred without their involvement. Weyland-Yutani knew that, of course.

And the people on the surface of New Galveston—they knew it, too. That posed quite a problem.

He needed to make sure that things were kept properly quiet. But it was hard, trying to be in charge of a situation when he was trapped beneath the surface, waiting for the lift.

One call in private, and he could get that taken care of.

Maybe.

Rollins answered almost immediately.

He looked around to make sure that no one was close enough to hear him. No one seemed to care, actually. They were justifiably interested in the creatures they were studying.

Nevertheless, he moved to the far side of the van, and looked back toward the dig site.

"Can you hear me?"

"Of course I can hear you, Mister Willis." Rollins's voice was calm, and carried a tone of authority that Willis found very attractive. He had always been drawn to strong women.

"We've acquired two separate active life-forms down here. We also have a much larger archeological find than originally believed."

There was a notable pause.

"How much larger?"

"Perhaps a full city. More than a town. An ancient, extraterrestrial city. Doctor Silas believes the ship we found might have been taking off when it crashed."

"Continue."

"We need to renegotiate, Ms. Rollins." He needed to be firm about that. Willis had plans, and those plans included moving much higher in the chain of command.

There was a long silence again, long enough to make him wonder if he'd overstepped his boundaries.

"I'm afraid I'll need more information than you've provided thus far," she said. To his relief, she didn't sound upset. "All you've told me is that there's a city. Do you have any details?"

"It's being mapped right now," he lied. "Before long, I can get you complete readings."

"Mister Willis, I already have access to those readings."

"You do?"

"You aren't the only person who is assisting me. I have the readings already." He peered back toward the group.

Who could possibly...?

"That said, you can still be of value to this enterprise. We will need data to back-up the information that has been transmitted. And there are certain... arrangements that will need to be made planetside. You make the appropriate arrangements, and I believe we can discuss a change in our business arrangement."

"Understood," he replied, and he smiled.

He looked back at the mercenaries and the expedition and their collected dead things. Whatever she required, he would provide it. There was always a way.

He'd learned that a long time ago.

28

They were awake now. Truly awake, not merely moving while they dreamed. In the darkness they uncoiled themselves from the places where they'd rested and gone into dead-sleep.

For some of them the dead-sleep had gone on too long. They had slumbered and withered and reached a true death, their shells cracking, their lifeblood burning away. For others the sleep was a painful thing and awakening was agony on a level they'd have never conceived.

But they endured.

They thrived. They did what was necessary for the hive.

Through their dark tunnels they heard the sounds of prey. Food, yes, but more importantly, hosts. There was still food in the older places. The desiccated remains of the creatures that had died long ago. It wasn't much, but as long as they spent most of their time in sleep, it sufficed.

But the dead could not host the young. It took life to make life.

And now, at last, life had come again. Soft, and weak and mewling life that would be reborn into the hive.

Eggs had hatched, the breeders had done their work, and now the hosts moaned and made their soft sounds as they prepared to birth new children. And all around them the adults waited.

Not all of the adults.

Some had been sent to locate the destroyer. They moved and hissed and their voices chattered in the darkness. The very thought of the destroyer *was enough to send shivers of rage through them. So many had been lost, and not even the long sleep could dull the pain. Most of the queens had been destroyed. Queens! Slaughtered! The lives of so many taken, including the sacred queens.*

Most of them.

Not all.

Life prevailed.

And as long as life prevailed, they would hunt the destroyer, and keep their queen safe.

One of the hosts let out a feeble moan and jerked within the confines of the birthing webs.

A moment later lifeblood flowed, and the face of a newborn broke through into the world.

They moved to protect it. The young were so vulnerable.

And the queen in her chamber let out a note of approval.

And all was right with the world.

Or it would be, when the destroyer had been dealt with.

Soon.

Soon.

They were patient. They had to be.

Life prevails.

29

DIGNITY

Dwadji and Cho were taking a break and eating, so Perkins settled back at the hub and listened to Manning's orders. The boss man was pissed off, but he was holding it in.

He was trying to find his way back to the mines, and she was trying to help, but there wasn't much she could do. The damned readings were all screwed up. His group was out there, but she couldn't read vitals or get a fix on their location. The best she could manage was to bring him up to date on what was happening at the hub.

And after almost three hours of that, Cho came and relieved her.

When she sat down for chow the tension was thick. Lutz and Vogel were keeping an eye on the landscape while everyone else crashed and burned for a time. No one was sleeping, but they were trying to rest—especially Piotrowicz, whose burnt face was causing him a good deal of pain. He'd opted not to take anything for it. Dulled senses seldom helped in a crisis.

Doctor Silas was staring at the alien remains, with deep worry lines creasing his face. She almost asked him what he was thinking when he spoke.

"Has anyone secured... Colleen's body?" he asked, keeping it together surprisingly well. A few of the mercs glanced at one another.

"Afraid not, Doc," Vogel said.

"I see." Silas nodded quietly, turned, and walked silently toward the ruined vehicle. Perkins grabbed a reaper and followed him.

The damage to the van was terminal. Two tires were flat, one completely shredded. Acid from the bugs had left several holes in the vehicle, and while they had stopped smoldering, they were simply too large to be patched. All the vehicle was good for now was spare parts—and not many of those.

Silas climbed into the van ahead of her, and seemed surprised by her presence when she climbed in behind him. He looked toward her for a moment and then managed a weak, apologetic smile.

"Colleen was a good person," he said. "I just want to show her a bit of dignity."

Perkins nodded. "Let me. Okay?" she said, and she slipped past him. "Let me, and when I'm done you can help me move her to a different location."

He nodded his head and his face twisted into grief. He struggled with it, trying not to show his feelings, but it was obvious to Perkins that the dead woman was more than a colleague.

She'd been down that path a few times over the years. Walker had been her "special friend with benefits" before he got himself killed, and D'Angelo had been something even more before he decided he simply couldn't live the lifestyle any longer. Sometimes, late at night when she was trying to sleep, she still hated him a little for that. She understood it, but she hated him just the same.

There were supplies on the vehicle, and among them she found a cloth sheet large enough to allow her to wrap the body. She was about to do so when Silas spoke, causing her to jump.

"Hold on a moment," he said, and he moved closer, peering at the corpse's chest wound. He reached out, hesitated for a moment, then rolled her over and looked at her back, frowning the entire time.

"What is it?" Perkins asked.

He frowned, grief replaced by curiosity... and something more. There was something else in his expression.

"It wasn't friendly fire," he said. "We thought it had to be, but it wasn't. Whatever... whatever happened to Colleen, it wasn't a gun blast at all."

"How do you know?"

He pointed with a trembling hand.

"Look carefully. That's an exit wound. But there's no entrance wound." His frown deepened. "Whatever it was that killed her, it did so from inside of her body."

He moved closer to the dead woman and his fingers carefully, ever so gently, examined her mouth and her neck. When he tried to move her face, she resisted. Rigor mortis had taken hold.

Nigel Silas cried silently as he continued to examine her body. Perkins stood with him and bit her tongue. She was a mercenary, and she fought wars for money. She refused to allow herself the luxury of crying for a woman she'd never met, or feeling pity for a man she didn't know.

No matter how much she wanted to.

He stepped back and let her finish the task of wrapping Colleen's body, and then helped her lift it from the van. With the lower gravity on New Galveston, it was likely she could have carried it by herself, even though it was a bit on the heavy side. But it wasn't about proving that she could do it herself. It was about letting the poor man say his goodbyes, and letting Colleen keep a few final dignities, even in death.

When they'd laid her down near the bodies of the alien things, Nigel thanked her and took her hands in his. His were soft. Hers were callused. They lived in different worlds.

He went back to the van and retrieved a case, opening it to reveal some tools. And then he moved over to the spidery thing. For the next fifteen or so minutes, Nigel the man disappeared. Doctor Silas the scientist began working on a puzzle.

Having examined the dead creature, he went back to the van. After a few minutes he emerged, carrying a long strip of translucent hide. It was small, it was wet, and it had several features in common with the full-grown alien—enough to point to a clear connection.

Silas looked it over carefully and set it down next to the spider-thing, still without saying a word.

She almost asked what he was thinking, but decided against it. Most likely it was beyond her, anyhow.

What good could it do?

30

WOUNDS

Exhaustion began to take its toll.

They traveled along the pathway that Manning thought most likely would lead to the mines, and they made good progress. But they had been hiking nonstop for hours, much of it uphill, and they needed to rest.

So they found a large enough chamber that they would be able to defend themselves from an assault. They placed lanterns around the area, lighting it as best they could, and dozed in shifts. Most of them, at least. Decker tried to sleep, but every time he began to do so, the nightmares came back more vivid than they had been since his original injuries.

Finally he drifted off, and in his dream he and Adams were locked in a passionate embrace. As he moved to kiss her, streams of spiders came spilling from her mouth and nose and ears. They swarmed over his face, biting him everywhere they landed.

He awoke with a jerk, and instinctively swatted at creatures that weren't there. Rolling over, he tried again to doze, but without success. He was simply too…

They're coming.

Decker bolted upright with a loud gasp, and scanned the area where the group had stopped. Easily half of the freelancers stirred, and several of them grabbed for their weapons.

Instantly alert, Manning looked at him.

"Where?"

Decker paused, then pointed. There was no sign of a tunnel where he pointed, but they awoke the few mercs who remained asleep, and cleared the area he'd indicated, training their weapons. Silent Dave pushed a button on whatever sort of cannon he had unstrapped from his back and the thing let out a long, barely audible whine as it warmed up.

"Won't do to leave our asses bare," Manning said. "Izzo, Simonson, and Foster—watch the tunnels, and make sure nothing comes crawling out."

While the trio moved to comply, the rest focused their weapons on the spot Decker had indicated. As prepared as they were, several of the mercs flinched when the surface opened up. What had been a solid wall swiveled open on an invisible hinge, and the first of the things came in fast, looking around as it stepped through.

It wasn't expecting them to be prepared, however, and instantly it encountered the business end of Bridges' shocker. The creature spasmed as the contacts hit it, and it let out a shriek that was painful to hear. But then it fell, half in and half out of the tunnel.

Another one followed, skittering over the body of the first and making a beeline for Decker. It hissed at him, drooling clear fluids from its mouth as it came, and he stepped back reflexively. Frozen by the hatred of the monsters and the emotions of the humans, he couldn't force his arms to raise his weapon. The sounds they made echoed in his head with a haunting familiarity. In his dreams he knew those noises were words and now those words were directed at him, hurled at him like curses.

Muller was the closest, and he raised his reaper. The first two rounds missed, but the third and fourth and fifth hit their target, blowing sizeable holes through the creature's exoskeleton. The merc danced back to avoid the splash of acid blood, cursing under his breath.

Then the dam broke. Monsters poured into the room in a frenzy. Claws and whipping tails and black chitin and teeth, so damned many teeth. Decker emptied the clip from his pistol and stepped back, seeking to reload but unable to find the extra clip.

"Damndamndamndamn*damn*!" he chanted, as if it would help.

Manning barked orders, and the mercenaries opened fire. Prepared this time, they were systematic in the massacre, carefully firing and decimating the creatures as they spilled into the room. Decker located his clip, slammed it into place, and joined in the fun.

Then one of the mercenaries let out a scream.

Decker spun and saw the black form of another monster—one that had to have come from another direction. It bit into the man's arm, and it was just a matter of seconds before he was down and the thing was jumping forward, heading for the next in line.

More followed.

The lanterns didn't last long in the melee. Whether they were knocked aside or the things were smart enough to target them, the chamber quickly fell into darkness, punctuated only by the dancing flashlight beams coming from a few of the mercenaries.

Manning was bawling out commands, and the members of his crew were doing their best to listen, but there was no opportunity to regroup. The creatures were relentless as they swarmed their prey. Decker shot another target, knocking it away, then grabbed at Adams, pulling on her arm. She flinched and turned toward him in the semidarkness.

"This way!" he shouted, and she seemed to hear. "Come on!" He pulled and she hesitated, then came with him, calling on the comm for Manning and the rest to follow.

And just like that they were making a tactical retreat. There was no choice really. Not for Decker at least. The flood of emotions from all around threatened to overwhelm him, and all too quickly he would be unable to defend himself. The two of them found a tunnel that was farthest from the swarm, and darted into it.

He heard the running footsteps of several other mercenaries behind them, but didn't pause to look around. The way became narrow, forcing them to crouch, and he worried that they would be forced to go back, but then it widened enough that they could stand.

Manning was nearby, cursing nonstop. And Decker knew why—at the same time as he knew there had been no choice.

Nevertheless, they had done the unthinkable. They left the rest behind.

31

The destroyer had escaped. But there were hosts, and they were still alive.

Three-fingered hands and six-fingered hands grabbed the bodies and dragged them toward the birthing chamber. Shape did not matter to the hive. Hosts from the distant past looked different from the hosts they dealt with in the now, but the offspring were all of the hive and the queen's glory. When one of the hosts tried to fight back, it was subdued. The hosts had weapons, but they could not see well in the darkness.

That was good to know. It was best to understand the weaknesses of the prey.

There would be time soon for finding and killing the destroyer. They had not forgotten the sins of the past. They would never forget. There would be no mercy.

The hate burned in them, accompanied by the adoration they felt for the breeders, and their worship for the mother. It was to the glory of the mother that they dragged their latest prizes, and set them before the eggs.

The eggs opened, and the breeders came forth. The hosts screamed with fear as the breeders joined with them, and offered them the life altering seed of the mother. And then the breeders died, as breeders do, that the hosts might be reborn in the glory of the mother.

3 2

PANDEMONIUM

"We need to go back to the city ruins," Silas said. "I think we have a bigger problem than we realize."

"How do you mean?" Cho asked.

"I don't think they're dead," Silas said. "Your men, and my associates. Not yet at least." He waved his hand toward the bodies. "I think they've been taken, the same way poor Colleen was taken."

Cho just stared.

"I don't mean to be cold, doctor, but isn't *that* Colleen?" He pointed to the body that Perkins had helped carry from the van. "How can she *not* be dead?"

Silas looked at the shrouded form and did a few rapid-fire blinks to fight back tears. He managed to hold his own.

"Yes, that's her," he replied. "But I mean I think they might be used the same way she was used." The man's throat worked for a few seconds while he struggled with the words he was trying to say. "I think they put something inside her, to incubate. It broke out of her when it had completed the process, and was ready to emerge."

Cho stared long and hard, and then said something under his breath that Perkins didn't hear. When he spoke up again, his voice was clearer.

"You make it sound as if we're dealing with a bunch of bugs," he said. He paused for a moment, as if a thought had struck him, then waved it away. "I don't have time for this shit. I need to see what's going on with the lift." He headed back for the hub.

Perkins stared after him only for a moment. She understood where he was coming from. All of the scientific information in the world meant less at that moment than the lives of the missing.

Vogel shrugged. "You need to go back to the site? Or only part of the way?"

"Part of the way would suffice, I think," Doctor Silas said. "The ship. It seems to cause the interference. If we can get past that, I can probably link into the readings from the probes. If they're still working, they've likely mapped enough to let us know what we're dealing with." Doctor Silas looked distracted, peering off into the distance. From what she could tell, he seemed that way most of the time.

"Then let's do this." Vogel rose up and headed for the flatbed.

"We need equipment." Silas stood, turning toward the van.

"I'll pull your sensor array, key it to our monitors, and load it onto the flatbed." Perkins sighed. "Let me read the frequency off your remote. Maybe we can make something happen."

She climbed back into the van and felt a chill that she tried to ignore. She didn't believe in ghosts. She did, however, believe in getting the hell out as quickly as she could. She checked the bottom panel of the sensor array for the probes, to see if the frequency was written there. It wasn't.

Of course not, she thought, still ignoring the crawling sensation that ran up and down her back. *Why should anything be easy?*

After about five minutes she climbed back out, carrying the entire sensor array. It weighed more than she wanted to think about, but she managed it. While an extremely impatient Vogel waited, she locked the array onto the dashboard of the truck and rigged a power supply.

While she was doing that, Vogel walked over to Cho.

"We're gonna drive the professor over to the other side of the ship," she said, "to see if we can pick up a signal from his probes. Shouldn't take long."

"Like hell you are," Cho responded. "The last thing we need is—"

"No!" Willis said. "That's *exactly* what we need, and I'm going with you. That information could be invaluable." He paused, and added, "The rewards we could reap might be more than you can imagine, Mister Cho."

The tech thought about it for a moment, looking as if he didn't trust what Willis was saying. Then he shrugged, and waved Vogel away.

"Take off, then," he said. "And get the hell back here as fast as you can manage."

They piled onto the truck, started it up, and headed toward the back of the spacecraft. Perkins had the wheel. Willis looked all around as if there might be more of the dark monsters waiting around every corner.

To be fair, there might.

On the flatbed, Silas watched his array, and Vogel kept her weapons ready.

We've gotta do this fast and easy, Perkins thought. *Only as far as we need to go, to get a signal.* She didn't like the idea of going near the place where Piotrowicz got his acid bath. *Upload the data, and get the hell out.*

It took them about ten minutes to reach the other side of the wrecked ship. Vogel was sweating by the time they stopped. She couldn't blame her. She'd actually fought them. Perkins hadn't even seen the things while they were alive, and they scared the shit out of her. She turned the truck, ready to make a fast getaway.

"We can go now," Silas said, breaking the silence.

"What?" Perkins's hand shot toward her gun before she realized what he had said.

"We can go now. We got what we came for." When he heard that, Willis looked ready to jump out of his skin.

She hit the ignition, and they lurched forward. Silas studied the display as they bounced along, Willis peering over his shoulder, looking as if he wanted to scream. Then they pulled up near the hub, the scientist set the display aside, and hopped from the truck and walked away without saying a word.

"No need to thank us there," Vogel said to the retreating scientist. "We're glad to have helped."

Willis picked up the display and studied it, a look of elation spreading over his face. Perkins craned her neck, trying to look.

"It's not complete, but the probes have been working the entire time," he said. There was an image that looked like the interior of the spacecraft. He tapped a command, and a cavern came into view. There were ruins—structures of every shape and size—stretching back as far as the image could go. "An alien city," he said. "This will keep the research and development people busy for decades."

"Has there ever been a find this big before?" she asked. He looked at her and shook his head.

"I don't know of any," he replied. "And we need to avoid getting ahead of ourselves. It might be that there's nothing down there." He paused and stared at the screen. "But I don't think that's the case. I think there's a lot down there. A lot." He sounded far away, and she suspected he was already planning how he would spend his portion of the earnings.

Despite herself, she smiled.

She left Willis with his monitor and climbed out. As she approached the main group again, there was a ruckus. The look Cho fired her way was one part exasperation and one part plea for assistance.

Silas was in the center of the mix, along with a couple of the others from his group—a heavyset man named Fowler, and a woman who was jabbing a finger into Cho's chest. Perkins picked up the pace, hoping to help the woman avoid getting her finger broken off at the knuckle.

"What's going on over here?" she asked.

They all tried talking at once. Cho bellowed louder than the rest, and for a moment there was quiet.

"Doc Silas thinks we should blow up this entire level," the tech leader said. "Like, right now."

"What?" Perkins looked at the scientist and he stared back, his eyes moist, his lower lip jutting out.

"It's not like th-that," he said, stammering. "Your man, Decker, he was the one who asked the question. Willis told me about it. He said he d-didn't know the answer. I just decided that it needed answering."

"What question?"

"What happened to all the aliens?"

"What?"

"What happened to all of the aliens? I don't mean those things." He waved his hand toward the assortment of dead things, and then waved his other arm toward the wrecked craft and the excavation that lay beyond it. "I mean *them*. The ones who lived here, once upon a time. The race that built the city, and this ship. What happened to all of them?"

Doctor Silas gulped in some air.

"I think I know the answer. I think those *things* happened to them." His finger stabbed in the direction of the dead aliens.

"But I thought the city-builders died off a long time ago." Perkins shook her head. The man's distress was contagious. She contemplated asking Piotrowicz to come over and administer a little something to calm him down.

But Silas smiled and nodded.

"Yes!" he said. "Exactly. And these others, the acid-blooded ones, they should have died, as well. Even if they are responsible for what happened in that city. But they didn't!"

Cho shifted his weight.

"What's the point you're making, doctor," he said. "Whatever these nasties are, they're far from dead, and our orders are to bring one back."

"But we're dealing with an alien species!" Silas answered, and it was his turn to be exasperated. "We don't know what sort of life cycle it has. But if they've been down here since the ship crashed, we must be talking centuries. And they're ready to do to us what they did to an entire *city*."

After that, everyone was silent. Finally Cho got up and waved an impatient hand.

"You handle this, Perkins," he said. "I have to check in with

Manning." He stalked off toward the hub.

Chicken shit, Perkins thought, but she didn't say it. "What do you mean, doctor?" she asked. "What makes you think these are the same creatures?"

"There shouldn't be *anything* down here that's alive." He waved his arms to encompass everything around them. "This area was sealed off for a long time. *Centuries*. And no one knew about that city. *No one*. That could have been abandoned for over a thousand years, for all we know.

"There are no water sources down here, less than ten percent humidity, no clean air. There shouldn't be anything bigger than a microbe down here. But when we entered the ship, we found bodies—so old that they were almost beyond recognition. And they all had one thing in common. They had holes in their chests.

"It seemed so impossible, I needed to confirm it, needed to see the data stored in the probes," he continued. "I prayed I was wrong, but it was all there."

"But it's not possible for something to live that long, is it?" Perkins said.

"Whatever we think is possible, something broke out of her body. The same way that something broke out of those old cadavers in the ship." There was real fear in his voice as he pointed at the spider-thing. "It lays eggs in a host. The host enables the egg to mature until it hatches. The thing that comes out grows bigger, until it looks like those things."

The woman with the pointy finger spoke up, but Perkins couldn't understand a word she was saying. Whatever language she was using, it wasn't one she'd heard before.

"To have destroyed an entire city, there had to be hundreds of them." Silas looked at Perkins with wide eyes and practically begged her to understand him. "If that's what happened—and I believe it is—then what happened to the rest of them?"

Perkins was about to respond, when she was cut off by a wail.

33

SURPRISES

Piotrowicz winced when Lutz peeled back the bandages on his face. Skin came away and exposed raw nerves, and he wanted to scream. They were out of sight of the others, some distance away. Petey didn't really want to share this particular experience.

Lutz stared at the wound with clinical detachment. He was good at that.

"Bad?" Piotrowicz asked.

"Well, you'll get to keep most of your face. You might want to consider a little plastic surgery when we're done here, though."

"What about the burns? Are they that bad?"

"No. It's just your face—it's ugly as sin." Lutz grinned. "Second degree burns mostly. You've got some blistering, and a little exposed meat, but I think you got lucky on this one." He sprayed chemical scrubbers on Piotrowicz's face that removed any chance of bacterial infection. It stung like hell. Then he painted the burned flesh with a thick salve, and reached for fresh bandages.

While he was questing for the sterile wraps, there was a sudden pain in his hand, as if it had been bitten.

What the hell? He jerked back, and peered at the spot where it had occurred. There he saw a large, black-shelled bug of some sort. The thing hadn't given any warning, and he hadn't even noticed it coming close. It just attacked.

The silvery teeth took most of his hand and wrist in one savage bite.

Lutz let out the tiniest little noise. He looked at the mangled wound where his hand had always been, and gave out a high-pitched wail.

Piotrowicz saw it all happen, but it was so damned fast, and he had his guard down. With people all around, he never thought anything might be able to sneak up on them.

The bug was smaller than the ones they'd fought and killed, and if he had to guess it was younger. That didn't make it any less dangerous. The fucker lashed out at Lutz, that nasty damn tail pounded into the big man's chest and he fell back, a soft sigh coming from the wound as a lung collapsed.

He heard voices nearby, alerted by Lutz's wail, but they still couldn't see him—didn't necessarily know where it had come from.

Piotrowicz reached for his rifle, and his hand found only air. No chance he was taking his eyes off the thing, though. No chance in hell. It jumped and he kept reaching, straining for what should have been right there, *damn it*, and the shining black thing hopped closer and hissed and sprayed wet from its mouth as it reached for him.

He kicked the bastard in the face as hard as he could. The bug snapped backward and hit the ground. He finally risked a look, and the rifle was nowhere to be seen. He felt a cold certainty that he was a dead man.

The thing came at him again, hunkering low to the ground as it scuttled closer. Baby or not, it was a fast learner. The tail lashed back and forth, sometimes rising above its body, and he found himself watching that deadly barb.

"Need a little help here!" he shouted, hoping someone was close enough to come to his aid.

Dwadji's voice came across the comm.

"What's going on, Petey? Where the hell are you?"

"Got a bug here and it's hungry!"

Vogel's voice came from his far left.

"I'm coming," she shouted. "Don't move."

"Don't tell me! Tell this little bastard!"

The alien dropped to all fours and charged, hissing and weaving. That damned tail jabbed for his face and he blocked with his left arm, feeling the ridges on the tail scraping layers of cloth and flesh from his forearm and wrist.

Dwadji was saying something else in his ear, but he couldn't pay enough attention to understand the words. The bug pounced on him, and he managed to catch its arms, but that wasn't enough. Seemed like every limb on the bastard was made for cutting, because the clawed feet walked up his legs and it kicked at his chest, carving trenches into his armor and sending him staggering backward.

The only noise he could make was a gasp. The hind claws kept kicking with enough force to stop him from doing much of anything else, and the unbelievably powerful arms fought to break free from his grip. He was trembling from the effort of holding the damn thing back.

Vogel bellowed at the thing, but it kept attacking, hissing as it tried for his face with that freaky ass secondary mouth. The tail arced up and over its shoulder and came for his skull.

Piotrowicz flinched back and waited to feel the blade at the end of that thing come pounding through his brain. Instead the creature let out a surprised squeal and he felt the hot body of the thing suddenly lifted from him as Vogel smashed it sideways with the butt of her pounder.

The rifle was a grunt's wet dream. It carried ninety rounds in the magazine that fired in single shot, three round, bursts or continuous streams. It sported four slots for artillery and two locations for bayonets. Though it was fairly heavy at eleven pounds, it was also perfectly balanced for use as a hand-to-hand tool. That was where the nickname came from.

Vogel knew how to use a pounder. The bug sailed back from the impact and curled in on itself for a moment as it rolled and skidded to a stop. When it looked back in their direction, Piotrowicz could see the broken shell of its skull. It was bleeding slightly, and the liquid sent up little puffs where it hit the ground.

Vogel flipped the weapon around and fired three rounds that hit chest, face, and the back of its elongated head.

The little bastard hit the ground, and twitched.

Piotrowicz was gasping and shaking as he climbed to his feet and looked down at the thing. It wasn't any more than three feet long. Less than half the size of the things that had been on the van earlier.

"What the fuck is that?" He was jazzed on adrenaline, and barely aware that he was shouting.

Vogel ignored him and shot it twice more, just in case. It stayed exactly as dead as it had been before, but leaked more of its acidic blood all over the ground. Dwadji was screaming into the comm now, asking if Piotrowicz was still alive.

Why don't you just drag your sorry ass over here to see, Piotrowicz thought to himself. "We got it," he said into the comm.

Vogel talked into her headset while Piotrowicz moved over to check on Lutz. The man was alive, but it wasn't looking great. His breathing was labored, and while they had a few medical supplies and he was a decent medic, the majority of their supplies were currently somewhere in the tunnels, far above. He cursed himself for listening to Manning when the man told him to give up his pack.

The rest of their group managed to get to the scene, and Silas moved to examine Lutz. While he wasn't a medical doctor, it turned out that the woman from his group actually was. Her name was Rosemont, and she got to work on keeping Lutz alive—give or take a collapsed lung.

"What the hell happened here?" It was Cho, just arriving, and Piotrowicz filled him in. The tech's jaw tightened, and he walked a short distance away, talking into his comm. Calling for the lift.

But there was no one. Nobody on any of the upper levels responded to his calls.

34

REGROUPING

Decker thought he just might start screaming and never stop.

The shaft they were in was narrow, and definitely underground. When they'd finally managed to get away from the ambush and stopped running for all they were worth, Manning called for names and they came up with a total of eight remaining survivors. Only a couple of them—including Decker—had functioning lights, so the darkness wrapped around them. It was one thing to be stuck in the darkness. It was another to think there might not be a light at the end of the tunnel.

Adams kept trying her motion sensors. She wasn't alone. But none of the damned things worked.

The comm was functional, and Cho had reported what was happening back with the rest of the group. It felt as if the hub was an unimaginable distance away.

Not far ahead of him, Manning had taken to tapping the walls with his knife's hilt. At first Decker thought he was just nervous, and wanted to keep a weapon near at hand. But the longer he kept doing it, the less that seemed to make sense. So he asked, and Manning explained as if he were talking to a very stupid relative.

"I want to know it the minute we're not underground any longer," the merc leader said. "We can't do much as long as we're beneath the surface, but once we're out, there's a chance we might blow this damned popsicle stand.

"Now shut the hell up, and let me get back to it."

Since the man was carrying a very large knife, Decker decided to listen to him.

Sometime later—it felt like days, but was probably only an hour or so—the sound of the tapping changed. One moment it was a dull *thud*, and the next it sounded hollow.

Manning stopped, and ran his fingertips over the entire wall of the tunnel, but there was nothing. No hidden door, no seam—nothing that indicated a weakness in the surface. Finally he swore and stepped back.

"Fuck this," he said, and he lifted his plasma rifle. "Close your eyes!" he shouted.

Even with his lids closed, Decker could see the flare of light. The stench of the melting silicon was acrid, and tasted of salt.

"Clear!"

Decker opened his eyes, squinting at the ghost of the glare, and saw the most wonderful sight he could remember in a very long time.

The wall was slagged. The tunnels were strong enough to resist the acid of the aliens' blood, but they weren't able to hold their own against the heat of the plasma discharge. The edges were still white hot, slowly fading to yellow, and beyond the wound in the wall, there were lights. After the pale illumination of the flashlights and lanterns, it seemed almost as bright as a clear day.

After a few moments, Manning tested the edge of the opening he'd made. When he was satisfied, he slipped through, letting the business end of the plasma rifle take the lead. Decker closed his eyes for a moment, trying to tell whether or not there were any of the things out there. It seemed as if they were safe for the moment, and he moved forward, quickly followed by Adams.

In short order they were gathered in a cavernous mine shaft.

There were lights. Lots of them. There was space and that was a blessing. The air was stale and recycled, and it still felt like a cool breeze and tasted sweet on the tongue. Decker took great, deep breaths, and the others around him did the same. A sense of intense relief radiated from the people around him, and mingled with his own.

Adams did several deep knee bends and stretched her body. After only a moment's hesitation Decker joined her and so did several of the others. Manning did not. He kept his eyes in motion, his face nearly expressionless as he scanned the area and assessed their location as best he could.

"Cho," he said into the comm link. "We're out of the damn tunnels and in a mine shaft."

"Any idea what level you're on?"

Manning shook his head. "No, though I think we may be above you. Are you at the console? I want to know if you can get readings off of us yet."

"Hold on." There was silence for a few seconds. "I'm here, but we're still not getting readings."

"Okay. Something's not adding up here, I don't care what's in the soil, or on that ship. Low level radiation wouldn't be causing this much trouble for our systems."

"I get you." Cho's voice was clipped and professional. "I've had Dwadji trying different frequencies, but so far we haven't found one to counter whatever is causing the interference."

"Well, keep at it. I want to know what's causing us all of this grief."

"Gotcha," Cho replied. "Maybe the radiation built up over time, the longer the ship was buried?"

Adams shook her head.

"I gotta cry bullshit on that," she said, and she looked to Decker for confirmation.

He shrugged. "I've seen terraforming disasters, and that level of radiation can cause heavy-duty infiltration, but I have my doubts about the ship. Any level of radiation that could reach more than few hundred feet from the wreckage would have to be much heavier, and likely life-threatening."

Manning listened, and his eyes narrowed.

"Yet Willis guaranteed that it was safe," he said. "And we took him at his word. Something is fucked here. I want to know what."

"We're looking into it, boss," Cho answered. "But it's slow going, and we've had a few shitstorms down here, too."

"Which reminds me. Are your motion sensors working?" When he said that Adams tried hers again, but had no better luck.

"Haven't checked 'em. The way Willis was talking, there didn't seem to be any point."

"Well, check. If they are it helps you know if any more of those things are coming your way."

There was silence for a moment, then Cho spoke again.

"Listen, about that," he said. "Silas, the guy who led the expedition to the ruined city, thinks we might have a major infestation situation on our hands here. If he's right, we may be screwed ten ways from Sunday."

"How so?"

"From what I can understand, he thinks the bugs we've run across might actually be hibernating down in that city." Another pause. "He thinks they might be waking up. We're not talking a couple of these things, if he's right. Silas thinks there could be hundreds of them, or maybe even more.

"He thinks they might have taken out the entire city, back in the day."

Decker looked around, at the other mercenaries. Where they had been letting themselves relax, just a little bit, they were alert again. Weapons at ready, peering in both directions along the mine shaft.

He looked at the hole they'd come through. It was dark in there. *Very* dark. Anything at all could be just a few feet away, and waiting to strike.

Then he looked to his left, and saw nothing but a long expanse of dirt road. To his right was a mirror image. There were no markings, no indications of which way they should go.

Looked inward again, and tried to focus past the background noise.

There... They were nearby. He knew they were close, because he could feel them. The catch was trying to figure out where they were, before they launched another assault.

Hundreds of them? His pulse sped up. He pulled his own plasma rifle from its spot on his back, checked the charge, and reminded himself of exactly where the safety was located.

Somewhere in the distance, something made a noise loud enough to echo down the tunnel. Decker couldn't tell which direction it came from, but he intended to find out.

Hundreds of the things. They only needed one. And then they needed to get the hell away from New Galveston, once and for all. *Eyes on the prize,* he told himself. *And stay alive.*

"Decker!"

He jumped a little at the sound of his name. It was Manning.

"What?" he responded.

"You getting any of your weird feelings?"

He nodded his head, and rolled his eyes involuntarily. He hoped Manning hadn't seen it. But the merc seemed oblivious.

"Which direction?" Adams asked.

"Not sure," he answered. "They're not close now, but I think they're more determined to find me now." It seemed as if their hatred was focusing. He didn't really know how the creatures worked, but it was as if they were homing in on him, like a compass points to the magnetic pole of a planet.

Decker licked his upper lip and tasted salt. He was sweating again. But he was determined not to panic—especially since it might get him killed.

"Okay," Manning said. "So which direction... *feels*... like our best bet to avoid the things?" His control slipped a bit. "Give me something to work with here!"

Decker closed his eyes, and that odd squirming sensation crawled through his scalp again. After a moment, he pointed to the left.

"Then let's go that way first to see if we can figure out where the hell we are." To the rest he said, "Light 'em up. Keep your attention where it needs to be, and don't let anything get near us that isn't wearing a company outfit."

Decker took a deep breath and spoke his mind.

"Listen, don't think I'm crazy here, because I'm not. But maybe we should go *toward* them." A couple of the mercs started to protest, but Manning shut them up, and Decker continued. "If we can find them before they find us, maybe we can get the jump on the fucker."

Manning looked him in the eyes and smiled very briefly.

"Look at you, growing a pair." Decker might have been offended, but he heard the admiration in the man's voice—even *felt* it. Manning was used to thinking he was a coward.

"I'd agree with you, but we don't know enough about the territory," the merc leader continued. "If they're hiding in one of those tunnels, we could spend hours with you looking for them, and never see them. And there's a lot less of us now. We need to keep our eyes open, and get back to the hub."

They started walking, moving with care and watching for anything out of the ordinary. The only good news was that there weren't too many places where the damned things could hide.

Manning got on the comm with Cho again.

"Get me Willis."

A couple of minutes passed, and the bureaucrat came on the line.

"What do you want, Manning?" Something in his voice bothered Decker, but if it affected the merc, he didn't show it. "Where the hell are you?"

"I think we're on a level above you, so there must be a secondary lift—no way are the miners going to wait for days just to hitch a ride." He paused to look around, then continued. "Any idea where we can find it? What should we be looking for?"

Willis tried to give him directions, but Manning cut him off.

"We don't know where *we* are, so directions aren't gonna do squat. What do the miners do, if they need to get out fast?"

Before he could answer, they felt the ground beneath them tremble slightly. Suddenly it began to rock more dramatically, building rapidly until they were knocked off their feet. In the distance, something rumbled loud enough to shake the walls. To protect himself from falling debris, Decker curled into a fetal position on the ground. Fragments of rock pelted them, and dust carried down the long corridor, a roiling cloud that billowed for a moment before it started to settle.

"What the hell was that?" Manning was up and looking back the way they'd come.

"Don't know, chief," Adams said. "But it was a long way off—and it came from the direction we're headed." She checked Decker, then each of the mercs, to make sure no one was hurt.

"Cho!" Manning bellowed into his comm. "What's the situation down there?"

No answer.

"Shit," he said. "Well, we'd better find out what the hell that was."

At Manning's command, they continued the way they were going, shielding their noses and mouths from the dust, which was only just beginning to settle. Decker found himself studying the walls and the ceiling. Whatever had happened could very well have caused structural damage. He wondered if they were in danger of having the entire mine collapsing around them.

As much as that concerned him, there was something even more pressing. He could feel the aliens on the move, that hideous sensation of their malignance creeping through his skull. Whatever had caused the tremor, it seemed to have stirred up the hornet's nest, as well.

His pulse was still too fast and his breaths seemed too small, so he focused himself. Anything else came for him, he intended to handle it as quickly as possible. He checked his plasma rifle again, and reminded himself of an ancient truism.

You're not being paranoid when something really is out to get you.

35

BOOM

Perkins stared at the bodies. She needed to get back to the comm. Soon, too, as her break was almost over. *Break*. That was a sad joke.

Just a couple of the creatures had thrown the entire group into chaos, and one of them hadn't even been full-grown. They were all spooked, and no one was following protocol. It was all Cho could do to keep up with Manning and his group, and it sounded as if they had lost a lot of good men.

Now everyone was just coming and going, without rhyme or reason. Hell, she had done it herself.

Cho should've had my ass in a sling, she thought. But he hadn't, and things were getting worse.

Her eyes drifted back to the spider-thing on the ground. What it had done to Colleen was monstrous, and the thing that had killed her from the inside had grown at an unbelievable rate. Only partly grown, it had taken off Lutz's hand, and put him out of commission—if he even lived.

And now, if Silas was right—and she really, really hoped he wasn't—there were hundreds, maybe *thousands* of the things out there. Waking up. Fuck, they had destroyed an entire *city*, killed everyone in it.

She hadn't seen Silas in a while. Willis was missing, too.

Maybe they're off somewhere, cooking something up, she mused. As quickly as she thought it, though, she dismissed the idea. It didn't seem like Silas's speed, not after everything he had been through.

Anderson was walking the tops of a couple of the larger stacks of supplies, doing her best to keep her eyes on the perimeter. Perkins climbed onto one of the shorter stacks and got her attention.

"You seen Willis or Silas?"

Anderson gave a half smile. She was never going to be anyone's idea of a model, but she was attractive enough. They weren't serious, but they'd spent a few nights together over the months they'd worked together.

"Silas was headed for the lift. Willis went off that way." She pointed toward yet another collection of building materials, this one stacked with lighting supplies and, *oh, hallelujah*, portable toilets.

Thinking that he'd had the right idea, Perkins nodded her thanks, and headed for the latrines. Nature was calling.

Halfway there she spotted Willis. He was closing a door in the cavern wall. Not a latrine, but a real door. It looked old— so much so that it blended in with the rock surface, making it almost invisible.

Where the hell does that lead, she wondered. Had she not been heading in that direction, she'd have never seen him.

She started to motion toward him, but before she could do so, the ground bucked under her feet, knocking her to the ground.

The sound was impossible to miss. Thunder hammered down the path leading from the lift, followed by a cloud of dust. A moment later it repeated, and then one more time. Each report was so loud that it sent spears of pain through her skull. Instantly her hearing was gone, replaced by a sharp ringing that pierced her senses.

She scrambled to her feet and headed for the rest of the group. Cho was moving, and so was Piotrowicz, and then they all were, every mercenary and explorer sprinting toward the truck. As they clambered into the cab and onto the flatbed, someone cranked the engine. But while she could feel the vibration, she couldn't hear it. She was vaguely aware of someone trying to talk through the comm, but she couldn't discern any of the words.

The comm would have to wait.

* * *

By the time the truck lurched to a stop at the lift site, most of the dust had settled.

Silas stood there, blood flowing in a rivulet down his arm, abrasions on his face and scalp, where the hair was thinnest. He was bleeding from a wound above his ear, but the cut looked superficial. The impact had knocked him to the ground, too. His body was coated with a thick layer of dust. In his hands he held a pulse rifle.

Perkins instinctively reached for her own sidearm. Then she realized his weapon was aimed at the dirt. He looked toward them and said something, but she couldn't hear him.

Cho jumped off of the truck and hit the ground running, heading straight for the scientist, murder in his eyes.

Behind Silas, debris clogged the entirety of the lift shaft. Three of the heavy support posts were shattered. There was no sign that they had been melted, but Perkins did the math. There were four slots on the pulse rifle designed to hold grenades. Even from a distance, she could see that three of the chambers were empty.

Cho reached him first, and grabbed him by the shirt. He drew back to throw a punch, but the scientist just stood there. The tech stopped, his fist still in the air, but then he lowered it.

"What the hell did you do?" Perkins demanded as she skidded up next to them. She could hear herself, but her voice sounded muffled.

Silas looked directly at her and spoke slowly and clearly, his voice loud.

"We can't leave here," he said, as if stating the obvious. "The contamination has to stop. There's a planet full of people above us, and we can't let them all be slaughtered by these things."

She stared at him, but couldn't bring herself to speak. He'd just effectively killed every last one of them.

Then she looked over at the lift, which had fallen down when Silas blew the supports. Mining equipment, raw trimonite ore, and heavy machinery now blocked the only possible exit available to them. She saw something dark, pooling, off to one side, and hoped it was oil. In another place she thought she might have seen an arm, sticking out from under the rubble.

The thought made her shudder.

Tons of raw materials and shattered equipment jammed the entire opening to the shaft above. Even if they could squeeze past, there was no guarantee of how far up the shaft was clogged with debris and ruination. There was no way that the people above them could get to them before they were dead.

"I had to do it!" Silas was screaming now, but even his outraged bellows sounded like they were coming through thick wads of cotton. "You were going to leave here! You might be contaminated!"

Cho drew his pistol. Silas looked right at him as he moved, and Perkins saw the motion out of the corner of her eye. She was still trying to put it all together in her head when Cho fired. The single shot blew Silas's intellect all over the debris that was blocking their exit from the tomb he'd built for them.

"You fucking idiot," he said to the corpse that crumpled at his feet. "You didn't save anyone."

He spat on the body.

She felt her lips press together into a tight line. She should have been outraged. She should have been afraid that Cho might have lost his mind. Maybe he had, come to that. But mostly what she was angry about was that the bastard beat her to it.

If she was going to die down here, she wanted the satisfaction of killing the son of a bitch who had guaranteed her death.

"That prick stole my rifle!" Piotrowicz looked at the wreckage, and the dead doctor and pointed.

Cho stared hard at him for a moment, and then turned away. No one else dared speak—especially not the doctor's former associates.

"We have to find another way out of here." Perkins looked toward the rest of the group. "Any suggestions?"

Rosemont looked back toward the excavation site.

"We could try the tubes." She didn't sound at all thrilled by the idea. "A few people have gone up that way."

Perkins scowled. "The one our team went up is blocked now. Has anyone gone up in those things, and come back down?"

The woman shook her head. "Not really." She was silent for a moment, then offered, "There's also an access tunnel, but it's narrow and it's a very, very long walk up the stairs. I don't even know if it's clear, or if it has those… things in it."

Perkins thought back.

"Would the entrance be off past the latrines?" she asked. The nod she got was all she needed. She nodded in return, and went to find Cho.

She'd just reached him when a crash made her jump. It came from the lift tunnel, and was loud enough to pierce the slowly diminishing deafness. There was nothing to see, but whatever it was, it had to have been heavy.

And then the lights above them flickered, and dimmed a bit.

"What the hell?" Piotrowicz looked around, and his eyes sought the power source for the lights. "Something in there must've hit the cables. I'll take a look and see if I can spot anything." He shook his head as he started to move. "I need to get my damn rifle anyway."

Anderson had given up her place on top of the building materials, and was standing on top of the truck's cabin. It was the best place for an unobstructed view of the surroundings, bleak as they were.

"See anything?" Perkins asked.

"Not yet," she replied. "But I will soon."

"Why do you say that?"

"Ever know anyone who could resist finding out the source of a loud noise? I mean, we came running, didn't we?"

"You think the bugs'll come?"

Anderson's eyes kept scanning the distance, looking from time to time toward the ruined elevator shaft.

"I'd bet on it," she said. "I'd win."

Perkins nodded. Unfortunately, she agreed.

"How do you think this is going to play out?"

"If that dead fuck was right, we're not getting out of this alive. It's seven thousand feet of staircase to get to the top of this mess."

Above them the lights dimmed a second time, leaving the entire area locked into a fading twilight.

Perkins was liking the situation less by the minute.

36

SHADOWS

The sun set, and darkness came over the Sea of Sorrows.

No one working on the dig site paid much attention, save to manually activate those few lights that didn't come on automatically. There were always a few, it seemed, regardless of how many redundancies were built into a system.

Luke Rand settled his considerable bulk into a chair in the dining hall. There were others around, but not many. Herschel and Markowitz were near the Hut, waiting while the engineers did what they could to unfuck whatever the hell had happened down there. The lift had crashed down, the teams on most of the levels had come up already, a good number of them shaken but no worse for the wear.

Rand was still working on reducing the toxicity levels in the Sea of Sorrows. The plans to build Laramie Township had been scrapped, but with the discovery of the trimonite, the location remained a priority. More so than before, really. Where there was a profit to be had, Weyland-Yutani liked to be the first on the spot.

Luke looked at his food, picked at it for a while, and decided he wasn't really very hungry.

Seeing Decker had done that to him. He liked Alan. He always had. He was a straight shooter, and that was a rarity. If the man liked you, you knew it. And if he didn't, you knew that, too. He was smart, and he kept an open mind.

So why had he screwed the man over? He couldn't get it out of his head. And to make matters worse, Decker didn't seem to mind. Or maybe he didn't know.

Either way, Luke didn't have much of an appetite. Of course that wasn't exactly a bad thing. He'd put on a few spare pounds, like enough to make an extra person.

The chaos down below made him uncomfortable, too. It seemed too much like Karma, and he didn't like that idea at all. Everyone working on the site knew about the alien ship—that wasn't the sort of thing you could keep under wraps. Not for long. He'd seen it. Not in person, just the pictures that the first couple of teams brought up, but still.

But what about the quarantine rules? Sometimes the damnedest things showed up when you were terraforming a planet. Like on DeLancy. It wasn't pretty, what happened to the people there when a spore frozen in the permafrost had thawed during the terraforming. By the time Rand arrived, he was in full environment gear, helping gather the remains. That was when he decided to get out of the business and retire.

And now he had a chance for that.

All it cost him was Decker's friendship. And a piece of his soul, maybe. It might be that Decker didn't know, but Luke knew. He could barely stand to be around the bastard. He knew what the company had done. He'd received the call from the home office, making damn sure he stuck to the "official" story.

Still, after DeLancy, losing Decker's camaraderie was a small price. He'd pay it ten times over, no problem, if it got him away from this shit once and for all.

He looked at his plate for another minute and gave up. The food all looked like crap and probably tasted just as good.

When he'd cleaned up his mess, he bought a couple of beers—these days he could afford the outrageous price—and left the building, heading for the barracks. A movie or two, and he'd get some sleep.

Off in the semidarkness of the night, he saw something moving across the sand. He squinted to try for a better look. Something was crawling out of the sand, and then it vanished. There were a lot of things wrong with Luke's health—even on a lower gravity planet, the whole weight thing caused issues—but there was nothing wrong with his eyes.

He tucked his beers into his pockets. He wanted his hands free. One hand touched the comm on his hip. The other reached for his shock-stick. Luke was a big guy, and he could certainly handle himself in a fight, but lately there was a lot of talk about security breaches, and he had a lot of money on the line.

He looked out over the sea, checking the mounds and the dunes and the mostly flattened terrain. The sky was getting darker, not because of the sun setting but because of the rain clouds moving in, and he took his time, trying to make sure he wasn't just being paranoid.

Damn. There *was* something out there. Fifty yards out he could see a couple of figures. They were trying not to be seen, but he spotted them.

"Hey, Bentley? You on duty tonight?" His comm crackled in response.

"Yeah. That you, Rand?"

"Got it the first time. Hey, we may have a problem out here. I think I see someone out on the sand."

"Where are they? Near the Hut?"

"No, they're a good ways out. Maybe like a hundred meters past."

"Wouldn't be the rescue team, then," Bentley said. "Might be somebody that found a way out, though."

"Well, you want me to check it?"

"Yeah, it's just me here right now. I can't leave the booth. Would you mind?"

Luke sighed. He'd rather drink a beer. On the other hand, if someone had found a way out from the site, he maybe should check.

"Yeah. I got this." Luke started walking, keeping his eyes on the spot where he'd seen the movements.

"Any news from below?" he asked.

"Yeah, and none of it's good," Bentley responded. "Far as I can tell, they can't get below level three. If there's anyone further down, we haven't heard a peep from them. They're trapped, and most likely dead."

Damn, that doesn't sound good, he thought. *It's hard enough getting a signal down there on a good day.*

"Well, I'll keep you informed," he said to Bentley. "You do the same, yeah? I got friends down there."

"So do I, buddy."

He kept walking, and as he got closer, the shadow-shapes were visible again, and becoming more clearly defined. They were definitely people, but something about them didn't look right. Were they wearing survival masks or something? He couldn't decide.

He covered another dozen yards, and then he stopped dead. The night had deepened further, but not enough to hide what he was seeing. These weren't humans. He didn't know what the hell they were, but humans didn't have tails, or whatever sort of weirdness was sprouting from the backs of those things. And their heads were too damned long.

He reached for his comm.

"Bent?" he muttered, automatically dropping his voice. When there was no response, he spoke louder. "Bentley? I *really* think we got a problem out here."

"What's that? Come again, Rand."

Then the two shapes turned toward the sound of his voice.

"Oh, fuck me." They started to move toward him.

"Say what?"

"Bentley! You gotta get the hell out here!" he said, and he was shouting now. "Bring a weapon. I mean it!" The things were coming faster, and they didn't move right. They moved like dogs or something. They moved so damned *fast*.

He reached for his shock-stick.

Shock-sticks were designed as a non-lethal alternative to firearms and other security measures. They were set to give exactly enough juice to drop a person temporarily.

He managed to shock the first one, and it didn't slow down in the slightest. Then the other one was on him, and he was screaming.

37

RED SAND

When he didn't hear back from Rand, Brett Bentley tried reaching him by comm three separate times, even as he armed himself. He started to call for backup, then remembered that damned near everyone on the site was down at the Hut, trying to get to the people in the mine.

This better not be a false alarm, he thought grimly. Like as not the dumb ass has gotten drunk again and then passed out on the sand.

Rand seemed like a nice enough guy, but he'd started drinking more and more since he'd been reassigned. Bentley decided that if he spotted the damned fool out in the sand, sleeping it off, that he'd let him stay out there.

Maybe a good rain shower will sober him up.

He grabbed a hand-held flashlight, and as an added measure lit up the perimeter security lights. Within less than twenty yards he saw fresh footprints, and he followed them about a hundred yards further. He stopped at a dark wet spot on the black sand—at first he couldn't make out what the source of the moisture was.

Maybe he stopped to take a piss, he thought. Then he flashed his light over the area, and saw the red tint that painted some of the black grains. Unless the man was pissing blood, something nasty had happened there.

Looking around, he found the signs of a struggle, then tracks that looked as if something—likely Rand—had been dragged away. Weirdly enough, there weren't any other boot prints—or anything resembling them.

Bentley pulled his pistol. His nerves were singing. Fourteen years he'd worked with the company. In all that time he'd never had to actually draw his weapon. He'd been trained, and he was a capable marksman. What he was not was combat seasoned.

He preferred it stay that way.

Just the same, he had a job to do. He called on the comm, and didn't recognize the voice of the person who responded.

"Talk to me," the voice said.

"I've got a situation out here," Bentley replied. "There's a guy missing—one of the contract employees—and there's blood on the sand. There's sign of an assault. Can you send someone to back me up?"

"Negative," the voice said. "We've got all hands on deck here, and that's still not enough. You'll have to check it out on your own."

"Roger that," Bentley said, adding silently, *Thanks for nothing, asshole.*

He started following the signs of struggle. The sand was dry and soft and held remarkably little detail. He could see a clear ridge where Rand had been dragged along, and there were indistinct marks on either side. So it had to have been two attackers. He followed the trail for about twenty yards.

"Damn it." The trail just sort of faded away. His light played across the soft sand. There was nothing after that. No indication that Rand had broken free, or that his attackers had gone anywhere.

Bentley turned and started back the way he'd come. Without clear cause, he couldn't go further from his post without violating procedure. Before he'd walked ten paces, however, he heard something behind him.

He turned and shone his light into the darkness.

So he had a good, clear look at the teeth of the monster.

3 8

WRECKED

Manning stood right next to Decker as they looked down the shaft at the smoldering ruins of the lift, and several tons of mangled equipment. The merc summed up his feelings by spitting a wad of phlegm down into the wreckage.

Decker looked at the shaft walls and shook his head. The entire thing had been carved from the surrounding stone, and the walls were damned hard. Despite that, he saw long cracks in the stone.

"Holy crap." Adams was looking up. "We're on level *five*." She pointed with the business end of her rifle, toward the markings at the upper edge of where the tunnel met the shaft. "Now all we have to do is find the backup elevators, and maybe we can get out of here."

Cho's voice came through on the comm, and Manning walked away, talking into his headset. The tech had killed the man responsible for the wreckage. It was a scientist from the excavation— he'd been convinced that they had to sacrifice themselves, to stop the creatures from getting loose.

The man had a point, Decker thought, but he kept it to himself. *But I'm not sure* anything *can stop them. Our own chance of surviving, on the other hand…* No. Screw that noise. He had every intention of getting home with his prizes intact. He had a life to get back to, and no intention of surrendering it to Weyland-Yutani, or to whatever weird monsters they might find.

The lights flickered again, and if the power failed them, they were in serious trouble. Then he had a thought.

He looked to Adams, who was scanning the way they'd come, and frowning.

"Hey, Adams?" he said. "Do you guys have anything that'll let you see better in the dark? I mean, as standard issue."

She shook her head. "No such thing as standard issue. We buy our own supplies. So, yeah, some of us have night goggles. They're no good in cramped quarters, like the tunnels—especially with all of us crammed in there together. And they'd've made targeting a bitch. But out in the open, they might just be of some use." She grinned. "I've got 'em in my pack."

"Seriously?"

"Yeah. The goggles work, but they aren't as good as the naked eye unless you're dealing with full darkness. Too much loss of peripheral vision."

"Yeah, I know what you mean." He'd used them on more than one assignment. There were sleeker, less intrusive models on the market, but they cost an arm and a leg. More than a grunt—or a paper pusher like him—could afford.

He didn't bother to ask if she had a spare set.

Something started to make his scalp feel tight, and the background noise ratcheted up a notch... then another. He pulled inward, and reached out with his senses.

"Manning?" His voice was low, and he kept it steady. When the merc didn't respond, he tried again, louder. "*Manning!*"

"What?"

"They're coming!"

Manning crossed the distance in an instant.

"Where are they?" His face took on harder angles. Decker took a minute, and then responded.

"They're coming from several directions," he said. "And they're not going to take long to get here."

"Then let's get our asses in gear, find the damned backup lifts, and get the hell out of here," Adams said, her voice shaking almost imperceptibly.

Manning nodded.

"Let's go. Keep your weapons ready, and check your armor. We'll follow the most traveled pathways." He took point again, carrying his rifle at the ready. This time Decker was in the middle of the group, with three in front of him and four to the rear.

Walking became increasingly difficult for Decker. *Everything* became harder to accomplish. As they approached the hole Manning had burned in the side of the tunnel, the sense of the creatures was so intense that it dragged on him physically.

Shit, he thought with sudden clarity. All he could get out was, "They're here!"

The first ones came through the hole, while other shapes charged from ahead of them, and some came from behind—most likely from the elevator shaft itself. He couldn't hope to count them. He didn't want to. All he could do was take aim and hope he didn't blow his own leg off when he fired.

The freelancers were in motion before he was. They were trained for combat. He was trained for filing reports. That thought had him half giggling even as he tried to find a target. But the mercenaries were in the way.

Four of the dark forms came in fast, barely even making a sound except for the skitter of their nails on the hard-packed soil and rocks. Adams opened fire while they were still a dozen yards away, and let out a grunt each time she pulled the trigger. Four little sounds from her, four loud booms from her weapon, and two of the creatures exploded.

The other two were better at ducking.

One of them leaped through the air, bounced off the wall and plowed into a dark-haired man who was already firing at another shape coming his way. The mercenary just had long enough to realize how screwed he was, before the shape rode him to the ground, clawing and biting the entire time. No one could help him. If they shot the damned thing, the blood would just burn the poor bastard.

He clubbed the thing in the face with his pistol, and tried to push it aside, but it didn't move. The creature's mouth opened and drooled out a slick of moisture even as the secondary mouth drove into the poor bastard's face and ripped at his cheek.

Decker looked away as another of the things leaped at Adams. She tried to track it, but failed. Before she could compensate for its speed, the alien was past the range of her weapon.

Decker didn't think. He just aimed, pulled the trigger, and got blindly lucky. The plasma from his rifle missed Adams and hit the fast moving demon in the upper back, burning through two protrusions that rose like frozen wings from its shoulders. The creature shrieked and bucked, trying to escape the pain.

Then it turned. Even through its agony Decker could feel it focusing on him, noticing him for what he was, for *who* he was, and the feeling of hatred was magnified a dozen times over.

Injured, possibly dying, the damned thing still came for him, clawing at the ground as it changed direction. There wasn't time to fire again, but he tried anyway, and launched a ball of liquid fire into the wall.

The thing had him dead to rights.

Manning caught it across the skull with the butt of his rifle, and drove the screaming nightmare into the ground. The blow was solid, but not enough. The thing was back up in an instant, and once again trying for Decker. He danced backward and ran into another person, but didn't dare look to see who was behind him.

The creature continued lashing out, scrambling to get to him with no concern for anything else. Feeling the creature's thoughts, the primal hatred, the desire to kill him, would have been bad enough, but the mind behind those emotions was so completely foreign that the raw emotions seemed even worse. He felt its single-minded rage, and his own fear rising as a counterpoint.

Manning kicked the thing in the side, and staggered it. Before it could recover a second time he fired, the barrel of his weapon flaring with each pull of the trigger. Four rounds pounded into the creature, and blew it backward with each impact.

It fell, and didn't get back up.

There wasn't time to celebrate as the next pack of the things appeared. The six mercenaries were ready, though, and had enough room to allow them to work in unison. Two opened fire with the explosive rounds that shattered the air and their enemies alike. The backsplash of the acid blood hit armor and flesh, but the splatter was minimized by distance.

Even as the first of the aliens went down, the ones behind them split up and attacked. They were fast and savage, quickly closing the distance and making ranged weapons ineffective. Manning directed his people and they listened, but all the commands in the world didn't change how brutal the attack was. The freelancers were pushed back, and Decker was pushed with them.

The things pushed their advantage without pause.

Adams and Manning and a few of the others quickly took to using their weapons as bludgeons. Manning slammed into one of the things and shoved it backward, grunting with the effort, and as it fell back another merc nailed it with a quick burst from a .44. She let out a yelp as the blood from the thing burned flesh, but instantly recovered and kept fighting.

One of the black-shelled demons jumped over Manning's head while he was pushing back against another. It cleared the distance effortlessly and came down on top of another mercenary, who was knocked flat and likely would have died on the spot, but the thing seemed far more intent on getting to Decker. As quickly as it landed, it jumped again and came for him.

Decker wrestled himself free of the crush of bodies and cursed, swinging his plasma rifle in a tight arc that just managed to save him from getting clawed to shreds.

Instead of carving into him, the creature's claws ripped the weapon from his hands. He didn't have time to think—he charged the creature and knocked it back toward the man it had flattened in its jump.

The mercenary was better prepared the second time, and brought up the double prongs of his shocker, electrocuting the thing with a jolt that should have killed it. He pushed the prongs into the thing's chest and fired voltage through it a second time, and then a third, until it was still. Its glossy black hide was cracked and bleeding.

Decker grabbed back his weapon and tried to catch his breath. They were everywhere.

"Fall back!" Manning bellowed, and his people did so. Adams pushed Decker along for the ride.

Suddenly a wave of force lifted him and threw him backward. His ears were pounded and a flash blinded him. Manning had dropped a grenade into the middle of the enemy.

He struggled to recover, and looked around. Several of the freelancers were clambering to their feet, shaking off the concussive force and continuing their strategic withdrawal. Manning tossed a small metal ball in a gentle underhand arc, toward still more of the things coming from the direction of the lift. He was a bit further back this time, managed to clear a few more yards before the detonation.

He kept his feet, and so did most of the other fighters, and then they were running—all of them. They moved hard and fast retreating from the scattered black shapes that littered the ground.

He couldn't see how many there were. He didn't dare take the time to find out. The survivors would recover, and they would be joined by more.

So they ran. Oh, they ran.

And the nightmares followed.

Panic was winning, and Decker had to stop it.

He forced himself to gulp in air and to actually look where he was going, because otherwise he would surely die. The things coming from behind made soft, low hisses and high, shrill shrieks, and the hard noises of their bodies in motion offered a sharp counterpoint. He tried glancing back, but all he could see was the mercenaries, several of whom were firing their weapons as they ran.

Adams had told him the rifle in his hands could be switched to automatic. He flipped the weapon over and looked for the control. But before he could do anything with it the terrain changed. The seemingly endless corridor started curving, and he had to pay attention to what was going on ahead of him.

Then they hit a fork.

"Which way, Decker?" He didn't recognize the voice.

Two choices: left or right.

The left fork looked more frequently used and he pointed in that direction, going mostly on instinct. The group went in that direction and he prayed he was right.

While he was praying he came to a stop and adjusted the settings on his plasma rifle. The mercenaries kept running. Heart hammering too hard for him to hear even the sound of his own breath, Decker aimed back the way they'd gone and waited.

The last of the freelancers, Llewellyn, charged past him—were there fewer than he remembered? It surely did seem that way.

The first of the things came skittering around the curve.

Their hatred was very nearly a living thing, another presence moving among the tide of chitinous bodies. They were charging faster than before, and he lowered the barrel of his rifle toward the center of their seething mass. Then he pulled the trigger.

And was blinded.

She had warned him. The air around him seemed to catch fire. One tiny burst of the stuff was enough to melt the flesh of the aliens. By the time he let go of the trigger, he'd unleashed close to a hundred times as much. The heat sent his hair rippling and the glare took away all but the briefest hints of the dark shapes ahead of him. They screamed, not only with their hideous voices, but also with their minds. The hatred washing over him disappeared in a conflagration of plasma and fear.

The walls where they had been were glowing. The stone was running in places and the darker lines—likely the trimonite—shone with a white heat.

"What the fuck is wrong with you?" Manning bellowed, startlingly close. He clamped a hand on Decker's shoulder and began dragging him backward.

Decker couldn't answer—he just allowed himself to be pulled away. His mind was overwhelmed by the brilliant, explosive light, and by the utter *silence* from the horde of things that had been trying to kill him.

Manning yanked the weapon from his hands, spun him around, and pushed him forward.

"Move!"

Decker obeyed, trying to breathe in air that felt too thin and far too hot. He stumbled forward and followed the people ahead of him. Behind him there was only Manning. The aliens were gone.

Just gone.

Up ahead the group slowed as they reached the mesh doors of the secondary lift. Adams looked back at him with wide eyes, and he felt more than he comprehended her shock.

He was feeling a bit shocked himself.

Behind them the heat was, if anything, actually getting worse.

"Ferguson!" Manning's voice cut through his thoughts. "Are the doors working?"

A lean, bloodied man nodded his head.

"Yes, sir!"

"Then get them open, and get us the hell out of here."

The metal bile of the aliens was replaced by the fear and disbelief of the mercenaries. They were in shock, and he didn't know if the bugs were the cause, or his own stupidity. *Probably both.* They entered the lift, and Ferguson closed the doors as the glow of the burning walls behind them lit up the corridor.

"Go!" Manning's voice snapped the order, and a moment later the entire platform they stood on lurched and began ascending.

Manning said nothing, but he stared bloody murder in Decker's direction.

"I stopped them, didn't I?" Decker offered. He hadn't planned on talking but there it was.

"You just dropped a miniature sun's worth of heat down a hallway made of stone and dirt! If we're fucking lucky, the entire thing won't collapse, you dumb bastard!"

He couldn't say he didn't know. He did. He just hadn't been thinking when he did it.

No, that wasn't true. He *was* thinking. He was thinking about getting away from the things that wanted to kill him.

"I shouldn't have given him a plasma rifle," Adams said, and that stung.

Manning turned on her in an instant.

"You think?"

Decker shook his head.

"No. This is on me. She told me not to switch over to automatic. This is all on me." He didn't want her taking the heat for his stupid move.

Manning took a deep, slow breath, and visibly calmed himself.

"Plasma rifles, for the record, tend to heat things up," he said. The lift kept rising, moving with all the speed of a tortoise.

39

COMMUNICATIONS

Rollins sat down at her desk and checked for new messages from the home office. There were none.

Good, she thought. Her superiors only sent responses when she posted a new query. Since she hadn't done so, their silence was the best news.

She began reviewing the various status reports, and Willis called. She didn't respond immediately, letting him stew a bit.

"Talk to me."

"We need your pilot back down here, as quickly as possible," he said, and he sounded out of breath. "I think things are going south in a hurry."

"What do you mean?" She checked the information that had come in, and the only glitch she could see was that one of the probes was no longer functioning. That was puzzling, since they were built for planetary extremes. It would take a lot to knock one out.

"The lift has been disabled," he continued. "There's been some sort of explosion."

"Where are you now?"

"I got myself to an access tunnel. I'm climbing. It's a long haul to the next level, but I'll get there." He seemed confident enough. She opted to let him keep his confidence. It would be short-lived enough, as it was.

"Very good," she said. "When you've reached safety let me know. Until then, good luck."

"Wait! What about the drop ship?"

"I'll be sending it down soon," she replied. "Have you managed to get all of the information I asked you for, Mister Willis?"

"All of the information they gathered on the city is with me right now. I also got pictures of those things."

"You've been very helpful," she said calmly. "Thank you for that. I'll look forward to seeing what you bring me."

"But—"

She killed the communication and called Pritchett into her office. The pilot arrived quickly.

"I need you down there," she said. "I expect we'll be getting what we wanted from this operation, and very soon."

"So they caught your aliens?" he asked.

"There have been complications, but I believe they'll manage. In the meantime, however, they'll need extraction, and it's going to come sooner, rather than later."

Pritchett nodded and left.

Rollins looked at her computer, and began to type.

To: L.Bannister@Weyland-Yutani.com
From: A.Rollins@Weyland-Yutani.com
Subject: New Galveston Acquisitions

Lorne,
It appears likely we will successfully achieve our
goals regarding the biomechanical data we have sought
for some time.

Regarding the dig site, we may only be able to salvage
data. Extracting the trimonite, and any other assets
located on the site, will likely be prohibitively
costly in many ways.

Please review the information encrypted in the
attached file. Due to the volume of data, the
compression rate has been increased by a factor of ten.
Expect white noise.

Best,
Andrea

She sent the message, stood up, and left her office. She wanted to think and the walls of the room didn't provide a view conducive to stirring her mind's enthusiasm.

Somewhere below her, the company's goals were coming within reach—closer than they had been in a very long time. It was within her reach to save the personnel who were involved, but that might risk the successful conclusion of the mission.

That wasn't an acceptable risk.

40

SEARCH AND RESCUE

The Quonset hut was a buzzing hive of activity, with about two-dozen people milling about. No one could figure out what the hell had happened.

The tunnel leading down was wide open, and everyone was very carefully avoiding standing too close to it. It was one hell of a drop if a person got stupid or clumsy. A few of the more adventurous rescue workers had already tried rappeling down the side of the deep pit to see what they could find. Next they were going to try maneuvering one of the rigs closer, and lowering a platform. Assuming they could find someone to work a rig.

The team that should have been doing that was lying broken and very likely dead at the bottom of the shaft. They'd been taking machinery back down to level five when the entire thing had fallen apart.

Lightfoot and Moretti were watching over the smaller, personal rigs of the rescue team, trying to get them low enough to check the next level down. They were there for the explicit purpose of making sure that if a rope got tangled, it got untangled as quickly as possible.

No one expected the ropes to go taut, and then go completely slack, but that was exactly what happened. There were four separate lines dropping down. They weren't connected to each other. Each was independent, and each fed out at its own pace. They had been working fast, but not so fast that it put them at risk.

According to the readout on the first line—the one belonging to Kirby—he had managed a little over five hundred feet when the line snapped tight and spat out a sudden extra thirty feet of high test silk before it came loose. Moretti saw it happen, and let out a little yelp of alarm. By the time he'd turned to Lightfoot to say something, the second line was doing the exact same thing.

Almost immediately, the last two lines repeated the process. Lightfoot hit the autofeeds to pull the lines back up. If any of the rescue team members were hurt, they'd be drawn up at a nice, steady pace and be back to the surface within a couple of minutes, max.

The lines came up quickly and smoothly.

They came up *too* quickly. And in all four cases, the members of the rescue unit didn't come up at all. The lines had been torn apart.

Several people got very busy shining lights down into the shaft and calling out for someone to respond.

But there were no responses. No unexpected noises, no signs that anything had gone wrong, there were simply no responses at all. And that bothered Moretti enough to start him pacing back and forth and chewing on his nails. It bothered Lightfoot enough to make him hunt down four more probes.

It was probably futile, though. All of the probes they had tried sending down had failed to transmit through the interference caused by the Sea of Sorrows. No one knew why—there wasn't any natural phenomenon that would explain it.

Lightfoot retrieved the probes anyway—they had to try. He linked their telemetry to the main console. This close, they were working just fine. So he dropped the probes down the shaft, and the four spherical sensors went to work, correlating information as they moved steadily downward.

Fifty feet down, the readings stopped.

Lightfoot let loose a stream of obscenities, and several others joined him. There had been a brief hope. Now there was nothing.

* * *

Moretti stepped outside of the hut to grab a smoke. He was stressed and he was angry and as much as he hated giving in to his temptations, the alternative was to rant as hard as Lightfoot.

Leaving the door open, he fought against the wind for a moment to light his smoke. Just as it was about to catch, something grabbed him and slammed him against the corrugated steel wall. His attacker was dressed in black armor of some sort, and impossible to see in the gloom. He grunted and started to scream, but a powerful grip caught him by the throat and stopped him with a strangled gurgling sound.

And while he struggled and fought and dropped his cigarette, other shapes came out of the desert and started into the hut, moving without concern for whether or not they were heard or seen.

Fonseca was the first to see them. She took in a deep breath and let out a positively epic shriek. While the people around her were doing their very best to jump out of their skins, at the unexpected sound, the monsters attacked.

There were seven of the things, all a shiny black with long talons, ridged tails, glittering blank faces, and rows of sharp teeth. They moved preternaturally fast, some on two legs, others skittering on four. They moved the wrong way, and made unsettling hissing sounds as they did so.

Few of the personnel were wearing comm-sets, and even fewer were armed. Most of the people participating in the search and rescue were technically off-duty. They were there because they needed to be there.

One of the bizarre creatures grabbed for Lightfoot, and he reacted strictly on reflex. He caught the thing by the wrists as it came for him, grabbing, seeking. He spun at the hip and hurled the nightmare past him and into the deep chasm of the lift tunnel. It screeched and fought for purchase as it dropped into the darkness.

He managed to fight off the second one that came for him, blocking several blows as it kept trying to get past his defenses. Those defenses were not perfect—they didn't take into account that the monster was armored, or that it had barbs along its prehensile tail. Or those damned *teeth*. Quickly he was bleeding from several wounds, even as the people around him were taken down.

Several of them fought, and they did their best, but most of the people were so terrified that they tried to flee instead of trying to defend themselves. Lightfoot was vaguely aware of a stampede for the door as the bug kept attacking, kept pushing him to the limits of his abilities.

And while he was focused on the thing in front of him, the one he'd knocked down the shaft climbed up the side of the deep tunnel and launched itself at him from behind. He'd never even considered that possibility.

One by one the workers, the rescuers, all of them fell. Their shouts and screams diminished, until they stopped altogether. And then they were taken, hauled out of the building and into the light rain that started falling from the night sky. Their unconscious and bleeding forms were dragged across the Sea of Sorrows.

And then the sea reached up and consumed them, until nothing was visible but the blackened sands, flat and unbroken.

41

GOOD NEWS

Four new data streams ran from the surface of New Galveston and straight up to the *Kiangya*, where the information was loaded into Andrea Rollins's computer. The news was unexpected, but not unwelcome. Information was power. Rollins knew that better than most.

She studied the new readouts and shook her head. For just a moment a smile played at her lips and then she crushed it.

Time for a new report.

She typed quickly, composing as she went.

```
To: L.Bannister@Weyland-Yutani.com
From: A.Rollins@Weyland-Yutani.com
Subject: Unexpected results.


Lorne,
It appears that the subject is substantially more
aggressive than we had expected, or even hoped.
Furthermore, data from the surface indicates that the
infestation is far more widespread than was originally
expected. I believe we are looking at a complete
involvement of all test subjects, and the very real
possibility that the team we assembled could actually
be infected before they have achieved their goals.

I have sent down a retrieval ship, in an effort to make
their return more feasible. Once we have procured the
appropriate samples, we may need to consider taking a
```

different course of action than originally planned, if
only to ensure that the property remains exclusive to
the company.

I believe the terminology used back before the
Expansion was "with extreme prejudice." Unless you
respond with a different recommendation, that is the
course I will follow. Failure could very well lead to
heavy sanctions, and penalties against Weyland-Yutani.

On a related track, the information gathered from
the examination of the dig site has been extensive.
While we cannot guarantee a complete analysis of the
biological-technological fusions, I believe we will be
substantially closer to a fruitful merging of biotech
and weapons manufacture, based entirely on the samples
that have been successfully scanned.

The alien vessel and the buildings found at the
dig site indicate similar—if not the same—patterns:
organically grown synthetic life. Biotechnological
structures, nurtured in a protective environment.
The implications are staggering, and I will do
everything within my power to ensure that we gain
physical samples of the structures, in the hope that
we might find sufficient genetic materials to warrant
a complete reorganization of the entire biotech
division, its goals and objectives.

As before the attached files are strictly encrypted to
ensure security. I will retain a full backup, should
data be lost in transmission, but I feel it best to
let you get started with the examination as soon as
possible.

Please advise ASAP should you feel a different course
of action is required.

All the best,
Andrea

She sent the message, and then settled back to wait.

And while she waited, she continued to watch the growing
wealth of details with a level of clinical detachment that would
have done her predecessors proud.

The Biological Technology Division was about to get a
very substantial boost, based on the raw data alone. If the

team succeeded in procuring live samples, the potential for advancement would be immeasurable, and would justify any sacrifice.

She hoped that Decker made it out alive, though. Whatever it was that linked him to the aliens, it seemed to have potential for further exploitation.

Somewhere far below, the independent multi-functional probes continued their task of reading information.

In front of her, the computer continued the task of defining and recording that information.

42

ESCAPE VELOCITY

The lights continued to fade. Perkins looked around in the near darkness, trying to see *anything*, and shivered. There was a fire in the lift, now, but it wasn't enough to help, and the smoke was beginning to be a problem.

"We can't stay here," Cho said. Perkins didn't like the alternatives any better, but she didn't have the energy to argue.

That was okay. Piotrowicz seemed more than willing to handle the task.

"Look, you can climb your ass up into those things if you want, but I think we're better off toughing it out here. Sooner or later, they're going to get someone down to our level."

"Yeah, but all they'll find is our corpses," Cho countered. "I'm not saying it has to be the tubes. I don't much like the idea of going through those things myself, but if Willis found a way out, then we can do the same thing." Cho was keeping his calm, but it was very obviously an effort.

Piotrowicz shook his head.

"It's not defensible."

"And this is?" Cho's voice rose again. Perkins sighed and ground her teeth.

Estrada spoke up.

"Look, I don't want to sit here with my thumb up my ass," he said. "It's getting darker, and I think those fucking things will come for us. We take the stairwell, and we block the access from below, and then we only have one way they can come for us, right?"

Anderson was back to pacing on top of the stacks of construction materials, where she had the best vantage point. Vogel and Dwadji were with her, making sure that they didn't get any more surprises. All three of them had switched over to their night vision goggles. No one was completely sure if they would help in the situation, but no one thought they'd hurt, either.

The problem wasn't just the darkness—it was that no one really knew if the creatures gave off enough ambient body heat to register. To that end each of the three had settings on a different level. One was using ultraviolet—Vogel, she thought—and that was working well enough. But Dwadji tried infrared, and it was seriously problematic. There was a fire in the lift, and if he looked that direction, it was nearly enough to blind him.

The fire had come suddenly, and didn't seem to be from the explosions. There had been a bright flash, like that of a plasma rifle, and burning debris had dropped down, setting fire to the wooden portions of the elevator and the mining equipment. It just compounded their problems, generating enough smoke to cause breathing troubles if somebody didn't do something soon.

Perkins was hot and she was sweating and she was hungry. *And tired.* So damned tired.

Bad as she felt, Lutz was doing worse. He kept fading in and out of consciousness. And when he was awake, he was in pain and bordering on delirious. The wound in his chest was still doing a slow leak and Doctor Rosemont had already intubated it. Even if he improved, she didn't think he'd be able to walk. They'd have to carry him. Actually, the scientific group would have to carry him, because every weapon needed to be available for use, and not a one of them was about to trust any of the explorers with a weapon.

If they tried to move him, especially up a narrow stairway, there was a good chance that Lutz wouldn't survive the strain. But his odds didn't seem any better if they stayed.

"Listen," Cho said. "The air down here is getting thick. My fucking eyes are burning from the smoke, and I think we need to move. As far as we can tell, there are lifts above us. They just don't reach this level. I know it's a bitch—I get that, and I don't want to risk Lutz either. But if we stay here, we're fucked.

"It's as simple as that."

"We can't stay here," Rosemont echoed. "With the fire, there's a chance the batteries over near the lift will blow up. If those things go, we're going to go with them. If the explosion doesn't get us, the fumes will." She looked to Piotrowicz with an apologetic expression on her round face. "I know you're worried about your friend—I'm worried about him, as well. But if we stay here, we're all going to die. I believe that." She gestured at the other members of the expedition, who looked exhausted and scared. "We'll have to carry him."

Piotrowicz looked at the woman for a long time. Finally he nodded.

"So let's get the hell out of here."

It wasn't long before they'd gathered Lutz and started along the way.

Lower gravity helped. They rigged a stretcher from two posts and a blanket from the van. It looked a little comical, watching someone smaller lifting the heavyset mercenary as they placed it under him.

While they worked, the trio of lookouts kept watch, seldom speaking.

Cho tried to get hold of Manning without success.

There was nothing else to it. They had to move.

They had to go.

So they grabbed everything they could carry, and began to make their way toward the door where Perkins had seen Willis emerge. The three sentries took strategic positions around the group of ten unarmed people. Perkins gave her night vision goggles to Rosemont, so she could guide her people while carrying the injured man.

Vogel called out.

"Here they come!" She pointed with the barrel of her pounder.

The black silicon tunnel, which had allegedly been sealed, vomited out several black shapes. No one saw them but Vogel. Then the other guards caught on and lined up with her.

Still carrying Lutz, Rosemont and her crew ran as best they could, and Perkins and Cho went with them. Piotrowicz, Vogel, Dwadji, and Anderson took their time and aimed for the vile things that skittered down the wall, moving in leaps and bounds, never staying in one place for more than an instant. Perkins slowed for a moment to see what was going on. She didn't want to. What she wanted was just to run. Fear clenched her stomach in a vice.

In the semidarkness, all she could make out was the forms of the aliens—no details. Two of the things got blown away as they descended, and fell to the cavern floor without any sign of life left to them. The others were faster, and got to the ground without being touched. They found cover in the stacks of supplies without anyone tagging them.

The group made it to the door.

Please let it open, Perkins thought. If Willis had—for whatever reason—locked it behind him, they were up shit creek without a paddle. But despite her fears, the thing opened. Cho stepped in first, lit his flashlight, and glanced around quickly. Then he gestured for the rest of the group to join him while he took point. There was no way of knowing what was above them, and it was best to be safe.

"Move it, folks!" Perkins said. "We've got company, and they'll be headed our way." Most likely they didn't need the reminder. She gave it to them anyway.

And then she was through the door and looking back, wishing she had her goggles, watching the others doing their best to fight off the damned things. She couldn't see the bugs. She could only see her four comrades where they stood on their perches and fired.

She spotted one, just as it came for Piotrowicz. He was standing several feet off the ground and the black shape charged, moving between two of the stacks. She only saw it because that barbed tail whipped fast enough to catch her attention.

She saw it.

Petey did not.

"Piotrowicz!" her voice called out and he turned to look at her.

The thing jumped, clearing the stack with ease. It hit him hard enough to lift him into the air. The monster's front claws landed on his shoulders and pushed him back. She saw the pistol in his hand as it sailed up and away, and even from a distance she thought she heard the sound of his skull cracking as he hit the packed dirt floor.

It seemed to her that she was looking right into his eyes when the beast came down, and bit him in the face. Then she couldn't take it any longer.

Perkins took aim and fired at the thing. She missed, but her charge blew a hole in Petey that was big enough to put her arm through.

"Oh, fuck, *no*!" Her voice cracked as she watched his entire body kick from the impact. She was still staring at him when the monster looked her way and charged. Adrenaline and instinct took over.

She still took the time to aim at the monster and fire.

The damned thing ducked under the blast. That was enough to make her focus. She aimed again, and realized she was too late.

The demon was on her, hissing and clawing, and then her head was slamming against the wall of the access tunnel and there was nothing.

Darkness ate her entire world.

Perkins hated the dark.

43

NESTS

There was a loud grinding noise, and then the entire affair jerked and stuttered and quit. The lift stopped working. They'd been rising at a nice, steady pace.

In that instant, Decker thought they were going to be stuck in the elevator forever. He caught himself breathing too hard and too fast. He needed to get away!

"You're freaking again." Adams was staring at him. "Are they closer?"

He swallowed as best he could, and tried to focus.

"I can't think," he said. "But I don't think it's them." He forced the words out. They didn't want to come. They wanted to stay locked in his throat.

Manning noticed the exchange and hissed out an order, telling Adams to give him a shot. She did so, and in the space of a dozen heartbeats he felt himself calming down. The bands around his chest relaxed, he gasped in a proper breath, and then another, a third.

"They're very close," he said. "They're serious, too. All I get is the sense that I'm the target."

"You mean they weren't serious before?"

"Shut the fuck up, Leibowitz," Manning growled.

"Yeah, they were serious before," Decker said, his resolve

hardening. "But I think there are more of them, and this group seems, I don't know, focused. This isn't a science, you know? It's a gut feeling. There just doesn't seem to be as much white noise coming from them."

Adams sighed loudly next to him. She was exasperated.

Tell me about it, he thought.

Manning called on the comm, but got no answer. No word from Cho. No one answered from any of the levels.

Grunting his own frustration, he turned his attention to the list. Bracing himself, he caught his boot on the railing and reached up until he could open the maintenance hatch above them. Less than a minute of looking around, and he dropped back down.

"It's maybe twelve feet up to the door to the next level. I say we take it." He looked around for a moment. "Any objections?"

There were none.

Manning was the first up, followed by Adams, and then Decker himself. One by one they climbed to the top of the car, and the two mercs pulled a pair of utility gloves from a pocket on their slacks. Like the gloves Decker often used on a work site, they were surprisingly thin, and equally effective, enabling the wearer to retain his sense of touch.

The merc leader used them to hold the cable, occasionally wiping some of the grease from the metal fibers to get a better purchase. In a matter of minutes he was up to the doors and wrestling with the locking mechanism. Adams watched him climb, and Decker watched Adams.

He forced his attention back to the bugs. The medication enabled him to deal with their increasing presence without pissing himself. They were close. They were so damn close he could almost smell them.

Decker glanced around the shaft just to make sure that last part was his imagination, because the bugs seemed adept at hiding in the strangest places. They might even have been the reason for the malfunction.

Seeing what he was doing, Adams pulled her flashlight and started scanning the area, frowning all the way.

Nothing. Then Manning dropped a line down.

"Make sure you use gloves," he warned. "The line is thin enough to cut flesh."

Decker shook his head. "I don't have any." A moment after that, two grease-coated gloves dropped on his face.

Adams stifled a laugh—though she didn't seem to be trying very hard—and started climbing. He was following a moment later, pulling his body up the line, straining with it. He was very glad of the lower gravity.

He pulled himself through onto the tunnel floor. They waited as the rest climbed, and Decker did his best to sort out the emotional tides swirling around him. Away from the claustrophobic lift, he could pinpoint details better, and there was another sensation—one he couldn't easily define. He tried concentrating on it, separating it out, but without success. It was more like interference than emotions.

"There's something down to the left," he said. "It doesn't feel like the bugs, but it's strong enough to get my attention. And in the midst of all this, that says a lot."

As with the previous level, this corridor was lit well enough, though the lights were less frequent here. Some of them had been broken and others dangled down from the ceiling where the anchors had given out and let go of their prizes.

"You think you can find whatever it is?" Manning asked, retrieving his gloves and shoving them into a pocket of his backpack. His expression had gone back to neutral.

"Yeah, I can." Decker nodded. "Like I said, it's strong. There's something familiar about it, too, but I can't put my finger on why."

"Then don't waste time trying. Lead on." Manning let him take point, but stayed close.

The differences between levels quickly became more evident. Where the fifth level had seemed empty, as if it had been deserted for a very long time, there were far more signs of activity here. Markings on the walls indicated they were on the second level, and some of the signs and notices looked to have been posted recently, over the course of the new activity.

The corridor was as well paved as the previous one, but there were far more chambers off to each side, and they had to check each one before continuing on. Several loaders and trucks were parked haphazardly in designated areas. Manning looked at them with interest, but said nothing.

A very large opening on the right hand side revealed a dark chamber. There were lights, but most of them were damaged or burnt out. The few that remained were dim, and flickered fitfully.

A quick look told them that this was an active mining site. The trimonite vein was very apparent, dark and glistening in the rough-hewn walls. The ceiling was close to twenty feet high in some places, and looked as if it climbed a good deal higher in spots. That must have been where the miners found a particularly rich vein of raw ore.

Decker peered up into the dark recesses, and shrugged.

"Of course," he said. "That's where the feeling is strongest."

"You just never stop being fun, do you?" Manning shook his head and held his rifle a little closer to his chest. "Bridges! I want you up here."

"What the hell did I do?" He was trying to be funny. Manning wasn't in the mood.

"Just think of yourself as the canary in the coal mine," Manning said. When Bridges looked at him without comprehension, he added, "I need someone to use as bait, and you're elected."

Bridges nodded and tapped the shocker against his leg. Decker winced reflexively, expecting the man to howl with pain. A moment later he lifted the weapon, and its light hum could be heard.

Adams stepped up next to him.

"Same routine." She handed Decker a metal baton. "Use the reaper first. You run out of ammo, use this. Hit 'em if they get too close. Otherwise, leave it to me." He wasn't quite foolish enough to ask for the rifle back, but part of him was tempted. Slowly but inexorably, he could tell that the bugs were closing in.

They moved carefully, and Decker advised where to look as the team ran light over the darkened surface of the walls. It wasn't long until they started seeing the same substance used in the construction of the black tunnels. Before long they were sprouting from every available surface.

The weird sensation grew. And then he saw the source.

Along the walls, sprawled in an uneven confusion, shapes stood out against the blackness. None of the forms made much sense until he understood that they weren't just *against* the blackness, but had been consumed by it.

No, not consumed—enclosed within it, woven into the black silicon. Here and there a limb jutted forth, a hand or a fist, a bone or a portion of flesh. Mostly what showed were the faces, some frozen in scowls of pain, others slack and lifeless. There were people here, a *lot* of them. They had been wrapped into the black silicon like flies in a spider's web.

"What the fuck?" He didn't know who spoke, but the emotions spiked for everyone in the group. Horror, anger, fear... all in equal measure.

Most of the trapped forms were unconscious, though some could be seen to be breathing. As the lights flickered over the shapes, Decker had to think that was a blessing. Several of them were dead. They hung slack in their glossy bindings, and universally the dead ones had holes in their stomachs or chests, complete with a thick drool of gore that ran down from the openings. He tried counting them, but the numbers didn't want to stick in his mind. He lost count after fifteen.

There were far too many for all of them to have been mercenaries. There had to be miners and other civilian personnel—he didn't want to know how many.

"Holy cow." Manning looked them up and down. His expression was no longer calm. His teeth were clenched. His gaze stopped on one of the dead ones, and he turned. "Adams? Didn't Cho say something about this?"

"Yeah, it was one of the civilians," she replied. "The scientist with a hole in her chest. Yeah." Adams shone her light over the deep wound and studied it carefully. Decker didn't want to look, but found he couldn't quite look away.

Then he realized something.

The dead weren't the source of the weird feeling, but they

were close to it. The unconscious humans weren't the source either. They were unconscious, and anything they gave off was muted by that fact.

"Fuck." He shook his head and stepped back. "It's coming from inside of them." His voice rasped. His whole body went numb. The *presence* of the things flared inside of his head, until his ears were ringing.

"What?" Adams asked.

"The feeling I'm getting," he said. "It's inside the people. Whatever it is, it's inside of their bodies."

Bridges glanced briefly over his shoulder.

"Trust me, there's nothing inside those people." He nodded toward one of the wounds as he said it. Decker couldn't decide if the man was trying to be funny, only that he failed.

"No, not *them*," he hissed. "I mean the ones that are alive. There's something else going on here. There's something *inside* of them." As he said it, the rest murmured oaths, until a gesture from Manning shut them up.

"That's sick!" Adams shook her head. "But it fits with what Cho said. I couldn't picture it before, but now it makes sense."

Manning started to say something, but instead he turned, aimed, and fired in one sure, fast move.

44

BREEDING GROUNDS

The result was a squeal of pain from one of the bugs as it got blown in half.

What they'd suspected became fact. The damned things were there. They'd been hiding in the black cascade of silicon, some of them near the trapped victims, and others further away. As Decker watched, the things unfolded themselves from their resting places and very quickly shifted into crouching positions, hissing at the human invasion of their territory.

One looked at him, and its rage increased exponentially. Immediately the sensation spread throughout the room, as all of the creatures recognized him. But unlike before, they did not attack. Instead they hesitated, and... taking positions.

"They're protecting the people." Bridges spoke with a genuine confusion in his voice. "Why would they do that?"

"No." Manning's voice was unsettlingly calm. "They're protecting their young. That's what Cho was saying earlier. They've planted babies inside the people."

Several of the mercenaries behind him let out noises of disbelief. But there it was for all to see. The corpses didn't add their voices to the argument, and neither did the living hosts to the unholy eggs. They could not. They were spared the agony of consciousness.

Through the noise, Decker recognized something. The *things* inside the bodies were keeping their hosts sedate. That's why there was no fear coming from them. They didn't deaden their pain so much as they numbed their emotions. Sedation for the spirit, not for the flesh. The very idea horrified him.

Manning gestured again, and with practiced ease the freelancers stepped into a closer formation. Each one that carried a ranged weapon paired up with another who stood with a bludgeon or some other close-combat device. They took up positions around Decker.

Without warning, the aliens attacked. There was no tensing to act as a forewarning, and they moved with the sudden speed and brutal efficiency of natural predators. And once again, they moved straight for Decker.

"Do this!" Manning opened fire and blew one of the creatures apart as it dropped down to attack. Others did the same, including Adams, who fired on one that was scaling the nearest wall and nearly hanging upside down as it came for them from above. The stench of the alien blood mingled with the rot of the dead and the industrial odors from the mine itself.

Decker tried to look everywhere at once. Despite their focus on him, the creatures seemed to be more careful this time, moving with greater purpose. Some of them seemed to be sacrificing themselves, but even in that there seemed to be a pattern—

Then it hit him.

"They're trying to get us away from their young!"

Manning paused for a moment, and then fired at one of the humans stuck to the web of black. The shot was either very lucky or amazingly accurate because he hit his target in the meat of the shoulder without managing to kill the poor bastard.

The reaction was immediate. The bugs turned their full attention on Manning, and moved to block him from having another clear shot.

"Damned if you aren't right again." Manning fired at the closest bug, and it whipped back and away, narrowly missing becoming another victim. "Now tell me what good that does us."

"You're the fucking tactician," Decker replied. "You tell me!" He could feel them clearly moving toward the area from different directions.

"There's more of the damn things coming from the main corridor," Decker added. "They're going to block us in here."

"Then let's open a path," Manning shouted. "Twelve o'clock, people—give it all you've got."

Manning opened fire, and the rest of his team did the same, concentrating on the ones in front of them, trying to clear a path. When the bugs came too close, Manning shot another of the victims, hanging on the wall. Instantly the creatures shifted toward that spot, as if driven purely by instinct.

Using that method the mercs began to move.

"I don't like this. It stinks of a setup." Bridges spoke and drew his pistol with his free hand. The shocker zapped attackers on his right, and the pistol kicked and boomed from the left. Another bug died.

And then one was on him before he could say anything more. It dropped from above and landed on the big man's shoulders, biting into the back of his neck and ripping its claws down the length of his body. He fell hard, and did not get back up.

The bug climbed off of him and scuttled toward Decker, keeping low to the ground. Adams fired and missed, and then ducked out of the thing's way as it came on. Decker let out a bellow and swung his baton at the glistening black face. The hard metal rod broke the thing's head open, but that wasn't enough. It kept coming, teeth bared and secondary teeth snapping as they dashed for him.

Someone pulled a trigger and the thing blew up, spraying a mist of its blood across Decker's left hand and chest. He wiped the burning viscera from his hand and then frantically pulled at the vest. The pain was enough to cast aside the numbing effects of whatever Adams had injected him with.

No one helped him. They couldn't afford to. Manning pushed forward and the things cleared out of his way, letting him go. Everyone who could do so followed, one by one stepping over Bridges' corpse as they moved.

From behind them came new sounds, the noises of more of the things coming their way. There was nowhere to move but forward.

Decker pushed past the dead mercenary and the web of living and dead miners. He wasn't the only one close to panic. He could feel it coming from several sources now, and much as he wanted to ignore it, he could not.

The pain in his hand grew worse, and he wiped it again and again on his pants, trying to remove it. But even with the acid wiped away, the enraged nerve endings did not care.

The creatures in front of them kept backing up, and Manning fired on one that wasn't fast enough. Several of the mercenaries were facing behind the group now, keeping their eyes on the way they'd come in case any of the damned things appeared. They would, too. No one doubted it.

One of the miners hanging from the wall bucked and twitched, and a moment later there was blood flowing down his chest. As they watched, something writhed there, and they could see the vague form of one of the creatures, its face pressing against skin and cloth alike.

Adams brushed Decker aside as he stared, and pumped a single round of plasma into the miner's chest. The human host didn't react. The parasitic thing in her chest let loose a weak yowl of pain, and Decker knew in that instant that she'd killed it.

The reaction from the bugs was immediate. They attacked *en masse*, the ones from the corridor coming in fast and prepared to kill every last person. One of the mercenaries called out a warning and threw something at the seething tide of dark chitin. A moment later an explosion tore the things apart. Many of the pursuers were shredded by the impact, but a few came out mostly intact, and continued on.

One by one, the freelancers blew them away.

Up ahead the narrow corridor within the silicon hall opened into a larger area, and when he reached it, Manning stopped dead.

"Everyone!" he shouted, a new edge to his voice. "Get in here now, and bring the plasma!"

Even before he caught up Decker, too, froze in place. The rest came fast, moving around him. But he couldn't do it—*wouldn't* take another step. He couldn't yet see what had stopped Manning, but he *felt* it. Felt the rage, so much brighter than anything he had felt before, so clearly defined. He did not see it, but he knew it. Knew it from the worst of his nightmares, the dark places he didn't want to remember.

The bugs were bad, but this thing?

This thing would be worse.

A noise came from that chamber, and it was vile. A deep, throaty hiss combined with a high-pitched squeal that screamed *stay away!* The sound dug at his senses and pushed into his brain and it was more than just a noise. There was something past the five senses in that screech.

But then the sound changed, and the new note almost sounded like the growl of a predator.

The thing knew he was close and it wanted him. It wanted him very badly.

Behind him more of the bugs were coming, moving along the ground and crawling over their dead brethren. Slipping along the walls and the ceiling above, lean and hungry. For a brief moment he blocked out the obscenity beyond the next wall. He let his survival instinct drive him toward Manning, and the rest of the mercenaries and their weapons.

Once he was past that final barrier, the pursuers seemed to *stop*, as if unwilling to carry the fight any further. And he saw why.

He saw his every nightmare given form.

45

MOTHER-OF-SPIDERS

Vast, ovular masses rose from the ground, wreathed in a low-lying mist that had no right to exist in a mine. He did not know if the shapes created that mist, or if it came from the abomination behind them.

It was so large, so vast, that he almost thought it had to actually be a construct—the cathedral where the demons worshipped. In his nightmares he had dreamed of spiders, but that had been driven by the limits of human experience. The thing had spidery aspects, yes, but was alien beyond comprehension. Massive limbs held the body upright. Vast legs spread above the main body, spreading far and wide, and braced the thing in mid-air.

If the body was the cathedral, then surely the vast head of the beast was the altar. There was a vulgar symmetry to it, a deadly, graceful shape that drew the eyes toward the mouth, where the lips peeled back and bared crystalline teeth that gleamed within that maw.

The great head of the beast turned as he entered the cavernous space and though he again saw nothing like eyes, he felt it looking at him, sensed the probing fingers of the thing's mind. If the rage of the bugs was a crawling heat, then the hatred emanating from this great beast was a swarming mass of fire burning into his mind.

He was aware of motion around him, but he could barely hope to comprehend the things going on at the corners of his eyes. He was too fixated on the thing that shuffled slowly to get a better view of him. It could not go far. The vast body was locked in place by a huge abdomen that writhed and heaved and pumped of its own accord, and vomited another glistening lump to the ground.

Lump. He felt himself edging toward hysterical laughter. Lump. That was rich. That was priceless!

Decker broke away from looking at the monster for a moment, because he had to share the joke.

"That's their mother," he said to Manning, and Adams, and the rest. "She's laying eggs. All around us. Those are fucking *eggs*." And the worst of it? He didn't think she was the only one. He couldn't see the others, but he felt a distant glimmer, an echo of what came from her in different places beneath the Sea of Sorrows. There was more than one of these great nightmares.

Not one of the mercenaries paid him the least bit of attention. They were transfixed by the monster. So he looked away from Adams, away from Manning and the rest, and stared at the eggs themselves. There were *things* moving in them, and some of the oval shapes were jittering as the crests at their tops split open.

Nightmares crept from those eggs.

They were not like the bugs or the great mother of all bugs. They were a different sort of demon entirely. These things did not hate him, did not care about him. They had one agenda that mattered, one desire that was brilliant and cold and horrifying.

"Facehuggers," the files from Weyland-Yutani called them. His mind screamed that they were spiders, the source of his recent arachnophobia. He knew what they wanted. Knew what they did, and that made the sight of them all the worse.

Decker stepped back and his back hit the wall. He tried to push his way through that unmoving surface, and was rebuked for his efforts.

"Oh, fuck me," he muttered.

One of the things scuttled across the ground and jumped, *jumped*, and even as it moved, the great monster behind the vast array of eggs let out a roar that shook through human and rock alike. Without fail they all looked—there was no choice really.

Long white legs like impossible fingers spread from the arachnoid body and a vast, thick tail whipped with deadly accuracy. Decker tried to reach Adams in time, but he failed. He lunged even as the thing wrapped its limbs around her face and that tail bullwhipped around her neck as tight as a noose.

Adams dropped her rifle, reaching for the thing on her face. Clawing at it.

Even as she did, another of the damned things jumped for Manning. He fired and the body exploded, washing across the ground and his lower legs as its remains pattered down.

The mercenary started to burn. He reached for the knife on his belt and pulled it free, rapidly cutting at his pants, sawing through the tough fabric. But Decker hardly noticed.

Adams!

Decker looked at the woman on the ground, fighting to free herself from the thing wrapped around her face. Odd bladders on the sides of the creature quivered and flapped and Adams bucked, her fingers failing to get any sort of purchase worth noticing.

He felt the horror she felt, lancing into his senses. A great, suffocating repulsion flowed from her, an utter inability to breathe, carried along the tide of her fear and violation.

The great mother of all nightmares let loose another roar.

The mercenaries didn't come to Adams's aid. Nor did they help Manning. Instead they opened fire on the enormous thing that screamed for their deaths. Explosive rounds and streams of bullets blasted into the shape, cracking through the thick hide and shattering chitinous armor. The mother-spider-beast reared back, almost shocked by the audacity of the tiny creatures that dared attack her. He was hit by the monster's surprise. She was meant to be worshipped. She was meant to be a queen and a goddess and mother to all.

Decker could feel that from her mind, if it could be called that.

The bloated demon shrieked and roared, and behind them the bugs reacted. There was no hesitation. There was no delay. She commanded and they obeyed, utterly willing to throw themselves between her and the enemies. They charged toward Decker and the freelancers and he did the only thing he could think of. He grabbed the plasma rifle from the ground in front of Adams and fired at the first of the things that got too close.

A tiny sun burned the air and missed the intended target. Instead the light cut through the surface of one of the eggs and lit the interior as the crab-thing inside it caught fire and boiled within its shell.

The queen lunged forward and snapped her face toward Decker. She glared at him and the heat of her hatred opened wide.

Images plowed through him, sent, he knew, by the thing that loomed above him. Ellen Ripley's face flashed in his mind, distorted by the Xenomorph's utterly inhuman senses. It saw but not with eyes as he understood them. It tasted and felt and heard, but none of those words were quite enough to show the differences.

In his dreams he had tried to interpret the minds of the Xenomorphs. Here, this close to the queen of the hellish things, the images were unfiltered, raw and painful.

He saw, and as much as he could, he understood. They were connected in ways that humans had often sought, yet failed to achieve. They were a colony, a hive. They shared thoughts on levels that people could not, and he was a part of that now. They had touched his psyche and marked him through his bloodline.

Ellen Ripley was marked in their minds. She was the Destroyer and because of their relationship, Decker too was the Destroyer.

He shut his thoughts down to the alien thing, terrified that somehow it might manage to learn of his children.

The great demoness screeched, her breath washing over his face. Decker aimed and fired, and missed.

All around him the mercenaries did a better job. Most of them took on the things that were closing in on them, but a couple— Manning among them, despite the burns now visible on his bared skin—attacked the largest of the creatures that were surging forward.

Decker fired again and again, and he found his mojo. Streaks of light ripped from the front of the rifle and buried themselves in targets. Three of the eggs exploded. He changed targets rapidly as the mother screeched and snapped at him. But he did not fire at her. He could not make himself look at her because seeing her made her too real, and his mind already wanted to go running away.

So he looked past her head and to her body, at the swollen collection of eggs she carried within her. And that was where he concentrated his fire.

Knowing his intent, her rage boiled over. The great beast broke free and lunged toward him pulling herself across the floor of the chamber, moving over her eggs in an effort to stop him.

Manning and the remaining four mercenaries kept firing, hitting her with round after round of destruction. Her body broke. Her face shattered. The great crest above her mouth split in two places and bled more acids that burned the soil, yet did nothing to the eggs it touched.

She roared and lurched forward again, reaching for Decker. He did not step back, however, and he prepared himself for death. He needn't have bothered. The great shape writhed and crashed to the ground. Even so, Manning didn't let up. He unloaded every shell he had into the still form, and then reloaded with the efficiency afforded only to longtime shooters.

For one long moment the bugs remained motionless, as their mother-queen collapsed. And then they went mad.

Decker did the only thing he could. He aimed and he fired. All around him the mercenaries did the same, as the tide of monsters swept forward. They attacked. They fought. And one by one they were dying. There was nowhere to go, no way to escape from them.

There was only the fight, as the horrors from his dreams came forth to drown them all.

46

Their rage could burn no brighter, but their sorrow was bottomless.

The enemy had killed the queen and he had to be stopped but instinct and hatred do not always mix. The feeling rose hotter and brighter and much as they wanted revenge, there were the breeders to consider. Without breeders the colony would die, and that could not happen.

Several of them fought instinct and defended against the invaders, attacking the enemy and the ones that sought to protect him. As if to prove their instincts right those that tried to attack were killed. Their deaths did not matter. The only death that mattered was the death of the queen. The only survival that mattered was that of the colony.

The breeders had to be saved and so they worked quickly, lifting the eggs, pulling them from the ground and moving with the heavy burdens, seeking another spot away from the flames of the enemy.

The queen was dead.

The colony would live.

47

FALLING

Pritchett called several times for permission to land, and had no luck.

Barring combat scenarios, he wasn't used to landing without permission. He didn't like not getting confirmation, because that sort of shit led to paperwork. Nevertheless, he knew where to go. He dropped from the sky and very carefully settled on the hard surface of the landing pad. The black sands had covered most of the markings, and they were revealed again as thrusters stabilized the ship and then slowed the descent to a crawl before he felt the great bulk come to a stop.

He made sure to do everything by the book, from checking the atmosphere and weather conditions to powering down into standby mode. No chance in hell was he giving Rollins an excuse to be pissed at him.

The engine went into sleep mode, and the lights dimmed appropriately.

No one came to greet him when he touched down. It was creepy. The damned place was too big not to have someone on duty, and by now they should have repaired whatever was wrong with their communications.

Looking out the window he could see the rain coming down, and guessed that might be a part of it, but it wasn't like they were dealing with a hurricane. Still, no one showed up. So he settled himself in his seat. For now he got to play the waiting game while the people around him continued with their mission.

He tried using several different frequencies to catch up with the others, but nothing came back. When that failed, much as he hated the notion, Pritchett called on his boss.

"Safely landed down here," he told Rollins over the comm. "It's just a matter of waiting now." At first there was silence, making him wonder if she had heard him. Then she responded.

"Keep yourself prepared, Mister Pritchett," she said. "The situation has heated up substantially."

What the hell does that mean? He didn't ask how she knew what was happening on the surface, and *below* the surface. He really didn't want to know. He just wanted this done.

He wasn't the sort to give in to superstitious ideas, but he had a very bad feeling about the whole situation.

After a few minutes his eye caught something. There was movement out on the sands. That was something at least. He didn't feel so completely abandoned any more.

Not that he was planning on going out there or letting anyone in who didn't knock first. In his experience, you couldn't be too careful.

48

LOVE

Perkins's jaw felt like it was ready to fall off. Her lips were swollen and tender. Her neck hurt.

Everything hurt, really.

Somewhere in the distance she heard shouting and weapons fire. There was the kind of screeching the bugs made, but louder.

The darkness wasn't complete—that was the first thing she noticed. She opened her eyes slowly, and felt the ache in the side of her head where she'd gotten her helmet ripped free by the thing that attacked her. She tried reaching for her head, and realized her hands were bound.

So she studied the darkness.

The black stuff from the tunnels was all around her. She could feel it touching her neck, her face. She could wiggle a few fingers on her left hand, and they touched something warm, but her right hand was useless and the attempt to make her fingers move resulted only in a new surge of agony.

The monster had bitten her hand. She remembered how fast it was, and the sudden explosion of pain that ran from her wrist to the tip of her middle finger. She was pretty sure all of her fingers were still there, but *damn* they hurt.

The warmth against her left hand moved a bit and she turned her head as best she could.

Piotrowicz's voice spoke out. He had an unpleasant, wet sound to his speech.

"Wondered if you would wake up."

"Petey? What the hell's going on?"

He laughed. It was a soft chuffing noise that broke into a small coughing fit.

"You probably can't see it, but the spider-things are all over the place. You had one on your face a while ago. So did I. Cho's got one covering his face right now."

"What?" It hurt to talk. She licked her tender lips and tasted something other than blood. She wasn't sure she wanted to know what it was, but the taste was bitter, almost metallic.

"We're done," he said. "We're already dead, Perkins. We just have to wait a while for the rest of it."

"What are you talking about?" Her voice broke. She felt the sting of tears and tried to force them back.

"That civvie from earlier, Colleen something-or-other. She had one of these things attack her. It put something inside. I felt it. I felt that goddamned thing in my mouth, in my throat." His voice was hoarse and he let out a long, shuddery breath. "I think I can feel it moving inside me. We're going to die. It's going to be bad."

"Fuck, Petey."

"I know." She felt the warmth move against her fingers. "Can you reach that?"

"Reach what?" She felt fabric. The cloth was wet and held the sort of heat she always thought of when she touched a kid with a fever. Her nephew Joe always got fevers. The kid was sickly as all get out. Then she felt a metal line slide across her fingertip. "Wait. I think I have something." She wriggled her fingers and strained hard, and felt the thin metal press between her fingers. "I've got it, I think."

"Good. That's good." Piotrowicz coughed. "I was wondering how smart those things are, you know? I mean, they're good hunters. They work together. I've seen whole units didn't work that well together, back in the Colonials. And you remember Phillips, right? Man couldn't even spell teamwork."

"Yeah. I remember him." She hadn't much liked Phillips. He

was a bitter man with a bad attitude. Also, he had the worst damned breath.

"Well, I think they're animal smart, not people smart. Know why?"

She didn't really want to play twenty questions, but, really, there wasn't much else to do.

"Tell me."

Before he could answer, another man's voice interrupted. She didn't recognize it—he wasn't one of the mercs.

"Can anyone hear me?" He coughed, a nasty, wet cough. "Something's wrong with me. Really wrong. I can't see, and my chest burns."

He stopped speaking for a moment and Perkins could hear him panting in the distance. When the man started up again, he was praying. After only a few moments of trying to make his way through what she thought was the Lord's Prayer, he started screaming. It was bad. His tone rose in octaves and decibels alike, and then faded away into whimpers.

Piotrowicz spoke again.

"He won't be around long. I think it's coming out of him. I was thinking they aren't very smart, because they left my belt on. I've been working for a while now, trying to get to my belt. Turns out I should have just waited for you."

She almost laughed.

"Petey, I don't care if it's the end of the fucking universe, I'm not taking off your pants."

And in response he did laugh. It was weak, but it was heartfelt, and the only reason he stopped was because the screamer started up again, wailing his pain out into the darkness around them.

From somewhere nearby she heard the sound of one of those things moving. They made a soft clicking noise when their parts rubbed together. Like plastic or glass.

When he could speak again Piotrowicz did so with a note of humor in his voice.

"I really love you, Perkins. But honestly, I always kind of thought of you like a big sister." He paused for a moment. "Doesn't mean I

535

wouldn't have, you know, if the circumstances were different. But no. I mean, they didn't take my belt. And they didn't take the grenade I was trying to reach. The one you've got your fingers on now."

Not far away the screamer spiraled down into sobs.

"Oh." It was all she could think to say.

"I think if I move my hip and you pull at the same time, we can probably get the pin out. After that I just have to wiggle around a bit to depress the striker."

"Are you serious?"

Piotrowicz didn't answer. He let the screamer answer for him. When he stopped, they were silent for a time.

"Okay, Petey."

"Good. I think we can end this a lot faster for all of us."

"Is the charge big enough?"

"Perkins, honey? Have you ever known anyone to accuse me of using anything less than excessive force?"

The screamer started up again and then stopped with a strangled gurgling sound, accompanied by a tearing that sounded like more than cloth.

"Let's do this," she said. "Petey?"

"Yeah?"

"Tell me you love me, one more time." She pulled hard at the pin. Her fingers strained and the wire hoop tried to slip free, but she caught it in time and after five of the longest seconds of her life, she managed to slip it free from the safety.

"I love you, Perkins."

The heat of his body pressed hard against her fingers, and she dropped the pin.

49

DIFFERENCES

Somewhere in the distance there was a sound, almost like a detonation, but muffled by the immensity of the rock walls.

Then there was silence.

Decker looked around and saw the dead bugs, the dead mother of all monsters, the dead mercenaries, and wondered exactly how it was that he was still alive.

Mostly that was Manning. The mercenary was still standing, and only a few feet away. He had looked considerably better in the past, but he was alive. There were four of them still standing, and all of them were bloodied.

"Adams," Decker said. His body was shaking from over-exertion and adrenaline, but he moved anyway. Adams lay where she had fallen, that vile thing wrapped around her face. She was alive. He could see her breathing. Like the people they'd seen stuck to the walls, she gave off a different emotional resonance. Being around her actually made his own mind calm down.

"One of those things is on Elway, too," Manning said.

He looked. Elway was an older guy, not exactly prone to speaking up. Hell, the man had never said a single word that Decker could recall.

"They're different."

"What?"

"The things on their faces. They're different." They were, too. The one on Elway was smaller. The one on Adams was larger, and seemed more elaborate. It had webbing between the front and rear legs.

"Whatever," Manning said. He looked around at the dead and the wounded. Then he reached for his knife, and looked at the thing on Elway.

"No," Muller said. "Acid blood. You'll burn his face off."

Manning looked at the thing on his mercenary, and finally nodded.

"We need to get out of this place," he said. "We need to get to the surface."

Decker stared long and hard at Adams.

"So let's go," he said. His hands caught her at the shoulder and at the knee, and he hefted her weight across his shoulders. She seemed to weigh almost nothing, but he knew that wouldn't last. They had a long way to go, and well before they reached their destination she was going to be a very heavy burden.

Manning grabbed Elway and hoisted him over one shoulder, slinging him like a duffle bag. In exchange he dropped most of his supplies, keeping only his rifle, and the belt of knives and assorted tools around his waist.

"Take the lead," the merc leader said.

Decker tried not to think about the people they were leaving behind. He didn't know them. They weren't his friends or his family. Objectively, they were his captors. It still didn't feel right. But there was no other choice.

They moved quickly, heading back the way they'd come. As they passed the bodies stuck to the walls, Decker looked away. Manning did not. He studied each face as they went past. He couldn't guarantee it, but Decker thought the man was memorizing them.

Muller—at least Decker thought that was the man's name— glanced over to where Manning looked and spoke softly.

"Want them left alive?"

Manning kept looking, but shook his head. There were no words.

Muller trailed behind the others. A few moments later Decker heard a series of detonations behind him. He didn't know what Muller had used, and he didn't care.

Eventually the man caught up.

"Where are they?" he asked as he fell into step with them. "Are they all gone, Decker?"

"No." He felt for them. "Not nearly."

"How many of those bastards are there?"

"Lots. Too many. More than I ever could have imagined. But right now they seem to be worrying about something else." He closed his eyes, focused. "They'll come for me again."

"Why?" Manning asked. Decker was surprised by his curiosity.

"I think hatred is the only thing they know. And they hate me. Maybe for what this Ellen Ripley woman did to them. Maybe just because I smell funny to them. I don't know for sure. I just know they want me dead."

"Well, I'm not so fond of you, either," Manning said. "But I like them less. Let's get the hell out of here."

The elevator was down and none of them wanted to climb that entire length of cable. It took them almost twenty minutes to find an access stairway. The damned thing wasn't hidden, but it was unmarked, and nearly lost in shadows.

The door was jammed, but Manning fixed that quickly enough. When they were through, he studied the hinges on the door for a moment and then rammed his knife into the spot between door and jamb. A simple wedge, but it would take a lot of effort to force the door open. For extra measure he looked to the last member of the group.

"Dave, glue that bastard shut."

The man Decker thought of as Llewellyn nodded and dug into his backpack. The goo he laid against the metal made door and frame both sizzle for a few moments, and then run together.

"Shit. How many feet down are we?" Muller's voice was justifiably exasperated.

"About one less with every stair, sunshine." Manning's voice wasn't as encouraging as his words. Just the same Muller took the hint and started upward.

One less foot with every step. Maybe not quite accurate, but it was true enough for Decker. He walked, doing his best not to complain each time Adams's weight shifted on his shoulders. Manning was walking ahead of him, and he made it look like carrying Elway was easy. He hated the bastard just a little more for that.

50

THE LONG AND WINDING ROAD

Willis was suffering from a serious case of the flop sweats.

His legs were shaking and his arms flopped uselessly at his sides, except when he tried to use them to pull him up another set of stairs.

Eyes on the prize. That was what his grandfather always said. *Keep your eyes on the prize and you'll get what you need out of the world.*

What did he need? Currently he needed to get to the top of the endless fucking array of stairs. Who the hell ever thought to drop an access tunnel down the full depth of the mines, without power?

He supposed he should be grateful, but he didn't really give a damn.

Willis first had climbed to the eighth level, planning to take a lift from there. Not the main lift, but one of the secondary or tertiary support lifts. It seemed like a good idea at first. It should have worked, too. But the door wouldn't open. He tried putting his shoulder into it, but all that gave him was a bruised shoulder.

He realized that he should have expected it. He'd taken the better part of a couple of hours to pry open the door on the bottom level. The shaft was part of the original complex, and even the stairs were falling apart in places. He had to be careful not to fall and break his neck.

The sixth level was as far as he made it before he had to give up taking the "easy way." None of the doors were going to open, and he could only pray that the one at the top was going to work.

He tried calling Rollins, and didn't get through. That didn't make sense, since she had given him a comm that was supposed to penetrate any barrier. Yet all he got was silence.

He'd stopped twice already to succumb to dry heaves because as much as he hated to admit it, a life behind the desk had left him in absolutely craptacular shape. His waist was broader than his shoulders and he counted higher than one when he counted his chins. It was easy to lie about that stuff when he was looking in the mirror every day, especially when he managed to find the occasional partner for his bed, but here and now, walking up a flight of stairs that was taller than a lot of skyscrapers, he was having a little more trouble arguing with the facts.

Eyes on the prize. When this was done he would be rich. Not well off, not comfortable, but disgustingly rich. He was a company man, and he liked working for Weyland-Yutani. But after this bloody insanity of a mission, he'd be taking early retirement.

He did, however, promise himself a good long session at a body remodeling facility. Modern science would fix what a bad diet and a desk job had done to him. He'd have the money to guarantee it.

All he had to do was get to the top of the stairs.

He almost wept when he reached the door for the second level. Someone had fused the door shut, for what insane reason he couldn't guess. Maybe to keep the monsters away. He didn't like that idea at all.

He took a moment to rest, to catch his breath, and to try to call Rollins with a progress report. Elation ran through him when she answered after only a few moments.

"I was beginning to worry about you, Mister Willis," she said. "I haven't heard from you in a few hours."

"I've been walking up a lot of stairs," he said. "I *tried* to contact you, but the damned comm wouldn't work." He didn't speak the words. He wheezed them. "I'm almost to the top. Do you have a ship on the way down?"

"No. It's already waiting for you and the rest of the team."

"There may not be a rest of the team."

"Several of them seem to be alive and well. We'll know soon enough."

"Where are they? Do you know?"

"Not exactly. They haven't access to the same communications devices that you do. They've been experiencing... technical difficulties." He nodded his head as if she could see him.

"Listen, it's bad down here. I haven't encountered many of them, but with everything that's going on, I think sterilization might become a necessity."

"We're already considering that option, Mister Willis."

He jerked his head up in surprise. He shouldn't have been shocked, really. He understood how the company worked well enough. Of course, that just made the data he was carrying all the more valuable. Rollins might have some of the scans, but he had the ones from the dig site, and there was no way she could have gotten the same level of detail that he had.

No way in hell. He kept telling himself that. With a grunt, he stood back up on watery legs and started up the stairs. *One more level.* How bad could it be?

"Mister Willis?" Rollins's voice actually startled him. He'd thought she had cut the link.

"Yes," he said. "I'm still here."

"You should be aware that this operation has been very costly to the company."

"Oh, yes." He paused to try catching his breath again. "I imagine it has. But the benefits, Ms. Rollins. They should be dazzling, shouldn't they? The biomechanical aspects from the ship alone should be worth whatever we've spent. If the information can be properly gleaned from the samples..."

"Do you still have the samples from the ship, Mister Willis?"

"Of course. They're in my office. In the safe."

"Wonderful. Please make sure you remember to retrieve them before you get to the drop ship."

"Oh." He stopped walking and caught his breath for a moment. "Do you know I would have forgotten them. Thank you for the reminder."

"Of course. Have a safe trip, Mister Willis. I look forward to meeting you in person."

This time he heard the barely audible click that indicated that the connection had been severed.

His breath was more a whimper than a sigh. He started moving. One step. One step. One step. Pause.

Just a little further.

51

A SIDE TRIP

"Mister Pritchett?" Rollins's voice came through clear as glass.

"Yeah. I'm here." He bolted upright in his seat. He'd been drifting. There was nothing to do but listen to the rain.

"Mister Pritchett, do you have access to a video pad?"

It took half a second to locate the screen from which he'd been reading.

"Yep. Right here."

"Good. I'm sending you a compressed file. On that file you will find a schematic of the offices. They're located in the largest building, in front of the barracks. Once you have those, I need you to locate the office of Tom Willis. He's busy right now, and I need you to collect some samples you'll find in the safe in his office."

"In the safe? Won't that be locked?"

"Come now, Mister Pritchett. I'm fully aware of your background. Even if I weren't, I'm also providing you with the combination. I've taken the liberty of overriding the retinal and DNA securities. This is company business, after all."

"You got it." Crock of crap was what it was. She didn't care about having the right to do anything. And he'd have bet his last paycheck that she'd acquired the combination without Willis's approval. The good news was that he didn't care. She wanted something in that safe, and he wanted his bonus.

"Mister Pritchett?"

"Yeah?"

"Arm yourself. There's a possibility that the life-forms we're looking to procure might be around in higher numbers than originally believed. If you should encounter one, I would suggest shooting first and worrying about the creature's intent later."

"You're the boss."

He took the time to arm himself. He also took the time to double check his armor.

He left the ship in standby mode, and locked it down before he left. No one was going anywhere without him.

52

The queen was dead.

Decker shook his head, trying to push the thoughts and images away. Still they came, unbidden and unwanted. The voices hissed and clicked in their alien thoughts and his mind interpreted them even as he tried to flee.

The enemy was still alive and the queen was dead. Their fury immeasurable. If they could have, they would have pursued the enemy, but they could not.

No! I'm not your enemy! Leave me alone! If they heard his attempts to speak back, to communicate, they did not react in any way he could understand.

The newborns were hatching, and they had to be protected. The enemy had proven to be as dangerous as their genetic memories had insisted, and for that reason the newborns had to be hidden away.

There would be no mercy from them. Mercy was as alien to them as their inhuman senses were to him.

* * *

They had already lost so much.

They moved among the nests and looked at the hosts. Some were conscious and some were not, that hardly mattered. Some were already giving birth, and others were close.

Then there were seven nests remaining. The past had taught them to be careful. They learned. They adapted. They survived.

The earliest of the new nests were no longer necessary. The hosts had served their purpose and their bodies were merely food now.

A new queen was already growing, carefully guarded and kept away from the enemy. She was taken down to the lowest levels of the hive to the great chambers where they had slept for so long, and remained untouched by the world around them as it changed.

The fear bloomed in his stomach and Decker shoved the thoughts aside. If he thought about the sheer numbers of the things he would truly go insane.

Two nests were gone, destroyed. The enemy still lived. The vile thing climbed away from the hive, and that was good. They would find him, and they would kill him.

They were careful with the new queen. She was so young, so fragile. She would grow strong, of course, but as with all things, time was a requirement.

Once she was secure, the ones who had seen to her safe escort turned their attention back to the enemy. It was close to the surface now, they could feel it crawling through the tunnels the hosts had cut into the ground.

They would follow.

The queen was dead. The queen was born anew. The queen would be protected, no matter what the cost.

53

PAYBACK

Karma was a bitch.

Luke Rand woke up not long after the monsters came and beat him into the ground. He'd tried to fight them, and they broke him. Three ribs and his jaw. He couldn't close his mouth, and every breath hurt like a fire being set just above his stomach.

He was underground, in near-complete darkness. And when he didn't think it could get any worse, they proved to him that he had no idea how bad things could get.

The area to which they dragged him was hot and damp, and covered in the glossy black deposits they'd been seeing all around the Sea of Sorrows ever since they'd arrived. He never guessed what they were. Never would have guessed, even if they'd given him a lifetime to figure it out.

The things held him down and when he tried to fight they effortlessly broke his right arm in three places. That pretty much ended his attempts. Still, that wasn't enough for the things. Two of them leaned over him and vomited gray-black goo over his body. The stuff started hardening as soon as it touched the air, and they spread it with their claws and slathered him with it until he was encased in a silicon straight jacket.

Even if he'd had it in him to fight any more, the glassy webbing quickly became too solid for his battered body to fight against.

There were other people around him, some of them were conscious and some of them weren't. He envied the ones who weren't.

Then the crab thing skittered over, and climbed up to his head. He tried to scream, painful as it was, but quickly his cries were muffled as it wrapped itself around his face. It was rape. That was the only way he could think of it and he felt tears of humiliation at the very idea. His jaw was already broken, but the thing didn't care. He tried twisting away, but he was glued down and the damned thing just didn't stop.

After a while everything just flowed into a dull ache, and then the pain went away altogether. He thought he should wonder why, but it didn't seem necessary.

Every bad thing he'd done in his life came back to him in that dark place. Stole a dollar when he was five. Stole a lot more than that when he was in school. He'd done some good things, like fighting for Aneki when the other kids tried to pick on him for being stuck in a wheelchair. But he'd also done his fair share of picking on the weaker ones.

There were people he'd done wrong, but he never thought it was enough to end up like this.

Those things were watching. He saw them moving now and again, and some of them were curled up in the blackness, lost in patterns that almost looked like parts of the walls of the cave. He had to look for them to see them at all, but he had time while he was stuck in one place, and thinking of all the bad things he'd done in his life.

He felt like shit about Decker. The man knew him for what he was, but he still stuck with him.

He felt like shit about a lot of things.

He didn't think he could feel any worse.

The pain came back in his broken ribs. It hammered his insides and moved around his heart and, oh, damn, but the pain was a living thing. It tore at his chest and then into his sides. His broken ribs were enough to make him howl past his broken jaw and bloodied lips.

The pain got worse, and worse again. So much worse.

In the end he couldn't think of a thing he'd ever done to deserve that much pain.

In the end it didn't matter.

Karma was a bitch, and didn't care what he thought.

54

BURDENS

The communiqué from the home office was short and to the point. It was also exactly what she had expected.

Andrea Rollins rose from her desk seat and stretched. She had things to do.

She called the bridge.

"Captain Cherbourg?"

"Yes, Ms. Rollins?"

"You should prepare the ship for departure. We won't be here much longer."

"Yes, ma'am."

"And Captain?"

"Yes, Ms. Rollins?"

"Be prepared to deliver your payload."

Cherbourg hesitated for a moment before responding, but only for a moment.

"Yes, ma'am."

Decker set Adams on the ground as gently as he could, and then sat for a moment.

True to his worries, she seemed at least ten times her original weight—at least if he listened to the protests from his shoulders. By comparison, Elway seemed to have only gained a few pounds.

He still hated Manning just a bit more for that.

"We get to the first level, are we going to try for another elevator or are we going to keep walking?" Muller asked. The question was a good one.

Manning looked down at the ground and shook his head.

"If this was a standard operation, we could take a truck back to the surface—there generally are ramps. But it's not. They were still rebuilding this thing, and I don't think they have an access road leading all the way up. So far these stairs have been clear of trouble and I like that, but it's not a guarantee." He paused to look around. "I am also very, very sick of confined spaces.

"When we get to level one, we don't have a schematic. We don't know the lay of the land. We don't know our way out of this place." He stopped talking, and seemed to be weighing the options.

Muller held up a hand and gestured for silence, one finger to his lips. Then he pointed to the stairs.

There was a sound from below.

Manning cleared his throat.

"So I think we have to consider which way is best, but I'm voting for exploring the first level. It'll give us more room to defend ourselves, if we need to."

As he spoke, he made several quick gestures. Muller nodded his head and moved, sliding to the edge of the stairwell and then carefully taking aim with his pistol. He tensed, and then Decker saw the tension leak out of the man's thick neck and shoulders, a little at a time.

"I think we're safe here." He stayed exactly where he was, and slowly lowered his pistol toward the floor.

A moment later they all heard the wheezing voice.

"Oh, thank God."

Manning recognized the voice.

"Willis?"

The bureaucrat was soaked through. His clothes were wet and clung to his bulk, his hair was pasted to his skull, and his face was a deep and unhealthy shade of red.

"Oh, thank you, God." He was climbing on his hands and knees, having apparently given up on the concept of walking.

Manning looked at Adams where she lay on the ground. His eyes flickered to Decker. The backpack she'd been carrying was gone. The backpack with the medical supplies.

"Anyone got a little water for this man?"

Silent Dave came to the rescue and tossed over a small bottle of liquid, rammed full of electrolytes and sugar. They were standard rations for most outposts. Willis's hands were shaking too hard for him to even hold the container. Once he'd calmed down, Manning opened it and handed it over.

"Sip it slowly."

He needn't have bothered. The man could barely even manage to sip. Still, after a few moments he had drunk half the bottle, and was breathing a bit easier.

"So, we're screwed. We need to get to the surface." Manning stared closely at Willis, who returned his look with a frown. "What's the fastest way?"

"There're elevators," he replied slowly. "The main lift is ruined, but one of the others, maybe."

"And you know where they are?"

"Yes. Of course."

"Then why the hell did you take the stairs?"

"Do you think I would have gone through hell like this, if I could get through one of the doors?" Willis answered testily. That seemed to mollify Manning.

"Well, finish catching your breath," the merc said. "We can't be here any more, and if what you say is true, the first level is our best bet."

"Ms. Rollins said she'd send down a drop ship." The words were almost mumbled. As soon as they were freed from his lips, Willis blinked as if slapped, and clammed up.

Decker felt the sudden shift in the man's emotions.

Manning didn't need to feel it. He leaned forward until he was close enough to kiss the man, and he spoke softly.

"Later, when this is over with," he said, "you and I will discuss how long you've been chatting it up with Rollins. For right now, though, get the fuck up. We're going to *move*."

"Wait. What happened to the others on your team?" Willis spoke as he slowly crawled his way up to a standing position.

Manning bared his teeth. No one in their right mind would have called it a smile.

"I didn't have any way to contact Rollins, you see, so things went badly." He cast his eyes toward the ground for a moment, and then back to Willis. "What happened to the rest of my people—the ones who were down on level nine with you?"

Willis looked away.

"I don't know," he said. Then his voice went up an octave. "I panicked, okay? I went for the stairs as soon as the fire started." He was lying. The man was a smarmy prick, and he was a lousy liar. At least from Decker's unique point of view.

Then that crawling sensation slipped weakly across the engineer's mind.

"I think they're coming again," he warned them. "But if they are, they aren't close."

The others made ready to continue to journey upward. Decker carefully slung Adams back over his shoulders, glad they weren't going all the way to the surface, while Manning hauled Elway onto his shoulder and checked the clip on his pistol.

"Can you tell where they're coming from?" he asked.

"No. It's not that clear." Decker shook his head. "Not yet, anyhow. And like you said before, I don't know the layout of the place. If I did, it might help me pinpoint them a little better."

Manning's hand caught Willis's shoulder in a fierce grip, and he bared his teeth again.

"Good news, then. We have our own tour guide."

Willis didn't look happy at the prospect, but he became more energetic as the energy boost ran into his system. Not energetic. Alert. He had probably been in a state of shock. Whatever it was, it enabled him to walk upright as they cleared the last flight of stairs, and reached level one. All that remained above them was the ground floor.

The door to level one opened easily.

This time Muller took the lead, looking left and right and then beckoning the rest of them into the corridor. The area was wrecked. Whatever had happened, it hadn't happened easily. There were broken lights and signs of a struggle, and a few pieces of people left behind.

Willis's eyes bulged in their sockets, but he remained silent.

Manning remedied that.

"Which way?" he demanded.

"There are elevators here—" Willis pointed. "—and elevators down that way." They moved toward the first set of doors, and discovered the same elevators that the group had tried riding up before. So he turned and led them in the opposite direction. After a hundred feet or so, they found a passageway that didn't exist on the lower levels.

"Where the hell does that go?" Manning asked.

"A new mining operation. It's got a lot of junk in the way, but it's got its own lift, and we used it to clear a lot of dirt and stone out of the way. The office and the compound are both in that direction, as well—up above."

"How far *down* does the lift go?"

"This is it," Willis replied. "This is as low as it goes. We found the main mining operation not long after we started here."

Manning shot Decker a glance, and Decker nodded. It was damned convenient that they found the original site that easily.

Damned convenient.

"Let's move," the merc said. And they were off.

Muller stayed in the lead, and they moved quickly. Decker did his best to focus on the minds of the bugs, and to ignore the cold detachment that emanated from the parasites clinging to Adams and Elway.

He wanted desperately to put Adams down, but wouldn't do that. *Couldn't* do that. She was good people. And he suspected she would have found a way to drag his sorry ass anywhere he needed to be taken. He made a silent promise to her that she'd get out of this alive. He intended to keep that promise, too. One way or another.

Despite the earlier signs of damage and struggle, there was little to see as they moved forward. No more bodies, no signs of a struggle of any kind. Indeed, to Decker's eye, it didn't seem as if the shaft had been used in quite a while. That seemed weird for what Willis had called a "new" operation.

"No one's dug here for some time now," Decker commented. "Why did they abandon it?"

"We didn't find enough trimonite to make it worth our while," Willis said. "It was too far out of the way to use for storage, so we just stopped bothering with it."

Ten minutes of walking got them to the elevator.

Manning looked to Decker.

"Anything?"

"No. Nothing." He pushed past the background noise. "Nothing close by, at least."

So Manning pushed the elevator call button, and double-checked his pistol again. Following his example, Decker checked the clip and the safety on the reaper.

Willis looked at the weapons with a mild hunger.

When the elevator chimed they waited for the doors to slide open and Decker found himself taking aim in that general direction. Anything coming out was going to get an unpleasant reception.

There were no occupants. Muller and Willis went first and the rest piled in quickly. The interior was battered, and large enough to let both Decker and Manning set their burdens down again. Decker rolled his shoulders and felt the muscles creak their gratitude.

He kept looking down the length of the rough corridor, half expecting to see more of the bugs coming their way. He didn't feel them, but he expected them just the same.

Manning seemed to feel the same.

"Damned things are like cockroaches," he muttered. "They keep popping out of nowhere."

Dave spoke up.

"Let 'em. I got three full clips and a serious need to shoot something." The rifle he waved had a big barrel, and looked like it had been designed to hunt small spaceships.

"That's what I like about you, Dave," Manning said. "Your optimism." The doors shut and the lift rose smoothly. The ride stayed smooth and then it jerked to a halt on the top level.

The doors opened into a hallway that was abandoned.

Muller checked anyway. Then he gave the all clear.

"Let's get the hell out of here, gentlemen," Manning said. "We need to find a defensible area and call the shuttle down."

Willis looked up and smiled weakly. "I think the shuttle is already here."

Manning frowned. "It is?"

"I could be wrong, but I believe that was the plan. It should be here already."

Manning nodded his head but kept that skeptical frown.

"If you're right, all the better."

Decker squatted and looked over Adams's still form. Then he very carefully lifted her and stood back up again.

"Let's go."

Willis cleared his throat. "I need to go to my office. I have files I need to retrieve." He pointed down the hallway. "Take two lefts and you'll be at the main doors. The landing pad is across from the barracks."

Manning lifted Elway.

"Don't be long. If it's you or my people, it's going to be my people. Understood?"

"Of course." Willis was still a little shaky, but he headed off toward his offices.

And they were off again, Muller and Dave taking the front and the rear while Alan and Manning carried their burdens. After all they'd been through, the silence seemed deafening, but Decker felt it. The growing sensation that the damned things were coming for him again.

"They're getting closer."

"Where?" Muller looked back at him.

"I don't know. I just know they're getting closer. Damn I hate this." His pulse was hammering, despite the odd calming sensation that emanated from Adams and Elway.

"Let's just move," Manning said. "We need to get to the damn shuttle, and *now*." He was doing his best to look everywhere at once. The strain from carrying Elway was showing itself now, and adding to Decker's discomfort. If Manning looked stressed, it was a bad sign in his book.

They made the two lefts with stops to check for the bugs. Nothing. Nothing at all, but instead of relaxing Decker, it made him stress even more. He knew they were coming, yet there was no sign of them.

"Where are all the people?" Muller mumbled—to himself, most likely, but Decker heard. He didn't answer, but he was wondering the same thing. There were no signs of a disturbance. The violence from below hadn't occurred here. There was no debris, and there were no bodies.

They reached a door, and there was the sound of falling water on the other side. They eased it open, and for the first time they saw the outside. It was dark out, and the rains were heavier than Decker had seen before.

The exterior lights were on, casting brilliant beams through the darkness and leaving the entire area in a dim twilight highlighted by the shining trails of illuminated raindrops. The air was clean, and smelled like a slice of heaven after the burning stench of the alien tunnels. The chill was enough to invigorate.

But it wouldn't last, Decker knew. The bugs were coming. No time to enjoy even the little things, because they were somewhere close by, and he needed to spot them before the damned things got close enough to kill them.

"Where are they, Decker?" Dave said. The man was getting positively chatty.

He looked around and saw the landing platform where the shuttle waited for them.

Of course.

"They're that way."

Manning didn't bother waiting. He started walking and expected the rest to keep pace. They did—even Decker, who had no desire to head toward the things that wanted to tear him to shreds.

The closer they got the more he felt his muscles tensing. They were out there. They had to be.

But damned if he could see them.

55

SAMPLES

The safe was exactly where he'd been told it would be, tucked into the floor at the base of a small desk that had delusions of being something better.

When Pritchett opened it, he found a small container with a biohazard symbol on the outside. He opened the seal and saw several small vials of gray and silver tissue samples. That was the stuff. He slid the package into his pants pocket, and took the time to grab a few papers that looked interesting. There was no money, nor any other valuables.

As he stood up the door opened.

The man standing in the doorway looked profoundly shocked by his presence.

That was fair. He felt the same way.

"What are you doing in my office?"

Pritchett looked the man up and down. He was stocky, and filthy dirty. He looked like he'd crawled his way across the entire complex on his belly. What he did not look like was a threat.

"Got orders from above to procure a few samples from your safe." He saw no reason to lie to the man.

Mister Business looked him up and down and scowled.

"Well, you've done your duty, and can hand them over to me." He actually held out a hand as if expecting Pritchett to surrender the package.

"Yeah. I don't see that happening." He took a step toward the man and placed a hand on his pistol's holster, just in case there was any debate.

"Now you listen here. My name is Tom Willis and I'm in charge of this facility. You need to hand over what you took before things get nasty, mister."

Seriously? He looked the man up and down. "Okay, get this. Your facility is screwed. I'm following orders. I'm also the pilot who's getting you out of here, unless you continue to give me shit. Give me enough trouble and I'll just leave your ass here."

Yeah, that got his attention just fine. The man went white.

"You wouldn't do that."

"Watch me," he replied. "Time to go. I'm just waiting on Manning and his team, and then we're out of here."

"Are there other shuttles coming, for more people?" The officious bravado was fading fast, and the man was looking less like a boss and more like a wage slave. Pritchett liked the change.

"Don't know. Don't care. It's time to go."

"But—"

"Listen, you can stay if you want. I don't care. I'm leaving."

The man looked at his desk, looked over his paperwork and office supplies like they were proof that he should be in charge. Pritchett just walked past him. Let the little bastard stay if he wanted to.

The sonovabitch sucker punched him. Hauled off and drove a fist into the side of Pritchett's head with all he could muster. It was a good punch, but it wasn't great. Pritchett staggered to the side and caught himself as he bounced into the doorjamb.

While the man was grabbing at something from his desk, Pritchett brought his leg around and kicked him in the thigh hard enough to make him scream. Whatever he'd been grabbing at fell from his hand.

Then Pritchett brought his open palm around and nailed his attacker in the jaw, hard enough to snap his head back.

Willis let out a grunt and tried for him again. Pritchett didn't waste time. There would have been some satisfaction in breaking the bastard's neck, but he was on a deadline. So he just drew the pistol and aimed it at Willis's face.

"No!" And just like that the fight went out of him.

"That's done. Move your ass before I shoot you." He pushed Willis ahead of him and let the man stumble. If he fell all over himself that was just fine.

Willis made four drunken steps into the hallway when he was hit by something big and black. It was fast, too, and it slashed a chunk out of the man's guts in one hard stroke of its fingers. The man fell back, a high keening scream leaking from his lips. He hit the wall, his eyes never once leaving the thing as it came for him a second time.

Pritchett opened fire.

Nothing happened. The safety was still engaged.

He cursed himself as he flipped the switch. The thing changed course and jumped at him, letting loose a few choice noises of its own.

This time when he pulled the trigger the pistol worked just fine. The thing staggered backward as he fired four times, blowing multiple holes into the torso and guts of the beast. It fell backward, kicked, thrashed, and died.

Its guts splashed over Willis, who let out a piercing shriek. His hands shook as his body smoked and burned—he didn't seem to know where to put them or what to do to make the pain go away. It must have been overwhelming. His skin blistered along his face and neck, bubbled over his arms and hands, and he shrieked again, looking toward Pritchett with eyes that seemed to blame him.

Pritchett just gaped, speechless.

Willis screamed again as a hole burned through his lips and half of his nose.

Pritchett reacted by instinct. One shot through Willis's skull—and then he moved for the door.

The ship wasn't that far away, really. He could make it in a couple of minutes, but suddenly it seemed like a lot further than that. The idea that he might run into any more of those things added miles in his mind. He kept his weapon drawn, and scanned his surroundings as he walked.

56

PLAIN SIGHT

Decker was happy to discover that Willis had it right. The drop ship was waiting on the landing pad, and the sight of it was like a boost of adrenaline straight to the heart. Suddenly Adams didn't weigh as much, and Decker felt as if he could sprint the short distance.

The mercenaries seemed to feel the same way. They moved faster and they were more alert.

"Where are they?" Manning said, and Decker's euphoria fell into check.

"Right there." He pointed toward the ship, and his voice rose. "They're right in front of us, and getting closer. But I can't see them!"

"You could maybe stop shouting, and telling them where we are, guys," Dave said. "You think maybe that's a good idea?"

Muller nodded and stayed quiet, but kept alert, his pulse rifle at the ready. When he glanced toward the sands, he muttered under his breath.

"No way."

Decker looked. He wished he'd managed not to. There were two of them at first, rising out of the sand. He had no idea where they'd come from until the next one rose.

The damned silicon.

Originally he'd thought they were just deposits, lumps of hardened sand, maybe caused by lightning strikes when the worst of the storms were still ripping the planet apart on a daily basis. Then he'd guessed that they might be debris from the tunnels the aliens were making. But as the sand erupted he realized the truth.

The bugs were craftier than he'd imagined. The silicon lumps he'd found were just the evidence of the trapdoors. Several of them popped up at the same time and the aliens crawled quickly from the tunnels they'd built.

Fully a dozen of the things came out at the same time, skittering across the sand, moving on all fours to better spread their weight and avoid sinking in the soft surface.

And the damn things *saw* him. He felt their anger rise as they did so, and they came faster. Behind them more were rising from their hidden tunnels, and charging toward him, the mercenaries, and their only hope of getting away from the planet.

Muller raised his pistol, aimed, and fired, and one of the bugs exploded. The others kept coming. They were focused on Decker to the exclusion of everything else. They wanted the Destroyer dead.

Decker set Adams down as gently as he could under the circumstances, and took aim with his pistol. Manning dropped Elway without ceremony, letting the man land roughly as he opened fire.

Not-so-silent Dave lifted the wide barrel of his weapon and fired. The noise was loud, a low roar of detonation, and out on the Sea of Sorrows there was a brilliant corresponding flash as several feet of sand and moving alien erupted in a wave of flames.

Dave let out a whooping battle cry and did it again, shifting his target a bit and blowing the shit out of another three yards of everything within range.

Still they came. The aliens moved faster now that they were in the open, and not dodging obstacles. Decker aimed, fired, missed. Aimed, fired and missed. He emptied the clip on the reaper, never certain if he'd hit anything at all.

Manning obliterated one of the things that got too close, and the monster rolled across the ground, leaving a trail of acid blood behind. Decker stared at the thing, suddenly unable to move.

It was dead, but the twitching parts still seemed to reach for him.

Another man came up from behind them and Decker spun, aimed and fired. Had there been any ammunition left in the reaper he'd have killed the stranger, but fate was kinder than that.

It was Pritchett, the pilot. The man slapped the weapon from his hands, pushed him aside and opened fire on the aliens.

Decker grabbed at the plasma rifle slung over his shoulder, but all he managed was to drop the weapon.

Dave fired a total of ten of his explosive rounds, and then switched clips with hands that were almost blindingly fast. The empty clip hit the ground and bounced, and by the time it had finished its short trip the mercenary was once again blowing holes in the desert and the aliens. He was careful to avoid getting too close to the shuttle.

Muller ran out of ammunition on his rifle, let it fall and immediately reached for the plasma rifle Decker had dropped. He grabbed it, his face pulled down in an expression of burning anger.

As Decker had done before, he set the weapon to automatic and unloaded the entire clip of plasma rounds into the approaching horde. Like Dave, he was careful about where he fired, giving the ship a wide berth. The night immediately became day, and the light revealed the monsters as they caught fire and burned, screeching and dying in the sudden conflagration.

Manning kept firing, picking off the shapes that made it through the sudden firestorm and got too close to the shuttle.

As the freelancers decimated the creatures, the panic that tried to eat through Decker's mind calmed, fading with each death. The heat from the plasma fires was almost enough to warm the chill that coursed through him.

Then Manning was reaching for Elway.

As Decker reached for Adams, Pritchett drove a fist into his stomach hard enough to drop him. While he was trying to get back up, the stranger aimed a pistol at his face.

"You lost your fucking mind?" he shouted. "You tried to shoot me!"

Manning reached over and put his hand on the pistol, slowly directing it away from Decker's face.

"Heat of the moment," he said. "Get over it. We need to leave."

"He fucking tried to kill me!"

"I said let it go, Pritchett! Now let. It. Go."

The pilot took a few extra heartbeats to stare blue murder at Decker, and then holstered his weapon.

"Where the fuck is Willis?" Manning barely even bothered to look around. "We need to leave. Now."

"He didn't make it." Pritchett didn't offer anything else.

Manning nodded and started walking.

The rest followed.

"What the fuck *are* those things?" Pritchett looked carefully around and avoided stepping on the burnt remains of the aliens. Then he slid back the protective case on his wrist and tapped a couple of keys on a remote. The lights on the drop ship started up instantly, and the door at the rear opened and descended, offering them access.

"Those are what we came here to find," Manning spat. "Aren't they great?"

Pritchett climbed aboard, and the rest quickly followed. The door began to close with a mechanical whine. Exhaustion tinted Decker's every move. He carried Adams into the seating area and very carefully strapped her into a seat. The thing covering her face shifted just a bit. The legs moved, the tail slid a few millimeters. It took everything left in him not to scream.

That cold feeling still came from the thing. A calm that seemed to promise that everything would be just fine. The sensation slithered into his mind from both of the spider-things, and he shivered. A lie. It had to be a lie. Nothing would ever be all right again. Not in a universe that had vomited these things into existence.

As if to prove him right, another of the bugs came through the door as it was rising back into place, pushing into the area with unsettling speed. Pritchett let out a tiny noise as the monster's claws opened his stomach and sliced through his thigh. The blood flow was immediate and heavy.

By the time he knew he was injured, the pilot was dead.

Dave grabbed the handrail above the aisle and twisted his entire body around. Both of his feet landed in the thing's charging body and sent it backward. While it was recovering, Muller looked around for a weapon, *any* weapon that might let him fight the thing.

It ignored him and went for Decker, silent and fast.

Muller grabbed a pistol and slammed it across the top of the alien's skull. It faltered, but did not fall. There was no room for firing a weapon inside the drop ship—not without risking hitting the wrong target.

Manning scrambled for the front of the ship.

Decker grabbed for anything that he could use against the creature and let out a bellow. Hard claws caught his calf and tore through the fabric of his pants, through the leather of his boot, and into the flesh beneath. He kicked the thing in its featureless face where the hint of a skull lay beneath the smooth back surface, above the gnashing teeth, once, twice, a third time, but it did not care. It just kept coming for him.

Muller hit the damned thing again, then a third time, and it ignored him too, as it pulled Decker closer, crawling over him. Its tail lashed sideways and slapped Muller in the chest hard enough to send him flying.

Dave reached for his pistol. All Decker could think about was how badly that blood was going to burn him, unless of course the monster got him first. He rolled over as best he could with the thing trying to claw its way up his body. Its mouth opened in what looked like a smile of triumph and the teeth parted, revealing a second mouth that drooled and steamed.

Just as those hellish mouths tried to take off Decker's face, Dave grabbed at the thing's tail and hauled it backward. Muller hit it again, this time with a full pack worth of gear. The force was enough to send it sprawling.

"Move!" Manning bellowed, and the mercenaries rolled out of the way, scrambling over seats and diving as far from the thing as they could. Decker pulled into a fetal position, ignoring the flaring pain in his calf as best he could.

A stream of silvery foam washed over the creature, splattering the floor around it and coating its body. It had the consistency of shaving cream, but even from a few feet away Decker could see how it stuck.

Manning kept a stream of the thick foam flowing as the creature fought to get back to its feet. Muller flung his pack as hard as he could and nailed the thing in the chest as it tried to rise. The pack was coated in an instant, and stuck where it hit.

The stream of foam stopped, the canister sputtering empty.

The bug screeched and flailed and tried to throw the pack away. And then it slowed down. More and more, the foam was hardening, sticking to the creature as it tried to get away.

Still the monster tried to reach Decker. It lunged and peeled itself partially from the floor, and pushed and came for him again, the hatred unending, a hellish hammering rage that would never stop until he was dead.

Or it was dead.

Maybe not even then.

Manning walked closer to the thing, dropping the bulky metal canister. It hit the deck with a loud clang and rolled a bit. Manning placed the two prongs of the shock-stick against an exposed part of the creature's head and hit it with enough volts to kill a man. It screamed and shuddered. It lunged and fell—or tried to. It never made it to the deck. Manning laid on the charge a second time and a third. And then stepped back.

"There's a cage in the hold. Let's move fast, before this damn thing wakes up."

Muller and Dave went to work with unsettling efficiency while Decker panted and stared.

"You're going to leave it alive?" His voice cracked as he spoke.

Manning's eyes scanned his face. He was once again like stone, his features unreadable. When he spoke it was with unsettling calm.

"The contract says alive pays better," he replied. "So we bring it back alive."

"You've got to be kidding me."

"No. This is a job, same as any other."

Emotion welled up inside of Decker, heating him with raw, primal anger.

"Manning, you've got to kill these things! All of them!" He was standing before he thought about it. His calf pulsed with pain but that didn't matter. He needed to make the man understand. The spider-things on Adams and Elway, the bug that Muller and Dave were putting into a heavy steel case, they had to die.

They had to die now.

Manning shook his head.

"Not happening. Not today."

Decker looked around, as if searching for something that would convince the man of how serious he was. The thing wanted him dead. It wouldn't stop. Couldn't Manning see that? Couldn't he *feel* it?

Decker's heart was hammering away and he was sweating again. This was never going to stop, not as long as any of the creatures were alive. They'd come after him. They'd come after Bethany and Ella and Josh! When the damned things were done with him, they'd still come after his children!

He looked to Elway and felt nothing, but when he looked at Adams there was a flash of regret. Still, it had to happen. They had to die. Those things would come out of them, and the entire goddamn nightmare would start again. They would find him, no matter where he was.

He knew that now.

"Put it down, Decker!" Manning's voice. He was bellowing. Decker realized then that he had a death grip on something. He looked down and saw the reaper in his fist.

"I can't," he said. "They have to be stopped."

Decker pulled the trigger, Elway and the spider-thing on his face were dead in his sights.

The hammer clicked on an empty chamber. He hadn't reloaded. That realization came to him at exactly the same time as Manning's fist smashed into his head.

"… lost your fucking mind!" He tried to shake away the pain, tried to find the words to explain, but before he could so much as wet his too dry lips, Manning's boot found his stomach.

57

DELIVERIES

Flanked by four security personnel, Andrea Rollins waited patiently as the drop ship's doors opened. Two of the mercenaries climbed out, their faces drawn. They looked at her and said nothing. A moment later Manning pushed Alan Decker through the walkway and let him fall. Then he disappeared back into the vessel.

Decker couldn't stand up by himself, as he was bound at the ankles and his wrists were strapped behind his back. She gestured to the two men with her, and they picked him up. He was injured. No real surprise there.

Manning came back a moment later carrying a woman. She was incapacitated and her face was hidden behind a mask of hard flesh and long legs that clutched her skull.

Adams. Her name was Adams. He set her on a gurney.

"How is she?" Rollins asked.

"You need to fix this." Manning's voice was as calm as ever.

"We intend to, Mister Manning. I've already got the chambers set up to monitor both Ms. Adams and Mister Elway. We'll take care of them."

She gestured to the other two men and they immediately entered the ship. They knew what to do. She'd explained very carefully. The two of them carried Elway out as if he were made of glass, and placed him on a gurney.

Manning watched carefully the entire time. Then he pointed to the ship.

"One live specimen. It's in the cage you provided and it's glued in place."

"Excellent work, Mister Manning."

He looked at the ship and then at her.

"Costly work."

"We knew that going in, didn't we?"

"Yeah. We did."

Rollins looked at the remaining mercenaries. Including Manning and the two hosts, there were a total of five out of the original thirty-five. But that was nothing compared to the loss of life among those who had been stationed at the base below.

"Do you need to rest right away?" she asked. "Or can I bother you to linger for a few more minutes?"

"I'll survive," Manning replied.

She smiled. "I just need to take care of a few details, and then we can finish this business."

He sat down and stared hard at the ground in front of him. He could have been a statue, if he hadn't breathed.

Rollins took care of arranging the placement of the alien's cage. It would be locked into cryogenic suspension in a chamber devised for exactly that purpose. There would be no chances taken. Weyland-Yutani had sought these particular creatures for a very long time, and she wasn't going to allow anything to go wrong.

Nor, frankly, did she much like the idea of anything that violent breaking loose.

When she was done she stood before the commander of the mercenaries and spoke softly.

"Walk with me, Mister Manning."

He lurched to his feet, and followed as she started to lead.

When they reached the bridge, Manning looked down at New Galveston and the speck far below them that marked the Sea of Sorrows. The flight crew was active, moving about and preparing to leave orbit. The captain, a dark-haired man with dark skin and an equally dark disposition, nodded a perfunctory greeting.

"How bad is it down there, Mister Manning?"

"You can't let them live. If you do, I can pretty much guarantee they'll own that planet in a year's time, perhaps less. The three cities the company put so much money into building will be ghost towns." He remained stoic as he gave his answer.

"Do you understand now why we warned about heavy losses?"

"Your pet, Decker, tried to kill my people at the end. He was scared that the things planted inside them would get out, I guess." He paused, and added, "I'm not sure he's wrong."

"Well, in his defense that was a possibility. But both of your people are now in hypersleep chambers, and already in stasis."

Manning nodded. He was silent for a long while.

Finally Rollins interrupted his reverie.

"So you recommend neutralizing the area?"

"Nuke it," he said without hesitation. "Wipe that mine and everything in there off the map."

"We'll take care of it."

"When?"

Rollins looked toward the captain of the ship. The man peered back at her and nodded his head. She turned back to Manning.

"Does right now suit you?"

"Yes. Right now is your best bet. Those things are smarter than you think."

Rollins knew better. She knew *exactly* how smart they were. Judging from everything that had transpired below, they were very nearly the perfect soldiers.

"Captain Cherbourg, please handle the matter."

The man nodded and spoke into his comm. What he said was too soft for her to hear, but the result was immediate. Four plasma warheads dropped from orbit and headed for the Sea of Sorrows. There was a time and a place for mercy. That time was not now.

The order to clear the area had gone out two days earlier, along with the statement that a viral strain had been located in the mines. No one on New Galveston questioned the instructions. The Sea of Sorrows was designated a hot zone, biologically speaking. It hadn't been hard to convince the local doctors of the dangers of a pandemic. Every city on the planet was connected by the tube system. The mine wasn't a part of that system, for which everyone was grateful.

The weapons would annihilate anything in the area to a depth of roughly twenty thousand feet.

"Within the hour the Sea of Sorrows will cease to exist, Mister Manning."

Manning nodded his head. He seemed perfectly fine with the notion.

"I'm just going to stand here and wait, if that's all right with you."

Rollins smiled. "I thought you might like to be here for that. I am sorry for your losses, Mister Manning,"

Manning just looked at her.

"Keep the rest of them alive, Ms. Rollins. And keep your part of the bargain."

"I always do, Mister Manning."

She left him there, staring at the small spot that would soon be removed, a cancer on the skin of an otherwise healthy planet. Some tissues had to be cut out in order to be sure the cancer didn't spread. Manning knew that.

58

PLAGUES

Decker tried breaking through the straps holding him in place, but it was a futile effort.

One of the men tending to his leg had been nice enough to inject him with a sedative that had him calm again. There was that at least.

He did his best to *remain* calm when Rollins showed up. She asked a few questions just out of his hearing range. One of the medics responded, nodded, and then they left. She pulled over a chair so she could be at eye level with him.

"You've been naughty, Mister Decker."

He looked hard at her and tried to get a reading, anything to let him know how badly he had screwed himself over. Nothing. He might as well have been staring at a wall.

"It was just too much," he said. "And those things… Those things were after me. *Are* after me. Do you understand that? They want me dead!" His voice was shaking by the time he was done, and he thought he might lose it, but he pushed that back.

She was a cold bitch. She simply nodded her head while staring into his face.

"I know," she said. "I know they are. You should know that the entire area is being cleaned. There won't be any of them left."

"Except the ones you have onboard now."

"That's correct." She stared at him. He looked away first, and he hated her for that. As if he needed another reason.

"You don't know how bad it is," he said. "You don't understand at all. They're insatiable."

"*Life* is insatiable, Mister Decker." She smiled thinly. He didn't like her smile. It made him think of lizards, and her lips reminded him too much of the very creatures they were discussing. "Life fights to exist," she continued. "Haven't you realized that? No matter what the universe wants, life insists on surviving. Not just human life. All of it. We've encountered diseases on a dozen different worlds, and they've been burned away, only to show up in other places. Typhen's Disorder, Arcturian Klerhaige, the Lansdale Plague. Doesn't matter what we do, they come back. And they're not alone.

"Life is persistent. Be grateful for that."

He remained silent. She didn't want to understand, and though he couldn't read a single emotion from her, he knew her type well enough. Nothing he said would change her mind.

Finally he broke the silence.

"So what happens now?"

Rollins patted his restrained hand.

"Despite a few bumps, you kept your part of the bargain, and so will the company. You get your job back. You get your life back. You get a nice bonus as a finder's fee. We get our prizes, and everybody wins."

"No," he replied. "As long as those things are around, everybody loses."

"You'll never see them again."

"How can you know that?"

"Because you're going back to Earth. They are going elsewhere." She smiled again. "We're not *that* crazy, Mister Decker. You don't take something like this and drop it into the most populated place imaginable. You study it very carefully in an isolated, controlled environment."

"What about Adams and Elway?"

She stopped smiling.

"I think that's enough questions. You're safe, Mister Decker. Your family is safe. Consider your debt paid."

"You're making a mistake," he said. "I know you think you're doing the right thing, Miss Rollins, but you're making a horrible mistake."

"You should rest now, Mister Decker. We'll be leaving orbit soon."

She left the room, and for a while Decker slept.

He woke up again when they came for him.

The two "escorts" were armed, but needn't have bothered. He was still restrained, and kept that way until they reached the hypersleep chambers.

Manning was stripped down to his underwear and sitting on the edge of his coffin-like chamber.

"They burned," he said. "I watched. I doubt there's anything left down there. Hard to see past the plasma fires, but I think they're all gone."

Decker listened without a word. Before he could think of anything to say, Manning continued.

"I know what you were thinking. I get it. But you even *think* hard about going after any of mine again, and I'll bury you on seven different worlds."

Decker didn't want to look the man in his eyes, but he made himself. He could have thought of a dozen things to say, but instead he just nodded.

Adams deserved better. That was the thing that kept going through his mind. Maybe they'd manage to save her and Elway, but he didn't think so. Manning was pissed, and Muller and Dave—two men who'd saved his life a couple of times each—were staring at him with murder in their hearts. They were resentful. They felt betrayed.

He couldn't blame them in the least. His actions at the end were purely selfish. Screw money and everything else, he was looking after himself and his kids. The mercenaries would never understand that. They weren't capable of that level of empathy.

One of the men who'd brought him into the chambers took the time to remove the restraints.

The other patted the weapon on his hip. It wasn't a shock stick.

"Lie back, Mister Decker." The man wasn't making a request, and he took the hint. A moment later the lid was descending and Decker took a deep breath, same as he always did, not that it made any difference. The chamber sealed itself, and cold sterile air began cycling over his body.

He closed his eyes and felt the gases change. They weren't taking any chances with him. He would be asleep and secured long before the ship left orbit.

He inhaled. He exhaled. He inhaled.

He slept.

LETTERS HOME

Rollins re-read her communiqué before sending it.

```
To: L.Bannister@Weyland-Yutani.com
From: A.Rollins@Weyland-Yutani.com
Subject: Success
```

Lorne,

I'm pleased to report what can only be called a
resounding success.

In addition to successfully capturing one of the adults
alive, we have also procured two separate parasites,
already attached to hosts. Though we can't be
completely certain of the maturation cycles, it looks
as if both have successfully implanted embryos within
the host bodies. Judging from the levels of activity we
recorded just before cryogenic suspension I would guess
that they are only hours from hatching.

If you look carefully at the two separate files I've
attached (See: Host One and Host Two), you will note
that the two parasites exhibit several differences, in
both size and shape. Of special interest, note that
Host Two, the female, has attached to her a parasite
that seems to have more than one embryo to administer.

The embryo that has already been implanted is
substantially larger than the implant in Host One, and
is structurally different. Judging from the accounts of
what the mercenaries encountered planetside, this could
very well be a "queen."

Imagine the possibilities.

Additional files include full information gleaned from all of the probes. There's simply too much information to properly correlate from here, and I imagine we will have much to discuss by the time I arrive at the offices.

Lastly, despite initial fears that they might have been left behind on New Galveston, the samples from the ship at the dig site have been safely secured and stored. I did not have time to ascertain whether there was any cellular activity as originally claimed by Doctor Tanaka, but the woman never seemed the sort to exaggerate or make wild claims. Per our previous discussion the samples have been halved, with parts being placed in stasis, and the rest being secured in a safe environment that doesn't risk further cellular degradation.

I wish I had been able to see the ship. Not just the pictures, but the actual vessel. And the city. But judging from what Manning reported, they were lost to us already. What a pity. All we have are schematics and readings.

Until I get back to the offices, good luck with the research.

All the best,
Andrea

She sent the encrypted messages and secured her computer for the trip. The *Kiangya* had already broken orbit and was heading for home, and she was glad of it.

For a moment she looked at the samples from the alien ship, and smiled. Infinite possibilities. That was what Weyland-Yutani was all about—at a profit of course, but infinite possibilities were a lovely thing.

She made her way to the hypersleep chambers and looked over the other figures, lying in forced slumber.

So many empty chambers, she noted. *So many assets, lost.*

Around her the ship was silent, and most of the lights had dimmed down into sleep mode, conserving energy. Some people were bothered by darkness and the quiet. Decker was likely one of them. That might never change for him. Rollins wasn't disturbed at all by the secrets the darkness might hold, or the mysteries that silences kept. Those were the very things on which she thrived. They were what made her feel complete.

EPILOGUE

The stars kept their secrets and the great ship moved between them, all inhabitants accounted for and locked in slumber. Most of them slept well.

Decker did not. In his dreams there were things chasing him.

No matter how hard he ran, how carefully he hid himself or what he might find as a weapon, he knew they would eventually locate him. It was as inevitable as the dark between the stars.

And in his frozen sleep, no one could hear his screams.

ACKNOWLEDGEMENTS

Every book has a foundation. *Alien: Sea of Sorrows* could not exist without the original stories and movies, and is linked directly to Tim Lebbon's *Alien: Out of the Shadows* and Christopher Golden's *Alien: River of Pain*. Those alone would make a powerful foundation, but *Sea of Sorrows* truly could not exist without the ideas put forth by Steve Asbell of Twentieth Century Fox and the support and efforts of Josh Izzo and Lauren Winarski and Steve Saffel. Thanks also to the rest of the Titan team, including Nick Landau, Vivian Cheung, Katy Wild, Natalie Laverick, and Julia Lloyd. My gratitude to one and all.

ABOUT THE AUTHOR

JAMES A. MOORE is the Shirley Jackson Award-winning, best selling author of over forty novel length works, including *The Seven Forges* and *Blood Red* series of novels as well as several standalone novels and licensed properties like *Aliens: Sea of Sorrows* and *Predator: Hunters and Hunted*. He has been both the Vice-President and the Secretary for the Horror Writer Association, and is an active member of the Science Fiction & Fantasy Association, International Association of Media Tie-In Writers, and the International Thriller Writers. He has written for Marvel Comics and several role-playing game companies including White Wolf Publishing. He currently lives in Northern Maine, with his wife, Tessa and a small menagerie of animals. He is currently at work on a new series of Sword & Sorcery novels, including *Korrigan Grimn: Warlord*, and *The Forgotten*.

www.genrefied.blogspot.com

BOOK THREE

RIVER OF PAIN

1

OUR GUEST

For a long time Ripley had tried her best to avoid the *Nostromo*'s medical bay. Its white walls and bright lights chased away even the smallest shadows. The air was full of electric buzz and the sounds of machines.

As warrant officer on board the *Nostromo*, she'd spent far more time in the gray gloom of its corridors and compartments, flickering work lights the only intrusion into the darkness. Strange, really, but in her time on board one ship after another, she had grown more accustomed to shadows than light.

All that had changed.

The *Nostromo* had been traveling through the Zeta-2-Reticuli system, carrying twenty million tons of mineral ore bound for Earth, when the ship's on-board computer, designated "Mother," had responded to a distress signal from a planetoid called LV-426. Mother had woken the crew early from hypersleep, with instructions to investigate.

Ripley was uneasy with the order from the start. They weren't planetary explorers or colonists. It wasn't their job.

But orders had been clear. The captain, Dallas, had reminded her that their "job" was whatever the corporation decided it should be. And so they'd gone.

Upon landing, Dallas had taken his executive officer, Kane, and their navigator, Lambert, out onto the surface to investigate the source of the distress signal—a derelict spacecraft that was decidedly not of human origin. At that point, all of Ripley's internal alarm bells had gone off. They had no idea what dangers might await them inside that ship, and the captain, the XO, and their pilot shouldn't have been the ones checking it out.

They walked into a nightmare.

Ripley no longer felt comfortable in the *Nostromo*'s shadows. She sought out the medical bay, not for treatment, but for its light. Ash was there—the ship's science officer. He had an air of superiority that pissed her off. Sometimes he seemed to be looking down on the rest of them, as if they were specimens viewed through his microscope.

It made her skin crawl.

Nevertheless, as the ship's science officer, he might be their best hope of figuring out what the hell had really happened down there in the raging atmospheric storms on the surface of LV-426... what had happened to Kane.

But Ripley wouldn't just blindly follow orders, not anymore. The company's demands had made her uneasy. Mother's focus on whatever xenomorphic life they had encountered down on that ugly moon had troubled her. But when she voiced her concerns, the others had been unwilling to listen.

Well, to hell with that. She wasn't going to give them a choice. She had a daughter back on Earth—she had promised Amanda that she would come home safely, and she refused to break that promise.

So she'd follow her instincts, ask whatever questions demanded answers, and not worry about whose toes she might be stepping on.

Ripley entered the medical bay quietly. It felt like crossing the border into a foreign land without the permission of the king. She surveyed the lab area, all screens and white walls and yellow buttons, the lighting subdued now.

She stepped through into a second compartment and saw Ash

off to her right, studying a vid-screen. A small man, his presence nevertheless held a certain weight. His brown hair had just begun to gray, and his eyes were icy blue.

Ash bent to peer through a microscope, diverting his attention enough that she managed to get within a few feet without him taking notice. The image on the computer screen made Ripley shiver with revulsion.

It looked like a scan of the spidery alien creature that had attached itself to the face of the XO, but she couldn't quite make out the details. The thing had some sort of tail that wrapped around Kane's throat, and it tightened any time they attempted to remove it. They'd cut into it, but the hideous thing had bled acid that had burned its way down through three levels of the *Nostromo*. Another deck or two, it would have eaten through the hull, and they'd all be dead now.

Ash was fascinated with it.

Ripley just wanted it dead.

"That's amazing," she said quietly, nodding toward the image on the screen. "What is it?"

Ash glanced up abruptly.

"Oh, this?" he said. "I don't know yet." He clicked off the screen, straightening his back, and attempted an air of courtesy that was unlike him. "Did you want something?"

So polite, she thought. *We're both being so damn polite.*

"Yes, I… to have a little talk," she muttered. To tell the truth, she wasn't quite sure *why* she was there. "How's Kane?"

The air between them had a buzz all its own, not unlike the persistent hum of electricity. From the moment Ash had joined the crew—foisted upon them by the company, right before they'd set off from Thedus with their cargo—she had harbored a dislike for him. Some people had that effect on her. They'd walk into a room and she'd be instantly on guard. If she'd been a cat—like Jones, the ship's mascot—an encounter with Ash would have made her hair stand up.

He avoided direct eye contact, and she could tell he wanted her to leave.

"He's holding. No changes."

Ripley nodded toward the darkened screen.

"And our guest?" That got her a glance.

"Well, as I said, I'm still… collating, actually," Ash replied. He picked up a micro-scanner tablet and studied its display. "But I have confirmed that he's got an outer layer of protein polysaccharides. Has a funny habit of shedding his cells and replacing them with polarized silicon, which gives him prolonged resistance to adverse environmental conditions." He paused, and gave her a little smile. "Is that enough?"

Enough, she thought. *Is that enough?* He might as well have asked her to get the fuck out.

"That's plenty," she replied, but she stood her ground. "What does it mean?" she asked, bending to look into the microscope.

Ash stiffened. "Please don't do that."

Ripley cocked her head, unable to keep from making a face. She knew he was more than a little persnickety about his lab, but why get so uptight about her looking into a microscope? She hadn't even touched it.

"I'm sorry," she said, her tone making it clear that she wasn't.

Ash recovered his composure.

"Well, it's an interesting combination of elements," he said, "making him a tough little son of a bitch."

A chill went through Ripley.

"And you let him in," she said.

Ash lifted his chin, looking offended.

"I was obeying a direct order, remember?" he replied testily.

Ripley studied him closely, and at that moment she knew exactly why she had come to the medical bay.

"Ash, when Dallas and Kane are off the ship, I'm senior officer," she said.

His expression went blank.

"Oh, yes. I forgot."

But he hadn't. She knew that, and so did he. He hadn't even attempted to sound convincing. What troubled her, however, was the *why* of it all. Was it just another example of Ash being a prick? Did he not respect her place in the command hierarchy? Or did it not have anything to do with her? Did he just feel like he could do whatever the hell he wanted, without facing any repercussions?

That stops now, she decided.

"You also forgot the science division's basic quarantine law," she said.

"No, *that* I didn't forget," he replied calmly.

"Oh, I see," she said. "You just broke it, huh?"

Ash bristled, peering straight at her, his right hand resting on his hip.

"Look, what would you have done with Kane, hmm? You know his only chance for survival was to get him in here."

His irritation pleased her. It was nice to know she could get to him.

"Unfortunately, by breaking quarantine you risk everybody's life," Ripley countered.

"Maybe I should have left him outside," Ash replied. Then he fell back to his usual air of aloof superiority. "Maybe I've jeopardized the rest of us, but it was a risk I was willing to take."

Ripley edged a bit closer, her gaze locked with his.

"That's a pretty big risk for a science officer," she said. "It's not exactly out of the manual, is it?"

"I do take my responsibilities as seriously as you, you know?" Ash replied.

Ripley cast another glance at the screen. She wanted a look at that computer, but she wasn't even sure she would understand what she was seeing.

Ash stared defiantly at her.

"You do your job," he added, "and let me do mine, yes?"

A dozen possible replies raced through her mind, none of them polite or pleasant. Instead, Ripley took a breath, let it out, then turned and strode from the room. All she had wanted all along was for Ash to do his job, but he seemed more interested in the creature attached to Kane's face than he was in saving the XO.

Why?

2

TREMORS

DATE: 11 OCTOBER, 2165

Greg Hansard stood in the raging atmospheric stew on the surface of LV-426, and wished he could scream. Above him, the atmosphere processor gave a shriek of grinding metal and shuddered so powerfully that he could feel the trembling of the machine in the ground underfoot.

"What the hell are you guys doing in there?" Hansard bellowed into his comm link.

His heart slammed in his chest, beating in rhythm with the banging of the processor, and he felt as if he was suffocating inside his breathing mask. The irony wasn't lost on him, but it didn't lessen the urge to tear the mask off. He wouldn't do it, though—he might be going crazy out there in the grit-storm, but not *that* crazy.

"Our best—that's what we're doing," one of the engineers shouted in reply. Over the roar of the wind, Hansard couldn't tell who it was. "There's a crack in the generator housing! If we bring it down to half-speed, we may be able to make repairs without shutting the whole thing down."

"Do it," Hansard shouted back. "Just get it done as fast as you can! We can't afford any more delays."

"Hell, boss, we didn't pick the damn planet," the engineer replied.

Hansard hung his head in exasperation.

"I know, man," he said. "And I'd like to throttle the idiot who did."

"Hansard, you better get over here!" another voice shouted over the comm. This one he recognized.

"What is it, Najit?" he asked as he began to circle around the machine. The atmosphere processor towered sixty-seven feet above his head, juddering and banging and spewing out breathable air.

"You'd better see for yourself," Najit replied.

There were three engineers inside the atmosphere processor, and half a dozen outside. Najit was a structural engineer. For six years the company had been trying to terraform LV-426—now called Acheron—even as they built the foundations for the colony to come. The main structure of the central complex was in place, and a dozen colonists were already living down there with the builders and engineers, all under the management of the colonial administrator, Al Simpson.

Barely a day went by without Simpson tracking him down to bitch at him over the speed of the terraforming efforts. As far as Hansard was concerned, Simpson was an idiot in the employ of people whose idiocy existed on a far grander scale.

The colony—dubbed Hadley's Hope, after one of its designers—was a joint endeavor sponsored by the Earth government and the Weyland-Yutani Corporation, overseen by the colonial administration and *supposedly* adhering to all rules established by the Interstellar Commerce Commission. Acheron itself wasn't really a planet, even though they referred to it that way. It was a rock in the middle of nowhere, one of the moons of a planet called Calpamos.

Its storms were near constant, a blinding torrent of wind and grit and dust. No matter how well Hansard sealed himself inside his mask and hood and exposure suit, the grit still got everywhere.

Everywhere.

Every damn day.

Of all the places Weyland-Yutani could have chosen as the cradle for a new human colony, why this one? Atmospheric conditions had prevented them from properly mapping the topography from space, and yet some asshole had decided it was prime real estate.

It seemed to Hansard as if the place itself didn't want them there. They had managed to place atmosphere processors at various intervals around the surface, and the most important one—the massive, cathedral-like Processor One—was under construction. But they had run into all sorts of problems along the way. Tremors cracked the terrain and swallowed one of the smaller processors whole. Accidents and surveying errors and faulty equipment had caused all kinds of delays.

And now... what?

He marched around the base of the processor, unnerved by the machine's knocking. The ground trembled, and Hansard thought he might have trembled along with it. He tasted dirt in his mouth.

"Najit?" he called, thinking he ought to have found the man already.

"Here!" came the reply.

Hansard peered through the blowing veil of grit and spotted three figures, but they weren't anywhere near the processor. They stood a dozen feet from the hull of the machine, staring down at the ground.

Oh shit, Hansard thought. *Please don't tell me—*

The processor shook. Hansard spun to stare at it, holding his breath. The machine shuddered so violently that he could see the hull shifting. Suddenly he realized that not all of the tremors were coming from the machine itself.

"Son of a bitch!" he shouted.

The grinding of metal inside the structure grew into a squealing thunder.

Turning, Hansard ran to the others. Three men outside, yes. But there were three men inside as well. Inside with that grinding, shrieking metal.

"What the hell—" he began.

"It's another fissure," Najit shouted.

As he drew closer, Hansard could see the crack in the ground beneath their feet, thick layers of atmospheric dust and volcanic ash spilling like sand into the fissure. Najit ran along the crack, following it away from the processor to determine its length, then paused and turned back to face the other two structural engineers.

"Fifteen feet!" Najit called. "And growing!"

Hansard didn't give a shit how far it went *away* from the

atmosphere processor. He ran to the outer hull and stared at the fissure where it disappeared underneath the machine.

"No," he whispered. "No no no no."

He gazed up through the curtain of windblown grit. The processor shuddered and the clanking from inside reminded him of an archival clip he'd seen of an ancient locomotive.

"Shut it down!" he roared. "Shut the whole thing down and get out!"

"Boss…" Najit started, caution in his voice.

Hansard rounded on the three structural engineers.

"Get back, you idiots," he said, waving them away. "Don't you remember Processor Three?"

On his comm he could hear the engineers inside the processor, shouting to each other—commands and profanities in a cocktail of panicked words.

"You think it's going to get worse?" Najit called.

The ground continued to tremble. The quake was localized, but there was no way of knowing how long it would last. They'd surveyed this sector for eighteen months before beginning construction, with no sign of localized tremors.

Until it was too late to stop.

"It's already bad enough," Hansard barked.

The processor gasped, and the hum inside it went silent, but its hull continued to tremble. A lull in the storm gave him a clearer view up the side of the machine, where he spotted a crack in the otherwise smooth metal, twenty feet off the ground.

Shit!

"Get out of there, *now*," he shouted. "Nguyen! Mendez! Get—"

Suddenly Hansard stopped, and stared down at his feet. The ground seemed to settle, and the tremor eased. He held his breath for several seconds until he felt sure it had ended. Not that it mattered.

The processor might be repairable, but there was no point. The next tremor—a day or ten years from now—might destroy it altogether. This machine would have to be abandoned, just a metal hulk that they would scavenge for parts as they built one on ground they deemed more stable. On Acheron, however, they would never know for sure if any ground was stable enough.

"Boss?" Najit said, coming to stand beside him.

Hansard stared off into the storm, buffeted by the wind.

Defeated.

Whoever had given LV-426 its new name had recognized the absurdity of it all. In ancient Greek mythology, Acheron had been one of the rivers that wound through the netherworld. The word had a grim translation.

River of Pain.

3

REBECCA

Russ Jorden stared at the beads of sweat on his wife's forehead and felt a tightening in his heart. She squeezed his hand so hard he felt the bones grind together, and he could see that she was holding her breath, her face scrunched into a mask of fury and pain.

"Breathe, Anne," he pleaded. "Come on, honey, breathe."

Anne gasped and her whole body relaxed a moment before she pursed her lips and began to blow out long drafts of air. Her face had been pale for hours, but now she looked almost gray and the circles beneath her eyes were bruise-blue. She let her head loll to one side and her eyes pleaded with him to do something, though they both knew the best he could do was be at her side and keep loving her.

"Why won't she just *get* here?" Anne asked.

"She's all cozy in there," Russ replied. "It's warm and she can hear your heartbeat. It's a big, scary universe out here."

Anne glanced down at her enormous belly, which had shifted dramatically lower in the past few hours. She frowned, her forehead etched with stern lines.

"Come on out, baby girl. If you're gonna be a part of this family, you've got to be courageous, and a little bit crazy."

Russ laughed softly, but he couldn't give in to the humor of the words the way he normally would have. Anne had been in labor for seventeen hours, and for the past three, her cervix had been stuck at seven centimeters dilated and sixty percent effaced. Dr. Komiskey had given her drugs to jump-start the process, with a warning that forcing the uterus into action might amplify the usual pain of labor.

Anne gave a deep groan, and her breathing quickened.

"Russell..."

"She'll be here soon," he vowed. "I promise." Silently he added, *C'mon, Rebecca. It's time.*

The nurse came into the room as Anne gritted her teeth and arched her back, her entire body going tense. Russ held his breath along with her—seeing Anne in pain made him want to scream. He glanced over in panic and frustration.

"Can't you do anything for her, Joel?"

The nurse, slender and dark, gave a sympathetic shake of his head.

"I've told you, Russ. She wanted to go natural, the way she did with Tim. Now it's too late to give her anything that would offer any significant relief. The painkillers she's already taken are the best we can do without endangering the baby."

Anne swore at him. Joel moved to the bedside and put a hand on her shoulder as she began to breathe again, easing down from another contraction.

"Dr. Komiskey will be here in a second to evaluate you again."

Russ glared at him. "And if she hasn't progressed?"

"I don't want a cesarean!" Anne snapped between gasps.

Joel patted her shoulder.

"You know it's perfectly safe. And if you're worried about scarring—"

"Don't be stupid. C-sections haven't left a scar since my grandmother was born," Anne said breathlessly.

"That's what I'm saying," the nurse replied. "For the sake of the baby—"

Stricken, Anne turned to stare at him.

"Joel, is there something wrong with the baby?"

"Not now," Joel said. "Everything we've seen looks perfectly normal, and all blood and genetic tests show a healthy child. But there can be complications if... Look, this is really something Dr.

Komiskey should be talking to you about."

"Damn it, Joel, we've known you two years now," Russ barked. "The colony's not that big. If there's something to worry about—"

"No. Just stop," Joel said, holding up a hand. "If you were on your own, you'd have something to worry about. But you're not alone. You've got the med-staff looking out for you and your baby, and the whole colony waiting for the little girl to show her face."

Anne cried out and squeezed Russ's hand again. He stared at his wife's beautiful face, contorted with pain, and realized that one of the beads of moisture on her cheek wasn't sweat at all, but a tear, and he knew they had let it go on too long.

"Get Komiskey in here," Russ snapped.

"She'll be here any—" Joel began.

"Get her!"

"Okay, okay." Joel rushed from the room, leaving the Jordens alone with their fear and hope and a baby who didn't seem to want to meet them.

Worried silence fell between Russ and Anne. Exhausted, she used the low ebbs between the agonizing crests of her contractions to breathe and rest and pray that when Dr. Komiskey returned, her cervix would be fully dilated so that she could push the baby out.

"I don't understand," she whispered tiredly. "Tim took four hours from first contraction to last. And my back... God, my back didn't hurt like this. What's wrong?"

Russ stared at the white smoothness of the monitors stationed above and beside the bed. If the baby went into distress, alarms would go off, but for the moment the monitors blinked green and blue and made no sound but a soft, almost musical hum. Beyond the monitors, quiet and dark, there stood a much larger machine, a huge unit with a mostly transparent hood.

If Komiskey had to surgically remove the baby, she would move Anne into that unit. It wasn't scarring that frightened Anne, but the idea that she would no longer be treated by human hands. The natal surgery unit would perform the C-section essentially by itself, and the thought terrified both of the Jordens. Humans might make errors, but at least they cared about the outcome. Machines did not understand consequences, or the value of life.

"Did we make a mistake?" Anne rasped.

Russ pressed a cold, damp cloth against her forehead.

"Timmy was so easy," he said. "We couldn't have known it would be like this. Trying to deliver naturally made sense at the time."

"Not that," his wife said, one hand fluttering weakly upward, moving her fingers as if she could erase his reply. "I mean coming to Acheron. To Hadley's Hope."

Russ frowned. "We had no choice. There was no work at home. We were lucky to get the opportunity to work off-planet. You know—"

"I do," she rasped, and then she began to stiffen, hissing breath through her teeth as another contraction came on. "But having children... *here*..."

The monitors flickered red, just for an instant, as Anne went rigid and roared in pain.

"That's it!" Russ snapped. He jumped from his seat, knocking the chair over behind him, and turned toward the door, but Anne would not release her grip on his hand. He turned to plead with her and saw that the monitor lights were all back to green. No alarms had sounded.

He didn't care. That one flicker had been enough.

"Komiskey!"

As he drew a breath to shout the doctor's name again, Dr. Theodora Komiskey came breezing through the door, a squat woman with blue eyes and a mass of brown curls. Joel followed dutifully in her wake.

"Let's see how far we've come," the doctor said, smiling and upbeat as ever.

"Halfway across the fucking universe," Russ growled.

He despised the false cheer so many doctors wore like a mask, and wanted to scream the smile off Dr. Komiskey's face, but that wouldn't have done anything to help Anne or the baby. Instead, he could only stand there while the barrel-shaped woman pulled on a pair of medical gloves, perched on a stool, and reached up between Anne's thighs, feeling around as if searching for something she'd lost.

"I can feel her head," Dr. Komiskey said, concern in her voice. "And now I understand the trouble. The baby's presenting in the posterior position—"

Russ felt his heart clench.

"What does that mean?"

Komiskey ignored him, addressing Anne instead. "She's facing your abdomen, which means the back of her skull is putting pressure on your sacrum—your tailbone. The good news is that you're fully dilated and effaced. Your baby is about to make her big debut as the adorable princess of Hadley's Hope."

Russ hung his head. "Thank God."

"What's…" Anne said, sucking in a breath. "What's the bad news?"

"The bad news is that it's gonna hurt like hell," Komiskey said.

Anne shook with relief.

"I'm ready when you are, Theo. Let's get the little newt out of there."

Russ smiled. They'd been calling the baby that for months, imagining her growing from tiny speck to odd little newt to full-fledged fetus.

"All right, then," Dr. Komiskey said. "When the next contraction hits, you're going to—"

But Anne didn't need to be told. She'd already given birth once. The contraction hit her and she shouted again, but this time her roar sounded less like a scream of pain and more like a battle cry.

Thirteen minutes later, Dr. Komiskey slipped Rebecca Jorden into her mother's arms. Russ smiled so wide that his face hurt, his chest so full of love he thought it might burst. As Anne kissed the baby girl's forehead, Russ touched her tiny hand and his infant daughter gripped his finger tightly, already strong.

"Hello, little newt," Anne whispered to the baby, and kissed her again. "Better be careful or that nickname's gonna stick."

Russ laughed and Anne turned to smile at him.

Newt, he thought. *You're a lucky little girl.*

DATE: 2 APRIL, 2173

When the new recreational center at the Hadley's Hope colony opened, nobody bothered with anything as formal or old-fashioned as a ribbon cutting. Al Simpson, the colony's administrator, unlocked the door and swung it open, and the party began. The Finch brothers brought some of their homemade whiskey, Samantha Monet and her sister had decorated the facility, and Bronagh Flaherty, the cook, put out a selection of cakes and cookies that she had made for the occasion.

The star of the evening, however, was two-and-a-half-week-old Newt Jorden. Al Simpson stood in the corner of the main room and sipped at a mug of hot Irish coffee, watching the rest of the colonists take turns fussing over the baby girl.

Swaddled in a blanket, cradled in her mother's arms, she was a beautiful little thing, no question about that. As a rule, Al had no fondness for babies. More often than not they were crying, crapping machines and looked like shriveled, hairless monkeys. Not little Newt, though. He'd barely heard a peep out of her since the party began, and she had big lovely peepers that made her seem like a curious old soul gazing out from within a ruddy, healthy baby face.

The Jordens' boy, Tim, had been an infant himself when they first arrived on LV-426, but Newt was a reason for the whole colony to celebrate—the first baby actually born on Acheron. Al thought that if all of the colony's future babies turned out like Newt, it wouldn't be so bad having them around. But he had a feeling that Newt would be an exception, and that he wasn't about to change his feelings toward newborns... or children in general, now that he thought about it.

"Cute kid," a voice said beside him.

Al flinched, coffee sloshing out of his mug. He swore as it burned his fingers and quickly switched the mug from his right to left hand.

"Don't sneak up on me like that," he said as he shook the coffee droplets from his fingers, and then blew on them.

"Damn, Al, I'm sorry about that," Greg Hansard said, wincing in sympathy.

Al shook his fingers again, but the pain had started to fade.

"Good thing I put a good dollop of Irish cream in there," he said. "Cooled it down a bit."

Hansard smiled. "Well, now, if you're not badly burned you might just have to show me where you're hiding that bottle."

Al didn't really want to share, but Hansard was the colony's chief engineer, and always good company. He supposed he could spare a few ounces of his private stock.

"I might be persuaded," he said, taking a long sip from his mug. Before he troubled himself to get Hansard a cup, he wanted to drink his own coffee while it was still hot. "You're right, though. The Jorden kid is kind of adorable. I don't know where she gets it, considering the parents."

Hansard uttered a dry laugh.

"They *are* pretty scruffy."

Al grinned, hiding the smile behind his cup as he glanced around. He had always been a man full of opinions, but the colonists were all stuck with each other and it would complicate relationships around Hadley's Hope if the colonial administrator started talking shit about people behind their backs. On the other hand, it wasn't Anne Jorden's wild, unruly curls that irritated him, or the fact that Russ always looked as if he'd had too much to drink the night before.

"Wildcatters are pretty much always scruffy, aren't they?" Al said quietly.

"They're trouble, is what they are," Hansard replied. He nodded toward the cluster of people still cooing and ahhing over the baby. Otto Finch had crouched down to talk to young Tim, the Jordens' son, and had handed him some kind of furry doll. "Nice enough people, the Jordens. But I worry about the boy."

Al frowned, turning to him. He didn't like the sound of that.

"What do you mean?"

Hansard grimaced, brows knitted as if already regretting that he'd spoken.

"Greg, you brought it up," Al said. "I'm the administrator. I can't let it go. If you think there's a problem—"

"Depends what you mean by 'problem.'"

Al glanced over at the Jordens again. Father and mother looked tired, but they both were smiling happily, so proud of their little family. They were surveyors employed by the colony, but like half of the survey team, they moonlighted on the side as wildcatters—prospectors—searching sectors of the planetoid's surface for mineral deposits, meteor crash sites, and other things of interest to the company. The colony's Weyland-Yutani science team used prospectors to retrieve soil and mineral samples, and to map out sections of the planet. The excursions were often very dangerous.

"It's not just that the lifestyle is crazy," Hansard said thoughtfully. "Yeah, colonists are going to have kids. That's the nature of what we're doing here. But wildcatting is risky, and Anne and Russ don't seem to recognize the dangers involved. Bad enough for most of them—who's going to raise their kids if something goes wrong? And the Jordens... well, they take it a step further, don't they? Just today, Russ took Tim out with him in the tractor, prospecting ten kilometers north."

Al stared at him. "You're sure of this?"

Hansard nodded. "I don't want to start something. Not tonight, anyway. But the kid's not safe out there. I've been in more of the damn atmo-storms than anyone, and if the tractor gets stuck..."

Al held up a hand.

"I'm with you, but there's no rule against it. I've mentioned it to several of the prospectors before, but they look at it the same way farmers do—it's a family business, and if they take their kids out into the fields, they're just teaching them for the future, giving them a sense of proprietorship."

"That's idiotic."

"I didn't say I agreed with them." Al scratched the back of his neck, suddenly feeling tired. "I blame Weyland-Yutani, if you want to know the truth."

Hansard arched an eyebrow.

"Dangerous opinion, Al. Talk like that can cost your job."

"We're floating on a desolate rock where they're trying to seed a little civilization. I don't think they're gonna care what I say as long as I do my job. And since when are you so in love with the company?"

"I'm not," Hansard admitted. "But I'm well paid, and when I leave here—when all the work is finally done—I'm hoping to get an easier assignment. Hell, since my first day on Acheron I've been wondering who I pissed off to end up here."

"Maybe they just had faith in you. Obviously not an easy job, trying to make this place livable." Al sipped his mug again, letting the coffee warm him and the alcohol loosen him up. No matter how high they set the heat inside the colony buildings, he still felt cold. *Just too damn far from the sun*, he thought.

He lowered his voice and glanced around to make sure he wasn't overheard.

"My point is that they tend to recruit daredevils and dimwits as colonists, not to mention people who are looking for a new start because they've burned all their bridges back home."

"You like the Jordens, though," Hansard said.

Al shrugged. "I like 'em fine, but they're too cavalier, too desperate to earn bonuses. The science team uses wildcatters because they're willing to take risks. I just worry they're going to put us all at risk one of these days. We've got a lot of years to go before this colony is fully established and populated. A decade or more. With that kind of time, anything could go wrong."

He looked over at Anne Jorden, who cradled her new baby close, kissing her soft cheeks and whispering love into her ears. Russ had knelt down beside young Tim, who pouted with his arms defiantly crossed, apparently upset over something to do with the baby.

"Mark my words," Al said, "if we ever have any serious trouble on this dirtball, it's gonna be because of people like them."

4

ARRIVALS

DATE: 16 MAY, 2179

For the first time in Jernigan's career, it looked like he'd claim salvage on a ship he hadn't even been looking for. He stood in the airlock that led into the retrieval bay and suited up, watching his two companions and wondering what they were thinking.

Not that it was hard to imagine what Landers would be thinking. The greedy bastard would just be eager to see what goodies the drifting vessel might contain. Fleet, though... he was an enigma. Jernigan had spent three years and four expeditions trying to figure him out. Landers laughed and said he should give up, that Fleet was almost an alien species. But Jernigan wasn't a quitter.

"Target ship gathered," a buzzing voice said in his earpiece. Moore, up on the flight deck. He was their eyes and ears right now, and Jernigan was comfortable with that.

"Any indication of its origins?" Jernigan asked.

"Negative. No beacons, no transmission, no signs of life. I've hailed another dozen times since you guys went to suit up. Nothing. No auto-response from on-board computers, no sign that it's even picking up my transmissions. Quiet as the grave."

"So what do you think?" Landers asked. "Some old military shuttle?"

"Not military," Moore said, and Jernigan saw Landers'

disappointment in the way he slumped. Anything military wasn't legally salvage, but way out here there was no one to police what they stripped out, packaged up, and sold to the highest bidder. Usually they went for ships or orbiting stations that they knew had been damaged or abandoned. The information was sent by the company who owned the wreck, or sometimes by private contacts who knew who to speak to, and how much a good salvage could net.

There was often dubious information passed on from shady sources, and several times he'd found himself boarding vessels that showed signs of forced abandonment or criminal activity. Once he'd found the remains of a firefight.

Deep-salvage had never been the most respectable of professions, but Jernigan really didn't give a shit what people thought. He had his own moral code, and he was quite proud to do a job that most people wouldn't.

Sometimes they'd reach a target vessel and find survivors on board. That changed everything. They still charged the company the cost of time and transport, but there was never a cut of anything larger. Even Landers had never raised any objection when they pulled back from stripping or towing in a ship that still had a living crew member or passenger.

Not quite respectable, never quite criminal.

"Not military," Jernigan said. "But no indication where it comes from? No ship's signature attached?"

"No, but it *is* old," Moore said. "Don't think I've seen anything like it outside of history holos." He paused, then added, "Right, just docking and pressurizing. Hold onto your nuts."

A soft vibration passed through the ship, and when Jernigan looked through the viewing port he saw moisture condense rapidly on the other side, turning quickly to ice. He made sure his suit's climate control systems were set to a comfortable level, then waited for all of the lights to turn green.

Landers and Fleet were experienced salvage workers, and Jernigan had no hesitation about working with either of them. They'd boarded at least twenty vessels and stations together, and seen each other through a few hairy moments. This one would go like clockwork.

He was sure of it.

As always, he felt the seed of excitement. One day, he was certain, they'd find something amazing.

When the lights were green, the three men left the airlock and entered the hold. Fleet fired up the remote cutting robot, trundling it across to the ship using a handheld control unit and igniting its cutting laser. He glanced at Landers, who'd taken position at a small panel close to where the salvaged ship had been gripped tight by a network of grappling arms.

Landers did one more quick check across all systems, then nodded.

"Clean as a virgin's pussy," he said. "Nothing in there to cause worry."

"And what would you know about virgins' pussies?" Fleet asked.

"Ask your sister," Landers said. Fleet didn't answer, or give any indication that he'd even heard. He steered the cutting robot toward the ship, used a scanner to measure the door and plan a cut. Then he hit *deploy*.

It took the laser a minute to cut through. Jernigan swayed slightly from foot to foot.

Weird-looking ship, he thought. *Old shuttle, maybe. Not a lifeboat.* There was evidence of damage around the door's exterior—scrapes and scratches, and a blast-scar close to the engines. Like everything they found and salvaged, this vessel had a story to tell.

The door fell inward with a heavy clang. Fleet withdrew the cutter and sent in a scanner. None of them expected that they'd find anything surprising, but they all knew the rules. Better safe than sorry.

The scanner did its work.

"Anything?" Jernigan asked.

"Looks like a hypersleep capsule," Fleet said.

"Oh, man," Landers said. "Anyone alive in there?" Jernigan hated the hint of disappointment in his colleague's voice.

"Can't tell," Fleet said. "Let's check it out."

The scanner withdrew and Jernigan went first, the other two following him in. There was a space suit splayed over the flight chair, and what looked like some sort of grappling gun dropped on the controls. The single hypersleep pod was coated in a layer of frost.

Jernigan brushed his hand across the curved canopy, revealing the striking woman inside. Hunkered down next to her was a cat. *Holy cow.* He hadn't seen a cat since he was a kid.

"Bio readouts are all in the green—looks like she's alive," he said. He slipped off his helmet and sighed. "Well, there goes our salvage, guys."

And that's a face with a story to tell, for sure, he thought.

DATE: 10 JUNE, 2179
TIME: 0945

The hum of the dropship turned into a metallic groan as it hit the atmosphere of LV-426. Captain Demian Brackett kept his boots flat on the floor and held onto the safety rig that kept him locked into his seat. The vessel slewed wickedly from side to side for several seconds before straightening out, and then it bounced like a speedboat skipping across high seas.

Alarms began to sound, red lights blinking all over the cockpit up front.

"What've we hit?" he shouted to the pilot.

The woman didn't turn around, too focused on keeping them on course.

"Just the atmosphere," she replied. "Acheron's never smooth sailing." She slapped a couple of buttons and the alarms died, though the lights continued to blink in distress.

Brackett gritted his teeth as the dropship filled with the noise of atmospheric debris plunking and scraping the hull. There seemed to be a *lot* of it.

"Am I missing something?" he called, raising his voice to be heard over the noise of the debris peppering the ship. "Haven't they been terraforming this planet for fifteen years?"

"More," the pilot shouted. "You should've seen what it was like trying to land here ten years ago, when I first got here."

No, thanks, Brackett thought. He had a stomach like iron, but even he had begun to feel queasy. His jaw hurt from clenching his teeth.

Gonna scramble my brains, he thought, as the whole dropship shook violently around him.

For a moment the barrage ceased. He started to relax, and then the ship plummeted abruptly, as if their controlled freefall had just become a suicide run. Cursing silently, he braced himself and twisted around to try to see through the cockpit to the outside.

"I'd rather not die on the first day of my command," he called. "Y'know, if it's no trouble for you."

The pilot glanced back at him, a scowl on her face.

"Take a breath, Captain. Seven crashes, and I've never had a passenger die on me."

"Seven *what*?"

They hit another air pocket and the drop threw him forward a second before the atmosphere thickened again, jerking him back so hard he slammed his head against the hull of the ship.

Son of a—

"Here you go, handsome," the pilot announced. The retro-rockets kicked in, lofted them up a dozen feet, and then began to lower them slowly. She guided the dropship gingerly forward and descended until it settled gently to the ground.

A hydraulic hiss came from the ship, as if it were exhaling right along with him, and Brackett released the catch on his restraints. The emergency lights shut down and the cabin brightened into a blue-white glow.

"Safe and sound, just like I promised," the pilot said. She disengaged the door locks and stood up from her seat, a mischievous smile on her face. For the first time, Brackett noticed her curves, and the way she looked at him.

"As good as your word," he said. "Yet I just now realized that I don't even know your name."

"Tressa," she said, holding out her hand. "At your service."

"Demian Brackett," he said as they shook.

She stepped over to the starboard door and entered a code into a control pad. The door hissed open, and a short ramp slid out with a rattle, clunking onto the planetary surface.

"So what crime did you commit to get stuck out here at the ass-end of the universe?" Tressa asked.

Brackett smiled. "I'm a good marine," he said. "I go where I'm told."

The wind began to howl, blowing a scouring dust into the ship. He took a look outside and his smile faded. Acheron was a world of black and gray, save for the growing colony whose buildings were mere silhouettes in the obscuring storm. After several seconds the wind died down again, giving him a better view, but there wasn't much more to see. Box structures, a glassoid greenhouse hemisphere, and in the distance the towering, ominous, hundred-and-fifty-foot high atmosphere processor, belching oxygen into the air.

"Home sweet home."

"Yeah," Tressa said, "you're not gonna get a lot of beach days. How long are you stationed here?"

Brackett picked up the duffel filled with his gear and slung it over his shoulder.

"Until they reassign me."

She tilted her head and cocked her hip and he flattered himself into thinking he saw regret in her eyes.

"Well, I hope we meet again, Captain Brackett. Somewhere far from Acheron."

DATE: 10 JUNE, 2179

There was somebody in the room with Ellen Ripley. She kept her eyes closed. The smell of disinfectant filled the air, and she heard the comforting sound of medical machines. The sensation of sheets against her skin and a mattress beneath her back was luxurious.

None of it prevented her from feeling like shit.

She felt no danger from the presence, no threat, and yet in her memory there was a deep, heavy weight of darkness striving to break through. It was a solid mass somewhere within her, and its gravity was relentless.

I'm so tired, she thought. But as she opened her eyes at last, she knew that she was lucky to be alive. A nurse bustled around her, checking readouts, fine-tuning the equipment, taking notes. As she watched the woman going about her work, Ripley caught sight of a window that had never been open before. It offered a wide, uninterrupted view out into space, the complex arms and habitation pods of a space station she did not recognize... and the surface of the planet below.

A planet she recognized as home.

Something warm flushed through her, spreading from her core and touching her cheeks. Happiness, and hope. She'd made it. She had survived the *Nostromo*, defeated the beast, and made it back home. She'd be seeing Amanda again soon.

Yet something was far from right. She felt sick in the pit of her stomach, and not just as a result of being clumsily pulled out of hypersleep. That darkness in her memory was pregnant with terror, bulging with nightmares waiting to be birthed. It lured her in. She thought of Dallas, Kane and the others, and the terrible fate that had befallen them, and in her mind their faces were old and sad, like faded photographs found at the bottom of an old suitcase.

She thought of the bastard Ash, and he seemed not so distant.

There was something else, too. Something... closer.

"How are we today?" the nurse asked.

Ripley tried to speak, but her tongue felt swollen and dry. She smacked her lips together.

"Terrible," she croaked.

"Well, better than yesterday, at least," the nurse said. She sounded so chirpy and upbeat, but there was something impersonal about her voice, too. As if she wanted to keep one step removed from her patient.

"Where am I?" Ripley asked.

"You're safe. You're at Gateway Station, been here a couple of days." She helped Ripley sit up and rearranged the pillows behind her. "You were pretty groggy at first, but now you're okay."

This is wrong, Ripley thought. Gateway Station? She'd never heard of it. She'd been away for a while, true, but unless this place was top secret, even military, she'd have known about it.

"Looks like you've got a visitor," the nurse said. Ripley turned around, and when the door opened it wasn't the man she saw, but the cat he carried.

"Jonesy!" she said, and her smile felt good. "Hey, come here." She reached out for the cat and the man brought him forward. "Where were you, you stupid cat? How are you? Where have you been?"

The guy sat as she made a fuss. She knew how foolish it looked and sounded, her talking to a cat. But it was Jonesy. Her link to the past, the *Nostromo*, and—

And?

That darkness inside, luring her in with its dreadful gravity. Maybe she just needed to puke.

"Guess you two have met, huh?"

Ripley looked at the man for the first time, and took an instant dislike to him. What he said next did nothing to dilute that.

"I'm Burke, Carter Burke. I work for the Company." He paused, then added, "But don't let that fool you, I'm really an okay guy."

Okay? Ripley thought. *Yeah, right. Smooth, shifty, slick, won't meet my eyes. Dammit, I still feel like shit.* She wanted him to go away, to leave her with Jonesy and her pains, and that thing inside—the memory, that terrible threat—which she had yet to understand.

But he was Company, which meant that he was here for a reason.

"I'm glad to see you're feeling a little better," he smarmed. "They tell me that all the weakness and disorientation should pass soon. It's just natural side effects of an unusually long hypersleep." He shrugged. "Something like that."

And there it is, Ripley thought. *The beginning of the truth. Nothing can turn out fine. I'm not that lucky.*

"What do you mean?" she asked. "How long was I out there?"

Burke's slickness melted away, and he suddenly seemed uncomfortable. She preferred him smarmy.

"Has no one discussed this with you yet?" he asked.

"No," Ripley said. "But, I mean…" She looked from the window again. "I don't recognize this place."

"I know," Burke said. "Ahh… okay. It's just that this might be a shock to you."

How long? Ripley thought, and Amanda stared at her from memory.

"It's longer than—" he began.

"How long?" she demanded. Amanda, in her mind's eye, was crying. "Please."

"Fifty-seven years," he said.

"What?"

No. No, no way, that's not possible, that's not— But in her memory her crew were faded figures, whispers on the tip of her tongue. Ash, though. He was almost still there.

"That's the thing, you were out there for fifty-seven years. What happened was, you had drifted right through the core systems, and it's really just… blind luck that a deep-salvage team found you when they did."

Ripley's heart beat faster.

Fifty-seven years.

Amanda turned away from her, fading, becoming a shadow of a memory just like her old crew.

No! Ripley thought. *Amanda! I came through so much to get back to you and—*

What *had* she gone through? That weight within her pulsed, almost playful with the promise of sickening, shattering revelation.

"It was one in a thousand, really," Burke said, but his voice was becoming more distant, less relevant. "You're damn lucky to be alive, kiddo."

Kiddo. She'd called Amanda "kiddo." She tried now, but her voice would not work, and her little girl was lost to her.

Lost.

"You could have been floating around out there forever…" His words faded to nothing, all meaning stolen by what was happening inside her. That weight she carried, beginning to reveal itself at last.

Ripley tried to catch her breath. Jonesy hissed at her. Cats saw everything.

But when the unbearable weight broke open at last, it wasn't a memory at all.

It was one of *them.*

She felt it inside her, invading, squirming inside her ribcage as it prepared to be born in sick, evil mockery of the daughter she had lost. She flipped back on the bed in agony, thrashing her arms. Burke tried to hold her down, shouting for help. She knocked a glass from his hand and heard it shattering on the floor. Her drip stand fell, ripping a needle from her arm.

Others rushed into the room. They didn't know what was wrong and there was no way she could tell them, no way to explain, other than to plead with them to help.

"Please!" she said. "Kill me!"

It pushed and bulged, cracking ribs, stretching skin, and through the white-hot blaze of agony she rolled up her gown and saw—

Ripley snapped awake in her bed, hand clutched to her chest. She felt rapid, fluttering movement, but it was only the beating of her heart.

Reality crashed in, and it was awful. She looked from the window and saw the beautiful curve of the Earth. So near and yet so far—but that no longer mattered. To Ripley it no longer felt like home.

The small screen on the med-monitor unit beside her bed flickered into life, and her nurse's face appeared.

"Bad dreams again?" she asked. "You want something to help you sleep?"

"No!" Ripley snapped. "I've slept enough." The nurse nodded and the screen went blank.

Jonesy had been sleeping on the bed with her. The medics didn't like it, but Burke had persuaded them that it would do her good. *After the shock she's had*, she had heard him telling them. She supposed she should have been grateful to him, but her first opinion stuck.

She didn't like the little fuck.

"Jonesy," she said, picking up the cat and cuddling him to her. "It's all right, it's all right. It's over."

But that dark, heavy weight remained within her, something very much a part of her and yet unknown. And in saying those calming words to the cat, she was only trying to persuade herself.

5

ROUGH TERRAIN

Two marines awaited Brackett on the surface. They saluted as he came down the ramp and he returned the gesture, striding hurriedly toward them.

"Welcome to Acheron, Captain," the first said. She was a tall woman with skin nearly as dark brown as Brackett's, and the pale line of an old scar across her left cheek. She gestured to the short, barrel-chested marine beside her, a pale man with bright orange hair and thick goggles covering his eyes. "I'm Lieutenant Julisa Paris. This is Sergeant Coughlin—"

"Nice to meet you both," Brackett replied. "And thanks for coming out into the storm to greet me, but let's continue this inside."

Sgt. Coughlin took his duffel with one hand, lugging it with an ease that bespoke notable strength, and the three of them hurried toward the nearest door, which led into a two-story gray building whose windows were long horizontal slits, some covered by heavy metal weather shielding.

"Hate to break it to you, Cap," Lt. Paris said, gesturing around them, "but this crap? This is a typical day out here." She led the way inside, stopped at the entrance to let them pass, and then slammed the door behind them. The sound of the scouring wind died instantly and the door sealed with a hiss.

White lights flickered and grew brighter. Brackett looked around at the clean, wide corridor that went deep into the building. Music played quietly from overhead speakers—early 22nd century jazz— and the captain decided he could have done worse. There were a lot of command posts where it would be almost impossible not to develop at least low-level claustrophobia. There'd be room to move here, and people to get to know—civilians and marines alike.

"Okay, let's do this right," he said, shaking hands with Paris and Coughlin. "Demian Brackett. Your new CO. And I figure since you two came out to greet me, that gives me three options. You're either good marines, suck-ups, or you drew the short straw. Which is it?"

Coughlin let out a barking laugh, his face reddening. "Oh, I'm definitely a suck-up," he said, hefting his burden. "I'm carrying your damn bag."

"And you, Lieutenant?" Brackett said, arching an eyebrow as he glanced at Paris.

A smile flickered across her features, but only one side of her mouth lifted. On the left side, beneath the scar, the muscles did not seem to respond.

"Give it time, Captain," Paris said. "I'm sure you'll figure me out."

"Fair enough. Lead the way."

As Lt. Paris guided him deeper into the building, Coughlin began to rattle off what he apparently considered the amenities of Hadley's Hope, including fresh greenhouse vegetables, a game room, vast, incomplete subterranean levels with plenty of room for running, and a cook who was—the sergeant claimed—a virtuoso when it came to Italian pastries.

The colony was only in its nascent stages. Someday it would be a sprawling hub, as Weyland-Yutani continued to promote expansion into this quadrant. Both the company and the government supported the scientific research that was already going on here, but eventually the real value of Hadley's Hope would be as a way station or port.

"I've gotta say," Coughlin went on, "it doesn't hurt that there are some lovely women among the colonists."

He seemed to catch himself, hitched Brackett's duffel higher on his shoulder, and shot a quick worried glance toward Paris.

"Say, Cap… our last CO was kind of a hardass when it came to, uhm, fraternizing with the colonists. That gonna be a problem with you?"

Brackett had given it some thought when he'd first received the assignment. While he didn't want the drama of romantic and sexual entanglements between his marines and the colonists, he didn't see how he could effectively prevent them. Better to have things out in the open than deal with the foolishness of people trying to maintain covert relationships.

"I'm not in favor," he said, "but I'd rather have you sleeping with the colonists than with other marines. There are regulations for a reason. I don't want you mooning over Lt. Paris in the midst of an op, and stumbling off a cliff."

Coughlin blinked, mouth gaping.

"Me an' the Loot? Nah, Captain, there's nothing like… I mean I wouldn't… well not that I wouldn't, but…"

Paris started to laugh and shook her head. Brackett had maintained a straight face, but Coughlin saw Paris's expression and blushed furiously.

"You're screwing with me."

"Yes, Sergeant," Brackett admitted. "I'm screwing with you."

Coughlin sighed. "Nice one, Cap. I see how it's gonna be."

"So, I'm not going to have any trouble with you, Sergeant Coughlin?"

"Not with him," Lt. Paris said. "But we've got our share of meatheads."

"Care to give me a heads-up?" Brackett said. "Let me know who to look out for?"

Paris didn't reply. Any trace of a smile vanished from her face. As she reached a door and keyed it open, she wore an expression that said she regretted having spoken.

As the three of them moved deeper inside the colony, they passed several civilians. Brackett heard laughter down a side corridor, and glanced over to see a pair of children doing cartwheels along the floor. That would take some getting used to—having kids around.

"What about you, Cap?" Coughlin said.

Brackett furrowed his brow. "What about what, Sarge?"

"You got someone in your life? Someone you left behind?"

Ahead, a row of high windows looked in on the spacious command block, where security and operations personnel sat at workstations and studied display screens. In the middle of the room, a heavyset white man appeared to be dressing down a scraggly, bearded young guy who held a blueprint scroll in his hand.

"Administration," Lt. Paris said. "That's Al Simpson. You're catching him on one of his better days."

Simpson's face turned red as he yelled at the young fellow. Paris didn't seem to be joking about this being one of the colonial administrator's better days, though. Brackett hoped the man wasn't going to be a problem. He didn't do well with civilian interference.

Paris caught Simpson's attention, and the man gestured to indicate that he'd be out in a moment.

"Seems like quite the charmer," Brackett said.

"He's not so bad," Lt. Paris mused. "But I wouldn't want to have to answer to him."

A companionable silence fell among the three marines as they waited in the corridor. Curious civilians smiled or nodded at the newly arrived CO as they passed. Coughlin slid the duffel to the ground and leaned against the wall.

Brackett turned to the Sergeant.

"The answer's no, by the way."

"What's that?"

"There isn't anyone I left behind."

Which wasn't a lie, but it wasn't the truth, either.

He'd had mixed feelings about this command from the very beginning. He'd been stationed on colonies before—each one maintained a small marine detachment assigned by the United States government, the same way the Colonial Marines offered protective services to all signatories of the United Americas pact.

In recent years, Weyland-Yutani—who owned or exerted influence over what seemed like half the universe—had gotten into the colonization business. The rumors about their business practices were utterly appalling, yet the realities were bad enough. Could you call it corruption, he had often wondered, if the malice and greed were purely intentional—part of the foundation of the business? Hadley's Hope was a joint endeavor between the government and the company, and he didn't like the idea of taking orders from corporate stooges.

There was another reason why being assigned to LV-426 had unsettled him.

Sgt. Coughlin had asked if he had left anyone behind, and Brackett hadn't been lying when he'd said no. He hadn't left anyone behind on Earth, but years ago, when he had joined the Colonial Marines, he'd been forced to break off a relationship with a woman he loved. She'd gone on to find a new life with another man. By the time he'd returned home for a furlough—hoping at least to say hello, to see her smile—she and her new husband had left the planet entirely.

Now, somehow, their paths were slated to cross again. His old girlfriend and her husband had been among the first colonists to arrive on Acheron more than a dozen years before. Brackett wondered if she still had the same smile, and whether or not she'd be happy to see him.

Her name had been Anne Ridley in those days.

DATE: 10 JUNE, 2179
TIME: 1105

Curtis Finch felt like strangling his brother. He might've considered actually doing it, except that if he took his hands off of the land crawler's steering wheel, they'd have been blown into a ditch.

"I want off, man," Otto said, bracing himself on the dashboard with both hands as the storm pummeled the six-wheeled vehicle with gusts of wind like the fists of a giant.

A burst of derisive laughter came from the back seat. The two Colonial Marines had been silent for long minutes while Curtis navigated them down out of the rugged hills, but now Sgt. Marvin Draper bent forward, icy eyes glaring at the elder Finch.

"You wanna get out here, be my guest," Draper sneered. "Nut job."

Otto flushed red as he whipped around to glare at both Draper and the gravely quiet, dark-eyed Pvt. Ankita Youseff.

"Shut yer trap, Draper. I said off, not out. Off, off, off. Off this godforsaken rock! I want to go home."

Draper let his restraints pull him back against the rear seat. He smiled, then spoke out of the corner of his mouth, addressing Pvt. Yousseff.

"Otto wants his mommy."

"Our mother's dead," Otto snapped, crying out as a gust lifted the left side of the crawler off the ground for a second before it crashed back down and the vehicle kept rolling. "But I'd dig my way down into the grave with her if it meant I didn't have to live here any—"

"Shut it!" Curtis barked. He'd had enough.

Otto stared at him. He had the blue eyes and dark red hair of their mother, while Curtis's brown eyes and hair favored their father, but no one could have looked at them and not known they were brothers.

Curtis peered straight ahead, lips dry, heart smashing in his chest as he tried desperately to maneuver the vehicle through the storm. He'd driven out this way a dozen times, but with the dust and debris, visibility had dropped to maybe ten percent in the past fifteen minutes. Continuing on like this—nearly blind—was foolhardy at best, but if he'd gauged their progress correctly, they only had a short distance to cover before they reached shelter.

It would be safer than trying to weather the storm inside the land crawler. They were still twenty miles out from Hadley's Hope, with no chance of getting back to the colony until the grit-storm had blown over.

"Curt—"

"I'm not joking, Otto," he told his brother, raising his voice to be heard over the screaming wind and the shushing roar of the dirt scouring the vehicle. "I'll put you out right here."

"Are you telling me you don't regret the day we set foot on Acheron?"

Curtis twisted toward him.

"Are you shitting me?" he said. "We wouldn't even be here if not for you."

"Here we go again!" Draper groaned in the back seat. "Yousseff, please put a bullet in my head so I don't have to listen to these two anymore."

Draper outranked her, but Yousseff didn't seem to take this as an order. Curtis almost wished she had. The hugely muscled Draper had a long scar on the right side of his face, going up from the corner of his mouth as if someone had tried to extend his smile. On his throat he bore a tattoo of a scorpion, and somehow the combination of scar and tattoo made Curtis very nervous. Like a scorpion, Draper seemed as if he might strike at any moment, his humor a cover for inner volatility.

Yet the same seemed true of Yousseff, who had no scars or tattoos. Her eyes were calm, and yet full of the promise of violence. Otto had once said that was just the mark of a soldier, but Curtis disagreed. He had known many other marines, and most of them hadn't been the type to take imminent violence as a given.

"Curtis…" Otto began warily.

"No." He didn't want to hear it. Curtis and Otto—the older brother by two years—had been on Acheron for forty-seven months as surveyors and wildcat prospectors. Their time with the colony might be nothing compared to people like Meznick and Generazio, and Russ and Anne Jorden, but some people were just cut out for this kind of work, while others were not. Otto had been the one who talked Curtis into joining the colony, but within the past few months, he had been falling apart.

Curtis understood, of course. All these years of terraforming had only partially tamed Acheron's violent atmosphere. Always turbulent, the weather patterns kicked up massive storms strong enough to overturn vehicles, kicking up so much soil that it became impossible to see, and for instruments to navigate. The environment could be deadly, and the substandard equipment seemed constantly on the verge of lethal malfunction.

As much as they liked the other colonists, the competition among the wildcatters—to find and stake claim on anything that would be valuable to the company—made it difficult to develop any real camaraderie.

Otto had been defeated by the oppressive nature of the place. Trouble was, they couldn't go home without earning enough money to pay for the journey, and for at least six months' rent back on Earth.

Curtis gripped the wheel even tighter and bent forward, slowing the vehicle. The gale raged around them, and for a few long seconds he could see nothing beyond the windshield. The lights from the crawler's control panel cast the interior in a green glow, turning their faces ghostly pale, but outside all was black.

He held his breath.

The crawler shook.

It rumbled through several dips in the landscape. He braked nearly to a stop, unwilling to risk the unknown. Then the wind lessened and he saw a familiar dark block silhouette in the storm ahead. Hitting the accelerator, he picked up speed.

"I can't do this," Otto whined. "I can't be here, Curt. It's like the whole planet is trying to kill us!"

Curtis took one hand off the wheel, turned, and punched his brother hard on the shoulder, as if they were small children again. Otto cried out, and clapped a hand to his arm.

"What the hell?" he shouted.

"Damn it, Finch!" Draper roared.

Yousseff spoke the only two words she'd offered that day.

"Stupid bastard."

Curtis looked forward again, grabbed the wheel tightly, and tried to turn—but too late to avoid the ditch. His heart sank as the left side of the crawler dipped and then dropped, and they scraped to a grinding halt, the right-hand tires spinning up dirt while the tires on the left spun at nothing but air.

"Gun it!" Draper said angrily.

"Won't do any good," Curtis told him, gunning it anyway. The crawler slewed a bit, the rear of the vehicle edging further over into the ditch.

"Stop!" Otto said, staring at him. "The undercarriage is caught on a ridge. We slide any more, and we'll roll right over."

Curtis took a slow breath, still clutching the wheel. The bedrock in the area consisted of stone flats and ridges buried in thick soil, with a top layer of dust and ash that shifted with the storms, so the visual details of the terrain changed considerably from day to day. Some of the ditches were as deep as twenty or thirty feet. If they rolled now, and managed to land right side up, he thought the crawler would be all right. They could make their way along the bottom of the ditch until they found a place where the grade wasn't too steep to let them out.

But if they landed upside down...

"We're bailing out," he said, and he killed the engine.

Yousseff swore.

As Curtis unlatched his restraints, Draper grabbed his shoulder from behind.

"What are you doing, Finch?"

"Don't be brainless!" his brother said. "You'll die out there."

Otto snatched up the handheld radio, stretching the cord. Wireless didn't work out in these storms.

"Admin, come in, this is Otto Finch," he barked into the radio. "Come in!"

They all froze, listening to the static that sputtered in response. For just a sliver of a moment the line cleared and they heard a burble of language—just a few unintelligible words. Until the atmosphere calmed down, communications would be nigh impossible. They might be able to get their message through, but admin would have trouble tracking them. With all of the mineral dust and volcanic ash whipping around, external instrument readings were always tricky.

"I'm not suicidal," Curtis said. He pointed through the windshield. "Look out there."

"What am I looking at?" Draper growled.

The storm had kicked up again. The crawler rocked on the ridge, then slid a bit further. The tower Curtis had seen before had been blotted out by the blowing grit.

"There's a processor tower about a hundred yards ahead," he said. "Processor Six. We hunker down there until the wind quits. Once we get through to admin, they'll send someone out to help. Even if we can't get through, they'll find us by tracking our personal data transmitters. We'll be fine."

He turned to his brother, saw the fear in his eyes, and actually felt sorry for him.

"Otto," he said. "We'll be all right."

6

THE LADDER

As they ran through the storm, scoured by grit and brutalized by the wind, Otto kept his head down. Goggles protected his eyes, but he felt safer looking at the ground.

A dreadful fear had been building in him for months, a kind of chasm opening up in his gut. In his nightmares, fissures split the surface of Acheron and dark things stirred down inside the planet's guts. Any time they left the colony, he felt as if he were standing on the edge of a roof a thousand feet up, looking at the ground far below. The urge to just fling himself over the edge, to plummet to his death, tugged at him. Every logical part of him fought that urge, but still it teased him forward, seductive as the voice of the serpent.

Thanatos, it was called. He'd read it somewhere. *The death urge.*

A tiny voice inside Otto Finch had grown steadily more convinced that Acheron meant to do him harm, and tempted him to surrender to its malicious purpose.

"I don't want to die here," he whispered, his words stolen by the storm.

He glanced up, saw Curtis's back, and kept trudging ahead. Draper and Yousseff were behind him, but he couldn't be sure they would pick him up if he fell. His brother, though—he had to believe that if he cried out, if he stumbled, Curtis would save him. They were brothers, after all.

Please, God, he thought. *Please, God. Don't let me die here.*

Yet it felt like a hollow prayer. He hadn't always believed in God, but if such a deity existed, he couldn't escape the feeling that He lived far, far away from here.

A loud scrape of metal made Otto look up.

Ahead, Curtis had reached the processor and as Otto staggered toward him, nearly blown off his feet by a gust, the heavy door rose up into its housing. It occurred to him that without Curtis they wouldn't have been able to enter—all surveyors knew the override code for these things, but Otto had forgotten it.

Thank you, my brother, he thought.

But then he staggered inside, out of the storm, and suddenly he felt a lot less grateful. He tore off his goggles and spun around, staring at the cylindrical ductwork that ran up the walls and overhead. The outlying atmosphere processors scattered around Acheron were tiny in comparison to the huge, arena-sized Processor One back at the colony, but the building was still impressive. The interior of Processor Six was fifty feet in diameter. In the corner was a small control room full of levers and gauges, a communications array, and a pair of computers that did most of the work. Pipes and ducts and ladders went up into a vast sphere—the core processor—and then into the darkness fifty or sixty feet overhead.

Otto didn't need to climb or use the control room to see that there was a problem. Steam hissed from the joints, and as he approached the nearest of the two-foot-wide ducts, he could see that the metal surface was vibrating. A clamorous buzz filled the interior of the station, the micro-rattle of thousands of feet of ductwork shaking against the brackets and rings that held it in place.

"Jeezus," Draper said, stripping off his coat. "Why's it so hot in here?"

Normally the innocent curiosity on his face—after what they'd just been through—would have made Otto want to laugh. But he wasn't capable of finding anything funny just then.

"Curtis," Otto called, loud enough to be heard over the hiss and rattle inside, and the roar of the storm outside.

Back toward the door, Curtis had removed his own heavy protective jacket. He stood with his goggles on his forehead, grimed with dust and sweat, and spoke quietly to Yousseff. The Colonial Marine sergeant seemed to ignore his flirtations half the time, and the other half she spent indulging him with the arch of an eyebrow or a slanted smile at some idiocy he'd spouted.

Otto hated her for that. He understood that his brother found the woman beautiful—with her dusky skin and those big, hypnotic brown eyes, anyone would have been captivated by her at first. But Yousseff had never seemed like anything but a cold bitch to Otto. Her half-smiles mocked Curtis for his lonely but hopeful heart.

"Curtis, damn it!" he shouted. "You'll have time to make a fool of yourself later!" He hated the crack in his voice, the edge of panic that lurked there.

Only when his brother glared at him, hostile to cover the sting of truth, did Otto realize what he'd said.

"You know what—" Curtis began, moving toward him.

"Stop!" Otto snapped, shaking his head and holding out a hand. "Just… stop. Be mad at me later, okay? We've got a problem."

Draper had dropped down to sit on the floor, knees drawn to his chest and his back against the wall. Now he laughed.

"Shit, just *one*?"

Otto felt like he couldn't breathe. When he and Curtis had been small boys, their father had punished them for misbehavior by locking them in the closet. The darkness had frightened him, but the closeness had been worse. Sometimes he had imagined that the thick air had a presence, that it did not like intruders—especially naughty little boys—and that it wanted to suffocate him. There in the dark, lying on a pile of his parents' shoes, with his mother's long coats brushing the back of his neck, he could feel it sliding over him in a heavy, dusty embrace. It would get warm very quickly and sweat beaded on his skin. He never dared pound on the door—his father had warned him many times about that—but he would cry and beg to be set free, and when at last he lay quietly on top of those shoes, he could smell the oil from the factory where the old man worked.

The inside of the processor had the same oil smell. Dark and hot, the air close. He stared at his brother as Curtis moved toward him, searching his eyes and wondering why Curtis didn't understand.

ALIEN

"Can't you hear it?" Otto asked, running a hand through his tangle of red hair. "Can't you *feel* it?"

Curtis froze, listening.

Draper glanced at Yousseff.

"What? D'you hear something?"

Then they all heard it. A chugging, grinding noise coming from overhead. Curtis pushed past Otto and put his hand on the same duct, felt the vibration, and then tried to see up into the darkness.

"It's machines," Draper said. "Just friggin' machines."

"Of course it's machines," Curtis said, shooting him a withering look. "Machines that are breaking down."

Yousseff perked up at that. No arched eyebrow or flirty half-smile now.

"What do you mean 'breaking down?'"

"Clogged," Otto said, his hands fluttering nervously. He pulled at the small curls on the back of his neck, a painful habit he'd picked up recently. "The unit's clogged. Too many storms lately, too long since the last maintenance. Draper said it's hot. Well, he's right, but it's more than that—it's overheating. From the sound of it, the unit's choking up there, all the filters need flushing and venting…"

Otto put his hand on the duct. It had grown hotter.

"…and it needs to be done in the next few hours, I'd say. Probably less, though." He tugged at his red curls. "I'm an optimist."

"Or what?" Draper demanded. "So the unit breaks down—that's not our problem. Soon as this grit-storm's over, we'll be able to get a signal through, and they'll send someone out from the colony."

Otto glanced at his brother and then lowered his gaze.

"Curtis?" Yousseff said, worry in her voice.

"Best case, Draper's right," Curtis replied. "The core's supposed to shut down if the filters clog enough—if the sphere is hot enough. But it's pretty hot in here already, and that hasn't happened."

"Do I want to ask what happens if the core doesn't do its automatic shutdown?" Draper asked.

Otto put his hands together and sprang them apart.

"Boom."

Yousseff cursed, turned to the door and unlatched it. She peered outside for just a second before shutting it tightly again.

"No sign of the storm letting up, I suppose," Curtis said. The look on her face was the only reply they needed. The four of them studied each other for several long moments. Otto saw beads of sweat on Draper's forehead, felt it on his own back, and knew the temperature had gone up just in the few minutes they'd been inside.

"Curtis!" Otto shouted.

His brother stared at him.

"I know, okay?" Cursing under his breath, Curtis hurried over to a ladder that was clamped to the wall just beside the door to the control room.

"Wait, what are you doing?" Draper demanded, wiping the sweat from his brow.

Curtis shot him a look. "You know how to flush the filters, vent the clog and send it outside?"

Draper threw his arms out, drawing attention to his uniform attire and his heavily muscled form.

"Do I *look* like a maintenance man?"

Curtis nodded upward. "That's why I'm climbing. I'm the only one here who knows how to do this. If I can clear the filters, this place doesn't blow up. If I can't, we take our chances with the storm."

"Well, hell, then... climb away," Draper said, gesturing toward the ladder.

Otto could see the way the rungs vibrated in his brother's hands as Curtis climbed the first few feet. *Must be rattling his bones*, he thought.

Yousseff came and stood at the base of the ladder.

"Be careful."

Curtis shot a grin down at Otto as if to say, *I told you so*.

The grinding and chugging grew louder above them. Otto could feel the place shaking under his feet, right up through his body. He clenched his jaw, watching his brother climb, and his teeth chattered from the tremor in the floor. His heart raced, and another bead of sweat ran down his neck.

"Hate this planet," he said quietly, convinced he spoke only to himself. "I hate this godforsaken—"

"It's a moon," Yousseff said.

Otto spun on her, practically snarling. "Hate this planet!" he screamed, eyes burning with tears he refused to shed.

Then something banged inside the core, metal giving way under pressure. The boom that followed rocked the entire structure, as if some giant had given it a thunderous kick from the outside. Up on the ladder, Curtis shouted and Otto looked up to see his brother slip, fingers frantically grasping for the rungs.

Otto shouted his brother's name as Curtis fell. He ran toward the base of the ladder. When Curtis hit the floor, the sound of it froze Otto in his tracks. He knew that noise from childhood—it was the sound of breaking bone.

Curtis let out a cry of pain—just one—and then fell so silent, so quickly that it seemed as if a guillotine had cut off his voice. He slumped there at the base of the ladder with the whole processor rocking and banging around them, more and more steam misting the already hot, close air, and Otto feared he might have died.

Draper shoved Otto roughly aside, saying *shitshitshitshitshitshit* as if in time with his racing heartbeat, and ran to kneel by Curtis.

Yousseff took two steps toward the core.

"Draper, this is not going to end well," she said. "We need to get out of here!"

With two fingers on Curtis's neck, checking for a pulse, Draper turned to glare at her.

"You don't think I know that?" he said. "What's your plan? Try driving in the grit-storm? If we don't wait for it to subside, we're dead out there."

"We're dead *in here* if we don't purge the throat of this beast!" Yousseff shouted.

Otto could barely hear them. He shuffled toward Curtis and fell to his knees beside Draper, shaking his head. His thoughts had been muddled with anxiety and fear for so long—a profound and growing sense that they were all in terrible danger—that it felt strange to have sudden clarity.

"Curtis?" he ventured, and he nudged his brother's shoulder. Curtis did not stir.

Otto's hands fluttered to his mouth and he turned to stare at Draper, breath hitching in his chest, horror spreading through him, eradicating all other emotions.

"Oh God," he said. "I did this. I did this! He didn't want to come to the colony and I talked him into it. This is my fault. I killed my own brother!"

Draper reached up and flicked Otto across the nose. The pain made him jerk backward.

"What the hell is—"

"Have I got your attention?" Draper shouted, and suddenly the sound of the storm sandpapering the outer walls and the thunder of the groaning processor flooded back into Otto's ears, as if he had somehow turned the volume down on the rest of the world for a minute.

Otto nodded.

"Moron's not dead," Draper said, nodding toward Curtis. "His leg's broken from the fall. Banged his head pretty good. If he's lucky, he passed out from the pain, and not brain damage. The big question is, can you do the job, Otto? Can you climb your ass up there and clear those vents?"

Shaking his head, Otto reached out to stroke Curtis's hair.

"Damn it, man, do you know how to do the job?" Draper roared, poking him in the chest.

"No!" Otto shouted, lower lip quivering. "I don't have the first clue!"

Draper turned toward Yousseff.

"I know the storm's causing interference, but you've gotta call us in. Get someone out here in the heavy-crawler!" Outside the wind howled even louder. The grit scouring the metal seemed almost to sing a high, mocking melody.

"No way we're getting a comms signal through this!" Yousseff barked at him. "We've got to go back out, take cover inside the crawler!"

"Keep trying, damn it!" Draper roared. "There'll be a lull in the storm. You'll get through."

Yousseff spun away from them and marched toward the far wall, covering one ear as she slipped on her headset. Otto stared at her, and he knew there would be no signal. They were going to die out here, and Acheron would swallow them up. The grit would strip them to the bone and the bones would be buried in dust and they'd slip down into the hell he always saw in his nightmares—the hell at the heart of this planet.

"I hate this planet!" he said loudly, trembling. He turned to look at the slack expression on his brother's face. Curtis's head lolled to one side and for the first time Otto saw the huge bruise on his left temple, red and swollen.

"Curtis!" he whined, unable to help himself. He shook his brother's hand, nudged his shoulder. "Curtis, please! I'm sorry. I'm so, so sorry!" He rocked back and forth, closing his eyes. "I hate this planet! I hate this—"

His eyes sprang open as Draper grabbed him by the front of his shirt.

"Shut your mouth!" Draper shouted, and he swung his fist.

The blow silenced Otto, bloodied his mouth, and broke off a tooth. Shocked, he stared at Draper, who still held him by the shirt, fist ready to land another punch. Tears sprang to Otto's eyes and this time he could not fight them off. They began to slide down his cheeks as he spit out his broken tooth and then used his tongue to probe the sharp edges in the hole where it had been.

"You're going up there," Draper said, gesturing to the ladder. "You and your asshole brother are inseparable. I don't believe for a second that you don't have at least *some* idea of how to stop this. So you're going up, Otto. Could be my life depends on it, which means you go up, or I shoot you in the head."

Otto's breath hitched. His shoulders shook.

"I hate this pla—"

Draper's fist crashed into his face again. Otto sagged in the marine's grip, sobbing, and spit out a big gob of his own blood. Then he nodded.

At least up on the ladder, he would be out of reach of Draper's fist. And maybe from up high, Curtis would look like he was only sleeping.

Regaining his balance, he went to the bottom rung. With the whole processor clanging and screaming around him, Otto began to climb.

On the third rung he froze, and then he let go, dropping down to land with a thud.

"What the hell are you—" Draper began.

Otto turned to him, tears running freely.

"Shoot me," he said as he flopped back against the wall and slid to the floor, anguish tearing him apart. "If you're going to kill me, just do it. I'd rather be dead than be here."

Draper swore and leveled his gun.

Yousseff grabbed his wrist, gave a quick shake of her head, and then walked toward Otto.

"Curtis is injured, Otto," she said. "If you don't do something, there's a good chance we're all going to die out here—your brother included."

Otto looked into her brown eyes, glistening and beautiful.

"Promise you'll make them send us home—me and Curtis—and I'll do what I can. Promise you'll make them send us on the next ship out."

Yousseff nodded. "I promise."

Otto sneered, nostrils flaring, and turned away.

"Lying bitch. You think I can't see it in your eyes?" he sobbed. And then he screamed. "I want to go home!"

7

TROUBLE IN THREES

DATE: 10 JUNE, 2179
TIME: 1110

In Demian Brackett's experience, the further out from Earth he was stationed, the more likely he was to run into troublemakers. People joined the Colonial Marines for a variety of reasons: some out of a sense of honor and duty, others to escape the patterns of their pasts, and still others because they had violence inside them and didn't want to hurt the people they loved.

What he'd found was that no matter what their rationale for enlisting, once they were in the Corps, they either turned into good marines or walking trouble. Whatever their intentions had been in the beginning, he'd found that most people had the capacity to go in either direction once they immersed themselves in a life as part of the Corps.

The other thing he'd observed over time was that the further from Earth a squad was assigned, the more freedom its troublemakers felt they had to stir things up.

Within forty-five minutes of his arrival on Acheron, Capt. Brackett had stowed his gear in his quarters, held a preliminary meet-and-greet with Al Simpson and the colony's senior support staff, and begun his first squad briefing. The Colonial Marines had a small muster room at their disposal, but it was large enough for the twenty-one men and women now gathered there.

Brackett stood at the front of the room, leaning on a podium that made him think of some sort of religious service, and studied the marines who stood before him. There were chairs stacked against one wall, but since this was his first meeting with the squad, he didn't want them getting comfortable.

Better for them all to stand, himself included.

Brackett kept it simple. Basic introduction and expectations, a hope that they would help him get up to speed, a firm instruction to adhere to protocol, and an appreciation of the welcome he'd already received from Lt. Paris and Sgt. Coughlin, who stood to one side, both slightly apart from the rest of the squad. As he spoke, he watched their eyes. Most of the squad seemed attentive, even curious about their new CO, just there to do their jobs. Several of them, however, did not seem quite as open.

One man in particular kept his eyes slightly narrowed, the corner of his mouth upturned, as if he might sneer at any moment. Pale and thin, with a hawk-like nose, the man radiated rebellion. Brackett had seen the sort before—defiant and hostile, the kind of man who would snicker and whisper and grumble. Hawk-Nose would warrant some attention, but he wasn't Brackett's only concern.

There were three others who stood nearby. While they didn't quite share Hawk-Nose's sneer, Brackett saw the tension and stiffness in them, and thought he caught several silent exchanges.

There were dangers on Acheron, but it ought to have been a relatively simple assignment. Brackett intended to make sure Hawk-Nose and his friends didn't complicate things for him.

"All right, that'll do for now," the captain said, surveying his squad. A tough-looking bunch, most of them alert and responsive. "Over the next few days I'll want to meet briefly with each of you. If we're going to be spending all this time together in paradise, I want to know who I've got watching my back, and I want you all to know that I've got your backs."

It might've been his imagination, but he was sure the slight sneer on the left side of Hawk-Nose's mouth deepened a bit.

"That's all. Dismissed." Brackett glanced to his right. "Lieutenant Paris. Sergeant Coughlin. Stick around a minute, please."

He waited while the squad filed out of the room, several of them unable to wait even until they reached the corridor before the quiet muttering began. Brackett wouldn't hold it against them. They had just met their new CO—it was natural for them to speculate about how much of a pain in the ass he was likely to become. He watched until the last of them had exited, and found himself alone with Paris and Coughlin.

"How did I do?" he asked, turning to them.

"You did fine, Captain," Paris said. "They don't know what to make of you yet, but they'll unclench soon enough."

"Not sure I want them to," Brackett replied thoughtfully. He frowned deeply. "The guy with the hawk-nose… what's his story?"

Paris cocked her head curiously. "Hawk-nose?"

Coughlin knew who he meant.

"That's Stamovich. Not much of a story to him, but if you're asking if he's going to give you a hard time—"

"The answer's 'maybe,'" Paris interrupted, and Coughlin nodded. "Stamovich is a prickly son of a bitch, probably punched his way out of his momma's womb, but he'll behave himself unless Draper tells him otherwise."

"Sergeant Marvin Draper?" Brackett asked, and his eyes narrowed. "I read his file. He's got a couple of black marks for insubordination, but that was years ago. Should I be worried about him, then? I mean, if he's the guy who might tell Cpl. Stamovich what to do…"

"Draper can be managed," Paris said. "He knows he's floating on an ugly little rock in space, and that pissing off the CO is a bad idea. As long as he doesn't directly disobey orders, best bet is to just ignore him as best you can."

Brackett frowned.

"If this sergeant has Stamovich on some sort of a leash, then how am I supposed to re—"

"Not just Stamovich, Cap," Coughlin cut in. "There are a few others who follow Draper's lead."

Eyes still narrowed, Brackett turned to study the muster room, repopulating it in his mind. He tried to summon the faces of his squad, remember where they had all been standing.

"Which one was Draper?" he asked.

Paris shook her head. "None of them. He and Youssef are out with a survey team."

"Why's that?"

"Standard procedure, sir," Paris replied. "Every time admin sends out a survey team, two of our people accompany them."

Brackett blinked. "Why are Colonial Marines needed on civilian excursions? The colonists have their jobs, and we have ours. We're meant to maintain security for the colony itself, not personal safety for each of its residents."

Paris glanced at Coughlin, but the stout little man just shrugged.

"Just SOP, Cap," Coughlin said. "Been that way since I got here."

"Al Simpson's been here from the beginning," Paris said. "If anyone has an answer to that, it'd be him."

Brackett took a deep breath. He hadn't intended to rock the boat on his first day, but it didn't sit right with him to think that marines were risking their lives on a daily basis, in ways that weren't part of their mission.

"Go about your duties," he said. "I'm going to talk to Simpson, and then get myself settled. Meet me back here at 1300."

Paris and Coughlin saluted, but Brackett barely noticed. His thoughts were on the absent Sgt. Draper. Had his superiors failed to sufficiently brief him on his posting on Acheron, or was the colonial administration utilizing the marines for corporate purposes without the authorization to do so?

He left the muster room and started to retrace his steps toward the administrative hub. The last thing he wanted was to get off on the wrong foot with Al Simpson on the first day of his deployment, but he hadn't spent years with the Colonial Marines—from firefights to bug hunts—and been awarded a Galactic Cross just so he could be some corporate lapdog in the ass-end of the universe.

Brow furrowed, lost in thought, he took a wrong turn and nearly collided with a man and woman headed the other direction.

"Pardon me," he mumbled.

The words were barely out of his mouth when he registered the little gasp that escaped the woman's lips. Initially, Brackett thought the near-collision had startled her, and he began to apologize again. He caught the strange look her companion gave her, but only when he refocused did he realize that her gasp had been one of shocked recognition.

"Demian?" she said, features blossoming into a brilliant smile. "What are *you* doing here?"

All of the tension and frustration slipped away. Brackett returned her smile and gave a delighted little laugh. One hundred and fifty-eight colonists at Hadley's Hope, not even counting the marines, and already he'd practically run her down.

"Hello, Anne," he said.

I'd forgotten how beautiful you are, he almost added. But then he cut his gaze to the left, caught the confused expression on her companion's face, and made the connection that had momentarily eluded him.

Brackett held out a hand.

"You must be Russell Jorden."

"Russ," the man said warily, shaking his hand.

"Captain Demian Brackett, Russ. Very pleased to meet the man worthy of being this one's husband."

"Yeah… thanks," Russ said carefully, but the caution behind his eyes did not disappear. Brackett couldn't blame him—husbands tended not to love having their wives' exes around.

For her part, Anne still wore her smile, but it had gone from bright to mystified.

"Seriously, Demian," she said. "What are you doing on Acheron? I never thought I'd see you again."

In the years since he'd seen her, age had added a few crinkles around her eyes, and the time she'd spent in the savage wilderness of deep space had made her seem somehow wilder herself. But time had only made her more beautiful to him. Tangled curls framed her face, and hard work had made her lean and powerful. Her eyes were alight with the intrepid determination inherent to those who chose life's more challenging paths.

She's another man's wife, he reminded himself. Not that he needed much of a reminder with the way Russ Jorden now studied him from behind slitted, almost reptilian eyes.

"This is my new post," Brackett explained. "The marines at Hadley's Hope are under my command."

"That's... that's..." Anne fumbled.

"Amazing," Russ said, now wearing a polite mask of a smile. "Welcome aboard, Brackett. It's rough living, but we've been out here so long that it just seems like home to us. I guess wherever your children grow up, that's always going to be home, right?"

"So I'm told," Brackett replied. "No kids myself, but I envy you two."

Anne glanced from Brackett to her husband, and a rigid sort of awkwardness descended upon them all. She looked as if she was searching for the right combination of words to alleviate that discomfort, when a voice called along the corridor.

"Captain Brackett, there you are!"

Brackett turned to see Al Simpson lumbering toward them. The man seemed afflicted with a permanent air of disapproval.

"I was just on my way to see you," Brackett said, letting his own tone inform the administrator that disapproval was an emotion available to both of them.

"Good timing, then," Simpson replied. If he'd caught the annoyance in the captain's voice, he didn't show it. "Look, we've got a small crisis on our hands, and it involves some of your people. I've called a meeting in the conference room, and you should be there."

"When's this?" Brackett asked.

"Now."

Anne glanced worriedly at her husband.

"Is this about Otto and Curtis?" Russ asked Simpson. "We were just coming to talk to you."

A flicker of panic passed over Simpson's face.

"The Finch brothers are fine. The storm is hitting hard in that sector, but they've taken shelter. All's well. Now, if you'll excuse us, I need Captain Brackett's consultation on a matter regarding his squad."

Simpson took Brackett by the elbow and abruptly steered him toward the administrative hub. The captain glanced back at the Jordens. Russ was staring after them, but Anne had turned her gaze to her husband, looking worried and pale. For an instant, Brackett regretted having accepted the post on Acheron, but then he shook off the feeling. He hadn't come to Hadley's Hope just to see Anne Jorden again.

Had he?

He shook off Simpson's arm and gave the man a sidelong glance as they hurried along the corridor, across a hallway junction, and into view of the busy, glassed-in administrative hub of the command block.

"You're not a good liar," Brackett said.

"Excuse me?" Simpson snapped, his face pinched with annoyance.

"I don't know who the Finch brothers are, but whoever they are, they're not fine." He paused, then added, "I seriously doubt Anne believed you either."

"She doesn't have to believe me," Simpson said. "She works for me. So why don't you let me worry about my people, and you can worry about yours?"

As they passed the command block and rounded a corner, Brackett studied him more closely. On the surface, the guy seemed like a hundred other low-level management monkeys he'd met, yet he wondered if Simpson was smarter than he looked.

A short way down the hall they paused at a door marked RESEARCH: NO UNAUTHORIZED ADMITTANCE, and Simpson punched numbers into a keypad that admitted them.

"You bring up an interesting subject," Brackett said, "the line that separates your people from mine."

Simpson made sure the door swung shut behind them and the lock engaged, then he set off for a white door a dozen feet along the hall, obviously expecting Brackett to follow.

"Whatever you've got to say, save it," the administrator sniffed. "We've got bigger problems at the moment than whatever dick-waving contest you feel like having to assert your authority."

Brackett quickened his pace, fighting the urge to grab Simpson by the scruff of his neck and smash his face into the doorframe. Then they were inside the white-doored room, and there were too many witnesses for him to do anything. He wouldn't have done it anyway—probably—but he sure as hell wasn't going to bloody the admin's nose in front of some young wide-eyed lab assistants in white coats and several older researchers in civilian clothes.

The lab coats clustered around the trio of older researchers, including a silver-haired Japanese man, a grim-eyed white guy with a wine-dark birthmark on his throat and jaw, and a sixtyish woman so slender that she reminded Brackett of the stick figures he'd drawn as a child.

The only guy in the room who didn't look like a scientist stood a distance back from the table, a deep frown creasing his forehead. An air of disapproval hung over him, like a man waiting for his children to get tired at a playground so he can take them home.

"Captain Brackett, meet Doctors Mori, Reese, and Hidalgo, and their team of brainiacs."

The doctors nodded. Simpson gestured to the guy standing away from the table.

"The moper in the corner there is Derrick Bradford, who's in charge of our ongoing terraforming operations."

"Captain," Bradford said with a nod.

Brackett approached the table for a proper round of handshakes.

"Welcome to Hadley's Hope, Captain—" Dr. Mori began.

"Enough of that," the grim-eyed doctor said, his birthmark flushing darker. "We haven't got time for niceties. Dr. Hidalgo, please bring the captain up to speed."

The stick figure sat up a bit straighter. Brackett noticed she had kind eyes. Worried eyes, at the moment.

"Two of our surveyors, Otto and Curtis Finch, encountered a level five atmospheric storm. They're fairly rare and localized, and the duration is hard to predict," Dr. Hidalgo said. "The Finchs and their marine escort were forced to abandon their vehicle and take shelter in an atmosphere processor."

Here, she shot a withering glance at Bradford.

"This processor hasn't been serviced in at least six months," she continued. "Records are unclear—"

Brackett grimaced and held up a hand.

"Look, I'm not even sure why my people are out there to begin with, but—"

"Later, Captain," Dr. Reese said.

Brackett glanced at Simpson.

"Later," the administrator agreed.

"They're in trouble," Derrick Bradford said, emphasizing the last word to make sure they all had their priorities straight. "The processor is malfunctioning—clogged—and the storm is making it worse. Curtis Finch is the only one with any engineering training among them, and he's injured."

Brackett tensed. "How long before the unit blows?"

"We can't be sure from here," Simpson said. "The storm's interfering, not just with communications, but with the monitoring signal from the processor. That's why we didn't know it had malfunctioned. It's not critical yet, but as far as we can tell, it's getting there."

Brackett stared at him. "You have a heavy-crawler, don't you? Why are we even talking about this? Get someone out there!"

Dr. Mori and Dr. Hidalgo exchanged an indecipherable glance.

Dr. Reese's smile reminded Brackett of a shark's.

"That's why you're here, Captain," Reese said. "There are two Colonial Marines out there, and you people never leave one of your own behind. We assumed that you and your squad would want to mount the rescue yourselves."

Brackett hadn't been at Hadley's Hope for half a day, and already he wanted to throttle most of the people he'd met.

"So, you send marines out to do your errands," he said, "and now you expect us to do your dirty work as well?"

Dr. Mori smoothed the jagged-cut lapels of his tailored jacket.

"While you're out there," he said, "the company would appreciate you retrieving whatever samples the team gathered before this mishap began."

Brackett stared at him, but remained silent. He'd wanted to hit Simpson earlier. Now he gritted his teeth and reminded himself that assaulting an aging Weyland-Yutani scientist would be frowned upon by his superiors.

"Mishap," he said, the word sounding like profanity to his ears.

Blank-faced, all of the scientists in the room just stared back at him. Only Bradford and Dr. Hidalgo had the good sense to look slightly uncomfortable.

Brackett turned to Simpson.

"Get the heavy-crawler outside."

"It's ready to go," Simpson replied.

"Fine. Call Sergeant Coughlin. Tell him he's got three minutes to pick five marines and meet me at my quarters."

He turned and strode back into the corridor.

Mishap, he thought.

Welcome to Acheron, indeed.

8

STORMS SEEN
AND UNSEEN

Anne and Russ Jorden strode down the corridor side by side, connected by long years of marriage and a web of tension that chained them to each other even as it forced them apart. Anne hated the sound of her husband's heavy footfalls, the way he seemed to stalk the floor when angry. She could feel the anxiety coming off him in waves, and it made her want to run away.

If only there were some place to which she could have fled, just for a little while, to regain her sense of self. But where could she have gone inside the colony of Hadley's Hope where Russ wouldn't be able to find her? Or where she wouldn't be intruded upon by well-meaning friends?

Nowhere.

"Still want to eat?" he asked, the words short and clipped, as if he'd barely opened his mouth to speak.

"If you're hungry," she replied warily. They'd planned to check with Simpson about the Finch brothers and then go to the mess hall for lunch. Now she had a stomach full of what seemed to be warring factions of butterflies.

"Game room, then?" Russ asked.

Still monosyllabic. Anxiety was giving way to anger. It made her want to punch him. Anne loved her husband from the scruff on his unshaven chin down to his almost comically skinny ankles. Over the years they had laughed so much together. They'd been courageous, and sometimes a little crazy. They'd crossed the galaxy, and had their children so far from Earth that they joked that the kids might qualify as alien creatures if they ever returned to their parents' home planet.

There had been difficult years, but Anne and Russ had been together—a team—and that had counted for something when the sameness of life at Hadley's Hope had started to make them both feel claustrophobic. On the day Russ had confessed that it sometimes felt like a prison sentence, Anne had cried until he'd sworn to her that her love, and the presence of Tim and Newt, were the only things that kept him sane.

They still had good days—wonderful days, even—but they both had frayed nerves. Some nights Anne couldn't sleep, and she felt as if she might be unraveling. Then she heard Newt laugh or saw Tim trying to model his walk after his father's masculine gait, and all would be well.

Not today.

Anne Jorden knew her husband's every tic and gesture. They weren't going to make it to the recreation center. Just as that thought solidified in her mind, Russ ducked into a maintenance corridor and turned to face her. Anne wanted to keep walking—maybe the dropship hadn't left yet—but instead she stepped into that quiet corridor with her husband. A worker passed by and glanced at them without slowing.

"What the hell is he doing here?" Russ whispered, almost hissing the words. He searched her eyes for a moment, and then looked away, as if bracing himself for the answer.

"I have *no* idea," Anne insisted.

His eyes narrowed.

"And I'm supposed to believe that? Think about how far we are from Earth, how many colonies there are now, and how few people had any interest in volunteering to come here in the first place. You want me to believe that this guy you used to sleep with just showed up here? *Here*?"

Anne felt her face flush. Her heart slammed against her ribcage, and she could feel her pulse throbbing in her temples. She took a step forward and punched Russ in the shoulder.

"Hey, what the fu—" he started.

She poked him in the chest once, then again.

"You get your head together, Russell," she hissed back. "Has your brain become so fuzzy after all these years out here that you've lost the ability to think rationally? How the hell would I know anything about what Demian's doing? I haven't had any contact with him since we left Earth." She stepped back and looked at him. "What do you think? That I've been carrying on some kind of intergalactic romance? Sure, that makes sense—its only thirty-nine light years away." She paused, then added, "Are you out of your damn mind?"

Russ just stared at her, fuming with anger and frustration. But then the words sank in, and he ran his hands over the stubble on his cheeks.

"No," he admitted. "Of course not… that's just—"

"Crazy."

"—stupid," he said. "But if this is a coincidence… now *that's* crazy."

Anne took his hand, ran her thumb over the ridges of his knuckles in an almost unconscious gesture. She knew it calmed him, and did it without even thinking, just as he barely recognized the effect it had. Their marriage included a thousand such comfortable intimacies.

"I'm not going to lie to you, Russ," Anne said calmly. "I'm delighted that Demian's here. We have friends in Hadley's Hope, but it's just such an unexpected pleasure to encounter someone who knows me well. Demian and I were together once, but before that we were friends for a long time. Real friends. He's a good man, and I want to learn about what he's done with his life since I saw him last…

"But you're my husband."

Russ exhaled, turned and slumped against the wall.

"I'm sort of an idiot, right?"

Anne smiled softly. "Sort of?"

Suddenly they heard giggles echoing down the main corridor, and then the sound of running feet. Together they turned and watched as several of the colony's children raced past the mouth of the maintenance corridor, scraps of paper in hand. Most of the children were seven years old or less, a band of tiny marauders who darted along in duos and trios. Anne saw the flaming red hair of Luisa Cantrell and then the familiar blond mane of their six-year-old, Rebecca.

"Newt!" she called to her daughter.

The little girl skidded to a halt. As she turned toward the maintenance corridor, she was nearly knocked over by her older brother, Tim.

"Rebecca, what are you—"

Newt smacked his chest.

"Look out, dummy," she said, walking over to her mother and father. "What are you guys doing here?"

Russ grinned. "We needed a private place for some messy kissing."

"Eeewww!" Newt cried, but she followed it with a little giggle. "You guys are so disfusting."

"Disgusting," Tim corrected, rolling his eyes.

Newt nodded. "Exactly."

"You're so embarrassing," Tim told his parents. He had the same blond hair as his sister, but at nearly ten, he had begun to look less like the little boy he had once been.

"We do our best," Anne told him.

Several other children ran past, including Tim's friend Aaron, who shouted out to him that Tim and Newt were going to lose.

"Tim, come on," Newt pleaded, trying to haul her brother away, anxious to return to whatever havoc they were wreaking.

"What are you all doing?" Russ asked. "Aside from running around like lunatics?"

"Scavenger hunt," Tim said as Newt took him by the hand and dragged him back into the main corridor. "Bye!" he called over his shoulder.

Russ shook his head in amusement as he watched the kids rush off. Despite whatever tensions had been growing between them the past few years, Anne's heart still melted when she saw how much her husband loved their children.

"Hey," she said, squeezing his hand as she rose up to kiss his cheek. She stared into his eyes. "There's nothing to worry about, okay? Absolutely nothing. This is home for us, and we're strong together, you and me. Our family is safe and sound."

Russ smiled. "Safe and sound," he said.

Yet she couldn't help noticing a trace of sadness in his eyes. As glad as she had been to see Demian, she knew her husband would continue to be haunted by the presence of her ex.

He let her hand slip from his.

"Hungry?"

"Starving, actually," she confessed. "My appetite's returned."

They walked together to the mess hall, hands by their sides, not quite touching. Russ grew quiet, and Anne could feel the frisson of lingering tension between them. Doubts and fears coalesced, pushing them apart.

Safe and sound, she told herself, not sure if it was a vow or a plea.

DATE: 10 JUNE, 2179
TIME: 1337

The marine driving the heavy-crawler was an aging jarhead named Aldo Crowley. He had skin like leather and gray in the stubble of his buzzcut, but the bright glint in his copper eyes suggested that he might not be as old as he looked.

He was. Aldo Crowley had turned forty-one in January. He was a grunt from a family of grunts, neither smart nor ambitious enough to rise above sergeant, and busted back down to corporal every time he disobeyed the orders of superior officers far greener than he'd been on his first day in uniform.

Brackett learned all of this in the first sixty seconds of the conversation he'd had with Julisa Paris about which members of the squad to bring on the rescue mission. Crowley was the first person she'd suggested, followed by a couple of hard-eyed privates named Chenovski and Hauer, who'd earned a rep for keeping their shit together when a situation turned ugly.

The captain took Lt. Paris with him as well, and the first three marines he could lay eyes on in the frantic moments of preparation—Nguyen, Pettigrew, and Stamovich.

"Not sure why you brought me with you, Captain," Paris said.

Brackett glanced around the vast interior of the heavy-crawler. The others were lined up on benches along the forward compartment. The back of the vehicle was used for equipment storage and cargo space.

He looked at Lt. Paris. With the rumble of the heavy-crawler's engines, and the way it rattled as it churned across Acheron's terrain, none of the others could have heard him if he'd replied. But what would he have said? That he wanted her there because he trusted her, though he'd only known her a few hours? That she knew the topography and the marines and the nature of the atmospheric storms? Any of those admissions would convey a kind of weakness.

Instead he turned the question around.

"Do you have concerns about Sergeant Coughlin's ability to command in our absence?"

Paris furrowed her brow. "None whatsoever!"

"Good, then."

She studied him a moment, the heavy-crawler rocking them back and forth, and then she turned away, trying to peer through the windshield ahead. Visibility had been shitty from the moment they'd rolled out of Hadley's Hope, and it had only gotten worse as they drove toward Processor Six. Aldo had an array of instruments on the dash that provided radar and thermography readings of the terrain ahead. Even so, Brackett had no idea how the guy could see anything at all.

On the bench beside him was an exo-mask. The black masks with their bulbous goggle-eyes made him think of giant, nightmarish insects. They were generally used for brief exposure on planets and moons where the atmosphere had toxins, but was otherwise suitable for humans. Exo-masks were commonly utilized during the worst of Acheron's storms, too, just to keep the grit out of eyes and mouths, making it easier to see and breathe.

"Tell me something," Brackett said, trying to break up the ice that was forming between himself and his lieutenant. "Has anyone ever asked why marines are sent along on these survey excursions? Is it as simple as free labor, or are our people supposed to keep the surveyors from slacking off on the job?"

"I did ask, when I first got here," Paris said. "My first CO on Acheron told me it'd been commonplace since the science team first arrived—we're talking twelve or thirteen years ago, now. But the surveyors aren't just taking samples and mapping topography."

Brackett arched an eyebrow.

"What the hell else could they be doing out on this rock?"

Lt. Paris cast a wary glance at Stamovich and the others who sat across from them. She tucked a stray short curl behind her ear.

"It's Weyland-Yutani, Captain," she said, as if that explained it all.

Brackett settled against the bench, his head bumping the wall as the heavy-crawler dipped into a shallow pit, and then climbed out of it. Maybe the involvement of Weyland-Yutani did explain it all. Standing orders from the corporation would include not only the study of the planetoid itself, but the company's ongoing interest in alien life, whether aboriginal or left behind by spacefaring races. Yet thirteen years after the science team's arrival, it seemed like a ridiculous idea.

If the surveyors had been likely to find anything of interest to their employers, surely they would have found it already. Maybe the Company was sending marines along for security, after all, just as a precaution.

He leaned forward, trying to catch a glimpse of anything at all through the windshield. Aldo never slowed down, no matter how much the heavy-crawler shook or how completely the storm blocked out any visibility.

"Can you see anything at all?" Brackett called to him, raising his voice to be heard over the vehicle's rumbling and the staccato scrape of the windblown debris against its shell.

Aldo glanced back at him.

"That's the trick, Captain," he replied. "You've just got to accept that there *is* nothing to see, and then you're all right!"

Brackett shook his head. "Why the hell did they put a colony on this damn moon to begin with?"

On the opposite bench, Stamovich caught the question and spoke up.

"The rest of the universe needed a place they could point to when things turned nasty and say, 'It could be worse—we could be on Acheron!'"

Nguyen and Pettigrew laughed at that, nodding in agreement. Stamovich high-fived Pettigrew, but the rest of the team Brackett had chosen for this mission didn't seem at all amused. He glanced at Chenovski and Hauer, saw the way they were averting their eyes, and then studied Stamovich.

The guy smiled thinly, an air of arrogance about him. Lt. Paris had told Brackett that Stamovich was loyal only to Sgt. Draper, but now he began to see that there was a deep divide among his squad, and it worried him. That kind of fractiousness in the ranks could get marines killed.

The heavy-crawler tilted hard to the left, and the engine roared as it climbed out of whatever pit they'd rolled through. As they leveled off, Aldo hit the brakes. The crawler skidded in the dust, rocking back and forth for a moment. He locked the transmission, and then turned in his seat to look back at Brackett.

"This is it, Cap," Aldo said. "But I'd make it quick if I were you."

"Is the storm getting worse?" Lt. Paris asked.

Aldo gave a tired laugh. "Nah. The processor's on fire."

9

OTTO'S WISH

Brackett swore and pushed forward, jamming himself between the front seats so he could peer out the windshield.

Off to their right, in the wind-driven swirl of grit, he could see the dark tower of Processor Six. Even from inside the heavy-crawler he could hear the groan and rattle of its core and vents, a kind of mechanical shriek. Black smoke poured out of the vents on top of the unit, and he saw the orange flicker of flames from inside them.

"Son of a…"

He grabbed his exo-mask.

"Move out!" he bellowed. "This thing could blow any minute, and I don't want to be here when it does!"

Aldo stayed in the driver's seat and Brackett ordered Pettigrew to stay inside the heavy-crawler—always good to keep someone back to play cavalry if things went from bad to worse. The rear hatch of the crawler could be lowered to the ground as a ramp, but in the midst of the storm, they exited through a side door and slid it quickly shut behind them.

Masks in place, Brackett and Paris led the other three marines through the blowing garbage, staggering against the wind. One step after another they made their way toward the atmosphere processor. Even inside his exo-mask, Brackett felt as if he were suffocating.

"Listen to that!" Nguyen called.

Brackett listened. Banging and grinding noises came from inside the processor. Every instinct told him to get the hell away from the groaning tower, but the noise bothered him much less than the stinking chemical smoke the storm swept their way.

"Have you started to rethink accepting this post?" Lt. Paris shouted beside him, her voice muffled and almost lost in the gale.

Brackett said nothing. He didn't like to lie.

They hit the entrance seconds later. Stamovich reached it first and released the latch. The wind blew the door in with a clang and Nguyen barreled inside. Brackett knew they were friends of Sgt. Draper's, eager to make sure their friend was all right, so he didn't worry about who had led the way.

Out of the raging storm, the noise level dropped so dramatically that he felt for a moment as if he'd gone partly deaf. Then Chenovski slammed the metal door closed behind them and the captain flinched in the gloom. Only dim emergency lights provided pulsing illumination. Red warnings flickered all over the core, and a cloud of thin black smoke filled the tower, thicker overhead.

Brackett pulled off his mask and glanced upward, but could not see whatever was burning up top.

"Draper! Yousseff!" Paris shouted, and all of the marines glanced around.

There were signs of the stranded team—jackets, a pair of goggles, and strangely enough, a boot—but nothing human in view. The core thundered, shaking so hard that the bolts locking it to the floor seemed to be trying to pull themselves out of their holes. One of the ascension ladders glimmered in red zoetrope shadows on the wall to the right.

"Marv! Sing out, ya bastard!" Stamovich barked. "Where are you?"

Brackett started around the core, nodding to Nguyen to proceed. They hadn't taken two steps when they heard a reply.

"Here! Watch yourselves!"

Then another voice, screaming.

"Send us home!"

Brackett hadn't run another three steps before he saw the burly bearded man lying on the ground. Blood streaked his face and caked in the hair on the left side of his head. His eyes were open and one hand rose to wave them back—or perhaps in a plea for help. He clutched his left leg, and Brackett realized the angle of the limb was all wrong.

Broken bone, and a bad one.

"Curtis!" Lt. Paris shouted.

Three more steps, and the whole scene came into view—it was the last thing Brackett had expected. He drew his weapon before his mind even had time to completely make sense of the dynamics playing out in front of him.

A ginger-haired man with mad eyes stood with his back to the wall, holding a female marine from behind with one arm, choking her as he held what had to be her own gun to her temple. A dozen feet away, deeper in the oily, flashing red shadows of the processor, another marine stood with his feet planted, his gun aimed at the ginger man and his hostage.

It wasn't hard for Brackett to figure out who the players were. If the guy with the broken leg was Curtis Finch, this had to be—

"Otto!" he roared. "Let Private Yousseff go!"

Draper—who else could it have been?—cast a quick glance at the new arrivals, but didn't dare take his focus off of Otto Finch for longer than that. He shuffled a bit to his right, moving toward the other marines. Brackett and Stamovich were side by side now, and rushed up to take position beside him. The rest found cover.

"Back off!" Otto screamed. His voice melded terror with the timbre of a child throwing a tantrum, and he stared around at the newly arrived marines as if the wrong twitch would make him explode. "Stay back or I'll kill her! I don't want to... I didn't ask for this, but I swear I'll do it!"

"Draper, report!" Brackett snapped.

The sergeant glared at him, then shot a questioning look at Stamovich.

"New CO," Stamovich called.

"I've got eyes, Stam," Draper sneered. He took a step nearer to

Otto, who shrieked until he moved back again.

Curtis Finch gestured to Lt. Paris, and she raced over to kneel beside him.

"Sergeant Draper, report!" Brackett ordered.

"What does it look like, sir?" Draper barked. "You need me to spell this shit out for you?"

"He wants off!" Yousseff shouted. Her expression betrayed no fear, but Brackett could see it in her eyes. Colonial Marines were tough as nails, some tougher, but no warrior wanted to die a hostage. It looked as if she was having trouble breathing.

"What the hell do you mean, *off*?" Lt. Paris called.

"Off the planet!" Yousseff snapped, then she coughed.

"Just send us home!" Otto shrieked, wild eyes darting back and forth, tears flowing. Snot dripped down over his lips. "I don't care about money anymore! I don't need a dollar of what we've earned up here! Just take me and Curtis and put us on a ship for home!"

The whole tower shook, as if the ground shuddered beneath them. A crack like thunder exploded in the air, and a fissure opened in the shell of the core, black smoke billowing out. An explosion rocked the unit high overhead and Brackett looked up to see orange flames gouting out into the swirling debris of the storm.

A quarter of the roof had just blown off.

"You got it!" Brackett said urgently. "Whatever you want, Otto! You want to go home, I'll make sure you get there!"

"Captain—" Draper warned.

"How do I know?" Otto screamed. "How can I believe *anyone* in this damned place?"

The grinding inside the core grew louder still. Brackett wracked his brain, trying to figure out what he could possibly say that would calm Otto Finch. The man had experienced some kind of psychotic break. There was no way he would believe any promise Brackett might make about getting him and his brother off-planet.

His brother.

Brackett glanced across and saw Paris kneeling with Curtis Finch. Sweat beaded on the man's pale forehead. From this angle, Brackett could see a small puddle on the floor beside him, where Curtis had vomited from the pain of his shattered leg. He looked desperate, gripping Paris's sleeve as if pleading with her.

Is this guy crazy, too?

One way to find out. Brackett ran from cover and slid to his knees beside the lieutenant. In the process he dropped his exo-mask.

Paris turned to him.

"Whatever you're going to do, Captain, do it fast," she said. "Curtis says we've just got minutes before this place tears itself apart."

Otto started shouting again. Brackett saw Draper motion to Stamovich and Pettigrew, who each eased a bit closer, as if they didn't really believe that Otto would kill Sgt. Yousseff. The wild-eyed ginger choked her harder, and screamed at them to stop.

"One more step and she's dead!" he screamed.

"Otto, listen to me!" Brackett said, rising to his feet again. "You won't just be killing Sergeant Yousseff—you'll be killing all of us, yourself and your brother included! Curtis says we've only got minutes before the core explodes. Look around, man! Half the roof is gone, all this fire and smoke… we're dead if we don't go now—"

"Take Curtis out!" Otto shouted, fresh tears cutting clean lines in the soot on his cheeks.

Brackett holstered his gun and held up his hands.

"We all need to go," he said. "Not just your brother."

"Take him out of here!" Otto screamed.

Brackett stared a moment at the profound fear in Otto's eyes, and then nodded, turning to Paris.

"Get him out."

He glanced around. "Nguyen! Hauer! Help Lt. Paris bring Curtis to the crawler!"

As the marines hustled to obey, slinging their weapons, Otto went still. Yousseff tensed as if to attempt to escape his grasp, and Otto jammed the gun against her temple.

"What are you doing?" Otto screamed, not at Yousseff but at the marines moving his brother. "Leave him alone!"

Lt. Paris snapped quiet orders to Hauer and Nguyen. One of the men rushed to a control panel, yanked it open and began to tear it from its hinge as the other helped Paris work Curtis out of his jacket.

"We're going to get him out of here, but we've got to stabilize his broken leg first," Brackett called to Otto, sweat running down the back of his neck. The temperature inside Processor Six continued to climb. "It's a bad break, Otto. He can't walk! Do you want your brother to die here?"

Torn, Otto stared. For several seconds he squeezed his eyes closed and then the words erupted from his mouth.

"Fine! Take him out!"

Paris nodded to Nguyen and Hauer, who worked hurriedly to slip the small metal door underneath Curtis's legs. Then they wrapped his jacket around both legs, tying them to the metal. Curtis cried out several times, and when Nguyen tightened the jacket, he screamed and fell unconscious. Even over the roar and rumble of the failing processor, that scream crawled under Brackett's skin.

"Go, go!" he snapped.

Hauer, Nguyen, and Paris hoisted Curtis off the ground and carried him in a rush toward the exit. If he hadn't already been unconscious, Brackett had no doubt the screams would have been hideous as his broken bones ground together.

"Captain!" Draper barked. "We don't have time—"

Brackett held up a hand to silence him, turning to Otto. He didn't like the look of Yousseff, whose gaze had begun to droop.

"We're out of time, Otto," Brackett said. "We're going to help Curtis, and we can help you too. I will do all I can to get you both sent home, but you've got to let Sergeant Yousseff go right—"

"I need to hear it from the Company!" Otto shouted, his voice cracking. "I want their guarantee!" The desperation in his eyes spoke of a profound fear that Brackett knew he could never assuage. Otto behaved like a man in a nightmare from which he could not wake. But he wasn't sleeping. This was all real, and deadly.

"Otto, we've got two or three minutes!" Brackett called. "Let Yousseff go now, or we're all going to die in here!"

"Captain Brackett, we're out of options!" Stamovich shouted.

"Damn right we are," Draper snapped.

He shot Otto Finch through the left eye, blowing blood and skull fragments and gray matter onto the wall. In death, Otto's fingers twitched and the gun in his hand went off. Yousseff shouted and pushed back, but the corpse's hand had already begun to jerk away and the bullet went astray, firing up into the smoke-filled darkness overhead.

Brackett stormed across the shuddering floor as the whole processor rocked and clanked around them.

"Dammit, Draper, what the hell was that?"

"Taking action, sir!" Draper called. "You said yourself we don't have time to waste."

Pettigrew and Stamovich nodded in agreement. Furious, Brackett felt his hands close into fists, but he forced them open again. Draper would have to wait until later.

"Move out!" he shouted, gesturing to the rest of them—Pettigrew, Chenovski, and Stamovich—as Yousseff staggered away from Otto's corpse, trying to catch her breath. "But we're taking the body back with us! His brother's going to want to bury him!"

"Screw that!" Draper barked. "Friggin' lunatic nearly killed Yousseff. We're not risking our lives for the guy!"

Despite the mounting danger—the seconds he could feel ticking away on his internal clock—Brackett stared in astonishment as Draper tapped Stamovich and the two of them broke into a trot for the door, with Pettigrew hesitating only a second before following.

Son of a bitch is mine, Brackett thought.

"Captain!" a voice called.

Brackett turned to see Chenovski trying to lift Otto Finch's corpse from the floor. Blood and gore had already baked onto the hot metal wall, but the pool on the ground around the dead man had widened and Chenovski slipped a bit as he tried to hoist Otto up. Brackett ran toward them. Something moved to his left and he glanced over to see Yousseff, who had at last recovered her breath.

Together, the three of them picked Otto up the way the others had carried Curtis, and they lurched for the way out. The whole processor seemed to tilt and they careened off the frame of the open door before bursting out into the darkness and the shrieking grit-storm. The wind swept them aside and they bent into it. Without his exo-mask, Brackett could barely make out the heavy-crawler. The three marines who had disobeyed his direct order were trudging toward it, fighting the gale. Seeing those escaping figures gave him additional motivation, and he shouted to Yousseff and Chenovski.

They made it to the crawler twelve long seconds behind Draper and the others. Aldo met them at the back of the vehicle, where the ramp was down, and helped Chenovski drag Otto's corpse inside, placing him beside his unconscious brother.

"Why did you help?" Brackett asked Yousseff, shouting to be heard over the storm.

Yousseff stared at him. "You gave an order."

Brackett knew that wasn't the real answer. Yousseff was one of Draper's cronies, or she wouldn't have been picked to accompany the Finchs.

"Let's move, Captain!" Aldo shouted, waving them along as he ran back toward the driver's door.

A pair of explosions came from Processor Six. Yousseff turned to stare at the tower, and Brackett followed her gaze toward the gout of flame rising from the shattered roof of the thing. He put a hand on her back, gave a little shove, and Yousseff seemed to snap from her momentary trance. They ran around up the ramp in a stoop, slamming down into seats even as the door ratcheted shut and the ramp retracted.

"Strap in!" Aldo shouted, and the crawler lunged forward, the grit-storm scouring its shell as it rumbled across the rugged terrain.

Brackett found a seat, glanced across the heavy-crawler, and realized he was directly opposite Draper. All eyes in the passenger section of the vehicle were upon him, the other marines wondering how he would react to Draper's insubordination.

Remaining silent, the captain ground his teeth so hard his jaw hurt. His first instinct was to put the bastard in the brig the second they returned to Hadley's Hope, and keep him there until he could arrange for Draper to be transferred away from Acheron. The trouble was that he didn't know how much backup he'd get from his own superiors. If he put Draper in the brig and then had to release him, it would undermine his authority even further than Draper's actions already had.

"Listen to me, you son of a bitch—" Brackett began, leaning forward and pointing.

At that moment, Processor Six exploded. The blast rocked the crawler to the left. Hauer and Pettigrew fell into the space between the facing rows of seats. Even muffled by the storm, the thunderous noise of the explosion made them all wince, and Youseff covered her ears. Something crashed down on the crawler's roof, and Aldo swerved to avoid a flaming chunk of metal that struck in front of them like a meteorite.

Stamovich swore loudly, and immediately the others began to taunt him for showing fear. That lasted only seconds, as they all returned their attention to the silent hostility crackling in the space that separated Brackett and Draper.

"You were saying?" Draper asked, his voice dry, tone full of disrespect.

"I'm saying it's been an ugly first day at my new command," Brackett said. "But I'm willing to bet the ugliness is just getting started for you, Sergeant. You, Stamovich, and Pettigrew are confined to quarters upon our return, and you'll stay there until further notice. If you think there won't be consequences for your actions today, I can only assume that your previous CO gave you the impression that rank meant nothing out here on the edge of oblivion.

"I'm here to disabuse you of that notion."

The corner of Draper's mouth lifted in what might have been a smirk, but otherwise he had no reply. The others were also wise enough not to speak.

The crawler rolled on.

They were halfway back to the colony, the storm at last beginning to subside, when Julisa Paris crawled from the rear of the crawler and slid into a seat beside Chenovski.

"Sorry, Captain," she said. "Hauer did what he could. Shock and blood loss took a toll. Curtis Finch is dead."

Brackett let out a heavy sigh and laid his head back against the juddering wall of the crawler.

"Crazy prick wanted off the planet, him and his brother both," Stamovich muttered. "Looks like he got his wish."

"How is that getting his wish?" Chenovski asked, sneering at him. "They're never getting off Acheron now. They'll be buried here. Whoever they've got back on Earth will learn they're dead, and just carry on. This place is so far away from home that these colonists might as well be dead already, in the minds of the people they left behind. If this was more than just a post for me—if I knew I was here permanently—I'd lose my shit just like Otto did."

They rolled on for a minute or two, all of them just taking that in. The marines began to stare at their feet, or tried to see out through the windshield, though Aldo waved for them to stay seated.

Yousseff nudged Brackett with an elbow. He'd been aware of her beside him, but had been too preoccupied with his anger to do more than acknowledge her.

"You asked me why I helped you carry him," she said quietly, so that over the roar of the engine and the whoosh of the diminishing storm, only Brackett could hear.

"It wasn't just you obeying an order," he replied, and it wasn't a question.

Yousseff dropped her gaze a moment, and then turned to face him.

"I could feel his fear," she said. "Otto could be a pain in the ass, but I liked him well enough. The guy just fell apart, Captain. He didn't want to hurt me—he was just terrified. I hate that it ended like this."

Brackett narrowed his gaze.

"What could scare anyone that much?"

Yousseff shrugged. "I don't think it was anything real. Nothing tangible. Acheron just got under his skin. He convinced himself there was something on this damned moon for him to fear, something that was gonna kill him. He was afraid he was gonna die if he didn't get off this rock."

Brackett glanced at Draper.

"I guess he was right. But it wasn't Acheron he should've been afraid of."

10

THE COST

DATE: 10 JUNE, 2179
TIME: 1648

Newt never minded being thought of as a child. She knew some kids who became very angry when grownups dismissed them as *little*, but Newt considered that a pretty silly thing to get mad about. After all, they *were* little. It wasn't as if the grownups were trying to insult them with the truth.

Really, she wasn't in any hurry to grow up at all. Adults were grumpy a lot. They got stressed out over things that didn't seem that important—sometimes about disagreements they assumed were going to happen, but which had not happened quite yet. Her parents were the perfect example. Lately they'd seemed all worried about things Newt freely admitted that she didn't quite understand.

What she did know was that there seemed no point to any of it. Stress made them both tense and edgy, and it crackled between them like that invisible energy that always gave her shocks when she dug through freshly laundered clothes in search of matching socks.

Static, Newt thought, proud of herself. *Of course—that's the word.*

The static electricity that sizzled unseen in the air between her parents over the past few months had kept growing stronger, but it had never been as bad as today. Newt had been in their quarters doing her homework, and had seen the way they navigated their way around the rooms, sometimes avoiding each other... and she'd had to get out of there.

Tim had been playing full-immersion *Burning Gods* and had ignored her when she'd asked if he wanted to go to the kitchen and see if Bronagh Flaherty would give them a freeze-pop. So she had gone without him.

Newt liked freeze-pops. Her favorite flavor was cherry, although there was a cherry tree in the greenhouse, and after tasting the fruit she had never understood why cherry freeze-pops were called cherry, when they tasted nothing like actual cherries.

Lost in such thoughts, she nearly ran right into the man who came hurriedly around the corner near the administration offices.

"Whoa!" he said, holding out his hands.

Only when Newt looked up at him, protecting her cherry freeze-pop from the imminent collision, did she realize it was Capt. Brackett. When he recognized her, the captain smiled.

"Hey! Rebecca, right?" he said, as if he'd somehow solved a riddle. Grownups were so weird. He had a nice smile, though.

"Newt," she said. "Everybody calls me—"

"Right, sorry!" Capt. Brackett said. "And I'm sorry I nearly ran you down. Just too many things on my mind, but that's no excuse for not paying attention." He looked down. "Is that a strawberry freeze-pop?"

He wore a smile, but it seemed tense to Newt, as if he wanted to be kind to her at the same time as he wanted to be angry at someone else. It seemed to create its own kind of static, a sort of cloud of frustration that surrounded him.

"Cherry," she answered. "It's my favorite."

"Cherry's nice," he allowed. "Do they have grape down there, as well?"

"If you ask Bronagh in the kitchen, she'll make you one, even if they don't have them in the freezer."

Capt. Brackett nodded as if this news pleased him very much.

"I'll have to do that," he said. "She sounds like a nice person."

Newt nodded. "Very nice."

He studied her for a second.

"You look so much like your mom. Do people tell you that?"

"It's because I have crazy hair sometimes. My mom has crazy hair pretty much all the time, but mine is only crazy sometimes. I have a doll—my brother says I'm too old for dolls, and maybe I am, but it's just one doll. Her name is Casey. She has crazy hair, too."

Capt. Brackett gave a soft laugh, and Newt noticed that some of the static around him seemed to have gone away. He didn't seem as stressed as he had been when he'd almost crashed into her, coming around the corner.

"Maybe I could meet Casey sometime," he said. "And maybe you could introduce me to Bronagh, too."

Newt smiled. "I can do that."

"Great! I'll track you down later." He looked down the hall. "Right now I've got to go talk to Mr. Simpson."

She gave him a thumbs up and bit the top off her freeze-pop. The icy cherry rush froze her teeth and made her talk a little funny.

"Okeydoke," she said. Her father always said that. "See ya."

"See ya, Newt," he replied, and he started past her, walking toward the command block with his shoulders set in a way that made him seem angry.

"Captain Brackett?" she called after him.

He glanced over his shoulder at her.

"Yeah?"

"You look like you're having a bad first day. I hope it gets better."

Capt. Brackett gave that same soft laugh and nodded.

"Me too, kid. Me too."

Brackett found Al Simpson in his office. Several people had given him strange looks as he strode purposefully toward the colonial administrator's closed door, but only after he had knocked and swung it open did he understand their wary expressions.

Simpson wasn't alone. He snapped his head around at Brackett's intrusion, bushy eyebrows knitted in irritation.

"Can I help you, Captain?"

Brackett stared at him, hand still on the knob, and then took a closer look at the other two people in the office—Dr. Reese and Dr. Hidalgo, the leaders of the colony's Weyland-Yutani science team.

The three of them looked to be in the middle of something, but what could be more important than the destruction of Processor Six, and the deaths of two of their surveyors?

"I thought you'd want a report on today's events," Brackett said, without trying to hide the accusatory bite of his words. "Two men died, in case you hadn't heard."

Simpson's gaze went even colder.

"I'd heard, yes," he said. "We were just discussing the failures in maintenance that led to the processor malfunctioning. Making sure nothing like that happens again is my top priority. The cost of replacing Processor Six alone is going to be—"

"Right," Brackett said. "The *cost*."

Dr. Hidalgo glanced away, unnerved by the insinuation, but Dr. Reese stiffened and raised his chin as if preparing for a fight.

"The Finch brothers knew the risks they were taking every time they went out there," Dr. Reese said. "If you wish to remonstrate with Mr. Simpson for his attention to the bottom line, I'll remind you that he is doing his job. Perhaps, Captain, you ought to worry more about your own."

Brackett thought of a dozen ways to wipe the smug expression off the doctor's face. He forced himself to take a deep breath.

"That's one of the things I came to talk about, actually," he said, turning his focus back to Simpson. "We need to get some clarity on exactly what the job is meant to be for the marines stationed with this colony. Before I address that, however, protocol requires that I deliver a report on what went down out there—and that's what I came to do."

Simpson sat back in his chair, tapping his fingers on his gleaming silver and glass alloy desk. The whole office was beautifully appointed with sleek, coldly metallic furniture and swirling light fixtures, unlike anything else Brackett had seen since arriving at Hadley's Hope. This elegance had to be a perk of the job, and yet Simpson had let the debris of his work pile up on every surface— dirty coffee mugs, cast-aside sweaters, tubes of soil samples, thick old paper files capped by more than one computer tablet. The man treated his surroundings shabbily, and Brackett could only assume that he treated his people the same way.

"Type it up and forward it to me," Simpson said, his fingers ceasing their drumming. "I'll get to it."

The tone implied a dismissal, but Brackett wasn't ready to be dismissed.

"You have two men dead, Simpson. You're not going to be able to sort out the events leading to their deaths without a full report—"

Dr. Reese sighed heavily, as if he tired of dealing with a simpleton.

"We've got a full report, Captain."

Brackett cocked his head. "But I didn't file any—"

"From Sergeant Draper," Simpson interrupted.

For a second or two, Brackett could only stare at them. Then he scoffed and shook his head as the significance of the statement sank in.

"Draper is confined to quarters," he said.

"Understood," Simpson replied. "But to my knowledge, you gave no orders that restricted his ability to receive visitors. You weren't immediately available upon your return—"

"I was debriefing my team," Brackett said, standing a bit straighter, his uniform chafing against his skin, "and seeing to the offloading of your two dead colonists. But I expect you knew that."

"Sergeant Draper's report was very thorough, and certainly sufficient for our needs," Dr. Reese said. "I'm sure there's a conversation that we all need to have, Captain Brackett—a conversation about the way operations are conducted here, and how the science team works hand in hand with the Colonial Marines—but I'm afraid it's going to have to wait until later. The destruction of Processor Six leaves us—"

Brackett coughed to clear his throat, which had the advantage of silencing the doctor for a moment.

"Yeah, doc," he said, "we'll discuss it over tea. Meantime, there are a couple of things I want to get straight, and right now. Things that *won't* wait." He held up a finger. "First off, from this moment forward you are to have no direct contact with any of my marines, aside from a thank you if they're polite enough to hold the door open for you in the hallway."

Brackett peered at Simpson, and then at Dr. Hidalgo, who seemed very uncomfortable.

"Captain, you must understand..." she began.

"Must I?" Brackett said. He shook his head. "No, doctor, I don't think so. My squad answers to me, and to me alone—and *you* don't get reports from Draper or anyone else. Sergeant Draper is a problem child. There's always at least one. But from now on I'm going to make him *my* problem."

"Noted," Simpson said, smoothing his shirt over his round belly.

Brackett studied the administrator for a second, then narrowed his gaze as he turned to Reese and Hidalgo. The birthmark on Reese's jaw and throat had turned so dark that it was almost purple.

"What about you two? Simpson may keep the lights on around here, but it's clear that the company has more influence than the government. So I need to hear it from you, as well. Is my message clear enough?"

Dr. Reese glared at him, the man's small eyes glittering with contempt.

"Quite clear," Dr. Hidalgo said.

Reese didn't argue with her. Brackett would've liked a more concrete response from him, given that he was the senior member of the science team, but his silence would have to be enough... for the moment.

"Good. That brings us to the other thing."

Al Simpson tucked his shirt in a bit tighter, as if it would give him greater authority.

"Can't this wait?"

Brackett just ignored him, and remained focused on the scientists.

"I'm told that it's standard procedure for Colonial Marines to accompany your survey teams into the field," he said. "That practice ends immediately."

Dr. Hidalgo flinched. "You can't do that!"

"Excuse me, doctor, but I certainly can." He stared at her, surprised at the sudden change that had come over her. She had seemed uncomfortable with Reese's attitude before, but now she'd adopted a similarly flinty air.

Brackett figured they saw him as some bristle-headed lunk in a uniform. Simpson and the scientists thought they were keeping him in the dark, but it didn't take a genius to understand why they wanted marines along on these excursions. Not once he'd had a little time to mull it over.

Most of the major scientific advancements of the past century had been made by organizations that had acquired and studied specimens from a variety of alien life forms. Sometimes it was a government, but most of the time it was a corporation.

Weyland-Yutani had long been on a crusade to find and utilize, monetize, or weaponize any alien species they could get their hands on. The company's efforts were hardly secret. Humanity had learned so much just from their Arcturian trading partners.

Brackett couldn't deny the value of encounters with alien life, but the Colonial Marines had never been meant to play security guards for a bunch of civilian surveyors... or to mount rescue missions for freelance wildcatters.

It had to stop.

"You're right, Captain—it *has* been our standard procedure," Simpson acknowledged. "It's been that way since the beginning of the colony. The marines provide security, and support for—"

Brackett held up a hand to stop him.

"No, we don't. This isn't something we're going to discuss. When I received my orders to take up the post of commander at Hadley's Hope, no mention was made of any such arrangement. The Colonial Marines aren't company employees, Mr. Simpson." He paused, then continued. "As soon as I leave here, I will transmit a query to my superiors. It will take approximately a week for a message to reach Earth, and for me to receive any reply. If I'm instructed to cooperate with your demands, I will of course comply with those orders. But unless and until I receive instructions along those lines, there will be no more marine escorts on these survey missions."

Dr. Reese sniffed, his face like stone.

"I don't think you'll like the answer you receive."

Brackett shrugged. "It's not up to me to like or dislike my orders, Doc. I'm a marine. For the moment, that means I don't have to give a shit what you think."

DATE: 10 JUNE, 2179
TIME: 1844

Hadley's Hope had been designed for communal living. The dining hall—what the marines called the "mess"—served three meals a day, and Anne Jorden would be the first to admit that the men and women who worked there were a hell of a lot more talented in the kitchen than she would ever be.

Russ had some skill with food prep—equal parts inspiration and intuition—but at her best Anne had never been able to do more with a meal than follow basic directions. Even so, at least twice a week the Jordens had a family dinner in their quarters, just the four of them sitting around the little table or sprawled on chairs in their family room.

Most of the colonists took at least a few meals in private each week. Communal living had its pleasures, but everyone needed private time now and again. The trouble of late had been that every time she and Russ had downtime—either alone or with the kids— they found themselves at odds.

Anne loved her husband. She hadn't come halfway across the universe with him on a whim. But the years on Acheron had showed them that living in such a small community meant there was nowhere for their daydreams to take them. Back on Earth, if she was irritated with her mate, she could have fantasized about moving out, getting a cottage in the mountains, and meeting a man who would look at her the way Russ had when they were first dating.

She could still remember that look, the desire and mischief in his eyes.

Here, her dreams had nowhere to run. It made her impatient with him, and sometimes unforgiving.

Not tonight, she vowed, as she stirred the noodles and spices frying in the pan on the small stove. The smell wafted up and made her mouth water. Three kinds of peppers, a cupboard's array of herbs… she might not be the galaxy's greatest chef, but she had perfected this one dish, at least.

Too bad the kids hated it.

Anne sipped her wine as she stirred, and glanced over at Tim. Her son sat in a plush chair, low to the floor, and stared studiously at the small tablet in his hands. Anyone would have thought he was doing homework or reading a book, but she could see the small black buttons in his ears that indicated he was listening to something. He was either watching some kind of vid, or playing a game.

Another day she might have admonished him—tonight, she took another sip of wine, smiled, and stirred the spicy noodles.

Demian Brackett, she thought, her smile soft and full of memories.

No. Tonight wasn't the night to get into an argument with Russ.

She wasn't about to rush off and have an affair with Demian—there'd be nowhere on Acheron she could hide from the consequences of infidelity. But that didn't mean she couldn't muse on the idea for a while. A good man, if a tad too serious, Demian was as handsome as he'd ever been. If anything, the small creases in the dark skin at the edges of his eyes made him even more attractive.

Anne sipped her wine, letting her mind wander. Russ was irritated with Demian's presence. She had wanted to punch him for his childishness earlier in the day. But if she kept letting her thoughts drift in salacious directions, she had the feeling that tonight her husband would be reaping the benefits of her ex-boyfriend's arrival.

Lucky Russ, she thought. *Lucky Anne, too*, because despite their recent tensions, she had a strong, intelligent, handsome and courageous husband who loved their children more than his own life. Whatever they might argue about, she knew they would still be together when the dust settled. Russ Jorden was her scruffy, wild-eyed man, even when she wanted to smack him in the head.

The door latch rattled, and then she heard the familiar creak. Stirring the spicy noodles, she lowered the heat on the burner a bit and turned to smile at Russ as he stepped into their quarters.

"Hey, honey," she began. "Can I pour you a glass of—"

The pale, haunted look on his face froze her tongue.

"Annie…"

She clicked off the burner, a dreadful numbness spreading inside her.

"What is it, Russell?" she said. "I know that look. Crap, I hate that look."

He crossed toward her. Anne noticed Tim's head swiveling to follow him—young as he was, he too must have been troubled by his father's mournful expression. The door still hung wide, open to the corridor, and she wanted to tell Timmy to shut it, but then Russ took her in his arms and held her tightly. He sagged into her, a ship lowering its sails when it had reached safe harbor, and she ran her fingers through the hair at the back of his neck.

"Tell me," she breathed.

Russ sighed heavily, pressed his forehead to hers, and then stepped back to meet her gaze.

"I just ran into Nolan Cale and he gave me the news... Curtis and Otto are dead."

The news staggered her, weakened her knees.

"No," she managed to say, shaking her head. "That can't..."

Anne turned to lean on the stove, shutting her eyes against her grief as a wave of anger swept over her.

"Idiots," she said. She slammed her hand down on the stove, rattling the still-sizzling pan. "Those dumb sons of bitches!"

"Hey," Russ said, taking her arm. "You know it's not like that. They took shelter in Processor Six. They'd have been okay, but Otto went stir crazy. From what I'm hearing, he just... unraveled."

Anne stared at him.

"They shouldn't have been out there in the first place. Those two were always taking unnecessary risks—anything to try to get ahead."

"They were our friends," Russ reminded her.

"Doesn't mean they weren't foolish," Anne said, refusing to be mollified. "The worst atmo-storms can be predicted within hours. Maybe they couldn't have seen how bad this storm would get before they left this morning, but they knew it was going to be a rough day."

Russ took a step back, glancing at Tim, who kept his eyes glued firmly on his tablet.

"But they're dead, Anne. You're going to hate yourself later, for—"

"For what? For being angry because they didn't have to die?" She let out a long, shuddering, tearful breath and dropped her gaze, staring at the ground. "They *didn't* have to die."

Russ touched her arm, slid his warm hand along her skin.

"No, they didn't."

Anne looked up at him, wiping her eyes.

"We're just as ambitious as they were, but we've never taken risks like that. We take our kids out on surveying trips, Russ. Our *kids*. Some of the administrators think we're crazy, but anyone who's ever spent time out there, surveying in the grit and the wind, knows how to figure out when the really bad storms are likely to hit."

"Otto just lost it, hon," he said. "You know he's been on edge."

Anne stiffened, then slowly nodded.

"Falling apart, Russ. The guy was falling apart. I've been worried about him and I've been worried about you, ever since the two of you started spending so much time together, the past few months. Thinking dark thoughts. Wishing impossible wishes."

Russ winced, then shook his head, running a hand over his scruffy chin.

"Now?" he said. "You want to do this right now?"

Anne felt as if she couldn't breathe.

"I don't *ever* want to do this. That doesn't mean I'm going to pretend it doesn't bother me that you and Otto have spent months convincing each other that your lives would've been better if you'd never come to Acheron."

"Wouldn't they have?" Russ barked, throwing up his hands. "Wouldn't things be better? For one thing, Otto and Curtis would still be alive!"

"You don't know that," she countered. "Otto was never the most stable—"

"Stop!"

"We came here because we dreamed of a life of discovery."

Russ rolled his eyes. "And how's that going for us so far?"

"We're on the far edge of the spread of human civilization," Anne said. "We have a good life. Make a decent living. Every night when I lay my head down, I think of all the people who would never have the courage to do what we've done!"

"None of them are stupid enough to take the risks we've taken."

"You have to take great risks to reap great rewards," Anne said, echoing the words he'd spoken when he had persuaded her to join the colony, years ago. Russ just cocked his head, staring at her as if she had grown two extra heads.

"When we go out on salvage runs, they control every step we take. They know where we are and what we're doing. Even if we found some artifacts, left there by indigenous life forms, or a vein of precious stone, they've got controls in place to cap what we can earn from any of it. That's not even real wildcatting... it's just risking our necks without the safeguards we've got when we're doing work for the company.

"And in all these years, what have we found of any real value? Nothing!" He glared at her. "We're wasting our time on this damned rock!"

Anne felt bile rise in the back of her throat. She wanted to be sick.

"I don't feel like I'm wasting my time here, Russell," she said. "I've got a happy little family and a circle of friends and a job that gives me the occasional surge of adrenaline. That's a good life."

"I didn't mean..." he said, then shook his head angrily. "That's not what I'm saying, and you know it."

Anne glanced at Tim, hunched over his tablet. No way the little black buds in his ears kept out his father's voice—not when Russ shouted.

"If you want to leave the colony so badly," she said quietly, "then do it. If you're that unhappy—"

"Oh, you'd love *that*, wouldn't you?" Russ said. "Perfect timing, now that Demian fucking Brackett has arrived!"

She glared at him. "Crap, you really are ten years old, you know that?"

"Play it off all you want, Anne, but I know you still have feelings for him. I can tell."

Anne covered her mouth with a hand. She didn't dare glance at Tim. What the hell was Russ thinking, having this conversation with their son in the room? They'd had plenty of disagreements with the kids around, but nothing like this. She only prayed that Tim was trying hard not to pay attention, that he had lost himself in whatever he was watching, reading, or playing, as he so often tended to do.

"You should stop now," she said.

Russ blinked and glanced back at Tim, understanding at last, but when he turned to Anne again, the anger still reddened his face.

"You're upset about Otto," she added. "So am I. Let's talk about this later."

"I'm upset, yes. My friend is gone. Otto may have been unstable, but that doesn't mean he wasn't right. This colony is a dead end for me—"

"For you?"

"For all of us."

Anne forced herself to breathe.

"If you want to go—"

"Fuck!" Russ shouted, throwing his arms up. He turned to storm out and they both looked at the door. Newt stood there, her mouth rimmed with a sticky red smear from her favorite popsicles. Her eyes were wide and full of pain and her lower lip trembled.

"Daddy's leaving?" she whispered.

Russ clenched and unclenched his hands, face etched with regret.

"Just for now, sweetheart," he said. "Just for now." Then he walked out.

Anne and Newt and Tim all stared at the door for a long moment, and then Newt ran into the corridor after him. Russ had turned left, probably heading to the rec center, but Newt didn't follow her father. She turned right, and vanished in an instant.

"Newt!" Anne called.

Tim shot up, plucking the buds from his ears and dropping his tablet onto the plush chair.

"I'll go after her," he said. Then he cast a hard look at his mother. "What is *wrong* with you two?"

Anne watched in silence as her son raced out into the hall in pursuit of his sister. She was left alone in the family quarters with her heart pounding in her ears.

The smell of cooking spices had gotten into her hair and her clothes, but she had lost her appetite.

11

NEW FRIENDS AND OLD

Brackett's quarters at Hadley's Hope were no more and no less than he'd expected.

A career in the Colonial Marines meant getting used to living a Spartan lifestyle. Bunk and sink, a chest of drawers, and a small closet if you were lucky. Living his life in uniform made it easier. On his off days, a plain t-shirt and regulation pants or sweatpants were all he needed, and he never had to worry about what he would be putting on—only whether or not he had clean laundry.

He never took a lot of personal items with him when he was reassigned. He had a photo-cube, a tablet full of music and thousands of books, his mother's dog tags, and a small wooden lion. It was a figurine carved by his father. These were the only pieces of his youth that he needed, just touchstones whose physical presence grounded him, so that even out here on the nascent edge of civilization, he was at home.

Brackett opened and closed the cabinets in the galley kitchen, saw glasses and plates and bowls. On the counter were a coffee maker and a toaster, and the sight made him smile. No matter how many things technology changed, certain others stayed the same. A couple of centuries after its introduction, a toaster was still necessary if you wanted to make toast properly. Sure, it had been improved, but it didn't play music for you or do research or boil your dinner—it made toast. In a strange way, he found that reassuring.

"Son of a bitch," he whispered, realizing just how exhausted he was.

Of course you're tired, he thought. On his way to Acheron, he'd had the fanciful idea that he'd arrive and meet the squad and the staff, settle in, have a nice meal, and just get to know everyone. Instead the day had started off ugly, and then turned deadly. He could still hear Otto Finch's desperate pleas as he walked across the anteroom and into his bedroom.

White sheets, white pillows, off-white walls, gray floor. A wave of familiar pleasure rolled over him and he sagged on his feet. Done. All he wanted was to put the grim day behind him and start over in the morning.

Brackett looked longingly at the bed. He needed to transmit a report to his superiors, and a request for clarification regarding the science team's co-opting of marine personnel, but he figured those could wait a couple of hours. He knew he ought to unpack, but what was the rush? His bags lay on the floor in the corner of the small anteroom, courtesy of Sgt. Coughlin.

So he crumpled onto the bed, boots still on, and dragged the pillow under his head. He could feel sleep rising up around him like some magical, enfolding mist, there instantly, ready to take him away. Draper and the other two assholes were confined to quarters, and Brackett decided that for the moment, he would confine himself to quarters as well. Just for a few hours… or maybe for the night. In the back of his mind, he knew he was hungry, but hunger felt disconnected from him. Far away. His thoughts began to blur.

A rapping came at the door.

"Oh, come on," Brackett groaned.

He clung to the pillow as if it were a life preserver, while the moment of almost-sleep dissipated. He'd left Lt. Paris and Pvt. Hauer as duty officers, unable to imagine another crisis rearing its head today. But the rapping came at the door a second time, and he knew he wasn't going to be able to ignore it.

Swearing under his breath, Brackett swung his legs off the bed and rose. Stretching, he twisted his neck until he heard a satisfying crack, and then strode through the anteroom toward the door.

"Who's there?" he called.

"Sergeant Coughlin, sir," came the muffled reply. "I'm sorry to disturb you, Captain, but you have a visitor."

Brackett frowned deeply. A visitor who required an escort? For a second he thought it must be one of the science team, but then he realized that Dr. Reese wouldn't need anyone to show him where to find the commanding officer's quarters.

He paused with his hand on the door latch, and a smile touched his lips.

Anne, he thought. *It must be.*

Unlocking the door, he hauled it open, head cocked at a curious angle. Coughlin stood smiling in the hall and Brackett blinked in confusion when he saw that it wasn't Anne beside him.

It was her daughter, Newt.

"She seemed lost," Coughlin said. "When she told me she was looking for you, I thought you wouldn't mind the intrusion."

Brackett dropped to a crouch so he could be face to face with the little girl. She still had a sticky red smear around her mouth from the freeze-pop she'd been eating earlier. She beamed at him, putting on her best smile, but Brackett could see from her red-rimmed eyes and the salty streaks on her face that she'd been crying.

Coughlin had surely noticed as well, and kindness had driven him to disturb his CO.

"It's no intrusion at all," Brackett said. "What can I do for you, Newt?"

The little girl shrugged. "Nothing for me. It's what *I* can do for *you*. See, I got back home and I thought to myself that you seemed like you really wanted one of those freeze-pops, and I wouldn't mind having another one, so I thought maybe I could bring you over to meet Bronagh right now instead of tomorrow or whenever. My mom always says 'don't put off till tomorrow what you can do today.'"

Brackett chuckled. "Well, she's right about that one." He glanced up at Coughlin. "I'll take it from here, Sergeant. Thanks for your help."

"Of course," Coughlin said. Then he tipped a wink at Newt. "If Bronagh has an extra freeze-pop, you know where to find me. My favorite's blueberry."

"Eeeeww," Newt said, scrunching her nose. "But okay. Mom also says 'don't yuck somebody else's yum.'"

"That's another good one," Coughlin told her, before saluting Brackett and turning to head back along the corridor.

The captain waited until the sergeant had gone before he went down on one knee, meeting Newt's hopeful gaze.

"I do like freeze-pops," he said, "but I don't think that's why you came to see me."

Newt pursed her lips, her brow knitted in disapproval.

"If you don't want one, you can just say so."

"Tell you what," Brackett said softly, "why don't we take a rain check and do that tomorrow, and right now I'll walk you back to your quarters. It's dinner time. Your mother must be wondering where you've gotten off to."

Newt replied so quietly that it took him a moment to realize that she'd spoken at all.

"They were fighting," she said. "I don't like it when they fight."

"I know what you mean," Brackett said. "My parents used to argue all the time. Sometimes it took a while for them to make up, but they always did." He stood up and reached for her hand. "Let me walk you back, and I bet you by the time we get there, all the fighting will be done.

"Tell you what," he added, "since I'm new here, you can show me around along the way."

Newt's lips were still pursed and her brow still knitted, but he saw her mouth tremble and then she nodded. No words, just that nod.

She took his hand and led the way, giving him her own little girl version of a tour of the civilian sections of the colony. Before long he knew which of the colonists had children, which of those children were bullies or babies, which air ducts made the best secret passages for hide and seek, and which of her neighbors made food that smelled disgusting. He almost reminded her of her mother's admonition not to yuck somebody else's yum, but decided not to tease her.

At a junction in the corridor, they encountered Dr. Hidalgo, who had surrendered her lab coat in favor of thick blue cotton sweatpants and a t-shirt. She had a towel around her neck and her face had gone pink from exertion. The aging scientist had appeared thin when Brackett had met her, but in this ensemble, her limbs seemed almost skeletal.

"Didja have a good workout, Dr. H?" Newt asked.

Dr. Hidalgo smiled. "I did, sweetie." She glanced at Brackett. "I see you've made a new friend."

"He's an *old* friend, actually," Newt said earnestly. "Of my mom's, I mean."

Dr. Hidalgo gave them a lopsided smile and glanced at Brackett. "Small universe, isn't it, Captain?"

Brackett nodded. "Smaller every day. But it hasn't run out of ways to surprise us."

"Let's hope it never does."

Dr. Hidalgo and Newt said their farewells, and then the girl continued to lead Brackett into the civilian quarters. He glanced back at the lanky scientist as she went around a corner and out of sight, and then turned to Newt.

"You like Dr. Hidalgo, huh?" he asked.

She shot him a curious glance.

"Don't you?"

Brackett grunted. "I guess I do," he said, surprising himself. Dr. Reese and Dr. Mori seemed like grim, arrogant, conniving pricks, and Dr. Hidalgo worked with them every day. Whatever they were doing here on Acheron, she was fully involved. But if a sweet kid like Rebecca Jorden liked her, surely she couldn't be all bad.

When they stopped in front of the door to her family's quarters, the little blond girl looked up at Brackett with her big, wise-beyond-her-years eyes, and sighed, steeling herself for whatever lay beyond the door.

"Thanks for being my friend," she said.

Brackett's grin was genuine, and so wide it hurt his grit-scoured face. "My pleasure," he said. "It's always nice to make a new friend."

Newt turned the latch and pushed the door open. When she stepped inside, Brackett stayed in the corridor, hesitant to intrude.

He could hear Anne call her daughter's name, her tone carrying that combination of love and worry and frustration that seemed exclusive to parents.

"You know you're not supposed to run off alone!" she said.

"Mom, I'm always running off alone," Newt replied. "Even when you make Tim go along, he hardly ever sticks with me. Nothing bad's going to happen. I know *everyone*."

A pause. In the hall, Brackett could almost picture the expression on Anne's face. In their time together, he believed he had seen every facet of her features on display. He took a step over the threshold and saw the boy, sitting on a broad plush chair on the floor, rolling his eyes at the fussing over his sister.

Tim noticed the movement and glanced up at Brackett.

"Hey," the boy said, raising a hand.

"Hello, Tim."

"Who's that?" Anne asked, and he heard her footfalls as she crossed their family room.

Brackett stepped into their quarters, leaving the door open behind him. To have closed it would have been presumptuous. As it was, he worried that he might be overstepping his bounds, but he couldn't help himself.

"Demian," Anne said, blinking several times as she brought herself up short, stopping a few feet away from him.

"Captain Brackett walked me back," Newt said happily, taking her mother's hand. The girl beamed proudly, as if she'd brought home an injured kitten to be nursed back to health. "I promised him I'd introduce him to Bronagh and get him a freeze-pop, but he said we should do that another day, that it must be dinner time—"

"It's *past* dinner time," Anne said, without taking her eyes off Brackett.

"Nuh-uh, 'cause Dad's not back yet," Newt said.

The logic seemed reasonable, but Anne flinched. Newt seemed to sense her misstep, and a sadness slid over her features.

Anne let go of her daughter's hand.

"Go wash up for dinner, please."

Newt hesitated for only a second before she thanked Brackett, promised him a freeze-pop the following day, and retreated down a short corridor to a door that must have been the bathroom.

"You too, Tim," Anne said, glancing at her son. Uneasy, uncertain.

Tim took a pair of black buds from his ears and set his tablet aside, then rose and made his way back into that corridor.

"Hello again, Annie," Brackett said once Tim had gone. Careful. Neutral.

Apparently at a loss for words, she opened her mouth to speak, but could only utter a short sound that sounded like half-laugh and half-sigh. She wetted her lips with her tongue and glanced away, shaking her head.

"I shouldn't have come?" Brackett asked.

"To my quarters, or to Hadley's Hope?"

"Neither, I'm guessing. Or both." He shrugged one shoulder. "But I'm here anyway."

Anne rolled her eyes, a familiar smirk on her lips.

"You're an exasperating man, Demian—always have been—but I'm glad you're here. It really is a wonderful surprise. I thought I'd never see you again—or anyone else from home."

He gazed at her a moment, so many things unspoken, demanding to be said. But years had passed, her children were nearby, and her husband might walk in at any moment. So all he did was smile.

"Happy I can still surprise you," he said, and he turned to go.

"Wait!" Anne said, reaching out to grab his arm.

The contact made them both freeze… both look down at the place where her fingers touched his forearm. Anne drew her hand back as if she'd been scalded, her eyes sad and uncertain. Then she gave that same sighing chuckle.

"Thanks for bringing Newt home," she said.

"She's a wonderful kid."

Anne nodded. "She is. A handful, though."

"Just like her mom."

A terrible sadness engulfed him, and he knew she saw it in his eyes, saw the way he deflated.

"Demian," she said carefully, "you knew…"

He waved the words away.

"Don't. I'm fine. I'd be lying if I said I didn't still feel something between us, but I didn't come here for you, and I damn sure have no intention of interfering with your life or your happiness. I just…"

"Just?" she echoed, her voice barely above a whisper, eyes full of history and could-have-beens.

Brackett gave her a lopsided smile.

"I've got to go. You've got beautiful children."

He wanted to tell her that it was impossible for him to look at Tim and Newt and not think that, if only they had made different choices years before, they could have been his. His and Anne's, together. He wanted to tell her that it hurt him, because he could so easily imagine the family they might have had.

But that wouldn't have been fair to anyone. Way back in boot camp, he had learned that sometimes there was no safe path, no decision from which one could emerge unscathed. In those cases, he had been taught to take the path of honor, even if it led to pain or death.

"I've got to transmit a report," he said. "See you around, Annie. Tell Newt I look forward to our date for freeze-pops."

Brackett left without looking her in the eyes again, not wanting to see if there were possibilities there. Not wanting her to see the possibilities in his.

12

NOSTROMO MYSTERIES

DATE: 12 JUNE, 2179

Maybe they're just doing this to torture me, Ripley thought. *But all it's doing is pissing me off.*

She'd emerged from hospital care, only to discover that she had become something of an oddity on Gateway Station—almost a celebrity, with her shockingly long hypersleep and tale of survival. The company had told her not to say anything, of course. Not to discuss anything of her experiences with anyone who might be unauthorized. But there were still whispers and rumors.

There always were.

And now they were showing her the faces of the dead.

She'd seen them a dozen times already today, but still she stared, trying to draw them nearer in her memory. It seemed the right thing to do, but they had all been dead and gone for more than half a century. However recent and fresh her grief might feel, they were fading into history.

Them and her daughter, too. Her whole life was informed by grief. *Screw it.*

"I don't understand this," she said, turning around to face the group who had gathered for the official inquiry. "We have been here for three and a half hours. How many different ways do you want me to tell the same story?"

Van Leuwen—another Company man, but smarter than Burke by a long shot—sat at the end of the long table. He was overseeing the inquiry, and sitting on either side of the table were eight others: Feds, interstellar commerce commission, colonial admin, insurance guys... and Burke.

He had tried to school her in how to approach this, what to say. *Bloody weasel.*

"Look at it from our perspective, please," Van Leuwen said. He invited her to sit once again, and Ripley, frustrated with the whole process but starting to see that perhaps playing it their way was the way to go, submitted. She sat, slowly, and listened to what she'd already heard several times before.

"Now, you freely admit to detonating the engines of, and thereby destroying, an M-Class star freighter, a rather expensive piece of hardware."

The insurance guy spoke up.

"Forty-two million in adjusted dollars." He smirked at Ripley. "That's minus payload, of course." *I could wipe that smirk off his face,* she thought, a little startled at the image of lashing out at him. He wasn't her enemy. None of these people were. Her enemy was dead, and the most frustrating thing was that no one here seemed to believe it.

The memory of her slaughtered friends demanded that she *force* them to believe. The undercurrent was that something suspicious had happened, something that she was trying to cover up with this outlandish story, and she was determined to put them right.

"The lifeboat's flight recorder corroborates *some* elements of your account," Van Leuwen continued. "That for reasons unknown, the *Nostromo* set down on LV-426, an unsurveyed planet at that time. That it resumed its course and was subsequently set to self-destruct, by *you*, for reasons unknown—"

"*Not* for reasons unknown!" Ripley said, again. *One more time,* she thought. The more she told her story, the less they seemed to believe it, and the more terrible it became to her. "I told you, we set down there on Company orders to get this thing which destroyed my crew. And your expensive ship."

A ripple seemed to pass through the people assembled there. Company people, some of them, but surely not all. She was essentially blaming the Company for what had happened to the *Nostromo*, so she could understand *some* of them feeling uncomfortable with that. Van Leuwen, the woman from the bio division, and that creep Burke.

But *all* of them?

"The analysis team that went over the lifeboat centimeter by centimeter found no physical evidence of the creature you described," Van Leuwen said.

"Good!" Ripley said, standing again. She was tall, imposing, and she liked the way a couple of the guys winced a little when she shouted. "That's because I blew it out of the airlock."

She sighed and looked down at her signed deposition, still feeling as if it lacked something. A story told, yet unfinished. She turned back to the screen to see Lambert staring at her—poor, scared Lambert who had died a dreadful death.

"Are there any species like this hostile organism on LV-426?" the insurance guy asked, turning to the woman from the bio division. She was sucking greedily on her cigarette, and it took her a few seconds to reply.

"No, it's a rock," she replied. "No indigenous life."

Now it was Ash staring at her from the screen, mocking her for being here with these idiots.

"Did IQs just drop sharply while I was away?" Ripley asked. "Ma'am, I already said it was not indigenous—it was a derelict spacecraft, it was an alien ship, it was not from there." She stared at the woman, who had something of a smirk on her lips. "Do you get it? We homed in on its beacon—"

"And found something never recorded once in over three hundred surveyed worlds," the woman said. "A creature that gestates inside a living human host—these are your words—and has concentrated acid for blood!"

"That's right!" Ripley snapped.

She was angry, frustrated, tired and hungry. But she could also see the looks on those faces around the table. Some were gently humoring her. Others looked aghast—not at what she was telling them, but at what they saw as a woman suffering a breakdown. Most of them seemed embarrassed to even be there.

"Look, I can see where this is going, but I'm telling you that those things exist."

"Thank you, Officer Ripley, that will be all," Van Leuwen said.

"Please, you're not listening to me. Kane, the crew member…" She had a flash memory of Kane, laconic and nice, a sweet guy just looking to earn a decent wage to help his family. "Kane, who went into that ship, said he saw thousands of eggs there. Thousands."

"Thank you, that will be *all*."

"Dammit, that's not all!" Ripley shouted. She couldn't get through to them. Could they not *see*? Could they not *understand*? "'Cause if one of those things gets down here, that *will* be all, and this…" She grabbed the papers, copies of her deposition, evidence sheets. "This bullshit that you think is so important… you can kiss all that goodbye!"

Silence. Some of them even stared. She knew she'd gone too far, but fuck it. Her sweet daughter had died believing her mother was lost forever. Ripley was adrift. And all she had left to do was to make sure no one, *no one*, had to go through what she had been through. Never again.

Van Leuwen sighed and clipped the lid onto his pen. Then after a longer pause, he broke the silence.

"It is the finding of this court of inquiry that Warrant Officer E. Ripley, NOC 14472, has acted with questionable judgment, and is unfit to hold an ICC license as a commercial flight officer. Said license is hereby suspended indefinitely. No criminal charges will be filed against you at this time…"

He went on. Official speak, technical terms. Ripley stared at him, trying to will him to believe her, holding back her anger and grief to prevent herself blowing up one more time. But Van Leuwen's mind was made up. He didn't look like the sort of man who made such decisions lightly, and it would take more than Ripley's gaze to change his mind.

In truth, she even agreed with him, partly. She wasn't fit to fly. She woke up from fresh nightmares two mornings out of three. That sense of dark, heavy dread was still inside her. Sometimes it threatened to pull her and everyone around her into its embrace.

But this wasn't about her.

She turned away, took a deep breath. As the others started to leave the room, the sleazeball Burke sidled up to her. She smelled his aftershave before she saw him, and both made her sick.

"That could have been… better," he said. But instead of responding, she dismissed him, and turned to confront Van Leuwen as he left the room.

"Van Leuwen," she said, doing her best to keep her voice level, to hold the madness down. "Why don't you just check out LV-426?"

"Because I don't have to," he said. "There have been people there for over twenty years, and they've never complained about any hostile organism."

No!

"What do you mean?" she asked. "What people?"

"Terraformers. Planet engineers. They go in and set up these big atmosphere processors to make the air breathable. Takes decades. What we call a shake-and-bake colony."

She slammed her arm on the door, blocking his exit.

"How many are there?" she demanded. "How many colonists?"

"I don't know," he shrugged. "Sixty, maybe seventy families." He looked down at her arm. "Do you mind?"

She let him go. She had no choice. That sense of dread within her was blooming, a terrible secret she should know but could not grasp, could not open.

"Families," she whispered, closing her eyes and seeing her sweet Amanda on those nights when the little girl had come into her bedroom, cold and scared of the dark, scared of monsters.

DATE: 19 JUNE, 2179
TIME: 1612

Dr. Bartholomew Reese kept mostly to himself.

Years before, at the urging of Dr. Hidalgo, the science team had arranged a weekly dinner, a sort of enforced socialization period for people who tended toward isolation and rumination. Dr.

Reese supposed the Monday night rituals were a good thing, even necessary in a way—for himself, at least, he knew that too much time alone made him more impatient and more irritable with the rest of the world than he already was, and that was saying something. Still, he never quite enjoyed the meal and considered it a distraction.

Fortunately, tonight was Thursday—the Monday gathering still days away—so he did not have to suffer the presence of his colleagues, or pretend an amiability he had never felt.

Reese sat in a reclining chair in his anteroom, a glass of Malbec on a side table and a two-hundred-year-old edition of Ray Bradbury's *The Illustrated Man* open in his lap. Most people eschewed the printed book, even scoffed at what they viewed as self-indulgence on his part for carting several boxes of books to Acheron when he had first been assigned here by the company. But in a savage, uncaring universe, Reese had always felt that a glass of wine and an open book were the best way to remind himself what it meant to be civilized.

A soft chime echoed through his quarters. He frowned and glanced at the door in irritation, wondering if he could ignore it. But no... nobody would interrupt him without good reason. He had no real friends, only colleagues, and they would not have come here without an urgent need.

Taking a sip of wine, he set the glass back down on the side table, slid a finger into his book to hold the page, and rose from the chair. As he crossed to the door, the arthritis in his knees singing out a painful reminder, the bell chimed again.

"Hang on!" he called.

He opened the door to find Dr. Mori on his threshold. In all of their time working together, Reese had never seen so wide a smile on the silver-haired Japanese biologist. The grin transformed him, and for a fleeting moment Reese had an image of what Mori must have looked like as a little boy.

"Bartholomew," Dr. Mori said, "may I come in?"

Reese stepped aside and Dr. Mori practically lunged into the room. He steepled his hands in front of his face as if to hide his grin. Dr. Reese closed the door and turned toward him.

"You look as giddy as a lovestruck teen," Reese said, with a hint of disapproval. "Whatever it is—"

"It *may* be the answer to the *Nostromo* mystery," Dr. Mori said, lowering his hands to reveal his smile again. He shook his head with a small laugh.

Reese felt his heart jump, but restrained himself. This might be nothing. Wishful thinking at best.

"Explain yourself," he said.

Dr. Mori nodded. "Al Simpson has just received a special order, copies of which were also transmitted to yourself and to me. In it, a Weyland-Yutani executive named Carter Burke has sent surface grid coordinates with instructions that a survey team be dispatched immediately to investigate the site. With that kind of urgency, Bartholomew, what else could it be?"

Dr. Reese lowered his gaze and stared at the floor a moment before uttering a small laugh.

He nodded.

"We've been here for years," Reese said. "There can only be one rationale for urgency." He narrowed his gaze. "Though you realize it may not be about the *Nostromo* at all. It might be some other indication—an atmospheric imaging array, revealing a geological depression that hints at the presence of ruins."

"Then why the suddenness?" Dr. Mori countered. "Why go directly to Simpson?"

Dr. Reese contemplated Mori's reasoning, and could not find fault in it. Still, he forced himself to breathe. Only a fool would allow himself to become overly excited before they truly knew the purpose for Carter Burke's special order.

Decades earlier, a Weyland-Yutani star freighter called the *Nostromo* had diverted from its course to respond to what the crew believed was a deep space distress call—one which could only have come from an alien ship—and subsequently vanished. It had long been believed that that distress call had come from one of the moons of Calpamos, with Acheron the likeliest candidate.

The science team's primary work with the Hadley's Hope colony had been to study Acheron and the way in which it had been changed by terraforming, as well as attempting to enrich the changing soil to support agriculture. At least, that was what the colonists, marines, and administrators had been told. Their less overt, higher-priority work was to examine all samples for any indication of alien life— native or visitor, past or present—on LV-426.

"Whatever has happened," Dr. Mori said, "new information must have come to light."

Reese nodded, his thoughts racing. He paced back toward his chair, considering the best way to handle the science team's relationship with Simpson. The man would follow instructions from Weyland-Yutani as if they had come from his own government. The government and the company had founded Hadley's Hope together, but Simpson's paychecks bore the Weyland-Yutani logo. He knew for whom he really worked.

Spotting his wine glass out of the corner of his eye, Dr. Reese set down his book and picked up the glass. He swirled the Malbec around for several seconds before taking a thoughtful sip.

"The timing of Captain Brackett's arrival is less than ideal," he said, glancing up at Dr. Mori. "I'm confident I know what his superiors will tell him, but until he is commanded otherwise, his orders on the ground here will stand as he sees them."

Dr. Mori frowned. "Why are you troubled by this?" he asked. "It isn't the marines who ought to be going along on this sojourn, but one of us. I should go with them, or you should. Even Dr. Hidalgo…"

Reese arched an eyebrow. "You want to go and investigate an unknown alien presence without a marine escort? Someone with guns and a willingness to use them, who will die protecting you?"

"Well, when you put it that way…"

"No, let's allow Simpson to send out a team of his wildcatters. Meanwhile, we'll get to work re-analyzing any data we've collected from that area. If the survey team returns without incident, perhaps one of us will go along the next time. By then, Brackett will have been instructed to cooperate, and the risk will be significantly decreased."

Dr. Mori smiled. "I like your thinking. We could toast to it if you'd offer me a glass of that rich red."

Reese's eyebrows shot up. "How rude of me. Apologies, my friend. A case arrived on this morning's dropship, and I don't mean to hoard it."

"Of course you do," Dr. Mori scoffed.

"Well, yes, but not so completely that I can't offer you a glass," he said with a smile. "I don't think we should start celebrating just yet—"

"Of course not."

"—but that doesn't mean we can't raise a glass in hope."

He retrieved a second glass from his small kitchen and poured several mouthfuls of wine for Mori. Reese handed it over and then raised his own glass.

"To the *Nostromo*," he said.

Dr. Mori nodded and clinked his glass against Reese's.

"To the *Nostromo*."

Dr. Hidalgo stood outside Dr. Mori's office, waiting for his return.

The news had torn her away from her dinner, and as she stood leaning against the wall, her stomach growled. She had been compared to a bird many times in her life—a stork, a flamingo—but the most accurate comparisons were to her appetite. She ate small portions, mostly nibbles here and there, but she ate all day long. Tonight she'd been in the dining hall with several of the lab assistants, eating vegetable dumplings with a chili sauce, when Dr. Mori's assistant had come to fetch her.

She'd wheedled the news out of him on the hurried walk back to the office, and now she waited like an errant schoolgirl sent to see the principal.

When she saw Dr. Mori coming down the corridor, she steeled herself for the encounter. She admired Mori for his brilliance and his dedication, but she had never liked him as a person. In her career, Elena Hidalgo had met many scientists whose company she had enjoyed—even here at Hadley's Hope, there were several lab assistants who were thoughtful and kind—but it had been her bad luck to end up working under Bartholomew Reese and the caustic, thoughtless Dr. Mori.

"I need to speak with you," she said as Mori approached. "You and Dr. Reese."

"He'll be along shortly," Dr. Mori said. "Is there a problem?"

"I think there is."

Dr. Mori unlocked his office door and gestured for her to enter. He followed her inside and closed the door behind him. The lights flickered on automatically, sensing their presence.

"Care to elaborate?" Dr. Mori asked, turning toward her and leaning against his desk. Everything about his tone and posture declared that he found her tiresome. "I presume this is about this evening's message from the company."

"From Carter Burke," Dr. Hidalgo said. "Whoever that is."

"Dr. Reese and I were just sharing our excitement about this development, Elena," he told her. "You don't seem as thrilled as I would have expected. This may be precisely the sort of break we've been hoping for since our arrival on Acheron. I don't know about you, but I've harbored a secret fear, almost from day one, that we had spent all of this time and effort, and built the colony in the wrong place."

Dr. Hidalgo shook her head.

"How can there be a wrong place? The colony doesn't exist just as a host body for us to nest upon."

Dr. Mori arched an eyebrow, gazing at her dubiously.

"Are you comparing us to parasites?"

"Of course not," she replied. "I love my work, I'm just… worried. That's all."

"There's nothing for you to be worried about, Dr. Hidalgo."

She thought of the children she had seen earlier, running in the hall; Newt and her little ginger-haired friend, Luisa.

"I'm not worried about myself."

Dr. Mori thoughtfully stroked his chin. The cliché of it—the wise old scientist in silent contemplation—was so condescending that it made her want to scream. But she held her tongue.

"My dear friend," he said, "the Company's had no secrets from you. From any member of our team. Yes, Hadley's Hope would have been built whether or not the Company had co-sponsored its construction, but there was a reason Weyland-Yutani bought into the idea in the first place. It used its influence to choose colony sites which would further its own interests. This is not espionage, Elena. It's business. More importantly, it's science."

She plunged her hands into the pockets of her lab coat, encountering a package of mints on one side and a wad of tissues on the other. Tangible, insignificant things, somehow they made her concerns more real.

"If we find alien life—" she began.

"Living creatures?" Dr. Mori scoffed. "After all these years, with all of the studies we've done of this planet, you know how miniscule the chances are of that. There's been no sign of any activity at all."

"My point is that it's *possible*. For the most part, other encounters with alien races have been benign, but there have been a few violent, bloody clashes. You know that. Our friends in the Colonial Marines must all have stories of friends they've lost. So I can't help but feel some trepidation about making contact with a new alien life form, with a colony full of people—including children—who have no idea that the chance even exists.

"What if the aliens are hostile?" she said. "What then?"

Dr. Mori blinked in surprise, lowering his arms to stare as if her question was the stupidest thing he'd ever heard. Then he frowned, his brow knitting with impatience.

"You know the answer to that question, Dr. Hidalgo," he said curtly. "Our research is too important for it to go to waste. That's why the science team was provided its own evacuation vessel, why we've all been given enough rudimentary training to launch the ship, and trigger the autopilot's homing system.

"You didn't think they were teaching us all of that for their own amusement, do you? Whatever else happens, our findings must reach Earth."

"Right, the evac ship," she responded. "A vessel even the colonial administrator is unaware of."

Dr. Mori flinched back from her, staring through narrowed eyes.

"I'm not sure where you're going with this," he said cautiously, "but I'd remind you about the contracts you've signed—specifically about the priorities the company has set for us. You didn't have to agree to those things. No one put a gun to your head, Elena. You chose this. It's a worst-case scenario—which isn't going to occur, remember." His voice softened slightly. "This is a dead planet. There is no threat here—only history to be unearthed, and perhaps alien remains. But in a worst-case scenario, that evac ship carries us out of here—the science team, our samples, and our data. Nothing more."

"But there are children…"

Dr. Mori glared at her for a long moment, took a breath and let it out slowly.

"Yes, there are," he said at last. "Children whose parents knew that their days and nights would be full of peril, from the moment they set off to join the colony. As did you. If I were you, I'd stop worrying about the worst-case scenario and start focusing on the task ahead of us, the wonderful opportunity we've been given."

He walked around the desk and took a seat behind it, drawing up his chair.

"A word of advice?" Dr. Mori continued. "When we meet with Reese, you'd do well not to bring this up. If he thinks you're not dedicated to the research, he'll cut you out of the process altogether. And then, if we *do* find something, all of the time you've spent on this godforsaken rock, with men you despise, will have been for nothing."

Dr. Hidalgo stared at him. She knew she ought to make some kind of argument, at least tell him that she did not despise him, but she had never been a convincing liar.

Mori opened his tablet and began to tap on a keyboard, perhaps making notes or consulting earlier files. After several long seconds, she turned and left, not bothering to close the door behind her.

In all her years, Dr. Hidalgo had never been more excited.

Or more afraid.

13

A FAMILY OUTING

DATE: 19 JUNE, 2179
TIME: 1857

Anne and Newt sprawled on the carpet playing *Kubix*, a puzzle game they had fallen in love with the previous year. The tiles were colorful, and played musical notes when being connected, but Anne liked it best because of the mathematical element that went into configuring them.

Newt barely noticed that she was learning anything, just enjoying the competition. In the beginning she had rarely won a game, but in recent weeks Newt had improved so much that she routinely beat her mother, which gave the little girl great pleasure.

Tim had gone off to the rec room to meet his friend Aaron, a burly boy with curly black hair and a chip on his shoulder. Anne would have preferred that Tim make other friends, but there weren't many children her son's age at Hadley's Hope, so she resigned herself to hoping Tim would have a positive influence on Aaron, and not the other way around.

Newt placed a triangular tile bearing a fuchsia smiley face into the design she'd been constructing, and a pretty melody began to play, emanating from the chips themselves.

"Yay!" Newt said happily, clapping her hands. "Gotcha!"

Anne laughed. "So you did."

The rattling of the door latch made them both look up, and Anne stiffened. A week had passed since the night they'd had their big argument, but the tension of it had echoed through every interaction they'd had since. She could still hear their angry words. So she drew a deep breath but did not stand up to greet him as the door swung inward.

"Daddy's home!" Russ said, practically bursting inside, a grin on his face. He clapped his hands as he saw them. "Hey, look at my girls. Newt, I hope you're kicking Momma's butt, as usual!"

Newt gave a matter-of-fact nod, eyebrows raised.

"Of course."

Anne realized that Newt had tensed up just as much as she had, and she felt her own relief echoing back from her daughter.

"You're in a good mood," Anne said with a tentative smile.

Russ slammed the door, crossed the carpet and knelt beside her. He took her hands and gazed into her eyes, and she remembered the same look in his eyes the day he had proposed to her.

"You're going to be in a good mood too," he said.

Anne laughed softly. "All right, how many drinks did you and Parvati have?"

"Three," he said. "No, four. Shots included. But it isn't alcohol fueling my mood, sweetheart. It's the promise of money. Simpson came looking for me in the bar. First thing tomorrow morning, you and I are headed out!"

Newt uttered a happy *ooh* and clapped again, her father's excitement infectious. Anne felt it, too.

"Out where?"

Russ snapped his fingers and pointed at her.

"That, my love, is the big question, and the best part. We're not supposed to discuss it, but he's received instructions to send a survey team to some very specific coordinates."

"Specific coordinates," Anne repeated, a pleasurable tremor going through her. "So this isn't random. This time we're actually—"

"*Looking* for something," Russ interrupted, nodding rapidly. He jumped to his feet and started to pace, his thoughts already racing ahead to the next morning. "They're not going to tell us what we're looking for, of course, but the company must expect us to find something out there."

"Native ruins," Anne cried. "It's got to be!"

"Or some kind of ancient settlement," another voice chimed in.

Anne looked over to see Tim standing at the entrance to the hallway, smiling happily. The boy hadn't smiled all day, and it lifted her spirits even further just to see it.

"Exactly." Russ snapped his fingers again and pointed at Tim. "*Non-human* settlement."

"It's like a gift," Anne said, but then a dark thought touched her. "*If* we find something. Let's not get ahead of ourselves, Russ. It might be that we go out there, and don't find anything at all."

Russ nodded. "Could be, could be." But she could see the glint in his eyes—a glint she knew so well—full of hope and plans for the future—and she knew he had already begun to spend the money in his mind.

"I want to come!" Newt said, standing up, her expression adorably determined.

"Rebecca and I *both* want to come," Tim confirmed.

"Absolutely not," Anne said, climbing to her feet.

"You *always* let us come," Newt said, crossing her arms. She turned to her father. "Dad, tell her."

"Well," Russ said, "we don't *always*, Newt. Only when it's not going to be more than a day."

Anne gave him a wary glance.

"Russ..."

He grinned. "Come on, Anne, they're excited. Tell you what, if we wake up tomorrow and the coordinates Simpson gives us are too far away, or if the weather looks ugly—"

"The weather's always ugly," she said, every trace of happiness draining from her as she thought about the Finch brothers. "After what happened with Otto and Curtis, I just don't think it's a good idea."

"Mom, we'll be fine," Tim said. "Come *on*."

"The storm has passed," Russ argued. "I checked on tomorrow's weather, and there's no indication of anything near that level of disturbance."

"That can change in an instant," she said.

"We'll monitor it."

"The calmest atmospheric day on Acheron is still dangerous. The wind and the dust—"

"We've been out with you *plenty* of times," Newt argued.

"Don't whine," her mother chided her.

"I'm *no*-ot."

Russ cocked his head. "Honey?"

Newt and Tim gazed at her expectantly. Anne knew she ought to say no, but their arguments weren't without merit. The storm that had led to the deaths had been an anomaly, and the atmosphere had returned to its ordinary level of violence—which they had all faced many times. Even the kids. And if she and Russ didn't take this job, it would go to Cale or one of the other wildcatters, and if they found anything truly valuable, she'd resent her own decision forever.

Still, she didn't like the idea of spending the next few days in a crawler with her husband. The specter of their week-old argument, and his jealousy over Demian's presence on Acheron, would be hanging over them. That didn't appeal to her at all. Once his euphoria passed, the conversation was sure to go places she didn't want it to go…

Unless the kids came along with them.

"Okay," she said finally. "If the stormcasting program doesn't show any major atmospheric disturbance—not just tomorrow, but for the next few days—then the kids can come."

"Yes!" Tim gave a triumphant fist pump.

Newt came over and wrapped an arm around Anne's waist, nodding her precocious approval.

Russ smiled at her across the room. It was a slow, sweet smile, with a look in his eyes suggesting that he might just have remembered what a great couple they were, and what a great family they'd made.

At that moment her anxiety passed, and Anne felt suffused by a wonderful contentment—a certainty that they had just passed some invisible hurdle. Suddenly she couldn't wait for the next day to arrive.

The coming morning promised a new beginning.

* * *

DATE: 21 JUNE, 2179
TIME: 0812

Al Simpson enjoyed mornings in the command block, despite the fact that "morning" was an elusive concept on Acheron. The constant swirl of volcanic ash and loose soil in the atmosphere blotted out any direct sunlight, but on a relatively calm day, morning took on a pleasant, twilight glow.

The colony buzzed with people hard at work. Outside the broad window—its storm shield raised—he could see six-wheeled crawlers moving about, emerging from underground garages and crossing the breadth of the growing colony. Simpson thought of them all as spiders, working together to construct a single web.

He'd been accused of being a curmudgeon, many times, and there was truth to that. But those who worked with him long enough realized very quickly that if they caught him in the morning, on a decent-weather day, and he had a cup of coffee in his hand, he might not bite their heads off.

He turned away from the window and took a sip. After years on Acheron, the shit that passed for coffee up here had finally started to taste good to him. He watched the technicians at their consoles, rushing around, tapping data into computers, and it felt good, especially when he reminded himself that unlike the people of Hadley's Hope, this was just a job to him. The colonists had signed on more or less for life, but Simpson was like the marines in one respect—any time he wanted, he could ask for a transfer.

His gaze drifted purposefully toward Mina Osterman, the most recent hire. She'd arrived two months earlier as a replacement for the plant architect, Borstein, who'd gone to work on a new colony Weyland-Yutani was developing in another sector. Mina had ginger hair and dark eyes, and she held herself always in a sort of relaxed pose that made people feel comfortable around her.

The previous Monday, Simpson had gotten a bit too comfortable with Mina and her reassuring smile and those dark eyes, and suggested certain nocturnal activities that had nothing to do with architecture. Now she seemed to feel his eyes upon her and looked up curiously. A frown furrowed her brow, and she rolled her eyes before returning to the paperwork in front of her.

Simpson took another sip of coffee, but it tasted bitter to him now. He knew he had overstepped with Mina, and it made him feel like an idiot. He turned to head back to his console and saw his assistant operations manager, Brad Lydecker, rushing toward him.

"You remember you sent some wildcatters out to that plateau, out past the Ilium range?"

Simpson grimaced. The Jordens.

And the morning had been going so well.

"Yeah, what?" he asked curtly.

"Well, the guy's on the horn from our mom-and-pop survey team," Lydecker explained. "Says he's homing in on the coordinates, and wants to confirm that his claim will be honored."

Simpson grumbled, cursing himself for sending Jorden out there at all. The guy had been on Acheron as long as Simpson had, and he needed to clarify the rules? Then again, Russ hadn't been chosen for his smarts.

Lydecker, on the other hand, didn't need to know that this was anything other than a routine wildcatting expedition.

"Christ," Simpson said, putting some drama into it. "Some honcho in a cushy office says go look at a grid reference that's in the middle of nowhere, we go and look. They don't say why, and I don't ask. It takes two weeks to get an answer out here, anyhow."

"So what do I tell this guy?" Lydecker said.

Simpson glanced at his coffee, but it had lost its magic altogether.

"Tell him that as far as I'm concerned, he finds something, it's his."

DATE: 21 JUNE, 2179
TIME: 1109

Russ Jorden felt alive. He gripped the crawler's steering wheel, and his heart raced as he hit the accelerator.

The vehicle roared across a shelf of furrowed rock, down a slant, and then blasted through the crest of a high drift of volcanic ash. With the dust eddying around them, it felt to him as if they were surging along the waves of a dead gray sea, with the promised land straight ahead.

In the back of the crawler, Newt and Tim bumped each other and bickered as siblings had done on journeys since time began. His children loved each other and played together daily, but they nipped at each other like growling, overgrown puppies. Sometimes he grew impatient with them, but not today.

"Look at that, Anne," he said, glancing over.

In the green glow of the magnetoscope, she looked ethereally beautiful, a ghostly, wild angel. The memory of their argument from the week before gave him a sudden jolt of sadness, but he pushed it away. They were together, now—really together—partners the way they were meant to be.

"I'm looking," she said, staring at the scope, which pinged again. The tone of the pings altered slightly depending on their proximity to the object they were nearing and the angle of their approach. Right now the sound was loud, and clear as a bell.

"Six degrees west," she told him.

"Six west," Russ echoed, turning the wheel to compensate. The scope kept pinging and he glanced over again, gleeful.

"Look at this fat, juicy magnetic profile!" he cried happily. "And it's mine, mine, mine!"

"Half mine, dear," Anne reminded him with an indulgent smile. His exuberance always amused her—it was how he'd won her over in the first place.

"And half mine!" Newt yelled from the back.

"I got too many partners," Russ joked, although the moment the words were out of his mouth, he knew they weren't really a joke at all. Weyland-Yutani would take the lion's share of whatever it was the scope had picked up.

Don't get greedy, he reminded himself. *This is still the find you've been waiting for.*

Whatever the scope had identified, it definitely wasn't any sort of natural rock or mineral formation. The ping was too strong, too regular, and he knew the terrain around here well enough to know what a huge anomaly they'd found. No, whatever it was, it had been built by someone… or something. Now he just wanted to see it. Sure, the payoff would be lovely, but he couldn't help thinking about what it would mean if he found the ruins of some previously unknown race. His name—their names, his and Anne's—they'd be written in history books, along with Burkhardt and Koizumi and the rest.

Newt poked her head up between the seats.

"Daddy, when are we going back to town?"

Russ smiled. "When we get rich, Newt."

"You always say that," she sulked. "I wanna go back. I wanna play Monster Maze."

Tim nudged her and put his face up close to hers.

"You cheat too much."

"Do not! I'm just the best."

"Do too! You go into places we can't fit."

"So what? That's why I'm the best!"

Frustrated, Anne spun to face them.

"Knock it off, you two. I catch *either* of you playing in the air ducts again, I'll tan your hides."

"*Mo*-om," Newt whined, "all the kids play it."

Russ would have defended them, reminded Anne that if they were children stuck in Hadley's Hope, they'd certainly have spent whole days exploring the system of ducts that crisscrossed the facility. But just at that moment, he lost the ability to put together a sentence—not to mention anything resembling a cogent thought.

All he could do was take his foot off of the crawler's accelerator and lean forward, staring out through the windscreen at the massive shape looming ahead of them in the veil of drifting ash.

"Holy shit," Russ said reverently.

At first glance, the gargantuan object rising out of the ground looked almost organic, as if it were the huge, curving remains of some giant alien beast. As the crawler slowly rolled nearer, he saw that the shape did, indeed, have some kind of organic influence in its design. And there could be no doubt that it *had* been designed.

But not by humans.

"Oh, my God," Anne whispered.

Russ felt his heart hammering in his chest as he pulled the crawler to a stop. They'd never seen anything like the object's horseshoe shape, or its strange, bio-mechanoid construction, but it most certainly was a vessel. A starship. Judging from the way the rocky terrain had been torn up, leaving great piles of debris clustered around it, he felt sure it had crash-landed here, digging up the stone and ash as it scarred the ground on impact.

"Folks," Russ said, "we have scored big this time."

The kids moved out of the way as Anne pulled on her heavy coat, helmet, and the goggles that would protect her eyes from the blowing grit. Russ shut down the engine and followed suit, all four of them keeping up a stream of excited chatter. They wore belts equipped with core samplers, flashlights, and short-range comms that would allow them to communicate without having to shout.

Hefting cameras and testing equipment, he and his wife climbed down out of the vehicle and dropped to the surface. A massive gust of wind buffeted against them and Russ stood to block Anne from the brunt of it. The wind reminded him of Otto and Curtis, and he silently vowed to be more careful than was typical of him, and to watch the skies for any sign that the weather might worsen.

Their breath clouded in the air. The temperature had dropped.

"You kids stay inside," Anne called to them. "I mean it! We'll be right back."

Clicking on his helmet light, Russ set off toward the derelict object, trudging through dust and then climbing onto a rocky ledge that protruded from the ash. Anne caught up to him as he studied the shape and the weird texture of the ship.

"Shouldn't we call it in?" she asked.

"Let's wait until we know what it is," Russ suggested.

Anne gave a soft grunt. "How about 'big weird thing?'"

It was a joke, but she didn't sound as if she was joking. She sounded spooked, and Russ couldn't blame her. Truth was, he was more than a little spooked himself, but he wasn't going to admit it. From the looks of the "big weird thing," it had been out here for ages—maybe centuries. Whatever it had been once upon a time, now it was little more than a creaky old haunted house, silent and remote.

Anne took the lead, trudging down from the jutting stone, through drifts of ash, and up a cascade of rocks beside the hull. Russ ran his gloved hand over the surface, its texture rough and lined when stroked in one direction, but smooth when he slid his palm across it the other way.

They began by attempting to walk the entire periphery of the ship, but just a few minutes after they'd begun, Anne froze up ahead of him.

"What is it?" Russ asked, as he came up beside her. Then he saw the thing that had caused her to halt. It was a large, twisted gash in the metal hull, blackness looming—almost breathing—within.

"What is it?" Anne repeated. She glanced at him, and he could see the wild grin behind her mask. "I'd say it's a way in."

She pointed the light attached to her belt, and turned it on. Russ did the same.

14

DERELICTION AND DUTY

DATE: 21 JUNE, 2179
TIME: 1121

Sgt. Marvin Draper and his cronies had spent Brackett's first week on Acheron testing the new CO's patience. They muttered to one another in the captain's presence, showed up late for duty assignments, and argued among themselves and with other marines. It made him wish he'd kept them confined to their quarters, but he couldn't have left them locked away forever, tempting as the thought might be.

Their latest antics, less than twelve hours earlier, had been to get drunk and enter the livestock pens, so that Cpl. Pettigrew could demonstrate his childhood pastime of "cattle-tipping"—knocking the cows over for a laugh.

All of it was behavior Brackett would have expected from college fraternity boys, but not from Colonial Marines.

He'd had enough.

"You've got a decision to make," he said to the five marines lined up in his office. "Either you fall in line, or you are going to spend the rest of your time on Acheron in your quarters, until I can have you transferred to somewhere even *more* remote than this hellhole."

Draper raised his stubbled chin.

"Sir, *is* there anywhere more remote, sir?"

Nguyen and Pettigrew remained blank-faced, but Stamovich smirked. As far as he was concerned, Draper was the alpha dog at Hadley's Hope, and the corporal had all the confidence in the universe that it would remain that way. Pvt. Yousseff, on the other hand, closed her eyes and pressed her lips tightly together, either furious with Draper and Stamovich, disgusted with them, or both.

Brackett wanted to slap the shit out of Stamovich, but he knew the only way to deal with an ass-kisser was to kick the ass he was so fond of kissing. He focused on Draper instead, moved nearer to him.

"What is my name, Sergeant?" he barked.

"Brackett, sir!" Draper barked in return, cocky as ever.

"Think again!"

"Captain Brackett, sir!"

Pettigrew, Nguyen, and Yousseff all shifted nervously. Stamovich watched the exchange from the corner of his eye, still half-smirking, sure that his asshole idol would win the day.

"Look me in the eye, Sergeant!" Brackett snapped.

Draper sneered as he complied, revealing his true nature.

"I am your commanding officer," Brackett said, quietly now, eye to eye, staring so hard he told himself his gaze was burning the core right out of Draper's brain. "If I order you to lick the floor clean, that's what you will do. If I want you to stand on your head in the corner, and stay there for a month, that's what you will do. If I tell you that you are confined to quarters, with zero human contact, then you will damn well stay alone in your quarters until you gouge your own eyes out with boredom."

Stamovich blinked and shifted a bit.

Draper still seemed too confident, though. Brackett knew he had been foolish to give the man an out, and now he took it away.

"You think it's going to be as easy as transferring out of here if you don't like your new commanding officer?" he continued, glancing at each of them in turn before coming back to Draper. He leaned forward, shuffled nearer, physically intruding on Draper's space until the marine had to take a step back.

"If you want out of here, *I* have to sign that paperwork. I have to be the one to *let* you out. So I'm not just your captain or your CO, Marvin.

I'm your jailer. I'm your warden. I'm your personal fucking deity. I can be a benevolent god, or I can be the devil you wish you'd never met."

The pink flush in Draper's cheeks pleased Brackett, but not as much as the uncertainty that appeared in the man's eyes.

"You see it now, don't you, Marvin?" Brackett went on. "You and your friends. The moment I arrived here you made certain assumptions, the stupidest of which was that a young captain with no visible battle scars might just be soft. You figured you could just go on with whatever—"

"Captain?" Yousseff said, voice quiet but firm.

Brackett rounded on her. "You've got something to say, Private? Do you not see me chewing Sergeant Draper a new asshole?"

"Yes, sir," Yousseff said, eyes front, still at attention. "And it's about time, sir. But you should know that this far from home, the company is the tail that wags the dog. They have far more sway than the government. It's been that way forever. We—"

"Maybe none of you is listening," Brackett said, fists clenching and unclenching. "So I'll say this as clearly as I can. I am a marine. I do not work for Weyland-Yutani, and neither do any of you. If the order comes down from above that I'm to reinstate marine escorts on these survey missions, so be it. Until then, we run the show by the book, and the colony's science team will just have to do without us!"

"They've already done that, sir," Pettigrew said.

Brackett frowned. "Done what?"

"Gone ahead without us. One of the wildcatters told me the orders came in from the company—something specific, which isn't how it usually works," Pettigrew replied, chin up at attention, rather than in defiance. "The family went out early yesterday morning, in a crawler."

Icy dread snaked along Brackett's spine.

"What family?"

Pettigrew shrugged.

"Do any of you know?" Brackett asked, scanning their faces.

Stamovich glanced at Pettigrew.

"It was Russ, wasn't it?" the corporal said. "Guy with the scruffy beard and the cute wife?"

Yousseff frowned. "They took their *kids*?"

Brackett stared at her a second, wanting to say something, but the words would not come to him. He had denied it to himself, pretended he was too pragmatic a man to harbor any romantic illusions, but now the truth was stripped bare inside him. He hadn't come to Acheron to steal another man's wife, but had he secretly hoped Anne would realize her mistake, and choose him at last? Put them back on the path they had once shared?

Damn fool that he was, yes he had.

He still loved her.

His decision—not to allow his marines to escort the survey teams—still felt like the right one. But he didn't like it, the thought of Anne and her family, sent out on their own. He could still picture little Newt, her mouth stained with cherry freeze-pop. If anything happened to her because he'd stuck to the rules, he wouldn't be able to forgive himself.

And how had he not known this? It had occurred to him that he hadn't seen Anne, or run into Newt or Tim in the halls—not in the past day or so. But he'd been so focused on getting his squad in line...

Just another reason to be pissed at Draper.

He worried not just because they'd been sent out alone, but because of the circumstances. If specific orders had come in, this wasn't anything routine.

"The order from the company," Brackett said, turning to Pettigrew again. "What did it say, exactly?"

"No idea, Captain," the private replied. "Sorry."

All five marines were watching him now, no doubt wondering why he seemed so troubled by this news. Brackett didn't care. His personal fears were not theirs to know.

"Draper."

"Yes, Captain?"

"For some reason, these friends of yours look up to you." Brackett stared into his eyes again, making it clear that there was no room for debate. "That means that I'm not only going to hold you responsible for your actions, but theirs as well. You've formed your own little tribe here, but you're not part of any tribe. You are a Colonial Marine. I leave it to you to decide whether or not you will begin to behave like one."

Brackett studied them all again.

"Dismissed."

The five of them filed out. He counted ten seconds after the last of them had gone, and then he rushed out into the corridor, shut the door behind him, and went in search of Al Simpson.

He needed answers.

And he couldn't get her out of his mind.

Anne.

DATE: 21 JUNE, 2179
TIME: 1122

When she was nine, back on Earth, Anne Jorden's brother Rick had persuaded her to swim with him in a pond in the dying woodland at the end of their street. The pond had a layer of rotting leaves on top, and a scummy surface tinted a sickly, unnatural green. Mosquitoes flitted across the surface, but never alighted for long.

Aside from the occasional eel they saw nothing else living in the water, certainly no fish. But Anne worked hard to keep up with Rick in those days, fought to be seen by him as his equal, though he was three years her elder. She knew how to throw a punch and climb a tree and fix a car, if the trouble wasn't too complex. And when Rick threw down the gauntlet on a dare, he could be certain his little sister would take him up on it... as long as he led the way.

Anne didn't need her brother to lead the way anymore, but as she stepped through the gash in the starship's hull, a shudder went through her, and she remembered that day at the pond with utter clarity. In only her underpants, she had walked into the water, the silt and muck squishing up between her toes and sucking at her feet. Wading in, she had felt the pond water slide over her skin in an oily, viscous caress. By the time the water was up to her waist, she felt filthier than she ever had in her life.

The interior of the ship reminded her of that pond. The air ought to have been dusty and dry, and the floor near the breach was piled with ash, but even through her heavy jacket she could feel a kind of cold, clinging, damp weight to the air.

"Do you feel that?" Russ asked, coming in behind her.

Anne glanced in either direction along the broad, tall corridor. The floors and walls were made of some otherworldly alloy, tubes like veins running along the ceiling and the innermost wall.

She switched off her helmet lamp to conserve its battery, gripped another light that was attached to her belt, and turned it on. Russ did the same. Streaks of some fluid had dried on the wall in several places. She reached out to touch the stain, but hesitated, then pulled her hand back.

"Yeah. I feel it." She looked to the right, staring along the tunnel. That direction would take them to the tip of the ship's horseshoe design—the one closest to the crawler—which suggested that the more significant finds would be to the left, in the bulk of the vessel.

Anne glanced at Russ.

"We should get out of here," she said, "call this in, and take the kids back to town."

Russ stared at her. His goggles had a mist of condensation on the inside. Even so, she saw the struggle in his eyes.

"We go back, and we'll never know what they really find out here," he said. "Honey, even our little cut of this find could set us up forever. Do you understand? But if we want to protect ourselves, keep the company from fucking us over, we've *gotta* know what it is we've found."

Anne's heart fluttered, but not with fear.

"Is that the only reason you want to go on?"

Russ grinned. "Hell, no. This is what we came out here for… something just like this! Do you want Mori or Reese or some company asshole to be the first one to see whatever there is to see?"

Nervous, afraid, but more thrilled than she'd ever been, she wetted her lips with her tongue.

"Hell, no," she echoed. "But we'll give it half an hour; no more. I don't want those kids waiting out there forever. I won't do that to them."

Her husband's eyes sparkled.

"Deal," he said.

This, she thought, *is why I married the man.*

She hefted her equipment and turned left, leading the way. The pond-scum feeling never went away. In fact, it increased as they trudged deeper into the derelict vessel. Her skin grew clammy and though the air felt cold, she felt flushed in a feverish sort of way. She would have thought she had fallen ill, except that Russ felt it, too.

Anne tried to keep her bearings, picturing the way the ship had sat on the ground, canted toward the back. It seemed hollow and dead, empty in a way that reminded her of an abandoned church she had entered once, as a girl. The small cemetery in the churchyard had been relocated, the bodies dug up and moved. The tabernacle had been taken out, along with several of the more elaborate stained-glass windows.

The place had felt haunted to her, not by ghosts, but by the absence of life… the architectural memory of voices raised in song and prayer, the echoes of footfalls on the stone floor, the clack of wooden kneelers, and the hope and surrender that always came with worship.

She'd never again felt such emptiness, until now.

Yet this was so much worse. The sense of the unknown, the breath of eons of alien culture slid around her, and she shivered with a dread she did not understand.

"It's just…"

"Extraordinary," Russ said.

"Ominous," Anne corrected. "I feel it in my bones, as if it's welcoming us and yet wants us gone, all at the same time."

"It's in your head," Russ said. "You're projecting. We can't even begin to imagine who the creatures were who built this—they must've been huge, though, far larger than any human. So your imagination tells you that we're intruders."

"We *are* intruders, Russell."

She could hear him laugh softly behind her.

"I don't see anyone sounding an alarm."

Anne flashed a smile, but it only lasted an instant. Her pulse kept racing, adrenaline singing through her.

"To your right," Russ said, voice tight. "Deep shadow. What's that?"

She twisted around and saw the shadowy cleft in the wall. Holding her breath, she edged nearer, and in the light from her belt she could make out an opening that was much larger than she'd thought. Floor to ceiling, it curved into the wall, a wide swath of shadow. Ducking her head into the cleft, she froze.

"Careful," Russ warned.

"It spirals down," she said.

"Their version of stairs?"

"Maybe. Definitely goes to another level, though." The spiral reminded her of the inside of an abandoned seashell, which underlined for her the strange bio-organic feel of the ship, as well as the emptiness that haunted her.

"Keep going. Clock's ticking," Russ reminded her.

Right, she thought. *Newt and Tim*. She had to get over the uneasiness that gripped her, and pick up the pace. Focused on her kids, Anne began to move faster, following her husband now.

"You sure we shouldn't have gone down there, to check out the sub-level?" she asked.

"Maybe, but I'm going to guess that whatever passes for a pilot's cabin is at the crux of the horseshoe. I could be wrong, but we don't have time to think too much about it. Whatever's down there, it'll be more than just corridors."

As he spoke, the ship's inner darkness seemed to deepen. Anne turned her head and shone her light on the wall, revealing scars in the strange metal. She stopped again.

"Anne," Russ prodded.

"Look at this," she said, staring at the pits and gashes in the wall. There were others on the floor. Something had melted right through, which made her stumble back and look up and around to make sure whatever had caused the melting hadn't continued to leak.

"Russ…" she said.

"Later," he told her as he passed by.

Anne fell in behind him again, but she kept her eyes on the walls and floor now, and she saw numerous places where similar scarring had occurred. Not just the melted spots, either. There were scorched holes blown in the wall, as if some sort of weapon had been fired. If not for the obvious age of the vessel, the way the dust and rock had eroded its hull and begun to swallow it, she would have begun to worry.

"Now this is weird," Russ said.

He clicked on one of the more powerful lights they'd brought in with them, hoping to take pictures to help establish their claim. The corridor lit up with a sickly yellow illumination and Anne gasped. The walls were different here. If the ship's construction seemed to hint at the organic, this was something else entirely. These walls were covered with a smooth, ribbed substance, black and gleaming like some mélange of insect cocoon and volcanic rock.

"What the hell is it?" she asked.

"You got me," Russ replied.

She ran one hand over the surface, grabbed a sharp ridge and applied pressure, snapping a small piece off in her hand. Chitinous and hard, its thinnest edges were brittle.

"Let's move on," she said, fascination guiding her. The clammy feeling had grown worse, but somehow she shrugged it off.

When they came to another open cleft, spiraling down to a sublevel, they stopped and stared at it for nearly a full minute. This cleft differed from the first. It, too, had been covered by that chitinous material, as if to adapt it for a different sort of species altogether.

"I don't like this," Anne said.

"Neither do I," Russ admitted. She could tell how hard it was for him to admit it. He sighed. "Look, let's just make it to the crux of the ship, to see if that's the engine room or pilot's cabin or whatever. We'll take footage of it, and then get the hell out of here. As long as we get that far, they can't shut us out entirely."

He started to walk away.

Anne stayed, staring down into that winding cleft.

"What—" Russ began.

"We go down," she said, not entirely certain why. "Whatever might be of value to the company—artifacts, technology, whatever— if it's down there, and we pass it by, we'll regret it forever." She turned and looked at him, letting him see a truth in her eyes that was painful to reveal. "I don't want to be here forever, Russ."

He shook his head with an incredulous laugh, put a gloved hand against his helmet. "Otto and I—"

"Were talking crazy," Anne said. "Abandoning the colony without a backup plan, with no exit strategy… that's foolish. But this… you're right. This could be it for us, the thing we've been searching for. The kids are out there waiting for us and they'll keep waiting. We've left them longer than this, and they know how to entertain each other. It's for their sake that we can't leave here without knowing what it is we've found."

Anne took one more look along the corridor, her light gleaming on the strange ridges and curves of the glassy black walls. A flash of connection sparked in her mind—cocoon to web to spider—and she shuddered at the inference. She didn't like the idea of them trapped inside some kind of spiderweb.

Not a web, she thought, frowning as she studied the walls again. *It's more like a hive. A wasps' nest.*

Either way, she didn't like it.

15

STRANGE CARGO

DATE: 21 JUNE, 2179
TIME: 1131

Brackett caught up with Simpson as he was coming out of the toilet, still in the process of cinching his belt. The man seemed to hear the heavy footfalls coming toward him, and he looked up, tensing immediately. He put his hands up as if he feared an assault.

"I've got a question for you," Brackett said, his voice firm.

"Whatever it is, maybe you'd better take a step back," Simpson said. Nervously, he smoothed his mustache and stood a bit straighter, trying to pretend he hadn't been afraid a moment before.

Brackett leaned in toward him, crowding the administrator so that he was the one who took a step back.

"You sent the Jordens out on a survey—"

"Which is none of your business, is it?" Simpson replied, trying to keep his voice level. "I mean, you made it pretty clear that, in your view, the Colonial Marines aren't to be involved with the Company's field work," he added, eyes narrowing.

"Their kids are, what, six and ten?"

Simpson shrugged. "Something like that."

Brackett tried to remind himself that he would be stationed on Acheron for years, and he had to be able to work with this man. But just the stale smell of Simpson's breath made him want to throw a punch.

"Look, Captain, I'm with you," the administrator continued. "I disapprove entirely of Russ and Anne bringing their kids out on this survey, but there are no rules against it. In fact, this is a wildcat job. Right now they're operating as independent contractors."

"Why now?" Brackett asked. "Why today?"

A pair of technicians hurried past them. They glanced uneasily at Simpson and Brackett, sensing the hostility there.

"It's really not your concern, Captain."

"You received specific orders. This isn't a routine grid search," Brackett said, and he saw the confirmation in Simpson's eyes. "Someone at Weyland-Yutani must have wanted that location surveyed immediately."

Simpson narrowed his eyes, a smirk appearing on his face.

"Presumably that's the case, Captain Brackett, but I'm not privy to the 'whys' in cases like this. Nobody tells me anything. If they *had* told me, however, you can be damned sure I wouldn't share it with you. It's company business, I'll remind you."

"And if something happens to the Jordens?" Brackett demanded. "To their kids?"

Simpson sneered. "Well, then it'll be a damn shame they didn't have any marines along to provide security."

He brushed past, and ambled back toward his office.

Brackett could only watch him go.

DATE: 21 JUNE, 2179
TIME: 1139

Anne led the way into the cleft, and she and Russ followed the spiral down into the lower level of the derelict ship.

Russ said nothing, but she could see from the way he held himself—the cock of his head and the slight hunch of his shoulders—that he felt the dark weight of the ship around him. Just as she did. Her heart beat faster and her breath turned shallow as they wound their way down, helmet lights throwing ghost shapes on the walls.

They found the first dead thing at the bottom of the spiral.

"Holy shit," Russ muttered.

Anne held her breath as she stepped into the corridor, staring at the thing in the juddering beam. She was trembling. In life, the alien had been very tall and powerfully built, with an extended torso and a long head. It seemed humanoid only in the sense that it had two arms and two legs, but otherwise it was entirely *other*. Something about it suggested an insect, which gave her an unnerving connection to her thoughts about the hard substance that coated the walls.

Yet this was no bug.

Its skin wasn't skin at all, but some kind of armored carapace. Richly blue in spots, it had faded to gray in most places, and the carapace looked to have gone thin and brittle. She felt sure the thicker, darker shell was closer to its living appearance. Its tail wound behind it, sharp and skeletal, with a tip that would have made a wicked weapon. Not quite a stinger, Anne thought, but if the alien used it that way it would have killed a person just as quickly.

"It's beautiful," Russ said.

Anne turned to stare at him in disgust.

"What?"

"Look at it," he said. "It's like nothing *anyone* has ever seen. Until now."

"It's horrible," she said quietly, staring at the blue-tinted jaws and the tail. "This thing was born to kill."

"It's been dead for a very long time," Russ said. "But I'll tell you what it was born for… to make us rich."

He gave a quiet laugh and turned away, moving down the sub-level corridor. Anne stared another moment at the dead alien, and then followed. Russ might be right, and she knew this thing couldn't harm her—its cadaver was little more than a shell, not unlike the derelict spacecraft they were exploring. But she couldn't escape the feeling of its presence. When she had first entered the ship, she had been sure its halls were as empty as that abandoned church. Now every shadow felt full of menace, of teeth and slithering, sharp-tipped tails.

The sub-level had been completely taken over by the chitinous walls she'd seen above, but still there were many spots where something had melted through, sprayed and burned its way into the floors and walls. They walked through the darkness, lighting their own way, and at a curve in the hallway they found three more of them.

One had been torn in half, its desiccated corpse a dried and twisted thing, half on one side of the hall and half on the other. Another had an enormous hole through its mid-section, and the floor beneath it had been melted away into a yawning chasm. A draft swept in from there, but whether from outside or from elsewhere in the ship, they could not tell.

There were doors all along the corridor. Some of them opened easily, while others were stuck shut by that strange, hardened, resin-like substance. The first two that Russ opened contained nothing more than dust and small, strange bones. In the next there were thick metal alloy shelves with mounds that were now rot. It was impossible to know what they had been before rotting.

"Cargo, do you think?" Anne asked.

"Of some kind," Russ agreed. "Food or some other materials. Those first two rooms were pens, though. Like stables. Alien livestock or something else... Whatever they were, these creatures were taking them somewhere."

That didn't sound right to Anne. Didn't feel right.

"I don't think so," she said. "Not the things we saw back there."

"What do you mean?"

"Whatever those creatures were, they weren't the ones piloting this ship."

He nodded, but didn't respond.

They continued on, discovering other massive alien corpses in clusters of three or four, perhaps twenty in all. Several minutes later, maneuvering through the claustrophobic underbelly of the ship, they encountered something altogether different. New remains.

Anne froze. Now she understood why the corridors were so high and so wide. They hadn't been built this size for the sake of grandeur, but simply for scale. The remains of this new creature were more humanoid than the first, but even larger than the others—nine feet, Anne guessed. All that remained of its body was its skeleton—bones inside some kind of exo-suit of the same design as the ship, with the same techno-organic texture.

This dead thing had been one of the ship's crew. She knew it.

"Where are the others?" she asked.

"Others?" Russ said. "You think there are other species here?"

"No, no... others like this one. Where's the rest of the crew?"

Russ had no answer.

"How long have we been gone from the crawler?" she asked.

"Dunno," he said, checking his watch. "Thirty-five minutes? Not more than that, I don't think."

Taking a deep breath, she reached out and took his hand, not liking the fact that their gloves kept their skin from touching.

"All right. Let's get some images of this guy and the others, and then we get out of here. Five minutes more," she said.

Russ agreed. They worked mostly in silence, both of them uneasy. Anne felt disappointed in herself—in both of them. By all rights they ought to have been ecstatic. He had been right. This was going to change their lives. Their share of whatever the company made from this salvage—from the ship and its tech, from the alien corpses and whatever Weyland-Yutani might learn from them—meant they would never have to work again. They should have been weeping with joy, screaming in celebration. Instead, Anne felt like she couldn't breathe, felt the weight of the air inside the ship as if it might suffocate her. She just wanted out, and judging from his silence, she knew that Russ felt the same.

It took them ten minutes. When they'd finished in the sub-level, they lugged their gear back up the spiral, then paused together and looked along the corridor toward the crux of the ship. Both of them. They had been married so long, knew each other so well, that no words were necessary for a decision to be made.

"This close," Russ said. "Five minutes or less, we'll be at the crux. See what there is to see. A few images, and we're back outside in fifteen, twenty minutes at most. The kids are probably napping by now."

"I'm sure it's been more than an hour," Anne told him. But Russ knew that it wasn't an argument. They both glanced back the way they'd come, toward the breach in the hull that would be their exit, and then he hefted his gear onto one shoulder and took her hand.

Together they walked toward the crux.

Around the next corner they discovered one of each of the two alien species, locked in a terrible embrace. This bug-like creature was different from its brethren. It was larger, and had a large, ridged plate on its bright blue head that seemed to be a kind of crest.

"What the hell happened here?" Russ muttered.

"War," Anne said. "The question is, where did the bugs come from? Were they on the ship, in the cargo hold, or were they already here on Acheron, and attacked the ship after the crash?"

"And what about this one?" Russ asked. "Why is it so different?"

Anne studied the deadly embrace again, studied that blue crest, and frowned.

"It's a queen."

"What, you mean like with bees?"

"Doesn't this all remind you of a hive?" She gestured at the crusted walls. "Maybe the others are like drones, and this one is like a queen." She shrugged. "Or maybe that crest on its head just makes me think of a crown."

The alien she thought of as a queen had impaled the crewman with its tail, but the crewman had given as good as he'd gotten. He'd thrust his left arm up inside the queen's jaws, as if he had tried to destroy its brain with a bare hand.

"Come on," Russ said. "Let's finish this up. I don't want to be here anymore."

They walked on.

Minutes later, they found a vast chamber where many of the crew must once have been able to gather. The dome curved high overhead, and it was crusted with the same chitin they had seen elsewhere.

"This is just creepy as hell," Russ said. "I feel like I can't breathe."

Anne could only nod.

There was a platform at the front of the chamber. On it stood a massive seat and some kind of gigantic apparatus that she felt sure must have been used to navigate the ship. In the seat was another of the crew, though this one wore a helmet that covered its entire head.

"The pilot, do you think?" Russ asked as they climbed up to investigate.

"Or the navigator."

"Look at its chest," Russ whispered, and she could practically feel his breath at her ear. But Anne had already seen the twisted, mummified bones jutting out of its exo-suit, and the hole behind its ribs.

"That's how they killed him," Russ said. "Must have used a weapon, or maybe one of their tails, like in the corridor back there."

"I don't think so," Anne whispered. She'd seen the way the bones twisted outward. Whatever had killed the giant had come from inside.

She stumbled back from it, nearly slipping off the edge of the platform. Catching herself, she grabbed the side of the navigator's chair and turned to face the back of the cavernous chamber. When they had come in, the platform had been the first thing their lights had illuminated. It had drawn them to it immediately.

Now she saw something else.

Many other somethings.

"Russell," she said quietly. A disquieting feeling came over her, not quite excitement and not quite fear. "Look at this."

Her light played over a low blanket of mist that hung just below the level of the platform. As she looked, she saw that the vapor itself seemed to have some small luminescence of its own. Below it, spread out all around the platform in a recessed area of the chamber floor, were dozens of large pods, each perhaps a foot or eighteen inches high. They were oval, somewhat egg-shaped, though there was something almost floral about the tops of the things. Ugly flowers that would never blossom.

Never, of course, because they had been here for eons.

"The mist…" Russ began.

"It's weirdly humid in here," Anne said. "Maybe the ship is drawing in moisture from the outside, and holding it in this chamber."

"What are they, Annie?" he asked, staring at the pods. "More cargo?"

Anne shone her light around and studied the chamber. A cargo space? It might have been, she supposed. She set her gear on the platform and moved down toward the objects.

"Should we bring one back?" she asked, pushing off from the edge of the platform and sliding down below the upper edge of the fog.

The pods appeared to have a leathery texture, yet they still reminded Anne of flowers yet to bloom. She frowned as she dropped to one knee, and studied the nearest one.

"Are they… pulsing?" Russ asked from behind her.

"I think so," Anne replied. A smile spread across her lips. It wasn't possible for them to be pulsing, of course, because that suggested that life remained in these pods, whatever they were. Centuries or millennia after the ship had crashed and the bloody battle that had killed so many on board, these strangely cool hothouse mists seemed to have kept these pods in some kind of hibernation state.

She reached for the nearest one, her fingers hovering only a foot away.

"Wait," Russ said. "We don't know what they are."

Anne turned to smile at him.

"If the surface is toxic, it won't get through my gloves."

"Let's just set up the camera, take some images, and Simpson can worry about them," Russ urged.

"Now where's *your* sense of adventure?" she asked.

She saw her husband's eyes widen at the same time as she heard a wet, sticky, peeling noise from behind her. Russ grabbed her arm and hauled her toward him.

"Get back!" he snapped.

Anne lost her balance and slumped against the edge of the platform. Beyond Russ, she saw the pod opening, strings of mucous hanging from the four petal-like flaps as it split apart. Something shifted and jerked inside the object.

"Russell…" she said, suddenly afraid.

"It's all right," he told her, glancing over at the pod.

The thing within launched itself at him, latched onto his face, and he tried to scream. The sound became a horrible gagging as he stumbled back into her. Anne cried out his name as she shoved and dragged and urged him up onto the platform. Only there did she see the back of the hideous spider-thing that had attached itself to him.

It's all right, he had said. But it was not all right. Nor would it ever be all right again.

16

BE CAREFUL WHAT
YOU WISH FOR

DATE: 21 JUNE, 2179
TIME: 1207

Upside down on the driver's seat of the crawler, Newt hummed softly to herself. It hurt her neck a bit, putting the weight on her shoulders and the back of her head, but she pushed her feet toward the vehicle's roof, extending her toes, trying to see if she could touch.

"Rebecca, sit normal," Tim instructed.

"This isn't normal?"

"You're upside down."

"Maybe *you're* upside down."

Her brother reached up and whapped her legs. She scrabbled for purchase but went over like a falling tree, tumbling in between the front seats. Her limbs flailed and she felt her right foot kick her brother's thigh. When he called out in protest, she kept flailing a bit longer and kicked him again, smiling to herself.

"Rebecca!" he snapped angrily.

She sat on the crawler's floor between the seats and gave him an exasperated look.

"Why do you always call me that?"

"It's your name," he answered. "And don't kick me."

"You pushed me over. I was falling. And I *don't* like that name."

Tim sighed and shoved himself deeper into his seat. He'd been drawing before, but put his pad aside fifteen or twenty minutes ago.

"Maybe I like being upside down," she muttered, pouting her lips.

"What?" he asked, glaring at her.

"I like being upside down."

He rolled his eyes. "Fine. Just do it in the other seat. I'm going to take a nap."

Newt raised her eyebrows and edged closer to him.

"Wow. You must *really* be bored."

Tim glanced at her. "Aren't you? They take us all the way out here, but then they don't let us do anything. What's the point?"

"I'm not bored," she asserted.

He sat up straighter, scratching at a blemish on his cheek.

"You're telling me you wouldn't rather be back at the colony, playing Monster Maze with Lizzie and Aaron and Kembrell?"

Newt scoffed and blew a lock of her hair away from her eyes. "Sure, that would be more fun than this. But Mom and Dad are here, and so it's okay to be here with them. It's an adventure, remember?"

Tim leaned toward her, cocking his head and studying her as if she were some kind of weird insect.

"Yeah, but it's *their* adventure," he said. "We're just sitting here."

"Maybe you are," Newt said, crawling back into the front seat. "*I'm* thinking."

Shifting around, she put her legs in the air again, propped on her neck and shoulders, and reached for the ceiling with her toes.

"Yeah? What are you thinking, then?"

Newt's stomach gave a little uneasy flutter and she shivered.

"I'm thinking Mom and Dad have been gone an awfully long time."

DATE: 21 JUNE, 2179
TIME: 1229

Brackett skipped lunch in the dining hall, heated himself a bowl of soup, and then turned to exercise to try to sweat out the worry that was gnawing at him. Two hundred sit-ups, two hundred pushups, and countless squats didn't do the job, so he switched to the pull-up bar his predecessor had installed over the bathroom door. Biceps burning, he drew himself up and lowered himself down, steady and in control of his pace.

His frustration began to leech away as his thoughts blurred with the effort. For the first time in well over an hour, he didn't feel the urge to check the clock on the wall, to count the minutes since the colony's last contact from the Jordens.

Sweat beaded and ran down the middle of his back. His heart thudded in his ears while he tried to remember how many reps he'd done, and decide if he ought to do more. The answer was easy enough—if he stopped now, he'd only go back to watching the time.

Whatever happens, it's not your fault, Brackett told himself, taking hold of the bar again. An image of Newt flickered into his thoughts. Newt, her mouth stained from that freeze-pop, those big eyes so earnest and wise beyond her years.

He hauled himself up again, pull-up after pull-up, trying to blot that image from his mind. It proved just as difficult as his attempts to forget Anne over the years. His life had gone on, and he'd been happy enough. Content enough. He'd thought that he would go the rest of his life without ever seeing her again, and decided that he could live with that.

For a brief period he'd been in love with a pilot named Tyra, but that had all unraveled, partly because of the demands of their careers and partly because each of them had experienced greater love before, and knew that what they had wasn't enough.

Then came his assignment to Acheron. Part of him wished he'd never been posted here. *River of pain,* he thought, remembering the mythological origins of the name. As far as Brackett was concerned, they had chosen it well.

Someone knocked at his door. He dropped down from the bar and grabbed his towel, wiping sweat from his face.

"It's open!" he called. The door swung inward and Julisa Paris stepped inside, straight-backed and formal.

"Captain," she said, by way of greeting.

"You have something for me, Lieutenant?"

"Sorry to say I don't, sir."

Brackett felt an uneasy tremor travel down his spine.

"So the Jordens haven't checked in?"

"That's what I'm told," Paris confirmed, her eyes grim. "As far as I can tell, Simpson hasn't even tried to reach them. He's playing it off as if it's no big deal, and maybe it isn't, but the shift supervisor I spoke to said people are getting jittery."

Brackett cursed under his breath.

"What do you want to do, Captain?" she asked.

"Nothing yet. But be ready. I stood on principle with this matter, and I'll look like an idiot if I throw those principles out the window. But if that family's in trouble, I don't plan to leave them out there. Thirty minutes, Lieutenant. If the Jordens haven't checked in by then, we're going out."

Paris saluted. "Yes, sir."

She turned on her heel and departed. Brackett closed the door behind her.

Where are you, Anne? he thought, as he hurried to the shower. He wanted to be suited up and ready to go if it came to that. The delay in reporting in could have been due to a communications malfunction, or they might be lost in the excitement of discovery. But a dreadful certainty had begun to form in his gut.

Call in, damn it, he thought. *Prove me wrong.*

DATE: 21 JUNE, 2179
TIME: 1256

Newt sat in the driver's seat, hugging herself.

The crawler's lights had gone on as it grew darker outside. The wind had picked up and it blew against the vehicle hard enough to rattle the windows. Though the heat ran, Newt still felt cold seeping in from outside, and she started to wonder how long the lights and the heat would work. Would the crawler run out of power? Her mom and dad wouldn't leave them here long enough for that to happen, would they?

Not on purpose, she thought.

For the first time, she grew truly worried.

The wind howled even harder as she glanced over at her brother, who had curled up in the passenger seat and fallen asleep at least half an hour before. She wanted to wake him, just so she wouldn't feel so alone, but he would only be nasty to her. Most of the time, Tim was a good big brother. They got along well and they played together and they laughed a lot, but when he was tired or nervous he could be short with her, even mean.

Newt didn't think she could handle him being unkind to her right now.

She sat staring out the window at the huge, curving spaceship. In the swirling dust and the gloom it was hard to get a clear view, but when there was a lull in the wind she could see it all right. The ship seemed quiet now, making it hard to imagine that anyone was alive inside it—walking around, having a Jorden family adventure.

She shifted in her seat, turning away from her view of the big , dark ship. It troubled her now just to think of it, silent and empty. She shifted again, and the wind whipped against the crawler so hard it felt like giant hands were giving the vehicle a shove.

She trembled and wetted her dry lips with her tongue. Tentatively, she reached out and nudged her brother. Tim grumbled and turned away, burrowing into the seat, trying to find a comfortable position.

"Tim," she whispered, shaking him a bit harder. "Timmy, wake up."

She hadn't called him Timmy since she was very little. He didn't like it, now that they were growing up, but at that moment she felt very small. Felt little again.

"Timmy," she said again, and he turned sleepily toward her, eyes opening.

"What?" he groaned.

"They've been gone a long time," she said.

For a second she thought he would snap at her, demand that she let him sleep. Then he sat up a bit straighter, and looked out through the windshield at the darkened landscape, listening to the wind. Nothing so far had scared her as much as the uncertainty she saw in her brother's eyes.

Tim looked afraid.

"It'll be okay, Newt," he said. "Dad knows what he's doing."

Suddenly she couldn't breathe. Tim never called her Newt. Why had he called her that now if not to comfort her, to try to make her less afraid?

Suddenly the door beside her whipped open, crashing against the crawler. Newt screamed as the wind roared in and she twisted just as a dark shape lunged in at her. Shrieking, she pulled back from the shape, her heart about to explode. Then she saw the face and with a shock realized it was her mother, panicked and looking so wild that Newt continued to scream.

Tim's shouts joined with her own as their mom reached inside and grabbed the handheld radio that was tethered to the dash.

"Mayday! Mayday!" her mother called into the radio, shouting over the wind. "This is alpha kilo two four nine calling Hadley Control. Repeat! This is—"

Newt looked past her mother and saw that she wasn't alone, that her father was there, too, but something was wrong with him. He lay sprawled on the ground outside the door and in the light from the crawler she could see there was something on his face. Some kind of disgusting thing that looked like a spider, its many legs like bony fingers, its body pulsing with hideous life.

Her screams turned to shrieks as her eyes went wide. She screamed again and again, her voice merging with the howling wind, so that it seemed as if all of Acheron screamed along with her.

DATE: 21 JUNE, 2179
TIME: 1257

Brackett strode toward the command block, full of grim purpose. Pride and principle had to be cast aside now. Too much time had passed. The Jordens had to be in trouble.

Lt. Paris walked beside him, perfectly in synch. Proving her wisdom, she hadn't said a word to him about the fact that it had been his decision—his desire to shake things up—that had led to the Jordens being sent out without an escort.

Simpson wouldn't have the lieutenant's discretion.

"You informed Sergeant Coughlin—"

"To gather a team, yes, sir," Paris finished for him. "Aldo will drive. We'll take Hauer and Chenovski—"

"Not 'we,'" Brackett interrupted. "I want you here. Anything goes wrong, I don't want Draper trying to call the shots."

"Yes, sir," she replied. "Only…"

"Only what?" he asked as they rounded a corner. From up ahead they could hear the sound of voices and the beeping of machines.

"It's you who should stay behind, Captain Brackett," she said firmly. "Sorry, sir, but you're the CO here. I'm your junior officer. If there's any risk involved—and we must assume that, until we learn otherwise—it ought to be me who goes."

Brackett didn't look at her.

"Except that you're right, Julisa," he replied. "I'm the CO, so it's my call."

They marched half a dozen steps before she replied.

"Yes, sir."

Simpson emerged from the command block before they'd even reached the door, one of his techs trailing behind him. They were in conversation, both looking deeply troubled, when the administrator glanced up and saw the marines approaching. Brackett knew instantly from his expression that something had occurred, and it wasn't good.

"Captain Brackett," Simpson said, concern turning to a sneer. "I hope you're happy now."

Lt. Paris swore. "You may want to rethink your approach right now, mister."

Brackett held up a hand.

"Stop," he said, glaring at the bureaucrat, who seemed scared even as he puffed himself up with arrogance and disdain. "Tell it fast, Simpson. What's happened?"

Simpson actually glanced around to make sure no one else was within hearing range.

"They found a derelict spacecraft," he said. "Ancient, according to Anne Jorden—"

Anne's all right, Brackett thought.

"—but even so, there was something on board. Some kind of leech, if I understood correctly. Hard to get a clear line with the constant atmospheric disturbance. Russ needs medical attention, and immediately."

"Shit," Brackett muttered. "What about the kids?"

"Okay, for now," Simpson said. "I'm getting a rescue together. Techs and volunteers."

"Forget it," Brackett said quickly. "We've got this. Sergeant Coughlin is gathering a team now. If you hadn't heard from them, we were going out anyway."

Simpson hitched up his belt.

"Oh, you mean it's not too much trouble?" he said. "We don't want to break protocol, after all. Don't want to put you out, Captain."

Brackett ground his teeth together, then took a step forward and poked a finger into the man's chest.

"Later, you and I are going to have a talk about how you could be *stupid* enough to get an order like the one you got from the company— an order that clearly implied a discovery of great importance—and still let Anne and Russ Jorden take their children with them."

He poked Simpson again.

"Until then," he said, "you can go fuck yourself."

DATE: 22 JUNE, 2179
TIME: 0402

Anne sat in the front seat of the crawler with an arm around each of her children. She had stripped off her jacket as if it had been tainted, somehow, by the vile mist surrounding the pods inside that ship. Sixteen hours after she'd dragged Russ back to the crawler, her ears still rang from Newt's screaming. It had taken forever for the girl to calm down, but she and Tim had finally fallen asleep.

Calmed down? Anne thought to herself. *She's not calm—she's in shock. And so are you, for that matter.*

She hadn't slept a wink. How could she?

Tim rustled in the back seat, coming blearily awake.

"Mom, why are we still here?" He sat up and rubbed his eyes, glancing out through the window at the darkness. "We need to get Dad back to the colony. Dr. Komiskey will help him."

"She *will* be able to help, right?" he added.

Anne kept silent. The words had woken Newt from a restless sleep, and now the little girl looked up. Her lips quivered, and then she buried her face in her mother's chest and began to cry again, a ragged, gasping sob that came and went in waves.

The wind shrieked around the crawler and the door banged because Anne hadn't closed it tightly enough. She shifted forward to look out the window on that side. In the glow of the vehicle's lights she could see the dust sweeping over Russ's still form. His goggles and jacket would protect him from the worst of it, but she'd tucked a blanket under his shoulders and used it to partially cover his face. It flapped in the wind, but so far it hadn't just blown away, and that was good.

Good, because it might keep him from suffocating, if the abomination hugging his face hadn't already done the job. Good, also, because it kept the kids from seeing clearly just what had happened to their father.

"Mom," Tim begged, "it's been too long! We need to just take Dad back ourselves!"

"We can't do that," she said.

"What are we waiting for?" Tim asked, his emotions fraying just as much as hers.

Anne glanced at Newt. She didn't want to have this conversation with Tim, and she sure as hell didn't want to have it with her six-year-old daughter beside her. Newt seemed to be barely listening, though. Even in the midst of her own shock and horror, Anne felt her heart breaking over her daughter's trauma.

You'd better be all right, Russell, she thought furiously. *You* have *to be.*

"It took all my strength to get him out here to the crawler, Tim," she said quietly, nuzzling her son's ear, hoping that Newt wouldn't hear her. "But even if I could get him inside, I wouldn't. And he wouldn't want me to."

"What are you *talking* about?" Tim cried. "He's... you saw him... he needs—"

"Tim!" she snapped, and instantly she regretted it.

Her son stared into her eyes, searching them for an answer.

"I can't have him in here with you and your sister," Anne said, hating the tremor in her voice and the hot tears that began to spill down her cheeks. She swiped at them angrily. "Whatever happens to your father, he would never forgive me if I did that. I don't know anything about that thing on his face—what it's doing to him, or what it might do to you and Newt if I brought it in here with you."

Newt shuddered and mumbled something into her chest, words muffled by Anne's shirt.

"What's that, honey?" Anne asked, glancing again out the window.

"So we have to wait," Newt repeated. Eyes red and puffy, she put on her brave face. "Daddy's going to be okay."

"Okay?" Tim asked. "Did you see that *thing*?"

Newt's breath hitched.

"I saw it before you did. But I also saw Dad when Mom was putting that blanket on him, and his chest was moving up and down. He's breathing, and as long as he's breathing, he's gonna be okay."

Anne smiled wanly at her, hating the screaming of the wind and the rattle of the door, but loving her children with all her heart.

"Of course he is," she said, with a confidence she did not feel. She kissed Newt's cheek, then turned and kissed Tim on the forehead. "Of course he is."

They sat wordlessly, and she clutched them to her.

"Do you hear that?" Tim asked.

Anne stiffened, listening hard for any sound from Russ or the creature. Then she heard the roar of an engine and her heart leapt. Newt sat up on the seat, facing backward, and headlights washed over her face. Anne whipped around to look out the back window, and saw the lights growing brighter.

Seconds later a heavy-crawler roared up beside them.

Demian Brackett was the first one out onto the ground.

Newt threw her door open, hopped out and ran to him, jumping up into his arms. Brackett staggered back a step but caught her, hugging her tightly. Over Newt's shoulder, he stared at Anne with those strong, reassuring eyes.

"Move it!" Brackett shouted as other marines climbed out of their crawler. He glanced over at Russ, the blanket still flapping over his face like some terrible shroud. "Get him aboard now!"

Anne stared at Russ as the marines went to him, watched the horror on their faces as they got their first glimpses of the thing attached to his face. A cold wave of nausea swept through her as she forced herself not to look at it, not to think about what it might have done to him.

"Sergeant Coughlin!" Brackett shouted over the wind. "Drive the Jordens' crawler back! Hauer, go with them!"

"No!" Newt cried, still in his arms. "You take us! Please!"

Brackett hesitated, cocking his head back to look into Newt's eyes. As the other marines put Russ on a stretcher and lifted him off the ground, Brackett nodded toward Coughlin and carried Newt toward her mother.

"All right," he said, handing Newt up into the crawler. He gave Anne a single nod. "Let's get you all home."

17

NOTHING ALIVE

DATE: 22 JUNE, 2179
TIME: 2101

Newt climbed out of the crawler and stood between her mother and Tim, watching numbly as the marines drove their larger vehicle into the underground garage behind them.

After so long with the wind and the scouring grit, it seemed strangely quiet in the garage... except of course that it wasn't quiet at all. Techs shouted to one another and a handful of colonists rushed over to talk to Newt's mother. Jiro, the botanist, wanted to know what had happened to Russ. Mrs. Hernandez, who had babysat for Newt and Tim many times, asked Newt's mom if they were all right. Then the nurse, Joel Asher, nudged past them.

"Give them room to breathe," Joel said, focusing on Newt's mother. "Anne, are you all right? Can you talk to me?"

Newt glanced up and saw that her mother didn't seem to have even heard Joel. Instead, she was staring at the marines' crawler as the driver, Aldo, and one of the others climbed up the ramp and into the rear of the vehicle.

"Mom," Newt said, taking her hand. She squeezed. "Joel's talking to you."

Anne blinked, and focused on Joel.

"Just look after Russ," she said. "The rest of us are fine."

"I need to check you all out," the nurse insisted.

"Not now. Just take care of my husband."

"Anne—"

"Not now!"

Capt. Brackett came around the front of the crawler, his eyes sad but kind. He held up a hand to the nurse.

"Please, just do as she asks. Worry about Russ for now," Brackett said, glancing at Newt and then Tim. "I'll make sure these guys come to the medical unit as soon as possible, but they're really fine. You want to make them okay, you need to take care of their father. That's what they need."

The nurse seemed about to argue when they all heard a commotion and looked up to see Aldo and Chenovski carrying Newt's father down out of the heavy-crawler on a stretcher. A ripple of fear went through the garage, and some of the people there recoiled in horror and revulsion from what they saw.

Newt's mother started toward the stretcher, but Brackett caught her by the shoulder.

"You want them to help him," Brackett said. "Let them do their jobs."

She brushed his hand away.

"He needs me."

"Anne," Brackett said, and something about his tone made her turn toward him. "He needs doctors. He needs the science team. You just said you and the kids can look after yourselves, and you're going to have to do that."

Newt watched her mother's face, saw the frustration and grief and even anger there, and she felt her own eyes begin to burn with fresh tears. It upset her—she thought she had been done with crying.

The marines paused at the bottom of the ramp, both of them staring at the multi-legged creature latched on to Russ's face.

"What is it?" Chenovski asked.

Aldo grunted. Newt had heard him talking many times about his past experiences. She thought of him as the bravest of the marines, but she saw the fear in him, and it worried her.

"Let's get it off him first, and then we'll figure out what it is," Aldo said. He glanced at Capt. Brackett when he said it, and a troubled look passed between them.

Newt took the captain's hand, gazing up at him.

"Help my dad."

Brackett went down on one knee beside her. They had ridden all the way back to the colony without any of them saying much, except for Newt's mom comforting her and Tim. Capt. Brackett had spoken kindly to all three of them, but she couldn't remember the words now—only the soothing tone. Mostly he had just *been there*, strong and sure that he could help them.

"I'll do everything I can," he said.

Joel, the nurse, laid a hand on the top of Newt's head.

"We all will."

They stood together and watched the marines carrying the stretcher toward the elevator. A door opened at the far end of the garage, and Dr. Reese came hurrying in with Dr. Mori and two of their researchers. Mr. Lydecker, from administration, strode in behind them. The group pushed past the colonists who had gathered in the garage, and raced to catch up with the marines carrying the stretcher.

Dr. Reese made Aldo and Chenovski stop a few feet from the elevator. He stood staring at Newt's father. Everyone there in the garage had seen the creature attached to his face by now, and all of them had turned away, some twisting their faces in disgust. Dr. Reese was the first person to see the nasty bug-thing with its long spindly legs—to see the way it had clamped onto Russ Jorden—and *smile*.

Lt. Paris walked over toward Brackett, glancing uneasily at Newt and her mother and brother.

"Why is he smiling?" Newt asked, a terrible, sour anger churning in her belly. "Is he happy this happened?"

"Of course not," Lt. Paris said, ruffling Newt's hair. "Dr. Reese is a scientist, honey. This is something he's never seen before. He may be excited about discovering something new, but I'm sure he's just as worried about your father as the rest of us are."

Tim snorted. "Bullshit."

Newt felt sure her mother would punish him for it, but she didn't correct him at all. Maybe she agreed. Or maybe she was just happy that Tim had spoken at all, since he had been so quiet on the ride back.

"Some people smile or laugh when they're nervous," Brackett added.

"I do that sometimes!" Newt said, squeezing her mother's hand, turning to look up into her face.

"He doesn't look nervous," Tim said.

"But he should be," their mother whispered, her eyes wide.

The captain patted Tim on the shoulder, then turned and picked Newt up off the ground as if she weighed nothing at all. Tired and sad as she was, she did not argue with him.

"Come on," he said. "Let's get you all back to your quarters so you can clean up."

Newt's mother nodded, and together they started across the garage toward the far door that Reese and Mori and the others had just come through. Mrs. Hernandez and a wildcatter named Gruenwald walked along with them, but the others hung back and just watched them. It made Newt feel bad to have these people she had known her whole life staring at them as if they were putting on some kind of show, when the only show was her family being scared.

"Simpson's going to be waiting for you upstairs, I'm sure," Brackett said. "He'll have to debrief you about what happened out there, what you saw—"

"I don't know if I can talk about it," Newt's mother said as they walked to the door, their footfalls echoing across the garage.

The captain reached out and squeezed her hand, holding it for only a second.

"You have to, and not just for the sake of the colony and any danger we might be in," he said. "Every detail you remember is another piece of information that might help them help Russ."

"Mom?" Tim said worriedly.

"Okay," Anne said, nodding. "Okay."

"I'll stay with you for the debrief," Brackett went on, "but you should ask a friend to run interference for you afterward, be the gatekeeper, so you don't have to talk to anyone you don't want to talk to."

"Can't you do it?" Newt asked.

Capt. Brackett hefted her a bit higher on his hip and met her eyes.

"I'm sorry, Newt. We're all going to have a lot to do now. That ship out there changes everything for the colony. My squad needs to be prepared for anything, and we need to provide security for the people Dr. Reese and Mr. Simpson are going to send out there, to figure out where it's from and to learn whatever they can about the aliens who built it."

"No!" Newt's mother said, suddenly fearful. "They can't! There are more of those things. A lot more!"

Newt stared at her. A fear she thought she'd beaten appeared in her belly. An image filled her mind of hundreds of those spider things, sneaking around the colony at night, trying to latch onto her face while she slept.

She hugged Brackett tightly.

"How many, Mom?" Tim asked fearfully.

"Did you run into anything else?" Brackett asked. "Larger creatures? Anything that looked more formidable?"

"Nothing alive," Newt's mother said.

Capt. Brackett glanced over at Gruenwald and Mrs. Hernandez, who were walking with Lt. Paris. All of them were paying close attention.

"We'll continue this with Simpson," he said. "Meanwhile, nobody's going to do anything stupid. Precautions will be taken."

Newt watched her mother thinking, saw her nod.

"Okay," Anne said.

"Lieutenant Paris," Brackett said, "post Coughlin and Yousseff outside wherever they're taking Mr. Jorden. Tell Dr. Reese I'm going to want to speak with him as soon as Anne and I are done with Simpson. Then send Draper and two other marines out to the site to stand sentry. Nobody enters that ship without authorization from whoever ends up with operational control of this fiasco."

"Yes, sir."

Newt felt a little safer. The captain's voice—his confidence and determination—reassured her a little bit. She could even believe that her father was going to be all right, if she didn't think about it too much.

She hugged the captain even tighter.

"Thank you," she whispered into his ear.

Then they were through the door and headed up the metal stairs, boots clanking on every step, and they had all run out of words again.

18

DARK TURNS

DATE: 23 JUNE, 2179
TIME: 1637

Nearly twenty-four hours after she and her family had returned to Hadley's Hope, Newt lay in bed, legs curled up beneath her.

Mrs. Hernandez had come in the middle of the day to look after her and Tim, and had made them a vegetable stir-fry. She explained that their mother did not want them to leave the family quarters.

Even at six, Newt understood that her mom didn't want her overhearing other people talking about what had happened to her dad, or about whatever the scientists and marines might have discovered out at that crashed spaceship. Another day, she would have been angry about being left out. But today she was too distracted by her fears for her father.

The night before, she'd had a terrible time getting to sleep. The memory of her own screams kept ringing in her head, and every time she closed her eyes, she saw the pulsing sacs on the body of the alien creature attached to her father's face. When she'd finally fallen asleep she had slept for ten straight hours without dreaming at all.

Waking, she'd been relieved that she hadn't had any nightmares… and then she'd remembered the day before, and thought about her father in the medical lab. That was when she realized that the real nightmare had been waiting for her to wake up.

Throughout the day, she'd tried to read and tried to nap. She'd tried to eat, too, but could only manage little nibbles. Tim had been sketching, but when she'd asked him what he was drawing, he told her she didn't want to know. Didn't want to see. So she knew exactly what it was he'd been drawing—the same thing she saw when she closed her eyes.

Mrs. Hernandez fussed over them, made sure they ate, but Newt didn't want to talk to anyone, so she retreated to her bedroom as soon as she'd cleared her dinner plate.

"Ssshhh," she whispered, clutching her doll, Casey, to her chest. She kissed the doll's head. "Daddy's going to be okay. Try not to be afraid."

Newt had been giving Casey that advice all day, but her dolly didn't seem inclined to take it. She couldn't make the fear go away, and neither could Newt.

"Just be brave," she whispered.

She exhaled and held Casey even more tightly. That seemed to work. Being brave wasn't the same as not being afraid. Her mom had told her that more than once. Being brave meant you faced your fears, and Newt silently promised herself she would do that, no matter what.

"You and me, Casey," she said. "We're gonna be brave."

She frowned. Had she heard a sound, out in the family room? A thump, maybe. Or a knock. Her pulse quickened and she burrowed deeper under her covers. Then she remembered what she had just told Casey. For a moment she held her breath, then she threw back her covers.

Holding onto Casey, she tiptoed to her bedroom door.

Before she could reach it, the door swung inward. Newt cried out and jumped back, clenching her right fist—ready to fight. Then Tim poked his head into her room. She hissed through her teeth and started toward him, figuring he deserved a punch in the nose just as much as any monster that might've come after her.

"Quiet," Tim whispered, putting a finger to his lips to shush her. He moved into her room, glancing nervously over his shoulder. "Mrs. Hernandez fell asleep in her chair, and we don't want her waking up right now."

Her hand unclenched. "Why not?"

Tim looked uneasily toward her.

"We need to go, Rebecca."

Newt frowned. "What? Where are we—"

"Dad's awake."

Her heart fluttered. "He's awake? Are you sure? Is he all right?"

A shuffling footstep came from just outside her room and she looked past her brother, noticing for the first time that they weren't alone. Aaron stepped in behind Tim, looking serious and anxious, both at the same time.

Newt held Casey down at her side. Aaron teased her about the doll almost every day, and she didn't know if she could handle it today. A year older than Tim and physically larger, Aaron usually acted younger.

"It's true," Aaron said quietly. No teasing. Not even a glance at the doll.

"I want to see him for myself," Tim said, studying his sister. "But I didn't want to leave you here, not without telling you where I was going, and asking if you wanted to come along."

Newt was confused at first, trying to figure out how they would get there without being discovered. Then she understood.

"Through the ducts?" she asked.

"Of course. We know which lab they're in," Tim said. "We've peeked in there before, when we've been playing Monster Maze."

"I don't know—"

Tim rolled his eyes in frustration. "Newt, are you coming or not?"

"But—"

"C'mon, Tim," Aaron said, "let's go without her."

Newt sat on the edge of her bed, laying Casey on her pillow. Indecision paralyzed her.

"Mom said we weren't supposed to leave our quarters," she reminded him.

Tim glared angrily at her. "I don't care. Aaron heard his parents say that Dad's awake, and I'm gonna see for myself."

"Let's go," Aaron prodded, turning to leave.

Tim followed him. "See you later, Rebecca."

Newt watched him walk out, feeling frozen on the outside but frantic on the inside. She wanted to see her father, too, but their mother had told them to stay put, and she didn't want to make her mother angry. More than that, she was afraid of what they might see if they crawled through the ducts and spied on the medical lab where her father had been taken. What if he wasn't really awake? What if that thing on his face had hurt him, or scarred him?

No way would their dad approve of them spying.

"Tim, don't leave me," she said softly, not wanting to shout for fear of waking Mrs. Hernandez. Taking a deep breath, she stood up, turned, and pointed at Casey, who lay against the pillow. "You stay right there and don't move," she said. "I'll be back."

Slipping on her shoes, she darted silently from her room, glanced once at Mrs. Hernandez napping on the sofa, and then went out the door. She caught up with the boys around the corner, moving down a wide corridor.

"Hey, you guys, wait for me!" she called.

Tim glanced back at her and smiled a little, slowing down until she reached him.

"We're gonna get it if Mom catches us," she said.

"Aw, quit your whining," Aaron snapped.

Tim glared at him, and Newt felt a little better. Her brother didn't always come to her defense, but she hoped with Dad not around they would stick together more than ever before. Aaron could be nice, but mostly he didn't seem to like having a little girl tag along.

Well, it's my *father in there,* Newt thought, *so I don't care what you like.*

She didn't want to get into a fight with him, or to have Tim end up in a fight with his friend. But she had been through too much in the past two days to put up with him being a jerk.

They took a side corridor on the left that was mostly used by maintenance workers. There was a service elevator at the back, and halfway along the hall there was a big vent. Tim and Newt kept watch while Aaron jiggered off the grate, then they snuck in quickly, with Tim bringing up the rear. When they were all inside, he pulled the grate back into place.

Enough light filtered through the vents and grates that they could see where they were going. They crawled quickly along the smooth, rectangular tube for several long minutes, turning this way and that, moving toward the science and medical labs. Usually they kept away from that part of the complex when they were playing—their parents had warned them to stick to the residential areas of the colony. But all of the children of Hadley's Hope had explored far and wide at some point or another.

Still, when they came to a duct that angled downward into darkness, she realized this was a way she had never gone.

"Do we have to go down there?" she whispered.

"What are you, scared?" Aaron scowled, then turned to Tim. "Maybe you oughta send your sister back, before she starts bawling or something." Then he went feet-first down the sloping duct, moving carefully. As soon as he was out of sight, Tim turned to his sister.

"You okay?" he asked. "Look, if you want to go back—"

Newt went head-first without waiting for him to finish. She slid on her belly, dragging the toes of her shoes and using her hands to slow herself, but she still crashed into Aaron at the bottom. He yelped in protest, then clamped a hand over his mouth.

"Sorry," she said, but she said it in a way—and with a smile—that made it clear she didn't mean it.

Tim came down behind them, but managed to stop himself in time. A dim light from ahead gave some gray illumination to the duct, and they quickly moved on. The metal felt cold to the touch, and the chill crept into Newt's bones.

Another few minutes and three more turns, and then Aaron stopped at a vent illuminated by bright white light.

"Here we are," he whispered. "I told you I knew the way. Keep it quiet, now, or they'll hear us."

They took a few seconds arranging themselves so that they could all see through the vent, the boys stretching out in either direction and Newt—the smallest of them—kneeling in the middle. One hand on the duct wall right above the vent, she bent to peer through the slats.

At first she could only see her mother and Dr. Komiskey—a curly haired, fortyish woman who gave all of the colonists annual checkups. But then Newt shifted slightly, cocked her head to the left, and she could make out a third person, sitting upright on an examining table, legs hanging over the edge.

Suddenly Newt grinned, a huge weight lifting from her heart. It was her dad, looking awful silly in nothing but his underpants.

"I know how you feel, Annie, but I just can't let him go," Dr. Komiskey said to Newt's mother. "He's not leaving here until we have a better idea of what happened to him. Even if I was inclined to discharge him, I couldn't. I'm not his physician—I'm just the staff doc.

"Dr. Reese is the director of the science team," she continued, "and there's no way he'd allow it." She looked at Newt's dad. "We're talking about a newly discovered, extraterrestrial, possibly *endoparasitoid* species. As yet, we know nothing about it."

Newt had no idea what Dr. Komiskey was talking about, but then she heard her father laugh quietly, and she grinned again.

Her dad shook his head.

"Honestly, Theodora, it's fine. Honey, tell Theodora it's fine. That thing was disgusting. If it was breathing for me—and it had to be, right?—I'd like to know what, if any, effects it had on me. It had its tongue down my throat, and only Anne's allowed to do that."

Newt twisted up her face, and she heard Aaron chuckle quietly. She elbowed him hard and he glared at her, but she kept her focus on her parents.

Someone coughed, and Newt shifted again, craning her neck the other way. She was surprised to see that Dr. Reese had been in the room all along, with Mr. Simpson beside him.

"Believe me, Mr. Jorden," Dr. Reese said, "we want to get you out of here as quickly as possible—get you back with your kids and back to work. But it'd be irresponsible to do that without making sure you haven't suffered any harm."

"That I haven't picked up some sort of plague or something, you mean," Newt's father said.

"That, too," Dr. Komiskey agreed.

Newt's mother took her father's hand. All this talk of ugly things made her anxious, but it soothed her to see the love between them. They squabbled plenty, but they really did love each other.

"Truthfully, Russ," Mr. Simpson began, "the science team wants their crack at you now. Dr. Komiskey has done what she can for you, but the team needs to study you, and for obvious reasons.

Meanwhile, we sent some men out to the site last night. Maybe they can bring back something to work with."

"You sent men?" Russ said, his voice louder. "That's *my* claim, damn it." Newt flinched at her father's anger, glancing away as he went on. "That's an authorized find, and nobody had better get any ideas otherwise."

Dr. Reese strode across the room to a wheeled table, on which sat a metal tray. Newt blinked and a sick shiver went through her as she saw the spider-like legs sticking up from the tray. Gray and dead, the creature lay on its back, stiff, and trailing the tail that had been wrapped around her father's neck.

The doctor picked up a scalpel and pushed back the legs.

"No one's arguing your claim, Mr. Jorden," Dr. Reese said. "But we all have our jobs to do. Try to remember that you had this thing wrapped around your head for nearly twenty-four hours."

Dr. Komiskey turned to Newt's mother.

"Look at him. He's half-dead after playing kiss-face with a lobster, and all he can think about is his claim."

Her father shot Dr. Komiskey an angry look, but Newt realized the doctor was right. He looked pale and exhausted, and more than a little sick. As she watched, her father clutched at his stomach and winced in pain. He groaned and lay back down on the cot, both hands on his belly.

"Please, Theodora," Anne said, "just let me take him to our quarters. I'll watch him every minute."

Dr. Komiskey glanced at Dr. Reese, who shook his head.

"I'm sorry, Annie," Dr. Komiskey said. "We just can't. Why don't you go and get some rest?"

At that moment none of them was looking at her dad, but Newt saw the pain etched on his face. He bared his teeth, and his hands seemed to jerk where they covered his stomach.

"What's wrong with him now?" Tim whispered into her ear.

Newt shook her head. She didn't know.

Her mother hesitated, glancing up at Dr. Reese and Mr. Simpson.

"Go on," Dr. Komiskey said. "I'll stay here with Russ, and wait for them to return from the site. Who knows, maybe they'll turn something up."

At that moment another man rushed into the room, a balding man with a thick brown mustache who Newt recognized as one of the mechanics who repaired the crawlers.

"They're here," the man said, breathing heavy from running. He looked worried and afraid. "They're back…"

Two other men hustled in, carrying someone on a stretcher.

"…and they've brought friends."

To Newt's left, Aaron swore under his breath.

"Oh no," Tim whispered.

Newt felt tears spring to her eyes as a fresh fear took hold of her. A sick feeling started in her stomach and spread from there, because the man on the stretcher had another of those face-hugging creatures attached to him, pulsing and breathing for him. The one on the metal tray was gray and brittle and dead, but this one was very much alive.

"Help me," her father groaned.

Newt bent closer to the vent.

"Tim, what's wrong with—"

Russ screamed and arched his back, roaring with pain. His chest bulged, right at his mid-section. He threw his hands to one side as he bucked again. Newt stared, wide-eyed, as something pushed up from inside him.

"Daddy?" she whispered, tears coming hot and fast now, burning her cheeks.

Her mother spun, staring at him. "Russ!" she cried.

Again he screamed and bucked. His chest burst open with a spray of blood and a sickeningly wet crunch of bone and splitting skin.

"Daddy!" Newt and Tim screamed together.

"Oh shit! Oh my God!" Aaron whimpered. "What is this?"

Then her father lay motionless on the table, but something moved in his chest, rising like a snake from the gory hole. Pale and bloody, it hissed, revealing sharp teeth, its head turning this way and that, eyes shut tight as a newborn's.

Unable to make a sound now, or even to breathe, Newt realized that in some way that must have been exactly what it was. A baby.

The people in the room shouted at one another to do something as the thing slithered out from her father's chest, slid to the floor, and then darted off into a corner where it smashed through a small plastic grate and vanished into the guts of the colony. Still painted with her father's blood.

Newt glanced around at the dimly lit duct.

It's in here now, in the ductwork with us, she thought. *Monster Maze.*

She started screaming again.

And this time she couldn't stop.

DATE: 23 JUNE, 2179
TIME: 1830

In the small exam room where she usually had her annual physical, Anne sat on the floor with her children huddled on either side of her. They burrowed against her and she held them tightly, whispering to them that it would be all right now, though even six-year-old Newt had to know that was a lie. Their father was dead, cold and bloody and already turning blue in the lab only twenty feet down the hall, where Dr. Reese had evicted Theodora Komiskey from her own med lab.

"Hey," a gentle voice said.

Anne looked up to see Dr. Komiskey standing in the open doorway. She'd been talking to several people, and arguing with Dr. Mori, but this was the first time the doctor had come in to speak with her.

"Theodora," she managed to say, and then her tears came.

She forced herself to cry quietly, and not to tremble too much, hoping to hide her tears from her children. Newt had fallen asleep against her, exhausted by grief, but Tim looked up at her face, his eyes red but his expression hard and grim. She hated seeing that look on his face—that look that said his world had broken in half, but he expected things to get even worse.

"I guess it's a good thing you didn't let me take him home," she rasped, looking at Dr. Komiskey.

"Can I do anything for you?" the doctor asked. "Reese is in my lab, and Mori and Hidalgo are looking over the others who've been brought in with those creatures on them."

"Have any of the others…" she began.

"Not yet," Dr. Komiskey said. "But they will. And there's been no luck finding the one who… the one that got away."

"Can't they cut the things off? Or do surgery to remove whatever's been implanted in the poor folks with those things on their faces?" Anne asked.

She couldn't believe such questions had to come out of her mouth.

"You know what happened when we tried cutting the one off of Russ. They bleed a powerful acid. Try to remove the thing and the patient is likely to die—never mind the way its proboscis wraps itself around the patient's…"

Dr. Komiskey faltered and glanced away.

"You know what, never mind," she said. "You shouldn't be hearing this. You should take the kids and go back to your place. I'll update you myself if we learn anything."

An icy ball of dread had been growing in Anne's gut, and now it doubled in size.

She shook her head.

"Not going to happen, Theodora," she said. "You've got marines out there. I want to be wherever they are. More of those things means more of the damn creatures in the walls or wherever they're going. We're in the middle of something no one's ever had to deal with before. With Russ…"

She stopped and glanced at Tim, saw the way his mouth had tightened into a white line as he forced himself not to cry.

"I'm on my own," she continued. "And I'm going to keep these kids safe. That means I want to be where the investigation is taking place. I want to know what you know, when you know it, and I want a marine or two within screaming distance."

She thought of Demian Brackett, but didn't mention him by name. Theodora wouldn't have understood, and Anne wasn't sure that she did, either. Given their history, she ought to have felt terrible guilt over how profoundly she desired his company just then, but she felt nothing of the kind. She loved Russ. He remained her husband in her heart, and she couldn't imagine the day when that would no longer be the case.

But Demian was still her friend, and a Colonial Marine, and she trusted him to do everything he could to look out for her and her children, partly because she knew he was still in love with her. Perhaps she ought to have felt badly about taking advantage of that love, but she was a mother, and her children's safety took precedence over everything.

"How many have been brought back so far?" she asked.

For several seconds, Dr. Komiskey looked everywhere but at Anne.

"How many?" Tim asked.

Newt rustled a bit in her sleep.

"Twelve or thirteen," Dr. Komiskey replied. "With more on the way."

"Are they stupid?" Anne said. "They need to get out of there now, and stay out!"

"From what I hear, they are," the doctor said. "All of these happened within just a minute or so of each other, in two waves... The first ones latched onto the marines who walked in among those eggs—or whatever they are—and the second wave attacked the people who were trying to rescue the first group."

Anne sighed, held her children close, and looked up at her.

"What are they, Theodora?" she asked, not really expecting an answer. "What the hell have we stumbled upon here? I mean, the company sent us out there, gave us specific coordinates and everything. Did they know what we would find?"

From the haunted look in the doctor's eyes, Anne knew she had been wondering the same thing.

"I wish I knew," Dr. Komiskey said. "But even if we did—"

"What, it wouldn't help?" Anne snapped, disturbing Newt. "If they know *anything* that we don't, I think it's time they clued us in. Don't you?"

The doctor exhaled.

"Whatever I learn, I'll share."

Then she turned and was gone, leaving Anne alone with her children again. They were the Jordens now, just the three of them. Without Russ, she was the only one who could protect them, and she intended to do that.

No matter what it cost her.

19

CAPTURE-FOR-STUDY

DATE: 23 JUNE, 2179
TIME: 1837

Brackett held tightly to his gun, trying to keep his frustration in check. He led the way for a lab assistant named Khati Fuqua and a surveyor called Bluejay. The origin of the nickname was a mystery the captain hadn't the time or inclination to solve.

Khati carried a three-foot shock-stick, while Bluejay lugged a light mesh soil sifter he intended to use as a net. They were approaching a junction on the basement level of D-Block, beneath the wing that held the med lab and operations. Though the hallway was quiet and abandoned, he was distracted by the voices coming through the comm unit in his ear. Al Simpson. One of Dr. Reese's assistants. Julisa Paris. Sgt. Coughlin.

"Did you join the marines to be a glorified exterminator?" Bluejay asked, his smile rustling his thick gray muttonchop sideburns.

"I'm not an exterminator," Khati snapped. "We're not going to kill this thing. Standing orders are that we take it alive."

"Not my orders," Brackett said.

"You may be stationed here, Captain Brackett," Khati said, "but this facility is under the operational control of Weyland-Yutani, and standing orders from the company are that any newly encountered alien species falls under the capture-for-study edict."

"Unless it represents a threat to human life," Brackett replied.

"There's nothing about that in the handbook," Bluejay told him, darting his head around a doorframe and peering into a bathroom where the door had been left propped open.

"You think this thing presents a danger to the colony?" Khati asked, arching an eyebrow. "From the way Dr. Reese described it, the creature looks like a fat snake with little arms. I don't think it's going to give us much trouble."

"That's if we can find the damn thing," Bluejay sighed. "Hold up for a second." The surveyor dashed into the bathroom, searched the stalls and glanced through air vents.

After the death of Russ Jorden and the escape of the alien parasite that had burst from his chest, Brackett had brought his squad into a room with Al Simpson and two-dozen colonists—some from the science team, and others from the colony staff. Dr. Reese had spoken to them about the parasite, given them a rough description, and asked them to search for it as quickly and as thoroughly as possible. It was vital, he'd said, that the alien be captured alive.

It had been Marvin Draper, of all people, who'd asked the most salient question.

"We catch this thing," Draper had said, "are you going to be able to stop the same thing from happening to those poor bastards we hauled back from that derelict ship?"

Dr. Reese had adopted a sad expression and nodded slowly.

"That is our hope, yes."

Somehow that had turned what Brackett would have expected to be a bug hunt into a search-and-rescue operation. Search for the parasite, rescue those who still had facehuggers attached to their heads.

"Come on, Bluejay," he said, starting along the corridor again without waiting for the surveyor. "We need to be faster."

Khati gave him an approving glance and caught up with him. In the bathroom, a toilet flushed and Bluejay came running out with his net over his shoulder, zipping up his pants. Brackett scowled as he reached the next door.

He rapped lightly on it and waited for a response. Simpson's number two, Lydecker, had gone onto the comm system and instructed everyone in the colony to shut themselves into whatever room they were in. They were to stay there until further notice, and to report anything out of the ordinary.

No answer.

"Open it," Khati said.

Brackett bristled. He needed to have a conversation with this woman. But it could wait.

Supposed to be a quiet post, he thought. *A nothing little colony on the edge of nowhere*. Instead it had been crisis upon crisis since his arrival. *Maybe I'm bad luck*. He thought of Anne Jorden and her children and their grief, and decided he didn't want to take responsibility for any of this—not even jokingly.

"Let's go," he said, turning the latch and pushing the door open.

Khati went in first, shock-stick held out ahead of her. Brackett and Bluejay followed, scanning the floor of what appeared to be some kind of stockroom. Lights flickered on as they entered, and Brackett crouched to look on the lower shelves as Khati and Bluejay did the same along aisles of lab and med supplies.

"Is this stuff manufactured here?" he asked.

"Some of it's brought with our monthly supply run," Khati answered. "The rest we make."

Brackett swore, peering into a vent.

"We've got maybe sixty people looking for this thing when it could be anywhere in the complex. No way are we finding this little bastard if it doesn't want to be—"

A scream tore along the corridor. Brackett ran for the door, but Khati beat him to it. Out in the hall they darted to the right, racing toward the source of the scream—a cry that had been abruptly cut off and now echoed only in his head.

Bluejay followed, but Brackett felt as if he and Khati were in a race until he grabbed her shoulder and shoved her back a step.

"What the hell—"

He turned on her. "That sounded like danger to me, which means you hang back, and I will investigate."

"Those aren't my instructions," she barked.

"They are now." Without waiting for a response, he hurtled down the corridor, gun at the ready, with Khati and Bluejay in his wake. At the junction he paused, trying to sort out whether the scream had come from the left or right, a question solved almost immediately by the sudden appearance of Sgt. Coughlin and two unfamiliar faces coming along the corridor from the left.

"You heard that, Captain?" Coughlin asked.

Brackett ignored him. The new arrivals were coming from the left, which meant the scream—that one, horrible, lonely scream—had come from the short corridor on the right. It ended in two broad, swinging double doors.

He ran toward them, and then stopped short. Khati raced up beside him again. Hot, humid air emanated from behind those doors, along with the thrumming vibration of machinery.

"What's through here?" Brackett asked.

"The laundry."

He signaled to Coughlin, who ran up to stand beside him. With his left hand, Brackett counted off three fingers, and together they burst through those double doors, gun barrels sweeping the room in opposite arcs. The churning noises of the washers assaulted them and the hot, damp scent of industrial cleaner made his eyes sting.

"Stay lively," Brackett said, motioning Coughlin forward and then holding up a hand to indicate that the others should stay back.

"For fuck's sake," Khati said, "it's an alien snake, not the bogeyman."

Brackett shot her a hard glance and she rolled her eyes, but did not advance.

The two marines moved into the vast room, where soiled clothes and linens stood in wheeled baskets below open ducts that Brackett realized must allow for dirty laundry to be dumped into hatches on the upper levels. An open doorway on the far side of that room led to another chamber, the source of the thundering machine noise.

Brackett and Coughlin hurried toward it.

Suddenly a laundry cart moved and a figure lurched up toward them. Brackett swung his gun around, finger on the trigger as he saw the wide, terrified eyes of a tall, white-haired woman staring back at him.

"What—" Coughlin began. Before he could react, the woman pushed past him, bolted past Khati and the rest, and vanished out into the corridor. The fear in her eyes was intense.

An alien snake, *Khati had said. The thing might be ugly as hell, but to inspire that kind of fear, it had to have done something terrible.*

At the broad open doorway that led into the humming, thundering room full of laundry machines, Brackett and Coughlin paused for a moment. Then Brackett nodded, and they went through.

At first he wasn't sure just what he was looking at. Machines washed. Machines dried. Machines folded and stacked. But stacks of clean laundry that must have belonged in carts like the ones out in the duct room had spilled onto the floor.

"Captain," Coughlin said, pointing at one of the huge folding machines.

White sheets made their way through the machine, stretched and creased and folded and then folded again. But one of the sheets wasn't purely white—it had a long red streak down the middle—and the next one had been soaked through with crimson.

Brackett's heart sped up. An ugly little parasite had done this?

"Move," he said, voice low, and he and Coughlin hurried around the other side of the huge folding machine.

Both of them froze as the machine started to whine and clank. Two huge rollers attempted to draw in the body of a slender man whose left arm and shoulder had been chewed up by the folding mechanism. The hole in his forehead, however, had not been made by the machine.

Blood and gray matter spilled onto the floor.

A second corpse lay fifteen feet away, near one of the thumping, swirling dryers.

"How many people normally work down here?" Brackett asked.

"Could be as many as four at a time," Bluejay said.

"Spread out!" Brackett shouted. "You see anything, don't approach. Just sing out."

The six of them moved among the various machines, the thrum and churn creating a blanket of gray noise that made it all the more vital for them to use their eyes. Brackett aimed his weapon up into the mechanical workings of the bloody folding machine, and then moved on to the other, while Coughlin began to search between and behind the dryers.

"Captain!" Bluejay shouted.

Brackett followed his voice, joining him in a corner where a massive fan in the wall drew superheated air out of the room. There were half a dozen of these spread out across the laundry. There were other large vents, as well, and Bluejay was staring at one of them.

"It's the return," he said. "Pushes cooled air back into the room."

Brackett stared. The grate had been destroyed, the metal latticework torn apart from within. The parasite had come through here.

"There," Bluejay said, pointing to the floor nearby.

But Brackett didn't need the surveyor to draw attention to the object that lay there, just a few feet from the torn grating. It was a bloody shoe, left behind. A sick dread knotted itself up inside his gut—no "little parasite" could drag a fully grown human into an air vent.

Weapon aimed at the ruined grate, Brackett backed away.

"All civilians, out of here right now!" he barked, glancing over his shoulder at them.

Khati shot him a dark look. She'd been moving around the huge washers, probing the shadows between and behind them with her shock-stick. Now she started toward him, that insatiable curiosity lighting her eyes.

"What've you found?" she called.

Brackett turned to Coughlin.

"Get them out of here," he said. "I'll call Paris, and get some reinforcements down here."

"If it went into the vents it could be anywhere," Bluejay said.

"Just go," Brackett said.

The surveyor held up his one free hand.

"You don't have to tell me twice. I don't wanna end up like those poor bastards."

Coughlin snapped orders at the two civilians who had accompanied him and ushered them—along with Bluejay and Khati—toward the duct room. Brackett kept his eyes on the torn grating, and backed further away. Had he seen something moving in the darkness there?

Somehow they were going to have to flush the thing out, but he had no idea where to begin.

He tapped the comm link on his collar.

"This is Brackett. I need Simpson on the line."

This time, the scream came from behind him.

Brackett spun, and saw one of the civilians dive back into the laundry room. The captain ran for the open doorway. A woman shouted frantically, and then Coughlin's gun barked, rapid-fire.

"Khati!" Brackett shouted as he barreled into the room, weapon up.

Something dark and swift scrambled up a shelving unit standing against the wall. He took aim and fired, bullets punching the wall and pinging off the metal shelving. Coughlin ran over beneath the alien and fired at it from close range, spattering blood onto the floor, where it hissed and smoked and burned straight through. Coughlin screamed and dropped to the floor, tearing off his left boot.

The creature leapt up into a laundry duct, and was gone.

Brackett took two more shots at the metal duct, and then he could only stand there, Khati at his side. She was whispering something that sounded like the most profanity-laced prayer he'd ever heard.

Turning to survey the room, Brackett saw Bluejay lying in a sprawl on top of a spilled cart of filthy towels and sheets, blood pumping out of a hole at the center of his chest. His eyes fluttered once and then glazed over, dark with death.

On the floor, Coughlin scrambled backward from beneath the duct and tore off a thick sock with a cry of fresh pain. He sat staring at his foot. Bloody, raw stumps were all that remained of his last two toes—the acid had burned right through his boot.

"Whatever that thing is, it's no snake," Khati said.

Brackett nodded. In the space of a few hours it had grown to the size of a large dog or a chimpanzee, though it didn't look anything like those creatures. It now had black skin, like a shell, along with a whipping, ridged tail, and its head was huge. He'd caught a glimpse of teeth in its mouth, and felt as if he'd seen something that belonged only in nightmares.

It's like a demon, he thought. But demons only existed in stories, and this alien creature was all too real.

How big would it grow? The question snapped him out of his shock.

"Simpson?" he said into the comm. "Simpson, this is Captain Brackett, are you there?"

"I'm here, Captain," the voice came back, weary and arrogant. "Doing my job. What can I—"

"How many are there now?" Brackett demanded. "How many people with those facehuggers on them?"

"There were thirteen," Simpson said. "Only nine now. Why?"

"What do you mean, 'only nine now?'"

"Four of the things have fallen off and died, just the way it happened with Russ Jorden," Simpson said. "We're keeping a close eye on them. Now, do you want to answer me?"

"You need to do a head count of the whole colony," Brackett said anxiously. "Make sure everyone is accounted for, top to bottom, and warn them to keep an eye out. We've seen the alien, down here in the laundry room. It's killed at least three people that we've seen, but I think it's taken others."

"Taken?" Simpson said. "What do you mean—"

Brackett silenced his comm and turned to Coughlin.

"Get to the med lab, right now. Keep watch over the patients there. If any of them have these things come out of them, you kill those damn snakes before they can get into the ducts, like this one."

Coughlin stood at attention, grim eyes gleaming through the pain. "Sir, yes, sir."

Khati bristled. "You can't—"

"Did you not see that thing?" Brackett snarled. "Fuck if I can't."

DATE: 23 JUNE, 2179
TIME: 1903

On his way to the med lab, Coughlin passed the research laboratory used by the science team, just as one of Dr. Reese's assistants came out through the door.

The sergeant glanced inside and stopped short, staring through the gap in the door as it swung closed. In a cylindrical glass tank in the middle of the room—one of a row of such tanks—one of the facehuggers floated in a bubbling bluish liquid. Just before the door clicked shut, Coughlin saw the thing twitch, saw its coiled tail snap out and strike the glass of the tank like a scorpion's sting.

The lab assistant gave him an admonishing glance.

"You're looking at *me* like that?" Coughlin asked. "What's going on in there?"

"Need to know, Sergeant," the young man said. "And you—"

"Yeah, whatever," Coughlin interrupted. "You're running tests on the thing, maybe to try to help, or maybe just because Weyland-Yutani wants their damn data. But what I want to know is *how* did you get it? From what I hear, there's no way to get one of those things off someone without killing the patient. Did you manage to get one of those eggs back from the derelict or did you murder someone for science?"

The assistant frowned disapprovingly.

"Every single one of those people with the stage one Xenomorphs on their faces is as good as dead already."

Coughlin clenched his fists. "What are you saying?"

The assistant smiled thinly. "I'm saying you don't need to know, Sergeant."

The guy walked on.

Coughlin wanted to shoot him.

When he reached the med lab, the sergeant found Dr. Komiskey sitting in a chair near the door with her arms crossed like a petulant child, but Coughlin could see why. Normally Komiskey's domain, the med lab had been taken over by the science team. Dr. Mori hovered over patients while Dr. Hidalgo went from cot to cot checking vital signs. One of their assistants sat on a cot, putting some kind of ointment on a nasty, ragged wound on his own arm.

Coughlin stared at the injured man and swore under his breath. Dr. Hidalgo looked unnerved, even frightened, but Dr. Mori's eyes were lit with a strange excitement.

"Pardon me, doctors, but Captain Brackett has assigned me to—"

"We've been informed," Dr. Mori said coldly. "Come in and stay out of the way."

But Coughlin didn't move. He counted seven patients with facehuggers, and two without.

"Where are the other four?" he asked.

"The morgue," Dr. Hidalgo said, blanching as she spoke.

"Son of a bitch," Coughlin whispered, cupping a hand to his skull. "And the parasites? Did you kill them, or stop them at least?"

The scientists said nothing, but Dr. Hidalgo glanced at the man who was now wrapping his wound. At least one of them had tried to stop the parasites from escaping.

"You people are lunatics," Coughlin said, shaking his head. "Don't you understand? The things growing inside them... they come out of there small, but they grow—fast. And now we've got, what, five of them out there? We're going to have to get everyone together for their own safety, or at least group them in certain locations, and with armed guards."

Dr. Hidalgo used forceps to touch the long, spindly legs of the facehugger that covered Saida Warsi's eyes, nose, and mouth. The thing slid off and flopped to the floor, dead, the trailing proboscis sliding from her open mouth as she coughed herself back to consciousness and began to scream. Coughlin wondered if she had been aware of what was going on around her, of the hideous fate that awaited her.

"Well?" Dr. Mori said. "What are you waiting for? Get hunting."

"Oh no," Coughlin said, raising the barrel of his gun, ready to kill anything that emerged from these poor afflicted bastards. "I'll call it in to Captain Brackett. Me? I'm staying right here."

20

THE WORST QUESTION

DATE: 23 JUNE, 2179
TIME: 2209

All uncertainty had left Demian Brackett's mind.

He moved along the basement corridors of F-Block with the military precision that had been drummed into him from the first day of training for the Colonial Marines, back to the wall, sweeping the barrel of his weapon in short arcs. Across from him, Pvt. Yousseff did the same, alert and on point. She might be one of Draper's cronies, but she'd proven more than capable of thinking for herself. Her eyes were alight with intelligence, courage, and just the right amount of fear to keep her on her toes.

Hours had passed since Bluejay's death and information had been coming in fast and furious. Coughlin had reported the activity in the med lab, the little science project Dr. Reese had going on. When this was all over and the aliens—what the science team were calling the Xenomorphs—had been eradicated, Brackett intended to have an ugly conversation with the doctor about how they had acquired the living facehugger. If there had been any misconduct—if Reese had endangered lives—Brackett would take the son of a bitch into custody himself. Weyland-Yutani might give their scientists a lot of leeway in accomplishing their goals, but not even they could countenance negligence that led to the death of innocents.

A quiet cough made Brackett glance back. Khati had stayed with him after Bluejay's death, still carrying her shock-stick. Yousseff shot her a withering glare.

"Sorry," Khati said. "I don't know why we have to be so quiet, anyway. If they hear us, these things aren't going to go scampering off. They're going to try to kill us."

Brackett grunted and turned to Yousseff.

"She has a point."

Still, they moved on in relative silence, traveling quickly from room to room, checking shadowed corners and behind furniture, carefully peering through grates and vents. Every time Brackett looked into one of the air ducts he felt sick to his stomach, knowing that Newt and the other children had routinely played there. Some parts of that air circulation system were wide enough for the growing Xenomorph, but other sections were narrower, and he thought the aliens would have trouble getting through there.

"Control, this is Brackett," he said into his comm. "I need a schematic of the ventilation system."

Static on the line, and then a voice.

"Captain, this is Lydecker. We've got it open now, actually. As we've been evacuating sections of the colony—isolating the population in more easily protected pockets—we've sealed off other areas as effectively as possible. Once your team has completed its sweep, you'll be able to access those areas one by one."

Brackett and Yousseff turned and entered an enormous concrete room full of pipes and chemical odors. Water dripped from poorly sealed pipe joints and stained the floor, and the smell of earth and growing things mingled with the chemicals.

"I owe your team an apology, Lydecker," Brackett admitted. "I underestimated you guys."

Static again, then a different voice.

"Save the hugs and kisses for later, Captain," Lt. Paris said. "I've got reports from three different relocation details. We've got the population temporarily settled into four locations, but there are people unaccounted for."

"Shit," Brackett muttered. "How many?"

No answer.

"Lydecker!" Julisa Paris snapped over the comm. "How many in total?"

Static. Then Lydecker replied.

"Fifteen."

The number stopped Brackett short. He froze inside the room with the dripping pipes, and tried to just breathe.

"What is it?" Khati asked.

Yousseff—who was on the same communications channel as Brackett and had heard the exchange—turned to her.

"Trouble."

Brackett exhaled and glanced around at the dripping pipes.

"What the hell is this room?"

"We're underneath the greenhouse," Khati replied.

Okay, Brackett thought. *That explains a lot.*

"Lydecker, this is Brackett," he said into his comm. "We're going to keep hunting, but hunting isn't enough. Once you're sure you've sealed off the population groups, I need you and Simpson to get Dr. Reese and his team in a room, and work on the only question that's going to matter pretty soon."

"What question is that?" No static this time.

"Where are they taking these people?" he replied. "There's got to be a reason they're taking them off somewhere, instead of just killing them and leaving the corpses. I'm going to guess that means they're all gathering in one place, like a nest or a hive or something. We need to figure out where that is, and take the fight to them there."

Many seconds passed with the crackle of static in Brackett's ear. He gazed at Khati and then at Yousseff.

"You think they're using those people to breed," Lydecker said at last. "But we're fairly certain none of the aliens have left the colony—none of the outer doors have been opened or breached in any way—and they'd have to go back to the derelict to reach those… eggs, or whatever they are."

"We don't know that," Yousseff chimed in. "We've never encountered this species before. We don't know what they're capable of."

"Those people might still be alive," Brackett said grimly. "So when you know the rest are safe, you start looking. If they can be saved, we've got to try."

"I'm with you, Captain," Lydecker said. "Mr. Simpson just came in and he wants me to assure you that he is with you, as well."

"All right," Brackett said. "Completing the sweep of F-Block's basement level and then moving upstairs to—"

Krrkk. A burst of static on the line. Then shouting.

"—got one! I've got one of the fuckers right here! Level one, northwest corner—"

Krrkk. Screaming in the background.

"Draper!" Yousseff shouted into her comm. "Backup's coming!"

Brackett was already in motion, racing out of the pipe room. Northwest corner of level one was practically right above their heads.

"Stairs?" Brackett called. Khati ran beside him with her shock-stick, a pitiful looking thing.

"Turn left, the door's on the right, next to the lift! You can't miss it."

Yousseff caught up, still shouting for Draper but receiving no reply on her comm. She swore several times. Brackett gritted his teeth, trying to remember who else had been paired with Draper for the sweep. They skidded around the corner, and he spotted the door with a huge B painted on it.

"Watch your ass!" he said. "There's more than one of these things."

Brackett turned the latch and banged the door open. Yousseff charged through, weapon ready, but the stairwell was empty. They raced up two steps at a time in the flickering, failing light, and could hear the shouts and screams before they reached the door into level one.

"Again!" Brackett said, grabbing the door and dragging it open.

Yousseff went first and Brackett burst through behind her, with Khati bringing up the rear. They nearly tripped over the bloody and broken corpse of a marine only recognizable by his uniform. For half a second, Brackett thought it was Marvin Draper, but then he heard the roar of a man's voice, and he and Yousseff ran to the corner.

Weapons up, they rounded the corner.

"Holy shit!" Yousseff barked.

Marvin Draper had braced his body against a door to keep one of the aliens from coming through. He had only a handgun for defense, his rifle on the floor half a dozen feet away. He roared profanities at it as the Xenomorph—so much bigger than it had been only four hours before—clawed at the door and slammed its head and body against it, knocking Draper back half a foot before the marine threw himself back again.

The alien hissed, spindly arms reaching through the gap. On the floor of the corridor, a man in a gray jumpsuit sat screaming and staring at his left arm, leg, and abdomen, where the alien's acid blood had eaten through flesh and even now eroded bone. Smoke rose from the wounds.

Brackett ignored the screaming man—he would be dead in minutes at best.

The alien banged its head through the gap, twisted and hissed. From within its jaws came a second set that slid out, punching toward Draper's face.

"Motherfucker!" Draper shouted as he darted aside. He jammed his gun against the alien's mouth and pulled the trigger, then spun away, using the door to shield himself from the acid spray before slamming against it to keep the furious alien from crashing through.

He'd never be able to hold it back for long.

"Draper!" Brackett shouted. "Let it out!"

He expected an argument, but he saw the flicker of understanding in Draper's eyes, and the marine gave him a nod.

"One!" Yousseff shouted, taking position beside Brackett. "Two!"

"Three!" Draper called, and he backed away from the door, darting along the corridor.

The alien crashed through, stood its ground, and glared at the newcomers.

Brackett and Yousseff opened fire. From a safe distance, Draper did the same. They blew the alien apart and it fell to the floor, twitching but dead, its blood eating through the floor in seconds.

Draper whooped triumphantly and shot the alien again. Brackett couldn't celebrate—not with the dead marine behind him and the dying civilian only fifteen feet away. The civilian lay on the floor now, bleeding out, eyes dull and glazed. He'd breathe his last breath at any moment. There wasn't a thing they could do for him, and Brackett didn't even know his name.

The man exhaled, a damp rattle coming from his throat, and then slumped.

His pain had ended.

"He got a few shots in with Valente's weapon after Valente went down," Draper explained. "Too close, though. The blood."

"We know," Yousseff said, turning to look back at the corner, beyond which Valente's corpse lay. "Damn it, Jimmy."

"He was a good marine," Draper said.

In Brackett's mind, that was the only eulogy any of them could hope for.

"Good timing, sir," Draper said, holstering his weapon and giving Brackett a salute.

Brackett casually returned the salute.

"Nice job staying alive until we got here." They stared at each other for a moment, united in mutual dislike, but both, Brackett thought, understanding that each had underestimated the other. From what he'd seen, Draper was a hell of a marine.

"What do they want with us, Captain?" Yousseff asked, approaching the dead alien, staring at its remains. "If they just want us dead, or want to eat us, why not just do that instead of taking people away?"

Khati walked over to the dead Xenomorph, studying it as closely as was safe.

"Now that we've got one to examine, maybe we'll start to figure that out." She noticed Brackett staring at her shock-stick and gave it a shake. "Yeah. I think I'm going to get myself a gun."

21

INCUBATION PERIOD

DATE: 25 JUNE, 2179
TIME: 0954

Coughlin liked Dr. Hidalgo. She could be cool and clinical, like any scientist he'd ever met, but she also treated people with courtesy and had a kind smile. She seemed to *notice* people, which her contemporaries never did.

Yet as he stood in the med lab and watched her work, he wasn't so sure. The doctor and her assistant—Wes Navarro—monitored the life signs of the people who still had those alien spider-things attached to their faces. But the medics made no effort to save lives. They had given up on the seven people who were still afflicted, surrendered them to imminent death, and it made Coughlin sick. One thing his parents had taught him as a kid was that you never surrendered, never gave in to despair.

Dr. Komiskey sat in a chair between two cots, drinking tea. The patients who'd been on those cots were dead now, carted off to the morgue by Volk, the orderly.

"You're just gonna sit there?" Coughlin asked. "These people are gonna die. Zak Li there, he can carve a flute with his own hands, and he plays the hell out of a guitar. Mo Whiting is like an exo-biologist or something, right? Nice lady. And you're just gonna let them die?"

Theodora Komiskey did not glance up from her tea. Her sorrow hung around her like a cloud.

But Coughlin wanted a reply, and so he forged on.

"All of you people with your medicine and your science, acting like you know everything, and you're not even going to try—"

"Sergeant!" Dr. Hidalgo snapped.

Coughlin looked up to see the older woman glaring at him. She had a small metal canister in one hand. Navarro had stopped, too— he held a pair of forceps and a steel tray. They were standing on either side of Zak Li, as if they'd been about to do something more than just observe.

"Let up on Dr. Komiskey, Sergeant," Dr. Hidalgo said. "We've all gone days with only a few hours' sleep. She's done all she can for these people—everything we can think of. Do you know the term 'triage?'"

"Of course. It means you figure out who's injured the worst, and in what order you need to treat them. We do the same thing in the field."

Dr. Hidalgo nodded slowly, gesturing at the half-dozen patients who lay on cots around them.

"It also means you treat the people who have a chance of surviving, and learn to recognize the ones who don't. We're in triage mode, Sergeant. We can't save these people. If we're to have any chance at all of saving the rest of the people in this colony, we need to learn everything we can about the aliens, and find a way to defeat them."

Coughlin stiffened, but as he glanced at Zak and Mo and the other people with those alien *things* on their faces, he began to see them not as patients, but as casualties. Only one of them—a fellow marine named Joplin Konig—had already lost the facehugger. He'd woken briefly and started to scream, his eyes wild, until Navarro had gotten a needle into him. Now Joplin was heavily sedated.

"That sucks," he muttered.

"I agree," Dr. Hidalgo replied, but she had already resumed what she had been doing. She bent over Zak Li and sprayed something from the canister onto two of the spidery legs on one side of his face. The legs turned white with frost, as did the patch of Zak's cheek that was visible between the alien's legs.

Liquid nitrogen, Sergeant Coughlin thought.

"Go," Hidalgo said.

Navarro used the forceps to pry one of the frozen legs away. It snapped off, and everyone in the room went still.

"No blood," Navarro said.

Dr. Komiskey stood up, sipped her tea, and crossed toward them.

"Might be a way to get the damn things off them safely after all…" she said cautiously, "but you've just killed the flesh on Mr. Li's cheek, as well."

The monitor began to beep loudly, and then to peal.

"Damn it!" Navarro shouted.

"The alien's cut off his oxygen," Dr. Hidalgo said, grimly resigned. "Back away. There's nothing we can do for him now."

So they stood there—the doctor, the scientist, her assistant, and Sgt. Coughlin—helpless to do anything. As the frozen portion of the alien's spidery legs began to thaw, the stub of the snapped one began to bleed. Acid blood burned through Zak's cheek, down through the cot, and into the floor beneath it.

Zak Li couldn't even scream.

"That's it," Coughlin said, lifting his weapon. "There *is* something we can do for these people, a way to stop their suffering. If they're going to die anyway, then let's put them out of their misery and kill these alien cockroaches all at the same time."

Dr. Hidalgo lunged forward, putting herself between Coughlin's gun and the patients.

"You'll do nothing of the kind!"

Coughlin frowned. "Why not? So you can continue studying your precious Xenomorphs?" He shook his head. "Do it without these poor bastards. I know Mori and Reese are over in the research lab, doing God knows what. Go join them, Dr. Hidalgo, and let me worry about the human end of things here. As far as I can see, it's something you and your team aren't very good at."

Navarro cleared his throat.

"Um, folks?"

Dr. Komiskey hurried over to Mo Whiting's cot. She took a pen from her pocket and used it to nudge the alien that was straddling Mo's face, and the spidery thing slid off, trailing the long dried gray proboscis that had been down her throat like it was some kind of withered umbilical cord.

Coughlin felt sick.

Fuck, he thought. *That's exactly what it is.*

"I've got a second one off over here," Navarro said. "We've got no consistent gestation period as yet, but these two are going to wake up soon. Someone's going to have to have 'the talk' with them."

On his cot, over near the door into the testing room, Pvt. Joplin Konig began to choke and jerk. Unconscious, he started to moan, and his body shook as if in a seizure.

Coughlin tapped the comm on his collar.

"Captain Brackett, do you copy? This is Coughlin."

Crackle on the line, and then Brackett's voice.

"Copy, Sergeant. Go ahead."

"It's going down now!"

"Do not let another one of these things leave that lab alive," Brackett snapped over the comm.

"Yes, sir!"

Navarro snatched up a complicated-looking device that he'd rigged with a net, still determined to catch the parasite as it burst from Joplin's chest.

"Back away, Navarro," Coughlin said. "This isn't a capture situation."

"Sergeant—" Dr. Hidalgo began.

Theodora Komiskey put both hands up, trying to referee, as if they had time to discuss it. Too many people were trying to keep Coughlin from doing his job. He needed reinforcements. He'd left Ginzler in the hall, guarding the lab from outside.

As Konig bucked on the table, eyes flying open as he gasped for air, Coughlin backed up to the automatic door and slapped the panel that slid it open. As he heard it shushing open, he spun to call for Ginzler.

An alien stood on the other side of the door, seven feet tall, ebon-skinned and ridged as if designed by some mad architect of the flesh. Stinking, viscous drool slid from its jaws as it reached for him.

Coughlin shouted in terror and brought up his weapon, but too late. As it grabbed him, its grip crushing his arms, he pulled the trigger and bullets tore into the floor and wall and killed Zak Li on his cot. Then the alien brought its tail around and impaled his heart with the precision of a swordsman.

Dying, Coughlin heard Dr. Hidalgo scream.

In his mind, he called for her to run, but he had neither words nor breath remaining to him.

Darkness claimed him.

Dr. Hidalgo shut her mouth, her own screams echoing in her mind. Fear surged through her, a terror unlike anything she'd ever known, but she shut it down.

The alien withdrew its blood-dripping tail from Sergeant Coughlin's chest with a sickening crunch of bone and the wet suction of a killing wound.

Navarro spouted frantic profanities and staggered backward, tripping over Mo Whiting's monitor and falling to the floor. The alien stalked toward him, almost bouncing with each step, its motion vaguely birdlike in a way that sickened her.

"Oh my God," Dr. Komiskey said. "Ohmigod." Her voice came from behind Pvt. Konig's cot, where she huddled now, thinking she could avoid death. A second creature crept through the door, stepping over Sergeant Coughlin's corpse.

The first one moved toward Mo Whiting, and Navarro screamed and jumped up, trying to flee. The creature caught him by the hair and dragged him back, regurgitating a thick liquid into his face. Navarro choked and flailed but quickly became sluggish, and the alien kept dragging him toward the door.

The second alien leapt onto Pvt. Konig just as the man's chest burst open and the newborn creature slithered out. The two monsters ignored each other. The parasite slithered off the cot and darted across the floor, just as the adult alien reached for Dr. Komiskey.

Dr. Hidalgo backed away slowly, keeping them in view. Gradually she picked up her pace. As the second newcomer stabbed its tail through Komiskey's shoulder—not a killing blow—the first paused and turned toward Dr. Hidalgo, and she froze a moment. It had no eyes that she could discern, but it cocked its head as if evaluating her, then hurried about its business with Navarro, dragging him from the lab.

Heart hammering inside her chest, barely able to breathe, she turned and fled toward an adjoining testing room, slapping the pad. When the door swished open, she darted inside, closed and locked it, and ran to the intercom on the wall. She held down the red button there, heard a wash of crackling static, and forced herself not to scream.

"This is Theresa Hidalgo in the med lab," she said quietly, the hushed words coming over the speakers above her head—and on every other speaker throughout the colony. That was the purpose of the red button.

"They're here," she rasped, her lower lip quivering as she glanced toward the door, wondering how long it would be before they came for her.

"Please, someone help."

DATE: 25 JUNE, 2179
TIME: 0954

Brackett reached the med lab with Yousseff, Hauer, and two other marines in tow. Silent and smooth, practically vibrating with adrenaline, he gestured for them to take up positions around the open door. Blood smeared the floor and had spattered the walls in patterns he read immediately.

Two dead, at least.

He scanned the corridor in both directions but saw no sign of aliens or any other personnel. The science team's research lab was at the far end of the corridor. He gestured to a tall, brutish marine whose name he hadn't even had time to learn, indicating that the man should check on the research lab. The door down that end was sealed up tight, but with the aliens using air ducts to travel, he thought it best to be sure.

"Cap," a low voice said, and he turned to see Hauer crouched in the elevator alcove fifteen feet away. Brackett held a hand up, palm out, to indicate that the private should stay put and wait for him.

With a nod to Yousseff and the other marine—a scarred, unshaven career grunt named Sixto—Brackett stepped into the med lab, sweeping the barrel of his gun in an arc across the room.

"Oh, man," Sixto whispered.

"Search it," Brackett said, and the three of them spread out.

They checked behind machines and kicked cots over, stepped around puddles of blood and shone lights into dark vents. There were three corpses in the room, Coughlin and two colonists who'd had facehuggers on them, but now had big holes in their chests. The rest of the people who'd been there, patients and doctors and marines, were all missing.

"Captain Brackett," Yousseff said, "what the hell is *this*?"

She knelt on the floor near a cot, touching a small pool of thick, sticky, resinous liquid that stretched between her fingers. With a grimace of disgust, she wiped her fingers on the cot.

Brackett heard a thump and glanced around to see Dr. Hidalgo looking at him through the small window set into a door at the other side of the room.

"Fuckin' miracle," he whispered as he rushed to the door and tried the latch.

The doctor stared at him through that little window, eyes wide, and it seemed to take her a moment to realize she had to open the door from inside. She shook her head as if coming out of a daze, and then worked the lock so that the door shushed open, sliding into a pocket in the wall.

"How are you alive?" Brackett asked her.

"Tes... th' tsst..." Dr. Hidalgo tried to speak but faltered, one hand fluttering up to cover her mouth. Her eyes filled with moisture, but as he watched, she seemed to force the tears not to fall. Steeling herself, taking slow breaths, she stood a bit straighter.

"The testing room," she explained, clearly now. "I said I was in the testing room." The words sounded like some kind of accusation, and Brackett frowned. They'd all heard her on the compound's intercom system, but Yousseff had told him that meant the med lab. Was the old woman angry that they hadn't come directly to her before searching the lab for threats?

Maybe she wasn't thinking clearly.

"I don't understand," he admitted.

"It's a sealed area. Sterile," Dr. Hidalgo said, hand still shaking as she tucked a gray strand of hair behind her ear. "My guess is that they couldn't get my scent in there."

"Or they got what they wanted, and didn't want to stick around and wait for the odds to shift against them," Pvt. Yousseff said, kicking at the desiccated body of a dead facehugger. "They dragged everyone else out of here, including the ones who were incubating more of the damn parasites."

Static crackled in Brackett's ear.

"This is Simpson for Captain Brackett. Do you read me, Captain?"

"Hang on, Mr. Simpson," Brackett said, poking his head into the testing room. He glanced around, then turned back to Dr. Hidalgo. The woman was tougher than she looked, but he could see she was still shaken. "Are you sure you're okay?"

Dr. Hidalgo exhaled. She reached out and put a grateful hand on his shoulder.

"Not even close, Captain, but thank you for asking. And for coming. I don't think I'd ever have left that room otherwise."

Brackett shifted his gaze back toward the interior of the testing room.

"Might turn out that you were safer in there." He turned to Yousseff. "Private, please stay with Dr. Hidalgo. I'll be back in a second." Then he headed into the corridor, where Hauer stood guard near the elevator alcove.

"I've got a feeling they're growing too big for the air ducts, Cap," Hauer said.

Brackett walked over and stared at the elevator doors, which had been forced open and now sat jammed at wrong angles inside their frame. The darkness of the elevator shaft yawned wide, a coldness emanating from within. He kept his weapon trained on the opening, but did not venture any closer.

He tapped the comm on his collar.

"Simpson, this is Brackett," he said. "You rang?"

"You sound pretty cavalier, Captain."

"I've had about six hours' sleep in three days, so I'm a little punchy. I've lost track of how many we've got dead, and how many have been abducted, and I'm trying to count up how many of these aliens we might be facing now. Everyone in the med lab is either dead or missing, except for Dr. Hidalgo—"

"Shit."

"—so it won't be long before their numbers rise significantly. We've got to locate these things, and I mean *now*."

"What about the research lab?" Simpson asked.

Brackett glanced along the corridor. The marine he'd sent to check on Reese and Mori walked out of their lab. He gave Brackett a thumbs up.

"All clear," Brackett said.

"Okay. All right, listen," Simpson went on, static fuzzing his words. "I want you to call in all of your people. We're moving all of the personnel together. I want your squad there protecting them." He paused, then added, "When the aliens come for us, you can kill them then."

Brackett scowled, staring into the dark maw of the elevator shaft.

"You're out of your mind, Simpson. They're breeding right now, and the ones already in here with us are growing bigger... stronger. We need to hunt the bugs down and wipe them out before there are more of them. It's our only hope."

"I disagree," Simpson said through the static.

"Yeah? Well, I've got a question for you," Brackett said, turning to see Dr. Hidalgo emerging from the med lab, stepping into the hallway. "Are you sure it's a good idea clustering everyone together? 'Cause if my squad can't track these bastards down, I think you may just be setting the table for dinner."

DATE: 25 JUNE, 2179
TIME: 1107

Anne jerked awake in the dark, gasping from a nightmare, her memory already splintering and skittering off into the recesses of her mind.

She caught her breath, felt the clammy sweat on her skin, and then exhaled as she realized it had been a dream. Glancing around, she saw Newt and Tim sprawled on a blanket that had been thrown on the floor, jackets and sweatshirts and seat cushions for pillows, and she remembered it all. The derelict spaceship and its abhorrent cargo, and what had happened to her husband.

"Russ," she breathed, eyes welling with tears that she quickly wiped away. She had to be stronger than that, for her kids.

Others slept around them, nearly a dozen people she had known for years but who seemed distant from her now. Some of these people were her friends, others her neighbors or co-workers, but her only priorities were Newt and Tim.

And Demian, she thought. No matter what else their past had held, once he had been her dearest friend. Whatever she intended to do, she ought to include him.

In the back of her mind she was aware that Demian Brackett hadn't made the rank of captain in the Colonial Marines without proving his mettle. She and her kids would have a much better chance of survival with him than without him.

"Mom?" Tim asked quietly. "Are you okay? You made a sound."

"Just bad dreams, sweetie," she said, hoping she sounded calmer than she felt. "Go back to sleep."

"I haven't been sleeping. I can't. Every time I close my eyes…"

You see your father die, she thought.

Whimpering softly, she grabbed her son and hugged him tightly.

"I know, Timmy. I know."

They'd been holed up in clusters for almost two full days, waiting for Simpson and Demian to give the all clear. From what Anne had heard, the reason that hadn't happened was that no trace had been found of the colonists who had gone missing, nor of the aliens that were presumed to have grown from the parasites. Then, last night, someone had noticed that some of the livestock were missing.

The door opened abruptly and she and Tim both flinched away from the light that knifed into the room. The two mechanics near the entrance jerked upright, aiming weapons at the figure that barged in, silhouetted by the glare from the corridor. Then the figure snapped the lights on, and the room flickered into illumination, people grumbling and shielding their eyes.

"Everyone up!" Lydecker said. "We're relocating all personnel immediately." He pulled the two armed mechanics aside for a private word while everyone began to rise, picking up bedding and pillows and other belongings. There were two other children in the room, and they had games and books with them. Anne wished she had brought such distractions for her own kids.

Food and drink had been brought to them over the course of the two days, and much of the detritus of those meals remained. Anne would be glad to leave the confined space.

"What's going on?" she asked, lifting a sleepy Newt into her arms, where the girl snuggled against her and went back to sleep. Two marines waited in the corridor, standing guard. A fresh wave of dread swept over Anne, and she pushed toward Lydecker with Tim trailing behind her.

"Brad, what's happened?" she asked.

Lydecker glanced at the others, saw they were mostly busy gathering their things, and bent to speak softly into her ear.

"Two of the groups were attacked," he said. "Four casualties, but everyone else is safe. Simpson and Brackett both think it'll be easier to protect everyone if we're all in one place. Everyone who can be armed will be, and it'll be easier to seal us off from the rest of the colony, as well."

Anne stared at him.

Safe, he'd said.

"Oh, my God."

Four casualties. She wondered who they were. Each would be someone she knew, perhaps a friend, but at the very least someone with whom she had shared a meal or a laugh over the years. Then Anne realized that she didn't want to know. *Four casualties*, she thought again. Better just to think of them that way. Better… because there would be more.

"Come on, Tim," she said. "Stay with me."

Anne and her kids were among the first people out of the room. She glanced around constantly as they followed Lydecker, but she stuck close to the marines, thinking that would make them safer if the aliens came for them.

With every step she was planning.

Help must be coming, she thought. *They'll have to have sent a report by now, a distress call. But how long would it take for anyone to arrive?*

The colony had a spaceworthy excavator ship on hand to mine asteroids, should the need arise. The question was whether or not the *Onager* had been here on Acheron when the shit hit the fan, or whether it was off-planet. She didn't know the answer, but she realized that she needed to find out—and quietly, because if everyone else had the same thought, there would be a huge rush to get away.

She wondered how far it would take them. Just to another moon, or out of the system? No chance for hypersleep on an excavator ship, she figured, but if they could just get to a safe orbit, they could wait in space for help to arrive.

And if the *Onager* wasn't there, there were always the crawlers in the garage. Out on the surface of the planet, she and her kids would have only whatever food and water they could bring with them, and they'd have to watch for storms, but at least they'd be away from the aliens.

Could they gather supplies and make it to the hangar without being caught? Without the aliens killing them or dragging them off? If the excavator ship wasn't there, and she ransacked the other crawlers for whatever supplies might be in them, how long could they survive if she drove out to one of the more distant processors? Long enough for help to arrive?

"I need to talk to Captain Brackett," she told one of the marines, a Pvt. Stamovich.

"He's a little busy right now," the private sneered.

Anne clutched Tim's hand in her left, carrying the sleeping Newt against her hip with her right.

"As soon as you get us all where we're going, I need you to contact him," she said firmly. "Tell him I want to talk to him."

Stamovich rolled his eyes and moved away, aiming his weapon around corners and through open doors.

The other marine was Boris Chenovski, who sidled up next to her.

"I'll make the call for you, Missus Jorden," Chenovski said. "But it may take a while for the captain to get back to you. We're in the middle of a bug hunt, y'know?"

"I know," she said quietly, leaning her head against Newt's as she walked. "Just please do what you can."

But in her mind, a clock had begun to tick.

22

SAFETY MEASURES

DATE: 25 JUNE, 2179
TIME: 1212

"Will we really be safe?" Newt asked.

Anne held her daughter's hand as they moved down the stairs, surrounded by fifteen or twenty others. Her heart fluttered wildly in her chest, but she forced herself to smile.

"Newt, I love you very much. I'm not going to let anything happen to you."

"Promise you won't leave me?"

Anne could barely breathe. Her smile thinned as she squeezed the little girl's hand.

"Promise."

They reached the next level. The door had been propped open and people were flowing through, joining others who were already in the hallway, streaming in the same direction. She caught a glimpse of Al Simpson walking by, pale and disheveled but still in charge, barking orders.

"Come on, sweetie," she said, picking Newt up again as she hurried to push past the crowd. Anne glanced over her shoulder and spotted Tim. "Let's go, little man."

Tim frowned. "I'm not little."

"No," Anne agreed, thinking that with his father gone, Tim would have to grow up very quickly indeed. "I guess you're not."

There was a pair of marines in the corridor, helping to guide people and make sure everyone got where they were going in an orderly fashion, but Anne saw the way they watched the vents and the doors and the way they held their guns, ready for trouble.

"See, Newt," she said, "these guys aren't going to let anything happen to us."

A group of mechanics, surveyors, and engineers had been busy welding doors and barricading them, closing off an entire section of D-Block not far from the med lab. Two doors had been left unwelded, but they were guarded by marines, and now most of the surviving colonists were moving to the huge storage area in D-Block, where they would hole up together until the marines and volunteers destroyed the aliens, or help arrived.

Anne tried not to think about the third option.

Tim hurried to catch up and moved in front of his mother and sister as if to shield them.

"Don't worry, Mom," he said grimly. "You and Newt can count on me to look out for you." Anne bit her lip and tried not to sob. She had no fear for herself, but the thought of her children trapped with these monsters made her want to scream. *Monsters we found*, she thought. *Monsters we brought back.*

"I feel better already," she said. "How about you, Newt?"

"Uh, sure," the girl said noncommittally. Her gaze darted around, on guard, just like the marines, and not for the first time Anne realized just how sharp her daughter was. Newt clutched her Casey doll to her chest, and clung a little tighter to her mother.

She caught up with Simpson a moment later. Flustered and sweating, he saw her coming and tried to ignore her.

"Mr. Lydecker," he said into his handheld comm, "do you have anything on the scans? Anything to help pinpoint their location?" This close to Simpson, Anne could hear the crackle of Lydecker's response.

"Not yet, sir. If there's a hive or something… well, we're working on it."

"Keep the doors sealed, Brad," Simpson said. "Stay safe."

Anne switched Newt to her other hip and stared at him as they walked. She wasn't about to let him avoid her.

"Do you really think we'll be safe in the storage area?" she asked.

"If we stay separated, those things will pick us off one by one," Simpson said. "Our best chance is to use all of our resources to secure this area, and hold out until help can arrive."

Anne felt a shiver go through her.

"Seriously, Al. Who could help us?"

"I've sent a message to Gateway," Simpson explained, puffed up and proud, as if he himself had just delivered them all to salvation. "They'll send more marines."

"But that will take weeks!" Anne said.

People turned to look at her. At her side, Tim glared at them until they looked away. Newt hugged her a bit tighter, upset by her distress.

Anne slowed down, letting Simpson get ahead. With her children, she dropped back to walk beside a marine.

"Can you tell me where Captain Brackett is?" she asked. "I really need to speak with him."

"I'll let him know, Mrs. Jorden. But as you can imagine—"

"Just tell him, please," she said. "Tell him it's important."

"Is Demian going to help us, Mom?" Newt whispered in her ear.

"Maybe *we'll* help him," Anne replied, wondering again how long she could afford to wait for Demian before making a break for it… and how long they could survive out on the surface, in the gritstorms, in a crawler.

"We can't stay here," she said to the marine. "There's got to be a way off this planet."

"The only way out of this is to fight," the marine said.

Anne glanced at Tim, so brave and handsome… so like his father. *Yeah, fight and die*, she thought, kissing Newt on the temple.

But perhaps the marine was right—maybe they could still get out of this. With everyone gathered together, there would be a limit to how many new hosts the aliens could abduct. The wildcatters were tough and most of them were armed. *Between us and the marines*, she thought, *maybe we can kill them all. Get back in control of the colony.*

Hour by hour. She decided that was the only way to evaluate their situation. *Hour by hour and day by day.* If Simpson and the rest of the staff could get them all settled in the storage area, Anne would give it a little time.

Is that hope, Annie? she asked herself. In her mind, it was Russ's voice she heard. The answer came to her immediately. It wasn't hope that drove her decision, not now. Her kids were exhausted—and not only the kids. Grief and fear had sapped all of the vitality from her. So for now, they would rest and put their trust in others.

Tomorrow morning she would reevaluate the situation.

Come on, Demian, she thought. *We need to talk, you and I.*

We need to run.

One thing Anne knew for certain, though. If she decided it was time to go and Demian disagreed, or she hadn't been able to find him by then, she and the kids would go it alone.

DATE: 26 JUNE, 2179
TIME: 0717

Newt's eyes flickered open. She rubbed the grit of sleep from them, and blinked as she stretched into a yawn that rolled her Casey doll out of her grasp.

The floor beneath the blanket was cold and hard, but somehow she'd been sleeping with her mom's jacket balled under her head for a pillow. Grimacing with disgust, she wiped drool from her mouth and realized some of it had gotten on the jacket. As she sat up, she tried to rub it off. Then it struck her where she was, and why she was there.

A terrible weight settled over her heart as she glanced around at the dozens of people who had gathered in the storage area. Only a handful were still sleeping, there at the back of the room with her. The rest were sitting together in frightened conversation or standing in worried clusters. A few marines and wildcatters were scattered around the chamber, carrying weapons. One of them—Chenovski—stood a few feet away from Newt, talking quietly with Tim and his friend Aaron.

"...think they're too big now to come through the air ducts?" Aaron asked.

Chenovski nodded. "Depends how long since they were hatched or whatever, but yeah. That's what we're thinking."

"Some of those ducts are pretty big inside," Tim said, glancing anxiously at a grate high up on the wall. "We've been in them."

"This is a storage area," Chenovski said. "It doesn't usually have anyone living in it. The vents will give us air, but they're really just there for ventilation. The ductwork leading here is narrower than most other parts of the colony. But don't worry, guys…" He slapped his rifle. "We're still on guard. You're protected, okay?"

Tim and Aaron glanced at each other, looking unconvinced. Newt didn't blame them. She had seen the thing that had punched its way out of her father's chest. She glanced nervously at the grating up on the wall, picked up her Casey doll, and hugged her.

She crossed her legs and just sat there, feeling so small with all of those people milling about. Her eyes roved over the many familiar faces and some not quite so familiar, and her heart began to quicken as she scanned in search of her mother. Her eyes darted from side to side and a terrible fear ignited inside her, burning higher and brighter with every passing second.

Newt closed her eyes for a second, but in the darkness inside her head she saw her father bucking as the alien creature burst out of his body, and she heard his scream of pain… the last time she had heard—or would ever hear—his voice.

How many familiar faces were missing now? Dead, like her daddy?

"No," Newt whispered, lip trembling as tears sprang to her eyes. She rose to her feet, holding Casey against her. "Mommy?"

She spun toward Tim and Aaron and Pvt. Chenovski.

"Where's Mommy?" she asked, but her voice came out too soft. She felt as if she were invisible to them.

Her breath hitched in her chest as she set off in a panic, pushing past people. Tim called her name and started after her but Newt didn't want her brother anymore, she wanted her mom. She bumped into legs and hips and backs, calling for her mother, but even as she did she caught sight of faces and tried to figure out who wasn't there in the storage area, and if they were dead. Where was Daddy's friend, Bill? Where was the cook, Bronagh, who always saved her a freeze-pop or a piece of cake?

"Momma?" Newt called.

A hand clutched her arm. Face flushed with heat and wet with tears, Newt tried to pull free but could not. She heard her name, words gently spoken, but she shook her head and turned angrily… desperately. All she wanted was her mother. Instead, she found herself looking into the brown eyes of Dr. Hidalgo. She had lines around her eyes and they seemed to have deepened, as if she had grown much older just in the past few days.

"Newt," Dr. Hidalgo said again. "It's all right. Listen to me. Your mother is helping to bring food and supplies to us. Just a few minutes ago she asked me to look after you when you woke, but I got caught up in conversation. I'm so sorry that you woke up alone."

The words seemed to come from far away.

"She's… she's alive?"

"Yes, dear. She's fine. I promise you." But something dark flickered across Dr. Hidalgo's face and Newt understood it, heard the hesitation in the scientist's voice.

"Someone else died, though," Newt said.

Dr. Hidalgo nodded. "Several were taken while we were getting settled here last night. Quietly."

Quietly, Newt thought. She knew she was young, but she would have been the first to declare that being little didn't make her stupid. Quietly meant the aliens weren't stupid either. They were sneaky and smart.

Tim and Aaron caught up to her.

"Rebecca," her brother said, "what are you doing? You can't just run—"

"I wanted Mom," she replied, wiping her eyes. That same heavy weight settled on her heart, and she felt suddenly as cold and hard as the floor she'd slept on. "I want Dad."

As Aaron glanced away, Tim nodded.

"Me too."

Newt felt herself going a little numb.

"Who else is gone?" she asked Dr. Hidalgo. "Who else is dead? Is Aldo okay? What about Lizzie Russo? Is Mrs. Flaherty here?"

Dr. Hidalgo blinked, taken off guard by the last name, and Newt knew there would be no more pieces of cake set aside for her in the kitchen. No more freeze-pops. Bronagh Flaherty was gone. She squeezed her eyes shut for a second, and again she could hear her father scream.

Newt turned to her brother and slid into his embrace. Tim hugged her tightly.

"I want Mom," she said.

"I know," her brother replied quietly. "She's coming."

23

ESCAPE ROUTES

DATE: 26 JUNE, 2179
TIME: 1111

Dr. Reese hesitated on the steps while Pvt. Stamovich opened the door and stepped into the corridor, gun at the ready. Stamovich looked pale and exhausted, but the man practically vibrated with potential violence.

Most of the morning had come and gone and there hadn't been an attack from the aliens since the middle of the night. Stam wanted to shoot something. Dr. Reese wanted a man who was ready to kill to protect him, but he did worry a bit that the private's itchy trigger finger might end up finding the wrong target.

Stam glanced back into the stairwell. "You're clear, Doc."

Reese followed him into the corridor and Stam led the way toward the storage area where most of the colonists were holed up.

"You sure they're not going to attack during the day?" Stam asked.

Dr. Reese frowned. "Not certain, of course. There isn't enough data. But aside from the 'births' of the newborn aliens, their appearances have mostly come at night."

"Mostly," Stam echoed.

"I don't think we can be sure of anything with the Xenomorphs, Private. In time, we'll know more about them."

"I don't know that we've got much time, Doc. And I gotta tell ya, I don't need to know much except how to kill 'em."

Dr. Reese tensed, but he nodded.

"We're working on it."

"I know, man," the gruff marine said as he swept his gun barrel in an arc that took in the corridor ahead of them, as well as behind. "Meantime, I still think we ought to be moving in larger groups. Just the two of us together…"

"I have work to do," Dr. Reese said. "And Captain Brackett has most of your squad searching for the creatures. If I had an entire army to protect me, believe me, they would be here now."

It troubled Dr. Reese that they had not yet found the alien hive. There had to be many of them now, and more gestating. Dozens of colonists had been taken away—far more than most of the people knew—and they hadn't just vanished. The aliens would be taking them to a place where there were eggs. His research had shown conclusively that one of the earliest facehuggers had been slightly different from the others. Dr. Mori theorized that its egg must have been selected by the aliens on the derelict, and bathed in special nutrients secreted in similar fashion as the cocooning resin the aliens produced from their throats.

But Dr. Reese did not concur. That meant one of those who'd gone inside the derelict would have had to encounter the one queen egg. The odds against it were overwhelming, and required far too much coincidence. Reese suspected some form of self-determination through biological imperative, where the facehugger itself underwent a metamorphosis in order to produce a queen, and perpetuate the species.

Whatever the case, the number of aliens that had already appeared inside the complex was the only evidence he required. Somewhere in the colony, the aliens had a queen that had matured to adulthood and had begun producing eggs with astonishing speed—yet another dramatic display of biological imperative. From what little they had already learned, it was clear that these Xenomorphs were the most extraordinary creatures he had ever encountered. They lived to perpetuate their own species, and were single-mindedly savage in the process.

A thump came from behind them, and they both swung around, Stamovich ready to shoot. Dr. Mori stood in the hallway with his arms up, his face almost as white as his hair.

"No, no!" Dr. Mori cried. "It's only me."

He seemed out of breath. Dr. Reese nearly barked at him for risking death, but then the stairwell door opened again and their lab assistant, Khati Fuqua, emerged along with a gun-bearing mechanic who had offered to defend them. The man thought he was doing a great service for the colony, since the science team was attempting to figure out a swifter way to kill the aliens.

Which, of course, they were not.

"Jeez, Doc," Stam said to Mori. "That's a good way to get a bullet to the head."

Dr. Mori exhaled loudly as he lowered his hands and hurried toward them.

"Dr. Reese, we need to speak."

Reese gestured to Stam.

"Lead the way, Mr. Stamovich. Give Dr. Mori and myself some privacy, please."

Mori gestured to Khati. She and the mechanic followed Stamovich toward the storage area.

"What is so urgent that you raced after me?" Dr. Reese asked quietly, glancing forward and backward to make sure they would not be overheard.

Dr. Mori knitted his brows. Reese might have been his superior, but he had never liked being spoken to in a tone that reminded him. Not that Reese much cared what Dr. Mori liked or disliked.

"I've only just learned how many of the colonists have been killed or taken," Mori said quietly. "It is time, Dr. Reese. I've done a computer model of the outcome here, but we didn't really need that, did we? You must make the call now. It is time for us to leave Acheron. The specimens are ready to be crated up for transport, and I have saved all of the data. We have everything we need—"

"Not everything we wanted, though," Dr. Reese said with a sidelong glance, eyes narrowed in irritation. "The company will want a living Xenomorph—one of the ovomorphs at least."

"And how do you propose we bring one of those back?" Dr. Mori hissed.

When Dr. Reese ignored him and kept walking, Mori grabbed his arm and forced Reese to face him.

"The model is clear—"

"I am in control of this situation, Dr. Mori," Reese said, jaw tight with anger at the other scientist's presumption.

"What you call control is an illusion," Dr. Mori whispered, both of them aware that Stam, Khati, and the mechanic had all paused to stare at them. "Time is running out. If we are going to save the data and ourselves, we must go."

"Soon," Dr. Reese promised. "Trust me."

DATE: 26 JUNE, 2179
TIME: 1117

Anne walked into the storage area carrying an enormous crate of fresh fruit from the greenhouse.

She'd spent nearly two hours picking fruit and vegetables with the greenhouse supervisor, Genevieve Dione, and a handful of other volunteers, and it had been among the most frightening times of her life. Despite the fact that they'd had a marine and two armed wildcatters along to watch their asses while they did the work.

She'd been proud to volunteer, glad to be able to help these people. Part of that, she knew, was guilt at the prospect of abandoning them. Some of them were her friends, and even those who weren't were still a part of the family the colony had become.

Now, though, she had done her duty. Her skin had crawled the whole time she'd been in the greenhouse and even on the walk back, waiting for the aliens to attack. She had expected the sensation to fade when she was back among her people, but no such luck. She set the produce basket down and glanced around, pulse quickening at each glimpse of a barricaded door or a dark vent where bars had been screwed in.

The thought of the *Onager* was like a bright ember burning in her mind. She glanced around and wondered who else might have thought of it, as well. Derrick Bradford, Nolan Cale, and Genevieve Dione were standing in a conspiratorial cluster, faces etched with determination. They were planning something, but she couldn't be sure what.

Most of the colonists would have discounted the excavator ship, even if they'd thought of it, knowing that it couldn't get them far. Others, however, must have realized that it all might come down to time, that floating around in orbit would buy them the precious days or weeks needed for rescue to arrive.

If it's even there, she thought. If it wasn't, there were always the crawlers. She could get her kids out of here in one of those metal beasts, should the need arise. But she didn't want to leave without Demian, if she could help it.

The clock was ticking.

"Mom!"

Anne turned to see Newt racing toward her, the Casey doll trailing from her left fist, clutched by its blond hair. She smiled and opened her arms, and Newt leaped into them.

"Hey, sweetie," Anne said, the shadows in her heart retreating for just a moment. "I'm glad you're up."

Newt pushed off so that Anne had to put her down, then punched her mother in the hip.

"Don't leave me alone again!" she said angrily. "You promised!"

"I was only..." Anne began, but she saw that her daughter was angry and afraid, and she cut herself off. "Okay. I'm sorry." She looked around. "Want an apple?"

Newt didn't want to be distracted or appeased, but after a moment's consideration she relented.

"I might like an apple," she admitted.

"Where's Tim?" Anne asked.

"Playing with Aaron," her daughter said, with obvious disapproval.

Anne's breath caught. "Not near the—"

"No, Mom," Newt said. "Not Monster Maze. Boys are dumb, but not *that* dumb. Besides, Private Chenovski has been watching them. I was playing with Luisa for a little while, but then her mom wanted her to eat something, so I've just been waiting."

Anne nodded as she bent to fetch an apple from the basket. As she handed the fruit to her daughter, she glanced over and saw Dr. Reese and Dr. Mori come in with several others, including Pvt. Stamovich. Her eyes narrowed. As Newt bit into the fruit, Anne fought the urge to confront Reese, to try to force him to tell her what he knew about the aliens. What had they learned?

Perhaps more importantly, what did Weyland-Yutani know about the creatures? Had the company known in advance what she and Russ would be walking into when they were ordered to investigate the coordinates where they'd found the derelict?

At the very thought, anger blossomed in her.

"Newt, do you see Dr. Reese right over there?"

"Sure."

"I need to talk to him for a minute. So I'm not leaving. I'll just be right over there—"

"I'll come."

"No, honey," Anne said. "It needs to be in private."

Newt looked suspicious for a second, then glanced over to gauge the distance between herself and the doctors.

"All right. But don't leave without me."

"Never," Anne said, kissing the top of her head. "Jordens forever."

Newt nodded once, firmly.

"Jordens forever," she said, with a mouthful of apple.

Anne strode across the storage area, moving around piles of goods and supplies that had been stacked up to make room for the colonists. Dr. Reese and Dr. Mori were talking to Al Simpson. She was so focused on Reese that when Demian Brackett came through the guarded door just beyond the scientists, also headed for Reese, she didn't immediately register his presence.

When she did spot him, she quickened her pace. It would be a mistake to reveal her plans in front of the scientists, so she would have to be wary. But she couldn't allow Brackett to leave before they'd spoken.

"Demian," she said, intercepting him. "We need to talk."

He must have seen the urgency in her expression, for his eyes filled with concern.

"What is it?" he asked. "Are the kids all right?"

The strength and kindness in him caused a wave of regret to wash over her. She knew she had made the right choice in marrying Russ— otherwise Newt and Tim would never have been born—but a pang of sadness filled her as she allowed herself to wonder where a life with Demian would have led.

"They're okay. I just..." She faltered as Simpson, Reese, and Mori approached them. The cacophony of voices in the storage area seemed to swell, and any hope of having a private conversation seemed like foolishness. "When you're done here, I need a word before you run off again."

Brackett gave her a solemn nod.

"Absolutely. Can you give me a minute?"

Anne started to reply, but then Simpson was there, looking aggrieved.

"Captain, what are you doing?" the administrator asked. "Have you found the nest?" His mustache quivered as he spoke.

"Not yet—" Brackett began.

"Then why are you here?" Simpson said angrily. "More than a few people are blaming the overnight losses on your refusal to dedicate your entire squad to the protection of this shelter. You told me those were unavoidable—that the most important thing was to track and kill the aliens—but you haven't accomplished that yet."

"Simpson," Brackett said, his voice low but dangerous. "I didn't come to talk to you. I'm here for Dr. Reese."

The administrator muttered something under his breath, preparing a retort, but Brackett silenced him with a glare.

"What can I do for you, Captain?" Dr. Reese asked.

"I received a communiqué from my superiors—one that I wanted to share with you," Brackett said.

Dr. Reese smiled thinly. "Please, go on."

"I asked about my squad being used as security detail on colonial surveying missions, making my objections clear. The reply came from Marine Space Force, Eridani command, on Helene 215," he continued, "informing me that my orders are to provide security for the colony itself—and that the safety of individuals traveling beyond the boundaries of the colony would *not* be the responsibility of the USCMC."

Dr. Mori sputtered. "That's absurd. We've always—"

"Hush," Dr. Reese said, holding up a hand. He looked grimly confident, and Anne didn't understand why. "Continue, Captain Brackett."

Anne looked at Demian's face, and she saw the anger there.

"Two hours after I received those initial orders, they were overridden by an eyes-only communiqué issued jointly by the command staff at O'Neil Station—"

"From the highest authority in the Marine Corps," Reese interrupted.

"Yes," Brackett acknowledged. "Jointly with the Chief of Operations for Gateway," he said, glancing at Anne to make sure she understood. He turned back to Reese and Mori, still ignoring Simpson. "I'm now instructed to put myself and my squad at your personal disposal, Dr. Reese. Whatever plan you devise to deal with the Xenomorphs, I am to support it in every way possible. And I will follow those orders, because I am a marine.

"But," he added, "I will continue to voice my opinions, and first among those is that the government and the company are far too cozy.

"I don't trust you, Doctor."

Anne watched Al Simpson deflate. The normally blustery administrator had just lost the last vestiges of whatever leadership he'd ever exerted over the people of Hadley's Hope. Blunt and snappish as he could be, she had always respected Simpson for his hard work and determination, but any control he'd had over the colony had always been an illusion. Everyone knew that Weyland-Yutani called the shots, and that meant that Dr. Reese had *always* been in charge. Brackett's new orders had only formalized the truth.

"What the *hell* is wrong with you?" she asked.

All four men turned to stare at her, the scientists blinking as if she had been invisible to them before. Several colonists had gathered around, spectators to the strange little power struggle going on.

"People are *dying*." Anne glared at them. "My friends and I… my kids… we don't care which of you is in charge. In fact, I'd venture to say that at this point, none of us gives a shit which of you *thinks* he's in charge. This place is falling apart. My husband is dead, along with a lot of my friends, and dozens are missing. The aliens are hard to kill and their number is growing. If you don't figure out a way to eliminate them, nobody will be left alive for any of you to order around.

"So stop standing around measuring your dicks."

A cheer went up around her, and a round of applause began.

"Mommy?" she heard Newt say, and she blushed, realizing her daughter had heard what she'd said. Anne glanced back and saw that Tim had his hands over his little sister's ears, and she smiled at both children.

"Mrs. Jorden is right," Simpson said, looking around at the gathered colonists. "We're already doing everything we can to protect you all, to track down the aliens, and retrieve our missing friends."

Retrieve? Did any of them really believe that? Anne heard grumbling voices around her and knew the colonists would not let Simpson go unchallenged. They were all afraid, and grieving, and there were no words that would soothe them. Only results would calm their nerves.

She glanced at Brackett, but he only stood stiffly beside the scientists as Dr. Reese muttered something to him.

"Are we all gonna die?" Luisa piped up, her red hair a messy tangle around her face.

Brackett's expression melted and he stepped forward.

"No, honey. I'm not going to let that—"

A commotion at the doors startled them all. People recoiled in surprise and fear, some calling out in alarm, but then Lydecker came bustling in with several other members of the administration staff. He saw that he'd frightened them, and apologized before hurrying over to Simpson, taking his boss by the arm and walking him into an isolated corner.

One of the people who'd come in with Lydecker was a young, clean-cut man named Bill Andrews who had often been responsible for assigning survey teams. Anne and Russ had gotten to know him well, and now she approached him.

"Bill… what's going on?"

He glanced around, clearly uncertain as to how much he could share. But then he blinked, as if remembering something he should never have forgotten.

"Annie, how are you holding up?"

She glanced over at her children. Newt and Dr. Hidalgo were seated on plastic crates, engaged in an animated conversation, but Tim sat alone on the floor, an air of sadness around him. When he was looking out for his sister he seemed all right, but when his thoughts weren't otherwise engaged, they naturally drifted back to the horror of his father's death.

"I'm doing okay," she said, exhaling slowly. "But I'm scared for the kids. I keep wondering when the nightmare will end, y'know?"

Bill cast a quick glance at Lydecker and Simpson, and lowered his voice.

"Maybe soon," he said, and she looked at him curiously. "We were stupid before, just not thinking properly. All of us have our PDT implants, and we finally realized we could track the missing folks that way."

Anne clapped a hand to her forehead. Every colonist had a subdermal implant—a personal data transmitter. In the years she'd been at Hadley's Hope, she'd only seen them used twice—when wildcatters had gone out of radio range and run into mechanical trouble—but still, someone ought to have thought of it earlier.

She should have thought of it.

"We think we've located the creatures' nest, underneath Processor One," Bill said. "Mr. Lydecker figures the marines will send an armed party over there now."

He smiled. "It won't be long."

Anne nodded, not daring to hope.

"One way or another."

DATE: 26 JUNE, 2179
TIME: 1221

"I don't think you understand me," Dr. Hidalgo said, tucking her hair behind her ears and fixing her colleagues with a grim stare. "I'm going with them."

Dr. Mori bared his teeth in a sneer of disapproval, but Dr. Reese seemed genuinely shocked. Dr. Hidalgo liked that—liked being able to shock him.

"That's not acceptable, Theresa," Reese said.

She laughed softly.

"Do you think I care what you find acceptable?"

When she had seen the clutch of conversation between Lydecker and Simpson, and then watched those two men approach her colleagues on the science team, she'd known that some sort of breakthrough had taken place. Then Anne had come back to collect her children, and told her that the alien nest had been found.

Dr. Hidalgo had known then that she couldn't stay here with the colonists. Not when she knew they were soon to be abandoned. So she had drawn her fellow scientists away from Simpson, Brackett, and the others for this conversation. It had gone about as well as she had expected.

"There is only one way to do this," Dr. Reese said. "The marines have to kill all of the aliens. One of the idiots suggested that they try to overload the processor core and hope that it will explode, just like in the accident involving the Finch brothers... the explosion that destroyed Processor Six."

Dr. Mori gaped at him. "But the entire colony would be destroyed."

"Precisely," Reese sneered.

Dr. Hidalgo nodded. "That's why Al Simpson volunteered to go along. They need a tech—someone who can guide them, and let them know what's safe and what isn't. He's gambling with his life, in the hope that he can help save the rest of these people." She peered at them intently. "I'm willing to do the same."

Dr. Mori gripped her arm roughly, fingers digging in as he came close to her, whispering intently.

"Are you dense, woman?" the silver-haired scientist asked. "We're taking our data and samples, and we are leaving Acheron."

But she shook her head.

"I can help them," she said. "I know enough about medicine to treat injuries, and I can advise them regarding the alien."

"Theresa," Dr. Reese said curtly, "if the marines seem unable to do the job, we are leaving, with you or without you."

Dr. Hidalgo hated even to blink. Every time she did, she saw the aliens murdering people in the med lab, then dragging others off to be used for incubation.

"Do what you have to do, Dr. Reese," she said, and then turned to Mori. "I'd tell you to look after yourself, but really, it's what the two of you have always been best at."

24

ALL FALL DOWN

DATE: 26 JUNE, 2179
TIME: 1332

Breathe, Julisa, she told herself. *You're armed and dangerous.* Even attempting to walk quietly, Lt. Paris thought her footfalls sounded like thunderclaps in the abandoned corridor.

Normally the thought would have made her smile, but smiles were in short supply this afternoon. So, for that matter, were marines. She wore MX4 body armor and a ballistic helmet. A VP78 pistol hung in the holster on her hip and she carried an M41A pulse rifle in her hands, with a battle rifle slung over her shoulder as a backup, all of them loaded with high-velocity rounds. She had enough firepower to take on an army by herself, but none of it would do a damn bit of good if one of those aliens got to her before she could kill it.

And that acid blood... she didn't even want to think about it.

Capt. Brackett had taken Draper, Pettigrew, and ten other marines off to hunt down the aliens in their hive, or whatever the hell it was, leaving her in charge of safeguarding the colonists in the sealed-off wing of D-Block. She'd stationed the rest of the squad around the inside of the perimeter, not just at every potential entrance into the storage area, but at every junction leading that way.

She herself had been patrolling the inside of the perimeter for the past hour, checking welds and barricades and the guards who were covering the two unwelded doors. She'd passed the door to the storage area a couple of turns back—left it guarded by three marines armed even more thoroughly than she was—but overall, they simply didn't have enough bodies to effectively guard the colonists if the aliens showed up en masse.

Her skin crawled every time she passed a doorway or approached a turn. As she approached the next corner, she whistled the signal she'd arranged. From around the turn came the reply, the same two notes, and she exhaled and quickened her pace. She rounded the corner to find Aldo Crowley leaning against the wall with his weapon cradled in his arms.

"Damn, Aldo," she said, "you look way too relaxed."

Crowley straightened to attention, but only for a moment before he chuckled and leaned back against the wall.

"Lieutenant, I'm one grunt with a gun. Those things come after us in force and I'm in the way, the best way for me to serve you is screaming like a little girl. Give the rest of y'all some warning."

She would have argued with him, but he wasn't wrong.

"Suit yourself," she said. "I'm not going to make you march in place out here. But I'll tell you this… these things *can* die. You just stand there with your thumb up your ass, you're liable to end up pregnant with one of their babies, or whatever the fuck that's about. Me? I'd rather be dead."

Lt. Paris walked on, but she noticed Aldo wasn't leaning against the wall anymore. He had his weapon in both hands, watching the corners and the shadows of the corridor ahead that branched off toward the command block.

Sixty feet further on she came to Pvt. Yousseff and a man called Virgil, who wore a face mask as he used a hand-welder to melt and seal the bolts on the stairwell door. That would leave only one door still unwelded—one way for Brackett and the others to get in and out.

Virgil had started from the bottom, liquid metal sparks flying out in all directions. The metal turned white-hot where the flame struck it.

"Anything?" Lt. Paris called over the noise of the welder.

Yousseff shook her head. Virgil didn't even look up.

Paris rose on her toes and peered through the small square windows set into the stairwell doors. Shadows and light played across the steps on the other side, but she saw nothing moving.

"You think they're going to be able to pull it off, Lieutenant?" Yousseff asked.

"I hope so," Paris said, then she grinned. "The new CO is easy on the eyes. I'd rather he not get his face bitten off."

Yousseff laughed and nodded.

"I'm right there with you."

Lt. Paris walked on, continuing her circuit of the perimeter, surprised that after serving with Yousseff for nearly two years, they'd finally found something they had in common. She thought about Brackett, off with that asshole Draper, and hoped they both came back alive. They'd already lost too many marines, like Coughlin, and she didn't want to lose any more.

Approaching the next corner, she whistled the signal.

Three more steps and she halted, frowning deeply. Breathing in and out, listening to her own heartbeat. She lifted the pulse rifle and took two steps nearer the turn. Then she whistled again.

The sound that came back was a wet gurgle, followed by the slap of flesh on floor.

Fuck.

Quiet and swift, she hurried to the corner. Back to the wall, she peered around the edge, leading with the rifle barrel.

The alien crouched above Chenovski, who lay on the floor, alive but somehow paralyzed. His face and body armor were covered with a thick layer of fluid, some kind of mucous, but his eyes were wide and aware as the alien dragged him toward another branching corridor.

Paralysis, she thought. *But he'll know it when they put him in front of one of those eggs and let a damn facehugger implant a parasite in his chest.*

She had kissed Chenovski once, drunk and maudlin because she was alone on her birthday. Mostly their friendship was based on her cheating at cards and him letting her get away with it.

Paris stepped out from the corner.

"Hey, shithead!" she barked.

The alien snapped its head up. If it had eyes, they stared at her.

"Lieutenant?" Yousseff called from off to her left, back the way she'd come.

Paris shot the alien twice in the chest. It staggered back, acid blood spilling to the ground, hissing as it ate through the floor. The acid spray hit Chenovski's legs and he moaned, but it could've been so much worse.

"Back off!" she shouted, taking a step forward, trying to scare it away from Chenovski while he was still alive.

It didn't look scared.

Instead, it advanced on her as if daring her to fire again—daring her to spill more acid onto her friend. Paris felt a nauseous twist in her gut.

How smart are these things?

She fired several times into the wall just beside the thing. From her left she heard Yousseff shouting... running her way... and then Aldo Crowley, coming as well, all the way from his post at the next corner, seventy yards away.

The alien didn't flinch. Its mouth opened and its jaws slid out, thick rivulets of drool spilling from its lips. Paris wanted to scream. Wanted to throw up. But mostly she wanted to kill it.

She pulled the trigger, a single shot aimed right at the center of its head. It twitched to the left so that the bullet punched through the carapace and struck its skull. It rose up as if in righteous fury, coiled its tail behind it, and Lt. Paris readied herself for it to charge, thinking that if she could open up with a full salvo from the pulse rifle, she could kill it before it reached her and maybe—just maybe—its blood would fall nearer to her, and Chenovski would live.

The alien drove the knifepoint of its tail through Chenovski's skull with a wet crunch.

Paris screamed and opened fire as the alien charged toward her. It took a dozen rounds as it lunged, and she backpedaled, slammed into the wall, and kept shooting until she blew its body apart. Its blood flew and she dove aside as it spattered and burned into the wall.

Sliding onto her belly, combat rifle clacking against her helmet and pistol jamming into her hip, she found herself on the floor as Yousseff reached her.

"Get up, Loot," Yousseff snapped. "There may be more."

As if Paris didn't know that. She scrambled to her feet and swung her plasma rifle up again.

"I don't know how it got in past the sealed-off door down that way, but it had to have come from that side corridor," Yousseff said, gesturing with her weapon. "No chance it got the drop on Chenovski approaching any other way."

Thirty feet along, the opening to that side corridor yawned wide. The two marines exchanged a glance. Neither of them wanted to go down there, but they had no choice. There seemed no question that the aliens knew exactly where the colonists were holed up, and were attempting to take out those who were guarding them.

Or they don't care, Lt. Paris thought with a shiver. *Maybe they just look at our storage area as their storage area now... And however that one got in, they figure they can come and get us a few at a time, whenever it's convenient.*

"With me," she told Yousseff, and she took a single step.

A crash reverberated along the corridor.

Aldo Crowley shouted filthy profanities to his God.

Paris and Yousseff whipped around to see Virgil on his ass with the welder in his hand, his face mask still down, almost obscenely impersonal. Another crash and the stairwell doors began to buckle on the top. The weld on the bottom, though still warm, held as the upper parts of the doors began to bow inward.

An alien slammed its head into the widening gap.

"Shoot it, Aldo!" Lt. Paris shouted as she and Yousseff raced back along the hallway. "Open fire, damn it!"

Aldo pulled the trigger, spraying the doors with plasma rounds that blew out the windows and stitched holes into the metal. The alien crashed into the doors again and the hinges shrieked, then began to give way.

Virgil sat up, scrambled forward, thrust his welder through the opening and let loose a stream of concentrated blue flame.

Lt. Paris heard the alien scream. She liked the sound.

Then the alien crashed through the doors. One tore completely free and fell on top of Virgil, knocking the welder from his hand. Its flame cut across his body as the door blocked their view of him, but Paris and Yousseff could hear him roaring in pain.

The alien ripped the gun from Aldo's grip and hurled the weapon aside, even as it punched its extended jaw through his forehead.

As Aldo slid down the wall, dead, Paris and Youseff opened fire, blowing the alien apart with dozens of rounds.

When they let up, the echo of gunfire ringing in their ears, Paris held her breath. They stared at the open maw of the ruined stairwell doors. After a few seconds they hurried past, not looking at Aldo, stopping only a moment to check on Virgil, who'd ended his own life with his welding torch.

They aimed into the darkened stairwell, lights flickering inside, and then hurried on to the corner that had until moments ago been Aldo Crowley's post.

Together, the two marines stood guard, watching the carnage-strewn corridor for sign of any further attack.

For the moment, the hallway was quiet.

"We are so screwed," Youseff breathed.

Lt. Paris said nothing. Instead, she prayed that Brackett and Draper could get the job done. She had known the risks when she joined the Corps, but she had decided that she was firmly opposed to dying on Acheron.

DATE: 26 JUNE, 2179
TIME: 1339

The enormous structure was labeled Atmosphere Processor One. The place was the size of an old-time sports stadium, at least fifteen stories high and several levels deep. Its inner workings included not only the most significant atmospheric processing units, but an energy reactor providing power to the entire colony.

A wide service tunnel ran from the main floor of the colony complex at an angle that led underground and connected up with sub-level one of the massive processing station. Walking through that tunnel, Brackett and his team saw clear evidence that the aliens had been using it to travel back and forth to the complex. The sticky, hardening resin that the demons secreted was everywhere, and they found streaks and puddles of human blood along the way.

Lydecker's staff had tracked the PDTs to a place under the primary heating stations, down in the guts of Processor One—sub-level three. The aliens were building their hive in the hot, humming belly of the place. As the captain led his team into the massive structure, he tried not to wonder how many of the monsters would be waiting.

Sub-level three was accessible via two elevators and long, narrow stairs. Brackett and Draper stood guard as Cpl. Pettigrew took Stamovich, Hauer, and seven other marines into the huge freight elevator. He didn't like splitting their numbers, but the speed of the elevator provided made it the best option. Taking the stairs all the way down offered too many dark corners from which the aliens could come for them.

Too many doors, as well, whereas the elevator only had one.

"Pettigrew, when you reach the bottom you sit tight unless you are under attack," Brackett said. "You read me? No one goes exploring. Just secure the area around the elevator and wait for us. We'll be right behind you."

"Yes, sir," Cpl. Pettigrew said. With the helmet hiding his blond hair he looked older. Or perhaps it was fear that had aged him.

"If you see any nasties, run faster than the other guys," Draper suggested, a mischievous glint in his eye. "The ones at the derelict."

Stamovich barked laughter, but then his face darkened.

"Hey. I'm one of those guys."

"Yeah," Draper said. "I know."

Brackett scowled. "All right, move along. We'll see you down there."

He stepped away from the elevator as the doors slid shut. As it descended, he glanced over to Al Simpson, who stood with Dr. Hidalgo by the other elevator. Simpson held a scanning device tied into the command block's systems. It showed a schematic of the sub-levels, pinpointing the location where sensors had picked up the cluster of PDTs.

"Go ahead, Mr. Simpson," he said.

Simpson hit the call button for the second elevator, and they heard the rattle and hum of its ascension. Dr. Hidalgo peered through the cage that formed the shaft, and watched the empty lift rising toward them.

When the elevator arrived, the cage and the inner doors slid open and they all stepped inside. The elevator rumbled and clattered as the doors closed and it began to descend. It occurred to Brackett to wonder just how smart the aliens might be. Were they capable of separating the sound of the elevator from the other industrial noises that filled this subterranean heart of the colony?

He thought they probably were.

When they reached the bottom—Brackett's thoughts drifting to *Paradise Lost* and the ninth circle of Hell—Pettigrew and the others had secured the area. Brackett was the first to step off the elevator, with Al Simpson a quick second. The administrator didn't so much as glance up, despite the danger they all expected to face. Brackett found himself developing a grudging respect for the man.

"That way," Simpson said, pointing across an open space toward a broad corridor that led between two massive generators. The lights were high up on the ceiling and provided little illumination, such that shadows were far more plentiful than the splashes of light.

"Can't we just let them have the place, and get our asses off-planet?" Hauer asked, a hint of seriousness in his voice. "Dust-off is my middle name."

"I thought your middle name was pussy," Stamovich muttered.

Several of the marines laughed.

Brackett swung his weapon up and aimed it toward the place Simpson had pointed.

"Maybe you assholes want to keep it down?" he suggested. "Y'know, on the off chance they don't already know we're coming?" That shut them up. Several of them took aim at the shadowy space between the generators, the way the captain had.

"Look, this is pretty simple," Draper said, glaring at Brackett. "We kill these things, or they kill us and everyone upstairs."

Brackett nodded. "For once we agree on something." He turned to Pettigrew. "Corporal, keep that elevator on this level, doors open. Dr. Hidalgo's going to stay here with you—"

"Oh no I'm not," the woman said, chin raised defiantly.

The marines all reacted in revulsion, but nobody said a word. The one who'd stepped in it wiped his boot as best he could on a dry section of floor, and they kept moving. A short time later, Draper pointed at the walls and Brackett shined his light around to discover that the resin had been spread everywhere. In places it seemed to have hardened.

"It looked like this inside the derelict," Draper whispered, "but way more extensive."

They really are building some kind of hive, Brackett thought.

Abruptly Hauer let out a cry of alarm, loud enough that it could be heard over the furnaces and generators.

"Hauer, what's… shit! They're here!" Sixto shouted.

Brackett spun to see Hauer being hauled upward, feet kicking. One of the aliens had its tail wrapped around his waist. In the flickering light Brackett could make out its silhouette in the darkness, on top of a rumbling generator. The alien drew Hauer toward it, wrapped an arm around him, and began to slip away.

"No!" Stamovich screamed, and opened fire, strafing the generator and the darkness above it with bullets.

Several others lost their cool and let loose with battle cries and volleys of bullets, shooting into the shadows above and around them.

"Cease fire!" Brackett roared. "God damn it, cease fire!"

Draper grabbed the barrel of Stamovich's gun and aimed it upward, shouting into his face.

When the gunfire died, Draper shoved Stamovich back.

"You idiot, you could have killed Hauer!"

Stam gaped at him. "Killed him? That thing just—"

"Took him," Draper said. "You don't know we can't get him back alive."

"You didn't even *like* Hauer!" Stamovich snapped.

"I don't know about you," one of the other marines said, "but I'd rather be dead than have one of those things on my face. You're dead anyway."

Brackett whipped around, swinging his pulse rifle in an arc, shining his light into the darkness. Simpson and Dr. Hidalgo moved closer to him, fear and doubt etched in their expressions. The captain nudged Dr. Hidalgo back toward the other marines. Simpson glanced down at his device. Beyond him, where a huge door led through into the reactor, the darkness began to unfurl.

"Movement!" Brackett shouted. "Twelve o'clock!"

They all began shouting then, as the shadows came alive. Stamovich screamed as an alien dropped from the ceiling and landed on top of him. Brackett turned, firing in bursts. He saw a marine die when one of the bugs impaled him from behind, throwing his arms out wide as if he'd been crucified.

Draper ran at Brackett, taking aim with his plasma rifle.

"Get down!"

Brackett hurled himself down and toward Draper, twisting as he landed on the floor, bringing his own gun up as the black contours of an alien lunged toward them. Draper shot the hell out of it, acid blood spattering the floor, its carapace cracking with a brittle crunch at every impact.

"Shit, it was there all along!" Brackett shouted. He'd been fifteen feet away from the thing, and it had clung so cleverly to the side of a furnace that he'd thought it was a part of the machinery.

Dr. Hidalgo appeared at his side, trying to help him up. She had his pistol in her hand and it looked pitifully small, totally useless. He glanced up into her eyes and saw a strange calm.

"There's something you need to know," she said loudly.

"Can't it wait?" he shouted, thinking she had lost her mind. They were in the middle of a firefight, people dying around them. *Marines* dying—his squad.

Brackett scrambled to rise as gunfire hammered at his eardrums, blocking out all other sound. How many aliens had been waiting for them? He tried to make sense of it, and while he did, he saw Al Simpson turn and run. An alien crept out from behind a generator to block his way. Simpson shouted and tried to backpedal, but too late. It took him, dragging him back into the darkness of the labyrinthine machinery.

Brackett shot him dead before the two figures could vanish. The demon dropped his corpse and whipped toward the marine captain, hissing. He and Draper both opened fire on it, but the alien ducked into the shadows. Brackett heard a clanking and scratching, and he caught a glimpse of its tail rising. The damn thing scaled the side of the generator. From up there, it could drop down on them any time.

"Fall back!" he shouted, waving for the squad to retreat. "Let's move!"

A quick scan showed him six marines still standing. Sixto held his side, blood spilling between his fingers, but he was still alive. They'd killed at least three aliens but there were others... the darkness seethed with their presence.

He turned to take Dr. Hidalgo's hand, and saw an alien standing behind her. She must have seen the shock in his eyes, because she spun around, took aim, and fired three bullets into its head. Blood splashed her, hissing as the acid ate into the flesh of her chest and right arm and shoulder.

Brackett bellowed, partly to block out the sound of Dr. Hidalgo's agonized shrieking. He wrapped his left arm around her waist and dragged her backward as he blew the alien apart.

"Go!" he shouted to Draper and the others.

They were marines. Retreat wasn't in their blood, but they went, swift and careful, firing shots into any darkness that might hold an enemy. Dr. Hidalgo staggered alongside Brackett and he helped her tear off her jacket and the body armor she'd been given. The acid had been slowed by the armor, but not stopped, and as he watched it sizzled into her flesh. The stench would stay with him for as long as he drew breath.

"Listen..." she said.

"Shut up!" he snapped. He slung his rifle over his shoulder and lifted her into his arms. She weighed almost nothing. That thin, birdlike body, chest rising and falling so quickly, made him want to scream again.

Brackett ran with her in his arms. Draper and the other marines shouted to him, exhorting him to hurry. As he ran, he looked down at her face and saw a single spot on her right cheek where the alien's blood had hit her. A hole had formed and even now it hissed and smoked, the acid eating down through her face like the slowest bullet in the universe.

She was going to die.

"Listen to me," she rasped.

More shouts came from ahead. The machinery vanished as he stumbled toward the two service elevators. The clanking and groaning continued but now all he could see was Draper and the others waving him forward. His heart hammered in his chest as he raced toward them, the dying scientist in his arms, and counted the heads of his surviving marines.

Six. Draper included. No sign of Pettigrew. They had left him behind to guard the elevators and the aliens had taken him.

Of course they did, Brackett thought. *I might as well have handed him over.*

Dr. Hidalgo began to choke. The acid on her chest had burned its way down into her lungs. She rasped and coughed.

"You... have to... *listen!*" she said.

Draper raced back to them, covering them as they moved toward the open elevator. The other marines were already inside, one of them keeping the doors from closing.

"There's a... ship," Dr. Hidalgo said, her eyes rolling in her head. "Science team... the company gave us... a ship. Authorized personnel door... between the med lab and..."

Brackett looked down at her.

"Here on Acheron? There's a ship here?"

He glanced up at Draper, who stared at her.

"An evac ship? Holy shit!" Draper said. "That son of a bitch Reese! How much room, Doc? How many passengers can she hold?"

Brackett felt her sag in his arms, and her head lolled back as she exhaled her last, rattling breath. For the first time it occurred to him that the acid might not stop, that it could eat its way through her and into him, and he dropped to his knees and placed her gently on the floor.

An evac ship, he thought. Somehow Weyland-Yutani had known. *Hell*, he thought, *maybe that's why they picked this place.*

No, they hadn't known for sure, he realized, or they would have brought a thousand people to scan every inch of the surface. But they'd had an inkling that somewhere in this system they might find something ugly. They'd given their science team a way off of this godforsaken moon, with the intention that everyone else—children included—was expendable.

Newt, Brackett thought. *Anne.*

They didn't have the firepower to destroy the aliens, not when at least a couple of dozen had already bred. The odds against *anyone* leaving Acheron alive were growing... anyone who didn't have an evac ship.

He was a marine. He had a mission and a duty to these people and the Corps. But if he could save the lives of a handful of them—including the woman he loved and her children—surely that was more noble than letting them all die here.

He touched Dr. Hidalgo's left cheek, wishing that she could be aboard that evac ship, silently thanking her. Now he understood the guilt he'd seen in her eyes earlier.

Brackett staggered to his feet and turned just in time to see the elevator begin to rise.

Draper gazed back at him through the cage, his eyes stone cold.

How many passengers can she hold? he had asked.

Brackett couldn't blame him really. Marvin Draper had proven his courage in combat, but if Brackett could have made a list of people to bring off-planet on that evac ship, Draper wouldn't have been on that list.

The elevator rattled upward and vanished into the upper levels.

Brackett hit the call button for the other elevator and peered up through the shaft.

Behind him, the darkness came to life.

26

ONE BY ONE

DATE: 26 JUNE, 2179
TIME: 1346

When Anne heard the hammering at the storage area door, she knew things had gone sideways. Half of the colonists flinched and scrambled away from the entrance, but she recognized it as the sound of a fist pounding to be let in. Aliens didn't knock.

Newt clutched her Casey doll and grabbed a fistful of her mother's shirt.

"Stay with Tim, honey," Anne said.

"Mom, no!" Newt cried, reaching out for her. "You said—"

"Just one second!"

Anne raced toward the door. Several people shouted for her to stop. Lydecker darted forward and beat her to it.

"What the hell are you doing?" he demanded.

She ignored him. Palm flat against the door, she called out, "Who's there?"

"Lt. Paris!" came a voice.

A twist of sick dread knotted itself in her belly, and her heart began to gallop. She swore under her breath as she shoved aside boxes that had been piled up, and ratcheted back the double locks. Lydecker didn't argue. He'd heard Paris's voice and knew the woman was alive and desperate, or she wouldn't have come knocking.

Anne threw open the door and Paris backed in, with Pvt. Yousseff behind her, both women training their weapons on the corridor behind them. Dressed in full body armor and helmets, they had sweat streaks on their faces and their eyes were wide with urgency.

"Any word from Simpson or Captain Brackett?" Paris demanded, turning on Lydecker.

The man shook his head.

Lt. Paris glanced around, cursing under her breath and not caring who heard her.

"Where the hell is Dr. Reese?" she demanded. "This is his show now, so where the hell is he?"

"Gone," Anne told her.

Yousseff snarled. "What do you mean, *gone*?"

"He and Dr. Mori said they had vital data that needed to be secured," Lydecker explained. "You want to tell me what the hell's going on?"

An icy shiver ran up Anne's spine as she saw the desperate confusion in Paris's eyes. Then the lieutenant slung her plasma rifle over her shoulder.

"Yousseff, the door," Paris said, and the other marine set about locking it up tight, sliding the crates back in front as a barricade.

"Listen up," Lt. Paris called, drawing the attention of the dozens of colonists clustered in the storage area. "None of the other marines set up around the sealed perimeter are answering on comms. At least three are dead that I know of, and we have to assume the aliens are inside the perimeter, picking us off one by one. They're taking their time, removing the people who were protecting you, and then they're coming in."

"How?" One of the wildcatters spoke up. "All but one of the doors have been welded and barricaded." He hefted a heavy shotgun, and frowned. "I'll blast the shit out of any one of those ugly bastards that tries to come near me or mine."

"Maybe you'll get lucky, Meznick," Paris said, "but I'm not sure your shotgun can do you much good. I'm telling you, I don't think this place is secure enough."

Anne felt like she couldn't breathe. *This* place wasn't secure enough? Where else could they go, where so many people could wait for rescue—where they could sleep and eat?

She glanced at her kids. Tim stood with an arm around his little sister, and she thought how proud Russ would have been of him.

People shouted questions at Paris. Some refused to go anywhere without word from Dr. Reese or Al Simpson. But when Yousseff glanced nervously at the door they had just barricaded, practically vibrating with the fear that the aliens would be coming through at any moment, Anne knew there was no more time for hesitation.

"I'm going," she said, dashing toward her children. "Kids, come on."

"I'm scared," Newt cried.

"Me too, Rebecca," Tim said. "But we'll be okay. I'll protect you," he promised.

"Anne, don't," Bill Andrews said, taking her arm from behind.

She shook him off.

"Don't be stupid, Bill," she replied. "Don't you see the fear in the eyes of these marines? You think Lieutenant Paris is wrong? This is a more comfortable place to hold out for rescue, but if we're dead when it arrives—"

"Where do we go then?" Andrews demanded, turning to Paris.

"We have a couple of ideas," the lieutenant said.

Anne lifted Newt into her arms, and then took Tim's hand as she barged toward the freshly barricaded door.

"Up one level and a hundred feet along the southwest corridor," she said. "The surveyors' operations center. It's right above the med lab, but it's basically a big box. One way in and out. We get in there and weld ourselves in—"

"And we starve to death in days," Meznick said.

"So carry what you can," Anne snapped, "but at least there we'd have days to try to figure something out. Better than dying here tonight."

"I ain't goin' nowhere," Meznick retorted. "We make a stand here, wait for Simpson and the others… far as we know, Brackett's team has exterminated the whole damn hive."

"Suit yourself," Anne said.

"What about Demian?" Newt whispered in her ear.

Anne swallowed hard but said nothing. All of her grand plans had gone up in smoke. She'd never make it to the hangar or the garage now—not with the kids, not if the marines who'd been guarding the perimeter were dead. Hell, she'd be lucky to make it to the operations center.

It's our only chance, she thought.

She glanced around for Cale, Dione, or Bradford, whom she'd seen quietly plotting together. None of them were in sight. She realized that somehow they—and who knew how many others—had slipped away without her noticing.

Probably going for the Onager, she thought. *Bastards*. But she couldn't really hate them for it. If she hadn't been waiting for Demian… hoping…

"Damn it," she snapped, marching away. She turned to Andrews. "You coming?"

He nodded. "Go. I'll grab some food and water, and catch up."

When people started milling about, some tearing open crates of supplies, Lydecker held up his hands.

"Calm down, folks," he said. "I'm staying right here, but I'm not going to stop anyone who wants to leave."

As if you could, Anne thought.

"We're only opening this door once, though. After that—"

"Out of the way, Lydecker," Anne barked. "Tim, help Private Yousseff."

Yousseff and Tim started pulling the crates away from the door again, aided by a couple of other colonists. By the time the door was hauled open—the two marines darting out, weapons leveled along abandoned halls—there were perhaps twenty people with armloads of goods, ready to make a run for it.

They'd barely gotten into the corridor and had the door slammed behind them when gunshots echoed from down the hall.

"Go, go!" Lt. Paris shouted as she and Yousseff raised their rifles and sighted along the corridor, toward the sound of gunfire.

Another marine came around the corner, limping badly and firing the last few shots from his plasma rifle before he ran out of ammo. Anne recognized Pvt. Dunphy, and cringed at the sight of the blood on the man's left hand, realizing that his sleeve was soaked with it. He'd been one of the marines on the perimeter, so they weren't all dead, but Dunphy didn't look far from the grave.

"Izzo's down!" Dunphy shouted. "I've got three coming this way!"

Julisa Paris turned and grabbed Anne's arm, staring into her eyes.

"Listen to me. Yousseff and I came from down there. That's where we killed one already. If they're coming from there, your path may be clear to the ops center. Go through the unwelded door, and we'll lock it behind us when we catch up.

"Go fast, and we'll take care of this," she added.

Anne nodded. "We'll give you five minutes before we seal the door to the ops center."

Paris touched Newt's blond locks and then gave them a small shove.

"Go! Tim, take care of your mom!"

Tim gripped Anne's hand tighter, and then they were running down the corridor, praying that the stairs up to the next level would be clear. Two minutes or less to get to the ops center, that was all they needed.

Anne glanced back, just once, at the doors to the storage area, wondering how long they could hold out. Even if they welded those internal doors, there were too many aliens. She felt sure that somehow they would get in, but it was too late for the others to follow them now. She and her kids, Bill Andrews, Parvati, Gruenwald and the others who'd followed her… they would live or die together.

She hugged Newt closer. Gripped Tim's hand tightly.

Live, she thought, almost a prayer. *We'll live.*

DATE: 26 JUNE, 2179
TIME: 1359

The thing moving in the darkness had a human shape.

Brackett stared at it, sighting along his rifle.

"Who goes there?"

"Captain?" the figure ventured as he emerged from the shadows.

"Pettigrew? Shit, I thought you were dead."

The corporal had his rifle at his side as he rushed toward the elevators, moving urgently now that he knew Brackett wouldn't shoot him.

"One of them came for me two minutes after you'd all gone," Pettigrew said, anxiously searching the shadows, alert and intense as the second elevator hummed and rattled on its way down. "I'd hit the hold button on the elevator and figured I didn't need to stand there waiting to die. It's not like the alien knew which buttons to push. I took off with the thing on my tail, managed to get into a maintenance closet just before it caught up."

"How'd you get away?" Brackett asked, glancing up through the cage at the descending elevator.

"Didn't have to," Pettigrew said.

Something shifted and scraped in the shadows above the nearest machinery. Pettigrew and Brackett both whipped around, taking aim. The lights flickered and Brackett saw the sleek gleam of something black, flowing like water in the darkness.

"The gunfire started—you guys were under attack—and it took off, more interested in the fight at hand," Pettigrew said. "I guess it figured it could come back for me later."

The elevator clanged as it descended, sliding into the cage right behind them and rattling to a stop.

"I think it has," Brackett muttered.

As the elevator doors opened, the alien leaped down from atop the groaning generator across the floor from them.

"Go, go!" Brackett said, firing at the alien as he backed into the elevator.

Pettigrew opened fire as well, but his rifle jammed and he swore, turning to slap the button for level one. The alien sprinted toward them, arms outstretched, tail wavering behind it, ready to strike. Brackett pulled the trigger again and stitched bullets across its chest.

The creature faltered and fell, blood melting into the floor only feet from the acid-ravaged body of Dr. Hidalgo. As the lift began to ascend, it hissed, whipped around to glare at them with that eyeless carapace of a head, and then lunged to its feet.

It struck the cage beneath them just as the elevator rose out of range. Before they were lifted out of view, Brackett saw others gliding from the darkness behind it.

"How do we live through this, Cap?" Pettigrew asked, slumping against the inside of the elevator.

Heart pounding, Brackett turned toward him.

"We get off this fucking rock."

Pettigrew narrowed his eyes in disbelief.

"How?"

"There's a way," Brackett replied, silently thanking Theresa Hidalgo. "We just have to get there before your buddy Draper."

DATE: 26 JUNE, 2179
TIME: 1359

Dr. Reese carried the silver case and Dr. Mori carried the gun.

They moved quickly and as quietly as possible, hoping not to be overheard by anyone, alien or human. Between the med lab and the research lab stood a single narrow door to which only the three primary members of the science team had access. On its metal surface were the faded words AUTHORIZED PERSONNEL ONLY.

Dr. Mori wore his key on a chain around his neck and used it to unlock the door as both men glanced anxiously around the hallway.

"I haven't been down here since the day we arrived," Mori whispered. "I never thought we would need to open this door."

Reese stared at him grimly, pleased with the weight of the case in his right hand.

"It was always a possibility."

Mori pushed the door inward and then stood back, covering the corridor with the pistol—the gun feeling so insignificant to him—as Dr. Reese entered. The key had activated the lights inside, and they flickered to life.

He frowned, glancing toward the research lab. Had he heard a sound there? The shuffle of footsteps? He listened for several seconds, and then convinced himself he'd imagined it. Stepping into the narrow passage, he pulled the door closed and flinched as it clanged shut.

"Idiot!" Reese groaned, the word rustling along the featureless gray walls of the claustrophobically narrow space. But there was nothing to be done about it now.

"Just move," Mori muttered. Technically, Dr. Reese was his superior, but just then Dr. Mori did not care. In the quest to survive, to escape

Acheron with their lives and their research, the two men were equals. The silver case held all of their data, as well as a single dead facehugger, and samples of an egg from the derelict and of the resin that came from the Xenomorphs' mouths. If they'd had more time they would have tried to take a living facehugger, but as much as they wanted to bring their research back to the company and reap the rewards, they could not do that if they hesitated too long, and ended up dead.

"Faster," Reese hissed quietly.

Mori gritted his teeth. "I'm not as young as I used to be."

They shuffled along the narrow corridor, shoulders brushing the walls, until they came to a slight turn where the hall widened enough to give them some breathing room. A dozen steps brought them through a low doorway where they had to stoop to pass through. Then the hall began to curve off to the right, leading to a second set of steps that descended at a right angle. The colony's first architects had designed this passage to be locked off and forgotten.

"Please, my friend," Dr. Mori said as he reached the bottom of the steps. "Give me a moment." Dr. Reese turned to glare at him, but then his expression softened.

"Only a moment."

Mori nodded. He'd been carrying the pistol, but there no longer seemed to be a need, so he clicked on the safety and slipped it into his rear waistband. When he glanced at the silver case in Reese's hand, he smiled even as he struggled to catch his breath.

He waited, nervously fiddling with a key hanging by a chain around his neck. The key they would need to get through the last door.

"Thank you," he said, taking a deep breath. "I'm all right."

Dr. Reese clapped him on the arm.

"Good. I don't want to go alone. It's a long journey."

As they started off again, leaving the stairs behind, there came a scuffing sound from back along the way they had come. The scientists froze and glanced at each other in frightened silence.

No, Dr. Mori thought. *Not when we've come so close.*

He drew his pitiful little gun as they stared back toward the steps and waited.

27

READY TO FIGHT

DATE: 26 JUNE, 2179
TIME: 1400

Jammed into the surveyors' ops center, the colonists who'd followed Anne moved quickly. At the back of the center there was a shop for repairing the equipment, and Bill Andrews located a hand-welder within minutes of their arrival.

Anne sat on a bench with her children and watched as Bill fired up the welder, the blue-white flame hissing as it scorched the air. She wetted her lips with her tongue, recognizing just how hard her heart had been pounding. They had made it here without anyone else dying, and now the sight of the welder and the box-like nature of the room made her feel immediately safer.

But others had felt safe before, and it hadn't helped them.

Across the room, Stefan Gruenwald and Neela Parvati were checking over the case of guns they'd carried from the storage area, handing them out.

"Tim," Anne said, "you and Newt stay here a minute."

Newt grabbed her hand, looking anxiously at the door as Bill tested the welder on the hinges on the left side of the double entry doors. Then she peered at her mother.

"It'll be all right," Anne promised her. "Protect Casey."

Newt glanced again at the welder in use, and then nodded and hugged the doll closer, kissing the top of its head.

Anne hurried across the room, weaving through the frightened people who were trying to settle themselves in some way that they might be comfortable, locked inside that room for however long they would be there. What supplies they'd brought were stacked on desks, and chairs were allotted to the oldest among them. Others made camp on the floor.

Anne glanced at the vents above the wall monitors, and though she felt sure the ducts were too narrow for the full-grown aliens, she wondered how many new ones might be bred. The one thing the colonists could not afford to do was cut off their own air supply.

When she marched up to the group with the guns, Parvati glanced at her.

"I want a gun," she said quietly.

Parvati arched an eyebrow.

Gruenwald cocked his head and looked at her worriedly.

"Don't you think we're all better off leaving the weapons with those who know how to use them?" he asked.

"The creatures got my husband," Anne said, then pointed across the room at her kids—at Tim, on the verge of tears, and Newt, clutching her Casey doll. "If things go bad, I need something to make sure *they* don't end up the same way."

Parvati opened her mouth in shock, perhaps thinking that Anne meant to kill her own children, rather than let the aliens have them. Anne wondered if that might really have been what she'd meant.

The question haunted her.

Gruenwald handed her the gun. She turned without another word and walked back to the bench.

The pounding on the doors began before she'd even sat down.

"Mom?" Newt asked.

Tim stood and came up beside her, ready to fight. A moment later, Newt did the same, and the sight of that six-year-old girl preparing to defend herself and her family broke whatever remained of Anne Jorden's heart. She tightened her grip on the pistol and watched as Bill stepped back, welder in hand.

Gruenwald rushed toward the door, Parvati just behind him, along with half a dozen others who were armed.

"Lieutenant Paris?" Bill called. "That you?"

"It's Draper!" boomed a voice. "Let us in, dammit. They're on our tail."

Gunfire erupted in the hallway.

"Open the damn door!" Draper shouted, and the banging resumed. "Where are Mori and Reese? They in there with you?"

"We've got to let them in!" Bill Andrews said, glancing around for support.

"No!" Gruenwald snapped. "We can't compromise our own security. They'll have to make it on their own."

Another burst of gunfire, and then Parvati surprised Anne by pushing past Gruenwald and going for the door.

"You aren't giving the orders here," she snapped at him. "We're not leaving anyone to those creatures!"

Two others rushed to help her.

"You morons!" Gruenwald barked, rushing to stop them. "Think about the children we've got in here!"

But Bill Andrews got in his way, pushing him back.

"We're thinking about the men and women out there."

Parvati and the others dragged the right-hand door open, its hinges not yet welded. Only then did Anne realize that the shooting in the corridor had ceased.

"We've got it open!" Parvati called.

"Oh no," Anne whispered, tears springing to her eyes as she pulled her children close with her left hand, and aimed the gun with her right. When she saw Sgt. Draper coming through the door—slumped, pale and bloody, but alive—she exhaled, all of her strength draining out of her.

Draper had bought them time.

But then the sergeant staggered and fell, and everyone could see the hole in his back...

...and the aliens barged in behind him, trampling the corpse and killing Neela Parvati before they were even through the door.

Newt and Tim screamed, and then Anne joined them.

They had nowhere left to run.

Nothing left to do but scream, and die.

DATE: 26 JUNE, 2179
TIME: 1400

Lt. Paris and Pvt. Youssef had killed two more aliens before they heard the worst of the screams, coming from the storage area.

Youssef broke into a sprint back toward the main doors. Anne Jorden, Bill Andrews, and a couple of dozen other people had left shortly before the aliens had attacked, and Paris couldn't help but wish she had gone with them—that they both had. Now she ran after Youssef, caught up to her at a turn in the corridor, and slammed her against the wall.

"Don't be stupid!" she shouted into the other woman's face, hating herself as she did it.

"But we've got to—" The private began to cry.

"What, die? 'Cause that's what we're going to do if we go that way!" Then Youssef laughed through her tears.

"Lieutenant, come on! We're dead anyway!"

Something moved behind them and they both spun around, fingers on the triggers. They nearly shot Brackett and Pettigrew.

"Shit!" Paris cried, heart crashing about in her chest.

"Anne Jorden and her kids?" Brackett yelled, rushing toward them. "They're in there with those things?"

Paris shook her head.

"No. A bunch of the colonists split off, went to the surveyors' ops center."

Brackett hung his head, breathing deeply.

"Thank God."

"We ran into Draper and a few others—they headed over there to defend that position," Youssef reported.

"Of course they did," Brackett snarled. "Son of a bitch."

"What's going on, Cap?" Lt. Paris added.

Brackett studied her.

"Yousseff said we were all dead. Maybe not."

"Maybe not what?" Yousseff asked, moving away from the corner now, away from the screaming and toward Brackett and Pettigrew.

"Maybe there's a way for us to get out of here," Pettigrew explained.

"You better not be messing with us," Lt. Paris said.

"I'm not," Brackett said, and his expression turned dark. He raised his plasma rifle, stepped away from the others, and opened fire as an alien came around the corner almost precisely where Yousseff had been standing moments before.

"Take us there, now!" Brackett yelled. "Take us to the ops center!" And then the four marines were all running and firing, and Lt. Paris was leading the way.

DATE: 26 JUNE, 2179
TIME: 1410

Dr. Reese took two steps back, putting Dr. Mori between himself and whatever shuffled through the corridor at the top of the stairs.

Behind him, the hallway narrowed again. If he remembered correctly, another fifty yards would bring him to a hatch through which there was a short set of steps, and then another hatch. Beyond that was the small hidden hangar where the six-passenger evac ship waited.

He took another step. Dr. Mori had the gun—Reese could do nothing to help defend them.

Run, he told himself, tightening his grip on the silver case. He had dedicated his life to scientific discovery—to the detriment of family, health, and any hope of real companionship. He had eschewed courtesy and personal grace for the quest for knowledge and advancement... for creation, regardless of consequence.

Reese knew that Weyland-Yutani put their greatest efforts into exploiting science, both developed and discovered. To find more effective ways to kill and conquer. He had never had a crisis of conscience.

But to abandon Dr. Mori...

Dr. Reese told himself that Mori was not his friend.

No, he thought, *but he's the closest thing I've got.*

Forcing all guilt away, he began to turn, just as a slender figure came around the corner and onto the landing at the top of those twelve steps.

Dr. Reese stared.

"Khati?" Dr. Mori said, and he started toward the bottom step.

Reese grabbed his shoulder.

"Stop, you fool."

The woman had been one of their researchers, but had vanished the previous evening. The science team had assumed that she had been dragged off by the aliens, but now here she was. The left side of her face had a huge purple bruise and multiple scrapes. Her hair was matted and wild and her torn clothes were in disarray.

Khati Fuqua looked down at them, eyes full of sorrow.

"Please…"

She shuffled toward the top of the steps, grunted in pain, and bent slightly as she reached for the railing. Her hand missed the rail and her foot missed the step, and she fell, tumbling end over end, reaching out to try to arrest her fall, but failing.

"Damn it!" Dr. Mori snapped, rushing to her side.

Dr. Reese approached warily, looking over Mori's shoulder.

"Is she all right?"

Groaning, Khati rolled over. She had one hand over her sternum and Dr. Reese wondered if she had slammed her chest on the edge of a step.

She bucked in pain.

"Oh no," she whispered.

"Oh no," Dr. Reese echoed.

Dr. Mori stood and stared at her.

"Khati, I'm so sorry."

Reese shifted the case to his left hand. With his right, he snatched the gun from Dr. Mori's grasp. Stepping over the researcher, he went halfway up the steps, back the way they'd come. He needed the vantage point.

"How did she follow us?" Dr. Reese demanded. "Didn't you shut the door?"

"I didn't lock it," Dr. Mori said. "I never thought—"

"Bullshit!" Dr. Reese swallowed hard, sweat beading on his forehead. "You couldn't have even shut it tightly, not and have her follow us. I don't want this, Mori, do you understand me?" His voice had turned shrill. He heard the edge of panic in it, but couldn't help himself.

"Do you think *she* wanted it?" Dr. Mori asked, staring down at Khati as she began to buck and cry out, hyperventilating as she tried to process her pain.

From halfway up those dozen steps, Dr. Reese pointed the gun at her and let out a long breath. He wanted desperately to pull the trigger, to just end her pain and any danger she might present.

"Do it," he whispered to himself.

But he couldn't pull the trigger, could not murder the young woman in cold blood, though to his mind it would have been a mercy.

Khati bucked again and he could see the skin of her chest push upward as the parasite burrowed its way out.

We don't have time for this, he thought.

But of course, it wouldn't be long.

28

MONSTER MAZE

DATE: 26 JUNE, 2179
TIME: 1411

In the midst of the screaming and gunfire, a strange calm enveloped Anne. It was as if the ops center had shifted into some parallel dimension, and she had been left behind.

Bill Andrews and Stefan Gruenwald were in the front line, strafing the aliens with plasma rounds that blew two of them apart. Acid blood splashed Gruenwald in the eyes and the man screamed and fell to his knees. He reached up and covered his face with the palms of his hands—and then screamed louder, in a melody of anguish and surrender, as the acid on his eyes also burned through his hands.

One of the Xenomorphs grabbed Bill Andrews and smashed him against the wall, breaking him without killing him. Saving him for later.

Those who weren't shooting were cowering, or searching for something with which to fight back.

Anne raised her pistol, exhaled, and fired three times as she backed up. She glanced over her shoulder at her children. Newt hugged her Casey doll so tightly that it looked like she might squeeze its head off. Tim had picked up a monitor screen, the only weapon he had close to hand.

No, she thought, the single word engraved in her mind.

No.

Then she saw the dark square on the wall behind her children.

"Tim! Newt!" she cried, her voice breaking. "Monster Maze!"

She saw them spin around, watched them realize what she wanted them to do. Then she turned back toward the screams and the carnage. The smell of blood and fear came at her like a stormfront. One of the aliens crouched above Newt's friend, Luisa. The little girl screamed so loud the shrieking seemed like a kind of madness that tore at her throat, and then the alien vomited its sticky resin into her face. The girl choked on it, and went silent. Her whole body jerked and then went still, driven into unconsciousness by shock and terror.

Something broke inside Anne.

"Leave her be!" she screamed, firing twice at the alien, her heart full of more hate than she had ever imagined it could hold.

One bullet cracked its carapace at the temple while the other punched a hole in its lower jaw. The small blood spatter missed Luisa, but Anne's heart stopped when she realized what she'd almost done.

The alien turned, and took a step toward her.

"Newt! Tim!" she shouted.

As the other colonists died or were dragged away around her, Anne's children were screaming for her. She turned and saw that they'd pried the grating off of the vent, but they'd paused, calling out for her to come with them. The anguish in their faces carved deep into her heart.

"Inside!" she shouted, running toward them. "Get inside!"

Tim shoved Newt into the narrow duct—much too small for one of the creatures—and then began to climb in behind her.

Anne heard a low hiss. She could practically feel the alien as it reached for her.

Russ, she thought. *I'm sorry.*

She turned, took aim, and fired once before its jaws punched through her forehead.

Newt heard her brother scream for their mother. He scrambled, banging against the inside of the duct as he climbed out again.

"Timmy, no!"

She grabbed his t-shirt but he tore free and turned toward her, furious tears streaming down his face.

"Go, Rebecca!" he roared. "Don't wait!"

But she watched him turn, watched him run over and bend to pick up the gun their mother had dropped.

"I'll save you, Mom!" Tim yelled.

But he couldn't. It was too late for that. Too late for their mother. Too late for Tim.

Numb, Newt turned away, but still she heard the scream—the last sound her brother—her best friend—would ever make.

She felt the alien coming for her and hurled herself deeper into the duct, crawling away as fast as possible. *Monster Maze*, she thought. But now these ducts were the only place the monsters weren't. She knew them better than anyone, but she'd never crawled around inside them alone.

Alone. The word echoed in her head the way her movements echoed along the ducts.

All alone.

DATE: 26 JUNE, 2179
TIME: 1411

Khati sucked air in through her teeth, breathing in the pattern taught to women who were about to give birth. Then she bucked again, blue eyes wide as she let out a scream that tore down the walls Dr. Reese had built inside himself to hide away his emotions. He'd known this woman, dined with her, enjoyed the sound of her laughter.

"Why are we still here?" Dr. Mori shouted from below him. "We should just go!"

Reese stood halfway up the steps, looking down on that small space and the entrance to the next segment of the evac corridor. Dr. Mori took another step into the corridor, hesitating and confused, and Reese knew he was right.

No delay, he thought.

What the hell was he waiting for? Khati was in agony and would be dead moments after the thing burst from her chest. His instinct had been to wait for the parasite to emerge, and to kill it before it could grow.

They ought to be running.

Khati's anguish kept him frozen there.

He remembered the way she had smiled at her first sip of coffee in the morning, the little hum of happiness she made when she tasted it.

He pulled the trigger, shooting her half a dozen times in the chest. Dr. Mori cried out and spun away. Khati slumped to the floor, falling still. The thing inside her body pulsed once, as if making one last attempt to break free, and then it, too, went still.

Dr. Reese exhaled, grieving for the woman as her blood and the parasite's pooled under her body, hissing as the acid ate at the floor beneath them.

"Son of a bitch!" Mori said, turning to look up at him again.

He'd been shot.

Dr. Reese frowned, not understanding for a moment, and then he realized that when Mori had spun away it hadn't been out of horror or disgust. A ricochet had struck him in the left shoulder, and now he clutched at that wound. He hissed up at Reese.

"Asshole!" Mori barked. "Let's go!"

Dr. Reese stared down at Khati and told himself that he saw relief in those dull, dead eyes. He lowered the gun and nodded, starting down the steps.

Mori whispered his name.

Frowning, Reese glanced up and saw the terror in his colleague's gaze. Then he heard the hiss behind him, the creak of weight on the stairs, and the dappling drip of liquid hitting metal.

He hung his head, not bothering to turn, knowing it was futile to try to run.

The alien's hands wrapped around his right shoulder and his throat, drawing him toward it like an insistent lover. Only when he felt its drool sluicing hotly down onto his neck did he begin to scream, thinking of the suffering he'd just witnessed in Khati.

He turned the gun upon himself, and pulled the trigger.

* * *

DATE: 26 JUNE, 2179
TIME: 1412

Brackett was the first one through the door. They'd heard the screams and gunfire coming down the hall, but by the time they reached the surveyors' ops center, the room had gone silent— except for the hiss of the aliens.

He slid along the corridor wall, then saw that only one side of the double doors stood open. Holding up a hand to halt the others, he raised three fingers, counted down, and then spun through the open part of the doorway. His eyes widened as he tracked the five aliens in the room, all of them bent to the task of covering living colonists in the sticky resin that slid from their mouths.

Brackett opened fire as Yousseff slammed into the other half of the double door, only to find it had been welded at the hinges.

"Make way, Cap!" Lt. Paris shouted. "Let us in!"

Brackett's plasma rounds blew apart one alien and wounded a second as they turned to come for him. Advancing would have been idiotic—trapping him in that small room with the demons. Instead he backed out, barking at the other marines, and all four of them retreated back down the corridor the way they had come.

"They've got to come out one at a time," he snapped, heart racing, his body flush with adrenaline. "We've got them!"

Pettigrew whooped in triumph as he realized Brackett was right. The four of them lined up across the corridor and shot the hell out of the aliens as they barged through the opening one at a time. Acid blood splashed all over the floor, burning holes in scattered patterns.

When it was over, the gunshot echoes still hammered at Brackett's eardrums. He took a moment to stare numbly at the carnage of shattered ebon carapace and limbs and tails, and then he started forward again.

"Watch 'em, Cap!" Pettigrew called, but Brackett knew they were all dead, or they would've just kept coming, following what seemed a genetic need to destroy everything they encountered.

He stepped carefully around the acid-eaten floor and the remains of the aliens and slipped back into the ops center. He took a deep breath as he scanned the bodies there, and then he started moving among them, checking for pulses, taking note of which were obviously dead, and who might still be breathing, having been intended for breeding by the aliens.

Those still alive had been in the process of being cocooned, and were unconscious.

"What are we going to do with them, Cap?" Julisa Paris asked as she came into the room and began following his lead, searching for survivors. The stench of blood and death made Brackett knit his brows. It hurt his head. He did not answer, because he knew they weren't seeing these people the same way. Paris saw friends and acquaintances where Brackett saw people who were mostly strangers. He sought three faces only.

Anne. Newt. Tim.

"There are other aliens," Paris went on. "More will come. How are we supposed to get these people free before—"

"We don't," Yousseff said, coming into the room behind them. With her helmet on, she almost looked like a little girl playing make-believe. The grim glint in her eyes revealed the truth. "It's a noble thought, Lieutenant, but as far as we know, there's room for five or six passengers on the evac ship."

"We'll make room," Lt. Paris said.

"Who will you leave behind for them?" Yousseff asked. "Me? Corporal Pettigrew?"

Brackett stopped hearing them.

He stood above a familiar corpse. Recognized her clothes and her hair. Not enough of her face remained for him to identify her that way, but he knew, and he felt ice sliding through his veins as a hollow opened up deep inside him.

"I'm sorry," he whispered, lowering his head.

He knelt beside her, putting down his weapon, and he covered his head with his hands as if he could trap the grief inside. In his mind he could still see the girl she'd been when they had first met. His body remembered her touch. His heart remembered the pain as he felt forced to break off the relationship when he shipped off to join the marines, and then the regret when he learned of her plan to marry Russ.

It would've been better if I'd never come, he thought. *Never seen you again.*

Pettigrew had remained out in the hallway, guarding their exit. Now he stuck his head into the room.

"Make it quick," he said. "I heard something out here. Back the way we came."

Yousseff came to stand beside him, staring down at Anne Jorden's corpse.

"I'm sorry, Captain," she said, "but we can't stay. If we don't make that evac ship, we're all dead."

Brackett nodded slowly. Blinking as if waking from sleep, he glanced around at the corpses and the cocooned, so many of them unrecognizable like Anne. Then he froze a moment, shook it off, and staggered to his feet. Six feet from his mother's corpse lay the body of Tim Jorden, a gun in his small hand.

"Newt?" Brackett said, glancing around. "Do any of you see Newt?"

"Holy shit, here!" Lt. Paris snapped as she ran toward a small, cocooned body.

Hope surged in Brackett, images of the little girl filling his head. He raced over and set to work beside Paris, the two of them tearing the hardened resin away from the little girl's body while Yousseff stood near the door and Pettigrew kept watch in the corridor.

When they broke away a piece of the material that had hidden her eyes, the hope withered inside Brackett.

"I'm sorry," Paris said quietly. "It's not her."

Brackett nodded. "Who is she, this little girl? You know her?"

"Her name's Luisa. One of Newt's friends."

Yousseff gestured to the far side of the room, where other bodies lay bloody and broken. "She must be one of those."

"Search," Brackett said. "Please, the two of you, see if you can confirm, one way or another." *Confirm that Newt is dead,* he meant, but they didn't need him to explain that, and he was glad. The words wouldn't come.

Brackett tore away more of the hardened cocoon, reached in and lifted Luisa out. Her red hair was matted with the stuff and she looked inhumanly pale, but as he stood with the little girl in his arms, she moaned softly and her eyes fluttered.

She would come around soon. She would live. He intended to make sure of that. There was nothing more he could do for Anne or Tim, but he could do this for Newt. He could save her friend.

Yousseff and Paris continued searching the rest of the room.

"Guys, we've gotta go!" Pettigrew called from the hallway. Gunfire rattled and echoed out in the corridor, and that was that.

They had run out of time for humanitarian acts. If they stayed and tried to defend those who were still alive, they would all surely die. There were simply too many aliens, too hard to kill, and the monsters were still breeding. Brackett glanced at the little girl in his arms.

You'll have to be enough, he thought. *If I can keep you alive...*

If he could keep Luisa alive, then he could live with the decision to run. To survive.

"You heard the sergeant! Move!" Brackett commanded.

Yousseff was the first to join Pettigrew in the corridor. Brackett followed, carrying Luisa, and Paris brought up the rear. As the lieutenant came through the door, Pettigrew shouted a warning and opened fire. Brackett turned to see two aliens rushing toward them from down the hall. Paris and Yousseff fired as well, tearing the aliens apart so that their blood sprayed and their carcasses crashed to the floor thirty feet away.

The little girl squirmed in Brackett's arms, whimpering but not regaining consciousness. He held her more tightly and shushed her as the gunfire echoes died away.

"Quickest way to the med lab?" Brackett asked.

Lt. Paris shot him a look.

"Why the hell would we—"

"Private passage to the evac ship is right next to it," Pettigrew said. "You know that door—"

"I know it," Paris interrupted, and then they were moving. The lieutenant took point this time, with Brackett carrying Luisa behind her and Pettigrew and Yousseff guarding their rear. The aliens had followed their trail, and they felt sure there would be more of them.

Brackett's legs felt as if they were made of lead and his heart thundered against his chest as he ran, the girl jostling in his arms. Paris swung her weapon in a sweeping arc as they ran past the elevator bay, its doors closed and quiet. They turned a corner, reached the stairwell door that would lead them up a level, to within spitting distance of the med lab, and Brackett turned to see Pettigrew and Yousseff hurrying up behind them.

"Anything?" Brackett asked.

Yousseff stayed at the corner, aiming her weapon back the way they'd come.

"Not a hint," Pettigrew replied. "Doesn't mean they aren't coming."

"Agreed," Yousseff said. "We're not safe until we dust off."

Paris ducked into the stairwell and motioned for them to follow. They raced down the stairs, Brackett flinching at the noise of their boots on each step, thinking of how far up and down the sound would carry. Luisa couldn't have weighed more than sixty-five pounds but his arms had grown tired. The temptation was strong to try to wake her, to get her to run for herself, but if the girl was very lucky she would sleep until they were well away from Acheron.

In the silence of space, they could all grieve together.

Paris left the stairwell at the next landing, sliding out into the corridor and scanning both directions.

"Clear!" she called, and they followed her out into the hall.

"Lieutenant, cover right. Yousseff, cover left," Brackett said. "Pettigrew, check the door." There was no questioning which door he meant. Set into the wall between the med lab and the research lab they all saw the narrow black door that hung halfway open, the AUTHORIZED PERSONNEL ONLY sign partly in shadow.

Yousseff slid down the hall first, with Pettigrew behind her. Brackett saw the ruined elevator doors across from the med lab, and directed Yousseff toward them with a lift of his chin. She nodded and padded along the corridor, clicking on the guide-light on top of her pulse rifle and aiming the beam into the darkened elevator shaft.

Pettigrew pushed the evac passage door open with the barrel of his rifle.

An alien burst from the shadowed interior, drove him to the ground, and grabbed him by the face. Its extruding jaw punched down through his chest, smashing bone and tearing muscle. As he died, Pettigrew fired half a dozen rounds from the plasma rifle, three or four of which hit the alien and spilled its blood all over him. The acid burned into his flesh, but Pettigrew was already dead.

"Paris!" Brackett shouted, backing away with Luisa in his arms.

Yousseff shouted Pettigrew's name, along with a string of profanities that cut off halfway after "mother." Brackett spun and looked down the corridor just in time to see Yousseff's legs flailing as she was dragged through the twisted opening in the elevator doors.

Lt. Paris saw it, too.

"This isn't going to happen," she said coldly. "We've got a way home."

"Then let's go!" Brackett snapped.

The alien Pettigrew had shot lay on the floor, struggling to rise. Its tail whipped around, the deadly tip trembling, ready to strike. Julisa Paris shot it three times, blew its skull apart, and then they were running again.

They darted through the narrow evac door, Paris watching the corridor ahead as Brackett kicked the door closed. He threw Luisa over one shoulder in a fireman's carry and heard her grunt, mumbling as she skirted at the edge of consciousness. Brackett threw both of the locks, bolting the door shut. It wouldn't stop the aliens for long, but he hoped it would be long enough.

Then they were running along the corridor, Paris out in front with her gun, praying that no more surprises waited for them ahead.

29

ENOUGH DYING

DATE: 26 JUNE, 2179
TIME: 1412

Dr. Mori ran, one hand clutching the bullet wound in his shoulder. The scraping behind him was close, but he couldn't afford to look.

The smell of his own blood made him want to vomit or faint or both. Tears ran down his face, his mind filled with images of Khati's hideous demise and of the alien killing Reese. Those memories were burned into his soul, and he knew he would see them every time he closed his eyes for as long as he lived.

For at least six or seven seconds, he fooled himself into thinking that *as long as he lived* would include more than just the next minute. But then he looked ahead, and saw that he had a hundred feet or so of corridor in front of him before he reached the door into the evac hangar.

A door that required a key.

And the time to use it.

A sob escaped from Dr. Mori. Regret washed through him—so many things he wished he had done, and so many more he wished he could take back. But he was all out of wishes.

He fell to his knees, weakened by blood loss and shock. One hand still pressed to his shoulder, where the wound began to sing with pain, he turned to watch the alien rushing toward him. He studied the smooth carapace of its enormous head and the nimble, darting predator's gait as it rushed after him. It saddened him that he would never have the chance to study it.

Beautiful, he thought. And it really was.

"Hey, ugly!" a woman's voice called.

The alien turned back toward the voice, its tail scraping the wall. It hissed.

"Get down, Dr. Mori!" a man shouted.

The bullets tore into the alien just as Dr. Mori threw himself to the floor. He scrambled away, staying down, as it juddered and then collapsed, twitching as it died. Dr. Mori stared at his shoes, one of which was steaming as several drops of acid burned through it. Shouting in panic he reached down and ripped the shoe off his foot.

Then he stared at his pitiful foot in its gray sock, the fabric thin at the toes, and he leaned against the wall, shaking.

Capt. Brackett stepped carefully around the dead alien, carrying a little girl in his arms. Lt. Paris followed behind him, gun still in her hands, ready to fight.

"Get up, Dr. Mori," Brackett said. "You're our ticket out of here."

Mori looked up at him, hollow and bereft.

"You'll take me with you?"

Brackett glanced at the little girl in his arms, but his eyes still seemed far away, as if he saw someone else there.

"I think there's been enough dying, don't you?"

Lt. Paris helped him to rise and he limped toward the door in his one remaining shoe, thankful for the key on the chain around his neck.

Dr. Mori opened the door to the hangar and cool air rushed around him.

He felt alive.

DATE: 26 JUNE, 2179
TIME: 1433

The evac ship shuddered violently as it passed through the debris-filled atmosphere of Acheron. Brackett had laid Luisa down in a hypersleep chamber but the lid remained open. The girl deserved to know what had happened, deserved to be a part of whatever came next for them. She was only a child, but Brackett wasn't going to hide the horrors from her. He would let her grieve, comfort her if he could, and hope she would be strong enough not to be destroyed by all she had lost.

He hoped that he was strong enough, too.

"We're exiting the envelope," Lt. Paris called from the cockpit. "Anyone want to have a last look before we leave this rock behind?"

"I'm good," Brackett said.

He glanced over at Dr. Mori. The man looked pale and weak, but he would survive. In a few minutes, when they'd cleared the turbulence and were on course, Brackett would remove the bullet from his shoulder and stitch up the wound. It would be painful, and there would be something in the medical supplies on the evac ship to dull that pain, but Brackett would not offer it. Mori deserved all that pain he had coming to him.

"What about you, Doc?" he asked.

Mori shook his head. "There's nothing for me back there."

Brackett nodded, a tight fist of anguish forming in his stomach. He breathed evenly and forced it away. He would grieve for Newt and Tim, for Anne, and for lost opportunities, but he could not allow himself to be broken. The hollow place inside him where his heart had been felt cold and dark, and perhaps it would remain that way forever. But he had work to do, and he could not let sorrow get in the way.

Use it, he thought. *Turn it into fuel.*

"Lieutenant Paris," he called, facing the front of the ship, "I assume the ship's navigational computer has a preset course."

"It does. Gateway Station. We'll be in hypersleep most of the time."

Brackett stared at Dr. Mori, thinking about how insidious the science team's behavior had been. They had known all along that there could be an alien threat on Acheron. Known enough that they had established their own escape plan. When word had come down from Weyland-Yutani to send surveyors out to those specific coordinates, they had known that the Jordens would have been in terrible danger.

Even when the worst happened, they had been more interested in studying the aliens, fulfilling their mission for the company, than in trying to figure out how to kill them—how to keep the people alive.

The colonists had been expendable.

Even the children.

But that protocol hadn't begun with Dr. Reese or Dr. Mori. It had come down from on high, from their employers.

"Turn it off," he said quietly. "Turn off the nav system."

Dr. Mori glanced up, brows knitted with surprise and worry.

"What's that, Cap?" Lt. Paris called back.

Not Lieutenant, he thought. *Not anymore.*

"Disable the preset course, Julisa," he said. "And figure out a way to keep them from tracking us, if you can. We're not going to Gateway Station."

"What are you doing, Captain?" Dr. Mori asked.

"I kept thinking of your Xenomorphs as demons, Doctor," Brackett replied, loud enough for Julisa to hear. "But they're not demons. They're merciless killers, and they're as alien as I can imagine any sentient creature ever being... but they're following their own biological imperatives. They're not evil."

Brackett smiled darkly.

"Weyland-Yutani, though... if there's evil in the universe, a scourge that needs to be exposed to the light and then destroyed, it's the company. From now on, that's my fight. That's my war. And if you don't want to be stranded on the first planet we come to, Dr. Mori, it's going to be your war, too."

In the open sleep chamber, Luisa began to mutter quietly, blinking her eyes as she started to rustle and wake. Brackett took her hand, and her small fingers gripped his larger, scarred ones.

"Now the real fight begins."

DATE: 26 JUNE, 2179
TIME: 1618

Newt and Tim and the other kids who played Monster Maze had always called it "the clubhouse," but she knew that the boxy space in which she had taken refuge wasn't meant to be a house, or even a room.

The rectangle might have been ten feet long by six feet wide, and while Newt could stand up there, a grown-up would have had to stoop or crouch or kneel. There were things there already—a blanket and various sweatshirts and jackets and books and old snack boxes left behind, as well as a handful of toys. Half a dozen air ducts led away from the clubhouse, while one blower fan pushed air in from above. Sometimes it grew too warm in there, and sometimes too cold, but it was hers and it was safe.

The aliens could never find her in here, which would be perfect…

Until she needed something to eat or drink.

Newt wrapped herself in the blanket and leaned against the metal wall of the box. She clutched her Casey doll to her chest, careful with it because its head had begun to detach from the body.

"It'll be all right," she whispered to Casey, heart pounding. Eyes wide, she glanced around at the ducts, knowing they couldn't come after her, but still afraid. Images flashed across her mind, striking like lightning, but she shook her head and forced them away.

Her mother.

Her brother.

Better not to think about them, or about the blood and the screaming. Better not to think at all. Just survive. That was what her mother would have told her. The Jordens had always been survivors.

"I'm quick," she whispered to Casey. It was true. Tim had said she cheated, but Newt had always been best at Monster Maze. If she was careful, and she listened well, she could avoid them when she needed to get food or something to drink.

"I'll protect you," she promised, and kissed the top of Casey's head.

Newt fell quiet after that, listening. When the blowers cycled off for a few minutes, she heard echoes making their way through the ducts from distant rooms and other levels within the colony. The sounds were strange and soft and sad, at least to her, but she thought that if she followed them back to their origins, the noises she was hearing might turn out to be screams.

She stayed where she was, and she tried not to cry.

Sometimes she succeeded.

30

BUILDING BETTER WORLDS

DATE: 5 JULY, 2179

On Gateway Station, every day blurred.

Every day of being no one, doing nothing, having little in her life. Every day of mourning her long-dead daughter—both the little girl she had left behind, and the woman who had grown, matured, loved, lived and died without Ripley ever getting to know her.

I told her I'd be home for her birthday, she kept thinking, always the last thing at night, and every day when she woke. That guilt was as rich and raw today as it was every day.

Every day blurred into one, into weeks, into months...

Sleeping. Waking. Working. Returning to her cabin. Eating, washing, drinking, smoking, watching the body of her cigarette turn to ash and flitter away like the years of her life, unknown and unmissed by anyone. A life without meaning was no life at all.

Today had been no different to any other day. Just one of many, all the same.

Until the door buzzer sounded.

It jarred Ripley out of her sad contemplations, and for a few seconds she couldn't place what it was. She hardly ever heard the noise. No one came to visit her, she had no friends. She was a woman out of time, and if people did speak to her—at the loading docks, in the mess—she always had the impression that she was seen not as a real person, but as a curiosity. An exhibit from the past.

She stood and went to the door, wondering who was there. When she opened the door and saw Burke, her heart sank.

He wasn't alone.

"Hi, Ripley," he said. "This is Lieutenant Gorman of the Colonial Marine Corps—"

She closed the door again. Burke, through all his efforts to ingratiate himself, had never come across as anything other than a slimeball working his own game. He pretended to care, and sometimes she thought he genuinely did. There were aspects to his personality that made him inscrutable, yet there was a vulnerability, too. Perhaps it should have made Ripley like him more, but he came across as weak.

As for the guy with him, he just looked like a grunt.

She turned away from the door, but Burke's voice came again from outside.

"Ripley, we have to talk. We've lost contact with the colony on LV-426."

She froze. Her heart stuttered. The heavy darkness within her seemed to pulse, and she turned slowly to the door. Opened it again.

On what? she wondered. *What am I letting back into my life?* She stared at Burke and the marine for a long time. Burke grew uncomfortable. The marine stared back. Then she let them both inside.

Jonesy grumbled and jumped from the stool. Ripley sat down slowly. She didn't ask Burke and Gorman to sit.

"So?" she asked.

"It's been a while," Burke said. "Last contact was pretty standard. A series of colonist messages and a request for equipment on the next resupply ship. Since then there's been no response to any Company requests or personal messages, no replies to scientific queries. Nada."

"Technical fault," she said, but her skin was cold, her insides colder.

"Distinct possibility," Gorman said.

Damn, Ripley thought, *he even talks like a grunt.*

Burke raised an eyebrow.

"What?" Ripley asked. She had a bad feeling about this. After everything they'd done to her, all that she'd told them and been ostracized for, why would Burke come all the way out here to the scummiest accommodation pod in Gateway?

With a soldier in tow.

"We're mounting a rescue mission," Burke said. "We want you to go."

Ripley's stomach dropped. A rush of memories flooded in—Kane's last supper, the *Nostromo*, the beast, the deaths she'd seen and those she had not. Dallas, her sometime lover.

She stood quickly from the stool, shoving it back so that it bounced from her cot and tumbled to the floor. Jonesy hissed and scampered away, hiding somewhere out of sight. She so wished she could do the same.

She went to the kitchen unit and poured coffee for the two men. Not because she wanted them to stay, but because without something to occupy her hands and her mind, she might lose it.

Did he really just ask me that?

"I don't believe this," she said. "You guys throw me to the wolves, and now you want me to go back out there? Forget it. It's not my problem." She handed Burke his coffee. She had to resist the temptation to fling it into the smug bastard's face.

"Can I finish?" he asked.

"No. There's no way."

She handed Gorman his drink, and he seemed to wake up.

"Ripley, you wouldn't be going in with the troops. I can guarantee your safety." At least it seemed he could say more than one word at a time.

"These Colonial Marines are very tough hombres," Burke said. She turned her back on him and poured herself a drink. Her heart was thudding as the memories grew more real. "They're packing state-of-the-art firepower; there's nothing they can't handle," Burke went on. "Lieutenant, am I right?"

"That's true. We've been trained to deal with situations like this."

"Then you don't need me," Ripley said. "I'm not a soldier." She hated the fact that her voice wavered, but the fear was rich and real. She couldn't hide it. Maybe she shouldn't even try.

"Yeah, but we don't know exactly what's going on out there,"

Burke said. "It may just be a downed transmitter, okay, but if it's not, I'd like you there as an advisor. And that's all."

Ripley stood and approached Burke. He was a company man, Weyland-Yutani, so he'd told her many times.

"What's your interest in this? Why are you going?"

"The corporation co-financed that colony, along with colonial administration. We're getting into a lot of terraforming now, building better worlds—"

"Yeah, yeah, I saw the commercial," Ripley said. "Look, I don't have time for this. I've got to get to work."

"Yeah, I heard you're working in the cargo docks."

"That's right."

"Running loaders and forklifts, that sort of—"

"So?"

"I think it's great that you're keeping busy, that it's the only thing you could get. There's nothing wrong with it."

Son of a bitch, Ripley thought. She was letting him get to her, and that made her even angrier.

"What would you say if I told you I could get you reinstated as a flight officer?" he asked. "The company has already agreed to pick up your contract."

She looked sidelong at Gorman—inscrutable, silent—then back to Burke.

"If I go," she said.

He nodded. "Yeah, if you go. Come on, it's a second chance, kiddo! And personally I think it would be the best thing in the world for you to get out there and face this thing. Get back on the horse—"

"Spare me, Burke, I've had my psych evaluation this month."

"I know," he said, standing and invading her personal space. "I've read it. You wake up every night, your sheets are soaking wet—"

He was reminding her of the nightmares, the dark places where she was chased by the beast, and that darker place that still weighed heavy within her when she was awake.

"Damn it, Burke!" she shouted in his face, "I said no, and I mean it! Now please leave. I am not going back, and I am..." She swallowed, caught her breath. "I would not be any use to you if I did."

"Okay," Burke said softly, as if suddenly he was talking to a child. Ripley lit another cigarette, shaking, and heard Burke drop something on her table. A comms card, she guessed.

Screw him. Screw him for making me feel like this.

"Want you to do me a favor…" he said. "Just think about it."

"Thanks for the coffee," Gorman said. He smoothed his buzzcut, put his cap back on, and led the way from her cabin. Burke closed the door softly behind them.

Ripley was shaking, and it wasn't because she was drinking too much coffee. She knelt and stroked the cat, and wondered whether he had nightmares, too.

DATE: 6 JULY, 2179

They were chasing her. No longer just one, now there were many beasts, and the corridors weren't just those of a dank spacecraft. She bounded from rough stone, slick with a viscous layer from which she shrank away. She tripped over coiled things that looked as though they belonged inside a body. She tried to scream.

I have to warn them. They're coming, they know we're here, and I have to warn the others!

She did not know what "others." Not Dallas and Lambert, not Kane—they were all dead and gone—but those other others who belonged somewhere else, somewhere deep in that dark, heavy memory that threatened so often to burst free and reveal itself fully.

So she ran. The beasts hunted her, and she knew without a shadow of a doubt that they would run her down and tear her to shreds before she found any friend ever again.

Ripley started awake, shouting, gasping, sweating, taking a few seconds to realize that she was no longer being chased and that, in fact, she was as safe as she'd ever been.

Almost.

Almost as safe, because the nightmares carried on. She was haunted by them, and as much as she hated to admit the psych evaluations—

desired to prove them wrong—she knew that she was damaged. Her mind was not her own. The gravity of that dark potential within her was slowly, inexorably crushing her to its will.

She splashed water on her face and down her neck, washing away the sweat of the nightmares, but not their taste. Then she stared into the mirror and knew what she had to do.

Burke's comms card was where he'd left it. She plugged it into the unit and buzzed him. He responded, sleep-addled and confused. It took him a moment, then he spoke.

"Ripley?" He glanced at the clock behind him, saw how early it still was. "You okay?"

"Just tell me one thing, Burke," she said. "You're going out there to destroy them. Right? Not to study. Not to bring back. But to wipe them out."

"That's the plan. You have my word on it."

She paused for a moment, and her life rested on a ledge. Stay as she was and she would eventually fall off. Confront her fears—face those nightmares—and perhaps one day she could move on.

"All right," she said. "I'm in." Burke went to say something else, but she broke the connection and sat back in her chair.

She felt lighter. Different. The weight from inside, that dark star… it was gone. Whatever it had been, it was lifted from her, and though confused, she did not mourn its passing. Whatever memories she had been reliving in those deep, dark nightmares were gone forever, and she was glad.

She looked at Jonesy, still sitting at the bottom of the bed.

"And you, you little shithead. You're staying here."

Jonesy looked very fine with that.

31

THE CRUELEST TRICK

DATE: 27 JULY, 2179
TIME: 0900

"We're on an express elevator to hell, going down!"

The ship dropped toward Acheron. Someone shouted *whoop*, but Ripley had her eyes squeezed shut, and she was concentrating hard to hold onto her dinner. The whole dropship rattled and shook, metal creaked, marines grunted, and she clasped onto her armrests so hard that her fingers cramped.

This was the most aggressive of atmosphere entries—an assault more than a landing—and Ripley had never trained for any of this.

But she'd been through worse. She opened her eyes, stared at the ceiling, and wondered what was to come.

DATE: 27 JULY, 2179
TIME: 0958

They'd done a fly-by of the colony. It still had power, the outer structure looked undamaged, and the giant atmosphere processors remained operational. Other than being so quiet, it didn't look like a colony that had suffered any mishaps.

But there was still no contact. If the colonists had heard the dropship circling around, surely they'd have emerged by now to welcome it?

Ripley was nervous as hell. The silence and stillness troubled her.

"Man, it looks like a fuckin' ghost town," one of the marines whispered.

She felt a chill go through her.

If they are all dead, then it's far from a ghost town, she thought. *It's a monster town.*

The lieutenant issued the order to land. Ripley, Burke, and the marines were in the ground assault vehicle held in the dropship's belly, with the android Bishop at the controls.

"I prefer the term artificial person myself," he'd said to her, but screw him. Bishop, Ash—different names for the same bastard, as far as she was concerned.

Seconds after the dropship ramp touched the landing pad, Bishop hit the gas. The atmosphere had changed now, going from bullish bravado to steady and calm, loaded with a readiness that almost set Ripley at ease. Almost. She'd seen the firepower these guys packed, and the professionalism with which they had prepared. But she also knew what could be inside this complex.

I should never have come, she thought for the thousandth time. But once out of hypersleep on the *Sulaco*, she'd decided to join the away team on their journey down to the surface. The *Sulaco* remained in unmanned orbit, and she had no desire to be left up there all on her own. She'd been alone for too long.

"Ten seconds people, look sharp!" another grunt bellowed. "All right, I want a nice clean dispersal this time."

The ground assault vehicle skidded to a halt and the door slid open.

Ripley held her breath. The marines streamed out and the door slammed shut. Gorman remained, along with Burke and Bishop. All she knew was what appeared on the display screens of Gorman's control centre. She felt immediately cut off from the rest, as if they were somewhere far away.

It was raining heavily, the ground thick with muddy ash. There were several abandoned vehicles in the midst of the complex. One solitary sign, BAR, glowed a steady red, the only sight that wasn't a bland gray.

The team spread out around a wide vehicle doorway labeled "North Lock."

"First squad up online," Gorman said. "Hicks, get yours in the corridor, watch the rear."

Ripley watched on various head-cam monitors as the first squad approached the door. They moved with calm, economical movements, quickly and calmly. Hudson ran a bypass on the door's locking mechanism, and then the heavy metal barrier started to slide open.

"Second squad move up," Gorman said. "Flanking positions."

The doors opened.

Inside, all was shadow.

The marines entered the complex grouped in close formation, checking corners, using attached shoulder-torches to illuminate their way. The inner lock doors were jammed half closed, and two marines pulled them all the way open.

Vasquez moved forward, and then Ripley saw what was revealed.

The corridor beyond had been ripped apart. Ceilings were down, wall paneling shattered, spewing guts of tattered pipes and hanging wires. Water dribbled from a ruptured channel.

Oh shit, Ripley thought.

"Second team move inside," Gorman said. "Hicks, take the upper level."

As the second squad moved up a staircase just inside the opened doors, the first squad edged deeper into the complex. The damage to the corridor was even more apparent now, and there were a few scattered piles of furniture that might have been blockades of some sort.

If so, none of them had worked.

"Sir, you copying this?" Apone asked. "Looks like hits from small arms fire, with some explosive damages. Probably seismic survey charges. Are you reading this? Keep it tight, people."

Ripley checked Hicks's head-cam and saw that he'd just reached the head of the staircase. The corridor beyond was equally dark, and also showed signs of damage.

"Okay, Hicks, Hudson, use your motion trackers," Gorman said. As Ripley saw the two men look down at devices in their hands, a chill went through her. Ash had designed units very like these to help them hunt the beast aboard the *Nostromo*. These units looked sharper and more solid, but she guessed that the technology was much the same.

The teams advanced. Ripley felt sweat trickle down her back. Burke watched with her, and Bishop stood back a little, observing the operation. She was stuck here with an android and two men she didn't like, and she started to wish she'd gone with Hicks.

"Quarter and search by twos," Gorman said.

It was Hudson who saw movement on his tracker. He called it in, and he and Vasquez advanced slowly along the dark corridor, guns at the ready. Hudson's heart rate increased. Vasquez's barely changed.

Pull them out, Ripley thought. She almost said it, but realized how panicked it seemed. They'd come this far, over such a vast distance, to discover what had happened here and to help anyone that had survived. So they had to go on.

But that didn't prevent her from being terrified.

Hudson kicked a door in and... gerbils. They skittered away in a panic.

"Sir, we have a negative situation here," Hudson drawled. "Moving on, sir." Ripley couldn't tell whether or not he sounded sarcastic.

Something caught her eye on another screen. The view from Hicks's head-cam swept across a corridor and Ripley saw something amiss, a series of dark, uneven patches on the floor.

"Wait! Wait, tell him to..." She snatched up a headset. "Hicks. Back up. Pan right." He did as she said and revealed the acid burns across the floor. Metal grill flooring, melted away as if it were made of ice. "There."

Like ice, her blood chilled. She felt sick.

"You seeing this all right?" Hicks said, looking at them through Drake's head-cam. "Looks melted. Somebody must have bagged one of Ripley's bad guys here."

Ripley glanced back at Burke. She didn't know why, wasn't even sure what she was expecting of him.

"Acid for blood," he said, apparently amazed at this confirmation of everything Ripley had told him.

"If you liked that, you're gonna love this," Hudson said. He and Vasquez had found a much larger burn site, a hole melted through several levels and wide enough for a man to fall through. *Maybe if one of them was blown apart*, Ripley thought. *Maybe then.*

"Sir, this place is dead," Apone said. "Whatever happened here I think we missed it."

Gorman scanned the screens and the bio readouts of his marines.

"All right, the area's secured, let's go in and see what their computer can tell us."

"Wait a minute," Ripley said, that familiar panic rising again, "the area's not—"

"The area is secured, Ripley," he said, dismissing her without a look. "First team, head for operations. Hudson, see if you can get their CPU online."

"Affirmative."

"Hicks, meet me at the South Lock," Gorman said. "We're coming in."

I bet they feel safer already, Ripley thought. She considered arguing with Gorman, telling him that there was no way the area could be declared secure until his teams had performed a full sweep. Though huge, vicious and violent, she also remembered how the beast had hidden itself away on board the *Narcissus*, remaining so still and quiet that she hadn't noticed it for some time.

Those corridors she'd seen on the head-cams—the warren of rooms, the stairwells—there could be a hundred Xenomorphs in there. But the assault vehicle was already moving, and soon they had skirted around the edge of the colony and pulled up at the South Lock.

I'm being drawn in, Ripley thought. *I should have stayed on the* Sulaco, *but I didn't want to be alone.* And now she should sit tight, right where she was… but she wouldn't. She would go with Gorman and Burke.

I can't not go.

She had to see what had happened to the colonists. Like it or not, she knew more about the Xenomorphs than anyone else on this mission.

It was still raining heavily as they exited the vehicle and approached the South Lock. Hicks and another marine was waiting for them there, and Gorman and Burke entered ahead of her.

Ripley slowed to a halt, still outside, a short distance from the open door.

I can still turn around, she thought. But in truth, she had come too far already.

"Are you all right?" Hicks asked. He'd turned, noticed her standing there, and come back for her. She liked him for that.

"Yes," Ripley said softly.

She stepped inside, and the doors slid shut behind her.

DATE: 27 JULY, 2179
TIME: 1003

In the maze of ducts, out scavenging for food, Newt heard voices.

They frightened her, those voices, but they also gave her hope and that made her angry. She had learned the hardest way imaginable that hope was the cruelest trick she could play on herself.

Hope might get her killed.

Still, she slipped through the ducts, following the voices...

...and she hoped.

ACKNOWLEDGEMENTS

I saw *Aliens* when it first hit theaters, right around my birthday in July of 1986. I was nineteen years old and it was the first time a movie ever gave me nightmares. Thanks to James Cameron for those nightmares. Deep thanks to my editor, Steve Saffel, for watching my six, and to the entire team at Titan for their dedication to this new voyage into the Alien canon. Special thanks to Josh Izzo at Fox for his passion and for reminding me to stay frosty, and to James A. Moore and Tim Lebbon for friendship and brainstorming. Finally, my gratitude, as always, to my fantastic family for their support, and to my agent, Howard Morhaim, for navigating the universe with me.

ABOUT THE AUTHOR

CHRISTOPHER GOLDEN is the *New York Times* bestselling author of *Ararat*, *Road of Bones*, *Snowblind*, and many other novels. With Mike Mignola, he is the co-creator of such comics series as *Baltimore*, *Lady Baltimore*, and *Joe Golem: Occult Detective*. Golden has edited and co-edited numerous anthologies, including *Seize the Night*, *The New Dead*, and Shirley Jackson Award winner *The Twisted Book of Shadows*. The author has been nominated ten times in eight different categories for the Bram Stoker Awards, and won twice. Golden is also a screenwriter and producer, as well as a writer of audio dramas and video games. He lives in Massachusetts.

www.christophergolden.com